WORLDS APART

Vol. 4 of the Three Worlds Saga

Carol A. Strickland

Other books by Carol A. Strickland

Touch of Danger– vol. 1 of the Three Worlds Saga

Lost in the Stars– vol. 2 of the Three Worlds Saga

Stalemate– vol. 3 of the Three Worlds Saga

Applesauce and Moonbeams– wacky soft sci fi

Nothing Personal– ditto but wackier

Burgundy and Lies– sweet historical romance

Published by Carol A. Strickland
www.CarolAStrickland.com

Publisher's Note: This is a work of fiction. Names, characters, places, and incidents are a product of the author's imagination. Locales and public names are sometimes used for atmospheric purposes. Any resemblance to actual people, living or dead, or to businesses, companies, events, institutions, or locales is completely coincidental.

Book Layout © 2017 BookDesignTemplates.com

Exterior cover by Strick. Interior cover illustration by Colleen Doran.

Worlds Apart/ Carol A. Strickland -- 1st ed.
ISBN Print edition 978-1-941318-19-5
ISBN Digital edition 978-1-941318-17-1
ISBN IngramSpark Print edition 978-1-941318-33-1
ISBN IngramSpark Digital edition 978-1-941318-34-8

My thanks to:

– Anselm Audley (that's his *nom de plume*; buy his books!), my patient editor. Where else could I find someone who keeps track so well of my constantly-changing character names? Besides, if I went with someone else I'd miss his snarky (but valid) Brit comments all over my manuscript.

– Kristine Cayne, who corrected my French and Québécois. Any missteps in this are my fault. To me, French just sounds so formal, and Québécois swearing seems backward in intent. With it, things aren't really awful until you involve the church. Where'd I put that Rosetta program?

1

Mmm. The bed was so cozy. She nestled deeper into the soft pillow, the blankets pulled over her head. A shivery wind swept her naked backside for a moment when the blankets lifted and the body of her new husband settled next to her. She wriggled over a trifle to let him in, but was still unwilling to come completely awake.

Let her have this delicious drowse for a few more moments. Time to let this new feeling completely soak in. How decadent, how rare: to feel safe.

Londo lay beside her, which meant that nothing could harm her. He was her protector. They were finally back on safe, secure Earth to stay– or at least for a while. There would be no scary trials today, no funerals, no rabid terrorists firing guns at them. Just time to get to know each other like ordinary people. And even better, like ordinary newlyweds. She smiled and turned over to cuddle closer to him.

Was that a fire crackling? The familiar, homey smell of wood smoke penetrated under the blankets to her nose. A fireplace in the master bedroom had been one of the few things finished in this mansion Londo called Starhaven.

Starhaven. And now they were both Starharts instead of one being a Rand and the other, an O'Kelly.

How wonderful touching was, the sense that had been denied her for years. Lon's heartbeat pulsed his warm skin under the press of her body. Feel his muscles bunch and slide as he pulled himself into a sitting position with her still under the blankets.

Mm, even his deep voice could touch her, thrumming down her spine as he spoke.

Someone answered.

Carolina O'Kelly Starhart's eyes flew open. She shrank into a ball, clutching to Londo's protection. Lon didn't seem alarmed. Neither his voice nor his mind reflected any threat. Cautiously, Lina stretched back to her full length again. She made a window between blankets and dared to peek out of her nest.

No phone; Londo talked to one of those weird mid-air screens, this one merely in 2-D, hanging over the bed right in front of his face. A sheet covered him, but only from the waist down. Onscreen sat Bolt in his flashy blue spandex parahero costume. Though she'd spoken to him before while in quarantine on far-off Sarastor, Earth's mega-speedster still awed her. He probably couldn't see her, thank goodness!

Lon patted her reassuringly under the sheets. "I'm back on Earzth now, Gary," he told the screen in his French-Canadian accent. "Checking in."

"It's an eff of about time," the Bolt companionably replied. "You missed a lot of action. Taking it easy in quarantine, were you?"

"Not for long. We had some action Out There, too."

What if he sees me? Lina telepathically demanded to know. **Not everyone here is an exhibitionist. Londo, you could've waited to call or done it in another room.**

I suppose. It's too late now, chérie. Relax.

"And what kind of action was that?" The Bolt leaned back in his chair with a grin, oblivious to their silent conversation. "Stuck in quarantine with that girl— Say, was that the Terran National Maria was talking about? Something about her being held under charges of mind control?"

"Didn't Maria get my message?" Londo hedged. "Those charges were dropped. Everything's okay now."

But they hadn't been dropped entirely. With everything that had happened, with Lina helping to save the world of Sarastor from a big invasion and then the Three Worlds appointing her and Lon and Jae as their Chosen, Stoan Kinrol, the highfalutin' commander of the Affiliated Systems Megaforce Legion, hadn't bothered to officially drop all the charges that had kept her under arrest for nearly a week. He'd left an opening through which she could be charged if the new forms of mind control that the Legion had been hearing rumors about, proved true. In that case, she'd be subjected to further testing and accusations. With maybe a lobotomy thrown in for laughs.

Stoan didn't even have the courage to charge her with what he really wanted: the crime of marrying Valiant, the most powerful, heroic man in the galaxy. Lina leaned into her pillow and sighed softly. The most wonderful, sexiest, kindest and most loving, handsomest man who ever lived. Her sweet Londo.

She stopped at that. What about Jae? Jae was also just as wonderful, just as sexy and loving and all the rest as Lon… but in different ways. How could she explain it if… no, *when*– be positive– Jae accepted their proposal of marriage into a full Feithi Triune? She didn't want him to think he was a third wheel. Her feelings for him might not run as deep as her feelings for Lon, but in time they would. Mm, they certainly would. Sweet Jae. All they needed was some more time together.

She determined that it was all right to use the superlative for both of them. After all, it was true: both were just the best men ever. If they didn't like her telling one that he was the best, and then turning to the other to tell him that he was also the best, they could just learn to lump it.

"An interstellar transporter." The Bolt was still talking with Lon, chuckling. "And Terran, too. I haven't seen Maria in the past few days, but Damon said she was in a real snit over it. She kept claiming that the Mega-Legion was going to snatch up this girl like they did you."

"No they didn't and yes she is," Londo replied in that deeply mellow voice of his. "She's gotten faster since you saw her. It takes about two minutes for her to teleport at interstellar distances."

"Two minutes!" Bolt's jaw dropped. "I don't believe it."

"*Oui.* And the two minutes are just because she has to prevent contagion. Otherwise it's instantaneous."

"I know I saw it, but it's an illusion of some kind. You've been drinking too much of Mike's wine supply."

"Just got in a little while ago. Haven't have time to visit Papa Mike yet. Besides, he'd slap me silly if I tried to touch his precious collection."

The two men grunted amiably at each other. Londo's grandfather, Mike Rand, was a norm and any violence he could direct toward Lon– if indeed he would ever bring himself to do so– would just bounce off Londo's invulnerable skin.

Lon rubbed Lina's shoulder under the bedding. "I thought the first thing I'd do was check in with the ParaNet," he told Bolt. "I didn't want anyone to gossip if they hadn't heard from me."

From her hiding place Lina fought back a grunt of her own. She'd hung around paraheroes enough now to know that they spent all their off-hours gossiping. Well, gossiping and making love. And of course the gossip about the mighty Valiant had always been that he was a virgin– or at least, he had been until he met her week before last. Now he was vulnerable whenever she touched him, and the outcome of that was definitely satisfactory. No wonder he behaved so possessively of her. He treated their lovemaking like receiving a trophy.

Of course. He'd been getting The Look all his life, as people not in the know wondered: was he or wasn't he? Now here he had a wife, practically a stamp on his head that proclaimed that he was Getting Some At Last. But no one on Earth knew about the two of them yet.

Londo was playing a game.

The only question was: did she have enough chutzpah to support her husband? She had duties to him. Londo was Goal A-plus always. Whatever Londo wanted…

She took a deep breath.

"I'll put you on the active duty list–" Bolt paused and then visibly boggled as she slid into what Lina hoped was his view of Londo. She wrapped her arms around Lon's neck languidly.

"Do you have to go on active duty right away, baby?" she purred into Lon's ear in her most sultry voice even as she tried to keep the sheet at a decent height. Lon stroked her arm and gazed at her with knowing eyes.

Bolt's gape turned into a sly grin.

"*Eh bien,*" Lon said, glancing back at the screen and Gary, "maybe you could delay scheduling me for active duty until tomorrow."

"Make it a couple days more," Lina stage-whispered to Lon, running her fingertip along his jawline.

"Or more," Londo repeated obediently.

Gary sat back in his chair, tapping his console with a pencil. He nodded at Lina. "Nice seeing you again," he said. "Tell you what, Londo you dirty dog, you just report in whenever you want to go on active duty. But I'm logging Valiant as being available for emergencies until then."

"Why don't you do that?" Londo agreed and turned his attention to Lina.

Gary broke into laughter as the screen blanked.

They did as well. "Jesus, Lina, I thought you were the shy type," Londo said when he could finally catch his breath.

"I have my moments." Lina hastily pulled the blankets around herself, allowing the shivers that had been trying to shake her for the past few minutes to catch up. "I figured you called while we were in bed, hoping to show off."

"Was I that obvious? Oh, you were perfect. *Absolutement.*" He lay back with just the sheet over his lower half, his chest bare to the frozen air, hands tucked behind his head. That crazy smile of his sat crooked on his face. He was off in his Never-Never Land, his mind whirling with scenes about how Gary's story would spread and mutate among the other members of the Terran Paranorm Network.

Lina couldn't help but smile back. "I want to buy you a tee shirt today that says, 'I'm getting some.' That way you won't have to pull stunts like this again."

He blinked out of his reverie. "I'll wear it. I promise. God, it's great to be back on Earzh."

"We need to buy a bed, too. I don't think this one's going to work. Who's having a sale this time of year?"

It was a queen-sized bed, but while Lina measured in at almost six feet, Lon had a few more inches than she, plus he was solidly muscled.

Londo wore his physique like a prince, unconscious of the personal power he radiated. His skin was the color of the tropics, all warm and toasty, his eyes a melting brown that could harden in an instant under regal brows into a scowl that could freeze villains in their tracks.

But to fit Londo into this banged-up bed he slept diagonally, and that didn't leave any real room for Lina. This was fine for honeymoons, but what about afterward? And what about when Jae arrived? Three would not fit unless they all piled on top of each other. Which they might. Jae was narrower than Londo, but beat him by more than a few inches in height. She still couldn't believe that Out There people thought Londo was *short!*

Of course Jae Rallene was still a question mark. Jae was right; a legal Triune marriage would involve complications. At least he had the sense not to barrel unthinkingly into life-changing situations like Lon and she had. Now they all had to do their homework on Triunes and the tricky balance of relationships therein. Plus they had to wait for Jae to return with his answer.

Lina's father had always accused her of being a whore, but Jae's people, the Feithi, had polygamous marriages as a matter of course. Theirs had been a telepathic society, which probably lent stability to the otherwise wobbly concept of three-ways: *Was I better than he was? You love her more than me!* And other scenarios she hadn't even imagined yet.

How would a Feithi marriage fare on Earth? In the one case Lina knew about, international law declared that a culturally-normal marriage from Out There was legal. Lon and she had been married in a Feithi dual marriage, and no one on Sarastor had raised a question about the possible illegality of that. But everyone else of Feith was now dead. Did that mean that Terran courts wouldn't recognize its culture?

"Don't worry about it," Londo told her. "All we have to think about today is getting a new bed. I know where we can get a custom one made. Jae can reinforce it for me."

"Will we have to buy expensive custom sheets for the rest of our lives?"

The full skylight above the bed showed that it was still mid-morning, the clouds ambling across a late-winter blue sky.

"Hum." Lon rubbed his upper lip as he considered those clouds and then eased down, his head against hers on the pillow. "I know. There are systems that endorse three-way marriages–"

"I heard about *them*." Lina wrinkled her nose. "Non-Feithi three-ways. The third's always a prostitute or a slave, and unlike the Civilized people of the Affiliated Systems, I don't approve of slavery. And *Civilized* people don't approve of three-ways."

Out There it was Very Important to be Civilized with a capital C and pointed pinky, especially if one were somehow related to the Mega-Legion like Lon was.

Londo nodded. "So we aren't buying a marriage, we're buying a bed. They make big beds and big sheets Out There. Okay?"

"Well… Are you sure we won't be supporting the system by buying this stuff? I do not want people to point at me and say that I'm pro-slavery."

"We need a bed, Lie."

"We also need walls. We need a lot of things. *Ca-ching*."

Two-by-fours and I-beams roughed in future walls of the bedroom. They supported a lot more wiring than just electricity could account for. Incomplete lengths of wallboard had been installed that separated this room from the one next door and from the hallway where an icy breeze blew with gusto.

The hall to the north had been carved out of mountainside. Opposite it a bowed wall of thermal windows overlooked a broad and deep mountain valley. On the east side of the room two logs merrily burned in the stone fireplace, barely cutting into the cold that hung like a light fog.

Londo hadn't finished the heat system yet. They were high in the Wyoming Rockies, and more than a few windows still awaited installation. Only the warmth left over from yesterday's late-winter sun through the passive solar design and thermal floor mass had kept the temperature from being far below freezing when they'd first arrived.

"We set priorities," Londo decided.

"Goals," she said. She had memorized her Zig Ziglar "Personal Goals" tapes long ago.

"Whatever. We need to sleep tonight. Sleep, not that other thing we do. Well, a little of that, too. Make that a lot." He stretched out on the too-small mattress. "I just dumped some old things here for temporary purposes. It's junk, most of it. We need a real bed so that I don't crash into you all night long."

"Oh all right, if they have some nice beds."

"I'm sure they do."

"Goal A, get bed. We need to write these things down."

Londo frowned at his wife as she pulled the covers around her head like a hood. "Is it cold in here?" he asked with concern. He'd given the room a good dose of heat breath just an hour ago.

"Only about freezing."

"*Maudite marde.* I'll get the heating system up and running before nightfall," he promised. "And the rest of the windows. Goal B. I'll need some thermostats, scatter them around so I can double-check the system."

"You can't tell when I touch you?"

Thanks to Lina's psychic work, his strength and invulnerability switched off whenever their skin met. That was how he was able to touch her like a human being, not like the megahero Valiant. Otherwise, he'd have crushed her to bloody mush long ago.

He shrugged as he reached for another blanket for her. "The touching affects me in different ways, kitten. It might be cool in here, but I can't tell the extent."

"Hmm." She thought for a moment. "Try this." She extended her hand in the air and crooked her finger as if she expected a bird to land on it, silently calling down etheric white light for protection.

"What?"

"You do it," she urged, and he obediently assumed the same position.

"Now what?"

She explained, "Imagine Tinker Bell there, a deva of temperature reporting." Devas were spiritual beings, usually in charge of animals or abstract concepts, as angels were often in charge of humans. The spirit world kept things loose, but that was how Lina organized her own thoughts about the unseen universe.

A couple weeks ago Londo had communicated with a deva of tropical weather, who'd provided them with a handy thunderstorm to escape a trap. Now Lon looked at his finger and screwed his mouth around in concentration. "Tinker Bell."

"You can get away with messy technique," she told him, feeling him trying to believe. "Intent alone will do it. Just relax. Have fun. Say hello to her."

He frowned but played along. "Hello, Tink," he said and blinked. "*Un instant.*" He squinted at his finger. "There's something there."

"Her name is Tinker Bell." Lina smiled. "What's she wearing?"

"She's…" He squinted harder.

"Relax. It's imagination, not vision."

"A jacket. No, a parka and a toboggan cap. Ski boots."

"It *is* cold in here, Lon."

"*Euh,* now what do I do? Does she mind?"

"Ask her."

"Oh. Oh!" He blinked and looked at Lina. "She just nodded her head and disappeared."

"And what do you say?" Lina prompted.

Lon gave her that great smile of his and turned to the empty spot over his finger. "Thank you, deva. I mean, thank you, Tink."

"Very good. Now make sure you're disconnected." At his blank look, she said, "Just sort of shake your head inside to clear it, make sure that your *intent* is that you're disconnected. If you don't, you might hang on to the deva longer than you or she wants to."

He nodded. "So she'll show me what the temperature is by how she's dressed? Was this just for this once, or will she come back later?"

"She seemed nice enough. I wouldn't bother her too much, but I'm sure she'll be available when you need her."

"*Très* cool." Londo Rand Starheart, aka Valiant, settled back, tucking the blankets around her as she snuggled against him. He loved this magic that she'd brought to his life, even though she said it wasn't magic at all, that it was just psychic work and anyone could do it with the right training.

He loved the way his lush, green-eyed beauty of a wife thought of him, as Londo and not just Valiant. The way she opened up her entire heart when she loved him and how she'd promised to do so beyond the end of time.

Life was good. And when Jae came on board, it would go from perfect to even more perfect. Jae was the love of his life; Lina was the love of his soul.

He paused in his thoughts. Jae and he had only so briefly shared minds last night and the night before. How much deeper was his love now for the beautiful

Feithi! How would things change as they shared minds more? Would he come to love Jae, whom he'd known since they were kids, more than Lina? Could you measure the two different loves against each other?

How the hell had those dead Feithi managed to run their damned Triunes? This was going to be difficult until they could figure things out. If only everyone hadn't been exterminated on the planet sixteen years ago. Now there was only Jae left, and what memories he had from his childhood. Those, and the records of Feith, buried in the network of the Interstellar Web. They'd all have to do a lot of research. Lon didn't like to do research; he pictured himself a man of action and adventure instead.

There were things to do today… but at least he could start without getting out of bed.

2

"Who reported this?" Emperor Yanist-Glory slammed his right fist onto the desk. "I want to know if this is true or just some bastard trying to make points with his command!"

As one, the group surrounding the desk took a step back. It was rare that the emperor lost control when he was angry, but once he did, heads could literally roll.

General Riant licked his lips and tried to look like he hadn't just been pulled from a sound sleep to come here to the palace's study. Though the emperor was in his bathrobe, his famous imperial hair standing on end like springs all over his head, his staff had hurried in full formal dress to his call. No one had dared report in holographic form.

Riant had dressed too quickly. One of his medals had slipped to the inside of his uniform and now scratched against his bare chest. He squared his shoulders. "This agent has furnished excellent information before."

"But twice has been completely wrong," Chancellor Bain said as he looked up from his padd screen.

Riant's upper lip automatically curled at the chancellor. "Only twice after years of solid reports. An outstanding record."

Emperor Yanist-Glory paced behind his desk, his eyes focused on the marble floor beyond his slippered feet.

Into the silence, Secretary Acksum spoke. "I–" He coughed to settle his voice to a lower register. "I hesitated to report…" He gulped as the emperor paused and looked at him. "Two other sightings. These from Deseed, not Jorter."

"When?" the emperor barked.

"Three days ago. From a single agent but spaced three hours apart. This man has only recently come into our employ, so we were waiting for confirmation from another source. We didn't get one."

"Until now." The emperor's voice was a low growl, but one kept to himself rather than directed at them.

"It is another star system entirely, your Glory."

"The next one over." The emperor didn't need to remind them. A meter-wide spherical map of the galactic sector floated over one end of his desk, showing the vastness of the Yanist-Glory Empire. Along the fuzzy edges outside the Empire sat the systems they spoke of.

There lay the great grain fields of Schwann, then the almost temperate, mineral-laden riches of Deseed. Light-years beyond them came the rich variety of both vegetative and technical resources on Jorter.

"Schwann," someone whispered.

The emperor fastened his gaze upon the speaker, a woman of middle age.

"It was last week," she said in a voice more solid. "Discounted. With all our mind control activity we sometimes find that an unprogrammed telepathic group hallucination will take hold over an area. It's a form of feedback. This was an illusion. Or a subconscious wish for, ah, freedom."

Yanist-Glory considered that. Finally he asked, "Which one was sighted there? Or was it both?"

The woman quickly replied, "Both men. But as I said, unreal. You know how it is, your Glory. We often get phantom reports of the Rands from the outer worlds."

"Deseed?"

Acksum said, "The informant there reported Maximus. He said there was a cape."

"Yes, that would be Hal Rand. Maximus," the emperor murmured. "And the Jorter report?"

"Our informant wasn't sure, just that it was a human who flew almost faster than he could see and then disappeared as if he'd gone into hyperspace without using a ship."

"Maximus or Valiant then, either one of the Rands."

The emperor used his fingertips to walk from star system to star system across his insubstantial map: Schwann, Deseed, Jorter… and beyond that, Earth, home of the Rands. Few seemed to recognize the uncut gem that was Earth and its secrets. The ignorance of Terrans was a joke out here among the stars. Let the other galactic sectors think so; let them forget the planet existed. That way they wouldn't put up a fuss when Earth became part of the Empire.

Primitive, self-sufficient Earth, with not even interstellar transportation facilities. Even so, it held the fabled Gateway to the Timeless Realms– probably the reason so many parahumans and their even more powerful counterparts, the megas, had sprung from that world. What unimaginable secrets lay beyond that Gateway, waiting to be plundered?

If he could just get past those Rands.

"Research and development," Yanist-Glory demanded.

Chancellor Bain didn't have to look at his padd for the results. "The last six quarters have focused on improving our mind control techniques. Per your command," he reminded his emperor.

Yanist-Glory frowned. "Yes." He paced again in a straight line and then changed into a circle that took up much of the room. "We need the mind control for this push."

Bain nodded. "After that we can return to finding a way to slow down both Valiant and Maximus."

"They cannot impede my plans," the emperor warned the group.

"They won't," Riant quickly said. "Once we have power points within the populations controlled and the rest cowed, the Rands won't dare interfere. They're notoriously soft-hearted when it comes to innocents."

"What about the parents? Maximus' parents?"

"Extremely well-guarded. We've tried and failed many times already. As you know."

"Hmf. Friends?"

"The same, though we still have hopes," Riant said. "As always, we watch them."

"And Maximus' wife?" After a beat, the emperor laughed at his own question. "No, I've heard the rumors about her. It must be difficult for a man to have that much power, receive that much galactic adoration, and have to settle for the likes of… whatever she is."

"Yes, your Glory."

Yanist-Glory clenched his fist around a projected star system in his celestial map. It did not implode under his touch but rather ignored his august presence. He almost snarled at its impertinence.

"If only the Rands had a weakness."

Lina was humming softly as she ran her hand over Londo's chest and arms, down to his belly and back up again. It was almost like a purr. The woman seemed to be made of lovely music that aroused and hypnotized him at the same time. Reluctantly Londo broke his trance.

"C'mon, Kitten, sit up. Hup hup." He used parabreath to warm the room again.

"Why?"

Lon tucked the sheet under her armpits, covering her modestly. "So I can concentrate," he told her. He fluffed pillows and scrunched them behind Lina, drawing a cover around her shoulders, then settled to use her most bountiful assets as his own pillows. The screen still hovered unfurled in front of them.

"We make phone calls," Lina surmised. "A John and Yoko redux, interviews from the bed. Where's your guitar? I'll be Yoko." She screeched a warble like a mule in heat and he chuckled at her.

"*Non.* Now hush, we need to check the news." Londo snapped his fingers at the screen using some kind of power– Lina wasn't sure which one or ones, but she knew he did *something*– and the screen turned into a three-dimensional affair with a logo on it. Lina recognized the language as Panlingua.

"This is a hell of a cable system you've got, love," she said. "Interstellar pickup."

"You bet."

"Oh no. Is this what I think it'll be?"

He pried her fingers from her eyes and held her hands away from her face as he settled back onto her.

The on-screen anchor had distinctly bluish skin tones, like Stoan Kinrol, making him look as if he were underwater. Shades of blue were very popular Out There for skin color, ranging from Wilder Mem-Bazer's aqua tones to Chim-rin Dinar's more lavender tint. Reds were also common and had a range all their own. So were peachy browns, although it seemed humans came in every color there was.

"Our top story," this blue man began, "concerns the Mega-Legion once again."

"Top story," Londo murmured with a nod of approval. He twined his fingers with Lina's and shifted for more comfort. This was for the entire galactic sector. Good, good…

"Just one day after the Affiliated Systems Mega-Legion paid a final tribute to one of its own, the megapara heroine Orenya, Legion Commander Magnos announced news of a decidedly more positive nature."

Lina groaned inwardly. Framed by all the flashing dots and triangles that allowed viewers to click for further information, the channel ran today's press conference from Mega-Legion HQ. And damn it, it would have to be His High Legion Holiness Stoan Kinrol, aka Magnos, who delivered the news with a pleasant expression.

Pervert.

God, he'd secretly filmed them having sex. Okay, maybe not an all-the-way perv. Maybe he'd had a supposed good reason, to witness that Londo's new, ahem, bragging rights weren't all in his mind. But that still didn't get him off for being a first-class slimeball. She shuddered at his invasion of the most private of acts.

Stoan-face announced the time and place of the wedding as if he approved of it, as if he hadn't sent Londo off to Earth today with a hint that any marriage could be easily annulled. Lina hoped his skin crawled from having to endorse them now.

He informed everyone watching that this Carolina O'Kelly person Valiant had married was a Terran who had recently become a paranormal. Powers: interstellar teleportation. Lina couldn't tell which upset the reporters worse: that her porting was so damned quick and far-ranging, or that she was from that backwater of the universe, Earth.

The video replayed a part of the wedding– not the songs, of course; song was a barbaric concept– and Lina again reached to cover her eyes, but Lon was too quick. He pulled her hands away.

"What a beautiful couple," he said.

He was gorgeous, that was true enough. That All-Canadian face could inspire confidence and loyalty in anyone. That build was spectacular. He was tall, dark and handsome; woof. And next to them, presiding at the ceremony, Jae was the most beautiful of humans, blond to Lon's brunet. Taller even than so-tall Londo, sometimes Jae seemed almost ethereal, but when he got down to business– yow. Watch out, hormones.

Between the two was her in her wedding gown. Lina cringed as she always did when she saw a picture of herself. Of course Legion PR had CGI'd her gown so the lace was now solid, and instead of being off the shoulder, it covered her up to her chin. Prudes.

She moaned in the agony of public exposure. *Muttbutt, Muttbutt,* Dad's voice in her head chanted.

"You'll like this someday," Londo promised. "Soon. I'll get Dr. Adam to find you a shrink to take care of that ego problem."

Right, as if Lina didn't know for a fact how insignificant she was.

Well, except for that Londo and Jae loved her. How strange and wonderful that they would pick her! And the Three Worlds– they'd chosen her as well. Maybe these were roles that they expected her to grow into. She certainly wasn't ready for them now. She was just ol' Lina Muttbutt.

Londo kissed her knuckles and Lina relaxed. Lon was more than enough for her. Had she ever been happy before she met him? Life was lovely.

Even if some people had to display her picture for others to judge. Stupid Stoan!

They'd ported back to Earth early this morning, sunbeams just starting to emerge from behind the mountain ridges. It being mid-March, Londo had insisted Lina wear her climalon jacket. He showed her how to notch up its heating system. The sun hadn't begun to make a dent in winter here.

Lon chose an arrival site with the best view of Starhaven and was rewarded when Lina drew her breath in stunned amazement. Proudly he wrapped his left arm around her.

The highest point of a snow-encrusted mountain towered above the mild slope they stood on. From east to west in the side of that mountain, as if it were giant crystals within the granite itself, hung an undulating curtain of windows punctuated by a rockfall– it had turned out to be the exterior of the main fireplace– its boulders caked with a layer of ice that added to the morning's glitter. The front door could double as the entry to the Hall of the Mountain King.

Unpicturesque boulders strewed the general vicinity as if a small asteroid had hit sometime in the recent past.

"You said it was a little place!" Lina exclaimed.

"*Eh bien…*" Londo shrugged. "I may have underestimated it."

"Oh, it's like the mountain just grew it," Lina breathed. With effort she tore her gaze from Lon's handiwork and looked all around this long valley within the mountain range. Wisps of clouds hung here and there, clinging to the ridges. At the bottom lay a misty lake and its river. "What a view!" She pointed. "Are those elk? Real elk?"

"Uh huh."

"I hope you don't have hunters for neighbors."

"No neighbors. No roads."

"No neigh–" She glanced around suspiciously and couldn't see any signs of civilization besides the unreflecting windows and doorway. "Londo, how much of this is yours?"

He waved to take in the entire vista. "As far as you can see. About ten mountains worth. The whole valley, plus a good barrier all around. There might still be some leftover nineteenth century explorers wandering around down there, but no one else."

Lina was so astonished she couldn't even swear, and he gave a boisterous laugh. Finally she said, "Maybe I shouldn't have quit my job."

"It's all paid for. There's even an annuity to cover taxes."

She shook her head, trying to grasp the concept of being rich. How wealthy was Lon, to be able to afford this? They had to talk finances soon. Mama Ruth and Chimrin had both mentioned the importance of that.

Lon took the opportunity to pick her up.

"Come on," he said. "Let's see the inside."

With all due ceremony Londo carried her over the threshold and set her down. From there he took her by the hand to lead her.

He'd told her maybe an hour before that this home he'd promised her might not be quite as finished as he'd let on. What it was, was a mammoth cave that stretched at least a hundred feet to the left before it disappeared around a bend, and three times as far to the right and back to a stone wall hewn from the very mountain. It was divided roughly in two by an array of skylights that brought light down to the ground floor, all the way to the back.

Piles of construction materials sat everywhere. A few rooms had been framed out with wood and metal I-beams. There were three stories roughed in; no stairs.

"We'll set up a security perimeter," Lon told her as he admired his work, "but somehow we've still got to welcome guests in style."

The sheer volume of the… house? mansion? palace? made the fireplace seem modest, but the thing must be twelve feet wide at least. Along the south-facing wall large vertical windows stretched up all the way to the ceiling. In here that was pretty high, maybe fifty or more feet. Morning sun blazed in as well as through the skylights, creating a great king's hall of light.

Lina asked, "How will everyone get here? Where's the parking lot?"

"For guests I guess we'll rig a teleporter–"

"For the regular hotel guests, I mean."

Londo crossed his arms over his chest and made a wry face at his wife.

She ignored it. "I think we should claim the apartment with the best view, just call dibs. Will we sell time-shares or rent the rooms? Do we put in a bar in addition to an in-house restaurant? I mean, it doesn't look like the guests can just go down the road to McDonalds if they're hungry. Do you intend this as a Motel

6, or one of those fancy Hilton affairs? Can we get room service? I love room service, but it's so expensive."

She seemed to have run out of steam, so Londo spoke. "No restaurant. No time-shares. No hotel. This is home. We do our own room service."

Lina blinked as noises rose from here and there, little hums, electrical breathing.

"The house recognized people," Lon explained. "I have a few circuits working already, and they're turning on for us. I don't keep the power on here all the time. Guess that will change now."

"Oh." Still, some of the noises weren't electrical. Faint scurries meant small animals in here– at least, Lina hoped they were small. The crisp breeze told her that part of a wall must be open to the outside world. She adjusted the collar of her jacket closer to her neck.

Just above his normal walking height, Lon flew slowly in a great circle with his arms out as he described the rotunda of an entryway, already circled with Egyptian temple-sized, three-storied columns. Using his hands as if he were directing airplanes into berth, he indicated wide future halls like spokes, funneling guests this way and that. It was clear to Lina that this was never supposed to be a true home, but a showplace or indeed a home-like hotel for Londo's friends.

Lon had been kidnapped by aliens as a child and held for years in a tiny room. These days, he liked his space.

Well, Lina's cats did too. Once there was some heat in here, they'd enjoy running around.

Here was the dining room, large enough to seat forty or more in elegance. *There* was the ballroom. Over here would be a man cave, as if this cavern needed a specific location for that. A library. Office, which he amended to "offices" and then "three of them." Interview area. Lina shuddered. Guest rooms. Special guest quarters for his father and grandparents, which even as Londo showed the area to Lina, he switched locations for to the other side of the mansion. "Privacy," he said. "Guests in the east wing; immediate family in the west."

She noticed he didn't provide for quarters for her family, which was just as well. And Jae was the last of his kind with no blood family to house.

Against the back wall sat a complicated if lonely-looking, modern computer desk grouping with what Lina recognized as a Sarastoran commonitor, landline phone, and a monitor set-up that didn't look like anything she'd seen in computer showrooms. Londo explained that it was a direct hookup to the ParaNet.

Other than that, what furniture there was across the entire cavern looked third- or even fourth-hand. "It's temporary," London kept assuring her.

Kitchen. Lina tried to picture it from Lon's point of view, but all she saw was the broken-down refrigerator. It had once been an avocado color, but someone had spray-painted it almond. Apparently they hadn't bought enough paint, for one side of it still showed the ugly original green with a little rust.

There was a make-do sink, a couple of swaybacked card tables, an electric stove that looked as if Lon had pulled it straight out of the dumpster… and a state-of-the-art wine refrigerator, a little larger than a dorm fridge with a see-through door.

Lon kept talking about restaurant-quality this and top-of-the-line that. Lina figured she could make do until they could get to a discount store. Was March a good month for appliance sales? Maybe she could argue a discount for a kitchenful of appliances. *Ca-ching.* Could they really feed forty (or more) people from a family-sized kitchen?

And just who would be cooking for that crowd?

"How long do you think it'll take to finish?" she asked, looking around at this municipal construction site of a home.

"I haven't even completed the design," Londo said. "I roughed this place out from the mountain last spring. I've just been goofing around with it. Didn't know you were on the horizon. Think of it as a large, three-dimensional doodle."

He recounted how a battle between him and the Mad Hacker and his Screaming Squad had left a hole in this mountain three years ago. Lon had come back again and again trying to figure how best to reconstruct the damaged wilderness, and had wound up not only buying the place but digging a little deeper.

"Would you believe it?" he asked her absently. "Starhaven's on a slice of land sandwiched between two national forests and a First Nations reservation. Someone in Washington must have forgotten about it, or hired totally inept surveyors. There's no ground access in or out. That's a huge plus for security right there. If I hadn't shoved money in the state's face before they could think to say no, they would never have known about it."

"Coincidence," Lina muttered to herself. She hadn't believed in coincidence in years. This was another present from the Three Worlds. **Thank you so very much,** she sincerely told them. The worlds had given the three of them so much already. **It's beautiful. We'll take good care of it.**

You're welcome, the planetary entities replied.

Lon hadn't heard. He turned in a circle, his vest hiked up over the hands in his back pants pockets as he scrutinized the place. "I haven't had a chance to work here for a while. Now we can adjust the plans to fit us and pick out what we want, *chérie*. We'll have only the best of everything. Furniture, built-in appliances, art… you name it."

Lina tilted her chin at him. "Built-in butler and maid," she suggested.

"Ah… *Non*. I'd like to keep security tight around here."

Why did she even bother to ask? "I'll need to get some more rubber gloves and orange cleaner. This is going to take a little work." *Cinderelly, Cinderelly…* she sang to herself. It was a good thing she'd quit work.

But oh, how she hated to clean! And then she corrected herself: *No way I'm going to clean all this by myself!* How to inform Lon of that so it would sink in?

Though she hated the idea of spending money, Lina decided that some way, somehow, they'd hire a cleaning staff. Goal… C, for far-off. There was far too much work to do elsewhere to spend time on tedious tasks here. They had three worlds to care for, and one of those worlds was under severe threat.

It would take years before this place would be ready to receive guests, or need complete cleaning. They'd operate piecemeal until then. Plenty of time to convince Londo of the necessity for that crew, and by that time their impending Doomsday Deadline would be past. Just nine months or so to go before the world of Aldierra made her final decision on whether to kill all her human inhabitants or not. After that, they could all breathe easier.

One way or another.

They wandered through stacks of lumber and wallboard, insulation and sawdust. The gym's ceiling was only two stories high. Unlike the rest of the house, which was insulated from the cold mountain rock, this room's decor was pure, raw granite. The chilly testosterone setting made the perfect backdrop for three gigantic pieces of exercise equipment that looked like they could take on the world's most powerful man. A mighty more-than-hydraulic array of tubing cocooned each.

Lon peeled off his vest and shirt and stretched out on one, pushing against two tons of force as he explained that his other equipment– the really big stuff– was at his apartment in Montreal and on the ParaNet satellite. He rolled into a sitting position, studying the room. "We can put some of Jae's equipment over there," he said, pointing to the interior cavern, "but I don't know. He needs an awful lot. Guess I can dig out some more." He turned to her. "What do you have?"

"Me?" Lina blinked as she came out of a fantasy starring a shirtless Lon lifting weights. Woof. "Mostly I like to run in the neighborhood. I go to the Sportsplex to swim."

He frowned at that. "You're not running alone. Start thinking about your personal security at all times. I'm not going to let anything happen to you. Again."

"You don't have any roads around here anyway." Lina shrugged. "I'll think about it."

Once again, as she had so very many times in the past two weeks, Lina changed her vision of her own future. Instead of a cozy cottage remarkably like her own house, just big enough for her and Lon and Jae and the cats, she'd be living in… well, construction. For a long, long while. There'd be no little love nest for ten.

It would be a big love nest. Maybe that would be best. Lina blew out a cold breath and followed Lon.

Scads of wires coiled both messily and in neatly-organized tracks in the utility room. Lights blinked on hot-water storage tanks and equipment with readouts that Lina didn't recognize. Lon explained that the house was on geothermal and atmospheric pressure power, or that it would be. It was only wired in a couple places now with a thrown-together solar display, and the passive heating system wasn't closed yet or tied into the active system that it would become. He hadn't finished the backup heat, which was why their breaths left long, frosty trails.

The house went on and on. It tired her out just taking the tour. At least she could port if she had to, and Lon and Jae could fly. Did those rolly Segways come in kitty-friendly size? They'd have to get some so the cats could get from Point A to Point B in under three hours without exhausting themselves. She could picture little Katie or maybe Bran-Bran poised upright on one, ears cocked back and spine arched in attack mode as they concentrated on catching some prey running for its very life from west wing to east.

Lon deposited her on the second floor. They passed a yellow and brown plaid sofa and matching chair with dark stains on them. One cushion looked as if it had been mauled by lions.

Before Lina could comment, Lon said, "Papa Mike gave it to me." Papa Mike was Lon's grandfather. "He had this in storage from when he and Mama Ruth were young. This was the first piece of furniture that they ever bought, the one thing– Mama Ruth says– that Hal didn't destroy while he was growing up." Hal was Maximus, Lon's adoptive father.

"That's funny; it looks like *something* ate it."

"They had a dog. When I told Papa Mike I was building here, he said that since it was a real house and not just an apartment, I needed some real furniture. So he got this out and gave it to me as a starter set."

Lina considered the furniture sourly. "That was sweet of him. Tell you what, Lon, we'll donate this to a museum, complete with the story. That way it can be preserved for everyone to see."

"You get to tell Papa Mike." Lon's eyes crinkled. "I'll stand by with the defibrillators after you break his heart." From the edge of the rail-less balcony he surveyed his kingdom. "We'll need to expand," Londo declared.

Expand! The man probably didn't even buy detergent in concentrate form, either. He reeled off rooms and equipment they'd need for their new mission of saving worlds.

"If you say so," Lina murmured. Cash registers kept *ca-chinging* in her mind for some reason.

More rooms. Many more rooms. They ascended to the third floor, which was all bedrooms. "…And if you figure in one bedroom needed for each kid, if we have six–"

"I thought I only signed up for two? Or maybe three." Lina gritted her teeth. What was she gotten herself in for?

"As I recall, you okayed the possibility of adoption," Lon said sternly.

"This is a subject that needs a lot of further discussion."

"Uh huh. Six kids at least, six bedrooms at least, maybe a nursery or play-room… More bathrooms… And I want to put in an elevator for handicapped use, just in case. You never know what's going to happen, who's going to be visiting. We'll expand, *bien sûr!*"

Ca-ching. Ca-ching. Lina wanted to sit down and hold her head. Maybe Jae could talk some sense into him.

Londo opened an installed door that seemed to be a little larger than the rest. She wondered what this room was and then stopped. "This is your room," she knew.

"Our room." He watched her. A queen-sized bed sat in the center, looking very small. It was made up in mismatched linens, covers thrown haphazardly over it all.

Like Lon's Legion bedroom, this was almost empty. Lina strolled the expanse to stand next to the windows. This would be where they'd sit on quiet evenings, watching the years go by as they grew closer together. This was where they'd talk every night in the dark. This was where she would be sleeping, waking up every morning with Londo by her side. And maybe with Jae.

It was the most glorious of rooms!

"And it's such a beautiful view." Lina gazed down at the lake so far below them. Cotton-candy clouds drifted by almost low enough to touch. It was like living in heaven.

Lon slipped his arm around her waist and leaned in to her. "Like it? I was thinking of adding a balcony."

"It's a castle in the sky," she told him, "fit for a prince." She ran her hands up his broad chest, rubbing her cheek against his. So happy. So content with her prince. "Don't wake me," she whispered.

"Wake up," he chuckled, delighted that she approved. "We've still got a little more of the tour."

"The dungeons!" Lina exclaimed. "And we haven't seen the dragons' aerie." Lon tugged on her braid and she followed him across the room.

The cavernous master bathroom boasted only an orange Port-a-let and more stacks of 2x4's, but Londo showed her the biggest closets– plural– she'd ever seen, complete with dressing areas. He gave her that dazzling smile of his and pulled her back to the bedroom, walking backward.

"So whatdya think? We'll go out tomorrow and start looking for furniture, real furniture. And we'll get some real appliances, not just this temporary junk that's here now, and some plants. Lots of plants. Jae likes 'em, and I think you do, too. I'll have this place sealed up tight in no time, the heat on line… Which room do you want finished first?"

"Ca-ching, ca-ching," Lina said out loud and laughed at him.

He knew what the sound was. "Let me worry about the money, honey." He turned it into a song. "Don't you worry 'bout the money, honey…" He swung her around, enjoying her giggles.

"At least we won't need to hire decorators," she said. "You may say you copied your rooms on Sarastor from magazines, but you've got more than a touch of the stereotype in you. You have so many talents."

"I've just got taste." He made a face at her. "Unlike the rest of the world."

"The decorator gene is a good one to have, fun for friends and family. You sure you aren't coming out of the closet anytime soon?"

"Lie, I thought we'd had this conversation," he sighed. "Secrecy. People just won't understand."

"Screw 'em if they can't. People have got to learn that they can't try to control others. Everyone should be what they want to be–"

"–So long as it doesn't hurt anyone, yadda yadda." Lon clapped his palms against either side of his face and rocked back and forth, rolling his eyes.

"We're going to be starting a gay pride movement on how many worlds? And you aren't willing to announce that Valiant is bisexual?"

"It would be counterproductive."

"Uh huh. But hypocrisy is okay."

He frowned and scratched the back of his head.

Lina said, "He will so understand."

"Hm? Oh. Hal." Shaking his head. "No way will Hal ever understand. This all is secret from him, forever, get that?"

She was silent.

"I mean it, Carolina. We all agreed."

"Mine was a temporary agreement. Until we come up with a way to go public."

"Until hell freezes over." He took her hand to gaze earnestly at her. "Promise, love. We can't have a weak link in the chain. We have to make decisions and stick to them."

"It's unethical."

"It's borderline. You can live with borderline."

She considered, troubled at the lie they had already moved so far into. He let her think. Finally she set her jaw and nodded.

"Good girl."

"Arf. Until we come up with something better."

"Agreed."

"And we revisit the problem often, not every ten years or so."

"*D'accord.* We'll have a long talk when Jae gets here and decide how often you can nag me. Here's something I really like."

He gestured to the air and guided Lina to the bed, where he lay on his back. Lina did the same and realized that the tray ceiling was turning transparent. It was a huge skylight. The sun shone in, revealing a beautiful blue sky with strings of clouds stretching across it. Birds flew overhead. Lina laughed with delight.

"Welcome home, Lina," Londo said, taking her into his arms.

"It's wonderful," she said. "It's all so wonderful." She kissed him tenderly. "Have I told you today how much I love you?"

"I think so."

"Well, I still do. And I love this place. It's fabulous, like a combination fairy tale and *Lifestyles of the Rich and Famous* on a really good day."

"I'm glad." He looked into her eyes. "What did I do to deserve you?"

She laughed and squeezed him. "I believe that's my line, sir. Stop stealing from me." She rolled him over, wrestling with him, and he happily wrestled back until they were wrapped in each other's limbs, sighing and chuckling as they kissed and fondled each other.

"It's so good to be home," Londo whispered in her ear as he held her. "I was just holding on, just thinking about getting home and nothing beyond that."

"Nothing?"

They had found something to think about and do, and now they were lying naked in bed watching Stoan's press conference. He finally shut up and the picture went back to the news anchor. who added some praise about Londo and how everyone wished him well.

Lina could feel the warm glow in Lon's stomach at the approval. But the reporter finished with, "So now the line of Maximus expands. We can all hope that this means there'll be a new generation of megamegaheroes arriving soon. The universe needs more of Maximus' line, and we can all be sure that the Big Blue's looking forward to becoming a grandfather sometime in the near future."

Londo let out an involuntary groan. Lina rubbed his shoulders.

"Maximus this, Maximus that," Londo grumbled. "He wasn't even at the wedding and they still treat it as if Hal were the one getting married."

"Now, Lon, it wasn't as bad as that."

"The line of Maximus. As if he were my blood father."

"Lon…"

"Okay, okay, he didn't deserve that. He's been the best father I could have wished for, but enough's enough. 'So, Valiant, you saved the entire planet. How would Maximus have handled it?'" Lon said in a fussy reporter voice. "'Hey, Valiant, nice job. Can I get a quote from Maximus?' 'Gee, Valiant, if you're here, where's Maximus?'"

"Poor Londo Starhart," Lina said softly. "Not Londo Rand any more. Tell me, has Maximus been named Protector of Earth? Of the Three Worlds?"

Lon grunted something that might have been "No."

"Does Maximus have a cool magickal shield?"

He looked at her out of the corners of his eyes.

"I'll take that as a no. Is Maximus the sexiest, most handsome man in the entire universe?"

Lon frowned at himself. Finally he said, "I told you to call him Hal, not Maximus. He'll want you to call him Hal."

"And Hal your wonderful father is different from Maximus the legend who casts his shadow even over the legendary Valiant," Lina said. "I know you love Hal, and you love Maximus as well. It's just the outer edges of the Maximus legend that get on your nerves."

He pulled his hair back tightly from the top of his head before he let it go. "Hell, Lie. I feel guilty even for that. Hal's worked hard for that legend. He deserves every speck of it."

"And you deserve every speck of yours, too. Tell me…" Lina played with the sheet over his chest. "When he was your age, 29– How had what he had accomplished compare with what you've done? How was his rep compared to yours now?"

"Well…" Lon frowned some more as he tried to think. Hal'd gone galactic when he'd been maybe… 26, maybe 27. That had brought the galaxy's attention to him, but he'd only been Out There for that year, and sporadically since then. Lon was always on the go, a well-ensconced figure on the galactic scene. "*Eh bien,* maybe I–"

"You have time to make an even bigger legend than his, honey, if that's what you want," Lina told him. "At the very least, on Three Worlds you're going to be engraved into the hearts of the populace. That's thirty billion people right there."

"I don't want to be bigger than he is. I just want… I want to be me. I want people to see me and not his reflection. I want to leave my own mark on the universe."

She kissed his cheek. "You already have, love. And you have so much more time."

"And I'm focused now. No more… folderol for me. I can just do important things from now on."

"Yes, darling. 'Folderol.' Is that French?"

Londo loved it when she looked at him that way, as if he could do no wrong. He squeezed her hand. "So, wife. What kinds of focused and fulfilling things will we do today?"

"Goal A was get a bed." She paused. "But Jae needs to be in on choosing furniture, too. Can we wait?"

Londo rubbed his nose in thought. "It would mean we'd have to squeeze together for a while."

"I can stand that."

"*Bon.* Goal A is hereby postponed until Jae's back. I'd like to go up to Montreal and say goodbye to the apartment," he said. "I don't think I'll keep it since we're moving in here."

"Why not? It's yours, right?"

"It occurs to me that we'll have to find a place on Aldierra to live while we're there, and that plus my Legion room, plus Starhaven, plus your place, plus Jae's place on Sarastor, plus Montreal seems just a bit presumptuous."

"My place we can sell."

"You're attached to it."

"I'll just get unattached. I was thinking of selling it anyway. It's too near the road for all the cats."

They planned small adventures, tiny steps into married life, for the day. Lina liked the planning alone, as she snuggled under Lon's warm chin, feeling his soft, deep voice vibrate all the way through her. He had the most exciting places to fondle, too. Touching was magic.

"I like this marriage stuff, Lina," he whispered. "All of the pleasure, none of the guilt."

"So do I." They necked a little before she spoke again. "We're on Mountain Time here, right?"

"*Ouais.* I suppose so."

"So that means…"

Lon patted her butt. "It means that we should be up and about if we're going to the East Coast, wife." He sat up in bed, smoothing back his hair. "But just remember, it also means that when we get done there, there'll still be a lot of night left here. For marital duties."

"Aye aye, Commander Honeybear."

3

It was crisp even in the early afternoon sunshine, but the reason that Lina hugged Londo so hard was because they flew low over the rooftops of Montreal, her in his arms. The breeze never touched her, never rifled a hair on Londo's head.

"You're using your ring," Lina accused him even as she tried to cover her eyes with the same hand that clamped around Lon's neck.

Though he was quite capable of flying by his own power, Londo wore a Personal Legion Array, centralized in his control ring, a stylish clutter of ultra-ultra Sarastoran human flight technology that, among other things, formed an atmospheric bubble around the wearer, allowing for quick travel through varying atmospheric pressures without causing nasty inner-ear or breathing problems. It also allowed the Legionnaire to arrive safely at their destination, unruffled by wind shear.

"I want to get down," Lina moaned.

"Over here's St. Joseph's Oratory," Londo said as they swooped low over the ridge of the mountain, dipping almost close enough to touch the towering green dome of the great cathedral.

"It's a shrine, not a cathedral," Lon said.

It sure looked like a classic cathedral to Lina as she peeked between her fingers. And high, perched up here on the mountain. Hundreds of steps led up to it. What must it be like when winter had really taken over and those steps were covered in ice?

"It's the biggest shrine to St. Joe in the world." Londo buzzed the dome in a long roll, hanging them upside down for more than a few seconds. "Just one guy did this, just imagine. Some guy who opened doors across the street and began healing the sick, he raised the money for all of this. They made him a saint."

"That's nice. Tell me all this when we're down, please. I want to go dow-wwn." She shuddered as again he swooped. The bare trees of the mountain bowed to them in their wake. "You need to walk down where the people are, too. You need the contact."

"But they'll mob me. You don't know what the paparazzi or crazed fans can do to spoil your day, Lie."

"Just this once, Londo, our first day here. They won't be prepared. Pretty please."

"Oh, *d'accord.* Just this once."

The jumble of city rooftops separated into a grid of neighborhood streets as he settled her on solid concrete somewhere downslope from where they'd been. Lina could unclutch now and open her eyes full to catch the sights of this new world.

Londo took her hand in his. This was still new for them, and they smiled at each other, at their hands interlocked. They walked leisurely down the narrow streets of Vieux Montreal, the restored heart of the city. Eighteenth-century architecture, mansard rooflines and limestone facades contrasted against the background of tall glass buildings. Every now and then Lon would point out Mont Réal or Royal, the long hump of a mountain for which the city was named, as it peeked between buildings. Funny; it didn't look nearly as high as it had a few minutes ago. It seemed downright friendly from here.

"Hello, mountain," she said, and she could just hear a far-off, sleepy greeting from the deva of the place.

Everywhere people spoke French. Signage was French. The smells of food that permeated these streets was French, French, French. It was a piece of Europe without leaving North America.

"Montréal," Lon instructed her.

"Mont-ree-yall," Lina repeated.

"C'mon, be serious. Mon'ray-al."

"Mawnt-ree-yaawl." Lina drawled and wrinkled her nose at him gleefully. "Uncouth *Americaine*."

"Uh huh. Ah mean, maize ou-ee. That's Frayunch, ain't it?" Lina snapped imaginary gum at him as he rolled his eyes.

Lon steered them along the cobblestones of Rue St.-Paul and pointed out the sights, seeing his city through her eyes as if it were all new. They stopped often to peer into antique store windows or watch a street show as jugglers clowned for crowds enjoying the sunshine. Down at the bottom of the wide, sloping Place Jacques-Cartier lay the St. Lawrence, rimmed with ice but open to river traffic.

"I thought it was just a little river port," Lina said weakly.

"It's the largest inland port in the world," Lon corrected her. "That isn't just a river there, that's the Saint Lawrence, central North America's outlet to the world."

"Not the Mississippi?"

"Never heard of it. Your feet are cold. Let's go in here." He pulled her into one of the quaint boutiques featuring sportswear and equipment.

Lina shivered at the sudden change in temperature as Londo motioned a clerk. "Boots for her, please."

Lina protested, but walked out with some chic yet comfy boots, gloves, and a hat that Londo said suited her. He carried her old shoes in a bag plus one with a box of ice skates. He still wore his light Canadiens jacket, but then the cold didn't bother him. Londo pulled Lina along the street, impatient to show her everything.

"Yo, Valiant!" Some man gave him the thumbs-up signal as he passed them. Lon nodded pleasantly and turned back.

"See, he didn't attack you or anything," Lina whispered.

"I noticed."

Lon also noted that Lina didn't gloat as he easily handled the people who stared as he strolled past. He even murmured "*Bonjour,*" a few times when the people looked truly paralyzed with celebrity fright. Only a few whipped out their phones to take a picture. Most people didn't even notice him amid the other pedestrians. Perhaps he could come down and mingle with the norms more often. It made him feel more human– and there were things to see down here.

They watched an extravagantly-staged toy railroad display in a window. "You think Hal would like that?" Lon pointed at one section that had a ski resort set up in miniature.

"How would I know?"

Lon gave a soft snort at that. "You will," and then realized that some Japanese tourists were taking their picture. They came up to Lon with autograph books open. He signed for everyone.

"*Arigato!*" they said with vigorous nods.

"*Do itashimashite.*"

Londo grinned at Lina's impressed look for his Japanese. He wouldn't confess that he only knew a few phrases. No need to tell her all his secrets at once.

A small steel drum band played in the cold along the almost ice-less walkways beside the river, so they stopped in the gathered crowd to listen. Some of the spectators danced. The beat was infectious, and Lina bounced her head to it.

"Kitten," Lon leaned to say softly in her ear, "let's dance. It'd keep you warm."

Lina groaned inwardly. Jae had warned her that Lon loved to dance, but he hadn't had time to really begin to teach her. "I don't–"

"OoOOOhh, it is, it is!" a girlish squeal came from behind them.

"I almost didn't recognize him at first. But it is! You got somethin' to write on? A pen! Who's got a pen?"

"Oo, Valiant! Valiant!"

Londo turned around: three women, older than Lina and acting ten years younger. Americans.

"Try to keep it down," he said pleasantly as they passed him some envelopes to write on. "People are listening to the band."

"Oo, Valiant, you're even handsomer in person than on TV!"

"Would you make that out to 'Valerie, the woman I love'?"

He walked slowly to the outer perimeter of the crowd as the women followed, scribbling, "To Valerie, a lovely woman" instead. One of them used a noisy camera to take at least a dozen shots in quick, motorized succession. Then he had to pose with each of the girls for a phone shot apiece.

"Do you always walk around like a regular person?"

"What's Maximus really like? Is he as tall as you?"

"I heard that you popped up every now and then, but I never believed this could rilly happen! Oh wow, they're never going to believe this back home."

"We were just about to go get some lunch. Oo. Valiant, you wanna come with us? I'll buy."

"We could get room service. We got a big hotel room, Valiant. Lotsa room for everybody, not one of those cramped things. It's a triple."

He signed for them all, including some other people who had been attracted by the outcry, and smiled kindly if distantly. "Thanks for the offer, ladies, but I already have a lunch date."

"Are you sure?" "Pleeease, Valiant! We'd have such a good time."

"I'm sure. *Merci* just the same." He reached behind himself and drew Lina to his side. The women eyed her warily. She returned the favor, perhaps with a little too much heat. "*À bientôt,*" Lon said and steered himself and her away from the crowd. The two jogged across the street as cameras and phones clicked behind them.

"Oo, Valiant," Lina cooed in his ear once they were alone again. "Did those women just proposition you for a little orgy, or was that my vivid pornographer imagination?"

"It was your vivid pornographer imagination, love."

"Um hum. And doesn't *à bientôt* mean 'see you soon?' Do you have plans for later? Does this kind of thing happen a lot?"

"Those are nice, aren't they?" Lon pointed at some paintings in a gallery window.

"Well, they were right about one thing. You are handsomer in person than you are on TV." She snuggled closer, almost burrowing her face in the collar of his jacket. "Are you ready to go now?" she whispered.

"Bored already?"

He glanced back at cameras pointed in their direction. Lina cowered beside him, using him as a shield. He realized she hadn't expected this. She'd thought all the attention would be on him.

"Please," she said.

He put his arm around her and steered her down the street. A few followed them at a distance. "You can take it," he told her. "You've taken a lot worse than this."

She shook her head.

"Talk to me," he told her.

She just clutched him harder.

He frowned and aimed for the artists' alley ahead, empty at this time of year. Around this corner and around that… and they had some privacy.

He turned her toward him and tipped her chin so she had to look into his eyes. She had such lovely green eyes. "*Chérie,*" he said, "let me have this day. That's all I ask."

"I remember another day I gave you."

His warm smile made her smile in response. "That was the best day of my life," he told her. "But we'll have even better days in the future. Today is my day for this. You understand, yes?"

She looked away and he knew she was considering his life, the one he'd admitted to so few people. His unwilling status as a virgin, untouchable and untouched. The subject of not-so-discreet jokes that lurked under the public adoration.

"*Chérie?*"

Finally she nodded and gave him a tiny smile. Her forehead wrinkled just between her brows. This was how she looked whenever she made these jumps out of her own life for his sake. "I give you this day," she said.

She was his. She was a wonder. He wrapped her in his arms and tried to show her how much he cherished her.

Behind them, a camera clicked. Someone applauded.

"*Maudite marde,*" Lon muttered against her lips.

"More pictures." Lina shuddered before shaking her head. "I can do this. They're only interested in you, right?" Taking a deep breath, she broke the hug enough to pat his back. "It's all right," she whispered to him. "We'll ask them for copies."

They disengaged, but Lon kept his arm around her. He could feel her hidden trembles. He gave the tourists what he hoped they'd take as a dismissive salute, and then turned to seek a new route with new people who knew when to quit scaring his dear lady.

Up a long slope that Lina didn't have to walk– Lon hopped over a few blocks to shorten their trip– Vieux Montreal gave way to modern Montreal. Bustling French-speakers passed them, politely going around the ambling couple. The change of scenery did the trick. Lina's tension ebbed as she took it all in.

"Cute!" she exclaimed at stuffed toy cats on display in one window. Londo began to pull her into the store.

"Wait!" Lina hung back. "Why are we going in?"

"You want it, I buy it."

"No, no!" She swung him around. "I like the toys. I love the boots, Lon, I really do, but every time I like something does not mean you have to buy it for me."

"I want to. It's something I want to do for you."

Again it hit Lina that this wonderful man actually loved her! Never in her life had anyone done that. She hugged him fiercely. "That's all you have to do, darling, just think that you'd like to buy something. I really don't want it. I've got enough junk as it is, don't you think? Bad enough that I hoard cats."

He touched noses with her. "But you *like* it."

"I like a lot of things. That doesn't mean I need to buy them– or have somebody buy them for me."

"I like things, I buy them."

"Maybe this is what's covered by that 'compromise' stuff we talked about."

His eyes crinkled as he took her hand in his and they resumed their stroll. "So I can't buy anything for you."

"No. Absolutely not. This Three Worlds thing is going to be expensive. We've got to start counting pennies."

"No, my accountants will have to do that."

Lina sighed. *Accountants.* Not just accountant, but plural. This was going to take some getting used to. Londo laughed to hear the thought.

Montreal continued to wend its exotic way past them as they circled. Down that street a ways was Chinatown and Little Dublin. *Là-bas* was Notre Dame. What people came up to greet him now were very polite, very positive. French-speaking. Londo translated to Lina what they said. She thought that there was a possessiveness in these people's attitudes, as if Valiant were the property of Montreal. Perhaps it was just that he was a part of their extended family, or perhaps again, their family's protector. They would always finish by nodding curiously at Lina, and she'd give a shy, smiling nod back as Londo's hand sought hers.

This wasn't bad, just a few people every now and then taking his picture. What do you know, she could handle this. After all, the attention was properly on him and not on her. What had she ever been afraid of?

"Hm," Lon said at the next window display.

"You don't have to–" Lina began, but he breezed past her to push his way inside.

"Londo," Lina said as she followed him, but he ignored her.

"One of these, and one of these…" He picked through a display of cat toys, shaking pink fuzzy mice to sample the little bells attached. "Do they like these?"

"I said, you don't have to get me–"

He leveled her a cool stare. "Did I say these were for you? These are for your– MY– cats. I am allowed to buy *my* cats anything I want." He snapped his fingers at an employee. "Where are the little treadmills? Fat Cat could use one. Did we feed them too much this morning? It sure looked like it to me. How often do they get fed? I need something to make that Molly like me. And the gray one, the shy one. What's her name?"

"Ember." Lina burst into a radiant smile. He glanced down at her, the slightest of twitches working at the corner of his mouth. "No arguments?" he asked.

She put her arms around him. "I love you."

His flat smile widened and his eyes narrowed as he exulted in his cleverness. The trick with Lina was that sometimes you had to work on her bit by bit. He'd have her not only accepting his gifts but rewarding him for them in that sweet, hot way she had that drove him so insane.

He pictured what she would do when he presented her with silk and lace frills. Diamonds. Rubies. All the luxuries she'd never had. Oh yeah. He should start conditioning her right away. Tonight.

"Are you sure you don't want to keep your place here?" she asked him as they made their way down the Boulevard Ste.-Catherine. "This is a great city. A little cold, but beautiful. Nice people."

"I'll think about it," he said, and pointed to an inconspicuous doorway between two stores ahead. "There."

She examined the menu posted next to the door. "Marcus Sous la Montagne" with the English translation, "Marcus Under the Mountain," printed smaller underneath, with a cartoon of a triumphant troll in a chef's apron and toque, bolts of lightning coming out from the pan he held. "Here what? Is there a phone inside so you can call for takeout? Is it big enough for a phone inside there?"

"No, crazy woman. You open the door, it signals a shrinking ray, and we're both shrunk until we're about one millimeter tall."

"Only a millimeter? Wow."

"Then we have to fight through the cockroaches to get to our tiiiny little table." He held his thumb and index finger close together to indicate the size. "Any roaches we kill get grilled for us, free. With lemon-kiwi sauce."

"Mm, kiwi roach. Crunchy. Over rice?"

"Saffron rice or noodles, your choice," he said. "It's a nice place; you'll like it. And don't worry about all the French. I'll translate what you don't understand."

He held the door for her. They went down a long, narrow stairway single file until the place opened into a cozy bistro decorated in deep reds and wood. A waiter looked up as they approached.

"Ah, Valiant!" he said softly, not to cause any attention. "*Je vous souhaite la bienvenue, et à votre très jolie compagne. S'il vous plait, veuillez me suivre. Votre table préférée est libre.*"

"*Bon,* Michel," Lon replied.

"I thought the only usual table you had was at McDonald's," Lina whispered as they followed the waiter.

"Hush. They throw you out for mentioning that name." Londo guided her with his hand at the small of her back.

In the dimness and under civilian disguise the presence of Valiant escaped the notice of the other patrons. Londo's usual table sat in a shadowy corner, behind some supporting beams that cut it off visually from the other seating.

"*Désirez-vous la meme chose que d'habitude ou voulez-vous voir le menu? Et pour la mademoiselle?*"

"*L'habituel, pour nous deux . Et du vin,*" Londo said. "I just ordered my usual for the two of us," he explained to Lina. The food was truly excellent here; she'd be pleased and surprised as well.

The waiter tucked his chit into his short apron.

"*Un moment,*" Lina said, and he turned back to her. "*Qu'est-ce que c'est 'l'habituel'?*" she asked Lon.

His mouth opened and she wrinkled her nose at him. He tried not to chuckle but just shook his head at her. Perhaps her grasp of French was better than he'd thought. "*J'avais oublie,*" Londo said to the waiter. "*Elle est végétarienne,*" he explained. His "usual" consisted of a beefsteak entree.

"*Est-ce que vous avez une soupe végétarienne?*" Lina asked the waiter.

"*Soupe aux légumes.* <It's very good,>" the waiter replied in French.

Lina looked at Lon.

"*D'accord,*" he said, trying not to look sheepish. Of all things to forget about his sweet wife. "<Vegetarian soup for her–and herbal tea,>" he remembered to add. "*Et un peu plus de salade que d'habitude. Avec du pain, du pain frais et chaud.*" Yes, hot, fresh bread and lots of salad for her. He'd take care of her well. He'd never give her a reason to quit loving him.

"*Mais oui, mais oui. Très bien.*" The waiter went to place their order.

"I didn't think you knew enough French to carry on a conversation, Lina," he said to her inward smile. "Did you study ordering in French when you were in school? You were quite good just then. You didn't even have an American accent."

"*Je suis désolée de te causer des ennuis, Lon, mais je ne crois pas que je fait manger le bifteck ces jours-ci.*" She tried not to smirk as she said it and didn't succeed.

He sat still for a moment, raised his index finger in the air as if to make a point, and then decided to mock-punch her on the chin. "And here I've been translating for you all afternoon. Since when do you speak French? Well, that is?"

"I found some linguatapes a few days ago. Suddenly all six years of plodding through French class came back to me and then some. Lon, do you know how much I would have paid for those tapes back in high school?"

He laughed.

"And I didn't want to be Lucy Ricardo to your Ricky, once the honeymoon's over and you start yelling at me."

She'd learned French for him. He took her hand and twined his fingers through hers. "I don't think it's ever going to come to that," he said, gazing in her eyes.

She smiled. "Neither do I. But I'm going to learn Feithi too, just in case."

He considered. "Good idea. Give me that program when you're done." He drew her into his arms and kissed her slowly. Yes, this marriage stuff was just fine.

They talked of setting up their home, perhaps a party to introduce Lina to the ParaNet.

"That's not necessary," Lina said as she tried her salad. It had violet flower blossoms in it. She'd never before had a salad with flowers. Nice.

"Of course it is. You've got to meet them sometime. You'll like them. Well, most of them."

She frowned at her fork. "How will they take the news? Will they hang me or just kick me off Earth?"

"Neither. If they try anything, we'll just refer them back to the Legion. Oh, Dragonlord will investigate you first thing; you can bet on that. He's a good guy, but suspicious to the bone. Cooperate with him as much as you can. Just be yourself."

"Dragonlord." She felt unreal. She was going to meet the heroes she'd seen on television for all these years! "What about Maximus?"

"Call him Hal. Well, maybe not at first, but he'll offer. Take him up on it at the first opportunity, or he'll think you're a snob after name appeal."

"When in reality I'm just quaking in my flip-flops."

"He's off Earth now, anyway. Still no word from him."

"Is he okay?"

"It's just part of being Maximus. When he disappears it's usually only a couple days at a time. Sometimes it's like this, weeks." Lon shrugged as he tore off more bread. "It depends on what he's doing. Hush-hush missions sometime call for radio silence."

"And you? Is that part of being Valiant?"

"I'm usually only gone for a day, maybe two at most. Except for when I'm with the Legion, about every three weeks, depending on how my team's scheduled. Then I take a week-plus. But now you can come along, and with the new schedule we shouldn't be gone for more than a day or two at a time, maximum. I'm thinking that most cases they'll just call me, I'll port in, and be back by suppertime."

He smiled so warmly at her. "Very convenient. My team will enjoy the regular hours. Mimik's been hinting that she's overworked, taking up my slack. I'll be able to reshuffle the team, only have Mimik take on Leader responsibilities when they're assigned long-range duty, which part-timers don't have."

"That's reassuring."

"So no worries there. I want you to concentrate on safety, Kitten. That news conference this morning marked the starting point for the need for security. From now on, that's Goal A. We've got to set up some basic contingency plans." Londo considered as he dug into his steak with gusto. "If I want you to port out somewhere to safety, I'll say… 'rhubarb.' That means you port *then,* no questions asked. Just you– out."

"'Rhubarb?'"

"Yeah."

"I like rhubarb pie. I grow it, rhubarb, that is, not the pie. Although that would be nice, growing pies. It would save a lot of time."

"*Rhubarb,* Lina."

"I was thinking that the next cat I got would be named Rhubarb. A big yellow male, you know, like in the old baseball movie. I suppose now the firstborn son will get the name."

Lon had to stop at that. "Rhubarb? And if it's a girl?"

"Rhubarbie, of course. And if it's non-binary, RhuPaul."

He cocked his head and pointed his knife at her. "Back to being serious. *Rhubarb.*"

"But *rhubarb* is a funny word."

"It'll be a deadly serious one now. I want you to practice with it. I want to sneak up behind you and say 'rhubarb' and see how fast you can port out. It'll be an automatic trigger. Anytime we're anywhere, keep a safe place in mind, ready to rhubarb just in case."

She sighed. "Yes, Londo. Do we have a word for us– all of us, if need be– to rhubarb? *Vaminos?*"

"We might actually use that in conversation sometime. I was going to learn Spanish this year."

"You don't know that yet? With Latinos the fastest-growing minority in the US? And you with a house in non-Francophonic Wyoming?"

"*We* have a house in Wyoming. That's why I want to learn. That plus I've been stumbling around linguistically in Spanish countries forever."

"'Oneferall.'"

"What?"

"Three Musketeers. Three Worlds. All for one and one for all. 'Oneferall,' all squashed together; it's something we'll never say otherwise. Unlike 'rhubarb.'"

"*D'accord, d'accord.* Not 'rhubarb.' What do we use?"

"'Shields up.'"

"And what if I want something fancy to say with my new shield?" Londo asked. "'Shields up!' I like that. I think I'll use that. 'D'Artagnan.' That's the word."

"D'Artagnan? D'Artagnan." Lina tasted the feel of it. "Okay. Michael York. He was so sexy in that movie. Not the lousy Disney one. And I've never gotten into that BBC thing, even with Dr. Who in it. Ooh, Michael in black with that big feather in his hat. Woof."

"Not Michael York. 'D'Artagnan' for you to escape, and 'Oneferall' for all of us. Learn the words, Lina."

"You're the one who has to remember the words, Lon. All I have to do is react to them." She gave him a sunny smile and then returned her attention to her lovely salad.

Toward the end of the meal, Londo fished out his cell phone. Within minutes he had two tickets to that night's sold-out symphony charity concert.

"I didn't think you liked classical," Lina said as they emerged onto the street again, back into the chill and hurrying people. "Aren't you more a rock and jazz man?"

"You said you love classical; therefore, we go," Londo explained.

"Oh, thanks. So who'd you bribe if the concert was sold out?"

He grinned. "One of the perks about being Valiant. Not only did I get tickets, I got great seats."

"Wonderful. Can I wear jeans, or–"

"D'Artagnan," he said.

A question passed over her face before realization set in. He watched her, felt her thoughts as she sought for what would be a safe place. She considered her own home, then discarded the idea. Then– she vanished.

Before he could suck in the breath he'd caught, she returned. "I'll get better," she assured him.

"I know you will. Good choice of Starhaven. I'll make it completely secure within the week." Londo checked his watch. "You feel like exercising off some of those lunch calories now, cabbage?"

"Mm… Define 'exercise.'" She wiggled her eyebrows at him.

4

Once outside, Londo lifted her and their bags up with one movement, as lightly as if she were a paperback book, and gave the smallest of hops. They soared hundreds of feet into the air as Lina grabbed him around the neck.

"Give me a little warning next time!"

He just laughed as they arced over downtown, its web of neighborhoods sprawling below them, the river circling the city with its central mountain. They descended next to a park that jutted into the river. "Bonsecours," Londo announced the name of the arena-sized skating rink. There had to be thirty people out on it, not nearly enough to crowd each other. An icy moat surrounded the area, overseen by an imposing domed building not far away.

Lon helped her on with her new skates, then expertly tied his own worn ones that she'd ported in, following his mental directions. She clomped around on the side of the rink, trying to get used to balancing on blades.

"You get me to do the strangest things," she accused him.

"And have you regretted any of them? You won't fall down," Londo promised. "Well, not much. Here." He took her hands in his and she held on for dear life as he towed her out to the middle of the rink, away from the circling skaters. A few people slowed down and stopped when they recognized him, but most weren't looking for a celebrity and thus didn't notice.

Lina took a few hesitant steps on the ice. Lon supported her every time she began to wobble. "You're doing great," he told her. She began to take tiny gliding strokes by herself. He skated boldly around her in circles, coaching her with his booming voice.

Lina colored. "Everyone's looking."

"Imagine that. Now make a big push here and stretch it out." She did and lost her balance, but he caught her before she could fall. "Do it again," he instructed, and kept at her until she began to glide across the ice in long rhythms.

"Look at me!" Lina exclaimed with a laugh. "I'm skating!"

"*Pas mal,* not bad at all," he approved, and they made a couple of leisurely laps of the place hand-in-hand. "I knew you could do it. Now try this."

Dashing away, he kept low, running the tips of his fingers along the ice, then bounding up to startle some couples skating close together. He arced around on the outside edge of his blades, spiraling through the thickest of the skaters. "<Coming through!>" he called in French.

"Londo!" Lina cried.

He raced down the other side now, skating backward with a merry grin on his face, not taking any note of who might be behind him. Somehow he managed not to collide with anyone, although once some people reacted as if he were about to and ended up really getting in his way. He popped up in the air and jounced over them, to resume his glide on their other side. He caught her eye as she clapped and laughed at his antics. He was showing off for *her!*

"Oh, but you're setting a horrid example for the children," Lina murmured, knowing that he could hear her. "What if they try to do that?"

Lon backflipped without breaking his lateral motion, and now sailed around on his fingertips, balanced on one hand. He circled her fast and tight.

"Let's see them try this," he told her. Then he was gone and buzzing through the knots of skaters. Most had stopped to watch the show and applauded. Lon gave them an upside-down salute as he passed. Now he tumbled across the ice like a gymnast, now he performed a triple-loop that hung for long seconds in the air.

Oh, my. Lina had fallen in love with Londo Rand and she adored him… but this was *Valiant.* She'd always been fascinated with Valiant, and here he was, in person! She watched his hijinks in breathless amazement, not noticing her feet sliding ever so slightly away from each other.

For the rest of her life she'd be able to watch him in action, in person. She hugged herself, knowing that rush would never wear off. Look at him– he was ever-renewing, springing energy that delighted in showing off. Any spotlight would naturally gravitate his way, and he would perform to it. Lon was a publicity hound, but he deserved every moment of– Whoops. Lina caught herself just before she could fall and cautiously maneuvered her wandering feet back to steadier positions.

She put her hands on her hips to disguise her embarrassment at getting into such a position. "What a Leo!" she teased her husband. Lon raced around her in dizzying circles until she suddenly sat down.

"I may be a Leo but you're an ice butt," he taunted, and returned to harassing and thrilling the crowd. Those who could, took videos of him. He paused every now and then to sign things that people held out.

Lina struggled to her feet in quite an ungainly fashion just in time for him to swoosh past her and send her sprawling again. His raucous laughs could be heard from here all through the Old Port. Halfway up to her feet, her butt the highest portion of her anatomy, she turned to shake her fist at him, but he was gone behind her. She hauled herself carefully to her full height only to find him rocketing behind her the other way. Whups– shouldn't have looked. He caught her as she began to fall and skated around the perimeter of the rink carrying her in his arms.

"Now this I could get used to," she said, laying her head against his broad chest.

"You could, hm?" Definitely a devil in those brown eyes today!

"I– Watch out, Lon!" He was barreling directly at a group of people, two of whom were filming them. There wasn't room to stop–

Londo threw her high in the air, screeched to an ice-shredding halt in front of the group, bowed to the cameras, and then reached out to catch Lina as she plummeted to earth again with a drawn-out, ear-splitting shriek.

It was seconds before Lina could find speech and coherent thoughts. "Londo Rand! You crazy lummox! How could you–"

"Now now, such language!" Londo smiled at the cameras and bowed again with her still in his arms. "What *will* the children think?" Three puffs of breath of varying qualities repaired the rink damage better than any zamboni could. Then he swung her up and over his shoulder, patted her rear end, and took off into the air.

Lina battered at the back of his jacket. "You insane— You put me down! Now!"

Londo swooped down to collect their shoes and packages, then arced high up again. "It's a big drop. You might go boom," he observed coolly. They climbed to a level with the highest stories of Montreal's tallest towers. He shifted her back properly cradled in his arms. "I think playtime's over. We have to get down to more mundane matters now. I need to see my agent."

Lina huffed before she decided that his mental gears had truly shifted. All thoughts of playing in front of the cameras were gone. He could do that, switch his focus 100% in the blink of an eye. Someday she might get used to it.

Like flying. It seemed a tenth— maybe a quarter— less frightening now. Maybe that was because Lon had just rescued her from a certain death-fall. "Just give me some warning next time. I almost wet my pants. You have an agent?"

"Sure." Lon laughed. "An agent, accountants, secretarial staff, an entire corporation full of lawyers, you name it. My agent coordinates appearances, handles press releases and interviews, things like that."

Lina thought of all the magazines alone that Londo appeared in, and realized that being his agent could probably be a full-time job.

"They have a staff that handles a handful of people," he said and looked at her. "You want to sign on?"

"With an agent? You're kidding," she said.

He chuckled. "You still haven't figured it out, have you, *chérie?* You're going to be famous in a little while, either as Speaker for the Three Worlds or just as— you should pardon the expression— Mrs. Valiant."

"Yeesh," she said.

"Yeesh indeed. Janet can handle it. We'll put Jae with her, too, as long as we're there."

"Do we tell her about the Triune?"

"Hell, no. She's one of the world's biggest blabbermouths. That's why she's so good. Let me think of her place for you. She's in town."

With the picture so clear in Lon's mind for Lina to build upon, they ported to an upscale reception room. Londo held the both of them inches above the carpet until they could switch footgear. The pert receptionist had been looking away as they ported in, and she jumped when she turned around.

"Oh– Valiant! I didn't see you come in. Good afternoon."

"Hi, Cathy," Lon said as he deposited his skates into their shopping bags. Lina had pulled that porting trick of hers, porting off the skates at the same time she ported on her boots, beating him.

Lina looked around, sliding out of her coat. Other affiliated offices and a hallway opened to the sides of the room. Judging from the view outside the wide windows, they were high in a downtown office building. Two people waiting in chairs stared unabashedly at the famous hero.

"Is she in?" Londo asked.

Cathy replied, "She was about to leave for the day, but I think she's still here."

"Yes, she is," Londo said, nodding his head at a wall as if he were peeking through.

"Then go on in." The receptionist smiled at him. She stared at Lina as she accompanied Londo. Valiant's arm was twined around Lina's waist. Cathy pushed her bag, packed to go home for the day, back into her bottom desk drawer.

Lon opened the oak door for Lina. "Janet!" he called into the room. "Got a minute? Or ten?"

A smartly tailored woman with a graying pageboy looked up from packing her attaché case and gave a genuine smile. "Londo! Where have you been for the past week? You've missed three major interviews." She took in the uncharacteristic informal clothing as well as the woman he was with, before she came around her desk for introductions.

"Janet Chinn, the best agent on the planet," Londo said with a grin, "this is Lina Starheart."

"How do you do?" Janet offered her hand to Lina, who shook it.

"My wife."

Janet's hand stopped in mid-shake.

"Very nice to meet you," Lina said. "I've heard good things."

Janet almost collapsed onto the edge of her desk. "Wuh–"

Londo rocked from the balls of his feet to his heels and back, not bothering to hide his grin. "I've changed my name to Starheart, too. You'll have to redo all your paperwork now. Sorry. That's S-t-a-r-h-e-a-r-t."

"No 'e,'" Lina declared.

"With an 'e.'"

"We have not made the final decision. Don't sneak your 'e' into this without a full discussion of the matter."

"I was not sneaking any 'e.'"

Janet looked from one to the other as they argued. "Where are my manners?" she asked. "Congratulations… Lina, was it? Short for…"

Londo snapped back to attend to Janet. "Carolina. As in the state."

"As in the accent, too. Valiant's wife. Oh, the press will eat this up." Janet looked hard at Londo and his broad smirk. "You could have told me before it happened. The entire world press corps would have been fighting to attend the wedding."

"It was rather sudden."

Janet's eyebrow went up and quickly back down as she shifted her gaze to Lina's stomach.

"No, I'm not pregnant," Lina said. "Things just happened quickly."

"And it was off-planet, too, at Mega-Legion Headquarters."

"She knows about them?" Lina asked.

"Sure. She's my agent."

"And you tell your agent everything," Janet assured Lina. "Simply every-thing. You have a video or something, don't you?"

"We do," Londo said, "and more. Lina's a parahuman, and she's just been named by the planet itself as Speaker for the Earth. Speaker for the Three Worlds, actually, but all anyone here will be interested in is the Earth. A friend of mine, Jan Rallene, has been named Minister of the Earth."

"And Londo's now Protector of the Earth," Lina added for Janet's information.

"*Oui. En tout cas,* we were wondering if you'd like to take both of them on as clients. I think they'll start getting a lot of press in a week or two."

Janet's eyes sparkled. "Sounds like an interesting challenge. If it's all that it seems, I'd have to hire another assistant or two to handle the load," she said. "And hell, Londo, I'll have to hire a temporary staff for the wedding news alone."

"We don't want to announce yet. We've just gotten back to Earth. We need to settle in, maybe take a honeymoon–"

"You have to announce before that! People will be mad enough that they missed the wedding. You have to give them the thrill of thinking that there's a chance of seeing you two sneaking around on your honeymoon."

"With the way things have been going, there might not be one," Lina said.

"Things have been… busy," Londo explained.

"You poor things," Janet commiserated. "Too busy to honeymoon and you aren't going to announce yet. Still, we'll need to have pictures ready for when you do. We'll take them today. Now. Let me get a photographer over here."

"Okay," Lon said.

"What?" Lina was aghast. "Lon… I…"

He took her hand in his. Her face had gone pale. "This is a part of this day," he told her softly. "You gave it to me."

She swallowed. Londo could feel her trying to find a way around fulfilling her promise.

"Remember?" he prompted. She wasn't the kind to welch on her word. It was a weakness of hers. A wonderful weakness in his ethical wife.

"Pictures."

For a moment Londo thought she'd be physically ill. Her fingers clamped on his; he could hear her heart pounding in fear. "It'll just take a few minutes," he urged. "We'll get it over with and it'll be done. C'mon, you have to admit that we need these."

She licked her lips, but the color did not return to her face. "We aren't dressed for it," she finally decided.

"We have some wardrobe here," Janet told her quickly.

Lon gave Lina a little booster hug. "They have a studio in house. It's efficient when you're doing shots on the run. We'll be out within the hour. Then you can breathe."

Janet was already on the phone. "Cathy, get Anthony here. Pronto. I don't care if he is; tell him that he'll throw himself off the nearest bridge if he doesn't get over here *tout de suite.* If I know Anthony, he'll be here in five minutes." She hung up, then turned back in her chair. "While we wait, Londo," she said, nestling her chin on her palm, "tell me everything."

Eight minutes later, someone knocked on the office door even as it opened. A fortyish man with curly dark hair poked his head inside. "This had better be good," he said before his eyes could tell his brain who was in the room. Mediterranean accented his voice. "Hello, Valiant. Good to see you again."

"*Salut,* Anthony. Got time for a quick session for the two of us?"

"Hm." Anthony circled Lina as Londo balanced on the arm of her chair. He scrutinized her face and figure. "Good mouth and cheekbones." Anthony nodded as if to himself. "Very nice eyes."

She watched him warily.

"Glamor shots?" Anthony asked Londo as he tipped Lina's chin this way and that. "What are we promoting?"

"*Non,* no advertising. Just something we can give the papers when needed. Plain and simple, us gazing serenely into the distance, that sort of thing."

Anthony's thumb dropped from Lina's chin, and he turned to Londo. "I do fabulous wedding photos, Valiant. Have you seen my portfolio? I can clear my calendar anytime."

"Right now we've got a half-hour, maybe forty-five minutes," Londo said. "Let's just get a shot or two today and come back for more later."

Before Lina knew it, there were hot rollers in her hair and she was looking as far up as she could while a strange young woman applied eye liner to her lower lid. Janet hovered nearby with a recorder in hand as Lon helped Anthony with lights.

Janet needed a bio. Lina gave her information as quickly, as succinctly as she could, while she tried to figure out how the beautician was applying the makeup so she could replicate it later. Age, place of birth, education, mascara. Janet winced when Lina told her she'd just quit the adult products business, but soon Janet tapped the recorder to stop it. Lina breathed a sigh of relief.

A painted woman stared uneasily back at her in the mirror as Londo and Anthony strolled over. She raised her hand to hide her rollers from Lon and then put it back down in defeat. He'd seen already and yet still smiled so encouragingly at her.

Lina closed her eyes as he left to change into a sweater. She tried to draw on her inner strength for courage to get through this, but still cameras pointed at her scared her to death. They brought up the voices of her parents telling her not to fidget, about how her hair was a mess, about how she was the ugliest girl ever born. *Muttbutt!* The pictures were always unacceptable because so was she.

This is not your parents, Lon said. **You look gorgeous. I want a billion pictures of you just like this.**

The makeup lady brushed Lina's hair vigorously as Janet fired questions at Lon. "This is so exciting," the woman whispered to Lina, but she didn't think so. *Please, Lord, make it be over quickly.* Could a person die from having their picture taken?

Lon took a few minutes to style his hair into perfection.

"That's it?" Lina asked. "No makeup?"

"Do I need any?" he asked her with a smirk.

She made a face at his outrageousness. "You're still the fairest of them all."

Janet laughed uproariously. "She's got you pegged, Lon," she said. "Lina, I've never seen a man preen so much. He'll stomp around in a pool of lava and go roll in a mud slide, but the only thing that really bothers him is that the camera might catch him at the wrong angle."

"Does not," Lon retorted, fixing a final flyaway hair in the mirror.

When they settled in front of the camera on two stools, wide silver lighting umbrellas to the side and front, Lina tried to do what Anthony instructed, but it was all she could do to keep her hands from rising to hide her ugly face. The constant clicking was like rifle shots, aiming at her gross imperfection.

"I'm sorry," she repeated again and again.

She trembled violently in Lon's arms. "Just a little camera shy," he said lightly and then gave her a squeeze. "Anthony, where are your car keys? Hold them over your head and rattle them for her. Janet, you make funny noises back there. Quack like a duck."

"I'm s-sorry," Lina said. She blinked hard. Her eyes glistened unnaturally in the spotlight.

Lon ran his thumb down her spine. "Maybe this wasn't such a good idea," he murmured in her ear.

"I can do this," she vowed, and bared her teeth at the situation and camera. There: a smile. Anthony's face twisted in dismay.

"These will be the outtakes," Lon decided. He made a gorgon face, complete with sticking-out tongue, at Anthony. "How's that? Let's see what you can do, Lie."

He puffed out his cheeks and pulled down his lower eyelids for her. "Wait, here's my Hal," he said, and pulled off an ultra-serious, hang-dog look that did slightly resemble his adoptive father on a very bad day. Despite herself, Lina laughed.

Lon told her jokes and was so dear in trying to put her at ease. Then he started telling Janet and Anthony about their little romp on the ice this afternoon, playing up how foolish Lina had looked sitting in the middle of the rink. At one point Anthony laughed so hard he had to lean over and support himself on his knees to keep from falling down.

Londo turned Lina to him and assured her that she'd get better at this. With a start she realized that Anthony's camera had been clicking the entire time.

"Perfect!" the photographer pronounced.

"Cheaters!" Lina said under her breath. But at least it was over. She was still alive. She'd had enough pictures taken to last a decade at least. No more photographs for her, not ever!

Emperor Yanist-Glory swept into the conference room without warning. It gave him pleasure to note how his councilors and ministers jerked to attention as if struck by a spark of lightning. He took his seat at the long table, ready for another day's work maintaining control over his mammoth star empire.

Yanist-Glory's mother had taught him to keep the bonds tight. Never allow exceptions, never show lenience. Fear could enslave even free men, and Yanist-Glory made sure that all feared him. His too-trusting mother certainly had, as he had supervised his man throttling her stringy imperial throat until she was dead and beyond resuscitation.

The ministers came out of their bows to take their places. In their eyes he could see the ever-present edge of fear. Was it sharper today? But there was a new, young face here, a cocky one, not fearful at all.

"Naril," he growled at the boy who looked so much like his younger self. "Why in blaze are *you* here? You overestimate your rights."

"Father," Naril-En began, and then corrected himself, "Your Imperial Majesty, I thought you'd be interested as to what Rikli-En has been up to."

"Rikli," Glory drawled out the name. "One worthless brat comes to tattle on another."

"He doesn't think he's so worthless." Naril-En tried to hide his triumphant smirk. Idiot boy, to think that no one else saw. "He's been using the Imperial Treasury to prepare for the great Joiry Balls next month. Last night all the networks covered his shopping spree. I assumed you'd have been too busy to watch."

"The Imperial Treasury? Who gave him access to that? We'll have their head!"

"Your Imperial Majesty." Old Gharma hesitantly lifted her hand for attention. "I looked into the matter as soon as I heard. Rikli-En approached the Treasury Master and brought to his attention that if he were representing the Empire and the Imperial House at the Joiry Balls, he should be dressed and attended suitably for the occasion. The Master made moneys from the public relations section of the Treasury available to the Heir."

"The Heir?" The emperor's left eyebrow arched.

"Forgive me, Majesty," Gharma said, "but he is widely considered to be the Heir until you officially designate otherwise. His position holds precedent."

The councilor cringed as the emperor sat back in his chair. "Here we are," Glory intoned, a terrible rumble in his voice, "trying to hold an empire together.

Increasing our borders, providing for those citizens who merit being provided for… And that pup of a boy is trying to bleed us dry! We will not have it."

His penetrating gaze took them all in turn. "Tell the Master of our Treasury to total how much that so-called heir of ours has stolen from us. Then tell him that he is Master no more, if we can't trust him with our own holdings. He is responsible for replenishing the Treasury out of his own pocket."

"But– But your majesty! That much money– I doubt if he makes that much in ten years!"

"Then sell him. Sell him into indentured servitude somewhere and confiscate his wages until everything is paid up. Sell his family, as many as you think it will take to repay the amount in… three years."

"Y-yes, Majesty. It is done." Councilor Sien-Velli touched the information onto her padd.

"And after the three years are up and the debt repaid," Yanist-Glory went on, "have him arrested and executed for stealing from the Treasury. But don't tell him that until then. No, no, don't tell him."

The emperor relaxed at his decision. He loved his irony, and it was his pleasure to find the irony in life even if he had to create it himself. Life held so few pleasures.

"Yes, Majesty."

"Is there any other *society news* before we get down to our real business?" Yanist-Glory's surveyed his people. But his councilors looked away from him, looked at each other and then down to the table. His son could not meet his eyes.

"Your Imperial Majesty," Gharma volunteered in a small voice.

The emperor blinked. Society news? "What could it be?" he asked.

"The boy. Rand."

Glory's eyes narrowed. "He's hardly a boy any more. As much as it would please us to count him among the dead, he's still alive and growing older."

"Yes, the man then. Valiant."

"Valiant?" he prompted.

"Apparently, Your Majesty, he has gotten married. We received a message out of our Sarastor embassy that–"

The sudden intake of breath frightened his ministers. "Married. Married!" The emperor broke out in a fit of laughter. "Valiant married! That's rich! Who, tell us, who is the girl? Or *what* is she? Is she something like what the wretch's miserable father got?" The emperor's lip curled up on the right and what could have been a laugh escaped.

"Majesty, she is Terran. A para, a megapara."

That stopped the emperor's smile. "A megapara. Invulnerable, too?"

"Unknown. One would suppose that if she were able to, ah, have relations with Valiant, she would have to be, wouldn't she?"

"That blonde one… Farthy? Fortee? We should have had her killed long ago, but we didn't think that–"

"N-no, Majesty. This is a new one."

The emperor's expression turned into a glower. He set his fists on the table. "Valiant married. Valiant enjoying life. We can't have that." He glanced around the room, picking… choosing… His eyes fell on Naril, his second semi-legitimate son.

"No," he finally decided. "Not you. Not Launch either. That insufferable brother of yours– Someone find Rikli and tell him that he has a new official duty. Something to keep him busy between parties. Let's make him earn his stolen keep."

"Yes, your Imperial Majesty?"

"Tell him that he is to take care of this wife."

"Sire… Your Imperial Majesty," Councilor Sien-Velli offered and he nodded to her. "Could this be the time–?"

"For our little surprise?" the emperor asked. A faint smile came to him but he shook his head. "No, no, we worked too hard too long waiting for that. When we finally set our sights on Earth and all its paraheroes–" he almost spat the word– "with the mighty Rands on the front battle lines, that is when we trigger that. That's when we set Rand against Rand. One, two… maybe three years more, no more than that, but not now, not now. All those paraheroes will be too busy hiding from that fallout to protect their precious world!"

He shook his head again, this time in wonder. "The mightiest beings in the universe, and yet they leave themselves so vulnerable. It seems to us that they ask for someone to hurt them, does it seem that way to you?"

Yanist-Glory was satisfied to see respect next to the fear around the table. He chuckled lightly. "So now young Rand has a wife. Lovely. Send Rikli to get her. Kidnap, a lingering incurable disease… No killing, not yet. We want to draw this out. Get something we can transmit to those Rands in bits and pieces before we send her body back the same way. Otherwise we don't care, so long as it hurts those damned Rands!"

The emperor leaned back in his chair and laughed softly. "It's not a question of if she gets it, but who gets her and when. We want to be the who. And we want it done now."

5

The sun hovered above the western horizon. Occasional headlights punctuated rush hour as they walked away from Janet's office. Londo felt Lina shiver even after he put his arm around her. It was chilly and getting colder. "You did great," he said.

"No I didn't."

"You did great considering what I put you through. I'm sorry."

That earned him a wan smile. "It had to be done. You were right. I think…"

"…That you'll be subjected to many photographers from here on out." He sighed. "It comes with the job, Kitten. We'll find a way through this. And in the meantime–"

"Mm?"

"I'll try not to surprise you with so many scary things."

"You love having your picture taken."

"*Euh…*"

"You take great pictures. I don't. Never have. Horrible things."

"These today were definitely not horrible. I'm going to take lots of pictures of you, and they'll all be *formidable*. You'll see." He rubbed his nose. "Ah, *oui*, fair warning: there will be more pictures tonight."

Lina let out a wounded squeak.

"Nothing to be done about it. Ignore the cameras if you can. I know; when the paparazzi descend, look at me instead. I like it when you look at me, not them. *Voyons*… You'll need a fancy dress. Do you have anything? *Not* the crappy suit."

"I've got the black dress from the funeral. Or the red with the little cape. Shoo, they don't wear capes here, do they? I've got to get back to a Terran mind-set."

"*Non,* those won't do. You don't have anything else?"

She shook her head as they waited for a light. "I'm not like you, Lon, not on the ten best-dressed list. I don't know what to wear. It's ignorance, not choice, and now I have you wearing the same thing."

He just smiled at her in that silly, crooked way of his. "I like showing the world which team I root for. Like you like showing what TV show you watch. How many *Star Trek* shirts do you own, anyway?"

"There's a time and place–"

"Including teaching you about clothes. We'll get to that. I know some people. The only thing you have to worry about tonight is a nice gown. A beautiful gown to do you justice."

"A gown. For me," she said. It made sense; she'd need a basic dress that she could wear to parties. Londo was probably invited to fancy parties all the time. Now she'd be invited, too.

She could wear those fake pearls she'd bought a couple years ago, but she didn't think that her scuffed black shoes would work. They needed resoling, too. Neither could she wear her black soled tights on Earth. Oh dear, she really wasn't ready for any of this!

"You trust me?" Lon asked.

His words jerked her back to the real world, just in time not to trip over a curb. "Of course. Absolutely."

"*Bon.*" The steady look he gave her reminded her that she'd promised to always trust him after he'd vowed to deserve that trust. "Trust me in this, then. Say it: you'll accept the dress I pick out for you."

This did not sound legit. "Ah…"

"Say it."

"Okay, deal. For tonight." A series of display windows with fashionable streetwear mannequins caught her attention. "Would that store carry some nice things?"

"We don't shop there," Lon said. "They carry furs."

Lina stopped dead in her tracks. "Furs!" she hissed. "Where's the nearest bottle of ketchup?"

Lon pulled her away from the front door of the establishment. "Down, girl. We aren't going in there." He steered her up the street until they got a good view of the block before them. He pointed at a down-arrow marking a Metro entrance. "We're going over there. I know a place where they've never sold furs."

"Well, good. I should hope they never sold furs on the subway. Wouldn't that get kinda crowded? I mean, having to elbow your way through the racks to get off?"

"Not le Metro. The Underground City. It has miles of stores and restaurants and theaters, everything you could want, and we keep it nice and cozy inside. Tink would be able to run around naked if she wanted."

"Really? It is kind of chilly out here. Is this as cold as it gets?" Lina tapped her coat to increase its heat.

"This is warm, Kitten. During winter it gets *cold* here."

"You're talking to a Southern girl. I'm allergic to cold weather."

"You're going to have to get un-allergic, living in the Rockies."

"I'll buy some long underwear, you know, the kind with the buttons on the flap in back. Just like in the movies."

"Crotchless." Lon panted at her like a dog. "Oh boy."

She swatted him on his shoulder. "You have one thing on your mind, Monsieur Parahero."

"Always."

"At least I'll never buy a fur coat to keep the cold away. Ketchup, Londo. Let's go get a case tonight and lie in wait for people. Or will it freeze in mid-air as you squirt it?"

He laughed and settled his arm more comfortably around her. "Paint works so much better than ketchup."

"Oil or latex?"

He bunched up her long auburn braid and tugged gently on it. "We can always experiment. What colors shall we try?"

"Hey!" She batted at his hand as he examined the situation. He avoided her easily.

"Maybe a nice green or a teal," he said critically.

"Maybe pink like Andri," Lina huffed as she tried to duck away from him. "Maybe Valiant needs a new look, too?"

He immediately released her. "I'm fine as it is," he said, but Lina already held a can, looking used, in her hand. The mixing marble inside it rattled loudly as she shook it.

"Crayon red," she pronounced. "That should make very nice work of you, shouldn't it?"

"Lina!" He tried ducking away from her, but she aimed the can at him. He ran down the street, laughing, with her in hot pursuit. People stopped to watch the couple. Lon cartwheeled and jumped up to hang above the pavement, then let her chase him on the ground some more. Another jump, a twirl in the air—and where did he get to?

He grabbed her tightly from behind and she gave a little shriek. "Even," he told her. "Say it. Get rid of it."

"Oh, all right," she said, porting the can back home. "Even."

He kissed her quickly. They laughed as they made their way down the street, hand in hand.

An escalator took them in the direction of the subway station, but an entire stainless steel world opened to the side, an expansive, modern shopping mall. Lina leaned over a balcony and started to count stories. They were midway up in the complex. A glass ceiling revealed the evening sky, and a stories-high fountain shifted its spray pattern as an elevator swept up the wall beside it. Kiosks and fast food and department stores– the usual made up the mall.

Lon took her hand and led her through the city beneath the city, stopping every now and then to look into windows at displays.

"Too chi-chi," he'd usually say, and move on.

"I would think someone who was on the best-dressed lists would like chi-chi," Lina said.

"*Mais non.* You want to take classic and give it a twist. You don't drip liquid latex on yourself and roll around in feathers and then go out." He paused. "Or do you like this stuff?"

She eyed the mannequins sourly. "I don't do drugs," she told him.

"Just for that I'm keeping you. There," he said, pointing ahead. "There's where we're going to find it."

He took her coat as they entered an elegant store called Mode Chaude. Lina took one look at the decor and knew this was going to be even more expensive than Abercrombie & Fitch. *Danger, danger, Will Robinson! Hide your wallet!*

Londo led them on a serpentine course between scattered customers and sedate displays. Real upholstered chairs, not folding ones, were grouped around low tables with flower arrangements. Those had to be silk, didn't they? An older man sat in one area, reading a sports magazine as he waited. There were no brand posters, no neon, no prices to be seen. The muzak was classical.

As Lon and Lina reached the halfway point into the store, a security guard stepped forward to follow the too-casually-dressed people. Lina stared him down. Then he stalked at a more respectful distance.

Londo squeezed Lina's hand. "Don't worry about it," he whispered to her. "He'll realize who I am soon enough."

"Oh. Just how many people simper around you anyway?" What must Lon's normal life be like?

"Too many. Here's what I had in mind." He stopped in front of a mannequin dressed in diamonds, pearls and red vinyl that plunged down to her navel in front and her butt crack in the rear.

"Londo! You wouldn't make me wear something like that."

"You said that you'd wear anything I chose for you."

She took a breath. She was married now, after all. Anything for Lon? "I… I… Wouldn't you call this chi-chi?"

He smirked with half-closed eyes. "Just testing you. How about this instead?" He pointed to a much more refined dress on another mannequin. This one was an electric purple sheath, and although it wasn't open to the navel, it only had two small straps covering the breasts.

"In case you hadn't noticed," she hissed quietly, "I'm a little more endowed than this mannequin. I don't think the style would work on me."

He kissed her cheek. "You, my darling Carolina, are magnificently endowed, and it is my pleasure to show off that endowment to the public."

"So it reflects back on you."

"So it might."

"So help me, Londo, I'm going to get you that 'I'm getting some' shirt."

"And I will wear it. I'll flash it to the press and give a V-for-victory sign."

"Honey," she said, twining her arms around his neck, "I'll be happy to wear something like this, but just for you. At home. After you get the heat working. Okay?"

"I'll take you up on that," Londo gave her that crooked smile as he rubbed her back. "Just wear something that I pick for you tonight."

She fumed, but didn't refuse.

"I saw what you wore during the invasion," he murmured.

"And I still don't see how Jae and Wiley got me into that," she pouted. "They said it was a matter of life or death for billions."

"Humor me, cabbage. C'mon." He disentangled himself from her arms.

"Argh. I can't refuse a 'c'mon' from you. Go ahead, Londo, do your worst."

Lon took his time then in choosing a gown for her to try. A smartly-dressed saleslady appeared. When she recognized whom she was waiting on, she quickly dismissed the security guard.

"What may I help you with today?" she purred, stepping in front of Lina to face Lon.

"Everything's in black," Londo complained as he ticked through the racks.

"They call it 'basic' for a reason," Lina said. She tapped on the saleslady's shoulder. "He's looking for himself," Lina explained as the woman turned. "Maybe something with a boa to wrap around his neck. He'll know when he finds it. Do you have anything with extra room in the shoulders? He likes to flex."

Londo paused to purse his lips at Lina. "What we're looking for is something for a black tie event," he said to the woman. "Not in black. She'll fade away in black, don't you think?"

The saleslady regarded Lina critically. "Not at all," she finally said. "A little extra color in the makeup, maybe some brighter highlights in the hair…"

"Maybe a tanning booth," Lina offered. Her deep though uneven tan of two weeks ago had disappeared completely, darn it.

"No time for tonight." Londo's voice came from deep within the racks. "Here." He appeared, dragging a pink gown with him. "This'll look great on you." He held the dress up to her. "What the hell size are you?"

"Not that small," Lina said. "Look, back home we didn't dress up for concerts. Jeans were fine. Some women wore dresses and pantyhose, but I always thought that concerts weren't an excuse for torture."

"Black tie," Londo reiterated as the saleslady bustled about trying to find a larger version of the dress.

"So I'll wear a black tie with my tee shirt," Lina said. "How about a plain black dress? These must cost a small fortune. If we find a classic little dress I can wear it a million times and get your money's worth out of it."

"*La voici,* Valiant!" the saleswoman announced cheerily. "I believe this will fit her quite well."

Londo held the dress against Lina and squinted his eyes. "On second thought," he said, "no. Let's try something in black. Com-pro-mise. You mentioned something about that, didn't you?" He stared at Lina evilly. "Yes, we'll paint your face like an Easter egg and wrap you in pearls. Black pearls." Glancing at the size of the dress, he retreated to the racks again.

"Puh-lease." Lina frowned at him before embarking on her own search. Here was a nice dress, floor-length. Simple, modest neckline and wide straps to accommodate a decent bra. She could find some short, colorful jackets that would make it look quite different when needed. They'd need tiny black buttons to match the dress, but these looked pretty standard. Ooo, a shawl would be a very classy accessory, especially if she sewed some beads or shiny somethings on it. Did this store have shawls?

Glancing at the price tag she quickly tucked the ensemble back onto the rack.

"Londo, let's get out of here," she said quietly, knowing that he could hear her wherever he was while the saleslady couldn't. "It's much too expensive."

"Nonsense!" Londo stood behind her with a dress in hand. The saleslady hovered behind him. "See? I found the perfect dress." He held it up to her and nodded. "*Absolutement.* Try it for fit and then we can go."

Lina tried to wipe the sour look off her face. "You must be joking," she said.

"Me? Joke? *Jamais;* not for this. This is the dress, Lie."

"Here's a nice one right here." Lina parted the gowns to show him the expensive black dress. If she could get him to agree to it, she was sure they could find something close to the same style at a more reasonably-priced store.

Londo glanced at her choice. "That's too plain for tonight. This dress, Lina. Hup hup." He met her eyes levelly. "You promised."

The saleslady showed her to a dressing room.

"I think I'll need some kind of push-up bra, just to give it the best effect. Oh, Looondo," Lina sang out through the dressing room half-door. "Could you go over to lingerie and get me a black strapless push-up bra? 36D, that's a dear." She grinned at his panicked face. "You might want to get some in slightly different sizes; they make bras all kinds of ways. If you could find an–"

"Can't you get it yourself?"

"I'm too busy getting undressed here. By the time you're back, I'll be ready for it."

Distressed, the saleslady regarded both of them and then hurried off to get it herself. Lina grinned over the top of the door at Londo, who grinned back.

"You're not going to get out of it this easily, *chérie,*" he told her.

"We'll see," she said, announcing a battle of the wills.

The saleslady quickly returned. His back turned, Lon heard a lot of material thrashing about behind the door of the dressing room. "No, miss," the saleslady said. "You can't wear that with this after all. See, it's open here. You'll have to take off the bra."

"Ohmigod," Lina said. Lon's soft laugh came from outside. "Okay, let's get it on. Uff. Watch it– I don't want to rip it!"

Lina emerged, clothed in a black floor-length skirt made of layers of sheer silk. There was a slit up to her hip on either side. Though the bodice covered most of her back, in front there were only two thin scarves from the waist to the neck. They weren't straps, but they were narrow enough– and close to transparent. The golden brand of the Three Worlds stood out loud and clear on her exposed cleavage.

"Now that's a dress," Lon said appreciatively.

"If you're living in a brothel in old San Francisco." Lina and the saleslady glanced at each other. The saleslady gave her a pitying look: *Men and the things we have to put up with.*

"Let me see how I look in it. Let's see how it feels to walk around in," Lina volunteered cheerily, which should have set Londo's warning signals off.

She sauntered out into the center of the evening wear section, ostensibly seeking a three-way mirror with better light. Two well-dressed young businessmen were strolling down the near aisle, and Lina ported one man's wallet out of his pocket onto the floor.

****Londo, use your telepathy now. Open yourself up, please.****

She approached the men. "Excuse me, did you lose your wallet?"

They turned at the sound of her voice. She knelt down to retrieve the wallet and hand it to them. "*C'est le vôtre?*" she asked sweetly, unobtrusively tucking her dress back from where it had shifted.

"*Ah oui, c'est le mien,*" one of the gentlemen said as he took his wallet, quite interested in *la mademoiselle* and her breasts. The other one quickly moved around so he could get a good view, too. "*Merci bien, chérie.*"

"Carolina!" ****Get back here, Lina!**** Londo bellowed silently, fists on his hips.

She nonchalantly swiveled back to him, an innocent look on her face. The saleslady giggled like a schoolgirl behind them.

"Jesus, Lina," Londo said. ****The things they were thinking!****

"What did you expect? You dressed me like a lady of ill repute, so that's the attitude they'd take when they saw me. I think with this I'd also need to get a big hat with big ol' feathers, just for that *classic* Sadie Thompson look."

He didn't say anything, but she could see the thundercloud over his head.

Lina turned to the saleslady. "How about something a little, tiny bit more sedate?" she suggested. "A tasteful bit of cleavage as a compromise?"

"Perhaps something strapless?" the saleslady suggested. She turned to Londo. "Men always like the strapless look. It suggests that an accident might happen."

"I could live with that," Lina said hopefully, studying Lon's expression. He still didn't say anything. "Okay, you don't have to wear the tee shirt. Just stay here for five minutes. We'll come up with something you'll like." She gave him a peck on the cheek and set him down in a comfortable chair.

She turned to where the saleslady was already gathering gowns. "The occasion is the symphony. I'm assuming narrow auditorium seats," Lina said, and the lady discarded some of her choices. Lina examined the remaining ones and stole a glance at Londo, who stared stonily at her. "Okay, let me try that one. It looks indecent enough to please him."

A glance in the mirror in the dressing room made her flinch. "Maybe something else?" she asked the saleslady. The woman cocked her head and raised an eyebrow at Lina. Lina sighed in resignation.

"We'll need to take in the waist a bit. The hem is wide enough to be let out…" The saleslady tugged and pulled the fabric as she studied the situation.

"Take in the waist? I won't be able to breathe." Bad enough that once again she couldn't wear a bra.

"Breathing and comfort are not the object of this dress, *mademoiselle.*"

Lina emerged from the dressing room with a fitted, gray-blue taffeta skirt that swished around her calves, and a matching velvet, flower-embroidered, boned (with pure steel packing straps, it felt like), strapless bustier that whittled her down where it didn't pump her up. The bustier rode lower than she'd thought it would. It partially covered her tattoo but the built-in corseting pushed everything up, practically to her chin. As far as she could tell, though, she was secure and safe.

The miracles of modern technology.

Londo perked up when he saw it.

"You need gloves for the symphony," the saleslady declared when she saw his reaction, and hurried off to find some.

Londo came over and gave a whistle. "Now that does you justice, Lina. I could live with this. Yes, very happily I could live with this."

"Oh dear. I hope I can. Are all your clothes choices going to be this risqué?"

"I'll be the picture of modesty with everything else. Well, almost everything." He grinned at her, touching foreheads. "Mm, the view is very nice from here." He wrapped his arms around her waist and kissed her, feeling the winner once again. Lina tangled her arms around his neck and they were lost in each other.

The saleslady cleared her throat. She displayed two sets of gloves: one a long, over-the-elbow opaque material, and the other translucent, elbow-length. Lina thought enough attention was being brought to her bustline, so she chose the shorter. Londo reached over her and took the long ones. "These," he said. "I have a friend who says these are coming back in style."

The trying-on drew the saleswoman's eyes to Lina's left hand and the elaborate ring and green diamond there. A glance at Londo's hand revealed the matching jewelry. Her eyes widened.

"We should be able to handle your entire trousseau here," the woman ventured when she could speak.

Londo had been standing back, admiring Lina with a silly grin on his face, but he stopped at that to frown at the saleswoman. Lina fiddled with the other glove, looking unconcerned.

"A trousseau."

"I think she means 'wardrobe,' Lon," Lina said. "I don't suppose this store approves of our tee shirts and jeans. The security guard certainly didn't seem to."

"You must forgive him," the woman assured them. "He didn't know who you were." She nodded to Valiant and looked pointedly at his ring with a questioning look on her face. "He thought you might be… just anyone."

Lina moved to a mirror. Her skirt made a satisfying rustle. She pulled her hair up and scrutinized herself, trying out the look. "*We got elegance,*" she sang softly. She saw Londo smiling devilishly behind her. "I'll need some accessories," she started. Those faux pearls from home might work–

"A necklace and some earrings. Maybe a bracelet. Gold and sapphires, I think," he said, holding an imaginary necklace to her neck and kissing her there.

The saleslady looked at her critically. "Blue topaz might be a better match," she said.

"Um. Actually, Londo," Lina said timidly. All this spending was dizzying. And really, unnecessary. "I was only thinking about some shoes. I've got some black tennies somewhere; I'll need to get some black shoelaces—"

"New shoes," Londo pronounced for the saleslady's benefit. "And hose, not tights. With a garter belt, *grr*," he added in Lina's ear. "Real jewelry, *chérie*. My princess is going to look the part tonight."

Lina whispered back, "*Ca-ching.* I'm wearing your dress pick. Now we compromise on everything else."

"Everything else except. When I give my wife jewelry, I call the shots. Completely."

She sighed. Him and his smile and that romantic heart of his. Maybe they could make an exception tonight, and tomorrow they'd be back on budget. There were too many important things they still had to buy. "Well. All right. But let me get some matching long underwear, too. This is a little breezy on top."

Then she saw the price tag as Londo pulled it out. "Holy—!" She clamped down on the expletive before it could leave her mouth. The saleslady was listening. "I'll put it back."

"This is no problem," Lon said easily. He addressed the woman. "We'll take this. And she was also looking at a black dress over there; we'll take that, too. But we need to get those accessories. Where's the jewelry department? Maybe some perfume *aussi*. Shoes? And evening coats?" He turned back to Lina. "You aren't going to wear *that*" he nodded at her perfectly good almost brand-new interstellar coat lying on the chair "over this dress tonight!" He paused. "And *you* get whatever underwear you need. Not long johns! I am not paying for long johns!"

"Londo! It's much too expensive! You have to start thinking about economizing—"

"I'll think about it tomorrow. Not tonight. Now be quiet."

She started to protest, but he put his fingertip on her lips. "No," he said. She tried again.

"*Non.* I am not compromising on this. If you say one more word I will buy something else as well. Something *really* expensive." He pressed his nose against hers, pretending a dark scowl. "Maybe a *fur.*"

She shut up. Lina didn't know what to think as Londo gave specific instructions to the saleslady. More employees were gathering to handle his orders. Finally Lina asked timidly, "Is there any place where I can get a quick makeover before the concert?" She'd washed off the thick makeup they'd used at the photo shoot.

"Certainly," the saleslady said. "We'll have one of the girls next door bring her things over here while you wait. We'll call for a hairdresser, too, while we get the alterations made on the dress. You'll need to try on that other dress as well."

Londo laughed at Lina's expression.

6

A dozen photographers and three TV news crews had set up at the concert auditorium. They were all fairly local, to judge from the signs on the vans parked down the street: Montreal and Trois-Rivières. Nothing national or international, Londo told her.

"So many," Lina said, staring out the tinted window of the limo.

"Not so many. You'll be fine. Remember the plan."

He had told her that the saleslady was thinking of calling the media about them and the concert. Lina hoped the woman had been paid a sizable amount of cash for all the embarrassment it would cause Lina. How had she ever agreed to go out in public in this dress?! Londo must be a mind controller. That was it. Those big brown eyes of his turned her brain to mush.

Londo (and his brown eyes) in a tux was stunning, though, worthy of being photographed and published so that every straight woman in the hemisphere could tack his picture to her office bulletin board. Tonight he dressed all in thrilling black, with a band-collared shirt that required no tie.

While he was dressing at his tony Montreal apartment, he'd adjusted his lapels, regarded her coolly, and announced himself as, "Rand. Lon Rand."

She'd broken out in global goosebumps. Somewhere between all this trust and holy love that marriage allowed them, there swelled a delicious flood of sheer lust. How nice that neither Lon nor Jae thought less of her for running wild with it these last few days! Sometimes just Lon's slow, hot glance suffocated her with desire. Sometimes the press of his broad hand sent chills of fire straight through her. It was thrilling how being near such a man made her feel like the ultimate woman.

He had bought a carnation-shaped diamond brooch for himself this evening, one that would go with his wedding ring. Lina had pinned it to his lapel in lieu of a real flower, and he'd admired the way it looked.

"Do you think it'll start a trend?" he asked her in all seriousness. She laughed to see him preen so, but then wondered when he tilted his chin down to examine himself in a mirror. He parted the hair on the top of his head in four or five different ways, studying it strangely.

"Come here and look," he urged her. "Is it thinning? Do you think I'm going bald?"

"Bald?" He was serious. Lina scrutinized his head.

"It looks good and thick to me," she declared. "Bald?"

A final, frowning rub, and Lon set to work on putting his hair to rights. "It looks thinner to me," he said. "It's genetic, baldness. How do I know that my father wasn't bald? Maybe my grandfather on my mother's side was. Maybe it runs on both sides of the family."

"It looks perfect to me," Lina said. Poor Londo, not to know his blood family. At least he had a loving adoptive one. "If it hasn't started thinning yet, chances are you aren't going bald."

"Ask your guides, will you?"

But even a thumbs-up diagnosis there didn't convince him. Luckily the doorman called about the limousine's arrival before he could fret more. It was time to leave.

La Place des Arts was only a short drive from Lon's condo on Robert-Bourassa Boulevard, but Lon had the driver take a detour first past UQAM ("Ookwam," he told Lina) and McGill University, his alma maters. Such diverse-looking schools: one was starkly modern and the other, oozing with gothic buildings.

Londo had wanted to attend a French-speaking uni, but the ParaNet had talked him out of Paris. They already had Europe well-represented among their membership. Lon's attention turned to the second-largest French-speaking city in the world, conveniently in a sector that needed a megapara since New York's

ElectroShock was about to retire. He chose UQAM and fell in love with Montreal. After he decided to major in architecture he'd transferred to McGill.

From there it was mere minutes to the site of the concert. Lina had time to check out only a third of the marvelous secrets of a fully-stocked limo. The driver asked if Lon wanted him to return afterward.

"*Non,*" Lon said, tucking his Sterling card back into his wallet. "I have something different arranged."

"Different?" Lina asked, still eyeing the members of the press outside the window. "When did you have time for all this?"

"While you were primping, *chérie.* I'm extremely efficient."

"I wasn't primping; I was being primped."

He offered his hand to help her out of the limo. As soon as the door opened the flash photography started. Lina tightened her long black coat around herself, and he gave her an excited grin.

Lon found this all so fun, a game to be played, a reputation to be recast. **They won't be inside. Probably.**

Then let's hurry. She gave him a rueful smile.

"Do we have to? You'll get used to it someday," he said.

"Today's not the day," she replied, "but handle it however you want, Lon." She was poured into the dress, and the entire point of that had been to show off her and his sexuality. He asked her if she was sure, and she smiled at him, patting his hand.

"How warm are you?"

"I'll give you warning before I turn into an icicle."

"That's my girl."

He took his time then mounting the short flight of stairs leading to a wide, well-lit plaza. At the top he turned her, slid his arm around her waist, and waved to the cameras below which went off like a cacophony of small lightnings. The flashes reflected in the windows of the hotel across the street. Lina tried to ignore them, tried to ignore the voice shouting inside her head to *get out of the picture, you ugly thing! Oh, that Muttbutt, why do we even bother taking pictures of her?* and the sound of beeping technology as Dad deleted her photos.

So she focused on Londo and found that the cameras tended to fade into the background.

Lon took her hand and led her to the main plaza, outlined with low piles of a late snow and large decorative light sculptures. They covered an empty basin where a pool would be in summer, Lon told her. A columned modern building curved in front of them, its wall of windows brilliant against the night sky and sleeping black mountain.

Away from the cameras Lina tried to appear calm and graceful to match Londo's slow strides. Only a few people entered the main building. The two of them were purposefully early. Even so, a couple stopped when they saw Lon and came over to say a few words. They were industry leaders who had worked with Lon on projects in the past. Lon introduced her to them as just "Lina" and didn't offer any more explanation than that.

"*Excusez-moi!* Valiant!"

Lina looked up to see a television crew pointing their camera at them. She hoped that the pleasant expression on her face hadn't changed. Lon ambled over to talk with them, pulling her along.

For some reason TV cameras didn't bother her that much. They never seemed to be scrutinizing her the way still cameras did. Maybe it was because Dad had never owned a videocam.

It was extremely convenient to be so fluent in French now, Lina thought with satisfaction. Lon had explained that there were pockets of the city in which no French was spoken, but they hadn't yet visited wherever those might be. This crew conversed all in French.

"So you're attending the concert tonight, Valiant? Are you just here for the charity event, or have you given up jazz?"

"Never," he replied. "I just seem to have developed a sudden interest in classical music."

"And your companion?"

"She's been a classical enthusiast for a long time," Londo evaded.

"Could we get your name, mademoiselle?" the reporter asked her.

Are you sure we aren't announcing tonight? she asked.

****Not to these guys. They ran a series on me last year that had me being the father of two of the screamingest little brats you'd ever seen. Tonight we play a game.****

"I prefer the title 'Ms,'" Lina told the woman pleasantly. She let her glittering black coat gape so it showed expensive cleavage, the gorgeous gold and blue topaz necklace that sparkled in the spotlight. "It's a little cold out tonight, isn't it?" She hugged the wrap back around herself.

She could hear Londo chuckling madly in her mind even as he handled a short interview about tonight's charity with outward seriousness. She gazed at him with amusement. She really was going to get him that tee shirt, if she had to design and print it herself. For too long he'd suffered the indignity of being thought an unwilling virgin, a victim of his own power. Which he *had* been until they'd met.

The TV woman addressed her. "Your name, please? Are you in the entertainment business? An actress? A model?"

Actress? Model? Couldn't they see beyond the glitter to the Muttbutt? Lina opened her mouth to give a vague answer, but Londo interrupted. "We need to be going now. Sorry. I don't want my lovely companion to catch cold, and there are other stations to talk to." He steered Lina away from the crew.

"Valiant!" the woman called out after them. "Is that a wedding ring you're wearing?"

They pretended they didn't hear her.

"Playing games." Lina tsk-tsked. "That was fun. How much longer can we keep that up?"

"Until it isn't amusing anymore," Londo decided. "Maybe a couple years."

"Valiant! Valiant!" Another news crew faced them down, this time with a desperate-looking reporter brandishing the microphone as he trotted forward.

Lon turned to Lina. "This guy has been razzing me for years about my lack of female social contacts," he told her. "He's had this slant to all his soft news stories about me that's always been… insulting. Snide."

"Ah. So?"

"So…" He met her eyes and raised one eyebrow.

The crew scurried to catch up to them. "Valiant!" the reporter wheezed.

"Been exercising hard tonight, Ross? Or was that little jog too much for you?" Londo smiled tightly.

"You've been away from Montreal a long time," he replied. He didn't bother looking at Lon. His puzzled attention focused on Lina. "Where've you been? Out There?"

"Way, way Out There." Lon's eyes narrowed in mischief at Lina. "But I'm back now. Just got in this morning. I'm about to take in a little culture and do something for the new First Nations Internet Scholarship Project at the same time."

"*Vraiment?* Please, introduce us to your companion, Valiant. We don't see you on the town with others very often. In fact, I believe it's been years. If ever."

Lina pretended astonishment. "*Non?* He told me he did this all the time."

"Well," Lon said, trying to look chagrined, "it may have been a while since—"

Lina lightly slapped Lon's coat collar. "Monsieur, you are playing games with me! How about the clothes?" She turned toward Ross. "Really, he told me he did this with all the girls he takes out. He bought me these clothes. Even the underwear. He picked it out personally. And jewelry, too! He said he always did that."

"Clothes?" Ross asked blankly.

"These," Lina slipped off her coat and turned around so they could get the full skin-tacular picture. "Me, I'm fine in tee shirt and jeans. But—!"

Londo put his hand over his heart. "I swear, I just didn't want you to be un-comfortable around people who were dressed better than you were."

Lina re-coated herself as fast as she could. As Lon gave her collar an intimate adjustment tug, she accused, "And I suppose you take every girl back to your apartment afterward? Hm?" She turned back to Ross. "He said he had some in-teresting paintings that I should see. I bet they're in the bedroom! I'd never heard that he was such a— a lothario!"

"Aw c'mon, baby, you'll really like these pictures. They're museum quality—"

"Black velvet bullfighters, probably. Tell the truth: are they in your bed-room?"

"I have very good lighting in there."

"Men! They're all alike!" Lina turned her back on him and glared into the distance.

Ross gaped at the two of them, Valiant looking flustered as if this woman were destroying his reputation. "But his reputation is exactly the opposite of—Ah… All you have to do," Ross told this glamorous woman, "is not to go back there with him."

Lina gave Ross an incredulous stare. "Do I *look* crazy to you?"

Londo let out a great laugh at that and put his arm around Lina's shoulders as the rest of the news crew joined in. Lina hid her mouth with her hand as she giggled.

Ross tried to frown at them and didn't quite pull it off. "Very funny. I take it you've been in his bedroom already," he said. "Give me something I can air. This could go national, maybe CNNi."

"Which bedroom?" Lina asked innocently. "He has so many. On different planets, even. And they have signs on the doors: NOW SERVING, and the number." She traced the imaginary sign in the air. "You have to have a number to stand in line, you know. There's no cutting allowed. Severe punishment for cutting in line." She shook a warning finger at Ross.

"Okay, okay." Lon grinned. "Enough."

"What, you don't think he believed me? I haven't even told him about the space harems and your league of slave girls. The six-year wait list."

Ross drummed his fingers on his crossed arms. "I take it you think I've been a little hard on you in the past, Valiant," he said.

"Just because you did five and a half minutes on who I *didn't* go with to the World Film Festival last year? I found that very amusing," Lon said without the faintest hint of a smile.

"You've almost always gone stag everywhere, Valiant. People can't help but wonder."

"Maybe I enjoy a private life."

Ross made a noise at the unlikeliness of that. "And maybe that privacy makes people come to certain conclusions about the strongest man in the world."

Lon's arm around Lina tensed. It was an old, embarrassing story for him. "And what would those conclusions be?"

"Come on, Valiant; you aren't deaf and blind. Tell you what; you announce what your status is on that question, and I'll give you ten minutes and run it on national. We'll dig up a picture of every woman you've ever been seen standing next to. It seems to me that there have been a number of women who say you've fathered children on them. Is any of that true?"

"Absolutely untrue, which is why every case has been thrown out of court. They're wasting my time. And you're wasting mine tonight."

Lon's ire had flashed hot as soon as Ross had mentioned those claims. "Now now, Lon," Lina soothed. "We're here for a lovely concert. Let's not spoil the evening."

"Ross has never reported on anything that I found particularly flattering," Lon said sullenly. He nodded at another group of cameras and sound techs closer to the concert hall. "It's time we moved on."

Ross's gaze returned to the woman standing next to Valiant, looking very familiar with him. "*D'accord,*" he finally said, "what can I do to make up for it so I can get a story tonight? Give me something I can actually air."

Londo pretended to consider. Finally he said, "Okay, I'll give you first crack at something."

"Yes?" The crew moved in closer and Londo faced the camera.

"I'm moving," he said.

"Moving?" Ross asked blankly before the import hit. "Moving!"

"From Montreal. If your viewers want the whole story, they'll just have to watch channel 4 over there. Or you can buy the story from them and air it yourselves." Again making sure the camera caught him full-on, he enunciated, "I watch Tele-4 all the time. 'Your news the way you want it.'"

The cameraman winced.

He flashed Ross a little salute and walked purposefully away, practically dragging Lina with him.

Lina scurried to keep up, trying to avoid the small runnels of ice that occasionally appeared on the pavement. "A little rough, weren't you?"

"I've been dreaming of that moment for years. Ah, life is good."

"Do you think you changed good ol' Ross's mind about you?"

"Sex lines and space harems. Lina, you're warped."

"Thanks."

Lon grinned as he slowed down and nodded in the direction of the next news crew, gathered next to the entryway in the majestic overhang between columns and glass. "Okay *d'ac,* how do we play with these people's minds?"

"Are we nice to this one?"

"He's one of the good guys, Lie."

"Valiant!"

"I saw you. Evening, Geoff."

"And good evening to you. You're all dressed up for the concert, I see."

"Trying not to embarrass myself in this elegant crowd," Londo replied.

"So would you introduce us to your fiancée?"

Lina looked behind herself, as if there could be someone else there.

"Fiancée?" Lon asked. "Where did you get that idea?"

"Fiancée?" Lina asked Lon. "Who's your fiancée?"

"Now, Lina." Lon turned her around and gave her a little push away from them. "Maybe you shouldn't listen to this."

"Are you saying that you aren't engaged?" Geoff the reporter asked warily.

"Who claimed that we were?" Londo demanded gently.

"Married?"

Lina slipped her arms around the crook of Lon's elbow as he stood there with his hands on his hips. "How could Valiant get married without the entire planet knowing?" she asked as a hint for the beginning of this game.

"Good point, Lina," Lon said. "Me, I always– in the rare moments that I considered marriage– I always thought that I'd announce a long engagement, followed by the biggest wedding this old world's ever seen."

"You're not engaged," Geoff said slowly.

"Not engaged."

You'd better be thankful that Jae hasn't given us an answer yet, or your tongue would turn green and fall off. "Londo, is there something the very nice gentleman thinks you should ask me?"

Lina batted her eyelashes at Lon.

Lon turned to Geoff. "I don't know. Is there something you think I should ask her?"

"N-no, Valiant! All our viewers want to know is… is… What's your relationship to this young lady?"

"Relationship."

"You know, Lon," Lina nudged him. "Like am I a cousin, or an aunt or a niece or your great-uncle twice removed…"

"But I really don't think we're blood related, Lina. At least not back any closer than, than…"

"At least ten, fifteen generations," Lina nodded at Geoff.

"Maybe more." Londo shrugged. "Sorry."

"Valiant," Geoff tried not to growl, "you aren't being very helpful."

"Oh. Sorry. How may I help you? I know. Lina, show him the dress. Seeing Lina in that dress would help any red-blooded man."

"It's awfully cold out here."

"Here, let me warm you up."

A wash of heat flowed over her. "How'd you do that?"

"Heat breath. Now model, *chérie*."

Lina slipped off her coat and turned for the camera. "It's definitely not something I'd recommend wearing at this time of year," she said. "At least, not without long johns."

"I don't know." Lon admired her from head to toe. "It certainly makes me feel warm all over."

Lina gave the name of the store they'd purchased the dress from, then included the makeup company and hair salon that had helped her get ready. They'd appreciate the PR. "We didn't get this from Sean-Chelster," Lina added as Lon helped her with her coat. "They sell furs there. Can you imagine! Furs! As if!"

"I told Lina that I never buy from anyone who sells furs," Lon told the camera. "They lost a lot of business this afternoon because of that policy."

"Many of the women here tonight don't share those compunctions, Valiant," Geoff observed as another group of well-dressed people entered the building. His head jerked at the distinct clank of a spray can being shaken.

"Where?" Lina asked, looking around, readying her weapon. "Ah. I see one. Banzai!"

"Lina." Lon grabbed the paint can from her. He handed it to Geoff, who gave it a dumbfounded stare. "For safe keeping. Lina, we'll go after a herd of fur-wearers tomorrow, maybe. But not tonight. I want to see a concert and then have a nice, quiet dinner somewhere."

Lina's fury melted. "At Marcus Sous? That was lovely."

"And we've already eaten there today. I was thinking about somewhere else for dinner."

Geoff almost grunted with frustration. "Okay," he said. "So you're seeing each other. Can I go out on a limb and say that much?"

"We're seeing each other?" Lon looked at Lina.

"I think that's fairly truthful," she told him. "There you are. I see you."

"Okay, we're seeing each other," Lon confirmed to Geoff. "We've been seeing each other for a while. We're going to be seeing each other for a while."

"How long a while?"

"Next question."

Geoff sighed and tried again. "How serious are you?"

"He's not serious at all," Lina said quickly. "He's always cracking me up. He's a very funny guy. I never knew that before."

"Funny? Valiant?"

"Valiant. Funny."

"Tell us some of the things he does. Miss…?"

"'Ms.' Let's see." Lina touched her lip, trying to call up a short specific.

"Can we at least get your name?" Geoff huffed in exasperation.

Lon rubbed the side of his nose. "Ah, I don't think so. 'Lina's' going to have to do for now."

"And you're from…?"

"Earth, and proud of it." Lina smiled innocently at Geoff. There were plugs to be made for security, paths to be blocked, Londo had explained to her, before her name or information about her could be given out. Not "Carolina"; there weren't that many in the world. And as for "Starhart"– they hadn't gotten used to saying it automatically yet. "O'Kelly" might slip out if they weren't careful.

Plus, not giving a last name would throw the focus away from the first name. Tonight she was a lady of mystery.

"We'll narrow that down," Lon grinned. "North America."

"You're a lot of help, Valiant," Geoff grumbled. "Well. Ms. Lina, about those funny things?"

"You know, I promised him I'd never embarrass him in public," she said. "I'm afraid that everything I can think of is terribly embarrassing. I'd hate to have Valiant mad at me. It could be painful."

Lon crossed his arms in front of himself. "Great. Now he'll think I beat up women."

"Funny things. Okay. Lon, why do you wear a coat out here when you can fly around in space *au naturel* if you wanted and not feel a thing?"

"Why–?" Lon frowned to himself at that. "It's not a matter of comfort, Lina, it's a matter of making others feel comfortable."

"Um hm. So style has nothing to do with it."

"Style reveals personal creativity." Lon addressed Geoff.

Behind him, Lina pantomimed the brooch and mouthed, "Ask him about it."

"Valiant, are you wearing a pin?" Geoff dutifully asked once he understood.

"Oh, this." Lon opened his coat so the camera could catch the ornament. "It's an idea I came up with. Flowers in lapels can be cumbersome to keep neat and fresh, so I thought, why not try a larger piece of jewelry instead? This is the twenty-first century; time to stop assigning sexual stereotyping to objects that have nothing to do with gender roles and everything to do with efficiency."

Lon went on for a few more minutes about it, extolling the elegance and masculinity of such a piece. Preening at his inventiveness. Geoff listened to it all and caught Lina's eye. She smiled back at him, her eyes merry.

"Funny," she said, and he chuckled.

"What?" Lon looked around at her, and then at Geoff.

"Nothing, nothing," Lina said. "Say, before we all turn to blocks of ice out here, why don't you tell Geoff what you wanted to tell him?"

Geoff came to attention. "And that is…?"

"*Euh,*" Lon began thoughtfully. He squared his shoulders and took a breath, looking straight into the camera pointing at him. "This is going to be abrupt, but

I want to take this opportunity to thank all the people of Montreal for being so kind to me throughout the years. Even in the heart of winter, Montreal is the warmest city there is. It's is my favorite city in the world, and *les Montréalais* are the best in the world. But I'm moving. Quite soon, I'm afraid. I would say I'd miss the city, but we're going to be back often."

"Moving? You're leaving?" Geoff blinked in shock.

"Certainly, I don't want anyone taking over my box at Le Centre Bell. They'll have to pry my season tickets out of my cold, dead hands." He turned to Lina. "They're out of town tonight or we'd be there instead of here. Some things are even more important than music."

"I take it we're talking about the Canadiens," she said quietly, hoping the crew wouldn't pick it up. She didn't want to appear ignorant of common hometown knowledge.

"*Mets-en! Les Habs*– my team."

Geoff was aghast. "Where are you moving to? Why are you moving? 'We?'"

"This has nothing negative to do with Montreal in any way," Londo assured him and the camera. "There are just times in your life when you need to move along. Montreal is still in my ParaNet territory; most of my friends are still here. My special charities are here and I'm not going to forsake them. I'm not going to forsake anything. I'm just going to live somewhere else."

Geoff tried to get more information out of him. Londo told him what he could without revealing the marriage or Starhaven or Three Worlds. He was trying so hard to tell the people of the city how he felt about them. He didn't want to leave. He was leaving because of her. Her and Jae. Lina knew he was beginning to tear up and he didn't want to appear less than Valiant in front of the cameras no matter what he felt.

She shivered and nudged Londo. "When does this wonderful city turn the cold machine off? It's freezing out here. Doesn't anyone know that it's almost spring?"

"This *is* almost spring."

"Seems more like midwinter to me. I'll go grab some long underwear somewhere, Lon, if that's okay with you. You stay here with Geoff as long as you need to."

"Wait, Lina; we should be going in anyway. Nice talking with you, Geoff. If you need any more, give Janet a call and I'll see if I can grab some time tomorrow. Maybe the next day would be better. We're really busy."

"Hold one minute, Valiant," Geoff begged. He turned to his crew and relinquished his mic. "Camera and sound off, guys." He used his chin to point at a dark niche and walked out of the crew's hearing distance. Lon and Lina followed. "So what is it, Londo? I've always been level with you. This is strictly off the record, just to satisfy my own curiosity."

Lon studied Geoff and then turned to Lina. "What do you say?"

"He's honest, but he's a reporter," Lina said. "Your discretion. How many more rounds of the game do you want to play?"

Lon sighed. "Okay, Geoff, you're right; you have always played straight with me. But I'm not going to tempt you on this one."

"There's something to tempt me with?"

"Look, when we decide to announce, you'll be in the first group we tell. Is that enough?"

"Announce. So you lied when you said she wasn't your fiancée."

"She's not my fiancée." Lon grinned at Geoff.

"But you said… All that about the long engagement and the big wedding…"

"Sometimes things don't work out the way we planned." Lon held Lina tightly to himself. "Sometimes the universe speeds things up."

Geoff's eyes immediately went to Lina's stomach.

"I'm going to start wearing a pillow, I think," Lina muttered. "Just so people will have something to look at."

"No, she's not," Londo answered Geoff's unspoken question.

Geoff was opening his mouth to ask another question when Lina subtly shook her head and put her finger to her lips. She saw that stopped him long enough to remember that Valiant didn't appreciate being asked what Maximus thought of his actions.

"Ah, about this move…" Geoff said instead.

"I'm only moving my residence. Lina's not a city girl, and I already started a house in the country, far from here. I used that as a bribe to get her to accept. I'll still be hanging around, like I said. And… there might be more."

Lina perked up at that. "More?"

"The Center. I was thinking about building it here. What do you think?"

"I hadn't really thought about it. I like what I've seen so far, Lon. Montreal's a nice place. But the Center will be too big to build in the city, won't it?"

"Nearby, a close commute."

"Oh… Why not? You love this town. It'll be good for you. But Jae has to agree."

"He will. I'll see to it."

"What Center is this? Who's Jae?" Geoff asked, looking lost.

"We're starting up something." Lon smiled kindly at his friend. "It's big. It's huge. And if I can find a nice property, it's going to go up here. Whatever you do, don't spread that around! Prices will go sky-high, and this project's going to take megabucks as it is. Megamegamegabucks."

"Ah…" Geoff's eyes flicked back and forth as he tried to figure it out. "Could I arrange for a long interview with you? This has to come out sometime. What's the project?"

Lina shivered within Lon's arms. He made what she first thought was a little kissy-face at her and suddenly she warmed up all over. Para-breath was a handy thing to have.

"Not tonight," Londo said gently. "Not tomorrow, and probably not for at least a week. Geoff, things have been happening lately, big things. Enormous things."

"At last you admit it," Lina murmured.

"Incredible things. We just got back to Earth this morning, and now we have got to take a few days to relax and figure it all out. From a number of directions. I'll give you a call when we're ready. You'll be invited to the press conference."

"In-depth interview, too? For the home-town press?"

Lon rubbed his nose. "Probably. We're not sure of what all we have to do at this point. I will try; I give you my word." He smiled in conciliation. "So, do you have tickets for the concert?"

"No. We just came to interview you. There was this call–"

"From a woman who works at Mode Chaude," Londo finished for him. "Okay, you got what you wanted. Time for me to make sure my wife doesn't freeze to death. Good night."

"'Night, Geoff. Nice meeting you," Lina smiled.

"Ah. Good night, Ms. Lina. Thanks, Londo!" He turned back to his crew, a little dazed, though his thoughts were clear enough to the two of them. *Valiant married. Good god, how in the world do they–?*

Tonight's throng included the mayor and other municipal officials as well as leaders of various local and national organizations. Lina tried to remember names, but Lon assured her that she probably wouldn't need or be expected to remember most of them. He had some tricks for names that he'd teach her later.

Apparently the mayor had been stopped on her way in by Ross the reporter, who had told her that Valiant was moving. She hunted Lon down like a rampaging bull.

"Mélanie, don't worry about it," Londo told her. "I'll still watch over the city, and we think–don't let this out–we think that we might be starting something big here. You'll like it, *c'est vrai.*"

"Londo, whether you want to admit it or not, you're a landmark of the city. We get a sizable amount of tourist dollars from you being here. People will lose jobs because of this."

"*Non non,* you're not going to lay a guilt trip on me. Listen, this something big could bring in a lot more tourist dollars, and for a better reason than people running around hoping to catch a glimpse of me through my windows."

The mayor's jaw jutted in disapproval. Londo promised an explanation within a week or two.

All around, Lina could hear murmurs of "Leaving Montreal!" People approached Londo to see if the rumor were really true. They studied Lina curiously. Londo introduced her as just "Lina," and his eyes crinkled at some of the ways they attempted to find out why Valiant was accompanied by a woman. His expression changed now and then as some man whom he was trying to talk with kept looking at Lina– or rather, her chest.

How Lina wished she had her coat with her so she could close it up! This was embarrassing. Should she smile pleasantly at such men or take them to task for being so rude? Londo scowled at some of them, but that only helped twice. She managed to get a program and used that as a shield for her cleavage, which amused Londo tremendously.

And there were camera phones. She shuddered every time she heard a click. She knew she was embarrassing Londo with her presence. Maybe if she stood away from him, the people could just take shots of him.

"Don't be silly," he whispered to her. "They want pictures of Valiant and the mystery princess. You're beautiful, *chérie*. Absolutely stunning. I'll show you the papers tomorrow and you'll see. Relax."

So she focused on him.

"Londo Rand!" A woman's voice cut across the room. Lon and Lina both turned at the sound.

"Trouble," Lon whispered to Lina. "You speak only French, get it?"

"*D'accord*," she responded as the brunette woman wove her way through the crowd. She wore a startling red dress with entirely too much cleavage. The people she pushed out of her way got no apology.

"Londo Rand!" the woman repeated as she approached them. She brandished a tiny digital recorder in front of her like a flashlight. "Imagine seeing you at a classical concert!"

"Eloise," Lon nodded at her. He turned to Lina. "*Je te présente Eloise Green du* New York Gazette."

"*Le* New York Gazette," Lina repeated obediently. "*C'est une plaisir de faire votre connaissance.*" She beamed beatifically at the woman.

"Um, *c'est... c'est...*" the woman began and failed. "Pleased to meet you... is it mademoiselle or madame?"

Lina blinked at her blankly; couldn't understand the language...

Eloise's face showed a moment of frustration before she turned back to Londo. "I haven't seen you at a decent concert since the Stones' Graveyard Tour five months ago. What the hell are you doing here?"

"My tastes have expanded. Are you here to support the charity or dig up some news?"

"I was just down the road when a call came in that you might be here tonight. Did you know that there's a rumor going around that you're married? Everyone's too frightened of you to ask about it."

"That's odd. A TV crew outside mentioned the rumor to me just a few minutes ago."

"And what did you tell them?" Eloise held the recorder high while she surreptitiously studied Lina. Her thoughts broadcast: Someone who didn't speak English in this day and age... obviously padded and pushed up for all she was worth.

Londo choked slightly.

"<Oo, *chéri,* did-ums catch that last thought?>" Lina said in French as she moved to mother Londo, straightening his lapel. She pouted saucily, wiggling like Marilyn Monroe just to irritate Eloise. "<You know, it's a shame you aren't wearing a tie. I could drive her crazy fiddling with it. You do know what ties symbolize, don't you?>"

"*Oui, ma petite,*" Lon replied.

"<She's got quite the crush on you. Possessive.>"

"<Your dress is turning green, cabbage.>"

"<Oh, pooh.>" Lina turned to Eloise and flashed her a dazzling smile.

"What was all that about?" Eloise asked.

"You really should learn French, Eloise, if you're going to cover French Canada," Londo admonished. He switched off the recorder she still held. Her eyes lingered on the fingers that brushed up against hers. "No interviews here."

"*Il est à moi;* <he's mine, he's mine,>" Lina chattered gayly but softly in French.

She gave Lon a wide-eyed look as he tried to shush her. What if someone–

"<No one around us heard, Honeybear.>"

"She doesn't seem to be as... intelligent as you usually go for," Eloise observed.

"That's pretty rude to say in front of someone." Lon's voice held more than a touch of steel.

"She doesn't understand me," Eloise said, and the pangs of jealousy within her stood out to anyone with an ounce of telepathy. "So what's with you and her,

Londo? You're acting awfully lovey-dovey. And that's a helluva ring you're wearing."

"Isn't it?" Londo said. "It goes well with my pin, don't you think?" He turned the lapel with the pin so it would catch the light.

"Lovely," Eloise said. "But you didn't answer my question. Are you married? To her? Engaged? Give me a direct answer."

"Eloise, this is a social evening," Londo said evenly. "I gave my interviews outside."

"Direct answer, please, Londo," Eloise repeated.

"<What a pain in the neck,>" Lina said in French. "<I see she's already started on her drunk for tonight. *They* say she's got a real problem with it. You might remind her about Alcoholics Anonymous– and tell her that she's wearing too much eyeliner.>"

Lon gave a wondering smile at Lina. "<Why, you really are jealous,>" he said.

"<Do you mind? I've never been jealous before–of a woman.>"

"<I like it,>" Lon declared, "<but don't let it go on too long.>"

"<Spoilsport.>" Lina undulated, letting her hand glide slowly down Lon's sleeve, watching Eloise with steady eyes. Eloise matched her glare for glare. "<We understand each other perfectly well,>" Lina said in a light tone of voice, as if she were chatting about the weather. "<Whatever did you do to encourage her, Lon?>"

"<Absolutely nothing,>" Lon declared. "<She's been behind the police barricades at every major disaster lately, ready to interview me.>"

"<A Valiant stalker,>" Lina observed. "<Creepy.>"

"Who the hell is she, Londo? Where's she from? Are you married or not?"

"Eloise," Lon said. "I can truthfully tell you that there's no record of my getting married anywhere on Earth."

"So you're living in sin, same difference. What kindergarten did she graduate from? And how long did it take her to do it?"

"Did we have some kind of arrangement?" Lon asked her. "I must have missed it. I don't understand all this 'tude." He nodded at the champagne glass in her hand. "You need to lay off that stuff. Now if you'll excuse me," Londo tucked Lina's hand under his arm, "I think it's time we found our seats."

"<So pleased to have met you,>" Lina said behind her. "<Let's not meet again.>"

Londo laughed softly. "<A little goes a long way, pet.>"

"<Arf. Warning noted and logged,> *mon capitaine.*"

7

The concert proceeded splendidly, and Lina lost herself in the glory of it. She enjoyed music now more than she ever had, if that were possible. And wonder of wonders, she felt Londo finding similar joy.

The evening's fare was twentieth century, which included Copland's "Fanfare for the Common Man." Lina watched Londo for his reaction to the song that they'd played at the funeral for his ex-love. His lips pinched tight. Taking his right hand between hers, she rubbed it. He looked at her hand over his and then met her eyes with a little smile of reassurance.

Afterward with the music still echoing in their minds, Lina excused herself to fix her hair and makeup. A swarm of minds– probably the press– surrounded the building. She didn't want to embarrass Londo in case anyone included her in their pictures of him.

The ladies' room held a vanity section. Lina commandeered a chair, ported in the makeup pouch they'd given her at the store, and tried to make a few repairs. Her gloves got in the way. The new bracelet took a moment to figure out how to get off. Lina began to ease her gloves down just to realize that Eloise was standing behind her.

"*Bonsoir encore,*" she said, hoping she sounded gracious instead of nervous, as Eloise eyed her hand sliding out of the glove. Lina ported the wedding ring to her index finger.

"How do there," Eloise said. Then she clearly spotted the ring that matched Lon's.

Eloise sat beside Lina, smiling in phony friendship. *"Cette... bague,"* Eloise said, pointing to the ring. Her breath was a rush of alcohol.

"Vous parlez francais!" Lina exclaimed, taking off her other glove.

"Uh, *non,*" Eloise said, proceeding syllable by syllable. *"Je no...* I don't speak French."

"Ah, quel dommage," Lina gave her a pitying look, reaching into the pouch to port in a comb. When Eloise looked down again the ring was on Lina's right hand, ring finger. The reporter performed a splendid double take.

"Waitaminnit," Eloise exclaimed softly. "Something strange is going on here." She grabbed Lina's hand, dislodging a hairpin and sending curls cascading down the back of Lina's head.

"Hey!" Lina cried.

"What do you think you're doing?" Another woman stepped up to take Lina's defense. "<Is she bothering you?>" she asked Lina in French.

"Merci," Lina replied in the same language, "<but I can handle her.>"

Lina whirled on Eloise, pointing at her. "<Listen here, you!>" she said firmly but softly, staying in French. "<Keep your hands off me. If you want to ask me a question, then do it. Otherwise, keep out of my face.>"

Lina?

I'm handling it, Londo.

"I bet you can understand every word I say," Eloise sneered.

Lina glared at her as she redid her hair.

"What do you have over him?" Eloise eyed the ring and Lina let it stay there for a while. Finesse, that's what was needed.

The harangue continued. "What does he see in you? Is he the kind of guy who's only interested in boobs? Miss No-mind? Do you do it with him? Do you go all the way? Good god, you don't suppose you really are married? No, he'd never do that with the likes of you. What does Maximus think about all this?"

She snapped her fingers in Lina's face to get her attention. "Look, girl, I can get you ten thousand bucks for an exclusive interview. More if you tell everything. I've got connections at *Playboy;* I think I can guarantee you a quarter-mill, Canadian, for an interview and a pictorial. How do you two do it? Can anyone do it?" Eloise paused. "I bet you've seen him naked. How big is he? Cut or not? Do you have pictures? *Playgirl* will put out a special issue. They'll pay their entire decade's operating costs just for one picture."

"<You're sick, lady. You don't even know what your mouth is saying any more. Does your editor know you go around like this?>" Lina tried to let her tone of voice indicate her disapproval of the reporter.

Eloise kept it up. "*Playboy.* Even you Frenchies have heard of that. *Plaaayboy,*" she drew the word out.

Lina glared at her. "<I've heard of *Plaaayboy,*>" she said in French. "<Have you ever heard of privacy? This is a free country; I don't have to put up with this.>"

"*Playboy,*" Eloise repeated, making the connection with her victim at last. "Ten thousand bucks, minimum. I bet you understand that, too."

Damn! She couldn't get her hair right. Her hand was shaking with outrage. Lina stopped and took a breath.

"They'll want to know all the details. I talked to the Three Rivers boys outside. They said you two have been together all today, maybe out on the spaceways. Is that how you do it? Are you some sort of alien bimbo with cast-iron parts? Come on, girl, tell me. Do you screw him? Or do you just take him up to a point? Blooow job?"

The woman from before came up behind Lina. "<Are you sure you don't need help here?>" she asked, giving Eloise the eye. "<She's saying some pretty awful things to you.>"

"<She's just confirming my view of reporters. *Some* reporters,>" Lina corrected, putting the final touch on her hair. She managed a bit of lipstick without her hand shaking too badly.

"<The things she's saying–>"

"<I can understand her,>" Lina said as she adjusted her dress. Eloise was frowning at her cleavage. "<Every word.>"

The woman laughed at that. "<Serves the bitch right. So tell me, if it's okay: are you guys married? Or engaged?>"

Lina gave her a kind, silent smile.

"*D'accord, d'accord.*" The woman smiled back as if she approved of the subterfuge. "<Well, if you are, congratulations and the best of luck. He's always seemed so lonely.>"

"<If we are involved,>" Lina said, "<thank you. And thank you for your offers of assistance.>"

"<Sure you can handle her? They have security guards here.>"

"<Her?>" Lina glanced quickly at Eloise. "<I can handle her with my hands tied behind my back. She may not like what I do, though. Let's hope it doesn't come to that.>"

"<All right.>" The woman nodded and was gone.

"Silicone. Sil-i-cone," Eloise repeated, pointing at Lina's chest.

In a way, it was pitiful. Lina's guides showed her strings of DNA, so the problem was hereditary; parents arguing, so the problem was nurturing, and a cartoonish picture of Eloise with her eyes crossed and tongue hanging out, which equaled basically "intentionally stupid person" in the imagery library Lina had learned over the years.

Lina put on the gloves again, transferring the ring to the proper finger once it was under cover. She tried to fasten the tiny buttons on the top of the gloves through her haze of irritation. It took three attempts before the bracelet was secure.

"Okay, a *Playboy* interview and a full hour of *ParaWatch*. E! will want two hours with you, maybe more. I can get you all that. Two million dollars, plus. That's American money, not this cheap Canadian stuff."

Lina got up from the table, straightening her spine. "*Bonsoir,*" she said frostily, hoping that that would shut Eloise up.

"And where do you think you're going?" Eloise reached for her hair, but Lina sensed the move and grabbed her hand before she could do anything. She leaned in to Eloise's face.

"Six words," she said softly in English. "Alcoholics Anonymous. You have a problem."

She straight-armed Eloise away from herself and strode out the door. Londo met her with her coat, his face tight.

I would have belted her, he told her.

Then it's good for her that you weren't there, Lina told him, patting his cheek. **We don't need a murder trial to hold us up.**

She let out a breath that she didn't realize she'd been holding. As she inhaled she felt the mood of the crowd: how fond and proud they were of Valiant, their own parahero. How happy for him that he was with a woman at last. Bubbling anticipation at the prospect that he might be married, excitement at the mystery of it all. She smiled and Londo looked at her questioningly.

"Feel the room," she said, and he sent his mind out.

"They love you," she told him. "Forget that Eloise woman. These guys think you're the greatest."

Lon tasted the mood of the room, a half-smile blooming on his face. "You're right," he said. He liked being liked.

"You fit in here," she said carefully so that he would sense it too.

"So I do." The cockiness was back. The laughter was back. "C'mon, pet, let's go outside. There are some people who want to take our picture."

"Arf. I'm nobody's pet."

"You're mine," he growled and took her in his arms to give her a possessive kiss.

She leaned back and sighed at him, oblivious of the crowd and their camera phones. "Well, maybe just for tonight. You're rather wonderful… tonight."

"Arf," he answered her. He held still while she wiped a tiny smear of un-set lipstick off his mouth. A few more cameras caught that. Then he helped her with her coat and put his arm around her waist. They moved outside with the crowd that had seemed to be waiting for them to move before they did, too.

Outside there was only a sea of people and flashing lights. "Valiant!" "Valiant!"

Suddenly everyone was shouting, "Valiant!" The night exploded with light, sometimes like twinkling stars, sometimes like supernovae as everyone took a picture at the same time.

Lina clenched. She tried not to cower behind Lon as she once more let her coat slip to reveal her cleavage. Anything for Londo. She kept her gaze on him. Wonderful him.

Someone with a microphone tried to edge to the front of the mob that was held back by two lines of arm-linked people wearing parkas. "Valiant! A word, please!"

"Valiant! Over here! CNNi!"

Lina could barely hear Lon's voice over the cacophony. "Don't worry," he told her. "I've got security working the crowd."

"Security?" Now she could see "ParaNet Security" written on those parkas in block letters, alongside the lightning-bolt ParaNet logo.

"Best in the business. You're safe."

Lon stopped and waved for the cameras, then eased them forward again. His grin revealed the happiness that poured from him. This was the night he'd always wished for. Lina couldn't help but smile at his joy.

Flashes went off in waves, catching the image of the sexy, well-dressed couple after a night at the symphony. The crowd parted like the Red Sea in front of Londo and they descended the steps to the street. Across from them, the glass wall of the hotel glowed white with reflected light. A limo stopped for them, but Londo moved farther out into the street, guiding Lina with him.

A horse and open carriage with tiny Christmas lights wrapping the trimwork waited for them. Amid all the confusion and high-tech recording, the sweet, homemade decoration seemed like blessed safety. Londo helped her into it and then hopped in beside her.

The driver pointed out a blanket to keep them warm in the cold night air before he turned back to urge his horse forward. Londo wrapped his arm around her shoulders, making it cozier still. The skittish horse *clop-clopped* away from the pandemonium, down a narrow alleyway to emerge onto an empty, four-lane thoroughfare.

"Oh my," Lina said. There were absolutely no cars on this street, unlike the cross-streets. "How did this happen?"

"I asked," Lon said.

"And they delivered?"

"*Mais oui.* I've never asked a favor of the Montreal Police before. They were quite happy to help, since I assured them that this was a one-time occasion."

"Oh." Lina took in the carriage: the silhouette of the driver sitting on his bench in front of them against the tiny multi-colored lights, the rear end of the horse. "<What's its name?>" she asked the driver.

"<She is Candy,>" he replied.

Every now and then Candy seemed a little excited, varying her crisp walk to trot, then slow down when her driver chided her. Her breath came out in small, frosty snorts. The sharp sounds of the horse's hooves echoed off the buildings of downtown.

No cameras. No crowd. Just Lina and Lon under their blanket in the chill night. They nestled cheek to cheek. "This is just too perfect," she said.

He tucked in a wayward tendril of her hair. "That's the way I want it to be with us. Forever." He drew her into a long, delicious kiss, and then another one. The driver drove on, slowly clip-clopping through the streets of Montreal, up toward *la montagne* and *le Parc Mont Réal.*

Londo pointed out historic sites and museums, interesting homes and shops. "Hungry?" he asked.

She rubbed his broad chest and sexy stomach. "I think I could stand skipping a meal," she hinted.

"And I wouldn't dream of starving you." He smiled. "We'll still have later." He looked around. "*Monsieur le cocher,*" he said.

"*Oui, monsieur?*"

"*Là-bas, s'il vous plait,*" he said, pointing.

"*Oui, monsieur.*" The carriage made a careful U-turn and stopped in front of an awninged restaurant.

"Oh my."

Londo declared, "A real date. It occurred to me that we've never had one. A real date includes a fancy dinner." He jumped lightly out of the carriage and helped Lina down. Lon paid the driver in actual cash– Lina was surprised that he hadn't produced the omnipresent Sterling card– and both bid Candy adieu.

They watched the carriage clop back, hopefully to a warm barn and dinner. Already traffic was resuming in the street they'd just left. Lina turned around slowly, taking in the bright lights of the big city and her handsome prince who gazed at her so lovingly.

"I feel like a princess," she said, and he squeezed her hand.

"*Bon,*" he said. "Now, sharpen up your French. We're going to an authentic French restaurant."

They paused under the velvet awning where a doorman gave a small bow before he opened the door for them. Londo and she stepped into the fanciest restaurant Lina had ever imagined. A tuxedoed maître d' studied the reservations book at a lectern. Just beyond was a sedate bar with no sports channel in sight, where everyone conversed quietly with each other. Somewhere a pianist played with cello accompaniment.

Several varied levels made up the restaurant, all brocades and polished wood; earthtones and reds. Lina could look down and see the candlelit tables with people dressed almost as well as she. The odor of savory herbs and roasting meats filled the air.

They approached the maître d', who apologized without looking up. "*Je regret, monsieur, madame, mais si vous n'avez pas de réservations, nous ne pourrons pas vous assoir.*"

He finally raised his chin. "Oh, Monsieur Valiant. <You're earlier than we expected. Your table isn't quite ready yet.>" He subtly signaled a waiter to move the offending customers along so as to make room for the hometown parahero. "<There will be but a short wait,>" he apologized.

"*Merci beaucoup,*" Londo murmured graciously and steered Lina toward the bar with its view of the lower city. Lina shook her head at him.

"I'm seeing a whole different side of you today."

"Glad I can surprise you." He turned her hand in his and pressed a kiss to the inside of her wrist.

"Stop it, Londo," she whispered. "You've got my heart doing flipflops as it is."

He kissed her lips lightly and turned as the maître d' announced that their table awaited them.

Lina hardly knew what she ordered, because she only had eyes for Londo. He had been cocky at the symphony, but now he was at his dashing best to show her the evening of her dreams. As they waited for their entrees they held hands and talked of inconsequential things. Someone walked by. A flash went off.

Even as she jumped in surprise, Lina cringed. A sudden rush of hot anger flooded her. How *dared* someone spoil this night? How rude must they be? The fellow had the audacity to grin at her, lining up another shot.

She ported him to the concert hall plaza.

"I hope he freezes solid," she growled.

"Whoa, whoa!" Lon quickly grabbed her hand. "You didn't port him off to outer space, did you?"

"Lon!" What kind of person did he think she was? She told him where the man had landed.

"Oh." Lon chewed the inside of his cheek for a moment. "Sorry. Guess I've been around too many people who wouldn't think twice about– Well." He rubbed her thumb. "Poor guy was just taking a picture of a couple of celebrities."

"Who were obviously trying to be alone. What gave him the right?"

Lon shrugged. "It's just very bad manners on his part. How terrible a sin is giving someone pneumonia?"

"You're saying I should forgive and forget? I don't do that."

Londo screwed his mouth around as he gazed heavenward. Finally he said, "With great power comes… Well, you know the rest."

"Oh, brother."

"Nothing I haven't been lectured about a thousand times."

Lina took a deep breath and released it. "Killjoy."

"You still have–"

"I know where he is," she admitted. She looked around the room for a suitable spot.

Lon, too, examined the situation and pointed a suggestion. "How about–?"

Lina ported the guy back. He'd pulled his fancy suit coat tight around himself, still clasping his camera in a deathhold. But now he sat shivering on the restaurant's small stage between the pianist and the cellist.

The boor let out a very satisfactory squawk. Or was it a honk? Whichever, it caught everyone's attention. The cellist's bow clattered upon the wood floor. Two off-key notes sounded on the piano before that instrument fell silent as well. Lon barked a single laugh as the crowd exclaimed over the sudden appearance, and then chuckled at the would-be paparazzo's bumbling escape from the spotlight.

"Not bad," Londo told Lina. "You reacted quickly to a threat. You're getting faster. Now all you have to do is to teach me how to do that."

"I will just as soon as I figure it out for myself, love." She craned her neck as two waiters surrounded the camera sneak to demand an explanation. Maybe she'd get to see the guy booted out of the place? She hoped they'd do it in the literal sense.

"Ahem."

Lina turned. The maître d' himself stood there and gave her a nod to acknowledge her attention. Then he presented Lon a long white box secured with a pink ribbon. In turn Lon handed it to her. "I believe these are for you,"

She knew what it was just from its shape, but she still gave a little gasp of delight as she opened it. The romance of the night returned, doubled. Faint perfume wafted out as the box opened. A dozen long-stemmed pink roses lay there, perfect in size.

"Oh, Lon..."

"You've never gotten flowers before." His eyes seemed to memorize her expression.

She gave her head a quick shake, fighting back public tears.

"Now you have. And believe me, they won't be the last."

What could she do but throw her arms around him and kiss him? So what if people were watching? She loved him so! He was so romantic. So masculine. So exciting. His gaze melted into hers; his smile reached out to touch her heart.

"I love you," she whispered, and he whispered it back as he twined his fingers in hers.

Did they talk at all after that, or did they merely gaze into each other's eyes and smile? Neither was aware any more of people watching them.

Entire gossip columns were written on the basis of that dinner alone, and people began to reassess what they'd believed about Valiant and his inabilities.

"We are coming back here for our fiftieth anniversary," Lon told her. "We'll rent out the whole place for everyone, maybe the shop next door, too. There'll be hundreds of people here."

"Including the thirty-six grandkids?"

"*Oui.* And the… um…"

"Two hundred sixteen."

"You *are* smart. Okay, two hundred sixteen great-grandkids. And spouses. Maybe it'll take the entire block to fit them all in. A couple dozen presidents, Legionnaires, maybe an interstellar leader or two. And french vanilla ice cream." He eyed her up and down as if she were what he wanted served on his plate. "You'll wear that dress. I love that dress."

She smiled at that. "You have it all planned, don't you?"

"You know me."

"And when did all this occur to you?"

He suddenly became very serious. "The first time I saw you through the smoke in that burning hotel. When you were pulling those damned sheets off the bed and talking to yourself."

She touched her fingertips to his fingers. He had such wide fingers, so sensitive. "Londo…" She paused and he waited patiently for her. "Darling, it's so different. I never, ever thought I'd be married. Never even considered it. And I'm not used to, to all this amazing stuff."

"Lina–"

"All I'm saying is, is, if I do anything wrong, or something you really don't like or something like that… Don't keep it inside. Just come out and say it, so I don't get any horrible habits. You promise you'll do that, won't you?"

"You'll do fine. You'll learn from your own mistakes."

"But don't you see? I can't afford to make any mistakes at all. I do not want to embarrass you. Or Jae. And I don't want to do anything to mess up the Worlds."

As hard as she fought it, the very edge of reality was just beginning to intrude upon her life. She'd had an idea of what she was getting into when she accepted Lon's proposal, but not only had she not imagined an awful lot of what his life was like, but her own life was further complicated by Jae and the Worlds. She could rail against fate, but she'd be getting her fifteen minutes– plus– on the world's stage. She wasn't ready. If there was something to be screwed up, she'd be the one to do it.

"You're not going to. You think of yourself as some kind of hick. You aren't. You're well-educated, you're cosmopolitan. People like you. Some of us even love you, Lina. You're going to do great."

"I just want to please you. I want to be the perfect wife for the perfect man."

"Perfect husband."

She had to smile at that. "Okay. The absolutely most perfect husband in the entire world. Galaxy. Whatever."

"You make me happy. Just Lina, my beloved. You were the one who told me this afternoon that you'd never had to think about things like how to dress. You'll learn. I'll introduce you to people who'll teach you. There are people who can teach you anything you need. I've been to them all." He took her hand in his. "You don't think I just popped into the world this perfect, did you?"

"Londo Starhart, you have a self-image I would kill for."

"So kill me, Lina Starheart. Kill me and I'll die happy as long as you were the one to do it. Let me love you. All I want is for you to be happy."

"I've never been anywhere near as happy as I am now with you. My dearest husband." She let their gaze heat the air. "Just one thing. Two things."

"Anything, *cherie.*"

"That plaid couch and chair at Starhaven. Gone."

He let out a laugh then, loud enough to make the people around them turn and look.

By now it was all over the national media. Two international tabloid and celebrity news shows had already changed their early-evening programs to include fifteen full minutes about the afternoon's antics. By tomorrow it would definitely be big news, only eclipsed by Valiant's announcement of leaving Montreal. Valiant publicly dating was confirmed, something that had only been caught twice before. He had escorted, he had happened to sit next to an occasional female celebrity at various functions. But this was obviously a very hot date– a first.

And that this should have been preceded by a tip that he was married made the parawatch editors worldwide scratch their heads and wonder. Was it possible? Could a human and Valiant–? Could the powers of Valiant be controlled to the point that–?

But all this was only speculation, just gossip column and tabloid material. The press was revving up to uncover the mystery. Hard-news reporters were already being dispatched to Montreal from news services all over the globe. Get some cold facts and the story, if there were indeed a marriage, would wipe everything short of nuclear war from lead position.

The newlyweds were oblivious to it all. Their waiter had to clear his throat to get their attention from each other's eyes. "May I interest you in some dessert?" he asked, signaling the dessert cart to approach. He began his descriptions of the sweets and drinks, but Londo interrupted.

"I don't think we'll be getting any," he said and then turned to Lina. "Unless you want something, *chérie.*"

Goodness, had she eaten dinner? She had no memory of food other than Lon's smile and his powerful, gentle hand on hers. She felt wonderful. Pleasantly full, warm, loved, and desired. "I'm fine, thank you." The corset was much too tight, but Lon would take care of that soon enough. So thoughtful.

He was certainly examining the corset situation thoroughly. She took the deepest breath she could and was rewarded by his own stopping momentarily. Then he licked his lips.

"Good. I had another kind of dessert in mind for later." He gave her the most lasciviously evil grin she'd ever witnessed. "Just the check, please."

Londo! We're in public. She turned pink with pleasure.

He kissed her hand as the waiter bowed and signaled another. As he got his wallet out of his coat pocket, Londo smiled mysteriously . "I think we'll take a limo again. Maybe it'll have the hockey game on TV."

"Hockey."

His eyes danced as they met Lina's doubting ones.

"Not port? It's a long ride to Wyoming."

"I thought maybe we might stay here tonight. If that's all right with you."

"Of course it is," Lina replied. "I just assumed... Well. Montreal's fine. Your place is very nice." But it was his place, not like Starhaven. Starhaven had a newness, an air of potential about it. It wasn't all his. It could be theirs.

"Starhaven's still a construction zone. I thought you might be more comfortable here. I haven't even started Goal A for today. You'll freeze if we stay there tonight. Maybe we can live here while I get Starhaven finished; it'll be easier all around. And just think: no horrible couches."

Until Starhaven was finished? How many years would that be? Still, he was here and wearing black, more dashing than James Bond could dream. They had time apart to make up for. Years of being lonely to amend. Oh hell, she just wanted to wrap herself around him and discover him anew. Now. "And you're already hooked up to cable. A hockey game, hm?" She played with her beautiful new necklace to draw his attention to the part of her anatomy that he particularly favored.

He squirmed in his seat. His left eyebrow twitched. "Well… Maybe I can watch it later. My system records all the games for me."

"So you don't want to watch les Canadiens tonight?"

"The game's probably over by now anyway. I'll think about it on the ride home."

"Even if it's just across town, I can still port us home. It's so much quicker." *Now, now, now.*

"We're relaxing for once. Taking it slow."

She opened her mouth in shock. What did he have up his sleeve? Besides those powerful arms, that was. "Who are you and what have you done with my Londo?"

"I've captured him and I'm holding him somewhere where you won't find him while I have my evil way with you tonight." He smirked at her. "We have to take the roundabout way to my secret hideout."

"Well. If you put it that way and as long as it's not too roundabout, maybe I'll come along with you. But no TV in the limo."

"I'll try to find something else to hold my attention." He leered at her once again, just to make her turn blush-pink.

Londo flashed his Sterling card to pay the check. A white limo was waiting for them. Paparazzi lined their route out, cameras madly flashing, but then it was into the warm car and soft seats, with Londo's arm around her and tinted windows to dull the outside commotion.

A too-convenient traffic accident snarled things so that the paparazzi stalled out far behind them. "Told you they were good," Londo told her and Lina remembered the ParaNet Security.

Two blocks away they transferred to a new limo, this one black and shorter than the other.

"We're taking a tour tonight," Londo told the driver. "Let's go everywhere." Lon leaned over her to point out the sights as they passed them. Le Centre Bell, home of hockey's Canadiens, of course, was one.

"Do we get out to pray?" Lina asked him.

"We would if it were the playoffs. They're not until next month. The pavement will be much warmer on your knees then."

They hardly slowed at Molson Stadium, where the Montreal Saints played. "Rands follow the Cowboys," Lon stated as if it were Newton's Fourth Law.

He spoke of the long history of the city, of the importance of Catholicism as they motored by impossibly gothic cathedrals. The distinct culture of the area combined with other pockets of ethnicism within it. They drove across a long bridge and stopped along the shore of the other side to admire the fairy-light skyline of Montreal.

"It's beautiful," Lina told him. "It is a truly beautiful city. And you should be getting a salary from the tourism bureau."

"I just want you to like it."

"I do. I love it. I'd love anywhere you were, sweetheart, but this is a lovely city."

He rubbed her as they watched a large ocean-bound ship glide down the St. Lawrence. She looked at him and he kissed her, then kissed her again and again.

"Lon," she whispered as his hands grew bold, "I am not going to do anything in a car with a strange driver sitting in the front seat."

"I haven't noticed anything particularly strange about him."

"Londo."

"He can't see anything with the partition up."

"And of course we can trust that the car comes with soundproofing and extra-strength springs. Lon, you have a choice: we stay here and just neck, or we go somewhere else for, um, something else. Let me warn you, it's been a very wonderful but long day, and you'll only get to act on one of those choices before I conk out on you."

Londo snatched up the car phone. "We'll be getting out here," he told the driver.

"Here?" The driver glanced around at the dark solitude of this midnight place. Then he shrugged and punched code into his trip meter. It churned out a receipt and copy for Londo to sign.

They stood in the cold to watch the limo drive off into the night. Lina clutched the box of roses to her chest.

Lon squeezed her hand. "Okay, now you can port us home, Kitten. Home."

Lina smiled at the combination of lust and domesticity that lit his face. But then her eyebrows contracted.

"What's wrong?"

"Lon, you have intruders. I don't think they're ParaNet Security."

8

Londo's shoulders straightened and his hands clenched into fists. "Fuck," he growled. That loving luster in his eyes sharpened into a military glint as he stared into the city center. His trademark Valiant frown creased his forehead even as his jaw twitched taut. "You're right. Let me check it out from a closer vantage. I know a place where you'll be safe. You be prepared to port out immediately without me if I tell you to. No arguments."

Lina bit her lip and nodded. He pictured it and she set them far down the hall from his apartment.

Lon used his paravision to scan his home. Six intruders. Three bombs– were they a suicide squad? Familiar-looking guns that reeked of Terry Rhodes' work. Those guns had killed him for a few minutes a few weeks ago.

"Get me a costume, will you, babe?"

Lina ported one in from his closet. She ported on her own jeans and tee shirt as he changed there in the hall, and then sent both their formal outfits to their bed at Starhaven, and the roses to her refrigerator in North Carolina. Londo hustled her down the hall in the opposite direction from his apartment even as he pulled a ParaNet communicator from his vest.

"Situation here," he said into the mouthpiece.

Who answered? Lina couldn't place the voice, other than to know it was male.

Lon said, "Three good-sized bombs in my apartment, along with six intruders. Several hundred people live in the building. I suspect that there are more terrorists lurking in the area. I'd appreciate some help."

"On it, Londo. Give us a minute; we have your position."

Londo tucked the communicator back in his pocket and pointed out the window for Lina. "There."

"What?"

"Go to that roof over there." He transferred the picture of what he could see to her mind. "Get your coat. Stay warm. I want you out of the way for this. Stay there until it's over."

"Can I port some stuff around if I've got a clear shot?"

He considered. "All right, but double-think everything. Your safety is most important. Promise you won't do anything crazy."

"I promise. And you be careful, too, real careful."

"I will." He gave her a kiss and a smack on the bottom. "D'Artagnan."

She ported to the rooftop. She could see him standing there by the window. Of course he could see her. He waved and she nodded, trying not to seem stiff with fear. As she drew on her coat, she settled in to scan the area closely.

Can I get rid of the bombs? she asked.

Not now. Terry might set off the remaining ones if she notices when one goes missing. Remember, she's got those computer-timed sensors, faster than human reaction. Let us evacuate the building first.

Okay.

Heroes materialized next to Londo in the hallway. She'd seen them daily on the news: Dragonlord, Olympia. Lina squinted to see the others. Bolt. Forte. Good; Londo had some muscle in there as backup. She wished Maximus were there, too.

They conferred for only a minute. Then they were off, running down the hall into the stairwells and out of Lina's view. In her mind she followed them as they went door-to-door, rousing people out of bed or from in front of their televisions, evacuating the building in a calm but quiet manner. They started at the top and worked down. Because Londo lived near the top floor, it didn't take long to evacuate down to his level, and then they moved through the next ten levels below that.

Lina.

I'm here.

Port the bombs now. Can you grab them all at once? Without blowing them up?

I'll give it a try. It was ten times more difficult to do a port when she didn't have a clear physical view of either end.

Here, he said, and linked his mind to hers even as he looked through the very walls toward his apartment. There they were. **If you can't take them all, then take 'em one at a time, as fast as you can.**

I'm starting now.

With people around she didn't want to risk all three at once. She'd blown up a compartment of Wiley's lab by not being careful. Instead she felt them out so she almost had all three, and then concentrated on one. On the next. On the next. Quick as a heartbeat, she sent them to Tiawa over the Pacific Ocean, where they fell harmlessly into the water to rot.

Perfect. Good work. He unlinked his paravision from her.

Guns next?

An explosion ripped through Lon's apartment like fire slicing the air itself. She saw it as it happened in her mind, followed some seconds later by a hollow, unnatural boom traveling at the speed of sound. Not a bomb; big guns. *Big* guns. The upper stories of the building went black.

"No!" Lina couldn't bear the thought of Londo losing any of his possessions. She ported everything she could, as fast as she could, first to her rooftop and then to Starhaven. If she could sense a gun, she ported it to there in two hops as well, but stored the guns in Starhaven's emptier spaces. Wiley might want to study them later. But things were happening too quickly for her to get a handle on moving objects. Her clairvoyance was not nearly as automatic or exact as Londo's clairvoyant vision. She couldn't pick up the terrorists, so she stuck with porting Londo's possessions.

Then there were things in apartments next to Lon's, things that she could dimly sense and fought to visualize. Two small dogs, left alone; they were certainly easy to picture. They went to North Carolina. The cats there would just have to cope. They were Starharts now, too.

Behind her excited voices emerged from the roof's service door. This building's occupants began to gather to join her at this safe viewing station. They rushed to her side of the building to watch the battle. They were mostly men, but also a few women, a few boys, one teenaged girl. Most had dressed hurriedly for the cold.

Lina moved back so she could make her two-step ports without them noticing.

They made comments and yelled as the battle progressed. Two of the young men started cheering for the terrorists as energy beams shot out of the windows of the apartments over there.

"Cool guns!" one of them exclaimed.

Londo reached *through* a wall to grab one sniper. He made a fist over the man's gun barrel. Even as it crumpled, he butted the weapon back into his chin with enough force to knock him out.

Lon turned to take care of the next one two rooms over, but out the window he saw a swarm of lights, like fireflies *en masse*. Twenty… thirty… More. They were wingless flying vehicles each the size of a Smart car, zipping through the sky toward him.

Armed.

Larger ones buzzed on the outskirts of the cloud. Those each held two people instead of one– and a cannon-sized weapon.

The first wave of them swooped by him, and the walls of the building dimpled under a hail of bullets. The ammo they were using penetrated the walls completely. Even as he heard one of the gunmen in his apartment let out a startled cry, Londo informed his fellow Networkers of the situation.

Overlapping conversation erupted on their frequency for a moment before order set in again. Dragonlord would continue evacuations, but on the lowest levels, since he had no way to protect himself against such weaponry. Bolt would take on the upper floors and Olympia would protect the residents as they evacuated. Forte held herself on standby, ready to support the building if need be, since she couldn't fly.

Londo would take care of the hovercars and their weapons.

They were likely the same weaponry that had temporarily stripped him of his powers mere weeks ago. Or they were the guns that had actually killed him.

A moment's panic gripped him– a sense of his own mortality, which he'd become so aware of these past weeks. Then he leaped out a broken window to meet the enemy. The innocent must be protected. This was his home. This was theirs as well.

He slammed into the first craft. It spun and crashed into the next. A domino effect took out a handful more before the formation opened to allow more space between the cars. Londo took the opportunity to push the affected cars to the street. With each one on the ground, he reached into its engine compartment and crushed the carburetor, then pinched the doors shut so there could be no escape.

The swarm had split in half: the first targeted him, down on the street, while the other orbited the building, firing into it. At least on those floors there shouldn't be anyone left to harm, other than the terrorists.

Oui, this was Terry's MO: destroy what was dear to Londo. She knew his attention would be divided between actually stopping her goons and protecting the civilians.

She must not know the ParaNet was here.

He disliked doing it, but Lon turned his concentration fully to the attacking craft.

Like a football, he flung himself into midst of the swarm, tackling and then following them down. As he pinched one door, he happened to notice the construction site down the block.

Girders.

Girders were good. It took mere moments to grab one by its center. He twirled through the sky, his weapon now a propeller of destruction. Satisfying crunching sounds of mayhem echoed all around him, bouncing off neighboring buildings. He made sure the cars didn't do so as well.

The smaller cars retreated quickly– ha! Not quickly enough for most of them!– and the larger ones eased forward. Using his paravision, he could see cannon and bazooka barrels swiveling to take aim.

Yes, they looked like those final guns on Tiawa, the ones that had ripped the life out of him. But Terry didn't know something else:

Londo had a shield.

The Three Worlds had gifted him with it. The Legion had put it through a few preliminary tests.

Lon extended his left arm, and the shield shimmered into view. Its ghostly surface bore the planetary symbols for the worlds he now served: Earth, Sarastor, and Aldierra.

Lina was worried, but he silently reassured her.

The nearest large hovercraft fired, recoiling in a tumble.

The white-hot blast illuminated all of this side of the mountain in its dazzle. Lon could see the red-hot barrel, see how the men inside the hovercraft not only panicked from their unstable craft, but from the heat.

And the shield soaked in the energy like it had been soap suds.

Oh, Londo liked this shield. Tucking the girder under his arm, he gave the shield a quick pat before bracing for another impact.

The shield took it all. Again. And again. And again.

Terry's troops would be blinded for a few seconds, no matter what kind of eyewear they were using. Lon kicked the careening vehicles to the street. Too bad if the men inside weren't cushioned enough for the impact. They were playing with the big boys now. He tried to aim for the parking lot behind the construction area, but in two cases he missed and the craft cratered the road instead.

Ah, now everyone in the sky was backing away from him. It took Terry long enough to figure that out.

The girder had become a twisted mass, its ends torn off. He ditched it, then took off after the retreating fleet. With outspread palms, he snapped cars like volleyballs high into the atmosphere. As they plummeted back down, Londo linked his hands and spiked them to the ground.

He noticed about ten of the small cars turning tail and streaking far across the sky. Using his com, he made sure that ParaNet tracked them.

Something made him turn around. Three of the larger cars had snuck back. One cannon began to lower its sights…

Lon's paravision melted the end of it even as it fired. A sheet of white plasma shot out in a wide beam. The walls of his building hissed as they disintegrated, melting at the sides of the blast.

"Forte!" he called on his radio. "Nineteenth floor, west side!" Even while sending GPS coordinates to the ParaNet transporters, he cooled the structure for her with his parabreath and was rewarded with the sight of the Russian heroine appearing in a room. She took a quick look around, then climbed onto the debris, right where a major structural beam should have stood. Stretching out her arms, she held the building in place.

"Go!" she shouted at Londo even as Olympia flew in to aid her.

Londo turned to the car that was about to fire next. If it had been him, he would have ordered simultaneous fire. Maybe the guns couldn't work that way.

They were going to fire down, into the heart of the building. There were still people down there. Lon swooped in time to shove his shield against the cannon's muzzle, braced by his shoulder.

Too bad you can't reflect, he silently told his new shield.

But it did. The cannon fired as soon as the shield went up, and the flash of the reflection blinded even Lon for a moment. White fire blanketed the sky. All of Eastern Canada must see it.

Of course not a shred of the hovercar survived.

Damned good thing the blast went up. Otherwise, half the city might have disintegrated. *I think I'll keep you on "absorb,"* he told the shield. At least until he'd trained more in using it.

Londo tested his shoulder. It was a little sore, but that was because he'd been batting hovercars around. Otherwise, the explosion hadn't harmed him.

Two more hovercars, the big kind.

They bobbed in the air, as if unsure what to do.

There was Terry in one of them. She was biting her lip as she glared at him.

Then she turned and pointed. Gave an order. Londo dove.

Lina wanted to strangle some sense into the idiots cheering for the bad guys, but she had to save her strength for porting.

People's possessions– They went to Starhaven in a big pile. An aquarium went to her heated North Carolina house. Refrigerators, ovens, a piano, clothing…

So many hovercars swooped out of nowhere to surround Lon's building. From this distance they looked like beetles swarming a tree. Lina knew in her bones that Terry was in one. Flashing red and blue lights began to roll up the street outside Lon's apartment.

A gun with a muzzle large enough to see from her position fired into the structure. Steel and concrete exploded outward. Olympia leaned out of a broken window to throw her snakeskin bola Ouroboros at the car. The vehicle rotated and sped away, but she gestured to the snakeskin. The car jerked once, then twice to a crawl as Ouroboros pulled back. The bola-snake stretched.

Olympia controlled her weapon like a horse's reins. The car stopped, bobbling in mid-air as if it were quivering. Then Ouroboros coiled around the hovercar, reflecting the night's lights upon its scales. Olympia jumped out of her window, landed lightly on the street, and then pulled it all down to street level as she would have a kite. As the police descended upon it, she gathered her snakeskin again and flew up to reenter the building.

The other hovercars had zoomed away at Olympia's presence but now they returned to circle. Lina noticed a spray of the vehicles plummeting from the sky behind the building. Must be Lon's work. Though she couldn't see where they crashed, she could certainly hear the metal-scraping thuds of the destruction.

One of the remaining cars fired at the building. This time it wasn't bullets, but blinding light. Before her eyesight had been blotted out by the glare, she'd seen Londo flash down to stand between another car and the building. She pressed her fists against her mouth in terror. These were mounted guns, as large as the ones that had killed him on Tiawa.

"Get 'em, Valiant!" someone called.

"I can't see!"

"They're going to blast him through to the Arctic Circle," another one said in a lower voice.

"Get out of the way, Valiant, you crazy bastard!"

"Do you think those things can hurt him?"

Lina tried not to breathe. She knew if she did, she'd scream in terror.

****I've got it; don't worry,**** Lon told her.

She saw it now: his Worlds-gifted shield materializing beside him, as tall as he was. It shone dimly in the night like ghosted silver.

"What the hell is that?"

"Hey, it's some kinda shield! Valiant's got a shield!"

"Get 'em, Valiant! Let 'em have it!!"

Lon hovered there, waving at the car with his free hand: *come on, come on and try your best.* The cannon let loose with a blast, but this time he braced the shield to intercept the attack. Blinding shot after blinding shot went off. Lina learned to keep her eyes shut.

When she was able to see again, she joined the crowd in trying to spot Lon. There he was– barreling through those retreating hovercars. Giving them what-for.

The crowd went wild with cheers.

Then Londo doubled back for some reason. Lina clenched her eyes shut and turned away just in time to see the world light up like high noon behind her eyelids. The crowd groaned as one, even before a deafening crash of thunder made their building rock. She heard a shriek of metal twisting nearby.

The bottommost floors of the apartment building lost power. The building stood black against the city. Smoke from extinguished fires poured out of the upper stories, light gray with a halo of dust.

Lina was exhausted. At least it hadn't been interplanetary porting. This had been just a matter of changing stuff's place, not of balancing pressures or electrical charge or screening contaminants. Still the sheer volume was enormous.

She couldn't do any more. Her guides told her, ****Enough,**** and she was relieved to obey.

Londo sank his fingers into the frame of the hovercar. He leaned into the side window, shattering it as his head emerged inside. "*Salut,* Terry," he told her with a grin. Her cannon sat beside her, melted. Sweat poured off her and her passenger, who held his hands in the air. A runnel of blood ran from Terry's left nostril, and it looked like some upset might have given her a black eye. Aw, *quel dommage.* "Lovely night for a drive, isn't it?"

Her expression was too dark to describe. Her knuckles were white as she clutched the arms of her seat. He chuckled.

"Hope you enjoyed it. I don't think they're going to let you out for a long, long time. If ever."

Then he dragged the car down to the pavement. He opened the door long enough for a policeman to take over, then jumped up to take care of the final hovercar.

After that it was all a matter of cleanup and temporary repair. Lon used the nearby construction site's materials to wedge the upper stories of what had once been his home into some kind of stability.

He heard onlookers from all around. "Look at him go!" "Go, Valiant! Awright!" And the cheers.

After a while he could check up on Forte. Gingerly she let loose her hold on the building, and nothing collapsed. Bolt flashed in with fire and water damage reports. Olympia said that all civilians had been evacuated safely. Dragonlord called in to confirm he was coordinating with the local police. Terry Rhodes was quite safely in custody. The remaining hovercars had been tracked, and Canadian forces were routing them even now.

"Guess the show's over for the night," someone behind Lina complained.

There were disappointed mutters of agreement. "It's too cold to hope anything else will happen," another said as they made their way to the door back inside.

"Do you think they'll give out autographs?"

Lina ported over to the remains of Lon's building. His expensive apartment was now a blackened shell with gaping holes in the scorched walls that provided no barrier to the freezing wind. A web of girders supported the ceiling. Water dripped from pipes there. The overbearing stench of burned plastic hung in the air. Silhouetted in the empty outer wall against the lights of the city stood Londo.

"Darling, are you all right?" she cried as she ran to him. She clutched him, trying to feel the live reality of him next to her.

"I'm okay," he said. "I'm fine. Not a scratch." He rocked her gently. "I'm fine."

"I'll get used to this," she finally said. "I will, I promise. I was so scared for you! Those guns–"

"I'm fine, *chérie*. They're out of commission now."

"We'll send the big guns to Wiley. He needs to study one, doesn't he? So you can come up with a defense against what they do."

"Funny; I was just thinking the same thing," Lon tried to smile at her. "I'm afraid I mangled the ones I came in contact with, but Wiley should still be able to reconstruct them. Let's give the people here a couple of weeks to take their photographs of the evidence. The police won't be interested in the mechanics. I'll pull a few strings."

"I don't want just anyone to be able to get their hands on those things!"

"They won't, they won't." He rubbed her back to calm her down. He sighed as he looked around the remains of his beautiful home.

Lina tried to cheer him. "It's a better view now." With all the exposure, you could see around to the mountain with its lighted cross as well as to Vieux Montreal and the south of the city.

He grunted at that. "*Mon coeur,* is it always like this? When the universe wants to make sure that you do something and don't back off?"

"Why? Were you thinking about forgetting about Starhaven and just living here?"

He was silent for a moment. "It began to occur to me tonight at the concert. Starhaven is still… so rough. I do love this city. I don't want to turn my back on it."

"So if we have the Center here, it'll still be home. Weren't you listening to yourself? We'll be here all the time. Living at Starhaven will make you value your time in Montreal all the more."

He surveyed the ruins of his home. "This was supposed to be my day."

"Oh, sweetheart…" She held him close and stroked his hair as if he were a child. "There will be other days. Better days."

"Promise?"

She kissed him, and therein lay deeper promises of forever. "We'll make a fresh start tomorrow."

"Yes. Tonight I still have some official business to take care of." He patted her butt. "So, what'd you think? Did you like it? Did you like me?"

She managed a laugh at that. "You looked just like that Valiant guy on TV. All brave and heroic and powerful… It gave me goosebumps on top of goose-bumps."

"Wait till later tonight. I'll give you goosebumps." His ParaNet communicator chirped from deep within his vest. "Gotta go for a while, *cherie.*"

Sipping at a steaming mug of caffeine, Lina watched Londo from the gathering throng behind the police barricades. Thank goodness Lon had used his shield tonight; it had reminded her that she had a Worlds-given flute she could use to calm the chaos at her house. It had also called back one cute pup who'd used the kitty door to escape.

It had taken a few phone calls to find snug spots for everyone at various Montreal vets. After that she had to port back to clean up the messes left by the sudden incursion and to reassure her own herd. Finally the cats had settled down for the night.

She'd fixed a large mug of chai, added a *Star Trek* toboggan to her winter ensemble, and ported back to Montreal. She was just one of the people who were flocking here by the hundreds, maybe even thousands, to see what they could see. Robert-Bourassa Boulevard was normally busy, but now cars filled with the curious jammed it to a late-night standstill, held up by all the road blocks and detours. The east side of the medianed street was entirely cordoned off; the west side stopped with the gawkers… and two fender-benders. Honking and raucous shouts filled the air.

City lights revealed wispy white clouds drifting heavenward from the gaps in the dark apartment building. The smell of char and burned plastic was almost overwhelming. Shattered remains of the upper stories that she had ported away from the street during the battle lay in piles. Lon and the others had added to them until they were quite the metropolitan mountains.

Lina neared the group of residents who gathered at the Red Cross trucks just outside the lines. As temporary quarters were arranged, they seemed slow to realize that they probably would be staying elsewhere for a long, long time.

Some of them tried to pick through the rubble for their belongings, but the cops ran them off politely. When Lina heard someone asking about a pet– a little girl was crying about her cat– she was happy to hear that the organization already had the information about the vets to give out.

It was freezing cold. Lina stuffed her free hand deep into her coat pockets. She'd let her hair down to add some warmth to her neck. Her coat controls were on full.

She watched Londo with the other heroes: Olympia, Bolt, Dragonlord, Forte, and some police officers, pointing to the damage, pointing to the trussed-up villains as they were hauled into waiting vans. Red and blue lights flashed all around them and the occasional spray of powdery debris drifted down from above.

One man drove up the east side of the street and jumped out of his car, waving his arms and pulling what was left of his hair. He had several choice words to shout. The police quickly ushered him away from the heroes. That must be the owner of the building, Lina surmised. *Hey guy,* she wanted to call to him, *it could have been much, much worse.*

Now camera crews trotted in from around the corner, avoiding the boulevard traffic jam. They formed a semicircle that invited the heroes to join them front and center. She could almost hear them asking their questions in English, sounding strangely foreign here. Funny how the night air carried– Oh no, that wasn't it at all. The sound came from an electronics store with two working TV sets in the display window. The local stations were covering this live, so she went over to watch the broadcast.

The eleven o'clock news had been extended to accommodate this. The Para-Net members clustered in a tight group so the cameras could catch them all. Lon handled most of the questions and certainly all that came in French, although he deferred to Dragonlord to furnish Terry Rhodes' criminal record in exacting detail. From the years cited, Lina realized that Lon must have been somewhere in his mid-teens when he first encountered Terry. No wonder she'd been able to seduce him. Well, to a point.

"Valiant," a reporter asked, "did this attack have something to do with your decision to leave Montreal?"

"You're leaving Montreal?" another interrupted. The Networkers turned to Londo curiously. Obviously this was the first they'd heard the news.

Lon sighed and shook his head. "After this attack I certainly have to live somewhere else," he said ruefully. "But since I didn't have any idea that this would take place, I can say that *non,* this had nothing to do with my decision. I have every intention of keeping close ties with Montreal. This attack tonight..." He tried to figure out the right way to phrase it.

"Terry Rhodes put innocent people's lives in danger simply because of my presence. We can all be thankful that no one was hurt besides her men, and we can make sure that our judicial system puts them all behind bars for a long, long time. My moving will ensure that something like this won't happen again."

Police called Valiant away from the group, so he wasn't there when one reporter finally asked: "Is it true that Valiant is now married?"

The camera caught Dragonlord's face as the question clearly hit him from out of the blue. Under his cowl he grimaced at the reporter, giving him a "that's the stupidest question I've ever heard" look, and said, "Next question."

Lina smiled; the game was still on. Londo would be pleased. And it *was* kind of fun, but she didn't really feel like having fun right now. She felt depressed, like Cinderella after the ball. Her prince wasn't with her. The overwhelming glamor and romance of the night was gone and she was just plain exhausted from porting and nerves and cold.

The press conference ended. The TV sets returned to late-night talk shows and infomercials. Reporters left and the television crews packed up. A van pulled up next to one of the barricades. One of the crews split off from the others to load it. Lina strolled over, curious to see what was kept inside. It looked like an amateur carpenter had set up a desk with a wall of electronics facing it.

"*Pardonnez-moi, mademoiselle,*" a male voice behind her said, and she stepped aside. "I mean," he said, "Ms., of course." It was Geoff the reporter from the concert.

"You keep late hours," she said.

"We happened to be close by when all this happened. So… you're keeping watch on him?"

"We were heading in for the night when we saw what was happening. Lon called the Network just before all hell broke loose."

"Are you a parahero, Ms. Lina? Off the record?"

"A hero? I've helped in some things." She smiled as she caught sight of Londo. Autograph seekers deluged the Networkers now. The police could hold some of them back, but many were getting through.

"But you're a para. You have to be. Maybe a megapara?"

"That's what people are telling me. Me, I think I'm just…"

"Just what?"

"Just a Speaker, Monsieur Geoff."

"Speaker? What kind of speaker?"

"Stop loafing, Geoff!" A man finished securing equipment into the van and looked up at the reporter. "That's the last of it. Let's do a final check-in and go home."

"In a minute," Geoff replied and turned back to Lina. "What's that mean? Speaker?"

"We haven't quite figured it all out yet." She ported in her padd. Geoff gasped to see it suddenly appear in her hands, then did a double take as the screen appeared above it. "Give me your full name again and phone number and I'll make sure he calls you once things have settled down a bit. The universe has been spinning like a top."

"I can ask you. What does Maximus think of all this?"

She gave a soft chuckle at that. "Don't *ever* ask him that question. Maximus? Maximus doesn't know. Lon's been leaving messages everywhere, but apparently Maximus is out and about and not checking in. Lon's really upset that he missed the wedding. Phone number?"

He looked over her shoulder as she scribbled on the padd, the writing magically transforming into print font. Then she ported the padd back to Starhaven.

"So why'd the Network deny knowledge of the marriage?" Geoff asked very softly, so no one could overhear. "Don't they know?"

Lina heaved a heavy sigh. "I think they will in a little while," she said, the first hint of new unease settling on her.

9

The frosted store window reflected the flashing blue lights of police vehicles along with the yellow strobes of barricades. The autograph hounds had thinned and the massive crowds wandered back to their beds.

Lina, the press is gone now.

She brightened up. Her prince was back with her. **I see that. Are you ready to go?**

Not yet. Come on over. But–

But what? What are you thinking up in that brilliant but twisted mind of yours?

I've been thinking about this for a few days now. Do me a favor.

She listened for a moment and had to laugh. **You are deeply disturbed. I can't do that!**

Sure you can. Please, chérie.

God. First the dress, now this. Okay, I'll try, she told him. **No guarantees.**

You're the best. Now let's go, love. Hup hup.

Lina reappeared on the curb, shivering as the sudden cold hit her again. She wasn't wearing her climalon jacket, but her old winter coat, which wasn't nearly as warm.

Lon spotted her the moment she arrived. **Oo, baby!**

She suppressed the urge to close her coat over the lowcut tank top. Lon had told her to make a vivid statement, so she'd chosen boobs again. Did she really want to make this kind of impression? To the ParaNet?

She made a face at Lon's far-off form, and dangly earrings whipped against her boa-wrapped neck. **I must be crazy. It's below freezing, dammit!** she complained. She couldn't recall ever buying it, yet here she was wearing a miniskirt in the frozen Arctic. Suddenly a blessedly warm breeze enveloped her. Lon had used his heat breath on her. **Thanks.**

No problem. I want pictures of this.

Lord, I hope not.

Could you fluff your hair? It'll work even better with big ho' hair.

Her reflection in the store window showed her dayglo red lipstick like neon against the window backdrop. She doubled over, ported in equipment and then back-brushed quickly. Her hair smoothed a good four inches from her scalp. Hello, Tammy Faye.

Yowza! Just perfect, Lie. I wish Jae could see this. Even as he said it she could feel him reach into one of his pockets. Knowing him, he'd released one of those floating camera deals. Embarrassing home movies for the Starharts, take 1.

She told him, **I'm only doing this because I love you.**

Yeah yeah. Hurry up and get over here!

Lina took a deep breath and tried to figure out what she was supposed to be. Jae did this all the time. He put up a false front and brazened it through. She knew a little of how his mind worked now; she could do this, too. She could.

She picked her way through icy spots and bits of glass toward Lon, giving a bulldozer attending to the debris a wide safety berth. She *would* do this. Arms fluttering, she ran lightly the last few yards to the ParaNetters.

Bolt saw her first. It was obvious that he had dealt with groupies before; she was no threat. He did give a good consideration to her cleavage. Oh well, that was part of the character. Dressed in the familiar blue spandex racing suit, a tight hood and goggles, the speedster glanced up at her face and started. She flashed a warning look at him before the others could turn around.

Lon's face was carefully neutral although his eyes twinkled at her.

"Oooo!" she cooed at them all. They turned to her. *Stay in character!* "That was, like, sooo spectacular! I've never seen actual paraheroes in real, live action before."

Oh lord, it was Olympia and Dragonlord up close and in person! Olympia's tunic-coat looked so much more ornate than it did on the news, woven with a primitive pattern of polka dots and ping starbursts. Her dark hair was tightly braided into a chignon, which added to the stern demeanor she gave Lina. Ouroboros settled around the legendary heroine's waist like a belt, though it rippled against her.

Lina had practically memorized Olympia's latest book. It held such an fascinating guess at to the future of twenty-first century feminism.

Lina decided that Dragonlord looked scarier on video than in person. His outfit invoked images of dragons, but the antennae attached to his cowl tended to bobble when he moved. Still, the black dragon wings that now folded to either side were impressive when he used his jet pack. She had to admit that overall he did have a gargoyle-ish presence.

If she looked at them too long she'd blush or do something stupid, so she skipped over to Lon. "And you, Valiant! Oh, you were just the absolute best!" She clapped her hands together in adoration. "Gosh, you're cute. I mean, so handsome!"

He gave her a thorough once-over and grinned. "You're cute, too. You liked it? *Vraiment?*"

Bolt snorted. Forte looked up at Dragonlord and significantly pursed her lips for Valiant's uncharacteristic actions. Dragonlord tilted his chin to assess the groupie/slut and shook his head back at Forte. He had no idea what was going on.

"OoOOoh yes! And that shield thing– that was totally kuel. I just had to tell you. How'd you do that?"

Lon let the shield appear for her. "What, this? Just a little something extra I added tonight. Maybe just for you."

"Rilly, Valiant? Then I have to thank you for the show–" Lina threw her arms around him. He leaned down for a long, long kiss. The shield disappeared so he could gather her in his arms until her feet left the ground. She let one pointed foot rise in the back for effect, and then his hand dropped down to her ass.

Londo! We're in public!

Stay with me, baby.

His tongue played with hers. She could feel him trying not to laugh. Bolt didn't succeed in masking his snorts behind his hands.

"OoOOoo." The kiss left Lina flustered. She could see that Londo was proud of his work on her. She giggled at him and his silliness, knowing that it would add to her character.

He set her back down on the ground. "You're welcome," he said gravely.

Twining her fingers in his hair, she ran her other hand over his broad chest. "Ooo. Um. Look, Valiant, if you'd like to… continue the excitement, we could go to my place."

"Hmm." His eyes crinkled appraisingly. "I think that could be arranged." Lon turned to the other heroes. "Could you finish here without me?" He turned back to Lina without waiting for a reply. "What did you have in mind for breakfast?"

"Anything you want," she cooed at him from beneath lowered eyelashes. "And afterward–"

"Afterward…?"

"Could I get an autograph?"

Lon broke into a grin. "Sure, babe," he said. "You have a pen in your apartment? I can find something to write on." He ogled her cleavage.

"Londo, you can't be serious," Olympia interrupted, her eyes darting back and forth between him and *that woman.* "Look, miss, we have work to do here. Why don't you just–"

"Now, Demi," Londo reasoned so coolly, "what I do with my life is my business, not yours. If I want to go out with… what did you say your name was, *chérie?*"

"No, my name's not Sherry," Lina told him. **Can't we end this now? I think I've lost any shred of dignity I might have had.**

Play along, pet.

"Arf," Lina replied out loud, to Olympia's great consternation.

"Excuse me," Forte said. The blonde Russian powerhouse was petite in height but solid in stature. In summer she wore red shorts and sports bra, but colder months brought out her tracksuit with the long, striped sleeves and pants. "If we could just interrupt this tender love scene, Londo, we still have some cleaning up to do." She eyed Lina frostily up and down, and Lina returned the favor, her arms locked around Londo's waist.

Forte shoved a clipboard at Londo so he had to drop his hands from Lina to receive it. "I hate police reports," he told her. "This will only take a minute or five."

"Hurry, Valley!"

"I will. And don't call me 'Valley.'" Londo flipped through the stack of paper, then began scribbling on the top piece.

Olympia muttered darkly as she filled out forms on her own clipboard. Forte and Dragonlord were giving Lina and Lon the evil eye. Bolt hopped behind them, unseen by the others, whirling his finger at his ear and sticking out his tongue to Londo. Lon glanced at him only a moment before returning, straight-faced, to his work.

Lina found a pack of gum in her coat pocket and wadded a stick into her mouth. As an afterthought she held the package out to the ParaNetters. "Juicyfruit?" she offered. "Juicyfruit, Valiant?" She snapped the gum loudly.

"No thanks," he said as Bolt blithely took a stick. The others just looked daggers at Lina. "Tara, is there some reason you can't fill out forms tonight? Or anybody else? I have an appointment here I'd like to keep."

"Oh really, Londo!" Forte, or Tara, huffed. She crooked an index finger at an officer clearing away another blockade, and the policeman trotted up to Lina and Londo.

"*Pardonnez-moi,*" he told Lina. "<Leave the ParaNetters to their work, Miss, or I'll have to remove you myself.>"

"*Ça alors!*" Lina exclaimed softly. "*Je suis ici avec Valiant.* <I'm with Valiant. Ask him if you don't believe me.>"

Lon looked up from his notes and nodded to the officer. "*C'est vrai,*" he said. The policeman nodded and returned to his barricade.

"What'd he say? What'd she say?" Tara demanded to know from Dragonlord.

"She's with him," Dragonlord replied and handed Lon another stack of paper, leaving his own hands free.

"No more reports!" Londo shook the paperwork at the gray-cloaked man and shoved all his paperwork at him. "Tonight I have had my home cruelly ripped from under me. Now this kind woman has offered me a place to stay for the night. Such a good samaritan."

Lina fluttered her eyes at him.

"So generous," Londo continued. "You don't find many like her in this world."

"Good god, Lon," Tara muttered, hands on her hips. "Someone get him a cold shower and me a pot to puke in."

Londo grinned as he hoisted Lina to sit on the crook of his arm. She might as well have been a feather. "No, not many like her at all. Such a pretty girl, too. How'd you like to be my girlfriend, my leetle cabbage?" He exaggerated his French accent for best effect.

"Londo," Olympia cried, "what has gotten into you?"

"Put the girl down," Dragonlord said.

Forte's eyes blazed first at Lina, then at Londo and back, this time cooler. "He's gone into crazy mode," she told the group, then addressed Lina. "Sometimes he gets a little– Um…"

"What do you get?" Lina asked Londo and broke into a quick grin before she could mask it down. Lon gave her a grin back and then frowned.

"Apparently not a girlfriend," Londo sulked, staring down his friends. "They don't want me to have one. Tell you what, *chérie,* how'd you like to be engaged to me instead? Would you do that? You could be my fiancée."

"My husband wouldn't approve," Lina told Londo firmly.

"You have a husband?" Lon innocently asked.

"But he wouldn't mind me being with you, Valiant. He's a big fan of yours. A big, *big* fan. Probably your biggest fan ever. Next to me. Is it true that you're the biggest megapara around?"

"Why don't I give him an autograph, too?"

"He'd like that a lot, Valley!"

"*Bon.*" Londo jounced her on his arm. "Do you think he'd mind if I married you, too? I'll make an honest bigamist out of you. I'm sorry, Demi–" He meant Olympia, who was sputtering at him– "but I've decided. I've just got to have this girl for my wife. She seems nice enough, doesn't she? Dresses like a tramp, but she's very pretty. She'll do." Lon pressed his nose against Lina's. "Marry me, *cherie.*"

"Really? I told you, my name's not Sherry." Lina snapped her gum again.

It was Forte who found her voice first among the ParaNetters. "Londo, you have gone clear around the bend this time! Look, you apologize to this girl right now and we'll call up that therapist of yours and tell him–"

"Wife," Lina said to Londo, ignoring these celebrities. It was easier to do this that way. "Does that mean I get a ring? A nice big one?"

"*Certainement, cherie.*" Londo grinned. "Here, I'll get you one just like mine. Do you like it?" He showed his wedding signet to her so that the others couldn't miss it.

"Why, it looks almost like the one I have," Lina said as if it were a surprise. She took off her left glove for Londo to inspect. He turned her hand so the others could contrast and compare their two rings: the white diamond on his finger and the green one on hers, both set in the symbol of the Three Worlds' Chosen. "My husband and you must shop at the same Walmart. They were having a sale."

"How about that." Londo gasped theatrically. "Imagine the coincidence!"

Olympia stood stock-still while Dragonlord regarded the two of them intently behind the slits of his mask. Forte still hadn't gotten it, but the Bolt shook with laughter, leaning against Olympia and slapping her shoulder. Ouroboros writhed with irritation around her waist.

Lon set Lina down. "I suppose we could tell everyone we're married now," he said. "I mean, since we both have matching rings. What did you say your name was, sweetheart?"

"'Starhart,' not 'sweetheart,'" she replied. "Lina Starhart. And your name would be…?"

"What a coincidence." Again Lon faked astonishment. "My name happens to be Londo Starheart. I just had it changed. Now this way we can have matching towels, too. Imagine how much money we'll save." He turned to the others and bowed while gesturing to Lina: "Everyone, this is Lina Starheart, my wife. The ol' ball and chain. The little woman. My old lady."

"This is not funny, Lon," Forte glared.

"F–," the Bolt declared.

"I don't think he's kidding," Dragonlord said slowly. "This is obviously a setup."

"A setup?" Londo's jaw dropped. He pressed his fingertips against his chest. "*Moi?*"

"One of your practical jokes," Olympia accused. "For a moment you even had me going. What are we going to do with you, Londo?"

Londo put his hands to his mouth in ultra-feminine shock and mimicked, "Oooh, Londo, you naughty boy! What are we going to *do* with you?"

Forte's jaw set in a determined pout. "Bamboozled again by Lon Rand. What we're going to do," she warned, punching her fist against the palm of her other hand, "is knock some respect into you."

"Excuse me," Lina said.

"You and which army?" Londo grinned. "So what, Gary, Demi– Are you going to hit me, too? Punish me for being a baaad boy?"

"I think we could take the effer if we did it all at once." The Bolt met Lon's grin with an anticipatory one of his own. "How are we going to do this?"

"Really, Londo." Olympia's voice revealed her pity at his childishness. "How long did you plan this? I'll hold him for you, Tara, if you really want to teach him a lesson."

"Excuse me," Lina said, louder this time. "But no one's going to beat up Lon tonight. Please. Not even for fun."

Forte ignored her and faked winding back for a roundhouse blow to Londo's chin. She disappeared, appearing instantaneously twenty feet away.

Londo stuck out that chin and pointed to it. "What's the matter, Tara?" he asked. "Is your reach getting shorter?"

"How'd you do that?" Forte demanded as she strode back.

"Yes, how'd you do that?"

"Can I please change now, Lon? I'm freezing."

"I like what you've got on."

"And it's the perfect outfit for meeting your friends. Now they think you've married the world's trashiest trailer trash."

Londo laughed. "Now, Lina, they're not–"

"Of course they are! You got your reaction; end of joke. Leave me some shred of dignity. Lord knows I don't have much left."

"You look great. I've got a permanent record of the outfit. What hooker did you grab this off of, anyway?"

"I'm going to burn everything when we get home. You're one sick puppy, sweetheart."

"Absolutely, *chérie.*"

"I told you, my name's not Sherry." Behind his back– just in case there was still a time-lag when she did it, though she was really fast now– Lina ported back into warm jeans and her Sarastor jacket. Rid of the bothersome earrings, she pulled her *Star Trek* toboggan cap roughly over her head, flattening her mall hair. "Much better," she declared.

He let out a full-body laugh and hugged her before releasing all but her hand. "*D'accord.* Ladies and gentlemen, I'd like to introduce you to Carolina Starheart, who is not trailer trash of any kind. She's my wife. My lovely and wonderful and amazing wife. As of, oh, about a week ago. A week? No, more than that."

He and Lina held a quick discussion of time passage, using their fingers as they ticked off the events of the past couple weeks. They were oblivious to the wide-open eyes all around.

"Eleven days," they decided together.

"For there," Lina said. "Wouldn't that be at least twelve, thirteen days Terran?"

Lon squinted calculation. "Maybe. We'll figure it out later."

Bolt laughed and gave a slow clap. "F–, Lon. You almost make me believe it."

Londo held up his ring again, holding Lina's left hand next to his. "Ta dah," he warbled.

"P-pleased to meet you," she said, terrified of what they'd say. She shivered– from cold or fear, she didn't know. Her jacket was still warming up anew.

"You're serious," Olympia said. "You're not serious."

Dragonlord said, "I should think that there would have been some news release issued, if nothing else. Let me see the marriage certificate."

"Video record only. It was done off-Earth."

Lina had drifted behind him again; he pulled her back.

"Great, Lon," she murmured. "Were you right about Hol vs. United States, too? That said that these things were legal, right?"

"Every bit is legal," Londo assured her. "*Voyons,*" he told the Networkers, "interstellar news broadcast the official announcement this morning. I've still got to check with my lawyer here to see what else we have to do, but as far as I'm concerned, and everyone Out There, we're married, and that's that."

"He's faking."

The Networkers discussed among themselves, with only Forte actually believing the possibility of a marriage.

"Boy Scout pledge of honor." Londo held up three fingers.

"You were never a Boy Scout." Olympia's eyes turned into slits as she considered him.

The Network discussion went on, leaving the two of them out of it.

Lina sighed. This was not anything like she thought it would be. And then she remembered. "Oh, Lon, I think I got all your neighbors' pets out, but I told the vets that you'd pay for their keep until they could be picked up. Was that okay?"

"Sure. I saw you dealing with the debris, too. Quite efficient, Lieutenant."

"Well, I couldn't have anyone hurt by the fallout, could I? Or lose their things to smoke damage. I put your stuff in the west wing and your neighbors'' things in the east. Is that okay for temporary?"

"Sure. Where'd you put the bombs? Not there, I hope?"

"You're so silly. Tiawa. Over water. I hope there weren't many fish below. They didn't go off anyway."

"Good target."

"You need to retrieve them for Wiley. I ported the small guns to Starhaven."

"We'll look into all that tomorrow."

Lina looked from him to Them and back, raising an eyebrow.

"No, I don't think they're going to say anything." He stood there and grinned at his partners, holding Lina tightly to him. She squeezed his hand nervously. "Well?" Londo prompted.

"Ah… congratulations," Dragonlord said, stepping forward to shake Lon's hand, then Lina's.

"You are serious. F–."

"Yes, Gary." Londo grinned at Bolt. "We're really married. Sorry you weren't invited to the ceremony."

"It happened a little fast," Lina admitted as she shook Gary's hand. "Thanks for calling the office, by the way. They were beyond impressed."

Forte hugged Londo. He squeezed her gently, a tribute to her own limited invulnerability. "Did you at least get a tape for us?"

"*Mais oui,*" he said. "I'm afraid that sooner or later, everyone this side of galactic center will have seen our wedding."

Olympia stepped forward to congratulate them. She picked up Londo's right hand curiously. He let her bend it back and forth to catch the light so that the mark there flashed gold. "I thought this was dirt at first. I didn't know that temporary tattoos would stick to you."

Lon gave her a lopsided smile. "It's not temporary. It's the real thing. I don't know whether to call it a tattoo or a brand or what. Lina says it's the Mark of Zorro." Londo considered it as the others watched him. "Starburst, circle, triangle." He turned to Lina. "That makes you the circle."

"I suppose there are worse things to be," she decided.

"This had to do with getting married?" Olympia continued her interrogation.

"It did and it didn't," Londo said. "No, I'd have to say that for the most part it didn't. I think. It just marks us as one of the Chosen."

"Chosen for what?"

"For Three Worlds. It's a new project we're starting up. Gonna make some changes around here." He looked around. "Man, it's good to be home." His breath left a frosty trail in the air, and Lina shivered again as it reminded her of how very cold the still midnight air of Montreal was.

Olympia turned to Lina. "Well then," she said. "Congratulations… Ms. Rand?"

"Starheart," Londo corrected her. "We're both Starhearts now. I like it. Good name." He looked inordinately pleased with himself.

Lina nodded thanks shyly to Olympia– the great Olympia!– as Lon gave the group a brief explanation of the Three Worlds.

The scope of the operation prompted Bolt let off a few more f-bombs.

Dragonlord took it all in, and then asked, "Does Hal know about this, Lon?"

"Where the hell is he?" Lon demanded. "I've been trying to get in touch with him for days."

"He left word a couple weeks ago that he'd be out galactic. Before you disappeared."

"So when are you going to announce?" Olympia asked. "There was a question at the press conference."

"There was?" Lon shook his finger at them all. "None of you can let out a word of this. Not before we tell Hal. Maybe a week or two more."

Bolt was about to ask more when he saw that they were being joined by a group of police officers. They spoke quickly to Londo in French, which Lon translated for the others. Lina followed it with no problem. The police needed final ParaNet statements before the last of the prisoners could be transported.

"*D'accord, on s-en vient,*" Lon told the officers. "Lina, stay here for a couple of minutes."

"Oh no, you don't." She grabbed his shoulder, which stopped him, to his teammates' consternation. "I have a few things to say to Terry the Bitch. After all, she tried to kill me, too. I take that kind of thing personally."

"Oh, *d'accord.* Tara, why don't you keep an eye on her and see she doesn't do anything rash."

Lina frowned at Londo. He crinkled his eyes at her and slipped her the floating spy camera thingie to use.

The others went ahead with the police toward the blue and red flashing lights. Lina's guides pointed out the prisoner van Terry was in, and Forte followed her.

Lina said, "You're going to have to ask for us to see her. These guys don't know me from Adam."

"I don't know a word of French," Forte said. "I managed two nights in a hot classroom before I dropped out. English was hard enough."

"I have a language program you can borrow. It's pretty painless, and it's quick. Besides, the officer probably speaks English."

"Or not. You go ahead."

Lina approached the police officer who guarded the back door of the van. *"Pardonnez-moi,"* she said hesitantly even as she released the camera. *"Mais Forte ici a besoin de voir la prisonnière Teresa... ah... Rhodes."*

"C'est ne pas possible. Les prisonniers sont–"

"C'est Forte," Lina urged, relying on the heroine's presence to get the man to break rules. She fanned out her hands to frame the famous heroine for his view. He could make an exception for a celebrity. *"Ne pourriez-vous pas faire une petite exception pour Forte? Elle ne veut que parler à Madame Rhodes pour quelques minutes."*

"Eh bien..."

"S'il vous plait, monsieur l'agent. C'est très important."

The officer looked around to see if anyone else was watching and then opened the back door.

"Merci beaucoup."

Lina peered inside. Trussed up securely with her handcuffs wrapped around a high bar, was the gaunt, bleached-blonde Terry, sporting a black eye, bloody nose, and who knew what else under the winter clothing. Terry glanced first at Forte's flashy costume, then at Lina. Her eyes widened even as she snarled.

"Bonsoir, Terry," Lina said with an evil smirk. "Imagine meeting you again."

"You're alive."

"And so is Londo. Alive and very well indeed."

"But I killed him; I know it," she hissed.

"So you did. Congratulations. I don't think anyone's even come close before. Too bad for you it only lasted a few minutes."

Forte started at that.

"Terry, I helped bring him back. And now–" Lina held up her ring hand in Terry's face so she couldn't miss it. "We're married."

Shock twisted Terry's features.

"So I just wanted to thank you so very much for your little plan to kill Londo and have his baby at the same time. Too bad for you that we turned it around. I'll be the one having his children now."

"*Manges d'la marde, grosse câlisse de chienne!*" Terry spat at her but Lina ducked out of the way even before the offending missile left Terry's lips.

"Don't get so excited. You have to admit it was all your fault. I wondered why you didn't just issue him a romantic dinner invitation as long as you had him powerless. It would have saved you a lot of trouble."

Forte's eyes took on a hint of comprehension after hearing Londo had been somehow "powerless" and now had a wife who was going to be "having his children."

Terry looked at Lina hard. "As if he would have–"

"He had a very soft spot for you still. Not exactly in his heart, but you know men."

Terry's face was unreadable.

"But I'm afraid that spot's not there anymore. Too bad. When you killed him, you killed any feelings that he had for you. He's not a masochist."

"So you've come to gloat." Terry snarled.

Lina grinned, baring her teeth. "I'm afraid so. It's something I don't get to do often. Tell me, what was all the blood for? I understand the… other sample, but why the blood?"

Terry looked away. "You'll never know."

"Para powers?" Understanding swept across Lina's face. "You thought you could give yourself para powers with his blood."

"I hate telepaths!" she hissed.

"Hell, I could have told you that wouldn't work." Lina eased against the van door. "You should have asked me. Of course, if you had– and if you had believed me– you wouldn't have set it all into place. And everything– *everything*– fell into place because of what you started.

"Your little plan was the keystone to– Well. We don't have time to go into all of that. You'll be finding out in the next few weeks, at any rate. Listen for word of the Three Worlds. That's us. We couldn't have done it without you."

"So get me out of here as a reward."

"No way. Terry– you don't mind if I call you Terry, do you?– look at it this way. Prison's going to give you a lot of time to think. Try to put it to good use."

"Get away from me! Trying to make yourself out so innocent and pure. I know what you are, you little tramp. I researched you. Does he know, know what you do?"

"Lon knows everything." Lina's voice dripped ice. "And you don't know what you think you do. You had me pegged 180 degrees wrong, and it almost wrecked that carefully-thought-out plan of yours."

"I hate telepaths. At least I hurt you good."

Lina ripped open her coat, pulling it and the sweater down to display her bare arm, her shoulders. "Better than new, Terry. No burns, no scars, no two-inch hole through my arm." She shook her head as she set her clothing to rights. "All that plotting, all that jealousy. And what did you get for it? You gave him to me." Lina stepped back from the vehicle.

"Go to f–ing hell!"

Lina turned to the officer. *"C'est tout. Nous avons fini ici."*

"Merci beaucoup," Forte managed with a smile. The officer nodded, dazed at her celebrity, and secured the van doors.

10

Jaeson Rallene scrutinized the tiny quarters Admiral Bracken had assigned him for the hyperspace journey to Aldierra with the fleet. He combed his fingers through his mop of blond hair, his startlingly blue eyes taking in every detail of the room, every possible hiding place for electronic surveillance.

They'd made a point about him having his own room as if solo quarters weren't the norm, even for high-ranking officials. From his duffel Jae pulled some of his Legion equipment and quickly found three A/V bugs. One was an E/M extractor. He turned it over. Not too small, but still interesting that the Aldierrans should have this kind of technology. They weren't that far behind Sarastor in a number of dangerous areas. Still, they were easy to decommission.

This trip would take longer than it should. Admiral Bracken wanted his entire fleet to arrive simultaneously around their home world of Aldierra, just as it had around Sarastor when Aldierra tried to invade, so they were crawling at Level 2 hyperspace instead of Level 3, to allow for those vehicles that couldn't attain the faster speed. Sarastor had been a hostile world to the Aldierrans. Why was Bracken treating Aldierra as if it were one, too?

According to Bracken, aside from the confusion the Ultimatum had caused, conditions were good on Aldierra. Even without telepathy Jae doubted that. The planet herself had mentioned the frightful state her humans had put her in. Lina had channeled images of civil strife over the world.

Jae sensed the admiral hiding facts and motives. Lina had said that he was a good man underneath it all, but Jae suspected that there was a lot of crap to clear out before he could find that man. Lina tended to see the good in people. Jae had been trained to be suspicious. Now he felt his suspicions confirmed and then some.

His preliminary investigation had already revealed that the orange-skinned Aldierrans were reticent about their world in the unlikeliest of areas, yet forthcoming in facts that he would have kept secret if he'd been head of a military force. They praised the regimental way they'd organized their society, as if it were all a military operation.

Families kept to themselves or in close alliances with select other families. Boys were put through family schools, but they were essentially military boot camps with sergeants playing teacher roles. There was no room for individuality or creativity in these house armies. Aberrant behavior was grounds for harsh discipline. How amazing that they expected some to break out as leaders– and that some actually did. Those who weren't punished for it were promoted.

A Great Council of military governors oversaw operations for the entire planet. It was they who elected a supreme Patriarch from their own ranks.

But oh no, these people assured him. Aldierrans weren't overly concentrated upon the military. They had the highest ideals to pursue; this was their goal in life. A significant portion of the population were supposedly involved in ecological concerns, so how could that have displeased the planet? What was wrong with them, that the planet should hate them so? they whined as Jae listened.

Londo could be territorial, but these people had taken possession and developed it to a paranoid artform. Every grammatical article was also a possessive pronoun. They spoke of taking things into personal possession when they were just picking them up. Of non-family anything being bad. Of women being wealth, and yet worth nothing.

Jae used the excuse of linguistic research to delve into familial relationships, which they were extremely reluctant otherwise to mention. Love and home were two words he never heard from them unless Jae dealt with them one-on-one. Then his subjects seemed shamed to say the words. But the love and the homes did exist. That was something.

There were few women on the world, maybe one in four. Was that an unlucky biological skew, or something more sinister? One of the lieutenants on board had a picture of his woman with him. He shyly revealed her to Jae: a nude shot, the orange-skinned woman's nipples and inner thighs painted gold, a gold sheen on her pubic hair. Her face held an oval of gold leaf with large, very red lips and heavy eye makeup. Dark hair hung down to her waist, looking very lush. It was the only non-artificial thing on her, Jae thought.

There were gold rings in her ears, in her nose, in her navel. A ruby stud in her lip. The lieutenant raved about her beauty and her ways of giving him pleasure. Jae tried to be complimentary about her and how much of an asset she must be to him. The lieutenant beamed with pride.

Then he asked Jae about Lina, if he had any pictures of her. Jae claimed he did not. Was it true that the Speaker was married to him? Jae told him that he was her fiancé; that was almost true. *Ah,* the lieutenant said. *Then you have been between the goldens?* The what? *The goldens, the golden thighs of the Speaker.* Jae blinked. The lieutenant said that everyone was asking about her, wondering what she was like.

"I'm assuming that you don't want to know what her hobbies are," Jae said dryly.

"A woman having hobbies?" The lieutenant laughed at the joke, at the very idea. "The only thought on a woman's mind needs to be how she pleases her husbands, how she runs their household, and when she will bear their next son."

There was a lot of food for thought there, and Jae didn't know where to begin. The lieutenant directed his questions for him.

"So, you have been between the goldens?"

Jae admitted that he had.

"And did she please you? Surely the Speaker for Aldierra must be very proficient in pleasing a man?"

"The Speaker is extremely proficient in pleasing a man. She knows the secrets of men that other women do not. To be with her is like being transported to an entire realm of, ah, bliss," Jae said with a straight face. He hoped that Lina never got wind of this conversation.

The lieutenant's eyes almost rolled to the back of his head, as if he were trying to imagine it. "It is said that her lovemaking would cause the very stars to explode in ecstasy." He turned to focus his gaze at Jae. "I would be the one to sign the final agreement with Aldierra," he said. "I would do anything, anything required to be the one."

Jae really didn't think that he was hearing what he thought he was. "When you say, 'sign the final agreement,'" he asked, "do you mean making a digitized record or a written agreement?"

"Absolutely not! Those things are temporary. A contract needs to be sealed by the soul. By a woman's soul. Women have the purer soul, so it is up to them."

"So when you say–"

"I mean that I wish to be the one to plumb the depths between the Speaker's goldens. To open her to me and write upon her inner soul with the ink of my self. I volunteer."

Such a brave lad, Jae thought. "I am unsure as to who will take part in this signing," he said through his translator, which was still having a difficult time sorting through the hitherto unknown language, "or what form of ceremony it will require. But we will keep you in mind."

"Anything," the lieutenant reminded him as he left.

The door closed behind him and Jae whooped with laughter. By the primeval Orb itself, was he glad that Lina wasn't along for this journey. Or Lon, for that would have been one dead lieutenant. Jae would have to schedule a long conversation with Lina before they got to Aldierra, so he could prepare her for this. Maybe Wiley had some blood pressure medication he could give her before they visited.

But the word "husbands" hadn't escaped Jae's notice, either. The next one-on-one conversation he arranged, he inquired about it. It seemed that since there were so few women, polygamous marriage was common on Aldierra. Many women seemed to die very young, mostly in childbirth or of mysterious women's ailments, so the ones that remained were shared.

There were extremely very few officers who had more than one woman in their immediate household. This was a sign of massive wealth and power.

So what of homosexuality? A culture with so many men in it; it must be common. Jae asked subtly and received a silent, stony stare in return for his effort. He questioned his next subject even more deviously.

"Men who don't have women… having sex," the man replied through the rough translator program. "Of course, there is jacking off. That is common enough. You go to parties and other than drinking and watching sports, or fighting between the guests, the main recreation is jacking off."

Jae nodded as if this were an everyday occurrence. He said cautiously, "I know this might be a delicate subject and of course I don't expect you to answer this from a personal experience, but is there any occasion whatsoever on your world… of men having sex with men?"

The older captain's eyes widened before his jaw set into a rigid jut. "Absolutely not! It is forbidden. A blasphemy!"

"Good, I'm glad to hear that," Jae encouraged him.

The man huffed indignation before he could collect himself to continue. "The very idea of a man weakening himself with that kind of behavior! We instruct our boys very early that such acts will stunt their growth and make them weaker than others. Make them ripe for conquest. No boy wants that. None. Life goes to the victor, and that kind of… heresy would weaken all of society. If we do catch anyone doing… *that*, he is beaten severely. Caught three times, and he is put to death."

Ah. Jae thought he might not come out of the closet on this planet. It might be more trouble than it was worth.

Icy darkness suffused Starhaven's master bedroom, but it was bone-chilling fear that snapped Lina awake.

****Lon!**** She shook him. "Londo!" she hissed.

His breathing pattern changed, but he didn't wake up.

****I heard something! Something's in the house!****

"Umm. Huh."

She shook him again as hard as she could and then froze. A figure stood silhouetted at the roughed-in door, watching them!

She ported out whoever it was just as Lon finally raised up. "No!" he cried, and then groaned as he realized the intruder was gone. He fell back onto the pillows.

"What—"

"Bring him back, Lie." Lon waved his hand in a tired circle. "That was Hal." He began to laugh in short spurts. Feet still under the covers, he rolled and half-fell out of bed as he groped for something in his discarded clothes.

"Ohhh shit. Bring him back?"

"Not yet, babe. Give me a second here."

Lina thanked goodness they'd been too tired to make love when they went to bed, promising to make it up to each other in the morning. At least they weren't naked, although there wasn't much to the silk chemise she had on. Londo turned on the one working room light, still laughing weakly.

"Okay, I'm ready." He plopped back on top of the bed. One of those tiny, almost-unnoticeable cameras rose to hover over them.

Lina pulled the blanket higher so that she'd be absolutely covered. Even better, she ported on her flannel nightshirt to replace the chemise. Then she ported in her new father-in-law.

Lina got her first good look of Maximus in person.

Good god, Maximus!

Clamping her hand over her mouth, she tried to make herself small. "Oh god."

Lon swiped down his face with a hand. "Hi, Hal," he said, grinning a little guiltily. He turned toward her. "No, it's not God. It's not even Santa Claus."

Maximus looked around the unfinished room until he couldn't avoid looking at them. His mouth kept opening and closing. "I seem to have been in Montreal for a moment there," he finally said.

He was the very figure of the magnificent hero: strength and confidence incarnate. His deep brown, almost black skin set off those steel-gray eyes that were the trademark of the legend. Not a trace of gray showed in his buzzed hair. He eased naturally into a hero's stance: feet apart, chest thrust forward. His shoulders were even broader than Londo's. Whereas Lon could model for a statue of Hercules, Maximus displayed the ultimate Mr. Universe physique.

The midnight-blue costume with its red, yellow and white logo slash across the chest and short white cape was unnatural in this setting. He belonged somewhere where a flag waved in the background and people cheered. *Not* in her bedroom!

He seemed to be searching for something to say. Could he be embarrassed, too? He was definitely avoiding looking at the bed. "You have some sort of new teleport security system? It's very smooth." he said in his deep, bass voice.

"S-sorry," Lina squeaked, trying to withdraw into the depths of the mattress. "I thought you were an intruder."

"Apparently I am." Maximus' gaze zeroed in on her and he gave a small bow. "I apologize."

"Ah. *D'accord,*" Lon began through some chuckles that were too masculine to be giggles, "I didn't think introductions would be made this way, but here goes. Carolina O'Kelly Starheart, this is my father, Henry Rand. You may have heard of him. Or I may have mentioned him before. Hal, Lina's the teleport security system around here now. Very, very smooth. Oh, did I mention? She's my wife." He rubbed Lina's arm and snorted as he watched Hal's reaction.

"Your–" Maximus' breathing stopped, his eyes first going wide, then narrowing. He drew back as he peered at first one, then the other occupant of the bed.

"Wife. Female married spouse. For about ten or so days now, I guess, although this is the fourth full day we've had together. *Voyons.* As of a couple days ago, she is also Speaker for the Three Worlds, of which one is Earth." Lon waved his hand grandly in the air. "You may genuflect."

"Speaker for… whatever that means. Wife."

"How– How do you do?" What did you say to Maximus? Oh god, what did her hair look like? Lina tried to brush it into order with her fingers without looking frantic about it.

Londo squeezed her shoulder. **Courage, Lina. It'll all be okay. You look fine, like a bride who's been properly bedded.**

"Pleased to…" Maximus said. He looked like he needed to sit down, but there were no chairs in here, so he leaned heavily against a sawhorse. "Married. Married?"

Londo tried not to laugh. He didn't succeed. "Oh yeah, I changed my name to Starheart, too. I know it's happened quickly. We have tapes of the wedding– at Mega-Legion HQ, Hal. We had practically a full house when we decided to go for it."

"You changed your name?" Then to Lina: "You're a Legionnaire?" Maximus asked. His eyes looked up and to the right; he was searching his memory for her name on the rolls.

The absurdity of the assumption hit her. "No, sir," she said with a little laugh. "Heavens, two Terrans in the Legion. They'd all keel over and die of embarrassment."

Maximus smiled a little at that, or maybe at the southern accent: *dah* instead of *die*.

"If we'd known where you were at the time," Lon said, "we could have brought you in somehow. But we didn't. Of course now with this surprise visit, we'll have something to laugh about at our twentieth anniversary."

"It's not so funny," Lina murmured darkly. Lon squeezed her again.

Maximus shook his head. "Else said that Damon left a message saying you were back on Earth, and that there was trouble—"

"Oh no," Lina groaned, covering her face with her hands. She could guess who "Damon" must be: Dragonlord. He was the only ParaNetter she'd met whose civilian name she hadn't heard yet. "More trouble."

Londo frowned at her. "Everyone's been congratulating us lately and then adding, 'Boy, are you in trouble now.'"

"She's not—"

"No! I'm getting tired of that question." Lina lowered her hands from her face. "And the 'how do you and he—' look. I'm sick of it already."

Lon slid his arm around her. "I've been getting a variation of that look practically all my life."

"And you don't like it either."

"No, I don't." He thought for a moment. "Maybe we could issue a press release, you know, Wilder's monograph. You could draw some diagrams for it." He tried to look studiously serious, but he had to break out into a laugh at her astonishment. She didn't know if he were—

She hit him playfully and to Maximus' obvious amazement he rolled with the blow. "I don't think so!" she laughed.

"Ow! Spousal abuse! Call the cops! Call the hospital!"

"Don't be such a big baby. I barely touched you."

"We have a witness. Who's the court going to believe?" Lon grinned at Lina as he took her in his arms and touched noses.

"What the hell is that?" Maximus demanded with a pointing finger.

Londo looked up to see what he was referring to– his right hand. "That's a tattoo. What does it look like?" Lon tried to make the answer sound as blasé as possible. He held up the hand to show it off. "Now all I need is a motorcycle. And a leather jacket, yeah. Lina can be my biker babe. You'd like that, wouldn't you, *chérie?*"

She was afraid to joke with him, afraid to look at Maximus.

****Sweet cheeks, he's just Hal. Relax for once in your life.****

"A tattoo. Wife. Starheart…" With a helpless expression, Maximus looked around at the bedroom, at the two of them in bed, Londo in his underwear, Lina shivering. "This may not be the best place for this conversation," he observed. "Perhaps we could adjourn to the living room?"

"Not a good place at the moment either," Lon said, his tone sour. "We had a slight influx of furniture tonight. We were going to straighten up tomorrow, get my neighbors' things back to them."

"Ah yes." Maximus scratched his head. "I was there looking for you, and all I found was a building with a very large hole in it and a quick patch job to hold it together. I take it that this move wasn't voluntary?"

"Not entirely. No."

Oh dear, how much worse could this get? Lina wrung her hands. "How about going to my place, then? Un-unless you don't like cats," she suggested. "Londo doesn't have a choice. Love me, love my cats. I may have some cookies or something if you're hungry." She put her hand to her mouth again, trying to think. What did she have that was good enough to serve Maximus? What did you serve a father-in-law? In the middle of the night?

"I don't mind cats," Maximus said as Londo reached for his robe.

Lina searched in her mind for some jeans and tee shirt, but Londo said, ****No. He woke us up. You don't have to dress up for him.**** So instead she mentally looked for a robe she could wear, a sedate one that would say nice girl instead of sex kitten. She chose the terrycloth one with the nap on the left shoulder that Molly loved to suck.

Londo frowned at her. "You don't have to go all Grandma Moses on me."

"Yes I do."

He shook his head and then pointed to the heavens. "Allferone," he ordered in royal command, and they ported out.

They appeared in the wee-hour darkness of her living room. A cold rain was falling outside, pattering on the skylight upstairs. Lina reached for a light switch as she heard various cats running to get away from the strangers.

"This is their third interruption tonight," She said as she turned up the heat, real heat at last! "Would you… Um, would you like something to drink?" she asked Maximus without looking him in the eye.

"Coffee would be fine," he replied kindly. He tilted his head at her, turned to Lon and raised an eyebrow as if to ask: *Does she ever look at people?*

Lina said, "I ah, I don't have any coffee." Stupid! Why hadn't she thought ahead? "I think I have some tea and some" her mouth said it before she could stop it, "Kool-Aid." She'd just offered Maximus Kool-Aid! Gah! "It's black cherry." Was she ever going to live this down? Damn Londo and those chuckles that he wasn't even trying to hold in!

"I think we can settle for tea," Londo told her. He patted her on the behind in front of his father! "You go into the kitchen and hide for a few minutes. Get used to the idea." He nodded his chin toward Maximus.

Without further encouragement Lina scuttled into the kitchen and washed at the kitchen sink before collecting cups and saucers out of the cupboard. They clinked in her trembling hands.

"Something's different," Londo said from the great room. "It smells of oranges in here. Aren't you missing some cobwebs?" He added to his father, "She's been gone for some time. Did you come in and clean when I wasn't looking, *chérie?*"

"Starheart," Maximus muttered.

Safe in the kitchen around the corner with a wall that Maximus and Londo could both easily see through, Lina replied, "I cleaned a bit after the unexpected herd left, but it's mostly because Sarah's been by today."

"Sarah?"

"Sarah Hunt. I do work for her and she comes by now and then and cleans for me. She knows where the spare key is."

"Oh." Lon picked up a spaceship model and wiped his finger on the shelf where it had been. No dust there. "So all this stuff you've been feeding me about being so destitute–"

"Destitute?" She poked her head around the corner.

"Poverty-stricken. Poor."

"I have never said–"

"And all this time you've had a maid." He shook his head at her, tsk-tsking at her counterfeit.

She returned to the sink. "An occasional bartered cleaning arrangement does not equal maid service."

Lon opened the door to what she referred to as a pantry. To him it was a small closet under the stairs with some cheap wire shelving to hold dry goods. He rifled around until he found two boxes of Girl Scout cookies.

Hal just stood there in the middle of the great room, looking around like he was lost. "Married," he muttered a few more times.

Londo stuck his tongue out at no one in particular, but in triumph all the same. He'd pulled one on Hal! This was very good indeed. Even better to have a hovercam recording the event for posterity– and so Jae could share in the laugh when he got back.

"Have a seat, Hal. Stay a while." Londo pointed to the tiny dining area between the living area and kitchen. It looked more like a breakfast nook to him, just big enough for a small circular table with three chairs. He set the cookie boxes on it.

"Okay, Lina, so you barter for people to come in and act like slaves for you. What'd you do for her?" Lon air-nudged a cat off one of the chairs and then sat, watching Lina fill the cups with water. Ten to one she'd forget that he or Hal could heat up the water for her…

"Sarah's a client. I got rid of her grandmother-in-law's ghost for her and she bartered by cleaning house. I make her use organic citrus cleaner. Grandma was a toughie. She didn't want to go. Well, she didn't *think* she wanted to. I convinced her otherwise."

"Got rid of a ghost?" Maximus interrupted.

Lina froze. *Stop your nervous chattering and pay attention to what you're saying!*

"Well… she was rattling kitchen cabinets and slamming doors. Scaring the kids." Lina tried to make it sound reasonable. "She didn't really bother any of them all that much, but I explained to Sarah that it's so much better for a ghost to go all the way over to the Other Side." Sheesh, this wasn't going well at all. She knew she was sounding like a third-rate Psychic Friend. She glanced at Londo. **Help me here.**

"Hell, hon, try to scare the bejeezus out of him if you can." Lon just sat there and grinned at her. Ha! She was putting the cups into the microwave.

"I'm trying not to. You'd be surprised how many people want to get rid of ghosts. I've had businesses hire me to do it. I have to go through the warehouse at work all the time and smudge out new arrivals. The place attracts them by the dozens, and the folks on third shift quit if they see too many strange things lurking in the back corners. The University hires me– well, I volunteer for them– to keep Memorial Hospital clear. You don't want to have stuck disincarnates hanging around sick people. You can get… problems." *Shut up, shut up!*

"Reassuring, Lie." Londo still held his maddening grin. "I'll be sure to tell all this to the nice men with the nets."

She almost stamped her foot. "Okay, it smells like oranges because… because I dropped a can of orange juice in here when I was making up a gallon of screwdrivers for the White Tea Party Ladies social this afternoon. We all play bridge and wear hats with plastic flowers on them over our sheets and gossip about whoever doesn't show up. And then we pray in front of an 8x10 glossy of the honorable Senator Jamie Stern. Is that normal enough?"

Maximus laughed at that, thank goodness. "Now, that's scary," he said.

The microwave dinged and Lina placed the hot cups of water on the table in front of the men. She paused, looking at the hot water. *Hot* water. She glared at Londo, who could heat up things with his breath.

Thanks for the help.

****Anytime, love,**** he grinned at her. "Hal, Lina's been a telepath a good part of her life. She's trained in psychic healing and stuff like that– and yes, apparently there're classes for that– and two weeks ago she got conked on the head and turned into an interstellar teleporter. Gorgeon says it's permanent."

"Gorgeon. Oh. Ah, okay…"

"She doesn't talk to ghosts all that much. Usually it's just devas and her guides. They're all invisible, but she says they're different kinds of beings."

"Guides." Hal looked like he wanted to say something else, but instead he reached for a cookie box and pried the zip strip on it open, notch by notch, as if that could set reality back to normal.

Lon cocked his head at Lina. ****Are you planning to sit down sometime and join us?****

****Give me an hour or two to get used to him.****

****Sit.****

****Arf.****

****Bad girl, bad girl.****

She pretended to look for something in the kitchen cabinets. Tea. She hadn't set out any tea for them to brew. She found five different kinds and dumped them all on the table, then scurried back to stand in the kitchen and hope that Maximus wouldn't notice her. Oh god, Maximus!

The deva of the house laughed at her trepidation. ****Do be quiet,**** she told it.

****We are all children of the universe,**** the deva reminded her. ****No one stands above or below anyone else.****

Impatiently Londo snatched the cookie box from Hal and pulled out the interior tray. He offered it to his father. Before he could react, one of the cats jumped up on the table and swiped at the plastic covering.

"Hey!" Londo snapped. "You! Get down!" The cat hissed at him before jumping down, leaving a small cloud of short hairs hanging in the air behind her. Lon gave the fuzzy orange cat a sharp nod. He was master of this castle now. Time for the cats to learn.

"Molly, are you hungry?" The orange cat turned at her name. Her tail rose to stick straight up. She trotted over to Lina and meowed.

"You have your food here." Lina pointed at the dish she'd filled before the concert with dry kibble. Molly meowed again, a long drawn-out affair.

"It's not time for breakfast yet."

Yeowww. Molly jumped up on the counter and patted one of the cabinet doors with her paw. Then she sat and turned her head to beseech Lina.

"Ohhh, all right. Just this once." It would keep her legitimately busy. Lina reached into the cabinet for a can of cat food. Molly immediately jumped down the floor to pace around one of two plates there. Lina pulled the poptop. It made a tiny *shuck* sound.

"Ick," Lina murmured.

Hal had been asking Londo a question, but now he stopped as a fast clacking came from upstairs. He glanced up to identify it as cat claws on linoleum as one cat made its way downstairs.

Plop, plop, and two previously unnoticed cats jumped down from bookshelves. *Click-click, click-click;* cats ran in through a pet door flap in the small utility room in back of the kitchen. Cats of all colors and patterns trotted into the kitchen, some of them meowing. All of them held their tails high. They pressed up against each other, circling Lina's legs and weaving between them.

Londo grabbed an imaginary cowboy hat to his head. Holding fast to his chair, he made it buck back and forth on one leg. "Run for cover, Hal! It's a stampede!"

"You can't be serious," Lina addressed the herd. "You can't all be hungry!"

"Good lord, how many are there?" Hal asked Londo. He looked past his son's head to see a decrepit black cat lying on a bookshelf. It lay completely still. "You may have one, ah, ah, deceased in the bunch." But as soon as he said that, the cat raised its head and slowly blinked toward the kitchen, then blinked at him.

Lon turned around to see what Hal was looking at. "That's Fafhrd. She's not dead, she's just old." The skinny cat got up from the shelf and stretched every way she could before she jumped down and ambled to join the rest, her tail rising. "That's the last of 'em, I think," Lon announced.

"Seven," Hal said slowly. "Seven cats."

"Ah! Ah! Ah!" Londo laughed like *Sesame Street's* Count.

Lina opened more cans and dumped food onto the plates. "Ick. Ick." There was meat in the cans, with accompanying dying animal impressions. Poor things.

The cats all crowded around their late-night dinner. The sound of munching and smacking cat lips filled the air.

11

Seven cats and a teleporting wife– *wife!*– who exorcised ghosts.

Hal studied his son's face as Lon watched Lina washing out the cans for recycling. Lon was smiling. That didn't happen much, especially around women. But here he was smiling at the woman, at the cats, at the situation. How had this happened?

Lon had never mentioned this "Lina" before; Hal would have taken special note of her and had her checked down to the last period of her CIA report.

How could Londo have gotten married without including him? Was Lon trying to leave him out of things, just because he was adopted? No, that couldn't be it. Mom and Dad seemed not to have been invited, either, and Londo doted on them. And Lon had left well over twenty messages on his phone, telling him to check in. The first ones at least must have been concerning the impending wedding.

"So this is the third interruption tonight?" Lon asked as he looked over his choices of herbal teas. He made faces at the selections. "Second was all the refugee animals. First was Sarah with the ghost…"

"Sarah doesn't have a ghost now. But she's a regular visitor here. She wouldn't have upset either the cats or the house deva."

"Oh yeah, your house deva. Where is he? He is a he?"

"Yeah, he's male energy for the most part. Look up there," she pointed to the ceiling above the open foyer. Maximus followed her gaze, as did Londo.

"What do I picture him as? Hal, I met this storm deva a couple weeks ago. And tonight when we came back to Starhaven there were snow devas– you should see 'em. Devas are like angels, but different."

"Excellent definition," Hal drawled.

"Okay, one thing they can do is guard things, not people. What does this guy look like?"

"Use your own imagination," Lina told him. "Don't force your mind into one image. He's sitting on the center of the roof." She watched Londo concentrate, and then his face cleared into a look of wonder. "There he is! I think. Hello, deva!"

Lina glanced at Maximus, who looked from the ceiling to his son and back. "I don't see anything."

"What's he saying?"

She glanced back up to her deva. He doffed a top hat and bowed to Londo. "He says he welcomes guests to his home. What a showoff you are!" she told the deva. "And here you'd just told me that no one was superior to anyone else."

Londo laughed. "What's he saying now?"

"He says that it's always proper to be polite to humans, or any other entities."

Londo dipped his head at the ceiling. "Absolutely; that's what I always say. Thank you, deva." Lon turned to Maximus. "Lina's told me that it's always proper to be polite to devas... and other entities. If it weren't for this fellow here–" he nodded in the direction of the ceiling, "a lot of people– and cats– would have been blown to bits by some bombs last week."

"What the devil are you talking about?"

"Now you're scaring him, Lon."

"I'm talking about this whole 'nother world right here that I'm just starting to discover, thanks to Lina. Devas for one. *J'te le dis!* Do you know that we actually got a thunderstorm to rain right where and when we wanted it to because we dealt with the storm deva? And Lina interrogated some prisoners of mine– after they'd committed suicide. That was spooky, Lie, I have to tell you. And then there's this Three Worlds deal we're involved in now."

"What do you see when you see this deva?" Maximus asked patiently, looking again at the blank ceiling.

"Ah, well, it's not like I see anything, it's more an… impression. That's it. Tall, skinny fellow looking like one of those chimney sweeps out of *Mary Poppins,* with a long scarf and a top hat. And pointy-toed boots. He's just sitting up there, keeping watch. Making sure nothing bad happens around here, I suppose. Checking in with Lina if anyone who's not supposed to be here comes in, right?"

Lina took pride in her new husband. "Pretty much," she said. He was amazing, being able to accept all that he'd been through with such faith. She wished that she could believe in things so easily. Maybe it was Lon's vivid imagination, the same one that had him spinning so many wonderful stories about faeries and magick kingdoms. He'd never had anyone tell him not to believe, never had anyone tell him not to believe in himself, either; not a word. As a child he hadn't had a mother or father for a long time, but then he hadn't had parents constantly telling him how flawed he was. Thank god.

She said, "Like tonight. He told me about Dragonlord– I take it that's 'Damon.' He was here earlier, checking the place out. Hope he's not allergic."

"How come you didn't tell me?" Lon asked her.

"It was almost right after we left Montreal. They sure started fast enough. We were watching the snow and then making a path through all the junk in the kitchen. I didn't think it was important enough to interrupt. Something… Oh. Say hello to Damon or Dragonlord or whoever, Londo, will you? And get rid of whatever he left behind, please."

"Hm?" Londo looked around. "Ah. I see it."

"I don't like people bugging my house. I have clients who have got to know that whatever they tell me is going to remain private."

Lon stood to reach behind the wall clock on the great room wall. He unclipped a small electronic bug and sang a line or two of farewell into it before he crushed it between his fingertips.

Some of the cats had finished their late-night snack, and Londo pointed them out to his father as they came around to wash themselves.

"That's Fafhrd and she's not dead; she's over twenty years old. And that's Moose, the other black cat. And over there is Fat Cat–"

"That's Katie. She's not fat. That's fur."

Londo nodded. "Fat Cat… And that's Fat Cat number two…"

"Molly. Don't call them Fat Cat."

"A few of them could stand to lose a little weight, Lie. The skittish gray one is Ember. I don't know who the hell that one is. Fa– Krazy Kat."

Lina looked up. "Obiwan."

"Oh yeah. Obiobiobiwan." The cat glanced at him and then went back to his bath. "The guy who likes to bat the ball around the track. And this is, is… Shilveshter." He spit the name just like the cartoon did, but Lina pouted.

"He's Bran!"

"*C'est ça,* Bwan-Bwan. Here, Bwannie-wannie-sweetie-weedie," Lon cooed in a high feminine voice. The kittenish tabby perked up and took a few steps toward him before Lon's boisterous laughter frightened him away.

"And there's only seven?" Maximus asked, amused.

"Just seven. Unless you've gotten some more since we've been back, Lina?" Londo picked up a small metal ball lying on the table. It tinkled like a thousand distant bells. Very nice. A crystal ball on a base decorated with dragons sat next to it, along with a large, rough chunk of rose quartz.

"Not that I recall," Lina said as she dug through the small pantry looking for napkins. She set them on the table and closed her eyes, gathering her courage. She couldn't put it off any longer, so she sat down rather abruptly next to them. Next to Maximus.

"Do you use this?" Londo asked, pointing to the crystal ball.

"It's artificial crystal, not natural." Good golly, the man oozed *presence.* They both did. The air fairly crackled with it.

"Which means…"

"No, I don't use it. It wouldn't work for anything. I just keep it around to impress clients who think that every proper psychic has a crystal ball. Showbiz. It makes a nice paperweight, don't you think?"

Lon's mouth took on his crooked grin. "Lina's been worried about what to call you," he told Maximus.

"'Hal' is fine," he smiled kindly at Lina. He looked just like he did on TV, only more so. As in: he was sitting right *here* more so. "So, what's all this about trouble?"

Lina looked at Londo and began, "Well, no one seems to think anything of Lon's becoming a telepath, but when they find out I'm one, they start having fits."

"You're a telepath?" Hal started, staring at his son.

"As of about two weeks now, yes," Lon answered. "Lina's been one all her life, though. Pretty powerful. That's what has everyone spooked."

"Discriminatory," Lina grumbled. "I should call the ACLU. Do they have a Sarastor chapter?"

"And you're also a teleporter…"

"As of about two weeks ago." She smiled. "Yes. Now that's fun."

"That's more than fun; it's handy," Lon said. "And she's Speaker for the Three Worlds as of two, three days ago."

"Londo's the Protector for the Three Worlds. Same time frame."

"We've got that on tape," Lon added. "With Jae."

"Don't tell me he's in on this, too." Hal began to tap his right ring finger on the table, which quivered in response.

"Yeah. Minister for the Three Worlds; and he's gone telepathic also."

"As of two weeks ago," Hal guessed.

"No, as of…?" Londo looked at Lina. She tried to think.

"Right after we stopped the invasion, but I think it may actually have occurred a little before that. His people were telepaths, you know, but it seems he repressed–"

"Invasion?" Hal looked from one to the other. "Perhaps we'd better start at the beginning."

It was mostly Londo who told the story, though he had Lina port in some *raaschen* crystals and a player and they watched the record where Lon lay dead within the heart of a hurricane inside Wiley's lab at Legion Headquarters.

Hal rubbed his lips as the lightnings roared around Londo, Lina and Jae. His jaw shook as Lina called Londo's soul back into his body.

"Pretty neat, eh?" Londo said, grinning at him.

Hal sat so still before he turned to her. "You saved my son's life," he said. "How can I ever thank you?"

Lina blushed.

"Perhaps this is a good time to mention where my dear wife works– I mean, worked," Londo said quickly. "I insisted she quit."

"You did not."

"Sez you. Take a peek over there," Lon pointed. "About two miles."

Hal's head swiveled. "Ah… The nursing home, the vet or the dentist?"

"Across the street from the dentist," Lina said weakly. "Keep in mind that I quit a couple days ago. I did, on my own."

Lon chuckled as he saw the puzzled look on Hal's face. "Look in the warehouse," he said, "and keep an eye out for ghosts."

"Good lord– porn."

"I'm hoping it won't be too much of an embarrassment to anyone," Lina said and tried not to blush any more. "Really, it's quite–"

"Do you mind if I ask what you did there?" Hal interrupted, his eyebrow raised.

"She wasn't in any of the movies, if that's what you're getting at," Londo said. "I'm going to have to study a lot more, just to make sure."

"Catalog coordinator." Lina sighed. "I was involved in the print and web catalogs."

"But no video work," Hal said, trying to get a confirmation. "No photos. Nothing in front of a camera."

Lina shook her head, unable to meet his eyes. "No, really, it's all very–"

"She's going to talk about healthy emotional balance and the First Amendment," Londo butted in. "Yadda yadda yadda, pure as the driven snow. So anyways, Hal, we were on Sarastor and…"

Lina got up to put some classical music on shuffle as Londo explained the events of the past two weeks. They were working on their third cup of tea– this time Lina remembered to have Lon heat the water– as Maxi– *Hal* walked around the room, examining her knickknacks, her *Star Trek* figurines and pictures, her books, the cabinet of crystals, the stack of mail on the coffee table. *Artists Magazine. Conscious Spirit Magazine.* A stack of Midnight Delivery catalogs. She could see him glance upstairs, likely peering through the ceiling to examine everything there, too. Probably checking to see if she had a little Red Room of Pain set up.

In his story Londo got to the invasion of Sarastor, then the trial, and finally the Three Worlds.

Lina sat so that Londo was between her and the pacing megahero as she watched him, trying to get used to the idea of Maximus as a real person. Here in her home.

Londo snorted.

If this were the first time I was meeting you, I'd be freaking out about that, too, she assured him. He considered the comment and nodded.

"I heard about Aiko," Hal said softly. "Such a terrible shock. I'm so sorry I wasn't there for you. You know I've been fond of her ever since we first met all those years ago. She was a great hero. And a good friend." His sigh was heavy. "I caught the funeral when it was broadcast. It was a moving eulogy, Lon. I watched it on Jorter with the president there. Volunteerism on the world tripled within the six hours afterward, and they said it was because of what you'd said. It's something when you can inspire people."

"Thanks." Lon looked down into his cup.

"I saw Mom and Dad had made it there; good. And I was wondering who the young lady with the voice was." Hal nodded at Lina. "A wonderful performance– although I hope you'll understand when I say that the people I was with were a bit… unenthusiastic about it."

"Scandalized?" Lina asked, expecting the reaction. He gave her a small smile.

"Maybe a little. They might let the Fanfare pass, but a vocalized song…" He shook his head. "Of course, I wonder now what they'd have thought if they knew that Aiko had requested it post mortem." He paused. "She really did?"

"We have it on tape," Lon said as he sorted through the raaschen and produced the one that contained the Investiture. "Somewhere she's still alive and happy. Wiley got it in special scans all across the spectrum. Genuine ectoplasmic energy patterns in classical configurations, but the strongest ones by far ever recorded."

"Don't worry," Lina said, "Stoan will find a way to show that all that energy really came from me when I was sitting there in that hyperspace chamber. It's all a clever mind control plan of mine."

"He's still accusing you of that?" Hal asked.

"He's still thinking about it," Lon answered for her. He got up and stretched. Katie startled awake at that and ran upstairs, knocking over something up there in her wake. "He doesn't do it out loud, not officially. He's going to be trouble for a while."

Lina fumed. "I'll just avoid His Legion Highness every time we're on Sarastor from now on."

"So, ah," Hal began, and then pulled his earlobe. "Mind control."

"Lina says it's hooks. Psychic hooks."

"If what I've run into is the same as what everyone's talking about," Lina added quickly.

Londo nodded. "But she's never controlled anyone. Ever."

Hal chewed his cheek as he listened to Lina explain about psychic hooks before he nodded. "So you have to get these– mind control hooks– before they, what, embed themselves in you?"

"Oh no. You can take 'em out after they've embedded. Everyone's got hooks of some kind of another. Most are harmless, but not all. I've gotten rid of thousands of malicious hooks from people. It's pretty simple."

Hal looked at Lon, who looked back at him.

"I thought mind control was permanent as long as the person doing the controlling maintained it."

"So did I," Lon said. "Lina, you told me how to mind control someone–"

"You did what?" Hal gave a start, suspicion etching his face.

"I told you how I *thought* it would be done," she said in her defense. "The right kind of hooks, aimed at the right places." She shivered. "As if someone would actually ever want to do it on purpose."

"Show me." Hal took a stance with his feet apart and firm on the floor, fists clenched by his side. He glared at her. "Show me how you'd do it."

"I don't do mind control," Lina said tightly. "Not even as a demonstration. I also don't play with atomic weaponry."

"Then… explain so I can understand. Say Lon there is trying to control me. What does he do?"

"Don't get any ideas," Lina muttered to Lon as he stood up. "Okay, Lon here is the evil Captain Control, and he's out to get Maximus. Chakras are energy centers within the spiritual, energy body. People have seven major ones." She pointed at Lon's throat. "Throat chakra, seat of personal power and will. When you're looking the other way, the Captain here goes *pwee*" and she used her fingertip to trace the path an arrow might take, "to send out a tendril of his personal aura to grab you here in your own throat chakra. The tendril hooks on the end and embeds itself in your aura, and the absolute concentration of the Captain over there overpowers your own unsuspecting chakra, which leaves it easy to dominate." She pointed at Lon's throat. "Another hook– *pwham*– but this time into your solar plexus chakra, the chakra governing communications between people. That would make the rapport with the victim easier to maintain as well."

She paused. "Now, what Erik did–"

"Erik?" Hal asked.

"Sunstorm," Londo told him. "He was caught doing… something… to increase his chances with girls. It seems to have been unconscious on his part. I'll tell you later."

They indicated Lina was to continue, so she did. "Erik hit the throat chakra, but also the heart and sacral chakras as well. Love and sex, as well as power. But he didn't realize he was doing it, and the weak hooks must have dissolved within a few hours. I never saw any controlling hooks on any Legionnaires when I was there, I mean, other than benign relationship ties."

"Sunstorm's a telepath," Londo explained. "Low level."

Lina said, "Let's face it, everything that lives is telepathic to some extent. It's a facet of life. That's why I get clients in all the time who have hooks in them from their spouses, their boyfriends, stalkers, parents, whoever wants to keep them in control."

"But these are weak hooks," Maximus said.

"Not all. If you think you've got a problem, there's usually some very powerful hooks there. And if you don't know you've got a problem, you might have worse ones. I've seen some cases where I was surprised that there was any independent thought left, where the spouse had had them under control for years and years."

"But you helped?"

"They're just hooks." Lina shrugged. "You get them to un-hook. You pull them out. It's almost beginner-level work. Almost. It helps if you know a few tricks."

"And then the mind controller can hook them again?"

"I teach my clients how to protect themselves." She paused. "Some clients return again and again with hooks. I finally tell them not to come back. Some people liked to be controlled, and if that's where they're coming from they don't need to be wasting my time with it. They need to see a shrink."

Hal looked at her, evaluating. "Do I have any hooks on me?"

Lina's eyes unfocused. "Nothing that has any evil intent," she announced after a few moments. She smiled. "There's a couple of strong ties there, though. Relationship ones."

"Where? Who did it?" Hal raised his elbows to examine himself as if he could spot something. Lon crossed his arms and waited to watch what Lina would do.

"Clear your mind," she instructed Hal. "Don't work hard at it; just easily blank it clear as you can. Let's see." She bit her lip, chose her target, and then plucked the air in two places, low and middle-height, about five feet from him. "Who comes to mind?"

Hal cocked his head. "Else. She asked me not to stay out much later."

Lina threw up her hands. "It's like I tell everyone. You already know the answers. You don't need me."

"But... Else?" Hal asked blankly.

"This is just one of the normal ways people maintain connections to others."

Lon laughed behind her. "That's pretty cool," he said. "Listen, Lina, every-one in the AffSys is running around saying that mind control is permanent."

"Maybe they should consult Chimrin then."

"She's one of them."

"Well, she and that Tishan Institute of hers should know better. Or maybe it's just that I've figured it out all wrong. Maybe Mind Control with capital let-ters isn't done like that at all."

"Maybe. I wonder if the technology involved– telepathic brains have to liter-ally be rewired to create a mind controller– has created a completely different type of control, or is merely able to prolong the effect." Lon rubbed his nose as he considered. "If there's no 'off' button…"

"But it could be done like that?" Hal wanted to know.

"I think so."

Hal nodded. "Then I want you to give the Network instruction in how to guard against it. And how to get rid of it. You said it was a beginner level–"

"Almost beginner." Lina thought. "Let's see. You'd have to learn centering, then white light protection, and then do a little aura balancing just to figure out how to feel things in the aura…" As she considered the exercises involved, she put her hands up to either side of herself and moved side-to-side as if within a cocoon. It looked like a type of slow Thai dance. "…And then actual hook work. Say, a four or five-hour class, with breaks."

"Five hours?" Lon asked. "For mind control?"

"An easy-paced five hours," Lina said. "Cut it down to three if everyone's hyper. I don't encourage caffeine."

Lon and Hal looked at each other and laughed again. Hal shook his head. "If that's true, then I know a lot of people who'll want to sign up," he said.

"I take small classes only. Maximum of fifteen people, so I can supervise."

"So you'll give lots of classes." Lon turned to Hal. "Have we terrified you enough tonight? With all the changes? All the powers?"

Hal chuckled. "Give me a chance to let it all sink in, then ask me. I'll tell you honestly, I know why the Legion might have had their doubts about you. About you two." He heaved a heavy sigh. "'Starheart,' eh? And I can see why Damon said 'Trouble.' You know him."

Lon gave a calculating smile as he strolled to the media side of the great room. He turned off the sound system and switched on the TV. "He'll do his white-glove investigation and Lina and I'll come out smelling like roses." He stopped at the blue recliner. "Down, cat. Ah, you're Ember. Down, Ember."

The gray cat took up the entire seat and gave him a bored expression. Hal joined them, propping himself on the corner of a nearby desk.

"I said, get down, Ember. They understand commands, Lina?"

"They do, but that was the wrong one," Lina informed him. "'Get down' is for when she knows she's jumped up somewhere where she's not supposed to be, and the command is given at full volume. But here she's in a chair, and she knows that chairs are for sitting and sleeping and shedding."

Lina bent over the recliner. "Excuuuse me, Ember," she said in a singsong voice. "Paar-don me." Ember looked at her as if to determine if she were serious. She stretched and eventually jumped down. "See? She knows that that means 'Get the hell out of my chair, because I'm going to sit in it even if you're still there.'"

Lon looked at her.

Lina said, "You have to learn how to reason with them. They have their pride."

"And you have seven of them?"

"You can't say I didn't warn you. *Our house is a very very very fine house…*" she reminded him.

"*D'accord, d'accord.* Did I remember to tell you about my ten rottweilers?"

"I don't believe so."

"Don't let him rattle you," Hal told her. "When he was growing up, all I would hear for months at a time was, 'Hal, I want a dog.' And I'd never let him get one because we were always going off somewhere. He should be happy now."

"I had that aquarium for a while," Lon said. "We set it up for automatic feeding."

"And then the damn fish all ate each other. I missed seeing how the last one managed to eat itself. I would have paid good money to see that."

Lina laughed. Maximus wasn't that bad. He was almost human.

She turned as she heard the word "Montreal" coming from the news. CNN was covering the night's top stories.

"I can never get used to them getting it on the air so fast," Hal said as footage from tonight's battle began. Heroes flying through the air, the sky turning white, the initial splash of debris splattering on the pavement below as people screamed and police shoved them back. Valiant looked even more wonderful and heroic than usual.

There was a captioned interview with that loud man, who indeed turned out to be Londo's landlord. He had a lot to say about the irresponsibility of paraheroes, and how he was now minus one huge building, with all those tenants and businesses. He was considering a lawsuit.

"*Trou de cue,*" Londo said. "He knows his insurance will cover it. I pay special premiums for him. And I assured him tonight that the lowest floors are perfectly safe and the inspectors will have a good number of tenants back in their apartments by… well, a month. I'll repair the rest of the building within two months. He'd better not sue."

"Why in the world did he ever let you in in the first place?" Lina wanted to know. "I mean, it was a beautiful home, nice location, wonderful view and all that. But Londo, if I owned an apartment building, the last person I would ever agree to rent to would be a walking, talking trouble target like yourself."

"Is that some kind of comment?"

"Only a statement of fact, honey. Starhaven, I assume, has a bit of impervion in its walls…"

"It's going to, total impervion. I've even got plans to lace the glass with it."

"You don't want anything to happen to it."

He nodded.

"How armored was that building? It blew apart rather easily."

"It's just an ordinary building. A little better made than most, nicer floor plan. I liked it. I wanted to live there. And LeGrand there," he gestured to the landlord on the screen, "he wanted to be able to tell people that he was Valiant's landlord."

"Some people will put up with anything, if there's a celebrity involved," Hal said as he watched Lina's face.

"Well they shouldn't if the safety of others is hanging on it," Lina declared. "People should have a little common sense."

"There's not a trace of impervion here," Londo said of Lina's home. "You're going to be getting visitors here, *chérie.* Many of them won't be friends, or they'll be friends you don't remember having. A lot of them will want souvenirs."

"The cats." She could hear the cat door going *click-click* as one either went out or came in.

"We'll transfer them to Starhaven as soon as possible, this week. You don't have a security system here."

"I've never needed one. The house deva–"

"I get the feeling that he might not be enough to handle some of your new problems." Lon gave the ceiling a salute. "But he did just fine with the warning the other day. Good work, deva. *Merci.*"

Hal studied Lina as she, too, gazed up at the ceiling, her eyes unfocusing. She stayed that way for a full minute. "You're right," she finally said softly. "What'll we do? Word's not out yet. Just rumors. Most people at work don't know where I live. Google just lists a mailbox route number, not a street address. Of course, that box is right across the street."

"It'll still help," Lon said gently.

"Tell you what," Lina said. "I'll get you that tee shirt and we won't announce. That way we don't have to worry about this house."

"Lina's going to get me a tee shirt that says 'I'm getting some,'" Londo explained to Hal, who snorted a tiny chuckle. "But Lina, we've discussed this–"

"I know, I know. It has to come out sometime." She put her head on his shoulder. "God Lon, I know it's no Starhaven, but I love this place." She sighed. "Maybe we could give it to Habitat for Humanity. There's still a lot left on the loan, but maybe they could turn around and sell it–" She shook her head. "Things are so different now."

"Disappointed?"

She brought her head up, wrinkled her nose at him. "Let's just say that I like the compensations."

Londo grinned back. **Let's get rid of him,** he said.

What? That's Maximus!

It's just Hal. We'll see him again. C'mon, Lina. We've got better things to do with the night. He took her for a deep kiss, then another, and despite Hal's presence, she started to get into it, too.

"So, you kids have been married for a couple weeks now?" Hal interrupted.

"In real, practical time, more like four days, with too many interruptions." Londo raised his eyebrows at his father. "Don't take this the wrong way, Hal, but get lost. We'll see you soon."

"Jae was right," Lina rebuked. "You aren't subtle at all."

Hal laughed even as his belt buckle beeped. He dug out a slender cell from behind it and checked the screen, suddenly serious. "I need to take this."

"Where is it?" Lon asked quickly. He turned to Lina. "We could give you a lift." At Lina's questioning look, he told her, "ParaNet emergency call."

"San Francisco," Hal replied.

"I've been to San Francisco," Lina told him. "I can port you there."

Hal looked from her to Londo, then back with a smile. "The ParaNet has our own transporters, but thanks for the offer. I'll call before I come next time." He nodded at Lina, gave Lon a grin, and then reached behind his belt buckle again. In moments he disappeared in fizzy dots. Transporter beam!

Lina blew out a breath once he was gone. "How'd that go?" she asked Lon. "Do you think he approved of me?"

"You were great." Londo nudged her. "Let's get things closed up here and head for home."

12

Lon and Lina slept in very late and then spent more time not-so-leisurely in bed.

"Why do I think the heat's not going to be finished today?" Lon smiled at his wife.

She rubbed his wonderful chest. "Let's work on it tomorrow. We've got too much to do today as it is."

"We can put some of that off until tomorrow, too. Who was to know we'd be bombed out of house and home? That wasn't on our goals list. Damned impolite of Terry." Londo finally declared, "I'm hungry. Let's get lunch."

"Kitchen's too full of junk to fix anything," Lina said.

"Tell you what," Lon said. "You get in that dress of yours– the sarong thing–"

"Pareo," Lina corrected.

"Whatever. And I'll take you out to lunch."

"McDonalds?"

He cocked his head. "I might be able to find someplace else. Let me think while we get dressed."

"Showers at my place. We'll need to go in shifts."

She ported back to Starhaven to find him in khaki shorts and sandals with a colorful, tropical-print shirt. Such a contrast to the mountains which now lay blinding white in a blanket of snow outside the bedroom windows. Dark sunglasses completed his ensemble.

Lina wrinkled her nose as she tried to guess. "I don't remember a McDonalds on Tiawa," Lina decided. Lon wanted to show her the world. How exciting life was now that he was in it!

"Not Tiawa." He reached for her hand. "C'mon, Lina. Let's port. Side trip first."

The picture he had in his mind was of his apartment building lobby. "Stay here where it's warm," he instructed her and trotted outside, giving some passersby a brilliant smile and salute before he jogged across the street to a news vendor in his sandals through a light snow shower.

The lobby swarmed with quiet confusion. It had been cut in half with yellow crime scene tape, and red "DANGER" signs hung from every door. Couples and families milled about in the untaped section looking lost. Some perched on plush chairs, luggage and small pets at their feet, waiting for something.

After last night, Lina was surprised that they were able to get this far into the place. But if Lon said the building wasn't about to fall down…

She recognized the small man in the safety helmet as he emerged from the stair well: LeGrand. He waved his arms and called in French, "Everyone! Let me have your attention over here! Everyone!"

The crowd flowed into a semi-circle around him.

"Okay, people. We don't know what's going on here. All I know is that it looks like the end of the world up there."

"How long before we can move back?" someone asked.

"I don't know," the man growled in a half-shout. "Valiant has left us high and dry on this one. Leave it to him to duck out after a fight."

"That's not true!" Lina exclaimed. She bulled her way through the throng, aiming for LeGrand.

"What, you know something I don't?" LeGrand rolled his eyes at the people. "I can't even get the officials here to give me an estimate. It looks bad, real bad. I don't see any of you moving back for months at least– if that."

A groan went up from the crowd. People began to shout questions and comments at LeGrand. Where was Valiant? How could he do this to them? Where was their furniture? Their pets?

Lina elbowed her way up next to LeGrand. "He's not telling you the truth!" she shouted above the roar. "Listen to me! Valiant told me!" The crowd quieted as she proceeded. "Valiant told me— he told LeGrand here, too, but apparently he chooses to forget. Valiant said that the lower floors are perfectly safe. He's arranged for the safety people to inspect today even though it's Sunday. If we're allowed in here they must have given partial approval already."

"What about the upper floors?" someone yelled.

"I'm not sure on the exact damage, but Valiant has arranged at his own expense to store what was salvaged for as long as needed. He thinks he'll have the building completely repaired within a couple months, but it may be a little longer."

The crowd murmured at that.

"Until then, I'd advise everyone to check with Monsieur LeGrand here, but make sure he tells you the *truth*."

LeGrand let out an indignant yelp, though Lina continued, "Valiant has paid for insurance all along that should provide enough money to let you live quite comfortably somewhere until your apartments are ready for you. Valiant pays those premiums out of his own pocket. And I'm sure that the regular insurance for the building will also be able to kick in some extra money, too. There'll be money to replace whatever it is you've lost."

"Is this true?" "LeGrand, why didn't you tell us?!"

"Because LeGrand just looks after LeGrand," a new voice boomed. Londo pushed through the crowd, newspapers in hand, to stand next to Lina.

"Valiant!"

Londo gave LeGrand a scathing stare before he turned back to the crowd. "My bet is that people from the ninth, some of the tenth floor down will be back in their homes by no later than noon tomorrow. It's Sunday; the inspectors aren't too crazy about rousing to come out here to look the place over, but they don't want you to be homeless either."

He detailed the damages for them and what he'd done the previous night as stop-gap so many could return to their normal lives.

"Twenty-eighth floor! Londo, what about the 28th?!"

Londo looked over at that and shook his head sadly. "Sorry, Marc. Your place and the MacKenzies'– all completely gone. We managed to save some of your things."

Lina whispered something into Lon's ear. He nodded.

"Those of you with missing pets; if you haven't yet gotten a call to pick them up, you'll be getting one today. They're all right. Even the fish."

Over in a corner several people hugged each other. A little boy jumped up and down, squealing.

"How long, Valiant? For the rest of us?"

Lon sighed. "Look, I can't guarantee things– I get these emergencies, you know, that mess up my schedule. I want to have everything repaired within the next six weeks, but I can't be positive. I will guarantee that by the end of three months everything will be done here. After that, however long it takes for the inspectors to okay everything, and you can move back. Until then, many of your possessions are being stored safely."

"Safely!" LeGrand sputtered. "How can anyone here be safe with you here, Valiant?! How long before the next crazy comes along and blasts everything to smithereens?"

"You haven't read today's papers." Londo gave him a sad smile. He handed two papers to Lina and kept one, unfolding it to display it over his head so the crowd could see.

"VALIANT TO LEAVE MONTREAL," the huge headline read.

The crowd stirred at that. "You can't," someone up front said. "You can't leave."

"I already have," Lon replied kindly. "I see now that it was a mistake to live in an unprotected place, surrounded by innocent people. Even if these things only happen once every ten years, that's too often.

"Thank you all for being such good neighbors, and I hope that all this doesn't disrupt your lives too long. I'll do my best to finish the repairs as soon as possible... but not today, if you don't mind. It's Sunday and I have some extremely important errands and some decompressing to do. I've had major upheavals in my life lately. A huge new mission to undertake. And like you, I'm trying to rebuild after the events of last night. So give me a few days and you'll see me back here helping to repair your homes. In the meantime, don't listen to LeGrand."

"Valiant, you grandstanding—"

"I may be a grandstander," Lon said patiently, "but you are a liar. I'll keep my eye on you. I'll make sure you don't cheat these people of anything else." He nodded at Lina and turned to the crowd. "*Au revoir.*" They vanished, leaving an astonished crowd behind.

"Ooh, Hawaii?"

"Molokai," Londo told her.

A breezy beachside patio surrounded by palm trees held dining tables scattered in an informal manner, their shade umbrellas still secured for the night. Few people were up yet. The sun had just peeked above the ocean's far edge. Flowers, the sea, and breakfast combined to perfume the air.

A sleek hotel stood behind them. Across the bay with mountains behind them rose high-rise hotels. Birds sang in the trees and over the ocean, some screeching, and the sky was beautifully clear and fresh with morning.

Lon led her to a beach-side table. While they waited for their orders, they read the papers and online reports. Lina scanned the pictures in them. The largest one was of Londo standing next to an elegant woman, surrounded by paparazzi and flashing cameras.

Wait. That had to be *her:* Muttbutt. She hadn't recognized herself.

Lon gave a snorted grunt and then spread his paper across the table, overlaying the one she had. It displayed a large color picture of him and Lina inside at the symphony. "Here," Lon pointed at the text impatiently. "'Valiant's startling announcement was made even more surprising because he was in the company of a beautiful woman whose identity he kept a mystery from the press.' 'Beautiful,' they said, so we'll have no more of this poor self-image of yours. You got that?"

Lina wasn't sure she was ready to make that jump. Did she really look like that?

"You are a gorgeous woman."

It was so nice that he and Jae thought she was pretty. Lina smiled at the morning, smiled at her husband. *Thank you, universe, for this. The entire lifetime's worth it, just for this.*

Lon scanned the stories, adding to them by searching on his phone. Finally he said, "*Voyons,* I count ten 'beautifuls,' three 'glamorouses' and one 'seductive.' Repeat, "seductive.' I don't see a single reference to any plain but honest faces here. I'm going to have a talk with that so-called father of yours, but you've got to move a little in the right direction, too."

"I want to get a print of this one," Lina decided of one photo of Lon. "James Bond doesn't hold a candle to you. I want it for my desk. Can we get it?"

"We'll order almost all of these; no problem." He paid attention to the new cup of coffee at his side before he went back to reviewing the stories. "No one's getting your name right. Here's a 'Linda,' and before I saw a 'Lana," but most of the time it seems to be 'Lena.'"

"I get that all the time."

"*Euh,* I suppose it's good temporarily for security. It'll keep 'em running in circles."

Lon continued to read through the stories: of the fight, accompanied by photographs that showed the fireworks against the silhouette of downtown; of him leaving Montreal with compilations of what he'd done for the city over the years; of his torrid date with Lena the mystery woman, interviews with the saleswoman who swore they both wore wedding rings, interviews with the waiter at last evening's restaurant who swore that they didn't...

He enjoyed the stories tremendously, especially the testimonials from the people sorry to see him go. He did a little dance in his chair. "Listen to this: 'Valiant has captured the heart and imagination of Montreal,' blah blah blah. 'We can only hope that he remains within Canada, for he is our greatest living national treasure.' That's nice. 'National treasure.' I like that."

"What are they going to do when they find out about Wyoming? Declare war?"

"We'll have the Center up there. Les Trois Mondes, headquartered in Quebec. They'll eat that up."

"If Jae approves."

"Of course he will. I'll make him eat dirt if I have to until he gives in."

"So you bully Jae, too?"

He looked over the top of the paper at her. "I do not bully people," he said. "I don't know where this rumor began."

"Yes, Teddy."

"Teddy?"

"Theodore Roosevelt." She batted her eyelashes at him. "Bully! Bully!"

"Teddy." He shook his head and went back to his paper.

"Also for my sweedie honey teddybear," she purred, and he tried not to smile.

"At least *I* do not control minds."

She took her paper and swatted it halfheartedly at him, but stopped when she saw the waiter approaching.

"Take care of that." Lon took the paper away from her and smoothed it. "These are going in a scrapbook."

Lina dined on tropical fruits and crepes as Londo dug into a Western breakfast of sausage, bacon, eggs and a large mound of deep-fried potatoes with onions… with a bit of fruit on the side as a deference to the place.

"Do you always eat that for breakfast?" Lina asked.

"Are you making a comment about my eating habits?"

"No, I'm just trying to figure out what to feed you. You're always talking about fast food, and this is the, what, third or fourth breakfast that you've eaten this celebration of cholesterol."

"You *are* making a comment." Londo pointed his fork at her warningly.

"It would be a comment if you weren't who you are," Lina defended herself. "But I don't have an idea in this world what's healthy for you, Lon. Are you making yourself sick eating this? Or is it just bouncing off and perfectly wholesome?"

"That sounds like a comment to me."

"I just want this to be a very long and healthy marriage." Lina took his hand. "I want what's best for you, darling."

He looked at her hand on his. "Wiley and Gorgeon did a complete workup of me years and years ago," he admitted. "They said that I could live on a diet of suet or raw iron and it probably wouldn't hurt me. This stuff tastes a little better than that."

Lina let out a satisfied sigh. "That makes me feel a lot better. Okay, you have my full permission to enjoy your breakfast. You may eat now."

He chuckled. "You know, Lina, you can be quite a tyrant at times."

She smiled indulgently at him. "Just trying to keep up with High Commander Valiant," she said.

"Oh come on," he protested. "I'm not that bad, am I?"

"Not usually. But someday… someday, Londo, someone's going to say no to you, and you're going to have to take it."

His eyes narrowed mischievously. "Hasn't happened yet. "

When they finished eating, they snugged their chairs together so they could check out the files Jae had given them about Feith, particularly how Feithi Triune marriages were supposed to work.

Not a word was included about having one in secret.

After some time they switched to the introduction to Aldierra that Admiral Bracken had given them. The electronics were still chewing their way through translations, though what they could make out did not give an optimistic outlook on the planet, either sociologically or ecologically.

Lina let out a sound that was halfway between a sigh and a moan, and Londo couldn't help but agree with her. It was going to be long, difficult mission, he knew. But for them it wouldn't begin in earnest today. Instead he offered his bride his hand, and they went out to explore the island.

Jae organized his notes and recordings of the trip so far, merging files on his studypadd to construct a better basic linguistic program. When he finished, the padd indicated that he could now leave it switched on whenever he was in the presence of someone speaking Farrani, the primary language of Aldierra, and it would update automatically.

He'd be very happy to leave the Aldierrans' stilted Panlingua behind. The excessive formality made him itch.

The tall, blond Legionnaire and Chosen of the Three Worlds reviewed his files as to what the admiral and his staff had said were Aldierra's primary needs:

food and raw ores primarily, along with certain medical supplies. They also requested women, but Jae didn't know how he could phrase that to the diplomats waiting back in the Affiliated Systems.

He studied political maps of the planet and had to ask how far the smaller oceans extended because he couldn't make them all out. Pink was usually the color that depicted sprawling mega-cities built on top of the seas, covering an astonishing percentage of their surface area. Sometimes the cities were built on or near the ocean floor, indicated in light gray. But now and then the sea cities were lilac. These turned out to be overlying cities: one on the ocean floor, and the other floating at sea level.

Twenty billion people lived on Aldierra.

Of all the Three Worlds, it had the least amount of solid surface area. Only land that had been too expensive or difficult to cultivate had been left wild or, better yet, a dumping ground. Jae scratched his neck as he reassessed that huge black spot on the map that had bothered Londo to see. It wasn't a landlocked ocean, but there were no cities built on it nor within several hundred kilometers.

Jae enlarged the notations. "Great Shit Flats," the map said. He drew back in shock. Maybe it was some twisted poetic term, but no. A quick search revealed many mentions of minor shit flats scattered across every continent, and the occasional Shit River and Shit Bay as well. There were even a few New Shit Rivers, as if the old ones hadn't been enough.

His fingers contracted into a loose fist. With the loss of fertile surface area, it was a wonder that the Aldierrans could produce even minimal food to feed their population. Couldn't they see their primary problem?

Too many people equaled too much demand for resources. Equaled a need to conquer new interstellar territory, but Aldierra herself had taken the steam out of that for a while at least. Everyone's attention had been forcibly turned back to the home world.

Shape up or die, the spirit of the planet had told them all. They had a shade over nine months to show improvement or the planet would wipe them out herself.

"Aldierra, what have you gotten us into?" he muttered to himself. Did he imagine a silent rumble in response?

Toward the end of his third day with the fleet, Jae strolled into the flagship's mess only to encounter a brawl. At least twenty men– there were no women he'd seen– lashed at each other's throats with knives, forks, chairs, and anything else they could find to use as weapons. Officers watched along the sidelines. One told Jae not to be alarmed, proud that his world had this exciting a life to offer, so unlike sleepy Sarastor. He explained to Jae that this was good training to become an officer or to be noticed by one.

Dodging blows, medics dragged three bodies from the battle. The officer shrugged. "Not officer material," he explained. "This way creates room for the younger men to move up. It's a recycling of manpower. It keeps the corps vigorous."

Jae stretched out his right arm. When his Worlds-given staff had fully materialized to his command, he banged it on the decking. The force resounded and then stilled into a silence that vibrated through everything. Everyone paused, even in their breathing, to turn their gazes to him.

"Stop!" Jae ordered them. "Now! Think about what you're doing. Aldierra has spoken. You need to learn to live together, or you will surely die that way."

His voice held them as it resounded in the room. "You have air, warmth, food. What is there to fight about? Are you children or men?"

He turned in a slow circle so he could catch them all in his sharp, eternal gaze. "What true man grinds his brother under his feet so he can use him as a ladder to advance? The bodies of your fallen brothers don't make a steady surface. They will begin to rot and stink under you. Sooner or later you'll fall as well. You will become the rot."

He swept his staff in front of him like a king. "Find a better foundation upon which to base your lives. Honor. Trust. Learn to build instead of destroy. And do it quick; Deadline approaches."

Sometimes the staff could become quite material. Jae used it to clear a way through the crowd to one injured man. "You," he pointed at the ensign he had seen kick this one unconscious. "See to it that he gets medical help. Organize a crew to assist you."

Jae moved through the debris, ordering the worst of the brawlers to lead the medical evacuation. He told them to report back to him about their victims' conditions. Then he returned to his quarters.

Jae didn't like to preach. He liked people who tried to preach to him even less. Example was so much better. How could he get his point across to these Aldierrans without talking down to them?

First he had to understand them. That would mean studying them harder than he'd ever studied anything before. Again he thought he felt that distant rumble in his mind.

"Patience, Aldierra," he murmured and thought that even through the void of hyperspace, the world entity heard him. He was one to talk; though he was the last member of the ever-patient Feithi, he'd never mastered the art.

He could fake it, though. With a long, controlled breath, he settled his features into his Feithi mask: the ultra-composed, non-judgmental pose that overlay roiling, intense judgment. He signaled his readiness to conduct another interview.

Fayetteville's Sunday traffic was thicker than one would expect. In their rental car, Lina and Lon passed a business district composed of low, cement-block buildings, their signs flickering on in the dusk, then began seeing more residential areas. Here North Carolina was flat; the ground, sand. Towering long-leaf pine trees lined the roads. A final sun beam broke through the thin overcast before dying.

"If they had spotted that fake license, we would have been dead meat," Lina said.

"I did a good job." Londo played with all the doodads on the car door, having exhausted the sound, temperature and electronics controls in the middle of the dash. "That was a terrible picture of you on it, Lie. We need to get you used to cameras."

He listed the various other IDs and cards they needed to replace now that they were married. "E or no e?" he asked of their new last name. Lina shrugged. Her mind was on other things.

Londo glanced at the rental agreement folded up in the glove compartment. Lina had had to fill it out, since she was the one with the old license, even though it had been his card that had paid. She spelled it "hart," though the license he'd doctored had said "heart." When they'd legally changed their name on Sarastor, they'd spelled it phonetically, using the Panlinguan alphabet. Earth was another matter.

"I think I've only spelled it without an 'e' once so far. I'll have my Terran lawyers look into the name, first thing."

"We should get Jae's input."

"Yeah, we will." Londo lowered the back of his seat to a lounging position and then righted it. "Is this a smooth ride?" Sometimes his insensitivity to the physical world blocked the oddest things.

"Yes, this gas-guzzler rides very smoothly and it's quieter than normal. I prefer my Civic."

Londo had insisted on a rental because he didn't want to be seen in Lina's ancient car. Besides, a rental fit their "just stopped in town between flights" story better.

He just had to get a car of his own soon! Where could he put a garage in Starhaven? There weren't any roads nearby. Maybe he should keep a car in Montreal instead. And he probably should learn how to drive. It seemed easy enough.

Would it look too odd if he drove around in the dead of winter with the top down? He knew that his car would be a convertible, a red— no, an electric blue convertible, yeah, custom painted, with all these extras and much more. Top of the line. Showy.

"You'll get road salt all over the inside if you drive it like that," Lina told him. "If we live in Wyoming, we'll need a sturdy car. Mine should do fine, or maybe we can get an electric pickup. Do they make those? I can't drive in snow or ice. Canada has schools for that, don't they? And drivers licenses are supposed to have rotten pictures. We'll have to muss you up for yours. My replacement license should probably be from Wyoming. What's our address? Do they have the same traffic laws as North Carolina?"

"No idea and no idea," Londo said, squirming in his seat. Then he poked around in the glove compartment. "Aren't they both states? Shouldn't they have the same traffic laws?"

"Who is this asking me about laws?"

He made a face at her against the glow of the dashboard. "I'm with the Para-Net, not the Highway Patrol. I don't do car stuff unless it's a police chase."

"You don't drive an inch until I teach you, do you hear? For some reason I don't trust Valiant with a car."

Lon grunted.

Lina was learning that a grunt meant he was trying to appear to be agreeing with her without really promising anything.

She turned the car onto the dark road off to the left. Well-maintained doublewides and modular homes packed tightly to either side of the street. Streetlights were few. In the darkness that swallowed up her brights, every house had a patch of sandy lawn, an azalea bush or two, and the occasional matching attached garage.

"They're all vinyl, cheap revival," Lina sang the old song. *"And they all look just the same."*

A carport with lattice was next to her parents' house, she recalled, but here were three other houses with lattice carports and– there. Familiar cars sat in front of the garage. A dark window held a sign: "Piano lessons." She parked alongside the street, right tires on the grass.

Lon looked up, his hand frozen in mid-air as he replaced the paperwork. *"Euh,* I take it this is the place."

"This is it." She groaned.

They sat there. Neither made a move to open the doors.

13

"We don't have to do this," she finally offered. "We can come up with some kind of excuse–"

"No." Londo swallowed. "No, we'll go in."

Her mouth opened as she realized he was scared.

"Look, this is my first time meeting my in-laws," he said. "Forgive me for being nervous. It seems to me that last night you were–"

"Last night was a surprise, Londo. Me in my nightgown and Maximus to boot. Give me a break."

"Give me a break, too. What do I call them? What if they don't–"

"At least we know they'll like you more than they like me."

He unclicked his seatbelt. "People can change, Kitten. Just think, you marrying me gives him another son-in-law, right? And isn't that the whole problem with him? Not having had a son?" He turned to look straight into a dark marble floating in the shadows. "And when you join the family, Jae," he told it, "that'll give him three sons-in-law. Won't that be cozy?"

"How long have you had that thing recording?" Lina demanded.

"Long enough. I like using it. I edit when I'm on downtime in hyperspace, and Jae needs to see this. Say hello, Lie."

"Hello, Jae, and God help us all."

"Amen. Just think: by the time Jae watches, we'll have survived this, right? Meeting your father is not going to be fatal."

Lina muttered unintelligibly to herself.

"And if it is," Lon added, "Hal will avenge us."

They sat there in the dark. Three minutes passed. "Lon…"

He looked at her. "What?"

"I'm serious. Don't divorce me because of–them."

That made him laugh, though this time it was a shaky one.

A pickup truck and a small convertible already filled the driveway. A new SUV took up the garage. Lina pointed them out: her brother-in-law's, her sister's, her parents'. A short cement walk brought them from the drive to the front door. Barking from within answered the doorbell.

"That's MacDuff," she explained. "I told you about him, didn't I? Oh– whatever you do, don't tell them you were just ordained."

"I won't." Londo placed his hand on his chest. "Reverend Starheart," he said wonderingly. "I don't feel any different."

"That's because you're still going to be doing what you've been doing all along. Ah, finally."

The inner door opened for a curly brown-haired girl, about nine years old, who jumped up and down when she saw them. "Aunt Lie! Aunt Lie!" she yelled and stopped. She stared at Londo. "Who are you?" she demanded through the clear storm door.

"Is that polite?" Lina asked. "I got married. This is your new Uncle Lon." They had agreed to refer to him just as Lon, a not-unusual Southern name anyway. "Londo" might remind them of somebody famous with the same name. He'd refused to go by "Lonnie," though. "Lon, this is Pegi, Barb's daughter. At least I think it's her. You cut your hair. It looks nice. Are you going to let us in?"

Pegi swung the door open with a flourish. "Sure, Aunt Lie." She drew her inside, peeking around her at Londo, up and up to his face. "He's awfully tall."

"Yes he is. And awfully handsome, too."

A border collie bounded around the corner, stopped for a moment when he saw Lina, and then galloped to her, wagging his entire rear end. He let out high-pitched *yip*s and cried as he ran around her in circles to butt her jeans here and there with his head.

She gave him a thorough rub. "Hello, Duffer. Aren't you a good doggie! Lon, this is MacDuff. Where's everyone else?"

Pegi gaped at Londo as Lina made up to the dog, who was trying to knock her down with kisses. "Hi," she said shyly.

"Hi, Pegi. It's nice to meet you. I like your hair, too." Londo smiled and held out his hand for her to shake. Kids always liked him. He liked kids.

A millisecond before her hand would have reached his, she turned and ran through the enclosed porch into the back of the house, flailing her arms. "Aunt Lie's here! Aunt Lina's here!" she screamed.

Lina sighed. "They must have the television on too loud again. Although they shouldn't be able to miss *her.*"

Lon squatted down and held out his hand for the dog to sniff. "At least you can say hello," he told the dog. "MacDuff. MacDuff, are you a good boy? Good dog?"

Duff's tail began to wag at him and he carefully scruffed the dog's head. His muzzle had distinct gray marks. "I like dogs, MacDuff. Do they have any cats around here for you to–"

"aarWUFF!" The dog came to attention and whirled around, twitching as he stopped at each of the cardinal points.

"*Mon dieu,* what's wrong?" Londo exclaimed.

"Don't say the C-A-T word around him. Easy, Duffer dog." Lina bent down to rub his neck. "Calm down. There aren't any C-A-T's around here. He gets all excited about those things, doesn't he, boy? That's it. Lon's not going to say the c-word again, is he?"

"I guess not." As an apology Londo rubbed up and down the dog's back, hoping his touch wasn't too rough or not enough. "I always wanted a dog."

"So you have seven you-know-whats instead."

He raised up again and the dog trotted happily in circles around them. "Let's get a dog, too."

"Let's get this over first before we make any more insane decisions." Lina closed the door behind them and leaned her forehead against it. Londo put his hands on her shoulders.

"We'll only be here for a couple hours," he said. "If things get out of hand, I'll take 'em outside and beat them up for you, okay *d'ac?*"

She laughed softly. "I wish. Well, maybe they'll be on their best behavior tonight. Wouldn't that be something?" She glanced up at the floating camera, hidden against the ceiling, and made a face for Jae. "'Into the valley of something rode the six hundred.' Come, Duff. Come, Londo."

"Arf."

They followed the shrieks of "Aunt Lie! Aunt Lie!" and "Quiet, Pegi!" For such a small house, Lon noted, it certainly wandered around a lot. The living room was in back. This had started out as an older single-wide that someone had expanded with stick-built rooms, enclosed porches, a converted garage, and makeshift halls. Maybe they were trying to keep remodeling costs down by tacking on rooms here and there as they got the money.

Nearby Pegi shouted incoherently.

The first strangers appeared all at once in a doorway. "Lina!" a plumpish, mustachioed man of early middle age said in a broad Texan accent. "Be quiet, Pegi! We thought you might not show up after all."

"We were held up at our last stop," Lina said. "Lon Starhart, this is my brother-in-law, Bubba Yates."

Last night Hal had laughed hugely when Lon had told him, "My new brother-in-law's name is 'Bubba.' I bet you anything he has a gun rack in his pickup." That had proved true.

"I've heard good things about you, Bubba," was all Londo now said with a straight face.

"Hiya," Bubba shook Londo's hand heartily. "Lon, is it? I can't say I've heard anything at all about you. It's a big surprise for everybody. Good to meet you, even if you make me look short." Bubba couldn't be over five foot six. "Let me just warn you in advance–"

"Mom and Dad are not pleased," a deeply tanned woman who bore more than a little resemblance to Lina said.

Her accent was southern, but it was neither the Texan accent of her husband nor the North Carolina accent of Lina's. It was something between the two, and it startled Lon to realize that he could differentiate it. All these years he'd thought of the American Southern accent as just one funny way of talking. Now he realized that there were all kinds of southern accents, just as there were for northern ones.

"You must be Barbara," he said, shaking her hand.

Barb's hair was straight, as opposed to the curls on Lina. Her eyes were brown as was her hair, and her nose, more pronounced than Lina's flatter one. Eight years older than her sister, Barb wasn't nearly as tall as Lina, though she was inches taller than her husband. But the oval face, the largeness of her eyes, the shapeliness of her figure– they were the same as Lina's. Bubba must consider himself a lucky fellow.

Barb was talking. "Yes, nice meeting you. Lon Starhart– Mom wasn't too clear if that was your original last name or not."

"We came up with it after we got married."

Barb nodded as if she had expected it. "They're not happy that y'all got married so quickly. And that they weren't invited. Did you at *least* get a video, Lina?"

"We didn't bring it with us." They'd both decided they would hold off on that until they saw how things went.

"Of all the things to leave behind… Well, we'll help you stage a retreat if you need it."

"We'll stand our ground," Londo told Barb before he turned to Bubba. "I'm dying to know: 'Bubba'–"

"That's the name I go by," Bubba replied with a friendly grin. "Call me 'Edward' and I'll be obliged to take you outside and teach you a few things. A man's chosen name is a man's chosen name."

"Absolutely." Lon nodded in Lina's direction. "If you hear her call me 'Lonnie,' you know there's going to be some yelling soon."

From behind her mother and father, Pegi darted forward and grabbed Londo by the hand. "Come on, Uncle Lon! I want you to meet Grandpa!"

Lina peeled Pegi's hand from Londo's. "Sorry. I get to do this. You can have him later, okay?"

Pegi's face twisted into a glowering pout. Stamping her foot with an "oh!", she ran down the hall to parts unknown.

Lon slipped his arm around Lina's waist for support– though he wasn't quite sure who was being more supported– and took a breath before entering the family room.

The television was indeed blasting, and a sharp-featured older man reclined in front of it. He looked up as they approached, his gaze quickly dismissing Lina to assess Londo: *Wet back!* The thought broadcast clearly to any telepath to hear it.

A woman who was an older, less tanned edition of Barb paused as she set the dining table. *Good heavens, he's not white. Kelly will have a fit.* She wiped her hands on a towel and started forward with a tremulous smile. Barb slipped over to the television to turn down its sound.

"This must be Lon," Lina's father said. He got up out of the chair, hand extended to shake. He was thin but tall, and Lina had gotten her nose from him. On her, it was a cute nub of a nose. It didn't work as well on him.

"This is my dad and mother, Lon. Emma and Kelly O'Kelly," Lina said, hiding behind a smile. "Lon Starhart."

Londo noted that no one in the family hugged each other in greeting. They shook a stranger's hand but didn't touch much– except for the dog, who went up to everyone for a pat and a rub. Bubba had his arm around Barb, but the O'Kellys themselves did not touch each other.

"Pleased to meet you, Mr. O'Kelly… Mrs. O'Kelly."

Lina's father nodded. "Emma and Kelly," he said.

"All right… Kelly," Londo said.

Emma hovered around him. "Can I get you something to drink? We have Coke, diet Coke, Sprite…"

"A Coke would be fine, thanks," Londo said.

"Are you sure? We have juice and beer…"

"No, a Coke is fine."

"And tea. I've got sweet or unsweet…"

"Here, Mom, I'll get it," Lina said. "Anyone else want anything?" She took orders and disappeared to the kitchen with her mother. Her sister came with them.

Coward, Londo accused.

Am not. I'm splitting them up, keeping them from working as an armed unit for as long as possible.*

Kelly was reevaluating him after hearing Londo speak. "You're French?" he asked.

"French-Canadian." Londo could almost feel the gears clicking in Kelly's head as they tried to figure out just what this man of color was.

Kelly eased back to his chair, and Londo and Bubba took the sofa. Pegi settled on the rug inches away from the television and turned it up to blast level, only to turn around and glare at Kelly when the sound muted. Kelly set down his remote control and pointed his finger at her. She ran out of the room into the front of the house, where most of the bedrooms were.

Londo listened for a moment to the women in the kitchen. "He's gorgeous!" Barb was whispering to Lina. He had a favorite sister-in-law now.

"We were put off to hear that you all'd gotten married so quickly," Kelly told Londo. He started to say more, but Bubba interrupted.

"So where did it happen? That island in the South Pacific?"

"We were in quarantine for so long," Lon evaded. "They even cut it short, just so we could get a nice temple ceremony instead of having it in the hospital."

"A temple?" Kelly said doubtfully. "What denomination?"

"Oh, it was non-denominational." Londo had been warned about touching on religious matters. He shouldn't make up things so quickly. "I was with friends, and they all attended. It was too bad that Lina didn't know very many there."

"Nondenominational." Kelly shook his head at that. "What business you in, Lon?"

"Self-employed for the most part. Security."

Bubba nodded his head at the news. "Dangerous work?"

Londo shrugged. "Sometimes. That's how I was in Tiawa. I wound up in the hospital and got caught in the quarantine. Lina was helping them out, and we… got involved."

Londo steered the introductory chat as best he could to simple backgrounds. Kelly worked for a tire company; Emma, for the post office. Barb was a dental hygienist while Bubba did home inspections. Unfortunately the talk about occupations brought up Lina's late one in porn.

"Porn. Filth. You have to watch out for her," Kelly warned, wagging a finger at Lon. "And she's involved these New Age people who worship crystals–"

"She got a medal once for saving someone's life," Bubba interrupted.

Lon lifted his eyebrow at that. "Really? She hasn't told me."

"It was when she was a lifeguard," Bubba told him. "She was just a kid–"

"Drinks," Lina announced, and handed them out. Lon noticed that she'd taken a Coke for herself– caffeine, which flummoxed her psyche somehow. Likely she didn't want to be too sensitive in this crowd.

Lina asked, "Where's Drew? I wanted Lon to meet everyone in one fell swoop."

"He's still working," Bubba told her. "He wanted to be here. Maybe the next time you show up, he'll be able to meet you. He's on double-duty now, you know. The after-school job plus community service."

"Yeah, I told Lon about Drew's little misunderstanding with the law," Lina said. Her teenaged nephew had been caught with friends spraying graffiti on their school.

"*Eh bien,* kids," Lon said, trying to be diplomatic. After all, he'd been a bit of a hellion when he was young, hadn't he? Well, he'd tried.

"That's right, Lina said you were from Canada," Barb said. She'd come into the room with Lina. Londo realized that he'd let some French slip. "You were in Montreal last night?"

"You must have heard about the trouble there," Londo said. "It was on CNN."

"I don't watch that," Kelly told him. "I get my news local, where I am. I don't need to know what's going on in Timbuktu."

"What happened?" Barb asked. "Was it something last night?"

"There was an explosion and fire."

"It was very close to Lon's apartment," Lina said quickly. "Traffic was snarled for hours. It made moving very difficult."

"I'll bet," Bubba said. "Explosions– What was it?"

Londo matched gazes with Lina. Okay, he wouldn't press his luck. "Arsonists."

"Criminals," Kelly said. "This world today. Criminals and terrorists and bad kids. I say string 'em all up and get rid of them."

Londo wondered if the man included his grandson in that statement.

"To top it all off," Lina interrupted, "Lon's father came looking for him in the middle of the night. He'd been out of the country for some time and we hadn't been able to reach him."

Lon shook his head. "A mutual friend left him a message, told him I was back. So he showed up after midnight… and let me tell you, he was more than a little shocked to see Lina there." He put his arm around Lina's shoulders. "I think he took the news well."

"So you and your father are world travelers, Lon?" Emma asked. She stood apart from the group, waiting for drinks to run low.

"I guess you could say so. He's in security, too. Sometimes we work together. It certainly takes us everywhere."

"So Lina will be left alone a lot." Was there a wistful twinge to Emma's statement? If so, for whom: Lina or herself? Or was he reading too much into some of this?

Lon caught Lina's eye. "We're going to do a lot of traveling together," he said. She gave him a faint smile at that, although it didn't last long.

"Traveling is a waste of time," Kelly said. "People need to stay where God meant them to be. Let those foreigners stay over there and I'll stay over here, and we'll both be happy."

"If I hadn't travelled to Tiawa I'd never have met Lina."

That got him a warm squeeze on his leg, though otherwise Lina sat stiffly beside him.

And yet the rest of the conversation went smoothly. Londo was surprised. Oh, he hadn't expected Kelly to meet them at the door twirling his moustache and flexing a bullwhip, but he did expect to see some more of the man who had so mistreated an innocent little girl.

Instead Kelly came off as reasonably intelligent– in some areas remarkably so– and deeply involved in his community and his church. Little by little, Londo relaxed. Each time he did so he could feel Lina tense up. She wanted him to hate her father for her.

I do not.

Don't you be the one to start anything here, Londo warned her. **If he's having a good day, let's just enjoy it.**

Lon tried to cajole Emma to sit, but every time she did Kelly ran out of tea and she had to hop up to get more. Sometimes a timer would ding in the kitchen, and Emma hurried off to take care of that. Lon couldn't tell if Emma had any opinions of her own, for every time she joined in the conversation, Kelly had a sudden recollection he had to add. The man did like to talk about himself, but Lon had seen many good people who did the same.

All in all, he thought that he could invite these in-laws to a party of his friends and not be embarrassed by them. Bubba in particular he liked. Bubba had been a carpenter in his single days and still liked to putter around the workshop.

"Maybe you could come out to Wyoming sometime and give me a hand with the house," Londo told him.

"I suppose you'll have it done soon," Bubba replied.

"It's a little on the large side. I'm thinking it won't be done until late summer or so."

"Three years from now," Lina said, and everyone laughed.

"This is terrific pot roast," Lon told Emma, helping himself to more. "It reminds me of my Mama Ruth's. That's my father's mother. The first thing she ever made for me was a pot roast."

"Why, thank you."

"Yeah, Ma, great dinner," Bubba said between enthusiastic bites.

Young Pegi didn't eat with them. She started out at the table but within minutes Barb told her it was okay to leave, and the little girl had reached out, grabbing food off serving platters with her fingers to load her plate and then run off. No one had corrected her. Lon could hear Cartoon Network playing in some bedroom with the door closed.

Like Helen Keller, but she doesn't have the excuse, Lina whispered to him.

Dinner conversation was pleasant and homey. Lon smiled at his new family and the news about what the neighbors were up to, who had sold what at the last church yard sale, and what great-grandfather Walt had done during the Great Depression: played the horses and by doing so, kept his family afloat.

Emma was up and down– mostly up, bringing in additions to the table– but finally she settled in her place.

"Grandma had to place his bets at the track in Chicago every week," Lina said, speaking of Walt. "She taught Mom how to do it."

"Always bet on the horse that winks at you," Emma said sagely as she passed around the green beans. "We had so much fun when Mom took me to the races, talking to all the jockeys and eating hot dogs and root beer. It's too bad we don't have those races in North Carolina. Horses are such beautiful animals. You know, I met Willie the Shoe once."

This had been her longest contribution to the conversation yet. Lon asked, "How long has it been since you've been to the track, Emma?"

"Oh my. I haven't been, well– since we got married, I suppose."

Kelly nodded. "People on my side of the family would talk. Had to get her out of the bad habit."

The green beans passed to Lina and Lon heard her sigh happily.

Something else I can eat. Wait, there's something– Oh no, Mom must have used bacon drippings on them for flavor. Poor dying pig vibes. Lina passed the vegetable bowl to Londo. She had only corn and plain mashed potatoes on her plate. She reached for a roll.

"Smells good to me," he murmured to her and dug in.

The mutter distracted Kelly's attention from his plate to Lina's. "What are you eating?"

She looked at her hand. "It seems to be a roll," she said.

"Get some pot roast."

"I can't; I've gone vegetarian. Guess I didn't mention it on the phone. Sorry."

Kelly's loaded fork stopped halfway to his mouth. "Vegetarian?"

"Yes. Not vegan, though. Pass the butter, Barb, would you? I wish I could make mashed potatoes like Mom. I cheat and use instant."

"Vegetarian? God put animals on earth to feed us. Why would you want to be a vegetarian?"

"I've been trying for a couple years now. I just finally did it."

"No member of this family is going to go ve-ge-tarian," Kelly growled. "Here, Emma, give me the roast. Think you're so much better than everyone else, do you?" He grabbed the platter from his wife, spilling meat juice on the crisp, white tablecloth, and stabbed his fork into the cow muscle as Lina grimaced. "You'll have some roast," he declared.

"No thank you," Lina replied icily. "I'm fine."

"I paid good money for this. You will have some meat like the rest of us," Kelly ordered and came away from the platter with two thick, dripping slices of roast.

"I said, no thank you," Lina repeated. "You're messing up Mom's nice table. Put it down."

"Lina likes to make up for me," Londo said easily. "I take two or three servings of the meat, and she fills up on the veggies. It works out nicely."

But Kelly braced to throw the slices onto Lina's plate. From this distance the impact would send her food flying onto her lap. Lon puffed very lightly as Kelly began the motion, and globs of meat juice spattered hard onto the sleeve of Kelly's shirt.

Kelly recoiled, gazing in horror at his sleeve. "Now look what you made me do!" he exclaimed. He dropped the platter back on the table and swiped at his shirt with his napkin. "Dammit, Lina–!"

"Don't worry about it," Emma said quickly, "I can get that out." She hustled to his side to dab a wetted napkin at the stain.

Through their link, Londo could feel someone kick Lina's foot.

"Why'd you do that?" Barb hissed at her under her breath.

"I didn't do anything," Lina retorted as she kicked her sister back.

Kelly sat and glared at Lina as he held out his arm for his wife to attend to. "You've always been trouble," he declared.

"I certainly always get the blame," Lina grumbled as she determinedly ate.

"She's clumsy, Lon; you watch out for her. Falling down all the time. Sneaking out at night, have you told him that, Muttbutt? She sneaks around, whores around the neighborhood unless you keep a close watch on her."

"I think that's enough." Lon set his glass down. "I think you're going to stop saying that about my wife. We're going to have a nice, pleasant meal here."

"This is my house."

"Or we could leave. We came because I wanted to meet the family. I'm well aware of all the accidents Lina had when she was younger– and I also have a pretty good suspicion of who caused them."

Emma blurted, "Don't leave! You just got here!" Realizing that she'd spoken out of turn, she glanced apologetically at her husband. "You don't want them to go, Kelly. Lon's a nice boy; you can tell that, can't you? Every bit as nice as Bubba, and you like Bubba. He's very fond of you, Bubba, you know that."

"I know that, Ma." Bubba studiously regarded the plate in front of himself.

"Good. There." She dabbed at the stains again. "I'll put it in the laundry and it'll be as good as new."

"She tries to blame her accidents on me." Kelly scowled first at Londo and then at Lina.

"Accidents– like the broken leg?" Londo asked.

"Change subjects," Lina said.

"Like the brain damage?"

"Brain damage!" Emma exclaimed. She clutched her napkin to her heart and gaped guiltily at Kelly.

Into the sudden silence Barb asked, "Brain damage? When was this? Dad, when was this? No one told me–!"

"There was no brain damage! Good god, what is the girl making up now–"

Lina set down her fork. "The doctor at the hospital– where we were quarantined– she did some tests and said I had suffered brain damage when I was a kid."

"Third-world doctors! Witch doctor, probably."

"Actually, Kelly, she's one of the finest doctors around," Londo said. "She ran tests. There was a long list of childhood injuries, but the damage to Lina's brain topped the list. The doctor said it had resulted from some kind of physical attack. If I did some research in police records, would I find a report? More than one? Just how often did you have to pack up and move through the years?"

"What kind of lies has she been spreading?!"

"Lon! Dad!" Lina was about to add something but set her mouth in a tight line. She deliberately folded her napkin and placed it beside her plate. "Things in the past are in the past. What we are going to do tonight is to sit at this table like civilized people and have a civilized meal. The conversation is going to be about the weather or sports or movies or, or whatever everyone can agree on without raising their voices. Is that clear?"

She looked at Londo. "Sit. Sit down, everyone. Mom, please sit down."

"I will not have you ordering me in my own home!" Kelly roared.

"Then we'll leave," Lon said quickly as he rose again. He held out his hand to Lina. It took a moment before she took it and stood as well.

Lon nodded to Barb, Bubba, Emma. "It's been a pleasure meeting you. I hope we can try this again sometime."

Lina let out a strangled sound.

"Soon," Londo said to everyone, including her.

"But we never see you," Emma told her daughter as the couple began to walk toward the hall that led to the front of the house. "You never come to visit."

"I'm here now. It didn't work out."

"Don't come–" Kelly began, but Bubba said something to him, and he quieted. He hunched over his plate and ate as Emma and the dog accompanied Londo and Lina.

"Come back soon," Emma whispered to them. "We miss you, Lina. He won't admit it, but he does."

"He doesn't," Lina said.

"And you love him."

Lina was silent.

"You have to love him. He's your father."

Londo opened the front door, careful not to let the dog out. "I'm glad to have met you, Emma. We will make a return visit, don't worry." He gave the dog's head a pat.

"Lina?"

Lina's upper lip curled. She looked at Londo before she did her mother. "Yeah," she said. "Maybe you could give him some drugs before we come, okay?"

Emma gave the direction of the dining room a quick glance. "I'll see what I can arrange."

14

They both jumped when Fear Factory screamed from the radio. "Who the hell set that thing?!" Lon demanded as he reached around to tap the snooze button.

"You the hell did, darling," Lina said as she came up from behind and kissed the side of his stubbled jaw good morning. "You mentioned something about needing to get out of bed sometime today? A lot of things to do, I believe you said. Can we find a better station? Soft rock, maybe? Something from this millennium?"

"Unh. Things to do." Lon settled himself back on the mattress and reached out to gather Lina to himself. She was soft and naked and warm. "I believe I'll just sleep in today," he declared. "I have some hard honeymooning to do, too." He growled playfully. "Very hard."

"Honeymoon? You mean, where no one interrupts you?"

"Uh huh." He brushed her hair back and kissed her shoulder.

"Where you lie around all day and just make love?"

"Sounds great." He kissed her chest.

"You mean like what we had on Tiawa?" She arched toward him. His lips moved lower, sucking and nibbling. He gave her a long, wet lick and then eased up, making her let out a mewl of disappointment.

"Not like Tiawa," he told her. "No Terry, no Menlo, no sand up my butt. Just warm bed. It is warm, isn't it?" he asked anxiously.

"It's heaven," she smiled, and slid down to meet his mouth with her own under the covers.

When the alarm had gone off four more times, they emerged, giggling.

"'Twas no lark," Lon declared, fishing for the next line. "Something something nightingale and we can go back to bed."

"'Twas Korn," Lina informed him. "C'mon, Londo. Out of bed. Responsible adult time comes after play time, right? I know; we'll institute a reward system."

Lon leaned on his elbow as he watched her stretch. And quake at the room's cold. She reached for that godawful terrycloth robe instead of the sheer silk one. Something had to be done about the heat. Work. He didn't feel like working today! But she was right. "You mean, after we get the whole house in order, we can meet back here?"

She turned to regard him and then plopped back on the bed. "Whole house, hell." She traced a design on his delicious stomach with her fingertips. "I was thinking more like after each room. Each *small* room."

He raised up to take her in his arms. "Much better idea. I like the way you think."

They installed the final two windows. As Lon finished off the last of the heating system, Lina sorted and ported furniture around the house. He certainly had a lot of furnishings at his old place. She felt a surge of pride that she'd managed to salvage so much of it.

Not so useless, Muttbutt, Lina told herself as she wandered over to watch him test the system. Lon had explained that it was based on geothermal and some kind of altitude energy, plus a healthy dose of solar. Whatever it was, it gave a soft whirr as it started, but then silenced.

"It's on," Lon assured her. "It'll take a while to warm things up, though. It wasn't made for instant heat." He strolled around the house using his parabreath to puff into the corners of the mammoth cave that was Starhaven. After each puff he'd wait a moment, then take a temperature reading with his padd.

It wasn't until Lina could pull off her winter coat that Lon began gathering his neighbors' furnishings into a stack. He used a network of teleported-in beams that he regularly utilized in his work to support the structure.

"Coat on again," he ordered Lina, and she watched him lift a twenty-by-twenty section of the skylight section of the roof off the top of Starhaven. He set it down outside, came in to lift the cargo, set that outside, then re-secured the roof. "The hole's temporary," he explained. "Starhaven's under construction, and I needed a way to get all the materials in."

Then he took off, towing the bundle behind him. It was the size of two large moving vans. Lina watched until he was a mere speck in the eastern sky. Then she began cleaning up the melting pockets of snow that had spilled from the roof.

She discovered that Starhaven's laundry room wasn't yet hooked to electricity. Instead she ported home to a pile of laundry into her own machines. By the time it was done, she'd given each cat individual attention and play time.

She arrived at Starhaven with folded sheets and groceries as Londo returned from his fifth and final furniture moving trip. They celebrated.

There were more ceiling drips to be cleaned up and laundry once again. This time Lina sent the rest, plus sheets, to Sarastor. Londo directed his automatic facilities there to take care of it. It would only take a few minutes. As they waited, Lina asked, "What room are we going to finish first? Can we bring the cats in now?"

Londo said, "Come on," and led Lina to what would be his study. Unlike most of the rest of the place, there were working electrical plugs here next to his Sarastoran computer center, which held a Mac to the side. He brought up the 3D plans for Starhaven. Lina sat on a stool beside him while he made rough adjustments in the blueprints, enlarging the pantry at her request. The new wine cellar had previously been assigned the pantry space, but now expanded to three times its original size. He made dozens of notes about other spots in the home.

Then he sat back to study the updated version. "Master bedroom, master bath and kitchen," he finally declared. "Those will have to come first."

"Kitty door."

He nodded and added that note. "Right. Plumbing, electrical, tiling, cabinets... Should we fix up a room so we can say that Jae's staying there?"

He indicated one of the bedrooms on the east side of the house, opposite the master bedroom.

"Opposite?" Lina asked. "Isn't that a little obvious?"

"*Peut-être,*" Lon said and chose a middle section. "Here. Here's Jae's official room."

"It's going to be for us, too."

"What's that mean?"

She rubbed his shoulders. "It means that three is fun for special times, but two is best, love. I can't imagine trying to get some sleep in the same room where you two are going at it. And besides, I wouldn't want to intrude."

"Hmm." Lon twiddled the stylus between his fingers. "You're right. We'll need more closet space over there as well to accommodate all of us, not just whoever has the rest shift."

"Rest shift?"

"You know what I mean. Hm. I don't like the idea of using twice the space to handle one problem."

"Lon, you know it's not always going to be hot & heavy honeymoon every night. A person's got to get some sleep on a regular basis."

"Bite your tongue."

Lina laughed and studied the plans. "Um, Londo, while you're at it…" She hesitated.

He turned to regard her. "What is it? Anything your heart desires, my love." He took her hand to encourage her to speak.

"Well, I've listened for years to the married women in the office, and they've all told me– now, we're talking each and every one, Londo– that separate bathrooms ensure a happy marriage. One bathroom and you have marital disputes. Two bathrooms… or in this case, maybe, three… and you have domestic bliss until the end of time."

Londo frowned. He'd heard Maria say the same thing, and some others as well. All women. What did bathrooms have to do with anything?

"Look here," Lina pointed. "You could have just one shower and that gigantic tub. No need to triplicate that. Bust through into the bedroom back here– that bedroom's big enough for the entire royal family, Lon, and you know it– and you've still got a central plumbing area without having to do any more excavating on this poor mountain."

He began doodling with the stylus, adjusting walls here and checking structural integrity there. He made a couple of nooks for linens and one corner labeled "milady's makeup table." Staring at it for three long, silent minutes, he turned the whole group on an axis. As he adjusted more walls, Lina could suddenly see the sense of it.

A circular pattern of half-baths opened up onto the shower and tub area. Arcing around those were a complex of three room-sized closets, then a room along the outer wall relabeled "auxiliary master bedroom." Its wall was punctuated with doors that connected to all closets in the master bedroom. Both bedrooms had direct access to the central bath, and were separated not only by the bathroom system but by all the closets, providing respectable positioning. Well, relatively so.

"Look at that. Lon, you're a genius! A regular Frank Lloyd Wright." Lina hugged him from behind and he smiled, knowing that he'd come up with a clever solution to the problem.

"We'll have to hit a plumbing supply store. We want Sarastoran plumbing, right?"

"Oh, Lon, can we?"

"And someplace where I can get some Terran tiles…"

"Oh– What about your building in Montreal?"

Londo pulled his hair with two fists. "I almost forgot!" Grabbing the cordless landline next to his computer, he hit a button that responded with a string of beeps. "Kurt?" he said into it. "Kurt, ah god it's the middle of the night there. I forgot; sorry. Of course it's me. Go back to sleep. But when you get up in the morning, start hiring a maximum crew. There's an apartment building in Montreal– oh you did? That's the job. I told them we'd have it done in three months, tops. Yeah." He turned to Lina. "This is Kurt Campbell. You remember; I told you about him."

Kurt Campbell? The only Kurt he'd ever talked about was– "The guy who was kidnapped along with you when you were a kid?"

"*Oui.* He runs my construction crews now." Lon turned back to the phone. "And after this job, Kurt, I need you to line up your best carpenters, I mean top of the line. We're starting the work on Starhaven. I want it done *tout de suite.*

That's where we're living now." He paused. "*Mais oui,* I said 'we.' Good night, Kurt. Give me a call when you're ready for transport." He switched off, chuckling madly. "That'll get him." The phone rang almost immediately. "Let's go," Lon instructed Lina and let the phone ring.

A twenty-minute visit to Sarastor garnered them all the plumbing materials they needed. It took almost as long for Lina to port everything to Starhaven. Lon checked his materials list, and then they were off for Terran shopping, this time alternating between a large home center and various specialty businesses that kept their stock on hand.

So this was marriage. Londo approved of the way his bride agreed with his basic decorating scheme for the bedrooms and baths. She added a few ideas, but she made her choices quickly and decisively. He'd been around women who would take three hours to settle on a specific shade of wall paint and then be dissatisfied at the results. Lina could see the finished vision of the house in his mind. He took her advice and went for lighter shades than he'd ordinarily have bought. Come to think of it, his colors usually turned out darker than he wanted.

But when he showed her the granite that would cover most of the surfaces of the bathrooms, she told him, "We need something wacky."

"Say again?"

The Arizona stone yard held a beautiful selection of marbles and granites, but the material he'd taken there a few months ago from the Starhaven site was the best-looking in the place, they both agreed. Their rock had been stored in a protected corner of the business. After Lon had given his cutting orders, Lina led him into the tile warehouse adjacent to the place.

"Something goofy," she repeated. "To break up all those squares and rectangles with organic shapes. It doesn't have to be front and center."

He frowned at her interference with his plans. If she'd just let him continue, she'd see that–

"Like this," she said, and held up a narrow edging tile. It portrayed a lineup of gargoyle heads done in a terra cotta orange, with tongues sticking out and crossed eyes. "Wrong color," she quickly told him, "but right idea. Just a bit here and there, to prove we're not machines."

The different planes of granite would butt up against each other in places. Perhaps they did need some boundary trim. Maybe his decorating ideas were more than a bit geometrical. Lon sorted through the available tiles.

He held one up.

"No," Lina said.

"But it's cats," he said. Three painted cats prowled per tile, with three variations providing nine cats in all. "Look, this one looks like Fat Cat," he pointed out.

"I don't like cutesy cat doodads."

But he convinced her that they'd hardly notice the tiles, and ordered some plainer but interesting trim as well to use for the majority of the job. Then he snuck a few of the dog version into his order.

"Yessir, Valiant, we'll have this ready for you asap," the head clerk assured him. In the back behind the shop, the sound of giant diamond-edged saws whined as they warmed up to cut slices of granite.

Lon didn't ask prices, and Lina was afraid to. She firmly told herself that these things were basic and had to be done. First things first: minimal quarters. If they waited, the cost would just go up.

And she didn't want Jae to be put off by having the house completely unfinished. He might decide he didn't want to live on barbaric Earth after all, and that possibility could *not* be an option!

Back at a home center, they passed a pet door display. Lina stopped. "Nothing in impervion," she noted.

Londo frowned at the flimsy plastic doors and then checked the area around themselves for nosy customers. He shoved their two big carts to one side, crammed the computer print-out of pick-up items in his jeans pocket, and said, "Let me take a look at that setup of yours again."

"Dragonlord is there."

"So we'll have a party," Lon told her. "Oneferall."

She ported them front and center into her living room so no one could say they snuck in. Daylight streamed through the tall, south-facing windows. The place was cheerily warm.

Dragonlord, in civilian clothes, jumped at least a foot into the air. Londo slapped his own stomach as he laughed. "I love doing that," he said. "Surprising Damon. It doesn't happen that often."

"You could give some warning," Damon growled.

"Sorry," Lina said. So Dragonlord had brown hair with a receding hairline. He eyed her warily, as if he didn't like to show his true face to people. She shrugged. "I'll work up some kind of fanfare or something. Give me a little time." She raised her voice. "And keep your fingers off the paintings! Body acids corrode paint. You break it, you bought it."

Londo glanced upstairs. "*Salut, Georges!*" he called.

"I know nussing, I see nussing," Lina said quietly, her hands in the air.

"We're just here to check out cat doors," Lon told Damon. "We're making a few adjustments on the house."

"You don't mind if I continue here?"

Lina looked heavenward and sighed.

"Keep on doing what you were doing," Londo said. "Cat doors."

"Out here," Lina said, and took him through the kitchen into the utility room.

"Christ, how many doors do you have?" He could see them all.

"I started out with the one on the outer wall," she told him. "But it's right next to the water heater and even with an insulating blanket, winter was just too much. So I boxed in the first one with insulation and put in another."

"An air lock."

"Exactly. And then I added the lean-to shed against the outer wall, so they had to be able to get out of that."

"I like the kitty stairs out there. But then, I like the kitty balcony in here, too."

"I notice you've already got cat balconies at Starhaven. They're going to love all the 2x4s. Scratching post heaven."

"Hm. I didn't think cat doors needed to be this size."

"Before the herd got so large, I was thinking of getting a dog."

Londo took off the plaid flannel shirt he'd thrown over his dark tee and got down on the floor to try to wriggle through the door. Was it big enough that a person could shimmy through? He could squeeze through down to his shoulders, but that was all.

"You're too big," Lina observed.

The air lock echoed his words loudly. "I haven't heard any complaints from you about that. At least, after the first time."

She was positive she heard a laugh from the living room.

She pressed her eyes shut to hide from the embarrassment. "Let's put it this way, love," she said, "I once caught a kid halfway through the air lock, trying to break in. If he'd had a lick of sense in him, he could have gotten through."

"Hey, get out!" came a shout from within the airlock. "I'm in here!"

Lina heard a cat growl and spit.

"Molly!" Lina cried. "Get out! Go outside!" She ported into the shed, its sudden darkness disconcerting. From this side the kitty door was waist high. Narrow cat steps led down to ground level. The translucent door gave her a view inside the airlock of the rear end of a ball of orange fur fluffed out as far as cat nerves could fluff it. A bushy tail stuck straight up as Molly stood her ground within her own domain.

Lina reached in and grabbed. Molly came out scrabbling and hissing. Lina secured her by the scruff of the neck as well as under her. The top of Lon's head frowned at her from within the airlock.

"Better, darling?" she smiled at him hopefully.

He glared at her. "I didn't want to kill her…"

Lina ported back into the utility room. "And she appreciates that. Really she does. Don't you, Molly-wolly?" She lifted the cat up to eye level to give her a little shake before setting her down on the floor. Spitting and growling furiously, Molly immediately jumped onto the top of the airlock where she could view the male body inserted into her door.

Londo pulled himself out, warily watching the cat above him. He hissed at her. She ran off into the recesses of the living room and then upstairs, judging from the sound of scrambling cat feet.

"Seven of them," he said as he dusted himself off.

"Seven," Lina confirmed. "Don't worry; you won't be invading their private sanctums all that often, will you?"

"Seven." He looked up to Lina's anxious face and had to smile. She did so want him to like the cats! "We'll have an airlock, too, but I see a security problem. A big one."

"How about if it had kitty-sized bends? Like a tunnel?"

"Do you think you can port a path out of solid rock?"

"No idea. I can try. Maybe if you did the looking– you can see through rock, right?– and I tied into you, I could port it."

"If you can't, I can rent a drill. But I still don't trust it. People could shove things inside. Use robots. And hell, I know people who could shrink and get in. You sure they need to go out?"

One look at her face and he rolled his eyes. He pulled himself up and went into the dining room to sit down in the sunlight. Reaching down, he scooped up Fat Cat and dumped her on the table. "Which one are you? Katie, right?"

The tortie meowed silently at him and tried to get down.

"Stay, Katie." He blocked her escape route.

Lina placed some kitty treats on the table. Katie regarded Londo warily. "He's okay, Katie darling," Lina told her, and Katie decided to eat the treats one at a time as Lina rubbed her chin.

"I've got it," Londo finally said. He made his hands a loose collar on Katie to demonstrate. "A collar with an electronic key–"

"Already been invented," Lina said. "They've got kitty doors like that. Just one problem." She opened a drawer in the kitchen and drew out a cat collar to show Lon.

"See? A proper cat collar has to have elastic or some kind of escape hatch on it, because a cat will get caught in it just as soon as you turn your back. As a result, you can't keep a collar on a cat– or at least, on any of mine– for more than twenty minutes. They're regular Houdinis."

Katie sat in the middle of the dining table and began her bath, starting at her shoulder.

"How would you like to get some kind of subdermal… transponder, or whatever the double-talk is, Katie darling?"

"Have the key implanted in them?" Londo looked hopeful.

"Poor babies. I wonder how much the operation will hurt?" Lina rubbed Katie worriedly. "Fafhrd can't take unnecessary anesthesia. She's too old."

"It's not an operation," Damon said, and they turned. "Your cats are already microchipped with ID, right?"

"Yes," Lina said.

Damon patted a pile of her files into order. "Just set up your kitty door so it only recognizes those microchips," he said.

"You can do that?" Lina asked her husband.

"I can. Problem solved, then," Lon declared. "When Jae comes in, we'll rig an impervion barrier or maybe a force field– *oui*, that'll work better– for the tunnel, and Starhaven will be a fortress again. Let's go back. *Une minute.*"

He leaned over to take an approximate measure of Katie, comparing her shoulder height to his forearm so he could choose the proper size cat door.

"Ah, Lon…"

He smiled at her. "What is it, *chérie?*"

"I forgot about all my messages. I need to get them cleared up." She pointed to her answering machine, which was blinking angrily. Lina didn't own a cell because out here she got no bars. "You're almost ready to go through the check-out lines."

"Which will take at least an hour."

"Not like Sarastor at all. I could handle all these by the time you were ready."

"Efficient. Very efficient," he approved. He stood and gave her a goodbye kiss. "Okay, beam me back, Scotty, or whatever it is. I'll give you a call when I'm ready."

"Take care, honey. Leave something for other people to buy."

He disappeared and she turned to Damon. "Is that okay? I mean, it is my house, if we want to get technical."

He shrugged. "Use this phone."

"That's where all my files– but you knew that. You've probably been through them all. Confidentiality out the window."

"The information won't travel any further," he assured her.

Lina jotted notes on a legal pad as she ran through the messages. She called the voicemail of eleven people and told them the same thing: she was moving quite unexpectedly, so very sorry, but she could recommend a couple of other psychics for them to use. Four got messages concerning civic affairs, a county planning committee that Lina had been on and now resigned from. Five others got a more personal message; she gave them her new phone number with a caution to use it for absolute emergencies only.

Damon listened in as she got hold of the next people, clients who needed to talk to her. One had to be told not to begin divorce proceedings until she saw a counselor, and Lina threatened to sign her up for that herself if she didn't do it. She made notes to follow up.

The phone rang. She glanced at Damon and he nodded. "On speaker," he said.

"Did you realize this is America?" she asked him as she punched the speaker button. He gave her a bored look. "American Civil Liberties Union," she answered the phone. "Carolina region here."

"Hey, Lina! You're back."

"Mace! How are you? What's the latest joke down there?"

The pleasant male voice laughed. "It's the craziest of 'em all. Seems there's this girl, you know? And she's running around with Valiant."

"Oh no. Who's telling these things?"

"Saw it on afternoon TV, girlfriend. On one of those cheesy Parahero Entertainment things."

"No."

"What's he like? Is he as cute in person as he is on the tube?"

"And then some. You may want to know that this conversation is being monitored."

"Oh, good! All right, how are a twelve-year-old girl in Alabama and the Heathrow Multi-Bomber alike?"

"God. Let me think…"

"Oh, it's obvious. They were both fingered by their brother!"

"Sick. That's sick." She noticed that whoever it was upstairs was chuckling. "That's sex humor about minors; you know I don't approve."

"Such a church lady."

"So how's the T-cells?"

"Unfortunately, they're getting better all the time. I may have to go back to work; I'm going to lose my disability when they reach 5000."

"And that's bad news? Mace, that's great! Told you, told you. Nyah."

"Nyah. As soon as I start work, the stress is going to send me straight back down."

Lina thought. "How much time do you think before disability ends?"

"Doc says about three months."

"Oh, that's great. We can't have you working at Sonny's again; you'll ruin their reputation."

"It can get worse? Lina girl, I'm never working as a waiter again!"

"They'll just have to learn to sell fried chicken some other way."

"Am I never going to live that down?"

"No. Never. I am going to keep that story alive as long as I live. It's just too perverted not to tell the world. Look, Valiant and I have a business deal that's starting up."

"Hm. Monkey business? You certainly looked ready for it in that dress, hon. How many hankies did you have stuffed in your bra?"

"Oh hush."

"And how many socks did he have stuffed–"

"I said, hush! There are normal people– well, semi-normal people listening. Look, Mace, we're going to be getting involved with the gay pride movement."

"Gay… You said Valiant is going to– But he's not…"

"He's extremely sympathetic to the cause," Lina said. "He believes in equal rights for all people and discrimination toward none."

"Should I salute as we talk?"

"And hum 'America the Beautiful,'" Lina instructed. "Would you believe there are entire worlds Out There, supposedly so much more advanced than Earth, that pretend that nothing's going on? People Out There are where gays were fifty years ago, with no movement in sight."

"You're kidding."

"No, I am not. Anyway, we want to start a Pride movement on a couple of worlds, and we need someone here who can start us off and get us in touch with the right people. You know everyone who's anyone, Mace."

"I do at that, I suppose. At least in North America and Europe. There's this guy I know who knows everyone in Australia, simply everyone! And I've been working on Asia…"

"Uh huh. You're the one who hands out the toaster ovens, right? So how's about, when you're ready, you start to work for us? You can name your own hours so you don't tire yourself out. You can hire an assistant to do the hard work. All you'll have to do is call up people all over and tell them dirty jokes."

"Lina, you're serious."

"I'm serious."

"You may be, but Valiant doesn't know me from Adam."

"We've been talking about you. Haven't you felt your ears burning?"

"Carolina Angelina O'Kelly, if this is a joke, tell me now. I'm actually starting to believe you."

"Serious as a church sermon, Mason Odell Lafayette. We want you to help us start Gay Pride movements Out There. Only one planet to start off with; we'll see how it goes."

"What– How– I don't even know where to begin. First, you'd have to create safe zones, I guess. Places where gays could go and know they were in the company of people like themselves and not have anyone haul them off to jail. Or worse."

"So you do know where to begin. You've got a little while to think about it, less if you want to go ahead and get started. I'm so glad you called. You were on our list. Talk to your contacts and get their ideas."

"Does this mean you've left Midnight Delivery?"

Lina twirled a lock of her hair and gave the phone a conspiratorial look. "Mace, they came up with this one product that they insisted had to go into the catalog. I mean, it was just disgusting and degrading. Even you would have been appalled. I *had* to quit."

"Tell me, tell me! I'm on pins and needles! What was it? Animal, leather or underage?"

"You know how people have all those lines of specialized athletic shoes. Pump ups and light ups…"

"Don't I know. I just priced some the other day."

"These were really expensive. I just said, tennis shoes in our catalog? And they said, spotlight them, above the fold on the homepage and top outside page three of the catalog. They were a ghastly pepto pink, not white, targeted specifically for lesbians. Velcro closures, very tacky."

"For lesbians?" He sounded confused.

"Uh huh. They had tongues twelve inches long, and you could get them off with one finger."

"Oh no! Oh no! I walked right into that one."

"Yes you did. Serves you right for that brother joke."

"Tastes like chicken, Lina. Let me think about this job thing."

"Tastes like fried chicken at Sonny's, Mr. Mazola. We'll be in touch."

She had to giggle quietly to herself. She'd gotten it out without messing it up, and he hadn't heard the joke before. That didn't happen too often. She glanced up at Damon, who had a disapproving look on his face. He'd taken out a tablet and was writing on it.

"Lesbian tennis shoes," he repeated gravely, shaking his head. "All right, for the record, what's the Sonny's fried chicken story?"

"About five minutes long. Longer, if it's told well." She grinned at him. "Lon's in line and I still have two more calls to make."

Lina had to think a few minutes before making the next call, writing things down as she got serious again. She reached for a huge unabridged dictionary, shooing one of the cats off it, and paged through a section, stopping to look up a word and write it down. A medical dictionary provided confirmation.

"This is private," she told Damon in a no-nonsense tone. Only then did she call the client to counsel them to get checked out at Duke Hospital. She said she thought they might have an eye condition called– she spelled it for them, referring to her notes– and told them to have a physician diagnose since she wasn't in the medical business and didn't have a license to practice medicine. She assured them that yes, they needed an operation and they would be relieved with its results.

"One more, honey; how're you doing?" she said to the air. She nodded at the silent reply and went to the last of the messages that the machine had recorded. It had reached its limit and stopped. The final message was dated one day ago.

"Hi, Sarah," she said into the phone. Skinny, black Fafhrd butted at her arm, and she picked her up to pet her as she talked. "I just wanted to tell you in case you hadn't heard– ah, you had. They are?" Lina sighed. "Could you spread the word that it would be very nice if people could wait a couple of weeks? Yeah, everyone can go on *TMZ* and spill their guts about me after we announce, not before. You have my blessing. But tell everyone to give us two weeks, please."

She paused, listening. "No, this was the last time, I think." She rifled through a small cabinet, pulling out a file. "Yes. Last time for house cleaning. We're all even now. Good timing, too. No, Lon got to see before and after. But guess who was here right after you cleaned? Guess. Guess. Maximus!" She gave a little shriek, and the answering shriek from the phone echoed in the room.

"Thank you, thank you, thank you for doing it. I would have been so embarrassed if it hadn't been clean. Oh, Lon– he already knows I'm a slob. And I think he might be a bigger slob, so it all works out." Pause. "He seems very nice, real down to earth. No, really." Pause. "Oh, he's… he's everything you've heard and then some, but at the same time he's nothing at all like you'd expect. Absolutely nothing at all. I could go on and on, but Lon's in a line at a hardware store right now and I've got to go pick him up in a few minutes. We're putting in some bathrooms. Right! His and hers.

"Of course I've been listening to you and Betsey and Claudia and all of the Married Women Club. Learning at the feet of the masters. I explained to Londo that this was the one and only true secret behind a successful marriage. Oh– there's his call. Gotta go. I told Sharon I'd get back there in a few days; I'll update you then. Bye, Sarah. Get back to work."

Lina disconnected the answering machine, plugging the phone directly into the wall outlet. She made sure that Fafhrd was sleeping soundly and then turned to Damon. "Have fun. We're off." She popped out.

A head appeared over the balcony upstairs, peering down at Damon. "So that's how a mind controller acts?" the man asked. "Funny; I don't feel any different."

Damon grunted and looked around. "I don't think we're going to find anything here," he said, "but let's finish up, Georges. No reason not to be thorough."

"I want to be particularly thorough when we go through her workplace." Georges chuckled, and Damon laughed, too, as he returned to work, setting a cat out of his way.

"It's a nasty job, but someone's got to do it."

The not-so-small mountain of building materials in the outside loading area was tightly packed but still took up twelve pallets. Lon looked up as Lina stepped from behind a column.

"Wow," she said, eying the load and estimating how much she could handle in each port. "I dunno. Maybe four trips?"

"You can pick up just the granite and then you're finished porting. You've done enough today. How many miles have you put in?"

"I don't port by distance, love."

He gave her one of those crooked smiles. "I can get this. Maybe you could help me pack it up?"

Two employees wandered up and studied the pile. "Hope you rented a delivery truck," one told Lon. "You're not going to fit this in a pickup."

"One way or another, we'll get it," Lon assured him. "Ah, here we are now."

Steel girders fizzed into view in the loading area, along with a collection of chains and wire. The employees stepped back hastily, but Lina had seen Londo do this already today.

Lon picked up the longest girder and slipped it through the bottom of the pallets. He threaded the others in the same direction as if he were putting in a quick hem with the pallets being the cloth. A push of a button on an end girder set off a series of clacks. The pile shuddered.

"They're connected now," Lon explained to the workers.

Three more employees joined the observers. They stared as Lon directed Lina to wrap the pile in flexible netting while he tightened chains around it. Finally, he chose four long chains and made cross-handles out of them, testing to see that the load carried evenly. The entire process had taken perhaps fifteen minutes, with five of those taken by Lina's unfamiliarity with the netting.

"Looks good," Lina said. "Guides are giving their thumbs-up."

"Thank you, guides." Londo flipped a half-salute over Lina's head as he stood on top of the cargo. "You get the granite– do it a little at a time– and then take the short way home, *chérie.* Put it in the auxiliary bedroom. I'll be there by the time you arrive."

Lina stuck around to enjoy the magnificent sight of her husband hoisting the truckload of building materials into the sky. He shot off to the northwest like a meteor. This way she also got to see the employees stagger back dumbfounded, the crowds of customers in the parking lot looking up and pointing at her wonderful husband.

Lon deserved to draw a crowd.

It took much longer to unload everything. Londo worked faster without her assisting him on the construction, so as the work progressed she concentrated on putting the kitchen and pantry to order. Every now and then Lon would call her in. She had to step carefully around equipment and wallboard to hold a chalk line for him, or to support some lumber or such while he worked on the other end.

She hummed in the kitchen as she worked. After she'd ported in her own small dining table to become the breakfast table here, she broke into song. Here was a home to last forever. She was moving in. Londo was building real bathrooms. Soon the cats would arrive and after them, Jae. Life was so good to her. *Thank you, universe!*

She made Londo some sandwiches and brought along two cans of Coke when she ported upstairs. He was singing the same song she'd been singing a couple of minutes ago.

"About ready for a break? I'm hungry," she said innocently as she held the tray in the doorway. He looked up and dropped his wrench.

All she wore was her bibbed apron.

Without bothering to pick up his equipment, he said, "I think I'll have dessert first," and jumped over his saw table.

It was his stomach that betrayed them later so they stopped to eat that late lunch. Then Lon noticed how far down the sun had gotten. "You're throwing me off my schedule," he complained with a stony but thoroughly fake pout. "At this rate I'll never get the tile laid by tonight."

She ran her hands around the base of his neck, then up into his lovely hair. "Do we really need a schedule for today? The tile isn't the only thing that likes to get laid."

"My schedule called for the cats to move in tomorrow."

She jumped up at that and ported on more than enough clothes, maybe even too many. "Then get back to work," she snapped. She ported off with his merry laughs ringing behind her.

Londo turned up some heavy metal on a boom box and sang along with it, pausing on occasion to play air guitar with his tape measure for her benefit when she was there assisting him. But he only needed her for a few minutes each time; he was very, very fast and worked with pneumatic equipment and compressors. "They can set the nails more precisely than I can," he yelled in explanation. With the nerve-jangling noise levels, Lina was happy enough to remain two stories down, accompanied by a soft rock Wyoming radio station that she listened to via Internet. Might as well get used to her new neighborhood.

By the time Lon had moved into the third half-bath to rough it in, she had organized what there was to the kitchen and was beginning on the grand living room, preparing supper as she went. She didn't trust the electric stove he had here. Was it the partial electricity or the stove itself that caused its deva to sit on top of it, arms crossed and scowling at her? Instead she ported back and forth to her house to use her reliable gas stove. Damon and the other guy were gone now. She could keep an eye on things clairvoyantly as she worked thousands of miles away in Starhaven.

"Lina!" Lon called from upstairs. Before she could react he yelled, "Don't port directly!"

So she ported into the bedroom and peeked into the bathrooms.

Londo held a cell phone to his ear and waved her to stay back. "No, Hal, I really have to go. We're laying the granite now. No, we don't need any help. You'd be embarrassed; Lina's standing here stark raving."

"I am not!" Lina cried.

"That way if she gets some thinset on her she can just shower it off." Londo paused, listening. "Sure, dinner would be fine, but not today. Not tomorrow either. We've got to get things started here. I'll give you a call when we get to a breathing point. *À bientôt.*" He slipped the phone onto his belt and turned to her.

"Here," Lon said and unscrewed his Legion ring from his hand. He tossed it to her. She barely caught it. "Don't tell anyone."

She put it on her third finger, same as he wore it, but it was too big. It fit uncomfortably on her thumb. This was the main control for the famous Legion Array.

"Like this," he said, and crinkled his finger slightly. Lina crinkled her thumb. "You should have the wrist and ankle bands, too, but I don't need them so I don't have any to loan you. Let's see if you can work this without them."

A network of linear distortions appeared in the air around her, so fine-lined she wouldn't have noticed them if she hadn't seen them in action before. They outlined a grid focused on twelve equidistant spots about a foot and a half out from her body.

Gravity felt funny. She seemed to be sloshing around ever so slowly where she stood.

"Just think about floating," Lon told her, leaning against the wall with his arms crossed in front of himself as he watched her. He hovered an inch or two above freshly-laid tile, the floor she would have landed on if she'd ported. "Think fairy dust and happy thoughts. Relax."

"Whoa!" Lina shot up to the ceiling, braking herself barely in time.

"Gently, dear," Londo chuckled. "Not so hard. Just a tickle in your mind about floating."

She fell, but he darted out of the bathroom and caught her in his arms.

"Don't worry," Lina told him breathlessly. "I'm still covered for insurance."

"Good. Feel where you are altitude-wise right now," he told her.

She smiled at him. "I like where I am. Altitude-wise."

"*Non non non,* no arms around me." She retracted her arms and he held her if she were just learning to float in a swimming pool. "You're in mid-air. I'll try to hold you as little as I can."

"But it's some kind of mind thing?"

"The mind thing comes from your unconscious eye movements. Think about flying, and the array reads the eye movement to shift into first gear from neutral, as it were."

"Oh."

"After that it comes down to balance. Shift your body and the ring accentuates the movement." He eased away from her. She could feel him holding her with just a few fingertips. When she tensed she began to tip–

"Easy," he said. "The array requires a soft touch. Balance yourself on my fingertips."

She swayed and balanced, swayed some more. "That's good," he murmured. "Keep yourself balanced. Just concentrate on holding steady, floating…"

She began to relax and then saw that he was holding both hands up to either side of himself. She was floating without him supporting her.

She hit the ground before he could catch her.

He shook his head at her as he helped her up. "You were doing it. Do it again."

Eventually she could hover and then swim through the air. It was enough for her to take granite tiles that he had cut and snug them into mortar along the wall and cabinets, along the floor, wherever the odd cuts were, without jarring those tiles already placed. Toward the end she hung upside down like Lon in a corner, giving the tile a little twist as she pushed into the thinset. Lon floated next to her with a soft mallet, tapping the tiles further into the mortar.

She did a slow, careful somersault to bring herself upright and then put her hand to her chest. "I'm going to take a Tums," she announced sourly. "All that stomach acid's coming up."

"So next time work levelly instead of upside-down," Lon told her as he tapped the final ones in. "Just because I work on my head doesn't mean you do, too. I can reach over you if I have to."

Lon had figured out patterns as he went, playing with the stone's natural markings. Cats and dogs subtly marched along the wall's intersections.

"Oh *maudite marde*," Lon said when they had finished. "I should have put in the melvins first. Now I'm going to have to watch myself while I'm hooking them up."

"Yes, you watch yourself because I won't be able to watch you." Lina gave him a peck on the cheek as she swam past. "I've got things to do downstairs."

She returned twice to help him hold large mirrors in place while he fastened them in. It was murderously hot in here now.

"I'm speeding up the drying," he admitted. "The tiles hold the heat in."

"In the meantime, we have a nice sauna here."

"I hadn't thought of that. Would you like a sauna?"

She wanted to hug him. He was so considerate. "No, no sauna here. Isn't there going to be one downstairs?"

"But that's in the gym."

"Oh gee, someone has to walk all the way downstairs to use the sauna."

He gave her a small smile as he set the final screw. *D'accord, d'accord. Maybe I was getting carried away.*

"I never lost anything in a sauna. It's hot and humid. I lived in North Carolina– same thing. Saunas are overrated by people who live up north."

"Jae will want one."

She thought about that as she floated. "So we'll call the one downstairs 'Jae's sauna.' I'll make a little sign. He'll love what you've done here, Lon. I love it. It's as beautiful and elegant as bathrooms get."

"It has turned out rather nice. Ring back." He began to pry it off her thumb.

"Must you? It's fun."

"Um hum. Just wearing it could land you sixty years in jail." His arm around her kept her suspended as he put the ring back on his own hand. "Things are far enough along here that I can grout now. See? Ahead of schedule even with you prancing around in your birthday suit. It'll take me maybe twenty minutes to grout all three, fifteen to clean the grout lines, and five more to clean in general. How's supper coming? I could swear I smell homemade cake. I liked the dessert we had for lunch."

She finished in the kitchen as he finished there. Her dishtowels were sopping by the time she finished drying the final round of mixing bowls. She'd used far too many dishes. She was showing off and not used to cooking for more than herself.

As she ported back with the broccoli casserole fresh out of the oven Lon was there, reaching around her, grabbing the dish without mitts. He set the pan down on the cooling rack next to the stuffed squash and then took Lina's hand. "C'mon," he told her. "See the finished product."

He held his hands over her eyes for the great unveiling even as they both floated over the drying tiles. The rooms really were splendid, complete with central shower and a lovely whirlpool spa that overlooked the valley. The talents of her husband amazed Lina.

Three bathrooms.

"He's just got to," Lon finally said, squeezing her.

Lina lay her head on his shoulder. "Heaven help us all."

It was all so wonderful. They were setting up the stage for their marriage— and their Three Worlds mission. Lina blessed the day not so long ago when she'd finally decided to break out of her shell and investigate the world. There'd been moments of terror— including some that few people had ever had to endure— but now there was this.

The mission ahead would be difficult, but they'd all decided that she'd best serve as a coordinator. She'd have a safe office and a staff. It was Jae and Lon who'd be out doing the tough work.

Lina didn't want to think about that. The horrors of the past two weeks were behind her now. They'd never hear from Terry the Bitch again. From now on there'd be clear sailing and blue skies.

Lon. Jae. Cats. Home. Happiness.

Neither the dining room nor the living room was wired for lights yet except along the circuit powering the TV. Lina ported in candles from her house. Londo set them on his long dining table, adding the roses as a centerpiece.

"Our first real dinner in our own home," Lon said contentedly as they sat down to eat. "I thought brides weren't supposed to know how to cook."

"You married someone who knows. Lon, I make a pot roast in beer with carrots and potatoes that people cry over, it's so good," she told him. "Spaghetti with meat sauce better than my mom's, and hers is great. Chili con carne and beef enchiladas New Mexico style, with a fried egg on top of a stack. Chicken a million ways, and all of them terrific, if I say so myself. Just one tiny problem…"

Lon paused in digging in, despite his hunger. "What's that?"

"Can't stand dead animal vibes now. I can't make any of that anymore." She laughed at his expression. "I can give you the recipes, but if you want to eat meat, you'll have to buy it and cook it yourself. Of course, you won't have to worry about that for much longer."

"I am not going vegetarian," he stated defiantly around a mouthful of squash and beans. "I'll eat it, though, especially if it tastes like this."

He made good on his promise, eating a lot more than Lina had estimated. But then he was Valiant, her growing boy. She'd just have to make portions large for him. Jae ate good-sized meals, too. She filed it in her head for future reference.

Later she sat in Lon's lap and fed him coconut cake by hand. "Tastes much better than off the tree," he told her, smacking his lips. They'd had problems with the coconuts on Tiawa. As they fed each other they reminisced about tropical evenings and passionate days, and how the future would be even better.

It was late. The large windows let in the faint light of a snowy night as Lon moved the candles and roses to the living room. He set them on the table next to the couch in front of the fireplace, and turned to the dark hearth. It lit at his sharp breath and caught, building into a sultry line of flames that occasionally popped with sparks.

Lina emerged from the kitchen, the dishes and food put away, to find that he'd brought down the quilt and some pillows from upstairs.

"Tink said everything was too hot up there," he told her. "We'll be more comfortable here tonight." He made them a nest on the floor and poured two glasses of wine.

Lina sniffed. "This isn't wine."

"You don't like it, so I got sparkling grape juice." He showed her the label. "To my beautiful bride." Londo clinked his glass against hers. They twined their arms together and tried to sip through their giggles.

"This is better than I ever imagined," Lon murmured in her ear as they lay together afterward. "The snow falling outside, wind roaring through the valley, and in here warm next to the fire, you in my arms…"

He kissed her again and listened to her soft sigh. She kissed his jaw and played with his hair. They slept until dawn there in each other's arms. In their dreams they both thanked the universe in their own ways.

15

"Uh oh." Lon wasn't surprised that he woke up before it happened; he often did that. An insistent buzz filled the air and Lon waved; the large TV screen clicked on. The two of them pulled themselves up to the couch to watch the report.

Personalized text scrolled across the bottom the screen that identified itself as ECN, the Emergency Call Network. It was Iowa: a head-on collision between a passenger train and one carrying hazardous chemicals.

"Puter, signal Network OOD to stand by," Lon ordered into the air. He received the two standard Sarastoran beeps of acknowledgement, though this time from across the cave's expanse at his computers. He streaked upstairs to the bedroom to get dressed. After a moment's consideration, Lina ported to her home bathroom, washed her face and gave her hair a quick brush as she ported on heavy jeans, tee shirt, sweater, heater coat and her new boots. She remembered sunscreen for her face.

She met Londo in his smart black Valiant uniform back in the living room as he sat at the computer desk. He gave her an up-and-down perusal.

"I can help," she said, and he nodded.

He'd Skyped into the ParaNet satellite. "I'm on the Iowa train," he reported to whoever was in their monitor room. Black Magnum, Lina noted as she came around to where she could see the screen.

"Right," Magnum said. "Gary's calling it, too." He looked up to see Lina in the screen and cocked his head at Lon.

"Lina's coming along," Lon said. "Kun-woo, Lina. Lina, Kun-woo."

"All right," Kun-woo said doubtfully. "Stand by for transport."

It felt fuzzy and more than a bit bumpy to Lina, not like her porting at all. The room started to act as if it were television reception that was breaking up, and then things went flat blue. The picture built up again rapidly to full-color and sharply cold focus, and they stood in the middle of the plains of Iowa.

Snow-blotted fields stretched to the far horizon with just the raised railroad track and a few straight lines of trees and telephone poles beyond to break the monotony. The sun was slightly up in the morning sky. The wind was calm: a peaceful if frozen day.

But in the midst sprawled two trains. The back cars of the lengthy freight train were still on the track, but all others weren't. They made a black and gray zigzag pattern on the white landscape, as did the ten or so cars from the passenger train. Some scattered sections lay as much as a hundred feet away from the tracks. The engines on both trains were completely crushed, hammered into crumpled masses of steel, and too many other cars showed the result of impact as well. Most lay on their sides. Shattered windows were the norm, and sprayed glass sparkled everywhere.

Like a cloud, fear hung in the air– panic and pain. Lists of contents marked the cylindrical chemical cars: sulfuric acid, liquid ammonia… A narrow fume of white smoke leaked from one of the middle cars.

Londo sprang into the air some fifty feet to survey the situation, then touched back down. "There'll be an ecological disaster unless I clear that away," he said. "You work with Gary and deal with the people. Look– there's the first ambulance." On the far side of the trees must be a road, because Lina could see the top of the vehicle and its flashing lights screaming toward them. "And here's my equipment." Piles of girders and chains had just materialized next to them.

Quickly he instructed Lina as to how she could best work. She listened closely.

"If you have to improvise, do it," he summed up. "Things change. Some of the situation may be different from how it first appears. Got it all?"

"Yes."

"Good. Now move." Londo grabbed an armful of girders without looking back, and snapped them into a grid.

Lina tore her attention away from him to the ambulance. **Don't be alarmed,** she silently shouted to the people inside the ambulance so they might hear. **Stop there.** It took two ports for her to see the right spot on the road to port to.

The ambulance swerved at her sudden appearance. Good thing they had been slowing down. Even so, it skidded to a halt. The driver threw open his door. Another man peered at her from the passenger seat.

"What the—"

"I'm Carolina Starhart," she said and then pointed behind herself. "Valiant's here already, and Bolt is on his…" A familiar sun bolt arced across the landscape from the east. "There he is now. I can teleport you to the train. I'm a clairvoyant and a teleporter. I can provide quick transport to hospitals. Okay?"

The two EMS workers opened their mouths a couple of times. Finally the passenger said, "Sure."

Lina said, "What do you need to take along with you?"

They scrambled to get their gurney and kits while Lina used her guides' help to scan the train. She couldn't help but notice that Londo was grappling with a chemical car to get it unhooked from its neighbor.

But the people were her priority. "The crew in the first locomotive on the chemical train are all dead," she reported to the EMS workers. "But there are survivors among the engine crew on Amtrak. *They* say they're the worst cases."

"Okay," the chief EMS said doubtfully. He looked like a farmer, spindly and tough.

The other was young, perhaps college age, with his long black hair drawn into a ponytail. "There'll be more ambulances," he said.

"Save them for the lesser injuries, please. I can give direct teleport to the nearest hospital. These first at least will need that." She waited while they reported the situation on their radio. "Ready?" Lina ported them to the Amtrak locomotive.

Bolt was there already, assessing the situation. They found him trying to worm his way into the collapsed husk that used to be a locomotive. He jumped when they appeared. "Whoa! Oh, it's you. Are you helping?"

"Yes. The people in the other locomotive are dead."

"Yeah, I know. We deal with the living first. There are crew in here."

"Two." She nodded her head, her eyes unfocused.

"Where's Lon? They're trapped. We need him to get them out."

"He said he had to attend to the chemicals." She turned to the EMS technicians. "I need one of you to picture in your mind an emergency room."

"Picture in our–?" the older man asked. He glanced for authority at the famous Bolt, who nodded to him.

Lina asked, "Where do you take them? I need a landing picture to teleport to."

"Leiner Memorial," the younger one declared. He squinted his eyes and his jaw jutted with concentration.

"Ah," Lina said. She built the picture up, felt it… There it was. People scrambling to get ready for the emergency. "Got it. I can get the ones here, Bolt. You won't have to dig them out."

"You've been porting how long?" Gary asked her doubtfully.

"Over two weeks now. I can do this."

He stayed there to make sure, though. Lina licked her lips. She had to be super careful with these injuries. "First one," she warned the technicians. They had their gurney set up and waiting, not sure what would happen.

That man, the man who was half-conscious even though he couldn't move, couldn't make a sound– feel him, all of him. He wasn't quite together; make sure she took everything… He appeared on the gurney. Within seconds his blood soaked it.

He lay there pulpy, purple and blue and black, runnels of blood and guts covering him like netting. Radiating such agony–! He sucked in a noisy breath and groaned before he passed out. The technicians exclaimed at his sudden appearance but gathered themselves and went through their life-saving routine. Check breathing, check heart, use pressure and compresses to slow the blood.

Lina stood pale and blinking, clutching at the collar of her coat as she stared at the victim.

"Get him to the hospital!" Bolt grabbed her shoulder.

She swallowed and took a breath. "I've got him," she said quickly. She ported the EMTs as well as the victim to the emergency room.

The younger tech looked up from his work and took stock of his new surroundings as if he traveled like this every day. "Get a doctor over here!" he shouted. "Get the primary team!" All through the hallway people looked up in shock at their sudden appearance, at the unexpected blood.

"Train wreck survivor!" the tech yelled as his partner concentrated on his work. "We're bringing 'em in the fast way! ParaNet's there!" People dressed in scrubs rushed up to them and the gurney rolled away into the curtained recesses of the emergency section, a circle of doctors and nurses around it.

The techs stayed behind with Lina. More doctors, or maybe nurses, gathered. The older tech pointed at Lina. "She teleports," he said. "She's with the Para-Net." The older tech grabbed another gurney.

Snap out of it, Lina! "Friend of the ParaNet," she corrected. "Not a member. I want to bring in more like this. How many can you handle?"

"Are they all like that?" One man asked. His nameplate said he was a doctor.

"He's the worst, I think. There's another one that's close. A lot who are real bad."

"How many in all?" "Was he really from the train wreck? We just heard about it." "How many are injured?"

One green-smocked woman examined Lina's pale face. "You okay?" she asked. "Sit down. Put your head between your knees."

"But I'm the one bringing them in." Lina brushed the hand from her arm. "I'll be back in a few minutes with the next one. Someone tell me when you get full here. No reason to stretch your resources thin; I can port people anywhere that can take them. We've got to go." She nodded to her aides and they braced.

Lina gritted her teeth at the bitter shock of Iowa winter as Bolt skidded up to them.

"You took long enough."

"Sorry. I'll get quicker."

He gave her a quick grin. "Don't put me out of business," he told her. "Now get back to work. Finish the engine, then take the cars one by one. I'll work on righting the cars so everyone can get off. If I see something that's priority, I'll either tell you or handle it myself. When you run out of steam, you tell me, okay? No heroics."

"Yessir." She turned back to the locomotive. The remaining crewman let out a cry and flung his arms outward as he appeared on the gurney.

The younger tech caught one of the man's bloody hands and eased it back to his chest. "Easy! Easy, man! We've got you! You're doing great," he reassured him. The lower leg hung by a thread of flesh. The other tech held on to the pressure point in the upper leg.

"Next one!" he called out to the hospital personnel as they arrived. They stayed only as long as it took to get a new gurney.

As they moved toward the first of the passenger cars, the young tech was the one who provided the mental image of the next hospital for Lina to use. His partner radioed the information ahead, then stopped to assess two passengers who had climbed out of windows.

Lina had to port into a half-open sideways doorway, then pick her way through the chaos. Passengers had been thrown about like chaff. She opened herself to her guides, who led her to the worst injuries first. Port outside with the next victim. Holding his hand, she trotted alongside his gurney halfway down a hospital hallway. He had a death grip on her and wouldn't let go.

His eyes tried to speak for him as his mouth couldn't.

Lina nodded. "If something does happen, I'll tell them," she reassured him. "Jolene and Rebecca and Tony. But you can tell them yourself. You're going to be fine." She hoped she wasn't lying.

She ported back down the hall to retrieve the two techs, who were surrounded by medical personnel.

"Look," the older one told her. "You don't need us. Can you take them directly from the train to here?"

"If I had someplace to put them," Lina said slowly.

"Here," the tech said. He patted a gurney. "They'll keep a fresh one right here for you. You put the worst ones here, people are waiting and they take 'em away.

Frankie and I can concentrate on some of the others at the accident, maybe help out the Bolt."

Lina nodded. "Let's try it," she said and then turned to a waiting nurse. "Someone should let me know when we reach your limit here." The nurse gave her a nod.

They were almost expecting her when she returned. She told them that she was going to be transporting someone with burns next.

"We'll call for air lift," the doctor who seemed to be in charge told her.

"There's no need," Lina told her. "Get me someone who can visualize the nearest burn center." She explained the process. "And call to tell them we're coming. After I get her taken care of, I'll send the next one here. Be standing by."

When she returned to the wreck, the techs were still struggling with the burn victim from the dining car, entangled in a heavy mass of fallen kitchen equipment. The Bolt had come forward to help. "Lina," he called. "I don't want to force her out with those burns."

Gingerly she felt the space in the universe within which the victim existed. "Got her," she said, and they both disappeared. Burn patients got private rooms, and her patient appeared directly onto the bed waiting for her, the one that the three people gathered by it were concentrating so hard on, trying to visualize it for Lina. She remained a moment but quickly ported out so as not to get in anyone's way.

Two more victims went to the previous hospital, then one more to the burn center.

Lina caught a glimpse of Bolt next to a downed car, alternating between turning into his namesake and transforming back to his normal body. *Whump. Whump. Whump.* Each brilliant *whump* must have had something to do with the pressure of light, because the cars raised a bit, then before they could fall again there'd be that blast of light, they'd raise some more, and he hit them again and again until the car rocked to vertical.

In the distance she heard the sound of metal screaming as it twisted. A few moments later, there was Londo, just a speck under a huge railroad car arcing across the sky.

She had her own cars to see to. These were still on their sides. She tried to clamber up to see inside a door to port in, but couldn't get a good grip and the window on the door wasn't placed right anyway. She couldn't see the outside top of the car, but she could port just above it. It was a few feet to drop, which she did with a thud, a sprawl and a curse– but there she was. Success. She peered into the windows.

People inside writhed on top of each other, trapped under luggage, skewed seating, and bodies. Only a few had managed to get to their feet, much less help others. Where to begin? There were badly injured people here. Which was which?

She ported off a window that felt like it was the emergency exit. "Rescue's here!" she called into the car. "Bolt and Valiant are working and ambulances are standing by. Stay calm and we'll get to you all!" She replaced the window to keep the heat inside.

Then she crawled down the line of windows until she could see her targets. One woman wasn't so bad off, but she was lying on top of another one who was, and if she ported the injured one, the woman would get hurt worse as she fell. So Lina ported them both to the hospital and they appeared piled together on the gurney. There, two nurses helped steady them as another gurney was swiftly brought in and Lina could port the grievously-injured woman to that.

The worst eighteen were taken care of as Lina switched to her fifth regional hospital. Even though the staff there had been contacted, they still jumped when Lina and her patient appeared. Their setup was always basically the same: a long hallway servicing individual areas. Sometimes those areas were curtained off, and sometimes were little rooms with windows that looked onto a central nurse station. A buzz of electronic machinery underscored the chatter of emergency personnel around each bed. Nurses and assistants scurried about efficiently; teams of doctors waited for all hell to break loose, then came up to ask her how many more?

Lina handled the injured while Bolt helped evacuate the people who were able to exit the cars on their own. By now almost all the cars were standing upright or mostly so. Crew that were able had set up steps as they could, but it was still a long drop from each car's doors to the ground. Some of the uninjured assisted. Five ambulance crews were also swarming through the cars, attending to the more minor injuries and sometimes instructing Lina to take a patient directly to hospital. She brought extra gurneys and stretchers in and set them in orderly lines in the freezing field by the trains for use as needed.

Lina's arms and coat were covered with blood. She left a red trail behind her as she hiked herself into yet another car. Everyone was shouting. People were milling in dazes, walking about, yelling at each other, yelling at her. Pulling at her coat and asking what they were supposed to go, where was their friend? Someone had set up a large, orange tent in the field that displayed the lightning bolt ParaNet logo. News helicopters clattered over the area. Sun bolts crackled all around, and out of the corner of her eyes Lina could sometimes see a flit of black in the sky that was gone before she could turn to see if it really was Londo.

But as she balanced on top of a makeshift step to peek into the next car, Londo appeared at her side.

"Take a break," he told her. "You're freezing."

"I'm in and out of the heat–"

"No questioning Team Leader. Now. Twenty minute break for you in the tent." Even as he jumped back into the sky, he was on the radio informing the people there of her size as he ordered heavy pants and more boots for her. She prayed he would add some gloves to that as well. With the rising breeze, her heated coat was having problems keeping out all of the cold, but by far her toes, fingers, and nose were getting the worst of it. Had she been in Hawaii just yesterday? She couldn't remember the concept of "warm."

"Was that Valiant?" A woman grabbed Lina's arm. "Where's my husband? He can find him! Tell him!" she demanded. "He'd gone up front to get some food when it happened."

A man stomped up to them. "I'm freezing! Where the eff is our luggage? Who's getting our effing luggage? We need a replacement train, buses at the least. Listen to me!"

Before she could reply, he shoved Lina backward onto the snowy ground.

"Hey!"

But the man just stood over her defiantly. "I have an appointment!"

Lina ported him into one of the vacated cars. One of the colder vacated cars.

"You're welcome!" she bellowed in his general direction.

It must have scared the hysterical woman, because she jumped and then took two steps back from Lina. She stared at Lina blankly. On the ground, Lina blinked back at her. Missing husband, right.

She jerked when lightning struck next to her and the Bolt appeared. "Status?" he asked.

"Ah, ah, the major injuries are all in the hospitals," she replied. "I think we only have the lesser stuff left."

"Good. Great. Why are you down there?" He glanced from her to the woman who was looking so expectantly at him.

Lina eased up off the icy ground, brushing herself off. "This lady's husband is missing," she said.

Bolt pointed at the ParaNet tent. "Information over there," he bawled, and the woman scurried away. When she was out of earshot, he told Lina, "Always refer them to the tent. For anything. Those people have a lot more effing patience than I do. Having problems?" He eyed her as she got the worst of the snow off herself.

"Someone objected to my priorities," Lina replied. "I'm afraid I wasn't very diplomatic." She checked the heat setting on her coat, but it was on maximum.

"Good. Keep your priorities in order, no matter what the bastards might say. And there are *always* bastards at these things. Crises might bring out the best in some people, but they also bring out the worst in others. We'll start changing over to Phase 2 now," he said, and he went on before Lina could ask what that was exactly. "Any left who need medical, port them to the ambulances, not to hospitals. Let the locals do their work. They like it. It's good for the communities. Besides, we don't do details. And if anyone hands you police paperwork, for eff's sake, find someone to hand it off to. *Not* a ParaNetter. We do *not* do paperwork." He mumbled something that included "Montreal" in it.

"Yessir."

So now Lina ported the prepared victims directly over to the ambulances, one, two, three. These were easy ports but there were so many–! Despite the larger threat of deep freeze, her head was beginning to pound as emergency vehicles roared off, lights flashing. Her back, arms and legs were sore. She hadn't lifted anything, but she felt as if she'd been raising a barn or climbing a mountain. Maybe she hadn't recovered fully from Montreal.

The wind picked up. Lina gave up on trying to adjust the heat on her coat. Sunlight dazzled against the snow cover. She gasped as she glimpsed Londo jumping with an entire railcar on his back. It was an amazing sight, but she kept going. Find the worst victim left and flag down the techs. Find the next-worse one; keep going.

The panic that crackled everywhere didn't help her headache. Over two hundred fifty passengers had been caught in the wreck, all crazy with fear and confusion. Some of them were walking dazed in the fields even though there was a big tent right over there. Thankfully, the cold seemed to convince most to try there for warmth.

Was there really an escape from the cold? Lina couldn't feel anything but agony in her fingers when she tried to move them. Her toes were a combination of numb and stinging pain.

Go to the tent! her guides yelled at her. **How will getting frostbite help you?**

"Okay, okay," she muttered as she ported to the plastic door of the tent. The heat hit her as she entered, and suddenly she couldn't stop quaking from cold.

She just stood there shivering, and realized she couldn't go on any more. Then a pair of hands took her arms. "You look frozen," a woman's voice told her. "You're bleeding. Are you hurt? Medic!"

The woman guided her to a gurney and helped Lina sit on it. Lina blinked and the world came back into focus. "I just want to h-hug a hea-heater," she said. "Get warm."

"Here we go," the woman told her, and wrapped her in a blanket that was so warm it must have been heated. Lina closed her eyes to savor it. She tried to draw the heat deeper within.

There was a man there with a red cross on his sweatshirt. The woman wore a ParaNet jacket. Together they helped Lina off with her coat, and wrapped the blanket around her.

The Red Cross guy tried to see where the blood from her coat had come from. "Where are you hurt?" he asked.

Lina shook her head. "N-not hurt. Another blanket? Puh-please?"

She struggled with her boots until they took over that process. They laid a heated blanket on her gurney, then her on top of it, then wrapped her like a mummy in new blankets.

Oh, that was so much better. "Wake me when it's spring," she declared.

She might actually have dozed, but it wasn't for more than a few minutes. Lon had only instructed her for 20. Well, he might insist on a little more than that now. She began to wriggle around, and the Red Cross guy helped her sit up.

"Getting warmer?"

"Yes, thank you. Where's my coat? And boots?"

They were covered with blood and general filth. "No dry cleaner is going to be able to handle that," Lina decided. So she ported them to the bathroom in Lon's– *their*– apartment on Sarastor and hoped the kol-vanaschen would clean them.

The Red Cross guy, Daniel, started at the disappearance. Then he scrutinized Lina. "You're Valiant's girl, the one he called in about," he decided.

Oh, that was nice. "Yes, I'm Valiant's girl." She beamed at Daniel and he looked confused.

"Va– Oh. Oh!" He gave a laugh. "I didn't mean it that way, but glad to hear it. Sommers!"

The ParaNet lady trotted over and after a discussion, produced a parka that had an orange stripe across the back that said "ParaNet" in big black letters, along with the lightning bolt. Lined pants and boots were also available. "Got any aspirin?" Lina asked, and had that along with a sandwich they removed the meat from, as well as a mug of blessed hot tea.

Inside the tent the shouting seemed to reverberate. More people kept coming in and Lina gave up her gurney for someone else. All of a sudden it seemed to her that there was no place to move to, that the crowd was elbow-to-elbow.

"Where the effing hell are those buses? We need those buses now!" she heard Sommers' familiar voice. "What do you mean, the school superintendent needs paperwork before she can release them? We're the effing ParaNet! Tell her exactly what she can do with her paperwork!"

Lina stood and stretched.

"Tell her we have our own insurance. It covers everything! Stupid, effing…"

Lina took a final swig of her tea. She'd seen porta-potties outside and made for one of them. Time to get back to work.

Crying, screaming, fear and curses greeted her as she climbed into another Amtrak car. Though it had begun heated, by now it was damned chilly in here. **Don't worry, we're here and we're helping,** she tried to beam to them as calmly as she could. Maybe they hadn't even heard her. There were a lot of children aboard and those wouldn't understand anyway.

They'd stayed aboard because they were afraid to go out into the cold and chaos. Through the windows she could see the sea of flashing blue and red lights that filled the state road, allowing a narrow path for ambulances to pass. The curious arrived, too, as well as people who wanted to help. Emotions piled upon emotions.

"It's okay to take a break." Bolt was suddenly behind her.

"I took one a while ago. There's got to be a way to calm them all," Lina said.

"Calming's the least of our worries."

"Maybe. If only we had some music." An idea came to her. "Let me try something."

She ported to the roof of the car and then pulled the flute that was always at her side, invisible and immaterial, from the air. It was her gift from the Worlds, and it faded into view, unlike something she ported. After a moment's thought, she brought it to her lips and began to play "Greensleeves." The peaceful notes traveled the length of the wrecks, its volume the same near her as it was at the end of the trains.

The almost-palpable panic now seemed to pause. **Don't worry; we'll reach you all. Just be patient. Help is here. Buses are coming to take you someplace safe and warm. You'll be fine.** Now they listened to her. They listened to the music.

She ended the song pleased. "That was interesting," she murmured to herself. The pounding in her head that had returned after her break now disappeared. She felt refreshed, maybe even warmer, and she ported back to the ground.

Bolt had been caught by the song's spell as well. "Eff, what am I doing just standing around? I've got work to do." And he was off to some other part of the train in a spark of pure light.

From outside, Lina could sense the presence of only minor injuries in one of the final cars. She strolled as she looked around to see that a line of people were walking from the ParaNet tent across the field. Two school buses sat at the side of the road, hurray. People who had stayed in their train cars now began to exit.

But some force gave her a push. What? It pushed again. She began to trot to the back of the car. People there climbed down from the door, tossing their carry-on luggage over the side. Some reached out to help each other.

Lina started to question her guides, but then sensed it: the small circle of particular panic. Lina began to run, porting as she went to shorten the distance.

"Excuse me. Excuse me." This car still tilted, but it was fairly upright. She fought the crowd pressing through the exits. She couldn't get a good picture of her target. "Let me through, please. Medical emergency!" She bulled her way through– a man cursed at her– and down the lopsided train aisle. Three passengers had gathered around one seat.

"I can help," she announced as she approached. An elderly gentleman sat holding his left arm. A silver-haired lady– his wife?– clutched at his other. Two younger women stood in the aisle next to them wringing their hands.

One drew Lina aside. "You're a paramedic? I think he's having a heart attack."

"Yes, I felt it from outside," Lina said. She moved to where the man and his wife could hear her. "Don't worry. My name's Carolina Starhart and you're going to be all right. Everything will be fine. Now, there's going to be a bit of a surprise here as we teleport. I'll take you along, too, ma'am," she nodded to the wife. "We're going directly to the hospital."

The man spasmed. He let out a gurgle. His wife screamed and clutched him.

Desperately Lina tried to remember the Kolaimni technique for heart attack: Peace and tranquility of mind. Obedience to the rightness of the universe. Connect to the etheric. Reach with her etheric hand to grasp the heart and picture it cold, cold, slowing down the heartbeat. "Here we go," she said as they ported, this time to that next hospital she'd been given an image of.

She set the man directly on a gurney and called for a doctor. She'd caught the staff by surprise. They just stood there gaping at the sudden appearance of three people in their midst.

She waved at a group. "Need a little help," she ordered. "A cardiac team."

One of the doctors, a middle-aged man with glasses, hurried toward her. Two nurses or assistants followed him, and they adjusted the old man on the gurney, then began taking readings.

Lina explained. "I'm holding his heart in hypothermia, but he needs immediate attention. And someone should see to his wife, please. Oh." She'd only briefly gone over this technique in class. She had known she should have reviewed it a few months ago, but there was no coulda, shoulda… "Could you get someone to assist me, please? Right now?"

The doctor looked at her like she was a lunatic, but he must have heard of the strange woman who'd been teleporting in patients to hospitals all over the state. Lina's face reflected her absolute concentration as she held her hand directly above the man's heart. The doctor called for nurses. One came running while he bent over his patient.

Let's move it, she said silently to the doctor. **I'm not precisely sure of what I'm doing here.**

She ported in her Kolaimni textbook and gave it to the nurse using her left hand as she kept her right in place. "Read to me the part about heart attacks," she asked. "It's toward the very back. Quickly, please."

The nurse immediately opened the back of the book and began to scan. She found the page and read to Lina.

The doctor snapped out of his shock. "Cardiac team to CCU!" he shouted to the emergency coordinator. He took hold of the gurney himself as Lina kept pace with it, her hand steady above the man's heart. "Nurse!" One came running up, and the doctor nodded to the panicked wife trotting alongside. The nurse took her by the shoulders and gently led her away.

"Okay," the doctor– his nameplate read Reddy– said, interrupting the nurse who was reading to Lina. "You say what?"

"I've lowered the temperature of his heart," Lina explained. "To slow it down, lessen the damage. The cold is beginning to work on the rest of him, too. I don't want to let it go on too long."

"How can you do that? You project cold or something?"

"No, I'm working on the etheric level. It's a psychic healing method," she said as she concentrated on maintaining her control. He listened to the instructions now as they swept past double swinging doors.

They turned the gurney into a section with EKG equipment lining the walls. Another doctor met them. Two nurses began to set up. Lina nodded at her own assistant nurse and adjusted her control to go along with the instructions. Oh, that's what she'd forgotten. Well, that made sense. She could feel the organs and cells of the old man's body relaxing now, calming from their clench and starting to recall their healthy function. Dr. Reddy shook his head at what he was hearing as he coordinated with the new doctor. Lina's nurse reached the end of the instructions and looked up expectantly.

"Are you ready?" Lina asked the cardiac doctor.

"Yes.

"Okay, you've got him… now," and she released her tight hold on the man's etheric field.

The team scrambled to the doctor's orders as Lina stood close but not in the way, working on the man from a distance, smoothing out the etheric field of his heart, relaxing the tensed and spasmed muscles there. She retraced the lines of structure the etheric body maintained for the physical one. Then she breathed light into him until she thought he was fairly stable. She saw a sink along the wall and ran water over her arms and hands to clear them of waste energy.

She left the area to ground and clear herself with earth energy, then went to see if she could find the victim's wife. She was just outside the room. The nurse was seated next to her, holding her hand.

Lina smiled. "I think he's going to be all right," she told the wife. "You just relax here and think good thoughts."

The woman clutched at her. "When can I see him?"

"I don't know. They're still working on him. I'm not a doctor, but he seems to be stabilizing to me. Now how about you?"

"What do you mean?"

"Are you okay? You got a nasty scratch on your arm."

She pointed to the torn and bloody sleeve. The attending nurse gave a small cry of alarm as the woman started; she hadn't even known she was injured.

"Oh honey," the nurse told the woman, "We'll get you patched up in no time so you can see your husband when he's ready. Okay?"

The lady smiled at the nurse. "Thank you." She turned to thank Lina, but Lina was gone.

After the heat of the hospital, the cold cut through her like an axe. A hard wind now howled across the snowy March plain, still stuck in winter. Lina saw more buses parked before the phalanx of police cars and ported over to them. A woman in a bright orange hooded coat and sunglasses was talking to the crew of one ambulance, come back for seconds.

"There she is." They pointed at her. The woman came over to her. Oh, she was the same one who'd been in the tent before. Her parka was emblazoned with "ParaNet Emergency Team."

"Ms. Starhart?" she asked and she nodded. "I'm Sommers. We hadn't been formally introduced. I'm head of ParaNet On-Site Auxiliary."

"What would you like me to do?"

Londo surveyed the condition of the passenger train. Gary'd done a solid job with it. They were all empty and upright. It didn't take long to place the handful of Amtrak cars on the tracks. Then he hooked the cars up to each other, gave a grunt, and towed the entire train north a few miles, where he triggered a switch to transfer it to a spur line. Coordinating with Bolt, Lon then began to straighten the remaining freight cars. He hefted them back onto the track. It took a while for the two ParaNetters to inspect them to make sure they and their contents were intact. One wasn't, and Londo air-lifted it to a containment area upstate. Linking the cars back together when he returned didn't take long.

Hal should be doing this part, Londo mused. *He's the one who gets such a kick out of trains.* Of course the trains Hal loved to play with were considerably smaller than these, but he was sure his father would still find amusement in rolling the full-sized models around on their track like this.

Then he studied the damaged tracks and added close-up footage to his visual record of the event. All evidence pointed to signaler error. Lon would bet that the Amtrak train was supposed to have waited on that siding while this one went through on the main track. Whether it was electronic or human error remained to be seen, but that wasn't an investigation he'd be involved with. Carefully he began to repair what he could of the tracks. He called in a list of needed materials. Techs and equipment were en route.

He looked up to see a locomotive slowing down as it approached the freight train backward. Amtrak's replacement was still an hour or so away. The tracks were clear on this side for the repair crews to get through. It would all be finished and cleared by end of day, but his work here was done.

Naked, Londo lay on his stomach, the lounge cushion cut out to expose his face. This was the life. He could see why people would like this.

Behind him a robotic masseur kneaded out knots he didn't know he'd gained during the course of the day. Rollers and wheels and thumb-sized pads comprised most of the floating machine's surfaces. He'd been anointed with oils that smelled good as they repaired and rejuvenated skin.

"What do you think of Legion Lifestyle?" he asked Lina, who lay in a similar position and exposure on the lounge next to him. They maintained contact by holding hands, so the masseur could work on him while Lon's vulnerability was nullified.

"It's warm," Lina replied dreamily.

"And?"

"I could get used to this."

"*Bon.* Get used to it."

"I skipped the Lifestyle chapter in the Legion spouse handbook. Is it all like this?"

The planet Sarastor was capital world of the Affiliated Systems, the next galactic sector over from that of Earth. On Sarastor was the artificial mountain of a complex that comprised AffSys Megaforce Legion Headquarters. This Lifestyle section took up several floors in the lower, less-regulated, levels. It was the middle of the night, and they were the only humans there.

"The spa is a good part of it, yes. I want you to use it. Pampering is a big part of my plans for you."

"Yes, Londo."

"They also handle parties and social engagements."

"Not Protocol?"

"Protocol tells you how to act at parties and social engagements, and whom to invite. Lifestyle finds you caterers, delivers your invitations, coordinates with your personal assistants…"

"I have a personal assistant?"

"You will in the next couple weeks. You should start interviewing, or you could have Lifestyle hire someone."

They fell silent to savor their treatment. Deeply relaxed, their hands slipped, and almost before Lon's masseur bleeped an error, their fingers scrabbled to find each other. After they locked into a secure grip, the robot masseur went back to its business.

"I understand this is all different for you," Lon told her, "so it's up to you to tell me when we need to back off and let you absorb the changes for a while. I'm going to remind Jae to give you some slack, too."

"I'm okay as long as you're along for the ride. And Jae."

"Good. That's my girl. Let's see how tomorrow's trip to Aldierra goes. Maybe Jae can take an hour or two off and we can all come back here for some R&R. Jae's got to be stressed out after all this as well. I–"

Carrying on without me?

Jae! they both shouted back at the unexpected call.

16

They raised up from their prone positions and their robo-masseurs backed off.

It's about time you got out of hyperspace, Lina said. **Are you okay?**

How's the situation? Londo asked.

Situation is not incredibly bad, and I'm fine.

You want to join us for dinner?

I've got a lot of ceremony to wade through here. No time, sorry. How about you two coming here later?

Sure, Londo said. **A late supper, maybe? I've never eaten Aldierran food.**

And you don't want to. You bring the food.

We have leftover cake from last night, Lina reported.

She made it herself, Jae. It's even better than Mama Ruth's.

Great. I'll give you a call when things cool down here. Love you, Lon. Love you too, Lie-Lie.

They sent him their warmest regards even as they sensed him setting down on the far-off planet's surface. Lon reached to the side of his lounger for his beer glass, and then clinked it against the glass of *laffez* Lina held out. "We'll be on Aldierra tonight," he said. "Here's to the beginning of the Three Worlds Project."

Something buzzed. "Damn!" Londo turned over to grab his vest, folded on a stool next to his lounge. He fished his ParaNet communicator from its pockets. It looked like a mouth harp in a plastic case, but it bore the golden logo for the group.

"Ran– Starheart here," he said, and Lina smiled at him.

"Londo. Emergency meeting. Where are you? We don't see your coordinates–"

"This had better be a real emergency," Londo growled. "Not another 'we need to cut back on expenses–'"

"We need you stat."

Lon let out a groan but set about getting dressed. Lina admired him for a moment before she ported on her own clothes.

"Give us a few minutes. We're on Sarastor."

"Kiss her goodbye, Londo. Just get the hell up here."

Lon clicked off the communicator and shoved it back into his vest. "Emergency meetings usually don't take over an hour, Kitten. Even if we have to leave directly from it, they'll probably give me a few seconds to call home. Hal's home now; he can probably sub for me."

"That would be so nice if he could."

"I might not even have to go anywhere. They may just need me for strategy."

"I'll cross my fingers."

"Why don't you go home and take a nap? Bring the cats in and let them look the place over, mountain and all. I want to install the cat door tomorrow. Best they get used to the place soon as possible. I'll be back in a while."

"I'll work the garden. I've been ignoring it. This way we can take Jae some pasta primavera for supper. If we have time tonight, we can bring the cats over then."

She could tell from his eyes that he was imagining himself the comfortably married man, with home and wife and supper waiting for him at the end of the day. Somehow now the idea didn't seem so Stepford-ish to Lina. She ran her hand over his. "I love you so much."

"And I'm certifiably crazy about you. I'll get my shrink to note it when I see him."

She laughed a little at that as Londo checked his watch. *"D'accord,"* he said. "Give me one hour or so." He bent down for a kiss.

Lina dropped more snow peas into her basket as Bran-Bran rubbed against her leg. Broccoli and cabbage, some asparagus and carrots; after all these ho-hum years of struggling with the hard clay, it looked like the garden had chosen this as the year to finally produce something. Well, she'd keep working on it until Habitat took the house. Was Lon right when he said that people would buy it at a higher price just because she had married him?

Her stomach clenched at the thought of saying goodbye to her home and clenched again at the knowledge of her imminent notoriety. She hadn't seen the last of paparazzi cameras. Could she stand to face them again? Maybe she and Lon could just port in close and unannounced to everything he had to attend.

But darn it, Londo loved that spotlight. He deserved it.

As the sun started to set in earnest, Lina chewed over the idea of herself as someone famous. She just couldn't picture it. Plus all this security stuff Londo was always talking about. She didn't want to think that someday there might be someone out there who wanted to harm her just because Lon was who he was, and she was his weak spot. Should she talk it over with Jae? No, the safety question seemed to obsess him as well. Even Wiley had lectured her.

Maybe she could discuss it with Rainj. She'd been a Legion wife for a few years now, certainly used to the spotlight and security precautions. Rainj would know what she should do when they were all watching–

They're watching, her guides told her.

"What?" Lina asked.

They're watching you.

Danger swirled around her like a encroaching dark fog. Lina eased up out of her crouch, trying to taste it. Whatever it was, it wasn't immediate, wasn't life-threatening. It was suspicion. Fear. And lingering on the outskirts– a sour undercurrent of hate.

Who was it? Where were they? Lina reached for more peas while trying to act as if she hadn't noticed. She struggled to get a fix.

Carolina.

****Londo?**** Why had he called her that? Someone else was clinging to Londo's thoughts. Who? Maybe– maybe Maximus. Lina wasn't familiar with the sense of Londo's father yet, but it felt like it could be him: curious and alert, non-hostile. Why would Lon let someone listen in?

She said, ****Someone's watching me here. I can't figure out who it is. Is the meeting over already?**** He couldn't have been gone more than forty-five minutes, tops. She'd only had time to feed the cats.

****Why don't you come home. Now.****

****What's up? You sound worried. Why are–****

****I'm sorry. I'm really sorry, cherie. I can't tell you.****

****That sounds ominous.****

****Now. Please.****

****Okay, incoming!****

Though she didn't have to do so on intraplanetary ports, Lina hung outside reality a moment while she checked Starhaven. She caught her breath. There was no way out of this other than not going at all. She appeared in the entry vestibule and kicked off her clay-caked shoes and socks, depositing her cold weather clothing there. That whatever it was was watching her again. They were here.

"Okay, okay," she said. She could feel a crowd waiting. She ported to stand next to Lon.

"Is there a problem, officers?" She raised her arms and then decide to place her hands on her head, prisoner of war style. This was déjà vu all over again.

The majority of the ParaNet stood in the bright living room area of Starhaven, staring at her. They wanted her surprised. Well, she certainly was. A wide red screen hung in the air behind them, her image centered upon it.

****The Wyoming Welcome Wagon sure wear funny clothes,**** she told Lon and then glanced at Maximus. It was definitely him linked telepathically to Lon like an echo. He'd heard.

The screen disappeared in a red glow, sucked back into the medallion belonging to the Galactic Guardian.

Hesitantly Lina lowered her hands. Keeping her movements slow, she took off her sunhat and tried to fluff her hair.

Lon cleared his throat. *"Chérie,* this is–"

****_The entire freaking ParaNet! Lon, you could've warned me._**** She didn't care if Maximus was listening in.

****_No I couldn't. I'm sorry. Couldn't be helped._**** "–The ParaNet. They don't want any telepathy between us." He stressed the word _us_.

"Oh. Sure, whatever." ****_Jae. Jae!_**** She ported in her basket of vegetables from the entry and set it on the table next to Lon. They exchanged a concerned glance. He nodded and jerked his chin up slightly; _trust me_, his body language said. She straightened, reached for his hand, and he took hers with a squeeze.

They all stood at alert like an enemy force in her living room: Maximus, Forte, Bolt and Blitz, the Galactic Guard, Olympia, Dragonlord, Dragonwing, Black Magnum, White Puma… All of the important heroes on Earth, all of the most famous of the most famous, here in person. The major North American non-para heroes, those without powers but almost as famous as the paras, mustered with their co-workers.

And Affiliated Systems Mega-Legion Commander Magnos, Stoan Kinrol, stood in front of the fireplace. Oh hell. His presence foretold that nothing good would come of this meeting. Wilder Mem-Bazer was with him, the two blue-skinned humans outside the crowd of Terrans. Wiley was a friendly, warm aqua, while Stoan's skin was cold ultramarine. Odd how they seemed so out of place here. On Sarastor they'd fit right in.

The fireplace behind them– oh god– Lon and her last night, right there. Someone– hopefully Lon– had messily rolled up the quilt and blankets they'd used. She could see a corner of Lon's jeans from yesterday sticking out of the pile. Good. At least there wasn't scattered underwear for the Networkers to gawk at.

But there were still the pile of blankets, the pillows, the almost-empty bottle of wine and the two wine glasses on the table next to the couch. All the candles she'd had going in this dark cavern of a living room last night. Anyone with half a mind could see what had gone on.

Damn it, she refused to be embarrassed. They were adults. She had other things to worry about.

Lina didn't switch to Panlingua for the two Legionnaires. Wiley understood English, and if Stoan hadn't brought along a translator that was just too bad. "Hi, Wiley. I see you made it to Earth the long way, Stoan. I assume that this is a social visit, since the Terrans on Sarastor told me that the Legion's never lifted a finger to help out here. Or am I mistaken; has the Legion's official jurisdiction suddenly expanded to include Earth?"

"Let me handle this," Lon said for her ears alone.

"Oneferall. Rhubarb," she suggested just as quietly.

"No. No rhubarb. Stay put and don't panic."

Lina realized that she had dirt from the garden on her knees and hands. She wore her ratty yardwork jeans and a frayed tee shirt that proclaimed that she was a cadet at Starfleet Training Academy. The cement floor was cool against her bare feet. This was not an impressive outfit in which to greet the world's mightiest heroes.

Stoan scowled at her. "Why don't you step away from Londo? I think we'd all feel better if you did." His words came out in English, though they didn't match his mouth movements. He had a translator after all, but there was no floating marble near him. Maybe it was built into his suit.

Lina checked Londo, who was looking daggers at Stoan. He glanced at her and gave a sharp nod, so she eased away from him with her hands raised. *I'm stepping away from the car, officer.*

Lina. What's up? Jae finally answered from Aldierra. **We're in the middle of a meeting here.**

She used the distraction of brushing herself off to cover her mental conversation. Besides, Stoan was talking to Lon, and Lon used gestures when he answered so that attention would automatically be on him, away from her.

I've got the entire ParaNet in my living room and Londo's not allowed to talk to me. Stoan and Wiley are here, too. I can't look like I'm talking to you.

I don't know anything about this. Lon hasn't told me. Hang on while I speak with him.

Lon would need to disguise his telepathic talk from Stoan, a distraction.

"You keep her in line." Stoan shook his finger at Lon.

Lina took a step forward, and felt every eye in the room except Lon's swing to her. "Perhaps you don't understand Terran or Feithi wedding vows," Lina told Stoan. "Londo is not my keeper or master. Slavery hasn't existed in this country for over a hundred years– unlike the Affiliated Systems, I believe."

"I am not going to argue cultural differences with you–"

"Of course not. You'd lose. This seems to be important ParaNet business here. I guess I should have changed on the way. I was working in the garden. Um. Hello," she said to the group, each and every one of whom seemed to eye her suspiciously, except Wiley of course. And Maximus. Not good. She hoped she had an ingratiating smile on her face when she said, "I'm Yoko."

At least that brought a small smile to some of them.

"Some of y'all I've met, but I think I know everyone's names. And I can take a wild guess at why you're here." She made a point of returning Stoan's scowl.

"Funny, I thought Londo said your name was Lina." Maximus stood up and came forward to shake her hand, making it a little friendlier by taking it between both of his. He touched her as if she were eggshells.

"It's nice to see you again, even though the circumstances may be strained." He gave her a smile, but his eyes glanced for a split second to Londo. He must still be monitoring Lon. How odd; Maximus wasn't letting on about Jae.

His dark cocoa skin made his gray eyes seem lighter than they were. Now in the late afternoon daylight he didn't seem quite as imposing as he had yesterday, but he was still a very large man, broader and even a bit taller than Lon and all muscles. This was her new father-in-law. How should she act toward him? Especially with people around? Maximus!

"Thanks, um, Hal," she said, and his smile became a mischievous crooked one at her shyness at using his name. It made him look an awful lot like Londo. "I suppose I should be used to this by now, but I'm not."

"It won't be long until we can leave all this behind us. I remember–"

The world went gray.

It wasn't the colors that had gone. All resonance disappeared, the telepathic sense that anyone else was in the room with her. But there they all were, just the same, though they could well have been holograms for all she could tell. The world had been drained of its lifeforce.

"It's good." Lina interrupted Maximus. He kept her hand in his steel-hard ones, his eyes narrowing as he considered her.

"Very good, whatever it is." She turned to Wilder. "Did you come all the way to Earth just to play with a new toy?"

Stoan stood defiantly between her and Lon, making sure that Lon wouldn't help her.

"I wouldn't call it a toy," Wiley answered. For once, both his eyes were focused upon her. "How did you know it wasn't some kind of anti-telepath?"

"Probably because I've never heard of an anti-telepath. And secondly, it just sounds mechanical."

"I don't hear anything."

"I do," Lon said.

Lina nodded. "Like nails on a blackboard."

"Or bad brakes," Londo added.

"Can you tell where it is?"

"So this is a test, like back on Sarastor." Lina looked around the room. "There. It's behind Olympia." And before he could ask, she added, "I can tell by the volume. It's starting to give me a headache. Anytime you want to turn it off is okay with me."

Wiley scratched some notes into his padd, probably about the time it took to start a headache. He was a Legionnaire, Lina told herself firmly, and this was a time when duty came before friendship. He was just doing his job.

She asked, "What else do you want to know?"

Many of the ParaNetters quietly sat down or leaned against the rough-framed walls from where they had previously been at attention. Apparently they now could sit back and enjoy the show.

She didn't relish being entertainment for the world's most famous people. Lina clenched her teeth against the sound and tried not to look at Lon. He could have warned her!

Wiley looked up from his notes (though his right eye had been on her the entire time). "Can you sense anything telepathically?"

"Nothing. It's a complete blank. No clairvoyance either. How about you, Lon?" She tried to keep the annoyance out of her voice, in case he had a very good excuse for putting her through this. Duty was one thing, but marriage superseded that. What they shared was more important than playing by the rules!

"Nothing for me, either," he said miserably from behind Stoan. Lina glared at the stone-hearted commander. Surely he was behind it all, forcing Londo to do this to her! She decided that she'd blame Stoan instead of Lon. It certainly made her feel better to do so. Yes, horrid Stoan played the only villain here.

Something buzzed. "We'll take the call," Lon told the air, which beep-beeped at him. A 3-D screen rolled down from nowhere, and some of the ParaNetters jumped. Jae leaned out of the screen, his tanned face and mane of golden hair such a relief to see.

"What the *skurny kick's* going on there?!" he demanded to know in Lingua. "Stoan, why are you harassing Lina?"

"How did you know what was happening?" Stoan asked.

Lina spoke up. "I called him telepathically after I got here. He was talking to Lon when the machine went off."

"But your instructions were–"

"Our instructions were that Lina and I could not telepath to each other," Lon said, "so we took a more roundabout way."

Wiley nodded at their logic, his mouth quirking into a resigned half-smile. Maybe he was on their side.

"Hal? You were supposed to be monitoring."

"They weren't talking to each other. Just Jae and Lon."

"I was promised cooperation. This does not seem like cooperation to me," Stoan declared. His steely gaze raked everyone in the room before settling on the screen. "Neutrino," he told Jae, "I'm ordering you to butt out. No telepathy to either of these two until you get an all-clear signal from me. Is that understood?"

"Perhaps now's the time to decide which has higher priority: Legion or Three Worlds," Jae began.

"Not now." Londo heaved something between a sigh and a grunt. "Jae, the quicker we can get Lina cleared here the quicker we can get our real work done. There's a reason for this, and I can't tell either of you."

Jae considered. "We've got at least twenty billion people relying on us. I can be in hyperspace today."

Lina stepped around Stoan so she'd be on screen. "Keep to your original schedule, Jae, please. I guess dinner tonight is out of the question. Is that right, Lon?"

He nodded. "Yes," was all he said.

She set her mouth before she continued, "But just because some people go off the deep end doesn't mean that we have to sacrifice making the foundations of the Three Worlds strong. We'll clear up things here. You attend to things there. I know we were all scheduled for that meeting on Sarastor in two days, but we'll take that trip whenever things calm down again. Does that sound right?"

"Do as she says, Jae," Londo urged. "We'll expect you here in six days now, I suppose. I'll postpone the conference call with the Eminence of Sarastor."

"All right; I'll arrange things on this end. But give me a call as soon as everything's blown over, or else I'll spend the entire trip to Earth worrying."

That's good, Jae. Show confidence. Lina smiled at him. "Safe journey, Jae. We want to hear what you have to report." She cocked her head and he understood the double meaning.

He gave them both a hard look. "You two be careful."

"We will," Lon said. "Starheart out." The screen disappeared.

Stoan strode up to Lina. "No more interruptions," he ordered. "And no more non-verbal communication to anyone until this test is over, is that understood?"

"Understood," Lina said quietly, dangerously. *Watch the attitude. Don't embarrass Londo, but get across to Stoan that he's not going to intimidate you.*

"Let's resume testing," Wilder said. "Try something besides telepathy. Can you channel?"

"Am I allowed to try?" she asked Stoan. He in turn looked at Wiley, who shrugged and then nodded.

"Go ahead."

Lina made certain her chakras were lined up, reached for the white light, and it shone faintly down on her. She searched for any spirit guides. Their shadowy presences were indeed there, giving her the OK gesture, but pointing to the Galactic Guard and shaking their heads. Apparently they didn't like something about him, but she wasn't going to be the one to tell him.

"Channeling's still on," she reported. "Nothing wrong there except for clarity. It's quite murky. Tentative, as if I were a beginner. All Three Worlds are checking in. No impression of Feith, but she's always difficult to sense since she's in some dimension beyond death. Aldierra is not pleased with events. You are interfering. Sarastor's telling her to take it easy. Earth… Earth isn't too sure about all this. I think. Like I said, it's murky. And a bad situation; I'm filtering through my emotions. You're not supposed to do that."

"Channeling?" young Blitz blurted. She couldn't be in high school yet. "You mean, like ancient Atlantean wizards?"

"I've never channeled one of those," Lina admitted, "but I know people who claim to. I just go with the run of the mill stuff, you know, angels and devas and spirit guides, and of course the earth and such. Visual and audio, both are on. And the guides tell me that this is okay for now, but they're warning about doing it too long. I'd have to agree; it really is giving me a headache. You could even add a little nausea to the list of symptoms."

"Run of the mill channeling," Bolt snorted, and some of the others smiled patronizingly in response. Still, they gave her a calculating eye.

Lina's gaze slid over to regard the Galactic Guardian, Paul Granger, dressed in the red-on-red uniform with its black and white accents, the slowly-spinning spiral galaxy symbol on both shoulders, the palm-sized ruby medallion at his throat. Her guides were really raising a fuss about him. Whatever for?

Galactic Guardians were– Galactic Guardians. Agents of a galaxy-wide organization, so much larger in importance than Legionnaires, who only guarded one sector. She'd met one at her wedding reception and had been dazzled. The Guard was to the Legion what the Legion was to the ParaNet, she supposed. They had the entire galaxy to patrol, linked by the communications and supervision of the Galactic Sentinels on Aum, who lived close to the huge black hole in the middle of the Milky Way. It was that black hole that powered all the rubies.

Lina knew Lon couldn't stand Granger, but… but he was a Galactic Guardian! She shifted her gaze quickly before he could think she was staring at him.

Wiley ran her answers through his padd, seeming not pleased but satisfied. Poor Lon looked miserable.

"Are you okay?" she asked him softly. He glanced up at her and then back down to the desk. Guilty. Or maybe sick. She wondered if the machine were physically affecting him more than herself. He was used to being invulnerable, but this affected his mind. Since his other powers were psionic, were they affected by all this? He wouldn't like that at all.

They wouldn't ask him about his powers, not in a group where not everyone had Unlimited security clearances. She'd ask him later. Best to know these things so they could guard against them in the future.

"Do you need some water?" she asked him. He could be a noobie in many ways when he didn't have powers.

He shook his head. Probably didn't want to seem weak here in a situation where he was cast as the offending party along with her. Londo wanted to be liked. He wanted respect. He'd fought hard to make his own place in—

Damn! This must be what a migraine felt like. Something in back of her eyes clamped down into a concentrated ball of pain, and she bit her lip against it.

"I really wish someone would turn it off. Please," she said as politely as she could. She felt like letting out with a string of curses, but this was the ParaNet, and she would not lower herself in their eyes. Lon had grown up with the Network, and likely they were looking her over as well as doing this test. Meeting the family for the first time, as it were.

At least her father wasn't here.

She could not be Londo's weak spot. *Stand up and show some strength, Muttbutt!* "Is anyone ever going to tell me what this is about?" she asked between clenched teeth.

"We have orders not to." Lon reached to take her hand but stopped as he felt Stoan's angry eyes on him. "You'll know in a few days. Stoan, can't we tell her anything now? The device works. You should be happy."

"I'll be happy when this is brought to a conclusion."

"A conclusion?" Was he trying for an annulment again? No, something else was up, something important or Lon wouldn't keep this from her. Londo would never betray her.

Maximus came to her, worry creasing his face. He could see that she was in pain. "I'm sorry, but some things have to be ParaNet and Legion secrets."

"Like—" She almost said "Like what Deegel revealed," but the Legion hadn't announced that yet. Was the ParaNet supposed to know about traitors within the Legion's ranks?

Apparently Maximus did and he'd guessed who she'd almost said, or maybe heard some echo of it through Lon. "Yes," he said. "Like her. And this is far, far above Level Four. Is it enough that we tell you that there's a good reason behind this?"

"Not really. But I guess I'm stuck, huh?"

Wiley walked in a small circle around her, his sensor still recording. "How about teleportation?"

Back to that again. Her head throbbed. "Port blind? Are you kidding?"

"Why?" He made a time note on his padd.

"Clairvoyance is off. You already know that I compensate for lots of stuff consciously. How about subconsciously? Suppose I port back to my house in North Carolina? Would I port through actual distance if I can't port normally? How fast is the earth moving through space? Do I wind up a thousand miles from where I aimed, in a vacuum? Or do I get in the way of the earth and arrive buried inside the core somewhere? No, I don't think so. I don't want to test space-time theory today." Besides, she had to visualize her destination clearly.

He looked at her with both eyes, and she knew that he could see her anxiety. He might have given her a reassuring glance, but she wasn't able to tell for sure. She'd never realized just how much she relied on telepathy to give her clues about people. And with Wiley's independently-wandering eyes, it was difficult to relate his looks to those of ordinary humans, even though the rest of him looked perfectly, suburbanly normal. Except for the aqua skin and purple hair, of course. At least he didn't look like *his* head was about to burst open.

Slow down, she told herself. *Breathe. Don't embarrass Londo.*

"This won't affect her permanently, will it?" Londo asked. "Can't you tune it down for her at least?"

Wiley shook his head and clicked on another screen. "How about using co-ordinates to port?"

"Huh. I don't know from coordinates. I have to be able to see something or see the place in someone's mind, or know where it is already in order to port. Maybe I could learn coordinates, but I'm new at this. Can I sit down? Can I get an aspirin?"

He scribbled in his Lingua handwriting. Olympia stepped forward. "Well then, something you can see? Something in this room?" She held out a small globe, silver and milky-white, with rivets and seams interrupting its surface.

"That's it, right?" She didn't really have to ask. Lina winced at the static it emitted. It drove straight through her bones.

"*Skurning merde,*" Lon hissed. Wiley scribbled some more.

"Yes." Olympia held it gingerly, as if she didn't know what Lina would do with it.

"A port. How about a simple one? Just a few inches." Lina visualized it to port about two feet above where it was. Instead, the globe rose steadily on its own to that position and held there, above Olympia's astonished hands.

"Whoa," Lina breathed. As her legs suddenly went weak, she sat on the edge of the comm table. "That's a new one." The globe started to wobble. "Steady," she urged, and it did. That was her doing that. When she visualized, it performed a loop-de-loop in the air. She would have laughed if her brain hadn't been pounding.

"Levitation," Londo said, almost too soft to hear, but Wiley and Olympia echoed him.

"I guess if I can port, there's little use for levitation. That's why I never noticed it before," Lina said.

Hal asked, "Have you ever moved anything before like this? Anything you couldn't explain, any kind of... I believe the word is *poltergeist* activity in your life?"

"Poltergeist?" That word clicked in her mind.

"Lina?"

"I'm not sure. Maybe when I was a kid. I don't remember. You'd have to ask my mother. I think I remember her saying something." She tried a small smile and failed. Gravity seemed too heavy even sitting. "But I doubt if she would admit to anything odd going on in the family." She felt weak and sickly. Everything from shoulders up was throbbing. Beside her, Lon put his hand on her shoulder to reassure her.

"Ow."

The small sound was like a gunshot in the suddenly-still room. Lon snatched his hand from her shoulder. She and he exchanged frantic glances. The bond was broken; the calibration gone. He was not matched as they had been, and now his touch was much too strong for her, even at its weakest.

Now he had to treat her like eggshells as he did all the others, controlling his strength consciously. No, he wouldn't even be able to do that; he couldn't trust his body to respond with control when it recognized her and thought it knew how to touch her.

"Wiley," he urged, and Lina hoped that only she could hear the desperation in his voice, "how much longer?"

"I still have a few tests to run," Wilder said, "but I'll try to get them over as quickly as poss–"

"Better do that within 3 minutes," Lina said, "because I'm going to be sick to my stomach in four, and I'm just not going to do that in front of the entire–" she still had the strength not to swear, but the deleted word was obvious– "Para-Net. I'm going to break your toy in three."

"You can destroy it?" The Guard stepped closer, curiously regarding first her, then the globe, still hanging in midair. Wilder scribbled furiously, not looking at what he was writing. One eye was on her, and the other on the globe.

"I can think of 2 possibilities. No, make that 3, thanks." She nodded to the helpful but foggy spirit guide who had pointed it out. "I can make the thing explode, but that would mean I'd have to vacuum. I hate to vacuum. We just cleaned in here yesterday."

"How would you do that?"

"Levitate everything out from the center in one burst. Or I could make it implode, same general idea but neater. And a guide just reminded me of a cute little trick I learned once at psychic school. My three minutes up yet?"

"Close enough," Wiley said.

Lina took a deep breath for strength. Do this and it would be over. Standing next to the globe, she had to set her jaw and squint from its hellish screeching. She circled it. It hung in midair at her command. There– The guide indicated the weak spot. Summoning the white light, she felt on the etheric level for the net of energies she could utilize, and then snapped her thumb, index and middle fingers next to the spot. There came a crack from inside, a small flash, and the smell of something burning.

Such blessed relief! The world washed over her again. Her vision seemed dimmer as other senses clicked on. "Now, that was something that an ancient Atlantean wizard taught a little old lady in West Virginia, who in turn taught me. My guides reminded me that she used the technique once to hot-wire her truck when she'd lost the keys."

Londo's hand squeezed her upper arm; she could feel the room again. She could feel *him.*

"Bond's back, Wiley," Lon reported, and moved in to hug her. She held him back, and she could feel the moment of surprise and hurt.

"Just a sec, love," she murmured. "Okay, Wiley, *now* I could transport out of here; took me a sec to get my bearings. Hang on… And *now* I think could take control of somebody's mind." She turned to Stoan. "That's what you were really wanting to know, wasn't it?"

"I thought you said you couldn't do mind control," he scowled at her.

"I did, and I can't. Just like you put a knife in someone's hand and tell them to stick it in someone's back. They can, but they can't. They can physically do it, but their ethics restrain them. Same thing." She clutched at Lon, very, very glad that he was there to hold her. Her legs felt like jelly, but his arms were wonderfully strong.

Lina, I…

I know, love. Don't worry about it. Everything's all right now. But the poor guy still looked miserable for her. Wasn't he sweet. **What's it about?**

I still can't tell you. There'll be more. Lon looked at Maximus. **That's strange. He can't hear us.**

Maybe it's because we're touching? If he can't hear us, can you tell me? I won't tell anyone.

Lon hesitated. **I don't know. I'm a Legionnaire, I'm a Networker. This is officially absolute secret business.** She could feel the tearing of his loyalties to them, to her.

But all you can tell me is that there'll be more.

I'm sorry, chérie. I'll make this up to you, I promise.

I trust you, darling. But I warn you, I'll want chocolate for this.

That made him smile ever so secretly, his eyes promising future rewards much better than chocolate.

Out loud within the room, Stoan had been berating her for mind control tendencies. She'd heard this enough times that she didn't feel she had to sit through the entire speech again.

"Wah wah-wah," Lon murmured to her in *Peanuts* mode.

But Lina didn't feel like joking. "If I did have Londo under mind control," she interrupted, "there'd be no way for you to stop me anyway. I could do it and we'd both be out of here in a nanosecond, out of your reach. I mean, if I were an evil telepath in Yanist-Glory's employ–"

"What do you know about this?" Hal asked sharply.

Lina blinked at him.

"Valiant," Stoan barked. "What kind of security breaches have you been committing?"

"Commander, I–"

Lina put her fists on her hips. "Well, *duh,*" she said. "Like I couldn't figure this out for myself. Wiley and Jae both said that mind control is right up Yanist-Glory's alley, and that there was some kind of current concern about a new per-mutation."

Stoan turned to Wiley, who stood with one finger pressed against his lower lip. Wiley glanced up to see the attention in the room focused on him.

"Ah, I believe there might have been a comment or two about that while she was under house arrest," he said. "Just in passing, no security breach for a Legion spouse."

Stoan turned to Lina. "And you just happened to remember it," he said. "Where did a Terran hear about Emperor Yanist-Glory?"

"I believe you know my husband…"

Now Stoan eyed Londo. Of course everyone here would know the true story of Lon's kidnapping as a child, ordered by the emperor.

Lon rubbed his nose. "All this is going to take a while, isn't it?" he asked rhetorically and then reached into his vest. He pulled out forty dollars, Canadian, handing it to Lina casually but quickly. "How about running out and getting people some reading material, hon?" he said.

"Hey!" Stoan yelled as Lina disappeared.

17

He whirled to face down Londo. "This is insubordination–"

"It is if she doesn't come back," Londo said evenly. "But she will. She knew who was here when she ported in, and she still came. She knows what's probably going to happen when Wiley gets through perfecting his gadget, but she'll come back. Have a little faith, Stoan."

"I don't think that was a wise thing to do," Hal told him sternly. "Things are in a balance here–"

"No, things are not in balance. Lina is getting run over," Londo snapped. "Stoan, back off. You've got her where you want her; be satisfied with that."

"Where is she?" Olympia asked curiously. She watched Londo as his eyes unfocused.

"Montreal," he said. "She's trying to decide what paraheroes would want to read. Go ahead, *chérie,* pick up anything that looks interesting. Keep it in English. Get some home decorating things, too. We've got to do some research." The furrow between his brows eased.

"I'd expect you to be swearing by now," Olympia told him. "What have you got up your sleeve, Lon? Or maybe she's the one who has?"

"Maybe true love has just mellowed me into a much nobler being, Demi." He put his hand over his heart and gave her an endearing expression.

"And maybe getting laid at last has," she replied sourly. He sniffed in condescension.

"A locator at the very least," Stoan was demanding of Wilder.

The multi-minded genius shrugged. "I had one on her while she was on Sarastor and she wore it faithfully. But it turned out that she could have ported it off at any time. Trying to chain up a teleporter– that's going to take some thought."

"Make sure the improved version of this thing doesn't harm her," Londo insisted. "No headaches, no nothing. We don't agree to this unless that much at least is met."

"I think I can provide that." Wiley tapped his padd at Londo as if to indicate that the proper data were there.

Stoan's eyes were dark. "Blood's ice and knife splinters."

"She'll be back," Wilder assured him, just as Lina popped back into the room.

"How about going out for some food now?" Londo said, as he dug into his vest pocket again.

"Londo!" Stoan bellowed. "Carolina– stay."

"Arf," she replied, dropping the pile of reading material onto the coffee table. She held up a couple of bills and silver. "Change," she said.

Lon held out his hand. It appeared there, and he deposited it back into his pocket. Lina brushed a few raindrops from her hair and took off the winter coat she'd had to port on. She ported it back into the utility room to dry out. Her sneakers were a little wet, but the unfinished floor could stand them. She didn't really want to be barefoot around these uniformed heroes.

"You don't do that again," Stoan ordered. "Consider yourself under house arrest."

"State your charges!" Londo demanded.

"Suspicion of using mind control."

"Lina was cleared of that days ago."

Stoan's lips pursed before he answered. "Not completely. This is a variant of that charge. You know what we're up against. Circumstances change; individual standings can morph during such times as this. I'm invoking Article…" Stoan glanced at his padd. "Fifteen, subsection 1.5."

Lon blew out a breath as he dug through his vest to get his own padd. He scrolled through. "Ah," he said. He didn't show the screen to Lina.

"Yes?" Lina asked hopefully, though his expression didn't inspire such.

"I can't tell you. But it gives him authority. Not here, but in AffSys space."

"Fabulous," Lina said. "Even if the charge were true, Stoan, I'm not aware of any law against mind control on Terran books. Where's your authorization to operate on this planet? I'll stay, but it's voluntary on my part."

She stooped to spread out the magazines and picked one up. "In the meantime I shall endeavor to be a polite hostess. See? I found a magazine that you don't have to be able to read to enjoy. And I'm sure it's right up your alley." She shoved a copy of *Hustler* at him.

Easy, love. We'll get through this.

He's such a stubborn bastard!

And no one else here is stubborn.

Lina rolled her eyes at Londo across the room and sighed. Stoan was speaking very loudly to Hal, poking the air in her direction, demanding that the ParaNet file official charges if that was what it was going to take. Hal tried to calm him down. Lina ran a hand through her hair, helplessly looking around the room, its inhabitants, and the situation. Shit. She was stuck.

Consider this a reception, Londo suggested.

Oh, ha ha.

Better than thinking about it as jail.

You know, there are more polite ways for them to do this. Are you supposed to be talking to me?

Now, Lina, just imagine if you really were a mind controller. Would this be too much?

She sighed again. **No, it would probably be too little. I hate to say it, but I see your point. But is this ever going to end? I mean, if Chimrin's sticking up for us doesn't count for anything, and apparently he's not impressed at all with the Three Worlds, what exactly will satisfy His Legionness over there?**

Londo scratched his head. **Maybe we could get someone to take over his mind using up-to-date methods? Then he could contrast and compare the sensations.**

And who would we get to volunteer? Nah, we'll have to hire a couple of big guys in pinstripe suits to make him see reason.

****I'll talk to some people about arranging that,**** Londo told her with a small smile. ****Just take it down a notch in the meantime, love. This too shall pass. We're peacemakers.****

****Blessed are the peacemakers.****

Wiley appeared at Lina's shoulder. "Before you two maim him, Lina, I need transport. We thought I had this figured out, but I was wrong. I need to return to my lab."

"I promise to be good."

Londo peered at Wiley's padd, then frowned when nothing made much sense. "How long will this take?" he asked.

Lina said, "When will I know what's going on?"

"Four, maybe five days," Londo told her. "Wiley?"

"An hour or two." Their friend snapped his screen off by flexing his ringed thumb. "It might take longer if my staff and I run into complications. I'm thinking of one troubling variable I hadn't taken into consideration."

"It takes a telepath to catch a telepath," Lina said in a low, conspiratorial voice.

"That's what we've told them." Londo held her gaze. "It's only a few who are doing this, *chérie,* but they're running the game. You don't have to like it, but you've got to play along."

"For four or five days. Okay. But time runs out after that."

"What will you do?" Wiley asked.

"I dunno. I'll find a way. If nothing else, I can be a royal pain and make life miserable for everyone else."

"Fair enough. Can I get a lift now?"

"Just a couple hours for this phase?" Londo asked Wiley again.

Wiley hefted the slightly charred globe of his inhibitor and tossed it a few inches into the air. "I'll have to break into Tishana records. Who knows how much time that will set me back?"

"Clock's ticking, Wiley."

"Yes. Maximum? Perhaps a half-day, Sarastoran. Eh, perhaps more. I'll divert all my people to this project."

Lina swallowed. "And when you come back…" He'd have a refined gadget to use on her. Probably to hold her until this whole thing was over. "How big a bottle of aspirin should I have standing by?"

"Aspirin?" Wiley's eyes moved as he sought the meaning. Then he glanced at Londo and gave a quirk of a smile. "No. That won't be necessary. Torture doesn't have to be part of this. I'm ready."

Lina ported him back to his main lab on Sarastor and turned to see Stoan glaring at her.

"Make yourself comfortable, Stoan," she told him sweetly. "It's going to be a while."

"Best movie."

"Uh." Lina thought. "*Star Trek IV,* but as a Trekkie I'm required by law to say that. There *might* be better movies out there. *Star Trek VI* has the all-time best closing credits, though."

"*Star Trek V?*" the Bolt asked.

"Doesn't exist. Never happened."

He snorted at that.

They asked her opinions and ratings on all kinds of things. More than that, they asked her the *why* behind her opinions. It was clear that they were trying to determine not only if she were a real Terran, but that she had a Terran viewpoint.

So Lina blathered on, delighted when Londo offered his own differing thoughts– he was so interesting!– and surprised when the other ParaNetters joined in.

"Best place in your area serving 24/7 breakfast."

"Omele–"

"That's not an Omelet Hut."

"Oh, but they have some nice food, as long as you have some Pepto for afterward."

Damon made a disgusted face. "I have a crew in the area who are hungry."

Lina nodded. "Then it's not that far for them to go to Chapel Hill. There are a few breakfast places that stay open all night. Good food, low prices."

"Address?"

"Uh. Dingo's is next to the Southern States store. I don't know the road name. Off of 54, right after the speed limit changes. The Rummy Tummy's just behind the big bank downtown, back where the old Library bar used to be."

Dragonlord crossed his arms over his laptop. "Addresses."

"I'm giving you perfectly good directions. Give me a map. Dingo's makes BLTs to die for, piled high on homemade bread. Vegetarian choices, too," she confided to Lon.

"I'm getting hungry myself," Olympia said.

The Guard stood grimacing behind Dragonlord. He pantomimed drinking from a tea cup, including an extended pinky. "Women can't give good directions," he declared. "They're always saying 'It's right next to the pansy patch by Marybelle's,' and they never come out with solid facts."

"I could find it," Olympia said. "It seemed fairly clear to me, if one knew the area."

"Point made," the Guardian said.

Once Lina had pointed out several locations on Mapquest, Dragonlord asked, "When I was at your house you were talking to a county commissioner. Who's the worst commissioner in your county? And why?"

Lina sighed. "Why can't you just ask me questions like 'Who won the World Series last year?' That's what they always ask in those World War II movies. Ask about things with straight answers. Of course I don't remember who actually won because who cares, it's not like it's basketball, but–"

"No one here knows the answers to these questions," Dragonlord said patiently. "You can't read our minds to find out the correct answer."

"Oh."

Eventually Damon ran out of questions and Lina went into the kitchen to consider the situation while Lon, Hal, and Damon spoke with Stoan. Apparently everyone was staying for the duration. Normal job rotation had been suspended, with the non-para, non-North American membership taking up the slack on the ParaNet satellite. Someone had brought in a pile of duffel bags alongside two new Port-a-lets sitting in the east wing.

More Port-a-lets in her home! Lina muttered darkly to herself as she searched the cabinets for the chips that had been in there before she moved in. She almost jumped when Olympia came up behind her.

"Playing hostess," she said. "You don't have to."

"No one's ever mistaken me for Martha Stewart," Lina replied. "I just need something to keep me busy. Frankly, I'm surprised that Stoan Face over there didn't take away all my knives."

"I think his magnetic powers can handle any knives, as long as they're metal." The corner of Olympia's mouth drew up into a pleasant smile. She had a Middle-Eastern skin tone and brown hair twisted back into the Scythian knot she always wore. Of course she looked perpetually late-twenty-something; she was Olympia, a world-class heroine since the Crimean War. Ouroboros, the jewel-patterned skin of the world-snake, wrapped around her waist outside her polka-dotted tunic coat, squirming as if it were still alive.

Lina blinked. Bolt had just been within her line of sight a minute ago, but now he reappeared, coalescing from a hand-sized spark. He set down two cases of assorted soft drinks on the breakfast table. "At your service," he announced to her. "Londo, Hal; one of you guys want to cool these down?" He'd no more said that than he was off again in a flash of his namesake light, to reappear a few minutes later with two cases of beer.

"What took you so long?" Olympia asked.

"They had to call for a price check."

"You got more plates, or do I eat this on my hand?" the Guard asked.

He stood next to the open fridge holding their coconut cake.

"No," Lina said. "Not that."

With the cake floating in front of him, the Guardian reached inside one of his gauntlets. He produced a metal strip that, with a flick of his hand, turned into a long-bladed knife.

"You heard her," Londo said as he came up at a fast walk. "Not that cake."

"Why?" Blithely the Guardian cut a large slice, digging his finger into the remaining cake's icing to sample. "It tastes okay to me."

"Put the thing down, Granger."

Londo's mouth set into a grim, almost deadly, line. Lina knew that this entire situation must be just as nerve-wracking to her husband as it was for her.

Londo?

You made this cake with your own hands. For me.

For Jae, too.

It's not Granger's. Coconut to remind them of their tropical island and what had blossomed there between them.

The Galactic Guardian, Granger, grabbed a saucer and plopped the large slice down on it.

"It's just a cake," Lina whispered to Lon. "I'll make another. This will go bad after a few days anyway."

"But–" Lon's bared teeth made him look feral. **He's been doing this to me lately. Sabotaging small things. Trying to make me look bad.**

Just a cake, darling. Breathe.

Someone's got to call him on it. I'm tired of it. I'm tired, his gaze took in the entire cavern, populated with the people who'd insisted on re-trying Lina, **of all this. It's got to stop.**

"We let them have this this time. There'll be so many other times for us, Lon. Better times."

His eyes darkened as he spared Granger a quick glance. "I'll pick my fights," he told her.

"Not over leftover cake. Not when you're already wrought up."

"No. Not now." He turned his back on Granger as the red-jacketed man sauntered out of the kitchen with his cake as if it were a prize. "He's a pig, Lina. Someday–"

Lina handed him the remaining cake and he took it to the dining room table. She ported in some paper dessert plates and determined not to tell the Networkers that they were for the cats' use.

"Men," Olympia said under her breath as those of that gender left the immediate area.

"You can't lump them all together," Lina replied.

"In some things," Puma told her. Somehow she'd been standing there and Lina hadn't noticed.

"Granger then," Olympia said. "In specific."

Lina started to chop her veggies with fervor into bite-sized pieces. Maybe Lon wasn't the only one agitated here. "I guess my guides agree with Londo."

Olympia turned to her. "What do you mean?"

"When you had that thing turned on and I was channeling, the guides kept pointing at him and making negative signs." She felt she had to explain further. "They do a lot of pantomime and symbology and such."

The Puma looked up from where she was trying out the dip with some celery. "You mean they gave him the finger?" She turned to Olympia. "It's not like that hasn't occurred to other people."

"Not the finger," Lina said. "They point to their heads and make 'crazy' signs, and then they showed me a picture. It's Janet Leigh in the shower, complete with creepy music. Oh, now its *Citizen Kane,* where Kane's on the podium with the big picture behind him. And there's a little Scrooge McDuck there, too, swimming in a vault of money. It's frustrating sometimes to figure it out."

Olympia grunted and her snakeskin writhed.

"He's not exactly Rico Carapella," the Puma said, referring to the legendary Guardian who had been Granger's predecessor, "but maybe it's that constant comparison that makes him the way he is."

Olympia looked at the Puma. "Do you really think so? I had such hopes for him when he was first assigned."

The Puma nodded. "Me too. He learned quickly and accomplished a lot of great things. The Argentine quake especially. That was amazing. Last year's floods in Bangladesh. But lately… Has it seemed to you he's become a slacker?"

Olympia took a breath before she spoke. "Granger likes his publicity. If nothing else, he works hard for that."

"Yes." Puma arranged the carrot sticks into a pretty container on the platter Lina was preparing. "That, too. I'm beginning to think that the Galactic Sentinels were too hasty in the recruiting department. Or maybe their training. We should ask that he be retrained." She glanced at Lina. "But maybe that's a conversation for some other time."

"I'm a Level Two," Lina said of her security clearance as Lon brought in the beer to be loaded into the fridge. "It comes automatically with marrying a Legionnaire, even if they put you in jail."

"Kee-rist, honey, they've run you through the ringer for marrying him, haven't they?" The Puma shook her clawed finger at Londo. "You do have some influence, you know. You could have gotten her off the hook."

Londo only murmured a growl. He was holding in his emotions, Lina knew. There were mantras going through his head that had to do with anger management techniques he'd learned through the years.

She could use some of that now, only for fear reduction. What were they going to do with her? There didn't seem to be any way she could get out of this without it reflecting horribly on Lon.

Breathe. Breathe.

Eventually they got around to the final exam.

"*Jeopardy?*" Lina asked as the computer game started on the TV. "What, you guys make a deal with Alex Trebek or something?"

"He's Canadian, you know," Londo said as he watched Dragonlord loading the arbitrary shuffle program.

Unfortunately, the five full games she had to play (with most of the ParaNet quietly giving their own guesses behind her, just out of her hearing; so much for them making sure they didn't use knowledge questions) never contained a *Star Trek* category. Instead they concentrated on sports– not her strong point.

"UNC! What is UNC-CH?" she shouted at one point, relieved to know one of the basketball answers at least.

"Why does she keep asking questions?" Stoan asked.

"Because it's *Jeopardy,* Stoan. Miami of Ohio."

Lina said, "I don't know that one, and I could hear you then, Londo. What is Miami of Ohio?"

"Doesn't count," Dragonlord declared. Londo made a disqualifying beeping sound as Lina switched categories.

"Ohh… whatshisface," Lina answered at one point. "You know, the guy. The guy."

"Lina, you know this one," Londo urged.

"Of course I do. A child would know this. It's…" Lina pulled at her hair. "He had hemorrhoids."

"Hemorrhoids? Ew."

"That's why the Battle of Waterloo was held up, because he couldn't sit in the saddle, and that's why he lost. Connie Willis kept harping on that in her book. It was about time travel, about time nexuses and why things go the way things go, and it rained just before Waterloo and that guy had hemorrhoids. Napoleon! Who was Napoleon? Shoo!" Lina slapped her knee in defeat.

"I think you ran out of time on that one," Dragonlord said dryly.

"Points given for hemorrhoids, Damon," Hal suggested.

"Hemorrhoids are never worth points."

Lina knew she was just awful. "I don't do well with names. Doesn't this game come in a multiple-choice version?"

She heard the end of a women-and-their-feeble-minds joke from Granger across the room.

But she didn't do badly overall, and there were four audio Daily Doubles that she bet to the hilt and won. She missed one Final Jeopardy but got all four others, following Lon's instructions for all-or-nothing betting. No, not bad at all.

He studied her totals. "I think we can finish up a few rooms with that," he said. "This is American dollars, right? Bedroom, wine cellar…"

"We don't do payouts," Damon said as he unplugged his console. "It was a game."

"Come on, honeymoon along the Riviera at least," Lon urged.

Damon clicked his briefcase shut over his electronic equipment. "Not with you." He patted Londo on the cheek. "But thanks for the thought."

"So. Am I Terran born and bred?" Lina asked.

"I never thought you weren't," Damon replied. He looked expectantly at Stoan.

"Final decisions aren't in yet," the Legion Commander declared, but a swarm of tiny beeps masked his final syllable. The Networkers' belts all chirped with electronics. Lon glanced to the flat-screen TV and it flashed on to ECN, the Emergency Call Network. The network's screen crawl reported an oil tanker sinking in a South China Sea storm. The crew was at risk. Fuel was leaking. It would be a good-sized job.

Hal reviewed the room, pointing out who would handle containing the oil, who would see to the safety of the crew...

"Lon, you patch up the tanker."

"Stoan can help me," Lon volunteered, glancing over at the Legion leader.

"Good idea," Hal said before Stoan could protest. "Thanks, Stoan."

"Who does that leave here?" Stoan finally asked, unamused.

"Me," Hal declared. "Now get to it, everyone."

Lina watched them all dissolve into sparkles. Lon raised his eyebrow at her, cut his eyes at his father and back to her. **Now for the grand inquisition,** he managed to say before he was gone.

18

Hal turned to her once the room was empty. "I wouldn't call it an inquisition," he told her. "Just a friendly chat between father-in-law and new daughter-in-law."

"Are you going to mind-monitor me, too?"

He gave her a bemused look. "Stoan's orders. I'm not supposed to mind-talk with you."

"No, we wouldn't want anyone to mind control Maximus."

In the background ECN had switched back to regular CNNi and the report of the morning's train wreck in Iowa. The on-scene reporter mentioned Carolina Starhart, who along with Bolt had saved the passengers.

Maximus turned the TV off remotely by using some combination of powers. "Not bad," he said. "Your third day back on Earth, and you've already made CNN."

"Um, actually, I think I was on there yesterday. For our date."

He nodded and sat down on the couch, motioning for her to sit, too. His gray eyes were sharp as steel shards, never leaving her. "You're right. I forgot that. I saw the celebrity shows with the mystery woman and Valiant doing the town. Let me guess; Lon picked the dress."

She shook her head. "Nope. I did. It was better than the one he wanted me to wear."

He gave a bark of a laugh at that. "So, are you happy with the coverage? On TV, I mean."

"What?"

"Are you happy that you're on CNN?"

"Why in the world would I ever want to be on CNN?"

Hal picked up a beer can and sipped from it. "Marrying someone like Valiant– You must have known there'd be lots of publicity."

"Well, no one knows we're married yet and I'm already on CNN. I wanted us kept private. Lon's the one who said we'd have to go public." She frowned. "And the Three Worlds make it kind of imperative, even though we think that I'll just be a glorified office manager." She looked up at him. "So that's what you meant."

"What?"

"The other night. When you said that some people would do anything to be linked to a celebrity."

"Maybe."

"Well, hell, if I wanted to be famous I would have… learned more things. How to talk in front of people. How to wear makeup, what clothes to wear. How to be a lady, for pete's sake. Lon knows I don't know any of that, and he still decided to marry me. What he should have picked was more the Princess Di kind: rich, glamorous, genteel. He picked D, none of the above. I think–"

Hal leaned back farther in the cushions, studying her. "What do you think?"

She hesitated. "I think that that's three-quarters of what Stoan has against me. He was rooting for Lon to marry Aiko. I had a chance to look up her record. I saw the biography they showed at her funeral. She was Princess Di and Olympia combined. And I know that Lon and she–"

"Lon never loved her. He was in serious like, but never love."

She hit the arm of the couch with her fist. "Tell that to Stoan. What the hell– I'm sorry; I cuss a lot. I'm trying to stop. What the *heck* is the Legion doing trying to tell the ParaNet what to do? This isn't their territory. Why don't y'all just tell him to take a flying leap? Of course, with that ring of his, it wouldn't do much good. Tell him to leave us in peace."

Hal grinned. "I'd like to see that. He does seem a little full of himself these days. But he's been under a lot of strain. There's something going on right now."

"Yanist-Glory and mind control."

"Yes. It's suddenly become a major problem. An immediate one. He's just being cautious, and in the process he's steamrolling you. And Lon."

"I hope their friendship can take it."

"Tell me about your family," Maximus said.

So he could switch subjects just as abruptly as Londo. Lina answered his questions about her father's fits of violent anger, about how her mother lived with it by making the family bend, to keep out of his way.

Hal wanted to know about her powers, why she didn't call them powers and thought everyone could do what she could– minus the porting, of course. He sat there openly, never crossing his arms or legs, never closing himself off from what she was saying. "So your parents choose not to believe you can do these things?" he asked.

"I learned to hide it early on. But every now and then they'd catch me. That's when the belt came out. And after Dad finally had his breakdown and found religion, then I got sermons on what a sin it was to try to attract attention that way." She blew out a breath she didn't know she'd bottled up. "It was so great when I could finally leave home. You can't begin to imagine."

"I can't imagine anyone not being thrilled to have a child. Not wanting to help them and support them all along the way."

Line smiled at him. "Well, they say that adoptive parents have the biggest hearts."

"I can't believe that anyone wouldn't–"

"Believe it."

"At least your mother loves you."

"Love?" Lina shook her head. "She's fond of me, yes. After all, I lived with her for a long time. She likes the family dog; she likes me."

Lina could feel the direction Hal's mind was moving in without reading him, but she let him say it out loud.

"So you didn't get any love at home. And then Londo came along–"

"And he loved me." She nodded. "We've discussed this. Talk to him. It probably started out with a lot of rebound effect, but it's become so much more than that."

"Jumping into marriage after only a few days–"

"We'd shared minds. We know each other. He said he couldn't live without me and I couldn't imagine living without him."

"You could have lived together."

"That's what he suggested after I turned him down. But we both knew that wouldn't be enough. Londo needs permanency. I need…"

Hal waited.

"I get scared and stop myself. Sometimes I need to be pushed."

"So he browbeat and harangued–"

"He out and out bullied," Lina declared. "I don't like to be bullied."

"He does that a lot," Hal observed.

There was a sparkle in Lina's eyes. "And some people let him get away with it," she said. "Some people seem to have spoiled him just a tad."

Hal met her gaze. "Maybe. He's had a difficult life."

"He has. And now it's time for him to learn that he can't go around bullying people. Leading them, giving them orders when he has to, yes. But on a personal level– no."

"So you're going to change him."

"The wife's first duty." Lina gathered some empty glasses that had been left on the coffee table. "No. He's going to change himself. He's going to see that there's more to life than being a parahero, and that during that other part he can mellow out. Relax. Enjoy." She took her load of glassware into the kitchen, knowing that Hal would follow her. "Goal A is to see he gets a chance to enjoy life."

Hal considered. "And is he going to enjoy his new duties as Protector of the Three Worlds? What is that going to entail?" he asked as she ran dishwater in the old sink.

She turned on the lamp she'd plugged in yesterday to this, one of the few working sockets on the main level. The last streaks of daylight had left the broad Wyoming sky that showed through the wall of windows, and the snowy slopes of the mountains had gone from blinding white to faint blues into deep purples. Now they lay dark under cold winter stars.

"Sometimes I wonder if we're doing what they really want us to do," Lina said slowly. "They gave us the authority to set our own agenda."

"With no paperwork, no official deputization in writing."

"That's a big problem," she sighed as she squirted detergent into the stream of water. "We'll be responsible for getting everything we do in writing to make up for it. Otherwise, I'm just a mind controller who's duped two of the most powerful beings in the galaxy to enforce some crazy scheme."

Hal settled at one of the chairs that she'd brought in with her dining set. "So this agenda of yours– what's the Terran part of it?"

"It seems to me– well, it seemed to all of us– that Earth's biggest problem is disunity. The inability to accept others' differences. Plus what Jae calls a "child-like impatience." The scramble to grab for everything right now, without giving a damn about tomorrow's consequences. Somehow we've got to bring people together and make them realize what they've got, what they need to preserve."

"So does that make you Nixon or Stalin?"

Lina looked at him sharply to see if he was joking or not. Hard to tell. "How about Martin Luther King? Rachel Carson? Eleanor Roosevelt or Thoreau?" she finally suggested, then grunted at herself. "I've got to start thinking more globally, less American. More galactically," she corrected herself. "We have a lot of research to do. So much to learn."

He nodded approval at that. Lina looked out the window, down the snow-covered slopes to the long, frozen lake below, barely visible now. "So if we're all Thoreau-ing up here– oh, that didn't sound right– that must be Walden Pond," she said. "Lon said it didn't have a name." She tried to look past the covering of ice. "I wonder if it has any fish in it."

"It does. Pretty good eating."

"Ack! We don't eat our pets!"

Hal snorted and then joined her at the window. "I noticed that the cats aren't here."

"We were going to move them in tonight or tomorrow now that the place is warmed up and semi-organized. I guess that won't be possible now."

"No. A few more days, Lina."

"I haven't given Faf her meds yet. I should do that before Wiley gets back."

Before Hal could offer his opinion, the elderly cat appeared in Lina's arms. She'd been asleep, and the port hadn't awakened her.

Lina set her down on the kitchen table, and the cat began to stir. Lina prepared the pill gun and then woke up Fafhrd completely just in time for the pill to go down her throat. "Once more, Faffy-taffy," Lina said and squeegeed some gel onto her index finger. Then she pried open the cat's jaws a second time to transfer the gel onto the roof of Fafhrd's mouth and what remained of the cat's upper teeth. Fafhrd worked on it as if it had been peanut butter stuck to the top of her mouth.

"That's a good girl. Yes, you are."

The cat smacked her lips with gusto. When she finished, she looked around the cavern and eyed Lina uncertainly. Then she met Hal's eyes.

"Blink slowly," Lina advised.

Without questioning, Hal did as he was told, and Fafhrd returned the motion.

"It's to calm her. It means you don't mean her any harm."

"Ah." Hal blinked again.

Fafhrd jumped down from the table. Lina returned to the sink to wash her hands before returning to the dishes. She asked, "Is all this security hubbub why Lon couldn't find you for so long?"

Hal was watching the elderly cat explore its new environs. She must approve of the couch, because she stretched up on its side and then began to scratch vigorously at it. "I was doing some recon concerning the problem, yes. It's spurred this push."

"Okay. He was frantic because you wouldn't check in. He wanted you to attend the wedding. He really did."

"Yes." Hal blew out a long sigh. "I understand now. But 'Starheart'?"

Lina's gaze took in the expanse of her new home, now fading into dark corners and caverns, and her eldest cat wandering. "Lon's going to like having cats. It's difficult to be angry at the universe when a cat is purring on your lap. Why not just send me to Aldierra and keep me out of the way with Jae there? I might be able to start Three Worlds working."

The sudden subject change stopped him for a moment. Maybe he was just shocked that she could do it, too. "That possibility was suggested," he said carefully.

"But Stoan nixed it." Lina's mouth was bitter. "So there's this *thing* that's going to keep me under control…"

Hal didn't confirm.

"Put me in a hyperspace chamber for a few days," she said.

"Also suggested," Hal said curtly. "Change subject."

Frustration and fear raged within Lina. "Would someone please tell Stoan that a little extra information never hurt any– Ohmigod."

She went white, clutching her hands into fists, her eyes unfocused. Hal felt the edge of communication through Lon.

Lina! Don't disturb him! He needs to concentrate.

Ohmigod, Londo. They're trying to kill him!

Kill who? Struggling to regain full contact with Londo, Hal slipped into the telepathic conversation.

Hal– It's Jae. He's in the middle of a battle on Aldierra. Some sort of coup attempt, maybe. Lina, can you get a picture to port? Don't port without me, whatever you do!

Oh god. If it hadn't been for that stupid machine we could have had a picture of Aldierra to port to. Damn. I can't go through Jae– he's got to concentrate. Maybe… maybe Admiral Bracken?

Hal watched as beads of sweat broke out on her forehead. Her eyes squeezed tightly shut as she searched. **I think he's unconscious. Or worse. Lon, you're going too deep. Stand back, don't distract him.**

Câlisse de tabarnac! Lina, get a picture!

I'm trying. That first officer– He's out, too. Aldierra! Aldierra, help me! Give me a picture of this. –What? A test? Aldierra, you crazy planet, he could be killed! This is no time for a test!

She slammed her fists down on the table. "Crazy planet!"

Get that picture!

I'm looking around for some friendly local devas. I can't get… Wait, there's one. Shit, she's backing Aldierra. Come on! Cut us a break! He's the freaking Minister for Aldierra, for pete's sake!

She pulled her hair back as she thought. **Let's try one of the ships. I can picture them—** Suddenly she gasped, falling backward only to have Hal catch her. "Holy shit! I didn't think anything could do that!"

What happened?

She cut me off, Lon. Aldierra's put up some kind of– wall or something. Almost like being in hyperspace or bumping into that thing of Wiley's. It's a complete blank out there.

Silence on his end for a long moment. **So Jae's on his own.**

She said it was some kind of test. Lina clapped her hands to her mouth, afraid that she was going to cry here in front of Maximus. That she was going to give things away in front of Hal, and it would all be her fault. That Jae was going to get hurt or killed.

Lon's warmth tinged with his anxiety reached her. **It's all right, chérie, drop it. You're not going to get by an entire planet. Jae's a professional. He's been in more tight situations than you can count. Just stay alert. Be ready to move when Aldierra lets you.**

All– all right.

And don't you move an inch without me in tow.

Yes, Londo. Hurry back!

19

Through the thin cushions of Jae's seat, the shuttle's engines shook and roared as they caromed in for a landing on one of Aldierra's ocean cities. The sky was overcast with inky black clouds that had also darkened their first landing site, a thousand miles from here. Jae remembered the clean green and white globe Aldierra had showed them at their Investiture. There had been no black.

He and the fleet's chief officers disembarked through a biotube and made their way to enclosed walkways. His escorts wore masks over their noses and mouths as well as tight-fitting eye lenses to keep out pollutants and acid air. They didn't issue him such protection, so Jae used his power to command the elements and wove a layer of fresh atmosphere around himself, securing it in place with his intention. The field would constantly renew itself with little conscious effort.

They met up with others, and then used a squadron of small flying vehicles to whisk them low across a bay to the conference center where this world's leaders waited for them. From his vantage point Jae saw people– men– in the streets throwing all manner of objects at buildings and ground vehicles. They attacked each other with weapons as well as their bare hands. There was no sign of authorities moving to control it.

"You can't tell me that this is business as usual," Jae said to Merson, the lieutenant who was assigned as his bodyguard. Merson had been the first one to volunteer to sign the agreement with the Speaker. Since then, dozens of others had volunteered as well.

"No, it's not," Merson admitted as he fumbled in a small compartment. His hand emerged with a mask for Jae, which Jae accepted but did not put on. "I shouldn't be telling you this, but ever since the Ultimatum some parts of society have crumbled. Some men have gone crazy with fear. Some claim that they were unbalanced by the very act of being contacted by the Speaker herself. It is said that they saw a light too bright to look at, the light of her soul reflected between her goldens."

Shards, but these people had one-track minds, Jae thought.

"Why isn't anyone doing anything about all this?"

"Hundreds of thousands died in the riots on the first day following the Ultimatum, Minister," Merson said. "Another fifty thousand at least have died since then. I've had a chance to see only a few reports; I don't know the entire story of what's gone on while we were in hyperspace. We're at a loss as to what to do about the violence, or whether indeed anything should be done. The Three Worlds must help us. The Blind Souls— those who saw the light too bright to look at— perhaps they are holy, a part of this new order that Aldierra wishes."

"And perhaps they're just unbalanced. Or using it as an excuse to break something," Jae replied sourly. "The first thing to do is to tell these people that they can't use the Ultimatum as an excuse to riot. The second thing is to order your police force to gather up the rioters and see that doctors pick out the ones who are truly mentally ill. Throw the others in jail for a few days until they calm down. Then have them pay off their fines in repair work."

Merson gaped at Jae as if he were the wisest person he'd ever heard. "I will relay your orders. Thank you, Minister."

They arrived at a building whose lower levels displayed ornate decorative architectural details. It towered into the sky to a domed cap, and Jae couldn't help but think he was entering a giant phallus.

A flight of broad steps led up to an airlock. Merson and the other officials pulled off their masks when they were inside. Here the air was warm and musty, but apparently it was preferable to the stuff outside. Jae chose to keep his own personal air conditioning on until he could study what it was that everyone else was breathing.

"The heads of state are expecting us on the third floor," Admiral Bracken explained as he joined them. Bracken, a broad man compared to most of the men around him, was resplendent in full, medaled uniform. Like all his people, his skin was orangish in hue.

Jae. Jae!

Jae held up his hand for silence. "I'm getting a message. It's the Speaker," he told the men. They bowed their heads in reverence and let him communicate.

Lina. What's up?

After hearing her situation of being confronted by the ParaNet and Stoan, Jae contacted Londo. Lon was being secretive. Jae hated it when Lon acted that way. His mind was structured by his intense loyalties and duty. When he didn't want to give up any information, he was uncompromising.

Damn it, Lon, tell me something. I'm Unlimited Clearance. What can it be that I can't know about?

Look. Hal's listening in.

Hi, Jae. You sound funny this way.

Hi, Hal. You're an Unlimited too, right? Give me something. Londo?

It's not just Unlimited, it's... Hal, can't I give him a clue?

Hell, he's on Aldierra. How's he going to interfere in the plan?

Jae tried to piece things together. **It's something to do with mind control. Does Stoan think that Lina's going to control someone new?**

Not Lina.

Is it bigger than a tool box? C'mon, Londo. Give me some hard information.

It's... it's... Stoan thinks Lina's part of this new conquest scheme of Gloryboy.

Still hovering over that? I thought he'd cleared her. Does he have proof of anything?

There's—

Londo cut off.

The others were watching him as if he were receiving communication from God. "A visual comm link," Jae snapped. "I have to communicate with Earth. Quickly!"

Men scrambled to make calls and set up the line. They knew the Speaker was from a planet called Earth; this must be important.

They settled Jae in a small room with a special subspace line that linked through four interstellar networks in order to reach Earth. Jae knew Lon's personal comsite and patched through the final connection. He also knew that at the very least, the line would be tapped on this end. He didn't care. Admiral Bracken and a few of his aides, including Merson, crowded the room, listening in.

The picture came through clearly: Londo, looking as if he hadn't slept in a week. Members of Lon's ParaNet were gathered behind him in a cavern.

"What the orb's going on there?!" Jae demanded. "Stoan, why are you harassing Lina?"

He argued with Stoan. Lina calmed him down. Jae didn't like the fact that Lina couldn't get a picture of Aldierra from him in case she or Lon needed it on an emergency basis, but what could he do? Stoan was in one of his moods again. He'd been in this one ever since Lina had come onto the scene. Both were as stubborn as the other. Jae fumed. He couldn't accomplish anything from this end, except to make Stoan madder at Lina and by association, angry with Londo.

"You two be careful," was the only thing Jae could think of to say.

"We will. Starheart out." Lina and Lon both smiled conspiratorially at him, and he couldn't help but smile back. Those two. Separately they were wonders; together they were dynamite. They'd be able to handle whatever was going on. He hoped. Something dinged at the back of his mind, trying to tell him something, but he didn't know what it was. Maybe it was just an interior signal to stay alert. That much he could do.

Jae tried to assure the admiral that the Speaker shouldn't be in any real danger. Valiant and Maximus, as well as Magnos, the Commander of the Legion himself, were all there to protect her. This seemed to satisfy Bracken.

They ambled upstairs using several grand staircases instead of the lifts. Perhaps the Aldierrans wanted to impress Jae with the grand craftsmanship of the building. It was overly large, but in a graceful way. Much of the architecture reminded him of trees towering overhead, like the trees of home on Feith, or maybe the trees of Earth. Funny that these people should destroy most of their trees and then preserve the memory in metal and ceramics. By the time they achieved the second flight, Admiral Bracken was puffing mightily.

The oval conference room they came to was spacious, a majority of its outer walls filled with windows that gave a commanding view of the city. For some stylistic reason its dark ceiling drooped in the middle, crushing the open effect. A square table of some size filled up that central space– precisely the spot Jae would *not* have located it– with rows of chairs just behind those that sat at the table. The walls were lined with still more chairs. Nearly every one was filled with uniformed men.

He wondered if they were all military, or if formal fashion imitated a military look. Could some be relatives of each other? Colors were important, he'd learned. The culture was divided into various houses and sub-houses, which used colors and patterns to identify themselves. The majority of these uniforms ran to greens, reds and violets. An occasional orange or yellow stuck out in the crowd.

At the table's largest chair sat the white-haired Patriarch Lupoff, his skin a deeply burnished bronze complemented by his blood-red uniform and gold medals. The Patriarch's Great Council flanked him, a dozen strong. Then came the regional governors. Heads of families of the larger sectors, all involved in some sort of supra-military government. At the end of the line of importance were aides to everyone.

Admiral Bracken and Jae stood before their assigned chairs on the opposite side of the table from the Council. Bracken introduced him to the group. They watched the Investiture of the Three Worlds as a holoprojection above the table.

The Patriarch nodded when it was through. Of course he had been informed of everything days ago. He made a lengthy speech about how this was a new era on Aldierra, and how the people of the world were prepared to work for the betterment of the planet now not just to save their own lives, but because they cared, they truly cared.

Jae didn't believe a word of it.

The man was a politician. He said things to make himself look good and to save himself in the bargain. He thought he could fool this planet, at least long enough to last his lifetime. Beyond that– he didn't give a damn.

One of the Council members rose and made a very pretty speech as well, with just as much honesty and commitment. There came another speech from another Council member, and another and another. Jae nodded at them, letting them ramble on to get their honor points from whomever they thought needed to give them some. They certainly wouldn't come from him. Blah-blah never accomplished anything but null-time gained. Time was one thing these people did not have.

Somewhere in the speeches he started to think of Lon's smile, the quiet one, and how his cheek had felt against Jae's neck. Lon had turned over and Jae lay on him, caressing him while able to feel that Lon really connected this time, really felt the touch of his skin, of his sweat. Of his lips on his, his tongue sliding over him, tasting him. The music of Lon's soft sighs, his deep chuckles. His gasps. The power and depth of their lovemaking.

During the next speech he thought of how Lon still was afraid to use his strength on Jae. He must somehow show Lon that he couldn't hurt him. They could play rough now and then. Londo would enjoy playing rough. Jae smiled to himself to think of some things they could do.

But none of that would get anything done here. After the speaker sat down, Jae saw another medaled politico prepare to stand up. Instead, Jae rose from his seat and brought his staff into reality. He did not knock it on the floor. He merely held it as a symbol of office.

"I'm grateful that you think enough of the Three Worlds to stage this ceremony," he told the group. "But is there anyone here who has anything of substance to say?" He looked around at the group. Some shifted in their seats at his words. One or two seemed amused. The others sat stonily where they were.

"I'm not hearing what Aldierra has ordered. She wants honest plans, long-range plans, and no tricks. What I'm hearing are empty words that will never be acted upon. I can only surmise that they are time-wasters to let the deadline pass and then be dropped. I'm not fooled. Aldierra isn't, either. How can we format a real, genuine future for Aldierra? If you help the planet, you'll be helping yourselves and your children. Your families. Perhaps you should think of it that way to get started."

The Patriarch lurched out of his chair. It took a little doing. Unlike most of the others, he was chubby and well past his middle age. His words were tinged with spittle. "Are you calling us liars?"

"Like all of the Chosen, I'm a telepath," Jae said, rather amazed that he could do so honestly.

The men around the table gaped. Some coughed in consternation.

Jae's jaw jutted as so much conspiracy now spun sideways in the room. Was it getting darker in here? The coughing increased.

"Danger," he barked. "Get down! There are people outside who–"

The bright orange beam of a blaster split the air to the left of him. Jae threw himself to the other side. Three men in blue uniforms and gas masks stood in the nearest doorway, two leveling guns at him. Jae summoned his wrist armaments. Instantly they clacked into formation from under his sleeves. He blasted the one gun with seifer coms, the energy running around his hand to focus in the direction he pointed. Jae missed his shot with the second gun, but it gave him time to dissolve the other weapon into pure oxygen using his own power.

Coughing filled the room like staccato gunfire. There was something in the air, some kind of gas– Jae could sense it clearly now. Not quite a poison, but one that felt like it could paralyze. Three men in his line of vision collapsed. His own aura of fresh air had kept the effects from him.

A wall blew open. And another. Soldiers poured into the room from all sides, some masked; most not. Two different colors of uniforms differentiated them: blue or green. Ready blasters whined with power. The men in blue fired at the people around the table. The greens scrambled to return the attack. Others seemed to be shooting just to add to the confusion. Another color came into play, white-orange crossfire that scored the room heated the air almost beyond bearing.

Londo's mind touched his, then backed off. Jae up-ended a chair and grabbed four more to form a barrier, commanding them into laser-resistant rezdar.

The blasters that he could see he ordered to gas. Solids were always more difficult to persuade to change, but the process raised the metal's temperature just before it converted. He could use that here. The gunmen's hands sizzled and they screamed.

He didn't know which army he was disarming. At least fewer shots crossed the air. He targeted dozens with both his own powers and the seifer coms. More people streamed into the room, already jammed with masked soldiers and conference participants. Ally shot ally just because they were all too close together. Jae piled more chairs around himself. Across the table, the Patriarch was protected behind a solid wall of bodyguards.

The air of the room was easy enough to convert into a fresh mixture of oxygen and nitrogen, with a balance of carbon dioxide. He ionized it as well.

With a sweep of his hands, Jae stood to his full height in the middle of his chair fortress. Tendril sparks of lightning spat across the room until a solid grid of pulsing, electrified runnels crackled just above everyone's head. Low thunder rattled the very walls.

Soldiers dropped to the floor, wailing in fright. Others stampeded for the doors.

"Secure the doors!" Jae shouted. Someone had the presence of mind to do so. Lightning sealed the open walls.

They were all locked in here with him now. Good. This many, maybe seventy armed men, he could handle.

Maybe.

Lina looked up from where she'd slammed her fist on the table. "I'm sorry about this. I really am," she said to Hal before she disappeared.

He jumped up. **Londo, she's—** Then he heard cursing from upstairs. He flew there in seconds, into their bedroom.

"You crazy damned planet," Lina muttered. She stood dressed now in a very clinging, open-sided tunic, obviously nothing on under it except tights, leaning over Lon's dresser and braiding a strand of hair in a stand-up mirror. "I don't care. It's not fair." She paused. "You're what?" She opened a drawer for some covered bands and slammed it shut. "Crazy planet. Yes, I'm talking to *you.* Oh, the big expert on human psychology, you are!"

"Lina," Hal said in his sternest voice.

"I'm sorry." She glanced at his reflection. "Tell them when they get back that I apologize profusely. I know this isn't making a good impression, but people's lives are at stake. We've got to go help out!"

Her eyes took on a misty look, and Hal heard her broadcast echoing through his link to Londo.

She says a few more minutes and then she'll stop blocking us. She claims he's fine. So far.

Good. I'll warn my team here that I'm leaving.

"I'm sorry, I'm sorry," she told Hal. Flowers appeared on the dresser, crocus and daffodils. She picked petals off them quickly, to pin into her hair.

"Stoan will be furious," Hal said. "He'll blacklist the Network."

"How many times can I say I'm sorry? But as I understand it, the Legion has no authority here, so the only thing I'm messing up in that respect is Stoan's attitude." She paused. "And it also reflects back on Londo. I'm sorry; I told him I never wanted to do anything that would embarrass him, but some things just can't be helped."

"The Network—"

"So you can haul me to court after all this. I'm operating on the fact that I am a citizen of the United States and subject to its laws and not to the ParaNet. That'll be my plea. I know y'all have some kind of international overrides, but well, dammit, if you're going to arrest me, arrest me. Don't just make me a prisoner in my own house. There are laws. Somewhere there are laws against this. I think I've been a damned good sport about it all, but enough is enough."

"You have to stay here. Jae can take care of himself. Or you can port Lon there—"

"We're a team." She turned to him, her face white and grim. "And like it or not, every last person on Aldierra knows me. If you must know the truth, they're a little terrified of me. If I go along I can speed things along, maybe prevent some bloodshed. They won't kill each other if they're too busy peeing in their pants."

"I can stop you," Hal said, and took her arm gently in his unbreakable grip.

She looked down at his hand there and ported, appearing three feet away from where she'd been. "I don't think so," she said. "You can probably knock me out, but then I won't be able to port Lon anywhere. And I don't think you really want anything to happen to Jae."

Lina's mind raced. "Look, we'll be back just as soon as everything's sewn up. If Jae's hurt, we'll need to take him to medical facilities. Five minutes, Londo. And if he's still under attack, we need to do something to help him."

They ported down to the kitchen. Londo appeared there a moment later, dripping oil and water onto the cement subfloor. He looked first at Hal, and then expectantly to Lina.

"Aldierra says that this is a chance for Jae to establish his reputation there," she said. "She doesn't want him to have to share the limelight. So if at all possible, we should defer to him."

"Defer to–?"

"They've heard of you there, Lon, across thousands of lightyears. They already respect you just for that. Him they've never heard of except as some kind of mythological Last Feithi."

Lon wiped oily water out of his hair. "And lord knows they know you. So if he isn't killed or permanently maimed–"

"She thinks that this will make the Aldierrans respect him as a warrior or something. They understand warriors."

"This is all for a show?" Hal asked in disbelief.

"Crazy planet," Lina muttered, shaking her head.

"Now look, *chérie,* it makes sense," Lon told her. "These guys have just finished trying to invade the capital world of the Affiliated Systems, for god's sake, and they thought they had a good chance. Hell, they had a great chance, if you hadn't spotted them. They weren't expecting you. These people are going to respect someone who can go up against huge odds and win."

"Wonderful," Lina said unhappily.

"If you're dealing with a mule, sometimes you've got to hit him in the head to get his attention," Lon declared. He switched his attention to Hal. "*Bon ben, s'il faut l'faire, on va l'faire.* We've got to do this." He made a sour face. "It'll probably get me a thousand demerits, maybe even suspension from Stoan, but there's no way around it. We'll be back when we get back."

"You won't get any demerits," Hal said. "I'm coming with you. As proctor."

Lina's eyes went wide. "You'd do that?"

"Someone's got to keep an eye on you two," Hal said. "So. What's our plan?"

Jae jumped out from behind his barricade but kept low to the ground. Deprived of their overheated guns, most of the soldiers had reached for knives to finish their work. Knives could be vaporized, too. And human metabolism could be slowed down. Jae had to concentrate so he didn't slow it too much. Killing should be a last resort.

Men collapsed in a great circle around him as he took them out one by one. He didn't care which side they were on, but most of the nearer knife wielders wore blues and reds. As each dropped, the men around them warily eased back a step.

He cleared a space twenty feet from himself, careful to avoid those at the conference table. Jae rapped his staff on the floor and stood up. The room fell silent. Everyone turned to him, not all of their own accord.

"Cease fighting," he commanded. "Everyone! It is useless to resist. There will be no more death here today. I am the Minister for Aldierra, and my mission is one of life."

No one dropped their weapon.

From out of the stilled crowd leapt a soldier, aiming himself at Jae. Jae stepped back over a body to take a fighting stance, and caught the assailant on the way down. He had a knife. Jae let him keep it. He wouldn't use his seifer coms yet, or his body armor. Time these boys were taught a lesson in basics.

They circled each other. The soldier feinted. Jae kicked him in the chin and he fell backward, but recovered quickly. He went in for a slash. Jae ducked out of the way and then lunged behind him. He aimed for the pressure points back there, a hard poke to the cervical meridian chi point. The man went down.

Another soldier darted from the crowd, joined by another and another. Three against one, but the others seemed content to watch and do nothing, even though their colors: green and blue, indicated that enemies stood side by side. All three new attackers wielded double knives. They wove around Jae, but he held himself like chained lightning, striking only when one got too near. Bobbing around another to kick him in the balls, leaving him down for the count. Wearing the last one out until he made a clumsy move. Jae kicked him in the gut, chopping into his jugular. He dropped.

Now more swarmed on him. As soon as one fell, another would join the fight. The bodies piled. Secure footing became more difficult. And apparently he'd missed some blasters. Jae ducked behind one knife-wielder just as he sensed somebody taking aim. He dispatched more than a dozen men by positioning them between the blaster fire and himself. He commanded the guns to gas, but this time held them a few moments at the metallic vapor points, burning hell out of their owners' hands. The answering shrieks were quite satisfactory.

Jae's vision blurred from a blow to his ear. A warm runnel of blood meandered down his forehead, but still he kept on through the almost unbearable heat and odds. The confines of the room, the unconscious and dead bodies on the floor, slowed the advancing enemy enough so that he could handle them. Barely.

He had to show these men their better. He was Legion. He was Feithi.

He fought until he could barely raise his arms. One of his sleeves was slashed and bloody from a knife. One of the buckles on his boot hung where someone had cut it, but the blade hadn't gotten through to his skin.

Still he didn't raise his body armor.

He half-crouched among the bodies, men waiting in a very wide semi-circle around him. They watched him calculatingly, well aware of the fallen, and heard the groans of the injured.

"Any more?" Jae asked, looking around the room. No one moved.

Time for his finishing gesture, the bold one he liked to use as an aperitif to scare the hell out of his enemies. This was not the fine sewing of electrons he'd done before. Now he steeled his weak arms to reach for the heavens, spoke to the sky– and jumped in spite of himself at the violence of the circle of lightning he brought down. It crashed just outside the room's windows, shattering them as it struck all around this building. The floor smoked, the air thundered in hundreds of echoes.

Angry planet. Very angry planet! He'd watch that in the future.

The men who were standing fell to their knees in terror.

"At last!"

Jae didn't have to turn to see that Londo, Lina– and Hal– had all arrived. The crowd of soldiers' eyes all widened as they shuffled farther back.

Watch it. Some of them are still armed, Jae warned them. Only then did he turn.

Londo looked soggy– oily, as if he'd been caught out on a mission. Lina was in that revealing Speaker outfit of hers, complete with flowers in her hair, her face torn between anger and anxiety. Londo held her firmly by her upper arm; otherwise it was clear she would have run to Jae. Hal was in full Maximus regalia, impressive as fuck. Jae was damned glad to see them all.

The warmup whine from a blaster was their only warning. Lon released Lina and then reached out to catch the hard laser light as if it were from a flashlight. "You missed one," he accused. Jae took care of it. The owner screamed as the gun flash-ignited.

"What in blaze is going on?" Lina demanded in Panlingua of the men who were gathered in the room. She knew that most of the invasion fleet had learned a smattering of that language. "Why has there been an attack against the Minister for the Three Worlds?"

"Speaker!" "The Speaker!" The awe-struck murmur swept through the room.

Lina strode as slowly as she could through the smoky haze and burning-flesh stench. She picked her way around and over the fallen to Jae's side, both distressed and relieved at the condition he was in, shocked to see all the bodies, and wondering what kind of warrior Jae must be to have done this. She didn't touch him, but stood by his side as he wiped the blood off his face in two hard strokes.

Jae's marble-sized translator for the Aldierran language bobbed next to her, but she emphasized her careful words with a wide-beam telepathic shout for all these non-telepaths. "This is Neutrino, the Minister for Aldierra. The planet has named him as one of her Chosen, along with Valiant and me. We three are now responsible to determine if you deserve to live, or should die at Aldierra's hand. It's fortunate that the Minister seems to be a match for– how many beaten men do I see here? He is more than a match for anything you can throw at him."

"Surrender to him!" Londo stepped forward now to take his place at Jae's other side, within range of the translator. "Any threat made against the Minister for Aldierra is a threat against your very survival as a race."

There were murmurs of "Valiant" as the men recognized him. Behind it all, the room whispered, "Maximus!"

The remaining soldiers dropped knives and other weaponry on the floor, their mouths gaping in awe at the four megas in the room. Jae stepped forward, glaring at them all until he was certain that the last weapon had been surrendered. He nodded and motioned. The doors to the room opened and soldiers dressed in green marched in to collect the prisoners.

"I have a feeling," Jae said to his partners, but loud enough so that the cowering members of the High Council could hear, "that unlike what we've been informed, all is not peace and idealism on Aldierra. I've seen city-wide riots. I've seen mortal fights breaking out within teams. I've heard reports of suicides by the thousands, which could have been massacres. And now we have this. The government of Aldierra seems to have several factions within it. It fights itself."

"A coup?" Maximus asked.

"Sounds like an attempted one to me," Lon replied. "You are Patriarch Lupoff?" he asked the man he recognized from Bracken's info-tapes. "Explain what we're looking at here, sir."

The Patriarch stood at his end of the table, his arms wrapped around himself. Finally he straightened and with as much dignity as he could summon, said, "This would be the work of the Kupsuhone Army. As the Minister said, a faction that wars constantly against the established government of Aldierra."

"How many of these factions are there?" Londo barked.

"Keep in mind that we're all telepaths." Jae smiled grimly at the Patriarch.

"Ah. Well, there are five major factions, and... and a number of minor ones," he admitted.

"So all's not well within Aldierran society," Jae said. He turned to Lina and Lon. "It's a continuous full-scale riot out there. They're using the Ultimatum as an excuse."

Lina circled the shattered conference table slowly, like a hawk its prey. Every eye was on her, the Speaker for their world. "These gentlemen have been quite full of themselves today, I see," she said.

"They've been making speeches," Jae confirmed.

"Speeches full of treachery," she added. "I can feel the vibes. Gentlemen, let me inform you of a little fact. The other day when your world spoke through me, I was along for the ride. She spoke to each and every person on this world, and do you know what?

"Aldierra knows every one of you better than you know yourselves. She knows your hopes, your dreams, your lies, your truths. If you make false plans, if you try to trick her– Just remember, she knows.

"And she's much, much more clever than you can ever hope to be. How many billions of years has she existed? You've only been here a few decades. You're little children to her, thinking you can get away with the obvious. She can see right through you."

"Damn it!" Londo's fist smacked on the now potholed and burned committee table, shattering it in half and startling them all to attention. "This is the chance of a lifetime, of a million lifetimes! You have the ability to make sweeping changes in this world! You can set an inspirational example to the entire galaxy, but you're throwing it away to feed your own vanity."

The Patriarch's mouth flapped open without any sound. Admiral Bracken stood up. "Protector, Speaker, Minister," he began, but then for a moment seemed not to know what to say. "What do we do?"

Lina? Your padd?

Lina nodded, and two minutes later her notepadd appeared in Jae's hand. He transferred the information from it to his own and vice versa. Lina turned to look for an empty spot in the room, away from all the vanquished soldiers being herded out of the room at gunpoint. She ported in a large, ancient blackboard kept in a forgotten storeroom corner back at her ex-workplace. It was mounted on a hefty stand that could rotate the board to show the back as well as the front, and there were several good-sized sticks of chalk still in the tray.

Lon moved to stand beside her at the board. "I like that," he said softly. "More solid than electronic notes. They'll have more visual import this way."

"I thought it seemed monumental," she whispered back, and he nodded.

"All right, gentlemen," Jae said, handing Lina's padd back to her. "Speeches are very nice for ceremonial occasions when you have time to make them. But there's no time to waste, so here's what we do. We three have come up with a list of what we think your plans of action should be, but we aren't well acquainted with your world. We need to see what you– honestly– think you should be doing. Let's start with overall goals first. What's your goal?"

Silence hung in the room.

Londo studied the men gathered there. "You people run this planet and you don't even know what your primary goal is?" He turned to regard his partners and Hal in amazement.

Lina grimaced at the men. "You." She pointed at Merson, and Jae chuckled to himself. "Take that white stick– it's called chalk– and write on the board. Capital letters, top of the board. Writing with your whole arm somehow makes the message sink in more, don't you think, Lon?"

"Absolutely. It's less ephemeral than a computer screen."

She waited for Merson to get into position and then she dictated. "Goal: To convince Aldierra through solid– *honest*– plans to let us all live."

Londo smiled at Lina. Always getting to the heart of the problem directly.

"How are we going to do this?" Jae asked them all. He pointed to Merson to keep writing. "We'll make the planet a better place to live for all the creatures that live upon her. Politically, socially, ecologically… Whatever it takes."

"Next comes the creative part," Londo instructed. "You fellows can all be creative, can't you? All you have to do is figure out how to accomplish your goal."

"And when we're done here, we'll compare it with the list we've come up with." Jae said, brandishing the padd in the air. Screens floated next to it with the notations they'd been compiling since the Investiture. "We assign start and finish dates to everything. And we call people to get the process underway, absolute top priority. We begin today. First of all, let's quell this riot you've got outside, just so everyone will be able to pay attention." He pointed to the Patriarch. "Ideas on how to stop it," he ordered.

The Patriarch looked around at his aides, his officers, the soldiers. He pointed at a man dressed in red with metallic frou-frou medals outlining his shoulders. "Deeve! Let's get some organization here. I want to see the armies, all of them, moving on this by sundown. Get the people off the street. Get them behind bars. Death to all who resist."

"No killing except in self-defense," Jae ordered, and Deeve nodded sharply, though clearly unhappy with the caveat.

Merson cleared his throat at his Patriarch. "Sir, if I could. The Minister has already suggested that medical personnel determine who the mentally ill are and to separate them from the others. And that those others should be forced to repair everything they've damaged."

"Good. You're on it, too," the Patriarch said. "Move."

Merson got up to leave, but he grinned at Jae and looked Lina up and down hungrily. She scowled at him as he left.

"See?" Jae said told his partners quietly. "We're doing fine now. Just a little bump in the road to world peace."

Another man took over from Merson with the chalk. People at the table offered suggestions. Secretaries set up their recorders again, and two computer-generated screens appeared to hover alongside the chalkboard, mirroring and expanding upon its content.

Hal finally stirred from his position of arms crossed in front of himself. "So it's started," he said. "Are we needed here anymore?"

"Just to tell me what's going on on Earth," Jae replied. They grouped together so the others in the room couldn't hear them. Lina turned their translator off and they spoke English.

Lon cocked his head at Hal, who sighed. "Both of them already know it's Yanist-Glory. Let's just say—"

"Hal, you are a blabbermouth."

"And these are your partners," Hal replied. "You've got new loyalties now, son. Learn your priorities."

Lon regarded Lina, then Jae and back to Lina. He had the awareness to look abashed before he said, "Yanist-Glory is staging a series of planetary coups, backed with a souped-up version of mind control."

"Shit," Lina said. "No wonder Stoan's spooked."

"Lina's not with Glory," Jae said. "Why's Stoan coming down on her?"

"Obviously because she had the bad timing to marry Lon right now," Hal replied. "A parallel event that Stoan thinks is congruent."

"Well, set him straight."

Londo reached into one of his vest's many pockets to retrieve a travel pack of cleaning wipes. He handed it to Jae, who used them to swab the blood from his face and hands.

"He's going to be. But it might mean a few days," Londo said. "He's invoked wartime command powers, which is why Lina's being subjected to detainment. And *chérie,* I don't think it's going to be too pleasant for you. They needed you to be a guinea pig, see if Wiley's machine worked. Stoan thinks that if it keeps you from contacting your so-called fellow conspirators, so much the better."

"I can take a few days of anything. It'll be worth it to get this all straightened out. How– what–" Lina licked her lips as she searched to clarify the image that was trying to form in her mind. With a gasp, she grabbed Londo by the arms. "*They* say it'll be war," she said. "That's not right, is it? Say it isn't war."

Lon eased her hands off himself and clasped them in his own. "It will probably be," he said and then interrupted her as she opened her mouth to protest. "A very quick, very decisive war. It's one planet, and it hasn't gone completely over to Yanist-Glory yet. There's still a majority of the population who will side with us." He took a moment to compose what would reassure her. "We are surgeons with scalpels, cutting out the rot before it can infect the entire body."

"No. Not war."

"A quick one. Tell her, Hal."

"Travel time plus a quick war," Hal nodded at her. "Four or five days."

"I've read about so-called quickie wars. They aren't."

"The Legion's done this a few times before, *chérie.* In and out– They know how to do it. We know how to do it."

Lina looked to Jae, and he nodded confirmation at her, though his features were troubled. What could she say? A war loomed that was going to set her husband in deadly danger, and he apparently approved of the plan. Her jaw shook so that she couldn't speak. Jae, Lon and Hal spoke among themselves for some minutes.

Lina finally turned to Jae. There'd be time to worry about the war later. Now she had to be strong in front of these Aldierrans, in front of her father-in-law. Deal with the immediate problem. "Are you okay? I don't think anything's broken."

"I just need to clean up, get some antibacterials."

Lon appreciated the piles of bodies. Some of them were waking up and groaning. Soldiers were dragging out the ones who couldn't walk. "Pretty impressive stuff, Jae. I bet they got a record of it. You should let Kuttr see it, see what he says."

"Uh huh." Jae wiped his mouth and checked his fingers for blood.

"So maybe she's not such a crazy planet after all," Lina said softly. "Yes, I'm talking to *you.*" She glanced down at the floor.

"What?" Jae looked at her curiously.

Lon raised an eyebrow at Jae. "She blocked us from coming because she wanted you to establish your rep here."

"She what?"

Lina made an apologetic face at Jae. "She has a flair for the dramatic, too."

"Great. Just great. Has she given you any hints as to what's up next?"

"All three worlds are being obtuse. Talks about tests and such."

"Tests." Jae looked from her to Londo to Hal. "That doesn't sound very pleasant."

"So everyone's on their toes for the next few days," Londo told them. "It seems we'll all be going our separate ways. We keep in touch with each other at all times–"

"That won't be possible with me, I don't think," Lina said. Wiley would have that infernal machine fixed.

"And you'll be in hyperspace for a while," Jae pointed out to Londo, who nodded. "No telepathy from there."

"I don't like this," Londo muttered. "What are our options?"

Lina sighed. "I bet any options we can come up with will be nixed in some way by the Worlds, like the way Aldierra blanked us out."

"Maybe the only thing we can do is for everyone who needs one to go take a bath. At least we'll all start off looking good," Jae said dryly. He tried to glower accusation at Londo's condition.

Londo rubbed some more oil from his hair, and then reluctantly smiled at his partner. "*D'accord.* If that's all we can do, that's it. Lina, the padd again?" He transferred something from it to Jae's. "Home movies," was the only explanation he gave to Jae. "For something to watch on the way to Earth. You might get back there before I do. Check in with Lina." His eyes flicked to meet Jae's directly, and then returned to gaze at his screen.

"Plan's in place," Hal said. "They'll start to miss us soon. We've got to get back. Jae? You want to–?"

"I'm staying," he replied. "We have to get this thing begun, tests or no tests." He turned to Lina. "And whatever you do, if you come back here before I can get the final cultural data to you– If someone asks you to sign a contract, don't do it!"

"What?"

"Tell you later."

"All right," Lon said. "We'll be back on Earth. Be careful, Jae. Watch your back."

"You watch yours," Jae said, and then they vanished.

20

The three of them appeared in a back corner at Starhaven. "I didn't think you'd want to get the living room all oily," Lina told Lon.

"I can *not* believe that's all the time it takes to go– how many parsecs?" Hal put his palm to his brow and shook his head.

"Aldierra's a little under 250 parsecs from Earth," Lon said. "Me for a shower." He started to take off in the direction of upstairs.

Stoan blocked his way.

"Where have you been?" he demanded. He glared at Lina in her Speaker outfit.

Lon said, "I told you, there was an emergency on Aldierra. We needed to help Jae."

"It's all right, Stoan," Hal said. "There was no security breach. It was strictly an Aldierran problem."

Stoan scowled at them all. "When I say to keep them apart, I mean it," he said. "Can't you Terrans take simple orders?"

"You should take another look at who you're talking to," Lina snapped. "Have a little respect."

"That's all right, Lina," Hal said. "It's actually refreshing to have someone not treat me like Maximus." He cast an appraising look at Stoan. "Legion Commander Magnos here certainly doesn't."

Stoan scowled again, but maybe this time he was scowling at himself. He finally looked up. "Clean up, Starheart," he ordered Londo, and Lon saluted smartly. He flew off toward the bedroom.

Bolt and Forte wandered over, looking the worse for wear though no spots of oil marred their costumes. Bolt glanced at Lina in her Speaker outfit and did a double take. She stepped behind the bulk of Maximus and quick-changed into her tee shirt and jeans. Bolt grimaced at her when she reappeared. She grimaced back.

"Anybody getting hungry?" Bolt asked the group. "I say it's time to call out for pizza."

In a corner was a red glow. The Galactic Guard was using his ruby to clean up his teammates one by one. Along with more futuristic electronic-related abilities the Galactic Sentinels mounted it with, the ruby could utilize the power of a black hole to manipulate gravity. Oil and seawater flowed off the various Networkers sideways, to stream upside-down into red-glowing buckets.

"Did someone mention food?" a woman's voice came from the darkness of the cavern. Night had been relieved by the two working lamps, a couple of camp lights, and Lina's candles.

"Dinnertime yet?" "Sandwiches at least." "We need more beer."

Lina brushed off her hands and headed for the refrigerator. People had already done a thorough job of cleaning it out. So much for that.

Stoan met with those gathered in the living room. They made him aware of empty stomachs. He raised his hand parallel to the ground, his Legion ring near his mouth. "Magnos to Mem-Bazer."

"Yes, Commander?" Wiley's voice sounded as if he were here instead of eighty parsecs away.

"How much time?"

"Estimate seven to eight hours, Commander. We've encountered some anomalies."

Stoan swore. Lina figured the rough conversion: ten Earth hours or more. She wondered if anyone had considered the irony that she'd be porting in her own jail cell when Wiley finished. She certainly didn't think it ironic. Stoan was treating her like a war criminal without just cause.

Well, someday he'd get his. In the meantime, she would have to bear it like a good Legion spouse. Don't embarrass Londo. Or Jae. Or Maximus, for that matter. Did that mean she had to smile while doing so?

Stoan signed off and informed the non-Lingua-speaking crowd. Olympia, Hal and the Galactic Guardian– obviously an official ParaNet delegation– ringed themselves around Stoan. The subject was dinner.

Londo landed next to Lina from upstairs, dressed in jeans and tee. His hair was dry but rumpled, which meant he must have cleaned up much quicker than normal. He pulled Lina close and she buried her head next to his neck.

"You heard the time?"

"*Oui.*"

"God. I think I'll go crazy."

"If you do, I'll go crazy with you." He used a fingertip to bring up her chin. "How are you doing, really?"

"I'll be all right. Will anyone mind if I take a nap? Lon, how will–"

"Londo!"

Lon turned at Stoan's sharp bark. "Yes, Stoan?" he responded nonchalantly.

"You. Away from her– now!"

"Yessir." Lon eased slowly away from her. "Ten hours at least, Stoan. Let Lina and me– and Gary, he's been going all day, too– grab some sack time. You others could go someplace interesting. A restaurant, an amusement center. Or at least go up to the ParaNet satellite. We have a snack bar there."

"No."

"Most of these folks have never been to Legion HQ. Lina could–"

"No!" Stoan stomped over to face Londo down. "We stay here, away from civilians, away from possible security leaks. It's bad enough that the operation has been held up with the damper malfunction. Stop treating this like some kind of party."

"A party." Londo considered. "We'd need refreshments for that. I'm starving. Anyone know a caterer? Gary, why don't you put on some dance music?"

"This is not a party!" Stoan commanded. The others had filed closer, and he turned to face the group. "I don't understand why I'm meeting such resistance.

This is a top-level, full-security investigation. Do any of you have a problem with that?"

"I do, sir," Londo said quickly.

Hal held his arms open as peacemaker. "We all understand the importance of the experiment," he told Stoan. "Some of us don't agree with your methods or your judgment of Lina here, but we'll go along with you– for now. But that's no reason why all of us have to stay on top alert. We can set guards; will that suffice? In the meantime, we're hungry and some are tired. There are no food replicators on Earth. We need to send out for food or make it ourselves."

Stone scowled at the rocky walls of Starhaven, his opinions apparent. Earth: a barbaric planet. No discipline or respect. "So prepare the food here. I read her bio. *She* can do it; it will keep her busy."

Lina's mouth dropped open.

"We'll take precautions with the food, of course," Stoan added for everyone's benefit.

"Wait. Wait," Londo said as Olympia began to voice her own objections. "Lina, cook for this crowd? She's exhausted. Do we even have any food here?"

"We've got a little." Lina looked helplessly at the three kitchen cabinets, the rusty fridge. The groceries she'd bought yesterday hadn't been all that much. A few staples, a few luxury foods to celebrate that were crumbs of leftovers now… "I hadn't expected on hosting a formal dinner."

"No one expects you to cook for us," Olympia said loudly. At her waist, Ouroboros writhed with indignation. "This is ridiculous. I've never seen an investigation like this." She stood defiantly in front of Stoan. "We'll call out for pizza."

"Whatever pizza is, no."

"We don't have enough food to go around," Lina said. "Someone's going to have to go out and–"

"No one goes out any more. You can get enough, can't you?" Stoan crooked his eyebrow at her.

She realized what he was saying. "So you're officially condoning thievery?" Lina countered.

"Just keep a list, *chérie*," Londo told her. "This is going on the Legion's tab. What's everyone want to eat? You can make just about anything, can't you, Lie?"

"Ah... Lon..."

"Oh, right."

"Vegetarian," Londo explained to the group. "She can't handle meat." That caught Stoan's attention while Black Magnum made an obscene meat joke that Londo haughtily ignored.

A ParaNet discussion ensued of various menus, some of which contained foods that Lina had never heard of. The group had members from around the globe and most major cultures.

While the discussion went on, Lina started to gather ingredients. She used to work in a Mexican restaurant. Years ago. She could remember how to make quantities of that, right? The biggest trick was to keep everything vegetarian.

She ported Lon's camera thing to her when he offered it and used it to scan barcodes and weights as she ported in groceries.

The ParaNet argued over submarine sandwiches versus grilled cheese versus casseroles. Lina had been in large groups who had no idea what they wanted to eat. Someone had to force a decision or they'd be discussing all day.

Londo pulled up a chair to the folding kitchen table as the arguments raged. "Whatcha got going?" he asked her, puzzling at the ingredients. "Grilled cheese?"

"Quesadillas," Lina told him. "Plain or spinach, or I could port in some soy meat substitute and try that. Not a good idea, blind experimentation on paying guests."

He grunted at her wisdom.

"First we get salsa and chips." She loaded her hand-cranked food chopper and gave it a short, energetic burst.

"Very efficient. What do you want me to do?"

"How about killing Stoan? Get down from there, Faf. Oh man, Fafhrd's still here. I want to wait until she takes a nap to port her back home so she won't be shocked. You could open these jars for me. How hungry are people? Can you grill things with your breath? I'm sorry, Lon, but I just don't trust your oven."

They both glanced over to the lopsided thing. "Its deva doesn't look very nice at all," Lina whispered to Londo. "He keeps making horrible faces at me."

"*D'accord,* just point me at whatever and don't go near the stove. You planning a salad with this? Raw vegetables are healthy, you know."

Now Lon recorded the barcodes and weights as Lina ported in everything. He used his paravision to search for the more obscure ingredients and for the proper brands of beer, then linked to her so she could port. Then he set up another table in the future dining room, this one a long one, as a salad and chips buffet. The Networkers' argument turned softer in tone as aromas began to emerge from the kitchen. Lina looked up from a food processor, hotplate, electric skillet, and Londo's fancy coffee maker, all sharing the same two outlets. "What did everyone decide on?" she asked innocently as the heroes approached the proto-kitchen.

Lon intercepted. "They decided on this," he told them, pointing to the buffet. "We have appetizers. Be prepared for a wait for your entree. Mild sauce is on the far end for the timid. Everyone dig in; sit where there's room. Drinks are over here unless you want some wine. That's in the back of the wine cellar. I guess it's the pantry now. Wait till you see what the final wine cellar's going to look like!"

He became the jovial host, guiding his guests around, turning up the music, suggesting drinks, stuffing plastic cutlery and paper napkins in people's hands.

When Lina looked around again, Lon was hauling a pool table on his back from one of the storage areas upstairs into the area just east of the living room. "No food on this!" he ordered. As he shifted more furniture downstairs, he juggled six chairs at once. Lina knew it was for her benefit. Londo was so thoughtful. And amazing. He twirled the topmost chair in midair without touching it! Lina clapped delightedly. He gave her a flamboyant bow and reached behind himself to catch the final chair.

"I found this." The White Puma strolled up to Lina with Fafhrd in her arms. "She's beautiful. How old is she? What's her name?"

"What the orb is that?" Stoan demanded as he investigated.

"It's a cat," the Puma said before Lina could reply. "And keep your voice down. You'll upset her. She's very old. A grand duchess." The elder Networker rubbed Fafhrd under the chin and the cat leaned in, closing her eyes in ecstasy.

"That's Fafhrd," Lina said. "We don't know for sure how old she is."

"Really old," the Puma replied. So was the Puma, though she didn't look a day over sixty-five.

Lina nodded as she loaded enchiladas into a baking dish. "Maybe twenty-five?"

"I thought she was twenty-one," Londo said from behind Stoan.

"I keep thinking older."

He nodded and reached for the cat. "Anything I can do with the duchess here?"

"We have to get you acclimated to them before you can handle them," Lina said, and Londo dropped his hands. Puma pulled the cat closer and cooed to her. Fafhrd blew a bubble from her mouth.

"A cat," Stoan repeated with a sour look. They'd threatened him with cats before.

"Some related species come as big as me," Londo assured him and then rolled his eyes. "But not housecats. They're usually, oh, twice as big as this one. Fafhrd's on the scrawny side. Sorry, Lie."

"And these… animals… live inside houses?"

"We've got seven of them," Lon reported. "We were going to move them in tonight."

"Not anymore. I won't share quarters with animals."

"There's probably a nice Motel 6 down the road for you then," Lina offered brightly. She piled chopped jalapenos onto one quesadilla and flipped the empty half of the tortilla to cover it. Then she slid it into her skillet. That would be for Stoan. Heh.

The Puma leaned over to whisper in her ear. "Subtlety is an art you need to learn. That'll be mine."

A third load of dishes were soaking, a sleeping Fafhrd had been ported back to North Carolina, and Lina was finishing preparing dessert. "My famous brownies," Lina whispered as she snuck Londo back from her house and the oven there. He carried the oven-hot pan in his bare hands.

He set it on a cooling rack and reached for a knife.

"Twenty minutes!" Lina rebuked him.

"Eh?"

"They have to cool."

He eyed the brownies with sheer avarice. "Rules are meant to be broken."

"Not my rules. Twenty minutes for my brownies. Six hours for spaghetti sauce. Twenty-four hours for fudge. There's a stiff fine for non-compliance."

The smell must have drifted into the main cavern, for appreciative speculation began there, with their "guests" glancing toward the kitchen.

"Dibs," Londo declared. "Corner piece."

Lina handed him another box of cinnamon granola bars to crush. "Duly noted," she said. "So that means you don't want my unfried ice cream?"

He watched her roll round scoops of vanilla in the granola he'd already crushed. She took a bowl, squirted a lacy abstract design of caramel and chocolate in it, and placed a finished ball of ice cream in the center, to be topped off with more ribbons of topping. Damon collected it and trotted off to the condiments table for whipped cream.

Londo watched him. "Maybe I'll have one of each," he decided.

"You'll get fat."

"I'll figure a way to work it off." He leered at her, his gaze sweeping down and up and then down again. "Maybe I'll take seconds."

She matched his grin, and he laughed. Then she wiped her hands on her apron, turning to take in the kitchen and the remains of the meal. "Do you think they'll want anything else? I've got popcorn, sandwich fixings, and fruit for later. Are y'all really allowed to drink on duty? There are three more vats of tea brewing in the fridge, but they won't be ready for another few hours. "

"Don't worry about any more for tonight. You've done great. They're very impressed– even Stoan. He had no idea there was so much to cooking. I know he'd apologize if he weren't in such a snit right now. You trundle upstairs after this and take a nap. I'll finish cleaning. Wait– did you get a plate?"

"Not yet."

Lon came around to the other side of the table, checking her electric skillet. "Here, I'm the cook now. I think I've watched you enough to make a quesadilla for you. Extra veggies for the chef."

"Thank you, Londo," Lina said softly. "Thanks for helping me through all this. I'm doing fine."

"It's my pleasure, love. Now you sit down and put your feet up. I won't have you fainting away from hunger later. Wiley will yell at me if you're not in optimum testing condition." He twisted a lock of her hair in his fingers and gave her a warm kiss.

She smiled with more than gratefulness at him. "Clean hands in the kitchen, sweetheart."

"Lina's rules."

"I'm afraid so."

They looked up as the Puma leaped (she didn't walk down the stairs because there weren't any yet) downstairs to the living room, complaining over the music about the plumbing on the third level. "How the hell do you use it? Why are there three?" she asked, twitching her false tail. With a snort, she headed to the portalets that Lon had repositioned in the future ballroom, far from the living area. "I call a corner piece!" she bellowed toward the kitchen before she closed the door on herself.

Half the Networkers took their camp bedding to the west wing and the rooms Londo insisted were future offices. Two Networkers were placed on guard duty. The rest settled on Lon's three sofas and a dozen mismatched chairs to channel surf. The main group quickly settled on a replay stream of a championship college basketball game. The screen's size made it appear as if they had courtside seats.

Stoan went off into a corner to set up three communications screens, which he shuttered from the rest with a privacy curtain. He conferred with Legionnaires or perhaps Affiliated Systems government officials.

"He is such a royal pain," Lina muttered to Lon as he drew up his black mission duffle to her kitchen table. She was mixing ingredients again.

"Look, *chérie.*" Lon pointed. Something small and round hovered in the air over the ParaNet crowd. "He's taping the game. He's intrigued by Terran culture. He probably wants to study it later."

Lina had her doubts about that, but Lon continued stacking underwear and two spare uniforms on the table, various electronic doodads and crystal seifer coms and vacuum-packed food supplies. He filled three thermoses with fresh water from the tap and then repacked the whole thing as Lina made a quadruple batch of chocolate chip cookies.

Again she snuck Lon to her house, where he set the controls on her oven. The finished cookies were eventually layered in waxed paper and packed in Tupperware for the war-bound group to take with them. Lon assured her that he could carry the package separate from his duffel and nothing would be crushed.

"My mom once told me how they sent cookies to friends who were in the Gulf War," Lina said and blinked back sudden tears.

"I'll be fine," Londo assured her. "They don't come much tougher than me."

Lina nodded but that didn't stop a tear from rolling down her cheek. She pressed some white tape on the plastic lid and raised a felt-tip pen. "'E' or no 'e' in 'Starhart'?" she asked.

He shook his head. "Whatever you want, Kitten."

She thought a moment and drew a star and a heart on the tape.

"That's us," Lon said. His broad, warm hand closed over hers and the pen. "Forever," he said.

Stoan woke too early. On this world night was still deep with no hint of dawn, but from his makeshift bed on the couch Stoan could hear Londo and the girl. He silently rolled out of his covers and crept to just outside the pool of light along the back wall of this level.

He'd thought he'd made it clear: no outside communications.

Londo and Carolina both sat in robes, watching a 3-D screen at the comm desk. It showed a street-level view of an urban center, buildings blackened by fire, weeds cracking pavement, and dozens of figures, some cloaked, squatting on the walkways with piles of belongings next to them. The people were gaunt and unkempt. All seemed to be men.

"Is this typical of residential areas?" Lina asked.

A voice– Jae's voice– came back to them, repeating the question. Another male voice replied that yes, most streets in this part of the city looked like this. Jae didn't repeat it to the screen. The view shifted and soared, taking in the entire length of the street. It came back around for a 360° view. The buildings along this block were three stories on average, with some higher ones seen over the rooftops, some much, much higher. Through the obvious signs of deterioration: broken windows, fire damage, compromised structure, people still lived inside. An occasional face passed a window.

"Look there," Londo said quietly and pointed. Stoan recognized it too as he moved closer, an archaic missile launcher positioned among the residential buildings as part of the neighborhood. Its lack of deterioration hinted that it might still function. Londo explained the same thoughts to Lina.

Jae spoke to someone and another voice answered while the camera zoomed in on a gunnery nest on the roof of the nearest building, and then on two small squads of what were obviously soldiers who patrolled the rooftops. Three more soldiers were posted down on the street.

Stoan frowned to himself. The Starhearts were listening in on Jae's tour of Aldierra, unbeknownst to Jae's hosts, and Jae had a spy camera recording.

A woman screamed. Jae turned quickly, the camera catching him in its picture, but the uniformed man next to Jae reached to touch his shoulder.

"It's nothing," he told Jae. "If it's real trouble, the woman will have her bodyguards protect her. Here, a good wife has guards; they do not travel alone like your Sarastoran women do. Very dangerous, that."

A shouting, laughing pack of boys ran into the street from an alleyway. They trotted around Jae, his guards and host, taunting them and pointing. From the camera's eye, they moved like a school of fish, darting and shifting about, yet always positioned in their own group.

Then a second group emerged from another alleyway. The first spread out and stopped. The boys in the second group stopped also, eyed the first, and went on their way a little slower, a little more wary than they'd been. Their formation was tighter now.

Stoan stood behind the Starhearts as the night guard Black Magnum leaned against an upright 4x4, sipping at a cup of coffee. The room was cool but not unpleasantly so; still, Stoan fastened his overshirt for decorum's sake.

This was the first look at the world that had dared to attempt an invasion of Sarastor. If successful, it might have escalated to war against the entire Affiliated Systems. As it was, it had resulted in a casualty important to Stoan: Aiko Fallow, aka Orenya. One of the greatest Legionnaires ever. He'd laid her to rest mere days ago.

If he'd been on Sarastor during the invasion, he'd have blasted these Aldierrans to spacedust if only for their impertinence. Instead he'd returned to find the forces in effect surrendered to the two Legionnaires who had remained staffing HQ. Somehow they and Carolina had managed without firing a shot.

Now the diplomats had rigged a shaky alliance with the Aldierrans. This Three Worlds hoodoo was also involved. Two of his best Legionnaires had been appointed caretakers of that world.

It was crazy. He didn't know what to think about it. He'd brought Andri Nemlor, his subcommander, and his predecessor, Chimrin Dinar, in for lengthy discussions. Mind control was rampant in this supra-sector of the galaxy, getting worse every day. It must have something to do with it. These things were not coincidences.

"What are they wearing on their faces?" he asked despite himself. All these people seemed to be men, and only the most raggedy didn't wear a partial face-mask that covered their mouths and noses. "Are they standard dress or–?"

Londo didn't bother to turn around. "Air filters," he explained. "All but the poor wear them. Air quality is pretty low."

"The children don't either."

Londo grunted.

"I haven't seen any women wearing them," Lina said. "I don't think they're allowed to."

"We haven't seen enough women to make that assumption yet," Londo told her. "Look, there's another one."

A figure draped in shawls from head to toe came into view. Just her left eye and cheek peeked out from under the covering. A gloved hand held the shawl tightly across her mouth. Four men shuffled in a formation around her.

"Four guards," said Lina. "That can't be a poor woman. She didn't have a filter, and that burka thing she's wearing is not going to filter out many pollutants."

As if in answer, the woman coughed hard three times. She leaned to support herself against the wall of the building they passed. Her guards paused with her but did not offer to help in any way. They didn't touch her.

"Women's health issues," Lina muttered.

Londo nodded but said, "Lots more here than just that."

Eventually Jae climbed into a floating car similar to what they had on Sarastor. In minutes he arrived in a large, open plaza, paved but containing a few sickly trees of medium size in front of a row of skyscrapers. A delegation waited to greet him while a much larger ring of guards stood back from them.

"Who—" Stoan began, but Londo waved him to silence over his shoulder.

A green-uniformed man introduced the officials to Jae, and Londo and Lina paid the gravest of attention. These were sub-continental governors. They all wore air filters that matched their outfits, and they tipped them out with one hand when they spoke, so their words were clear. When they finished speaking, the masks clicked back into place.

The camera eye zipped back to Jae's side as he got into an individual mass-transportation vehicle that followed the others cross-country, perhaps the equivalent of a couple counties over. They were taking a preliminary tour of the area's ecosytem. This gave Jae privacy at last.

"Relax, Stoan," he told the camera. "I'm bouncing this through Legion communications to Earth. You'll have a record of everything."

"Are they still considering invasion?" Stoan asked.

"It's all they can do to hold things together on their own world. After their big fail last week, we can count invasions out. Did you see the power plant in the distance? Fission, can you believe it?"

"Where do we start?" Lon first rubbed his nose, then his chin. "How do you sort through everything to find what's the most wrong with the world to work on first?"

"We make sure everyone has the basics," Lina declared, but Jae shook his head at the camera.

"We give them hope," he said. "They probably look around their world and see the same things we do, but more. This is all they've ever seen, all they expect. First of all, we've got to convince them that they can change, that a better world is possible. Then we get to the basics. And then–" Jae sighed and shook his head– "food resources. Breathable air. Tackle the overpopulation question."

"If they're so overpopulated, where are all the women?" Lina asked. "We aren't seeing half the population, and I want to know why. Do they keep them locked up in nunneries, or do the men just clone themselves?"

"If they do, we shut down the cloning systems immediately," Londo said. "We've also got to get this civil strife under control. Redirect their frustration so that they're building and cleaning up, instead of battering each other's brains out. Or planning interstellar invasions."

They discussed until the vehicle slowed down. "You guys get to bed," Jae said. "Lina feels like she's about to drop, and you aren't far behind, Lon. We'll have these records to look at when I get back, and I'll have a better frame of knowledge to study them."

Londo and Lina returned to their room while Black Magnum stationed himself at the base of where the stairs would someday be to go to the third floor. He never noticed them making desperate but muffled love on the eve of interstellar war.

The sun came up with no word still from Wiley. In their bed, Lina lay in Londo's arms watching the sky brighten overhead. "Is that bad?" she asked quietly.

"I don't know. I just know that every minute we're held up is a minute more that the enemy has to find out about the Legion's plans. Look, Kitten, if something goes wrong at either end, you wait for Jae and tell him Operation Fantôme."

"Op–?"

"Fantôme. No questions. It may take him a while to remember, but he will. I'll go over all these contingency plans we have when I get back. For now, just trust me and do it."

"Yes, Londo."

Breakfast had been catered. It sat on Lon's long serving table in lidded silver chafing stations: scrambled eggs, oatmeal, ham, bacon, sausage, fruits, fish and rice…

"I was going to make pancakes, not Denny's breakfast sushi bar," Lina whispered to Londo. At least she didn't have to cook it.

"I like pancakes. Ah, there's some over there," he whispered back. "Bet you Stoan ordered this through Hal. I tell you, he didn't have any idea how much work he was putting you through last night. This is his way of apologizing."

Lina looked doubtfully at the Legion commander, who sat across the room behind privacy screens talking with someone. She turned slowly to take in the unfinished cavern with all its semi-framed levels and piles of lumber, the glass outer wall with the magnificent Christmas-like view of the morning mountains, and clusters of world-famous paraheroes scattered here and there, mostly watching the news. Someone had set a privacy screen blocking the sleeping area in the west wing for those who had either been on late shift or were from different time zones.

Was this how it was going to be forever? Slightly-controlled chaos? Eternal suspicion?

"So where are you two registered?" the White Puma asked from behind her. Next to her, young Blitz rubbed sleep from her eyes. She still had enough youthful energy for her dark ponytail to spin in her wake.

"The wedding's entered into the legal record on Sarastor," Lina said automatically, responding to the test.

"No, hon, *registered.*"

"Registered." Lon scratched his head.

Oh. Wedding. Registered. The meaning finally sank into Lina's mind. "Um, I don't know. I mean, we're not registered anywhere."

Lon gave Puma a lopsided smile. "We'll get registered soon enough. We're going to do this marriage thing properly, sooner or later." He squeezed Lina's waist. "What all do we need, *chérie?*"

"A whole lot of nails and wallboard and paint. Do lumberyards do wedding registrations?"

"What kind of nails?" Puma asked. "I still have big boxes left over from the Sixties when Carlos and I built our house. You two can have them. I'll even wrap them with a bow."

Blitz's lower lip protruded. "Nails aren't presents," she informed her ignorant elders.

Lina knew she and Lon and Jae had so much to do in so many areas of their lives. Their energies were scattered, what with wars and construction projects and getting to know one's husband and maybe fiancé. They had to be firm with their goals and make sure priorities were in their proper place.

She said, "I don't think the cats are moving in today."

Lon took note of the new topic and shook his head. "Better off where they are. We need to feed them before we go. Old Cat needs her medicine."

"Her name's Fafhrd. They're supposed to be fed twice a day. They haven't gotten that treatment for a long time."

"Fat Cat and Fat Cat Two don't need to be fed twice a day." He took her hand and squeezed it. "Don't worry, *chérie*. Things are going to get back to normal in a while."

"Things are never going to be normal again."

He patted her hand and didn't say anything.

Still no word.

They beamed some of Lon's gym equipment down from the ParaNet satellite. Many of the Networkers helped set it in place as well as try it out— at low power, of course. Others trooped outside to test the ski slope Lon cleared last fall.

Maximus— no, Hal— stopped in the kitchen for some coffee after his shower. Lon's equipment could tax him as well.

"It just seems to me," Lina told the leader of the ParaNet, "that whoever you're going after, I can help. At the very least, have me channel for you. You never know what'll turn up that way."

"I don't think Stoan would like me discussing this with you. But I have already mentioned it. Lon brought up the channeling. He thinks a lot of your guides. But Stoan doesn't want you along on this trip."

"Well, at least you'll have a telepath with you for this," Lina sighed.

Hal looked at her sharply. "Who?"

"Londo, of course."

"Oh, Lon. Right." He shook his head. "I can't believe that Lon's a teep now. Is he any good?"

"Yes. He doesn't know his own strength sometimes, but he's sure caught on quickly enough. Try him as a telepath to catch whoever it is. Oh– remind him every now and then to shield himself with the white light. I kept forgetting to do that when I was starting out, but I had guides who reminded me. Lon doesn't have that luxury. I haven't taught him yet how to channel. If he looks like he's getting in trouble, just tell him to ask for the white light. My guides say it won't be long at all now."

Hal took a sip and then nodded his head. "I'll remind him."

"Thanks." That made her feel a lot better about whatever it was that was going to happen.

"Londo won't be using any telepathy where we're going," Stoan's voice said.

"Your loss then." Lina didn't look around. "I would think that's a serious tactical mistake, not using all the resources available to you."

"Since I'm leading this mission, I'll decide tactics. I want to talk to you, Carolina. Alone."

She turned at that to the tall, blue-skinned, blue-haired Legionnaire in his full Magnos uniform. His chest displayed pulsating symbols that bounced around two poles, attracting and repulsing each other in turn, sometimes setting off sparks. It was his ordinary uniform; there were no distinctions for his being Legion commander. Everyone– at least everyone Out There– knew that Magnos was Commander of the AffSys Mega-Legion.

She asked, "Any particular place? Planet?"

"Earth will do. Someplace well away from here. I don't want Londo to listen in. I've already told him not to listen telepathically. Don't broadcast to him."

"As gracious as always, Stoan. All right. My place, then." She ported them to North Carolina. She didn't want Stoan inside her house, so she set them outside in the garden, near the small fishpond. It was cool but not cold, a pleasant mid-March day. She ported on her jacket.

Stoan blinked in the sudden noon light, taking in the still-leafless forest that surrounded the garden and house. Birds sang in the trees, lured by the feeders. The breeze whispered through all the branches, a background behind the birdsong, sparkled by a small windchime hanging by the back door. He scowled as he realized that nature itself provided music on this planet.

Lina ported a can of fish food from the house and tossed some into the pond. It was a little early in the season to feed them, but a school of tiny orange fish rose to the surface just the same. Maybe it had been warm here lately.

"We're reasonably close to being on the opposite side of the continent from Starhaven." Likely Lon could hear them well even if they were on Sarastor.

"Good enough." Stoan took a stance, feet spread, arms crossed. "I want to know what the hell's going on. Between you and Londo. Between you and Jae. I saw you kiss Jae."

She rolled her eyes and turned away. "I thought we'd been through this already."

"Our two most powerful members, and you seem to have both of them firmly in your control."

"Mind control, of course."

"Or emotional control. When it boils down to it, one's as bad as the other."

Lina threw more food into the pond. She never liked to lie; she was terrible at doing it anyway. Bending the truth was more her forte, but she had to be sure to bend it in a way that the others wouldn't contradict her.

"Lon told you–"

"Number one, that you were quite a demonstrative young woman. That, it turns out, is entirely incorrect. In fact, until lately it seems as if you've had an actual phobia about touching. The only person you've been demonstrative to is Lon… and of course, there's Jae."

"Londo's my husband. Jae's my partner now. And Lon cured me of the phobia."

"Number two, Lon said that it was traditional on Earth for Terrans, and especially Terran women, to be emotionally demonstrative. From what I've seen, that's incorrect."

"So he stretched a point. Besides, you haven't seen that much." She whirled on Stoan. "Do your Legion personnel files go as far as to specify sexual preference? Here on Earth they usually don't. And here on Earth, it's not usually considered a plus if someone is homosexual. Do your records list Jae that way?"

Stoan's lips parted and then closed into a grim line. "No, our records don't list preference. But Jae…" He paused again. His eyes moved up, then to the right.

"Just how well do you know him? How well do you know the Feithi culture? They accepted gays. A lot of them were bi, did you know that?"

"So you're telling me he doesn't like women so he wouldn't go after you? I've known him with lots of women."

"And do you know of all his affairs with men? I don't know many Legionnaires, but already I've had a couple confide that Jae's partial to men. I already know about his infamous two-week affairs." She popped the plastic lid back on the can with a slap. "Do you know about your other members? You did, for example, know about Lon and Aiko?"

"I knew about them, yes. I usually know what's going on, and with whom. I have to know."

"So you claim to know about Deegel and her little bedroom party the other night as well?"

"Eh…"

"But you didn't know about Jae. How does that happen? Do you automatically close your eyes to the abnormal? How about the truth?"

She barreled on, diverting the subject. "Jae's told me that homosexuality in the AffSys is regarded about the same as it is on Earth. No, worse. Here, there's a gay pride movement, people coming out of the closet, as they call it, revealing themselves when they're gay. People's attitudes are changing. They realize that homosexuality is just another aspect of humanity. I don't think that's the way it is on Sarastor."

"No, it's not. You're not to tell anyone about this, if it's true."

"Jae doesn't want to disguise his sexual preferences any more, but he's afraid that with the importance of the Three Worlds he will have to. It's not fair to him not to be honest, not to be himself."

Stoan's eyes narrowed, weighing her words. *Thank god he's not a telepath,* Lina thought. Stoan said, "That kiss… was not a friendly kiss."

Lina laughed. She had him now. "Jae is notorious for having two week affairs. That's one thing I will never indulge in. I sign up for life, Mister Legion Commander, sir. And as for that kiss– I don't know about Sarastor, but here a lot of comedies have been written about people misreading an innocent kiss, especially when a third party wants to see something scandalous."

Stoan caught her hand. He pulled her against him so that their eyes were inches apart as he leaned down to glare. Lina could feel something– the magnetic field?– around and through them both increasing. It made the hairs on her arms stand on end. He twisted her arm behind her back and held her there, unable to break loose.

"Can you port away now?"

She gritted her teeth, unwilling to show a weakness in front of this man. "You have a damnably intricate aura when you do this. I could– but you wouldn't like it. And Lon and Jae wouldn't like it if I hurt their friend."

He smiled in satisfaction that he had her. "All right. Now listen to me. I am commander of the Legion, and I'm telling you to stay away from Neutrino."

"And I am Speaker for the Three Worlds. If I wish to express affection to my close friend, the Minister for the Three Worlds, I will. We have incredibly important work to do as a team. Do you hear me? Jae's my friend. I will do my best to protect him and provide him with what he needs to be happy."

"And what does he need?"

Lina paused. "Jae needs Feith."

The scowl on Stoan's face blanked. "Feith is dead. How are you going to get him that?"

"There's going to be a lot of Feith in the Three Worlds projects. Jae wants to use it as a template."

"And what does the Protector of the Three Worlds think of all this?"

"Londo knows everything there is to know. Everything. He's a telepath, no matter how much you want to deny that. Jae is a telepath, no matter how much you want to deny that either. We know everything about each other. We are a unit. Closer than Legionnaires; the best of friends." She tried to shake off his hold but could not.

"And all this closeness, the telepathy– How long will it be before you wind up in bed together? How long until you betray Londo?"

Lina's eyes spat fire. "I will never betray Londo, not ever!"

This was getting them nowhere. War would break out by tomorrow. She tried to calm herself. "Look, Stoan, I've told Lon that I'll try never to embarrass him in public. If you think that me being around Jae will embarrass Londo, then I will avoid him– as long as he's on Legion business. But otherwise, Jae's my friend. He's with the Three Worlds now, and you have to accept that. We're going to be seen together often, with and without Londo. It's going to be part of our duties to work together."

He released her arm with a shove and turned away. The magnetic field vanished. "So if I tell you to stay away from him while he's on Legion business, you will."

"I will."

"Then do it."

"I hope you'll tell both of them your reasons."

Bran-Bran pranced up to Lina, then spotted Stoan. He hid from him behind Lina's legs as she leaned down to pick him up.

"Cats," Stoan grumbled.

Lina chose to coo at Bran before he squirmed out of her arms and ran off into the woods.

"So who do I have guard you while we're away?"

"Well, you could finally come to the conclusion that I'm not a threat–"

"Not now. You'll be guarded." Stoan studied her. "Are you bisexual?"

She laughed at the suddenness of it. "Y'know, everyone keeps telling me, 'Stoan's a great guy. You're just catching him on a bad day.' When are you going to have a good day, Stoan? When is this all going to stop? I'm tired of it."

"Are you bisexual?"

She rolled her eyes. "No, I'm quite happy being entirely heterosexual. Is that good enough?"

"It will do. And Olympia is heterosexual, too? Great orb, I can't believe I'm asking these questions."

Lina smiled and shook her head. "I believe she's quite happily lesbian, although the news gossip would have her involved with men on occasion. She may be bisexual; I'm not sure. But definitely lesbian. Are you afraid I'll seduce her? Put her under my emotional control?"

"I don't know what you're capable of. How about the Galactic Guardian? Paul Granger?"

"No. I refuse to have him for a bodyguard. Don't misread my apprehensions about him as some sort of signal that oh, yes, he'd be the perfect bodyguard, she's not interested in him. I think from the few moments I've been around him that he's a, an egomaniac. With other problems."

"He's a Galactic Guardian."

"Then ask the ParaNetters. Londo thinks he's incompetent. I know Olympia doesn't like him. Look, she's got Ouroboros; are you familiar with its properties?"

He looked at her sideways. "No."

"Then ask her about what it can do. If you're determined to use up a megapara's valuable time, she'd be your best choice. I don't understand why you just don't slap me in a hyperspace chamber and be done with it."

"I'll inquire about the object. And I'll get both Londo and Jae to corroborate your story."

"I know you will."

He frowned at her. "Are all Terran women like you?"

She smiled grimly. "God uses a cookie cutter so we all turn out alike."

He took a breath. "I want you to stay away from Jae. Now take us back, Speaker."

She ported them both back to the kitchen and without a word said to him, ported upstairs into one of the storage areas to work through his negative energy by sorting through things. No sooner had she settled than Bolt slid into the room.

21

"Not having a good day, hum?" he said lightly.

She picked up a couch pillow and tried to throw it the length of the future room. It just didn't have the right heft. "Damn," she said and flopped onto a computer chair. "Pompous asshole. Pardon my French."

Bolt sat on the half-eaten plaid couch. "I believe the title is Commander of the Mega-Legion, not Pompous Asshole. Problems?"

"He's a jerk. Anything I do, he takes it the wrong way."

"Oh? He does something besides saying you're a mind controller?"

"He's got a whole list. And the thing is, I can actually see his point of view. Maybe. He's protecting the Legion, protecting Londo, protecting… a lot of things. Unfortunately, his idea of protecting things is to be an asshole as far as I'm concerned."

Apparently Stoan felt the need for her to have two guards, for now the Galactic Guardian wandered in.

"Speaking of which…" Bolt said.

"Is there a party in here? Was I invited?" The Guard turned an ingratiating grin at Lina. His hair, moussed to sit up, had been dyed a deep red to coordinate with his costume. A fringe of slight beard in a similar hue framed his face. He sat in a chair and put his feet up on a desk, noisily eating an apple. "So it's Lina, is it? You can call me Paul. You can call me anytime."

"Granger…" Bolt started.

"They all call me Granger for some reason. Never Paul," he said between crunches. "Say, you're a telepath, right, Lina?"

"Yes." What was he getting at? He was staring at her breasts. He looked up to her face and his eyes changed from brown to red. Suddenly she saw images. They weren't telepathic, but she thought only she could see them, as if they were polarized to her retinas like security computer screens on Sarastor.

He broadcast the vision through a red haze, through his ruby, and she could dimly see the room beyond what he fed her: images of him kicking Bolt out and then throwing her down on the sofa, tying her tight to it. She could hear it now as well: him ripping off her clothes. Making savage sex in Valiant's own house. She was certain of the phrasing of that as he whispered. *Valiant's own house.*

"Stop that," she hissed. Bolt looked at her curiously.

The images kept coming.

"I said, stop that." Desperately trying to ignore the feed, she stood up and faced Granger. "Get out of this room. Send someone else in, if you must have two guards."

He stayed in his seat, looking at her and grinning. Still he ate the apple, sucking on its core. Images: her tied up to the sofa arms. shrieking in terror as he thrust inside her. Him pressing his fingers against her windpipe until she passed out. Urinating on her afterwards. "Hey baby, it could be so good…" whispered in her ears.

"Get out of my house!" She ported him away.

Bolt jumped off the bed. "What did you do?"

"I ported him. I will not have that kind of person in my house. The images he was sending me were– disgusting. He wouldn't stop." She turned to Bolt. "He's a Galactic Guardian?!"

"Jesus. Where did you send him?" Bolt took her by the arm and almost dragged her out into the hallway, but she followed him willingly. He gave a hop, the world blinked for a moment, and then they were on the bottom floor.

She answered, "To Tiawa. It was the farthest point I could think of on the planet." Bolt pulled her into the living room.

The others looked up at the commotion.

"How long before he comes back?" Lina demanded. "I want him out of here permanently."

Bolt said, "If he uses his ring, maybe a few minutes. If he uses the ParaNet teleporter…" A soft glow and hum appeared in one corner of the room. "…About now."

The Guardian materialized fully. "Didn't you like my company?" He leered at her. At least the images had stopped. Maybe that was due to the quorum of Networkers here.

"What's going on?" Maximus came barreling out of the kitchen area, Londo in tow. Stoan was right behind them, with Olympia bringing up the rear.

"I was just guarding her with Gary."

"He was using his ruby to beam filth at me," Lina declared. "Bondage and rape. He wouldn't stop. So I ported him." She turned to Maximus, chief of the ParaNet. "I want him out of here. I may have to put up with Stoan's rigmarole, but I don't have to put up with this."

"I don't know what she's talking about. She–" The images started again. Candlewax dripping on her. Piercing her nipples, making it slow and painful. Her blindfolded and gagged, not knowing what he'd do next. This time there was no sound that some of the others might pick up.

But she didn't need sound for Londo to see the images through their link. "What the *skurny*–" he began.

"Are those coming from–" Maximus could see them too.

Not a hint of the panic that overwhelmed Lina shook her voice. "I warned you, Guardian. Stop it. I swear I'll port you to Sarastor next. I know a nice little locked, impervion-lined room there. It'll take you longer to get back. And there are other places I know of, even farther away. Rimhold, for one."

The off-planet threat stopped him. The silent movie vanished. Granger looked from her to Maximus. "Who are you going to believe, Hal? A Galactic Guardian, or the bitch who's controlling Londo?"

Even as Londo lunged forward, Maximus planted his hand on Lon's chest, a hand that could stop freight trains in their tracks. Londo brushed it aside and grabbed Granger by his throat amulet to slam him into the wall behind him. A blinding flare of ruby light immobilized Londo's arm. Granger halted before he went all the way through the wallboard.

"Say that again, *enfant d'chienne,* and you'll regret it. What the hell are you trying to do to my wife?!" Lon snarled at the Guardian.

Pieces of the wallboard flaked off to settle on the red-glowing man. The ruby's light concentrated at the point where Londo's fingers wrapped around it. The whites showed around Granger's eyes, but he gathered his wits quick enough to sneer at Lon.

"Hey, boy," he drawled, Londo's fist still at his throat. "You wanna step outside? We can settle this right here and now."

Granger grinned with anticipation as Lon's eyes narrowed in fury, his teeth bared. He was almost blind with rage. Londo strained against his restraint, his hair standing sideways as gravity shifted around him, trying to pull him away.

"Valiant versus the Ruby. This will be a fight that people will want to see for years to come." Through the bravado, Granger's voice was raspy. "One miserable para versus the futuristic science of the galaxy's most advanced beings." His fingers curled in a "bring it on" gesture. "Let's do it."

"Valiant!" Stoan barked. "Guardian! Break it up!"

Maximus reached a hand between them to force them apart. "Granger, you're on monitor duty *now* until notified otherwise."

The Guardian stayed where he was. "It was just a joke. A joke!"

"I mean it," Maximus said. "Now. Londo, release him."

One finger at a time, Lon did so. Granger grimaced and reached behind his belt buckle. He vanished in a blur of dematerialization.

"Jesus," Lina whispered into the sudden silence. She sat down as her legs gave out.

"What happened?" Maximus demanded of Bolt.

"He came in and proceeded to hit on her. He asked her if she was a telepath and then stared at her and she told him to stop it. She gave him a couple of warnings, told him to send in another guard, but he kept smiling at her and staring. Then– poof– he was gone."

Lina couldn't stop trembling. "He was projecting– perversion."

Londo stood in a cloud of black anger. "I knew I had to guard her from my enemies," he said, "but I didn't know I had to protect her from my so-called friends." He gave Stoan a look of pure fury.

"We have to do something about that *ublyudok*," Forte said. The Russian para had recently wakened and didn't look quite together yet as she held her half-loaded breakfast plate. She stood by Lina. "He's getting worse."

"I agree," Olympia said from behind Maximus. He turned to look at her. "It's time we either kicked him out of the Network altogether or contacted the Sentinels to see if we can get a new Guardian assigned to Earth. At the very least, his attitude in a number of areas has become inappropriate of late."

"Inappropriate?" Lina said. "The man needs major therapy. The thought of him having that ruby under his control gives me the creeps."

Londo wrapped her in his arms. She sank into their solid protection.

"Are you all right?"

"Yeah. He's a jerk, but he's gone now." She lay her head on his shoulder. Lon had crossed a Galactic Guardian for her. He was wonderful.

He rocked her gently in his arms.

Stoan's ring buzzed.

"Londo," Lina whispered.

As the others watched Stoan and listened to the conversation between him and Wiley, Lon and Lina sneaked to the East Wing and the partial walls there.

They wouldn't be able to do this again for a few days, maybe forever, so they made these long kisses count. When they finally broke apart, Lina stroked Lon's cheek, gazed into his brown eyes and said, "You be careful. You can track these mind controllers; just look for someone who feels wrong. Trust your gut. Remember to ask for the protection of the white light."

"Tell me how."

She showed him how to invoke the light.

"You'll be safe with Demi," Lon told her. "This security escort we've set up is more to protect you than to protect someone else from mind control."

"Am I going to be in danger?"

"I don't think so. But word's been out in the AffSys about us for four days now, even more if you count that the people in the Terran Zone could have been talking. I don't want to risk anything. I don't like leaving things to chance. I don't like the sound of those tests the Worlds were talking about."

"Sometimes all you have left is to trust in the universe," Lina said. She never took her own advice. The future loomed in menace. "Promise me something?"

"I'll promise you the sun, the moon… Anything you desire, my darling Carolina. We'll get rid of the plaid couches. What else?"

"I don't care about the couches. Just one thing." She grasped his vest to pull him close. To make him understand how very important this was. "Promise me: You'll come back to me. Whole. Alive. And soon. Londo, you must promise!"

He crushed her to him and swore into her hair, "I promise, I promise!"

He kissed her long and hard. "I'll be back soon. I promise I won't stand for any of this if they try to accuse you again. If the war lasts for more than a week, I'll send a message or come back long enough to explain things myself. If things look safe, I'll bring you back with me." He took her chin in his hand so she'd look directly into his eyes. "You be here when I come home."

She nodded and tried to smile. "My path will always lead back to you." She swiped back the tears and took a deep breath. Hand in hand they walked into the living room.

As soon as Wiley arrived he scanned what he had brought: a wide bracelet, sickly gold in color with tiny blinking lights scattered over its surface. It would reach loosely from her wrist almost up to her elbow, with a slight overhang over the back of her hand, like a sleeve a size or two too big. Unfortunately, not large enough to slip out of.

Wiley examined it with sensors. "It's in exactly the same condition now as when I left."

Of course, Lina thought. *They might think I changed it when I ported it here.*

Just the sight of the bracelet made Lina feel sick. *Danger! Danger!* Her insides screamed. She physically felt spirit guides try to push her away from it.

"You can do this," Londo whispered to her. "Courage."

She nodded and willed herself to believe. "*They* really don't like it," she reported to the group. "I don't either, not one bit. Put it on." She held out her arm, turning toward Lon. ****Be careful,**** she repeated. Grimly Wiley fastened the shackle in place.

The room went white. Her legs buckled.

Someone caught her as she went down. Everything was empty white: sight, sound, touch… telepathy. The world was dead.

Lina's head swam. She fought to stay conscious. She might have blanked out for a second or three, but how would she know in this? *Breathe,* she ordered herself. *Breathe.* Somebody spoke to her, but she couldn't make out the words.

Her brain pitched and wheeled on overload. She had to concentrate like she never had before. Bring her chakras in line. Pull down the white light– anything to help her! Energy to her root chakra, to the next chakra, to the next. Breathe. Breathe.

"Jesus," she whispered, and it was a half-plea. She pressed the heels of her hands to her forehead and rested her head on them. Bad energy out, good energy in. Balance.

Now she had to slow down her breathing; hyperventilating wouldn't help. She leaned back. She was fairly sure she was in a chair now, and shook her head trying to clear off this whatever it was. When she opened her eyes faint shadows moved around her. The voices sounded a little clearer, but the words still eluded her.

"I'll be okay," she told them. She could barely hear her own voice. "Just give me a few minutes. Please."

She spread herself to the blinding white light, pouring into her like it never had before. Then she opened her eyes again. Here was the room, but she had to squint against the brightness of it. Lon hovered over her. *"Chérie,"* he said. She winced at the volume of the words. He hadn't dared to take her hand.

"I'm back," she announced between shaky breaths. Her words sounded slurred to her. Concentrate! Concentrate! "I'm not okay, but I will be. Don't worry, Lon honey." He let out a breath and sat back on his heels, watching her warily.

"Can you describe the effects?" Wiley asked from somewhere. She looked around; he stood at her side, recording. He seemed paler than usual, a minty blue.

"I'll… try." When she licked her lips she realized she was panting. "No concentration at all. It's like I'm high and about to faint at the same time. Total disorientation. No headache. You talk. Let me… get myself together."

"Right." He ran his sensors around her, around the bracelet, and reported readings to the group. She ignored him as she fought to stabilize the world. But he was talking to her again. "Let's go through the drill. Telepathy?"

She shook her head, feeling her brain swishing. "Not a bit. Vision, hearing and touch affected, too. Don't know what else. Those last are getting a little better, though."

"But no telepathy?"

"Zero."

"Londo, how about you?"

He touched his finger to her hand, so cautiously. "Mine is working. It's just that when it comes to Lina, there's a big blank."

"Very good. Lina, clairvoyance?"

"Hell, Wiley, I can hardly see the room for the glare. No, no clairvoyance."

"Teleportation?"

"Dream on." She became aware of Ouroboros winding up her other arm as if it were a snake. She shivered.

"She won't hurt you," Olympia said softly. Lina nodded and tried to be brave, like when you went to a doctor's office and got a procedure for the first time without the doctor explaining it. You never knew when the pain would come, or how long it would take. You survived by remembering that they'd get in trouble if they killed you.

"Channeling?" Wiley asked.

"Give me a minute." Lina closed her eyes, still inside the white light, and looked around. "They're there," she reported. "Very faint but here, whispering light shadows. They don't like this one bit– *danger, danger Will Robinson…*" She shook her head again. "And they still don't like *him*."

"Who?"

"The Guardian. Boy, were they right. They–" She licked her dry lips.

Demi's soft voice came from behind her. "She said earlier that the… guides had been pointing at him and using disparaging signs."

Lina nodded. "They're still really agitated about him. About everything. Don't know what it means. No concentration at all. And there's nausea. I can't feel gravity to figure out where 'down' is."

Wiley made more notes. "Right, let's leave that. Levitation?"

"I can't even get myself out of this chair, let alone levitate. Give me some time to get my bearing again, and we can try. But not now."

Ouroboros bit her. It was like a thin needle instead of a fang, but it still hurt for a moment.

"Ow." Heat spread out from that point, coursing through her veins.

Demi took firm hold of the mystic snakeskin. "You can concentrate," she commanded.

An electric shock sparked through the conduit of the snakeskin and its venom. "Whoa!" Lina exclaimed. She shook her head and the room cleared. Now she could plainly feel herself sitting in the chair with its corduroy fabric, her hair sticking to her head with a layer of sweat. The sound in the room seemed just a little louder than normal.

"The venom will not harm you," Olympia assured her.

Lina let out what had been a held breath and looked first at Ouroboros coiled around her arm, then at Olympia. Not electricity; magick. "Too cool," she said, amazed. She turned to Wiley. "It's just like one of your high-power stims," she reported, wiping the sweat from her brow with her free hand.

Lon sat on the floor right in front of her. "I'm okay now, darling," she said with a brave smile. The one he gave her in return was shaky, but the tension in his eyes relaxed.

"You've ruined the control of the experiment," Wiley complained to Olympia.

"I've expanded the limitations of the experiment, by making her more powerful than she would ordinarily be. This will actually serve us better. But first," she held the weighted tail of the snakeskin firmly in her hand. "Carolina, I command you to tell the complete truth. Are you involved with any invasion plans for any planet?"

"No."

"Are you in contact with any telepathic race?"

"Just us humans. And I've met Chimrin and Erik and Jae with the Legion. People there talked about the Tishana, but I never saw any."

"Humans aren't normally telepathic," Stoan said.

"Explain about humans," Olympia ordered.

"What, about humans being telepathic?"

Olympia nodded.

It seemed like Ouroboros squeezed her mind, making one series of memories stand out, but Lina gave them up willingly. She explained that humanity had always had its telepaths and psychics: the Delphic oracles, Nostradamus... Now that the Aquarian Age had begun things were accelerating as humanity geared up for a jump in spiritual consciousness.

"A hundred years ago psi was a rare thing," she told them. "Or maybe those who could use it were just in hiding. Now we're everywhere. Lots of people that you wouldn't expect are into this stuff. And when you start on the spiritual journey, you find that the farther along you go the more psi ability you get.

"Telepathy is a natural part of spirituality. A telepath is going to naturally be a spiritual person. Of course, there's different kinds of spirituality–"

Olympia interrupted. "Can one make an unnatural telepath? How did you make telepaths out of Londo and Neutrino?"

"Maybe the Three Worlds just gave us a good kick in the pants, bumping us all up a level. Terry the Bitch mentioned that she'd thought Lon was a telepath all along. I gave him someone he could practice with, so he started to use it, like he was ready for it anyway. Jae's people were naturally telepathic, but he must have blocked it after the Great Disaster until he started hanging around me. Maybe. Maybe it was because he and Lon are close. If Lon was ready for the jump, then maybe that made Jae ready as well."

Lina paused, thinking of other ways. "Wiley has his device that can un-make a telepath. It shouldn't be possible. It's highly unnatural, whatever it is."

"That's true enough," Wilder muttered.

"But if he can do that, maybe someone can artificially make a telepath. I don't know. Let Wiley tell you that. But a natural telepath– They aren't going to cause you guys any trouble. A natural telepath is just not going to be that kind of person. Not off the deep end, that is."

Olympia turned expectantly to Wilder. He sighed. "Mind controllers are artificial constructs. I believe that the discovery of how to make them was quite accidental. After the last day's work I'd be willing to bet I understand how it's done, but then…" He shrugged. He was the brilliant Dr. Mem-Bazer, that's why. "I know how the brain is re-structured. Just as it's clear that the Empire now understands it as well."

Lon rubbed his chin. "The spirituality… ethics part is now left out of the equation entirely."

Wiley frowned his confirmation. "They've short-circuited a natural counterbalance to the problem of telepathic misuse."

Olympia clenched the snake rope in her hand. "Lina, are you in league with any artificial telepaths?"

"Never met one to my knowledge. Definite no. And I've never practiced any form of mind control either, so there. Are you satisfied?"

"I am," Olympia began to uncoil Ouroboros from Lina's arm when Hal reached out to stop her.

"Lina, you showed me how a non-telepath could control someone's mind," he said sternly, and some of the people in the room gaped in astonishment. "You said it was possible."

"Yes. Just as people speed up their breathing when they're frightened, they can reach out with their aura to influence people as an unconscious thing. They aren't aware they're doing it, but when it works they keep on unconsciously doing it. Those are the kinds of mental controls I usually work on. The hooks can be very powerful, very binding. I've never seen any bad hooks from anyone I'd consider telepathic."

"So if a natural telepath's sense of ethics will deter them from mind control, we'll find that most controllers are norms without ethics? Norms perhaps who have trained in aura control?"

Lina chewed on her bottom lip as she thought. "That makes sense. But they'd have to be pretty screwed up to think that taking another's will from them was right. They'd have to believe in the rightness of slavery." Lina glared at Stoan, who was pacing the area, his arms behind his back. "Like people of the AffSys do."

Wiley tapped his chin thoughtfully. "Suppose that you have an unethical person and someone artificially increases their telepathic brain centers. Shorts out any remaining ethics centers."

"Well…" Lina tried to think hard as Ouroboros squirmed on her arm. "That would give them instant feedback when they utilized mind control, wouldn't it? Maybe provide pinpoint precision."

"I believe that's what we're after," Wiley said.

"Oh. Then you'd want to scramble the telepathy part of the circuit. You could knock the controllers off-balance long enough to drop their hooks or defocus them at least. But that's all they are; they're just hooks, Wiley. No matter what kind of generator they might be connected to to soup them up, the mind control I'm thinking of is just hooks. At the worst, it might make the person's aura a tangled-up knot. But knots can be untangled. The controlled can be cured. I wish I could see one of these controlled people. I don't understand what all the fuss is about."

"You cannot cure mind control," Stoan growled from behind her somewhere. "You can only hope to permanently disable the controller."

The snakeskin still wound around her arm. Lina could feel its hot venom tracing her veins.

"Try it with me," Maximus said. "Let's see if this is the same kind of control we're talking about."

"No. I told you."

"Order her," Maximus told Olympia.

"Lina, I command you to mentally control–"

"No. Don't do this."

"You can't refuse. Just a light control. The suppressor only negates your telepathy. I want you to–" Olympia's brow contracted.

"No!" Lina sucked in her breath. *Think of something else!* The influence from the snake pressed in upon her. She began to focus on Hal's aura.

Though she usually only felt auras, the colors that surrounded him brightened into dim view.

"No. No! Stop it!" Think of anything else. *A B C D E F...* Hal's aura fluctuated with lights, the blue web of the etheric. The dry coils of Ouroboros contracted into her arm. *Utilize the left brain instead. Two to the first power was two. Two to the second power was four. Two to the third power was...*

It hurt. The lasso squeezed her arm down to the bone, but it also squeezed her mind. Arithmetic fled. It was like someone propping her eyes open to focus them on Hal.

"Just a light control, Lina."

"Don't make me!" She wouldn't! She couldn't! Never, ever, take someone's will away from them! "Stop it!" She clawed at her arm, trying to peel off Ouroboros.

The snake rope opened slitted eyes at her. Its horrible mouth yawned in her face, hissing. Lina drew back with a cry.

"Stop it, Demi!" Londo cried. He reached for the snake, but it bucked a threat at him. Automatically Lon stepped back, but in an instant he reached out to grasp—

Londo would rescue her!

"Tell her to return to normal. Now!" Lon's fingers wrapped around the snake's head, which bulged under his grip as if it had been an empty ball. It was only a snakeskin, not a real snake.

Lina writhed in the chair. The snake didn't budge. Sweat soaked her; her heart pounded loud enough for anyone to hear.

Olympia stood steadfast as Lon kept pulling on Ouroboros. "Back off, Londo."

He did. His hands twitched at his side, his face contorted in agony. The muscles in his legs trembled. It was clear he couldn't move.

Ouroboros was magick.

"Don't fight this, Lina," Olympia soothed. "Just a very light mental control. You want to do this," she urged.

The snake squeezed and bit Lina hard in the bicep.

"I've never had to urge anyone before," Olympia told the group. "You can do this, Lina."

"Shut up! Make it stop! It's evil! It's anti-life! God! Make it stopmakeitstopmakeitstooop!"

She arched up and shrieked. Despite the magick Lon lunged for her, but Gary caught her and held her as she screamed again. The snakeskin crackled with tiny lightnings.

Lon roared, restrained now only by his father. "Stop it, Demi!"

"Another seizure coming up!" Wiley shouted. "Stop it, Olympia. Now!"

"Return to normal!" Olympia blurted. Quickly she unlooped the skin from Lina's arm, hissing as it snapped with static electricity against her. A deep red, scaly burn stretched around and around Lina's arm where Ouroboros had lain against the skin. Two deep indentations purpled against the burn.

"She's not breathing. Clear away!" Wiley whipped a flexible rod out of his medikit and pressed it against the side of Lina's head even as Gary eased her back into the chair. Hal held Londo back in an iron grip as Lon clawed against him.

"You'll hurt her if you touch her," he whispered into his ear. "Let Wiley handle it."

"I'm sorry, Londo." Horror etched Olympia's face. "I didn't think it would go this far. I've never seen that happen before. I–"

"Wiley–!"

"Take it easy, Lon. She's coming back now." Wiley saw the shudder of an inhale and nodded. He checked his sensors with two minds, keeping the rod against her head for two minutes more. "What is that rope?" he asked Olympia with another mind.

"It's the discarded skin of the World Snake. It's 2500 years old." Olympia licked her lips as she saw a hint of color returning to Lina's cheeks. "I found it and sewed it with the thread of Fate."

"Of course," Wiley replied dryly. World Snakes and threads of Fate. Well, he was on Earth after all. "It's a means of mind control, correct?"

"Its venom is a potent command serum. When combined with my suggestions, then yes, I suppose you could call it mind control." She gave a tiny shrug. "It warps the weave of Life."

Wiley exchanged a glance with Stoan. Terrans and shamanism.

"The combined effect is extremely powerful," Hal said. "I had it demonstrated on me once."

"Everything was normal when we began," Olympia declared. "I felt it. There was no adverse reaction."

"And have you ever given anyone an order that went against someone's every instinct?" Londo hissed at her. "How long would you have let it go on, Demi?"

"I'm sorry, Londo. I'd never seen a reaction like that. I thought…"

"You thought what?" Stoan asked.

"I thought that maybe she was taking control of Ouroboros. If she was a mind controller, that's what she'd try." Olympia grimaced. "But she wasn't. I could feel it. She was trying to escape the command, not counter it."

She looked over at the seething megapara. "No, Londo," she said. "I've never before given an order that was completely counter to someone's ethics. I've never told anyone to kill anyone else. I've never told them to hate someone. I don't make many mistakes these days, but apparently I just did."

"Make it the last time," Wiley coolly said as he detached the rod. "This almost killed her." He administered an injection to Lina's neck. More color flushed into her face. He ran his sensors over the arm, the peculiar burns there. Neural and cell disruption but very little actual heat damage, centered around the two bites. High magick? Could be, could be. Well, it was gone now. He could heal the physical damage. He spread some regeneration cream on her arm and returned to scanning her neural nets.

"How is she, Wiley?" Londo asked anxiously. "Is there permanent damage?" He searched Lina's face for a sign.

"I got to her in time," Wiley replied. He turned to Ouroboros and scanned it. Yes indeed, magick on a mega scale. Of course he couldn't read specifics; magick didn't function that way. But it was a huge focus of power, centered along all the decorative stitching. The thread of Fate. Hmm. And Lina had come out of countering it alive.

"All she needs is a little rest, say a week-long honeymoon– with no supernatural events. I wouldn't think I'd have to mention that, but anymore with you, Londo–"

"She's not going to get it right now." Londo shook off Hal's restraining hand and kneeled beside Lina's chair. She did look better. Her breathing was regular, her color was almost back. She was still pale. "I want to bring her with us, make sure she's all right."

"No," Stoan said sternly. "She stays. I don't want your mind distracted during the heat of things, Londo."

"I'll keep her under the best of care," Olympia promised softly. Lina was coming around now, trying to open her eyes. "Don't worry."

"*Chérie,*" Londo said. "It's okay now. You're okay. They aren't going to make you try to do that anymore."

Lina tried to speak and failed, but her eyes fluttered open all the way. Her fingers slid to Lon's arm.

"How many?" Wiley held up three fingers in front of her face.

"F-forty-two," she told him in a hoarse whisper. "I can see, Wiley." She straightened in the chair. Wiley ran his scanners down the length of her again.

"That's twice in less than three weeks that I've had to bring you back from death," he accused her. "I'm going to start charging you for my services."

She managed a wan smile. "I'm still covered for the next month with Blue Cross. Take it up with them." She looked over at Londo. "I'm okay, love. I'm okay. How much more?"

"Just this thing." He tapped on the shackle. "Five days maximum, and I can take it off you." Londo didn't even glance at Stoan. "Yes, Jae, she's all right now. She's going to be fine; Wiley says so. Go back to your meeting. We'll tell you all about it later." He kept his eyes on Lina's. "Until then you're to take it easy. Doctor's orders."

She relaxed in the chair with a faint smile for him. "Yes, Londo."

"Get some more decorating magazines and look through them. Badger Demi until she gets you some Blu-rays of all those *Star Treks* you missed. Read some science fiction."

"Yes, love." The room started to spin again, but Lina caught it before it went out of control, gripping the arm of her husband fiercely, and brought everything into focus again. She was not going to get sick! "Do… Do you want to go over the checklist again, without Ouroboros in place?" Lina suggested to Wiley.

"Do you feel up to it?" he asked.

"Don't, *mon coeur.* Not after that."

"What can it hurt, Lon? If y'all are going to use these things out wherever you're going, Wiley needs all the information he can get, right?"

"You still don't have to do this. I can put one on on the way."

"Londo," she tried to reassure him with a smile, "you're one hell of a strong telepath. But you gots no finesse. You ain't been trained in anyt'ing. And those other powers of yours would probably mess up the test from here to kingdom come. It's bad enough that I had caffeinated tea this morning. I'm sorry, Wiley. I forgot, or I wouldn't have drunk it."

Londo looked from her to Wiley and back. "Are you sure? You can take this?"

"I can take anything as long as I know there's an end to it someday."

"Five days tops, Lina love. And then I'll sit down and tell you everything I'm allowed to tell."

"Five days. I'll hold you to that." She sighed. "Could you get me a glass of water? Do we still have a clean glass left?"

"I'll get you one if I have to wash it personally."

Channeling was still barely on, still more confusing than helpful, though. She was able to levitate things, but nothing else worked. The guides shook their heads when asked about weaknesses in the shackle. An attempt to implode the device failed.

"Oh well, at least there's no headache this time. No noise, either. This one's a keeper. Are you sure you don't want to take it with you?"

"Sorry, Lina." Wiley didn't look at her.

"Well. I could hope." She turned to her troubled husband. "Don't forget to tape your hockey games while you're gone. And if you can, the NCAA games with the Heels."

"I will. Thanks for the reminder, Kitten. I love you."

"I love you, too, darling. Be safe. Remember your promise– and the white light. *Qapla'.*"

"It's time for us to go," Olympia said as she picked up Lina's jacket.

"We have to make a stop to feed the cats," Lina said. She reached for Londo one last time, willing to chance one last touch. They almost made it. "Forever,

Londo," she said as they faded into that pixelated blur the ParaNet's transporter made of the world.

He tried to smile reassuringly at her.

22

L on stared at the afterimage of the beamaway, feeling as helpless as he could remember. Angry that it had come to this. Furious at himself to have allowed this to happen.

What kind of man was he?

He could do nothing now but pace and wait. And win a planetary war, the quicker the better. *Time to determine your loyalties,* Hal had told him. He tightened his hands into fists. At least this way she'd stay on Earth, stay safe. Especially if Demi were with her.

"What did she say?" Stoan asked Hal. "It didn't translate."

Hal shrugged, but Gary spoke up. "*Qapla'*. It's Klingon for 'success,' success in battle."

"Klingon?"

"From *Star Trek.*" Gary glanced around the room at the people regarding him and declared defensively, "They say it all the time. '*Qapla'*.'"

"It's a dramatic entertainment series, Stoan," Londo said as he paced.

The Network had discussed a guard for Lina. They'd agreed with Stoan that a guard was needed, but instead of watching to make sure that Lina didn't betray anyone, Hal had pointed out that the Legion had already announced the marriage, and the shackle would leave Lina defenseless. Lon had immediately suggested leaving her with Jae, but Stoan had nixed that idea.

What were they going to do about Stoan?

Too many questions. Too many things already set in motion. As Lina would remind him, there was no woulda, coulda, shoulda. Deal with the cards you were dealt. Londo was good at that; he was the best there was.

He turned to find Hal next to him. "The quicker we handle Yanist-Glory, the quicker you'll be back," Hal said, and Lon nodded grimly. He had a bad feeling about all this. He could feel the universe rolling with turbulent waves.

Stoan established communications to Sarastor. "The suppressor works," he reported to his subcommander, Andri. "Go ahead and replicate it. We'll use the dampers, too, so copy Wiley's improvements into the replicators for those as well.

"Tell all remaining teams to disembark now. We've lost too much time here as it is. We're taking off for Jorter; we'll rendezvous with you on Deseed in twenty hours. We'll have the information."

"Yes, Commander," Andri replied. "Three full teams here haven't left yet. If we wait, we could get another one together. The team to Shogarna 4 is due back in a few hours."

"Don't wait for them," Stoan ordered. "Leave them a briefing and have them follow. Have the HQ replicators spit out more dampers and suppressors until they return. They can bring those with them."

"Yessir. Nemlor out."

Stoan turned off the screen and swung to face the heroes gathered at Starhaven. He held them all in a stern gaze. He knew they disagreed completely with his views on Carolina, with one exception: the Galactic Guardian, allowed back now that *she* had gone. Hal kept him and Lon on opposite sides of the room.

The Guardian was on Stoan's side, but he didn't think that this was a man he particularly wanted there. He'd never met a Guard who set him on edge this way. This one had a too-sly smile, a greedy glint in his eye. Still, members of the Galactic Brigade were carefully chosen by the Galactic Sentinels, and the Sentinels just didn't make mistakes. It was impossible. This must just be a conflict of personal style. Stoan could rise above it and work with him.

Stoan had made the mistake of allowing the Terrans to see too many of the Legion's records of that woman. He'd shown them that first night at the Romaki

Club, automatically assuming that her singing performance would make her appear freakish. He'd forgotten that song was an integral part of the planetary culture here, not just an individual aberration.

The Network had begun with justifiable suspicions of Lina. She'd attached herself so quickly, so mysteriously, to one of the most powerful beings in the sector. By the time they'd finished their investigation, they'd been ready to throw the new couple a party! Stoan had never had a plan go so askew. Well, this was where it stopped. The rest of this mission had to proceed as planned, with no room for error. Worlds were in the balance; lives, at stake.

"All right," he said, and he had their full attention. "We've got one team here. Mega- and advanced-parapowers only." He saw the sour look on some of their faces. They liked to operate as a complete team when they could. "This will involve quick strikes on a planetary scale. We can't compensate for non-mega-powers then. I'd like to," he said, to assuage their resentment.

"Lon, Gary, Tara, Jelena, Toshi, Granger…" Hal ran down the list, including almost a dozen on his ParaNet team. "Becky, you're staying behind. Your mother told me that if you missed any more school she'd pull you out of the Network for good."

"Yes, sir."

Gary nudged his young protégé on the shoulder. She gave him a quick, embarrassed grin of relief that she wasn't going to war.

Stoan shook his head at the numbers. Earth certainly had more than its share of mega-powered heroes, enough to form a reserve unit for the Legion. The extra power they offered could decide this war.

"I'd prefer Londo work with Legion teams in this," Stoan told Hal, who glanced at Lon and nodded.

The Guardian's ruby buzzed angrily. "Hold it a minute," he told them. He concentrated distantly as the ruby glowed upon his throat for about thirty seconds. "A Brigade emergency, two sectors over," he reported, looking up. "They're calling adjacent Guards. I have to join in on this. Tell you what, I'll catch up to you on Deseed. I have the timetable."

Stoan grimaced but nodded. "If it's unavoidable," Stoan said. "Brigade emergencies supersede even our own."

The Guard inclined his head crisply at Stoan and then flew out the front door. A comet tail of red light marked his route streaking off into the upper atmosphere.

"Down one already," Stoan muttered. "Let's hit hyperspace before we lose any more."

It was a long six hours to Jorter, with the thirteen of them crowded in a linked ship that combined the Network's sole small hyperspaceship with Stoan's roomier Legion hypercraft. Hal was interested to find out that while telepathy couldn't penetrate the hyperspace barrier, it worked within their own bubble of hyperspace.

Lon pointed out ways that they might be able to utilize the situation as an alternate to the dampers. Hyperspace could snap mind control by cutting the controlled person off from their controller's influence. If they ran out of dampers, controlled world leaders could be brought on board to have their orders relayed by jump-shuttles to normal space. Stoan and the others agreed to his contingency plans.

"How do you feel now?" Stoan asked him privately.

Londo tried not to snarl. "She's not controlling me."

A grunt was all the apology he received.

Wilder fiddled with the ship's special replicators on the way. Toshi and Tara assisted him. They produced more of the psi-nulling globes that he'd originally used, the dampers. Those could be used to dull an area from outside control, whereas the shackles, or suppressors, would be for individual use, to stop augmented telepaths from controlling.

The group went over maps and military organizational charts. They studied photos of major military figures on Jorter who were suspected as being part of Yanist-Glory's plot. Hal led the briefing. He'd been the one who'd first become suspicious as the balance of power in this neighboring galactic sector shifted.

He showed the Terrans on the sector map how four star systems bordering on Yanist-Glory's empire had suddenly declared themselves vassal states of the empire. Here, then a few months later here, then here and here. It was a pattern in which Earth could be involved if it kept up for, say, five years more.

Hal reported that in each instance top military personnel had begun to act strangely. It hadn't been enough for anyone to be officially questioned, but just so people had noticed that they weren't their usual selves. Then those brass had used their positions to mount coups and declare themselves for Yanist-Glory.

It was hard to believe that any world would willingly come under the emperor's "protection." He had a history of executing half the military personnel of the worlds he added to his empire, replacing them with loyal troops of his own. But here it was, world after world. Troops had gone willingly to be slaughtered to make room for the Imperials.

Government officials would be replaced by Yanist-Glory's own toadies, usually to drain resources for their personal benefit.

Logically, Jorter was next in line. Hal had already discovered a deviation: a Colonel Sey-Yune was postponing priority meetings as well as changing his aides and headquarters staff. He'd just returned from an extended vacation. Most people around him put it down to reinvigoration.

Except for a few, who had sent urgent messages to the legendary Maximus of Earth.

Hal had warned the Mega-Legion Commander of the security threat. They'd agreed that he should take his own recon of the situation. Hal decided not to warn any of the other military leaders of Jorter for fear that some of them might be infected as well. Instead he had prowled, asked discreet questions of people he thought he could trust, and then headed back to Earth to report both to the Network and the Mega-Legion.

Stoan had seen Lina as the obvious plant. He'd insisted on coming to Earth personally to make sure that the threat from her was neutralized while they were occupied elsewhere. As Legion commander, he would head the mission instead of Maximus. This was a matter of Affiliated Systems security.

Hal finished his report with suggestions for their approval. The group discussed strategy until everyone knew their roles.

Then there was nothing to do but sit and wait to arrive at Jorter. The Networkers organized a quick poker game, but Lon uncharacteristically stayed out of it. He lounged in a chair, looking at nothing, his chin on his fist. Hal breathed a sigh of relief, much to his own consternation. This was Lon being moody; this was Lon acting like himself.

But when Hal sat down beside his adopted son, he saw that Lon's face held a secret smile instead of a scowl. Hal shook his head; Lon bitten by the love bug. He'd given up hope that this would ever happen.

"I can read minds now," he joked in a quiet voice. "Let me tell you who you're thinking about."

Lon gave him a half-grin. "No great trick to that," he said. "And don't let Stoan hear you say you can read minds."

"I can't believe you've gone telepath," Hal said. "Do you have any idea how it happened?"

"I think Terry was right," Lon said slowly. "I can remember now, over the years, the times when I almost knew what people were thinking."

"You've always been able to size up people quickly, see situations before anyone else could."

"Maybe that's a part of it," Lon agreed. "Being around Lina, talking telepathically and sharing minds, that must have brought it all into focus."

Hal began to laugh softly. "Sorry," he apologized. "I was getting suspicious because you didn't join in the game over there. Now I realize–"

"Telepaths spoil the odds." Lon regarded the group at the poker table. "I figure I've got maybe four games left with the Legion before they figure it out. There are some people I've been wanting to fleece for a long time. Let's see how long it takes for the little light to come on in their heads."

They were silent for a while. Then Hal said quietly, "I like Lina. I think she's a good choice for you."

"Good to hear," Lon said.

"Are her parents really as bad as she says?"

"Worse." Lon scowled. "If I'd been in her shoes, I'd have run as far away from them as I could. Don't tell her I said that."

Hal nodded, considering it. "The in-laws need to meet."

"Not yet. They think that you're some kind of international security expert, a jet-setter of sorts. They won't be suspicious if they never meet you. And although they might not be able to place my face, yours is one they'll recognize."

"So you really think they shouldn't know?"

Lon groaned even as he heaved a sigh. "Lina's got them pegged right. They'd go straight off the edge of the earth. I wonder how long it'll be before they figure it out on their own. When that happens, we'll have a big family get-together, *d'accord?*"

"All right." Hal paused. How to put it? How not to show the hurt and surprise? "So you're Starheart now..." he began, and didn't know where to go from there.

"Ah. Yeah. That's something that Lina and I both came up with." Londo knew what Hal was asking. "Look, Hal, it's nothing against you. I know how much I owe and love you. And Mama Ruth and Papa Mike, too. I'll always owe you for my life. Rands are family. But... I just wanted to be me, by myself, for once. Not under your shadow." He shook his head. "This isn't coming out right. I'm always grateful to you, and I'll be there whenever you need me, but it's just that–"

"It's just that it's always Maximus and Valiant, and never Valiant and Maximus," Hal said softly. "I understand."

"If I'd known about the Three Worlds," Lon said slowly, "maybe we would have gone a different route. It's going to point me in a different direction than the one you've taken. But Lina didn't want to be called Rand, and I can't blame her."

"It's not that bad a name," Hal countered.

"But in her mind that would have meant I owned her. You know how women are nowadays. Can I say that? So we played around with names. 'O'Randly,' I think, was when we decided that we'd have to go for something totally new." He gave a grimace that was supposed to be an apologetic smile. "It could have been worse. I believe 'Lon and Lina Startrek' was getting a lot of support from one of the team members."

Hal had to chuckle at that. "All right," he conceded. "Starheart it is. A little flashy, but I suppose I can live with it. It'll take a while to get used to it."

Lon grunted.

"So… about this Three Worlds stuff. You've got a big agenda to fulfill. And there are only three of you to do it. You're going to need a lot of help. I volunteer."

"We *are* going to need help," Lon nodded. "But we're the Three Worlds, Hal. I know you, you're doing this because you care about me and you care about those worlds out there, but–"

Lon swallowed. "But I don't want this project to be Maximus and the Three Worlds. It's got to be us. We were the Chosen. It's not that we won't welcome any input you want to make," he added hastily as he saw Hal's frown, "but like I said, this is a different direction than you're aiming yourself. It's going to be even more different as time goes by. We've started working on a lot of ideas. A million ideas, and they're our ideas. It's our project, and it's important enough that I don't think it should have to lie in Maximus' shadow. You've got one hell of a big shadow."

His father considered him.

"I'm almost thirty," Lon said. "Time I stood up and became my own man."

"I thought you already were. A long time ago I looked at you and said, my boy's a man now. A long time."

"Maybe others haven't seen it that way. They'd have to be able to see around you to see me."

Hal nodded slowly. "All right. If you need me, just call and I'll be there. You can't get around that."

Lon gave a small smile. "Thanks. I really appreciate it. You know we three will be there for you, too, right?"

"Else," Hal said abruptly. "How will Lina take her?"

"I'll give her a warning. I don't know if she just treats everything like she's in some *Star Trek* show, or if it really makes her a little more accepting of the unusual, but when someone throws from left field, she catches the ball."

"Always a plus," Hal said and looked up. "Jorter just ahead. We're coming out of hyperspace." He looked to Lon curiously as his face screwed up in pain.

"Augh. *Merde.* Damn it to hell anyway." Lon shook his head and took a breath. He blinked and exhaled. "God. Chimrin's always complaining about this, and I know what she means now. The telepathic impressions all descend on you at once."

Communications flared to life. "This is Jorter Control to unidentified vessel," an orange-skinned woman in a dark uniform declared. "State your origin point and purpose or prepare to be boarded."

"Easy now," Hal sat in front of the screen with the others out of view.

"Maximus!" The woman's eyes went from wide-eyed surprise to narrow suspicion. "In a hyperspace ship?"

"This is the Paranorm Network ship TPN-1 out of Earth. Aren't our transponders working? Or are you in some sort of emergency mode, jumping the gun out here?" He toggled a switch to make it seem like their communications were on the blink. They hadn't wanted to come in with all flags flying.

"We're getting static from you, Maximus," the traffic controller confirmed. "You might want to have someone look at that while you're here. We just got confirmation of your ID."

"We don't want to show up unannounced, " Hal said gravely. "Are you on military alert?"

The controller nodded. "Third stage, with second stage looming."

"Darn. Here we've come to see if we can get some assistance from your forces for a Terran emergency."

"I wouldn't know anything about that, TPN-1." She consulted her screens. "If you give me a destination, I'll clear you for landing."

23

Only Hal went out in uniform. Lon had been here many times, so Wilder gave him his illusion projector to fasten onto his belt. After it was programmed, Londo appeared blond and lankier than before. He rumpled his hair, checked out his new, narrow face, and loosened his clothing.

The three of them: him, Tara and Gary, went in civilian disguise. Initially Stoan had been hesitant about including Lon in a subterfuge mission, but he couldn't argue the point that Lon was now a telepath and thus might be able to point out other telepaths or evidence of mind control. Even so, it would be reassuring to have his muscle there if the situation got too hot.

The legendary hero Maximus and his attachés were admitted into Planetary Military Headquarters despite the Level Three alert. Aides escorted them into an inner conference room dominated by a black table. Three Jorterti officers joined them.

"Ordinarily, Maximus," Major Radley began, "I'd be delighted to see you again, particularly at this time while we're under alert. But I'm told there's trouble on your world?"

"We're having problems controlling some dissidents on Earth," Hal explained. "We're in the process of setting up a world government and– well, you can understand that there are a few people who have problems with the concept. Unfortunately they've achieved access to some military arsenals."

"And your Network can't handle it?"

"Without help we may cause many more unnecessary deaths than we would if we had, say, three or four units operating with us." Hal went on to detail specific logistics that the ParaNet couldn't provide.

The Jorterti took notes on their padds. The table turned into a communications screen as they attempted to find some available units who could be spared. Major Radley shook his head. "This is tough. We have no idea if our own situation will escalate or not."

"We understand," Hal said. "These things happen. Emergencies arise. We'll try Deseed, then. Maybe they'll be able to free up some troops."

"You knew that they've gone over to Yanist-Glory."

Hal sank back in his chair with a shocked expression. "Yanist-Glory? You must be joking."

The major grimaced and leaned heavily on his elbows. "It just happened. One of our own men, Trey Sey-Yune, barely got away from there in time before they locked down the planet."

Hal considered. "So he was there. He'd have gotten a look at how it was accomplished."

One of the Jorterti aides was listening closely but not bothering to take notes. She looked up to see the standing Terran attaché gazing at her. Why was he staring? His gaze moved slowly down off her face and then back up. Then he smiled a wickedly bad boy smile.

She looked away and then wondered why. He certainly looked interesting; the fact that he accompanied Maximus was intriguing. He must be a man of power. These days she was free again. In the old days she'd have taken a chance if he were going to be here when she got off duty. But that seemed like a different person now, not her any more, and it didn't occur to her to wonder why. Instead she listened intently to the conversation about Deseed and Yanist-Glory. She forgot about the blond man.

Soon Colonel Sey-Yune joined them, nodding amicably to the others. He was medium height with skin a subtle shade of mango, and dark rust hair. A crisp uniform accentuated his lean physique. His eyes shown bright as he shook the great Maximus's hand. "Yes, I was there just before it happened," he told the group. "Funny thing– the local news reported that they'd just had enough of living between empires and republics, and that the Empire could afford them the greatest protection. So they swore allegiance to the Emperor."

"Just like that?"

The general cocked his head at Hal. "It's tense living on the frontier. You Terrans should realize that. You're as caught between everyone as we are. Of course, Deseed was practically in Imperial territory already."

"And now they're officially there." Hal leaned over to consult with his attachés. The blond attaché leaned down to hear, putting his hand on Maximus's shoulder. The other two attaches muttered back and forth. Finally the standing man straightened.

"Falcon," Hal said to him, "see if you can get some information on this sudden change of heart on Deseed for us to take back and study. Colonel Sey-Yune," he nodded to the ranking officer, "could you assign my aide Falcon here someone who could show him where to download your non-classified files about this? Or as classified as I can qualify for? We certainly don't want Earth to fall into the emperor's clutches."

"I can arrange that much," the colonel replied and motioned to the woman aide. "Lieutenant Latreas, please show Falcon what files we have. Anything we can do for Earth is our pleasure."

"We are most gratified, General," Hal said graciously. "Now, about your alert here…"

The aide Falcon followed Lt. Latreas out of the room.

Lon brushed absently at his hair back in the ship, glad it was combed again.

"There was only a tiny core of Sey-Yune's mind even there anymore. Like someone had piled a dumpload of dirt on top of a marble. The control was that overwhelming."

Stoan sat back in his chair, rocking it as he tapped his chin. "And the aide?"

"She wasn't nearly as bad. It was so strange to read her: two entirely different sets of thoughts were in her mind, and one of her was totally unaware that there was anyone else there."

"Were there… hooks?" Hal asked. He looked directly into Lon's eyes.

"I don't know. I've only been doing this for a couple of days. Lina's been doing it for years, and she's taken classes. When we get to Deseed I'll try looking for hooks."

Tara was trying to figure the consequences. "So if you can see hooks, Lina can get them out. Eliminate the mind control."

"So she says."

"And if you can't see hooks…"

"Then either I'm just blind and they really are there, or they're doing this by some other means."

"But this aide—" Stoan prompted Lon for more information.

"She was one of Sey-Yune's people. She took me back to his sector of Headquarters. I'd guess I passed about three dozen personnel, and every last one of them was like her, but to a lesser degree. Instead of being controlled, I'd call them… highly influenced."

"Do you think we can trust the information we got from them?" Stoan asked.

Wilder answered. "I've already examined a large part of it. Because it originally came through Sey-Yune, we can consider it propaganda. It is an incomplete view of what's going on, and skewed considerably from what our ships already around Deseed have relayed."

Stoan nodded. "Let's have it then. We'll take the final four hours of the trip for rest period." Everyone turned to the main viewscreen within the Legion ship, getting comfortable. The authorities on Jorter thought they'd returned empty-handed to an Earth in planetary turmoil, not guessing that they were going onward to Imperial Deseed to wage war.

As the others settled down afterward, Stoan drew Hal and Londo aside to finalize the kinds of initial intelligence they'd need about Deseed. The two Terrans would begin as scouts, but then Hal would have his own solo mission to attend to, and Londo—

Stoan kept his options open on Londo. The ability to spot controlled people was certainly a plus, but had emerged from suspicious circumstances. He'd wait to see what was truly happening on Deseed before he committed himself to a plan of action with Londo.

Stoan couldn't help frowning at Lon as they discussed possible tactics.

"Why don't you trust me?" Lon finally asked.

Stoan considered his hands, then gave Hal the courtesy of a glance before he regarded his son. "I don't know who you are any more," he said. "A telepath. Protector of the Three Worlds. A… husband. All within a week of each other. You've even changed your name."

Stoan's mouth worked around the sourness of it all. "Circumventing my orders on Earth. That's not like you. I don't trust people who are suddenly not who I thought they were, not when we're battling mind control. I need people who'll work with me, not against me."

"Chimrin's cleared us," Londo stated. How many times must he repeat this?

"He's clean, Stoan," Hal told the Legion commander. He certainly seemed to believe it. "And so is she. I know Lina must seem very strange to you, but believe me, she's pretty run of the mill for a Terran psychic. Not in what she does, but in her attitude. Psychics pride themselves on being mysterious and spooky, I think, and artists make a point of being non-conformist. You don't have anything to worry about with her."

Maximus was a towering heroic figure in the galaxy, in history. Valiant wasn't far behind him. But mind control– Stoan had had too personal an experience with it to trust these two all the way. It was uncontrollable. It was evil. There was no way Stoan would ever allow it to spread if he had anything to say about it!

Hal looked up as Tara motioned to him. She and Wilder were still fiddling with some of the suppressors and needed help. He nodded and joined her.

That left Stoan and Londo alone.

"Quit harping about her," Londo said. He was trying not to get angry. They faced a tense situation. This was no time to fritter away energy negatively. No time to break ranks. "Be happy for me instead. If you can't, then just think of her as a great Legion tool, just another piece of equipment. She's going to increase our efficiency enormously. She's willing to port people as needed."

"She's ambitious," Stoan said carefully. "And look who she married."

"She's been thrown against her will into circumstances I can barely begin to comprehend," Londo countered. "She's adapting amazingly well. And Stoan, I had to beg her to marry me."

"So you're saying she didn't marry for love?" Stoan's eyes narrowed.

"Oh, she loves me," Londo said, unaware that he was smiling warmly as he said it. "I understand how it is not to know for sure. But I'm a telepath now. Her love for me– it's there, and it's forever. I knew that before she even realized. Trust me in this, Stoan."

Stoan drummed his fingers on the desk.

"Neither of us is controlling the other," Londo reassured him. "And I can tell that no one on this ship is being controlled, either."

"Let's talk about someone else, then." Stoan's scrutiny never left Lon's face. "Good old Jae, your best friend."

"Lina's too, now," Lon said carefully. "They got to know each other well– as friends– while we were away."

"As friends," Stoan repeated.

"Yes."

"Isn't it funny how the three of you were all chosen?" Stoan mused, apparently to himself.

"Lina says there's no such thing as coincidence," Londo said. "She sees the universe as having a purpose, an infinity of purposes that build on each other. The universe knew we three would be partners, so you chose Jae to guard her so they could become friends first."

"I didn't. I had no idea," Stoan said.

"Maybe subconsciously or super consciously you did." Londo quirked a mischievous eyebrow. "You're taking part in the Cosmic Game."

"Don't go all existential on me, Rand."

"Starheart."

"That, too. By the orb, you changed your name. Your idea or hers?"

Londo thought. "I knew I said I wanted the both of us to have the same name." He looked around; Hal was talking to Wilder and Tara. "And I didn't want it to be Rand," he said softly. Stoan stuck his tongue in his cheek at that but nodded. "She obviously isn't the type to take her husband's name…"

"Not the type? It would be logical to take the more prestigious spouse's name."

Lon shook his head. "Wrong culture, Stoan. Earth– or the countries there that we're from– is going through a gender-equalization movement. Traditionally women have taken their husbands' names to signify themselves as property, or at least subservient to the man. Lina's a modern woman. She believes in symbols having power, and names are very powerful symbols."

Stoan sighed. "So it's Starheart." He paused for a half-beat. "And Jae is a homosexual." He watched Londo's eyes widen at that, watched Londo set his teeth.

"Which one told you? Lina or Jae?"

"Does it matter?"

"I suppose not. Yes. Jae's gay."

"And you've known all along?" Stoan could see Lon's eyes move in an arc as he remembered.

"Pretty much. Why didn't I ever tell anyone? Because it's none of their business. Sexual preference is a private thing, or at least it should be." Lon's gaze measured Stoan. "So tell me, are you going to give Jae grief about this?"

"Is he planning on going public?" Stoan asked.

"He probably will, and before not too long." Londo smiled to himself. "Lina got him a pile of rainbow literature– that's for the homosexual rights movement– while they were on Earth. She has a lot of gay friends, she's very supportive of the movement, and she thought Jae should know about it."

"Shards." Stoan shook his head. "Lon, Legionnaires are supposed to uphold an image–"

"There's nothing wrong with being gay," Lon declared. "It's a biological imperative. If you're gay, there's nothing you can do about it, except learn to accept yourself. Maybe even celebrate it." Lon rubbed his head. The irony of what he was saying hadn't escaped him. "I know there are support groups on Earth for families of gays, to help them understand. The Legion is a family, Stoan. Maybe I need to get some of that literature and leave it lying around Headquarters."

Stoan clenched the edge of the table. "You think there are other gays in the Legion?"

Londo shrugged. "I know of a few bisexuals–"

"Bisexuals?"

Londo nodded.

"Great shards of plasma, what else is going on that I don't know about?"

"Nothing that would seriously impair the Legion's image if it were ever discovered," Londo assured him. "We all know and respect our duty to the Legion. We're all behind you, Stoan. Just don't go voicing public disapproval of what we do in private."

"All right; we're speaking privately now, so let me tell you one more thing." Stoan's face hardened. "There's something going on between Jae and Carolina. I know it through sheer instinct. I don't know if it's mind control or human nature. But something's–"

"Stoan–"

"Listen to me, Ra– Starheart. If you want this marriage of yours to last more than a month, I'd suggest you sit down with both of them– separately– and remind them of the facts. Jae's a Legionnaire. Carolina's now a Legion spouse. I don't want even a hint of impropriety."

Stoan's voice softened. "Lon, you're my friend. We've known each other for years. I trust my life to you, and I've had to do it in the past. *Skurn* it, I want you happy and I'm ecstatic that you finally got laid. But make sure *she* knows what's at stake. If she loves you, she shouldn't mind being loyal to you. It comes with the job of being a spouse. Tell her what's expected of her."

"I'll tell you what I told her when she asked," Londo said. "I expect her to be herself. She and I are Terran, and there's nothing you can do about that."

"Try to be a little less Terran, can you?" Stoan asked.

Londo grinned at him. "Hell, Stoan, we're going to be the most Terran Terrans the AffSys has ever seen! No one will be embarrassed by it unless they choose to be embarrassed."

"And Jae?"

Lon considered. "Jae's going to be more Jae, I think. I don't know if that means more Feithi or what. Jae's a creature unique to himself."

Stoan had to admit that Lon was right about Jae. As the last Feithi and sole survivor of the Great Disaster, Jae Rallene was beyond rules.

Stoan was trying to be fair, but he was Legion commander. If there was something to be nipped, better to nip it before it could grow. He still wasn't sure about Carolina. Chimrin had cleared her, reporting that none of the three were controlled or controlling, but had also explained that Carolina and she operated on different frequencies, or the psi equivalent. They weren't attuned in many areas.

Stoan had taken it upon himself days ago to contact the Tishan Institute. Chimrin was one of their best, certainly their best telepath who was also a cunning and resourceful combat leader. She'd commanded the Mega-Legion for years, just before Stoan achieved the same position. But she wasn't the Institute's strongest teep.

He'd run tapes of Carolina for the provost-general, the famed telepath Engrade, a rather old man who had murmured a continuous "humm" as he'd watched, especially the one where Carolina had deflected Erik's mind control.

Engrade reran it several times.

"He's a controller, all right," Engrade reported. "Not major scale by any means, but it's there. I wouldn't have caught it if it hadn't been pointed out. I just can't quite see what it is she's doing. Oh, I can see it on the readout– very interesting electro-magnetic readings there. I've never heard of someone being able to record this kind of phenomena."

"Doctor Mem-Bazer recently developed the technique," Stoan said.

Engrade nodded absently. "It's not quite telepathic. She's using clairvoyance to monitor the process, but the actual process is not telepathic in nature." He looked at Stoan. "I have no idea what to tell you it is. What planet did you say she was from?"

"Earth," Stoan replied.

"Earth." Engrade had given a funny, puzzled look. "What's ever come out of Earth?" The old man gazed unfocused at the woman on his screen and then looked up suddenly. "Great shards," he said, "she's Valiant's lover!"

Telepaths. Stoan tried not to look rueful. "Yes, they're married," he confirmed. "We haven't announced it yet. We're waiting to see if she's a controller or not."

Engrade shook his head. "Not in this instance. She's actually stopping the control before it starts. The first time–" The professor let the screen split to show the first meeting between Carolina and Erik. "It goes so quickly. I can sense the control starting, and then I don't know if she's deflecting it or decontrolling– I know that sounds ridiculous. Maybe overriding it. Very quick, whatever it is."

Stoan scrolled through Wiley's lab records. "Could you take a look at this and tell me what's going on? Paying attention to possibilities of mind control in particular."

"Of course." Engrade had nodded, obviously honored to be of service to the Mega-Legion.

Stoan ran the tape of Lon and Lina suddenly appearing in the main lab in a blaze of light, colors and streamers of stars behind them, clasped in each other's arms.

"Great blazing grigach. Great blazing–! Look at that!" Engrade gasped. His mouth flapped open again and again as he watched the scene. Then he shook his head. "I'm sorry," he said "Let's run that again. Shards and splinters!"

They ran through it several times, Engrade exclaiming each time he caught something new.

"It's… It's… I don't know," he said. "Like nothing I've ever seen. It's like– the mind of the Infinite opening up and allowing a peek inside, if I may be poetic. There are presences here– at least three huge minds, extremely powerful, but having nothing to do with the humans. And it's as if there's a… background, a backdrop, if you will, of more distant minds, just as powerful. They're curious as to what's going on." Engrade rubbed his upper lip and then his chin, trying to make sense of it.

"How about Valiant and Carolina there?" Stoan asked. "I'm looking for mind control."

"Oh, them," the provost almost dismissed the two main participants. "An extremely high level of physical attraction. They resonate to each other; that's interesting enough. You don't see that happen often, not even for two people in the throes of a marriage proposal." He squinted at the screen. "They've shared minds. That's a very advanced technique, and they've done it deeply." His eyes went to Stoan's. "I'd never heard that Valiant was a telepath."

"He is now, as of a few days ago."

Engrade shook his head. "No one *becomes* a telepath. They either are or aren't, but they can suppress the ability. Sometimes it suddenly breaks loose. It can happen when a latent is around a functioning telepath for a time."

"And the Feithi were telepathic, weren't they?"

"Feithi?" Engrade's eyebrows contracted in puzzlement. "Yes, Feith was a world of telepaths. But Valiant's not from— Ah. The Legion has another new telepath?"

"Neutrino, yes," Stoan had informed him. Suddenly a thought struck him and he played another tape, one of Jae and Carolina stopping the Aldierran invasion. Londo hadn't been there then.

"Any mind control here?" he asked Engrade. "Any evidence of shared minds?"

Engrade shook his head. "Absolutely none," he reported.

"All right," Stoan said. "Just one more, and let me warn you that this is a little more strange that the other one."

Engrade chuckled weakly at that, wiping his eyes. "Stranger than what you've already shown me? I wish I had the authority to show these to my colleagues, to stupefy them as you've done me." He took a breath and said, "Bring it on, Commander."

He watched as the ghost of Orenya appeared in Legion Headquarters and the Three Worlds appointed their Chosen.

Engrade was silent for a long time afterward. Stoan let him think.

Finally he spoke. "They are the same minds here, the enormous minds, towering so far above human understanding. Absolutely unreadable, but their presence— Could it really be planetary entities? Of course there have always been the ancient myths, but no thinking person would really believe— But here they are. Here they are!"

"Carolina chats with them on a regular basis," Stoan reported dryly.

Engrade's eyes were sharp on his. "Valiant's become a telepath. Neutrino's become a telepath. These... Worlds have communicated to humans. All since this Carolina woman has come on the scene."

"Valiant's new wife."

"I can see why you're concerned." Engrade leaned back in his seat, rubbing the bulb of his nose. "First, let me tell you that I don't detect the taint of mind controller on her. Not at all. But someone who can communicate with planets, if indeed that is what these minds are— Well, I'd like to gather a full Tishan Council to examine this woman. Just to make sure she's not operating so far above us that we can't detect what she's doing. A new kind of mind control, perhaps. Psyche has already given you her opinion, I assume. She's had a chance to observe her?"

"Only a little. She's told me that she's not controlling anyone."

Engrade nodded, and leaned over to a keypad/screen on his desk. "Could you arrange to bring Mrs. Valiant here sometime on the 8th? Or 9th. The entire faculty and Council will have completed students' exams by then. They'll be able to devote their undivided attention to this."

A single finger went over his mouth as Engrade thought. "And it would be interesting to have some patients from the hospital— the mentally-controlled ones— on hand to see how she reacts to them. That would be telling in and of itself. We'll need to prepare a battery of sensors. Could I communicate with Dr. Mem-Bazer about this?"

"The Legion is yours to command for this project," Stoan told him. "Though Mem-Bazer's assistance won't be available for a week or so."

Engrade nodded. "I'll begin to arrange things immediately," he said. "Please inform me as to when she'll arrive. Ah. This would probably work best as… a surprise." His eyes met Stoan's.

They understood each other.

"Mem-Bazer's come up with something else," Stoan said guardedly. "He's working on a telepathic damper field generator."

Engrade sucked in his breath. "To keep her in the dark until she faces us," he said. "If it were to actually work, it would render the entire Institute helpless— telepathically speaking."

"I realize that," Stoan had said. "Perhaps we can localize the field to the individual. I'll arrange for her to be brought to you as soon as possible. The ninth latest."

Now in hyperspace and back on schedule, Stoan smiled to himself. Carolina was on Earth, all wrapped up nicely with a suppressor. Helpless. Not so cocky now; no threats from her direction to worry about. After they'd finished this mission, it would be easy to transfer her to Tishan for her examination.

"Were you planning to tell her about this? Tell me?" Londo rose on his knuckles to tower over the sitting Stoan. "Or would you arrange the kidnapping while you assigned me Legion duty somewhere else?" As he glared at Stoan, Londo's teeth ground audibly.

He'd read Stoan's mind.

"Broadcasting," Lon said in a hiss. "Proud of your plan, aren't you? You aren't going to take my wife, Stoan Kinrol. She's already talked to Chimrin, and we've discussed going to Tishan when we have the time and inclination. But I will not stand still to have her taken against her will."

"If I order you to let us—"

"Enough!" Lon's teeth bared, and unveiled rage burned in his eyes. "You will not do this— period. If you order me as Legion commander to permit it, I will resign. You won't have any power over me then. I've let you do too much as it is. You won't take advantage of me again. Lina will get to Tishan; we'll all three get to Tishan. Eventually. After this plot, I think we'll push back our schedule. But whenever it is, it will be on our terms, of our own volition. Not because you're upset because Lina doesn't treat you like a god incarnate!"

"Don't try to make something of—"

"It's true. There might have been something to worry about at first, but now it's personal with you, Stoan. Your pride's been hurt because you've been treated like a person and not the commander. I married who I wanted to and not your choice. People aren't acting precisely like you'd like, perfect little Legion robots. Things are happening that you can't put your Legion commander finger on and explain. Well, tough. These things happen. Face it like a man. Don't blame everything on Lina."

Londo almost struck his fist against the desk, but stopped. The desk would not have held up to him. Hal and the others still up were watching as it was.

"Tell me you won't kidnap her. You won't cart her off to Tishan without her permission. And mine."

Hal rose. **Stay back,** Londo ordered. **This is my affair.**

Stoan regarded Londo. The secret was out of the bag anyway. There'd be no element of surprise. "All right," he finally said. "No kidnapping."

Londo nodded, but he didn't relax. "Lay off Lina. Pick something new to harp about."

Stoan was silent. "No more singing in public," he countered. "No gay literature in Legion HQ. No more 'innocent' kisses in public parks. No more threats against me, no more threats about quitting."

Hal came over anyway. "Let's let things cool down over here, shall we?" he said equably. "We've got to be in top form in three hours. You're beginning to get a little too loud over here about things that I want to ask about. Kidnapping and threats—"

"It's between us," Stoan said, his voice a low growl directed at Londo. "But you're right. We'll settle this later, Londo. I'm going to get some sleep." Stoan pushed himself away from the desk and left the room. Hal turned to Londo, but Lon didn't offer any explanations.

24

Olympia scrunched in the office chair. Once again, she pushed her mirrored sunglasses as close to her eyes as possible. She had wedged herself between the file cabinet and the window so as to be the least obtrusive and still have a good view of the open end of the cubicle. The blinds had been closed for security.

Lina didn't bother to hide her sarcasm as she worked at her computer. "It's not bright enough in here to wear those. You don't have to be ashamed. It's honest work, a fairly honest office."

"So you say."

"Since when are Europeans such prudes?"

"Asian. Scythia is in Asia."

"Asians then. Londo was fine with where I worked."

"He would be. Lon can be–" Abruptly Olympia shut her mouth.

"A perv," Lina finished for her.

"I didn't say that."

"A sweetie perv. He has some very strange ideas sometimes. But you know, sometimes he comes up with something that's quite interesting. And no one's going to recognize you, Olympia, not in that getup."

"It's Demeter. Call me Demi. For *them* I'm 'Ms. Smith.'" Demi had dressed in black jeans and leather jacket over a white tank top, an all-American look as opposed to the traditional Scythian patterning and style of her uniform. She wore a long black wig that was scraggily but looked real, and a white scarf tied into a hairband helped hold it secure. Every once in a while Lina could see a glow when the jacket eased open, with movement from where Ouroboros was stuffed, still crackling with those tiny lightnings. The gun holstered at Demi's hip had required many levels of permission to be allowed in the building.

Demi wore a badge on her left breast pocket that said "ParaNet Security: D. Smith" and under that was the blue VISITORS badge from Midnight Delivery. It might as well have been a scarlet "A." The famous feminist writhed under its seal and thrashed about yet again in the office chair.

"If you do that all day, so help me, I'm going to find a camera and take a whole album of you here," Lina threatened. "And then I'm going to send it to N.O.W. and–" The Macintosh blooped in front of her and she hit some more keys. "Leigh!" she called. "It's in your folder now!"

A voice from a few cubicles down answered: "That was quick."

"Just throw money. Since when do we use high school kids?"

"High school?" Leigh's head and part of the hot pink boa she had wrapped around her neck, peeked around the corner into Lina's cubicle. She gave Demi a quick glance, but that was all.

Demi would swear that was the same boa Lina had worn the other night in Montreal.

"I was being generous," Lina said. "To tell the truth, he looked middle school to me. We sure we have proof of age?"

Leigh shrugged. "Craig said everything was okay."

"I'd feel a lot better if you double-checked. You know Craig. He's in such a hurry to get back to–" Lina covered one nostril, gave a huge sniff and Leigh nodded– "that he doesn't check the fine print. Five minutes extra here can save five to ten years down the line."

"Sure, I can check," Leigh said and trotted past them.

"Thanks."

Thank goodness Demi had agreed to them coming here. As expected, things at Lina's ex-job had begun to fall apart. A couple hours' work was needed to set things back on track, but it was all she could do to re-organize her files with all the people coming up to her. "I know you're being here is a secret," they'd whisper, "but let me take just one picture!"

"What in the world for?" Lina would demand. "You've seen me every day you've been here. I haven't changed that much, have I?"

"Is *HE* coming?" they'd ask. "Can I get your autograph?"

Lina guffawed at that one and wrote a rude remark on a piece of Midnight Delivery note paper, finishing with a flourish.

Everyone looked uncertainly at her shackle. "What the hell is that thing?"

"Don't answer," Demi would tell her every time. "It's classified."

Lina would then shrug to whoever it was and give a half-smile, except the time when idiot Deb had asked if it was a cast from where Valiant had, you know, *hurt* her while *you know.*

"Get out of here!" Lina yelled. Behind the fleeing woman, another co-worker, this one a chubby blond man, sauntered up, hands in his pockets.

Lina smiled. "Hey, Shark. How's it going?"

"Not as good as you. We saw you on CNN. The guys in the warehouse all want autographed pictures. I haven't seen you flash that much skin since… Hell, I've never seen you flash that much skin. Hubba-hubba."

"Lend me your gun, Ms. Smith. Just for one shot."

"We deserve something for all the trouble you put us through. Half the building was running around thinking we were about to get raided."

"Raided?"

"Valiant had been here." Shark let out a chuckle through his nose. "But then Kaya said he'd just placed a fifteen-page order. We didn't think he'd raid us if he wanted to get his stuff. Just what are you doing with him, Lina? Isn't perversion of a major mega a felony?"

"Oh god." A snort sounded from Demi behind her. "Tell everyone he's just gathering evidence. Yeah, that's it." Lina instructed Shark to spread the "corrected" rumor.

"Your security system's really tight," Demi would mutter every time a new stranger appeared. She'd jump out of her chair and brace herself for action when they were particularly sudden, her hand sliding to her holster.

This made a few of them flee, but for the most part they regarded her curiously. "Can I take your picture, too?" someone asked.

"No! Go away." Demi considered setting up traffic cones to keep all these gawkers at bay.

"Are you really with ParaNet Security? Do you know any of *them?*"

"I'm not here to gossip."

Gilroy from Accounting asked Lina, "Not much fun to have around, is she?"

"I'm not supposed to be fun," Demi growled. She clicked the safety back in place on the hidden gun she's just reached for.

He nodded at the movement. "What ya got there?"

"My lunch. Move along." Something caught her attention out of the corner of her eye: a flash of red. She ducked to the window and cracked the blinds. Did a trail of red light hang in the air, disappearing even as she tried to focus on it?

Red light. She would swear to it.

"I don't like this," Demi muttered to herself as she chewed over recent events and possibilities.

Lina reached into her purse for some coins. "Gilroy, could you do me a favor and get me a Coke? And something for Ms. Smith, too." She stage whispered, "No caffeine for her, please."

"Sure," Gilroy said. When he came back he tried to sneak up on Lina's cubicle, but Demi had the gun ready when he poked his head around the corner.

"Good way for you to get your head blown off," she growled at him.

"So how many people have you killed?"

"Today? More than you can count, probably."

"Is she really in danger?"

"This is standard procedure."

Lina fought back a groan at that. This had better not be standard procedure. This had better be a once-in-a-lifetime thing with lots of apologies afterward. She'd apologize to Olympia, that was, Demi, too, for wasting such an important parahero's time. Stoan had better do the same. Jerk.

At least she now had all organizational procedures filed and in the Cloud so that any moron could follow them, if they took the time to read them. She didn't think she underestimated her fellow employees, she just thought that once most of them entered the building they just didn't give a damn until they left for the evening. To her, a job was a sacred responsibility. You did your best no matter what.

Once again Demi jumped to her feet. This time a cow poked its head around the corner.

"Don't shoot the cow!" Lina cried.

A cowboy followed the lumbering cow. The animal wasn't a very good costume. The person in front had a much better time of it than the one forming the be-uddered rear section, who had to walk bent over, their head near the lead's butt.

Demi gaped. "What the hell is this?"

The cowboy tipped his hat to them both. "Just a reminder that if we exceed our goals this week on upsells, there'll be a steak dinner next month for the whole department." His eyes fell on Lina. "What the f– is that on your arm? Wait– is that a gun?" He squinted at Demi. "ParaNet Security?"

Demi secured her gun and scowled at the cow. The guy in back must be sweating and tired. He lurched from foot to foot as they stood there.

"This isn't the Call Center," Lina told the cowboy. "This is Marketing." She held her left arm up with its blinking lights. "New interface for the computer. Very ergonomic. And we have permission from Jolly for ParaNet Security."

"Oh. Sorry, ladies," the cowboy said as he tipped his hat again.

"No steak for anyone here?" Leigh's disappointed voice came from two cubicles away.

"Afraid not. Just upsell. C'mon, Bessy!" The cowboy swatted both parts of his cow and muttered protests echoed from within.

"That was a department supervisor," Lina whispered to Demi as the cowboy moved out of earshot. "Isn't it a good thing that porn sells itself? I'd like to see the sales around here if Management actually knew what they were doing."

Lina returned to final filing. She coordinated with Leigh and added two more similarly-experienced coworkers as backups, running them through the folders about operating procedures.

"LINA!!"

"Wonderful intercom system you have here," Demi muttered darkly. She picked up a magazine to thumb through and realized the subject matter. "Ew!" She threw it back on the pile.

"Still here!" Lina called out.

Lina's ex-supervisor, Sharon, appeared. "I can get everyone together now," she said. "Meg's gone for the day. We can meet in the war room."

"War room?" Demi asked.

"Not that kind," Lina told her and then turned back to Sharon. "Are you going to invite Kim?"

"Of course."

"Don't. She's your leak. She's the reason things went to hell in a handbasket around here. It only took her two weeks, too." Line wove back and forth, her arms stiffly extended. "Dee-stroy. Ex-ter-mi-nate."

"Aw come on, Lie. Just because you don't like her…"

"I don't like sneaks. I don't like liars, either." Lina leaned back in her chair. "Look, I know she's your friend, and good for you. She's got a lot of good qualities. But you know as well as I do that she lies about everything. And somehow you've got to know that she's got her nose as far up Meg's butt as she can get it. Anything you say to Kim goes straight to Meg's ears. Via the digestive system, I suppose."

"Aw, come on. She doesn't–"

"Of course she does. That little incident of the personnel records getting out last year? Kim. Meg finding out that Alton was doing work for his church during work hours when he had nothing else to do? Kim. I even have witnesses for three really big events last year but if I told you what they were, you'd know who told me.

"Kim was behind it all, stuff that got a person canned once, one person demoted, and here she is getting promoted when she doesn't do that great a job except to act perpetually overworked. She should get an Oscar. She doesn't show up at this meeting, Sharon, or I'm not going. It would be a waste of my time and yours to try to fix all this just so she could screw things up again to make herself look good."

"But–"

"No Kim. She doesn't even get to know that a meeting is going on."

The small woman bit her lip and then said, "All right."

Lina clicked some files for printout. "Tell you what. We get this catalog moving again, and then in a couple months you can do a control experiment on Kim. Do the catalog one way, and then tell Kim that you're doing it another way. See which way you get called on the floor in Meg's office for. I'll bet you a dinner downtown." Lina glanced away from her Mac screen to watch Sharon's face. "Ah ha! You won't bet against me."

"She's not the leak, I tell you."

Lina gathered up a pen and pad of paper. "So prove it to me in two months. Meeting time, Ms. Smith. I don't like it when people dawdle to meetings. Sometimes I fine 'em; time is money."

The "war room" was a small interior conference room with no windows, no openings other than one door. Over a dozen people packed it.

"My secret team," Lina explained to Demi as they shut the door behind themselves. Large dry-erase boards lined the walls with codes on the top, dates below the codes progressing through the year, and notations: "Boobilicious Package", "Lesbomania", "12 Lays of Christmas", "In Your Face," "Kiester Parade," "Straight Guys, Gay Guys," along with "postage test," "hi-lo pricing test," and so on. The war this company waged was in marketing.

"Everyone here?" Lina asked the room and nodded. "As usual, I'd like to emphasize that no one talk to anyone else in any way about this operation. Especially not Kim."

"*That* snitch. Sorry, Sharon."

"No personal comments, please," Lina instructed. She moved to an easel with a large writing pad on it, consulting some notes. "Our problem is that two sections of our undercover catalog production line have been discovered. We need to find a way to reinstate them– or improve them– without management finding out. Ms. Smith tells me we've got ninety minutes before she drags me out of here. Hope no one has to take a potty break. We've got work to do."

Demi noted that Lina kept the meeting rigorously on track as she received a more specific report of the situation and what they had been doing that was now un-salvageable. As the minutes passed, Demi relaxed. It was actually intriguing to hear what kind of skills and data management porn required. Most important were continuous, stringent safeguards to protect against children gaining access to their materials or, worse, *being* in them. The focus was to keep the products eye-catching enough to create sales. More sales equaled better salaries and job security.

Lina directed her group like a general her troops. She made sure they gave the information she needed to guide the group to make decisions. She arranged workarounds to skip over the heads of those who would impede the work. She set up employee teams from different departments that would bring up problems as they developed and solve them before they could create a catastrophe.

Interestingly enough, Lina not only kept stressing the need to cater to the customers, but to keep her group inspired by the jobs they were employed to accomplish.

Demi cocked her head at it all. Now she could see Lina operating in an efficient coordinating position with this Three Worlds thing Londo was involved in. Still, the scope would be exponentially larger. Could they really accomplish a fraction of what they'd pledged themselves to do?

Lina checked the easel tablet that was now covered with her scrawl. Filled pages had been given to Sharon, who would dispose of them off-property. "I'm going to play Hitler today because of the time squeeze," Lina told the group as she began numbering phrases. "Usually I'd ask for input on priorities, but this is quicker."

"What about the proofing?" the older man in back asked, pointing at the board. "Why doesn't it have any priority?"

"Because if we solve this problem," Lina pointed at #3 and then circled it with her Sharpie, "it goes away."

"Ah. Oh yeah."

She took five minutes to go down the list, instructing her operatives of what they were to do, how they were to report to each other, how they had to get slackers' actions down on paper and reported to a specific person in Personnel in order for it to do any good. Everyone in the room scribbled their own notes as fast as they could.

"There will be no electronic record of this meeting," Lina reminded everyone. "Bonnie, you need to make up the work if and when Oliver's canned. You can do it fast and dirty, keep your own work going, and make the mailings on time."

"Right," the woman who must be Bonnie said, a little smile on her face. Everyone liked being recognized.

"But when the replacement comes in, you take some time off. Scream for comp time and not vacation time. Do not compromise on that. Tell them that you're beat, or they'll expect that kind of work out of you every day. We don't want you to burn out. Sharon, can you back her up on that?"

"No sweat."

"Is that it?" Lina asked the group, who were pouring over their own notes and checking others'.

"I think so," Sharon said and stood. "Let's all guard our notes, people. Secrecy saves your job."

"Can we come back here, or do I have to arrange something?"

"We may not be able to return." Demi watched Lina pouring cat food onto paper plates on the kitchen floor. Demi had changed back into costume, Ouroboros crackling around her waist. She didn't know how long the effect would last, but it seemed to her that the snake was enjoying the sensation.

Lina had pulled on a tee shirt to match her mood. It said, "Klingon Ambassador" over her jeans and on the back was some funny script that Lina told her said, "Death to the Empire's Enemies" in Klingonese.

"I have to call my neighbor to get her to cat sit."

"Do it."

Lina checked that the auxiliary key was hidden in the front column but still accessible. Notes had been taped all over her door from friends and strangers. The bench on the front porch was missing.

Demi didn't like it. She accompanied Lina to her mailbox across the street, making sure there was no traffic to see them, and frowned some more when they found the mailbox full of notes. One of them was threatening.

"All this is without us even announcing on TV," Lina said with a sick expression. "Can we– can we take the cats with us? People can do really rotten things to animals. Please."

"Let me make a call," Demi said. Three minutes later a big, burly man in a gray uniform and matching duffel appeared, shimmering into the living room. He looked around curiously.

"ParaNet Security, Olympia." He nodded at her. His pocket badge said the same thing, as well as his name, Ragin.

Demi nodded back "We need around the clock security."

"For the lady?"

"She'll be coming with me. For the house. And there are cats here."

"Seven," Lina said.

Ragin nodded. "I've got cats of my own. Don't worry; I'll take good care of them. Inside or outside?"

"They have a kitty door."

"I'd like to keep them inside. Are they litter-trained?"

Lina told Ragin where the cat supplies were, how to give Fafhrd her medicine, the closest quickie-marts, and the phone numbers for pizza delivery. She called her neighbor to cancel.

"There shouldn't be any trouble, ma'am," he told her kindly. "We handle these kinds of things all the time for the Network."

"There could be reporters," Demi told him.

"And my story is…?"

"You're the housesitter. You're an old friend of Lina's and you'd love to tell them all about the old days, but she's asked that you say nothing. No comment."

"A lady of mystery, eh?" Ragin considered her. "No mention of Valiant at all. I can handle it."

They hadn't mentioned Valiant to him. He must have seen her on TV. "What name do I use for you?"

"She's Lina Starhart," Demi said automatically.

"O'Kelly," Lina corrected. "Anyone around here will call me that."

He nodded as he made notes. "And if family calls?"

"They won't." The guard seemed quite professional and at ease with the cats. Lina breathed a sigh of relief. "Thank you, Mr. Ragin." She nodded at Olympia, ready to teleport.

Something invisible shoved her back. "Wait," Lina said.

Danger, one of her guides whispered. Maybe. Hard to tell. Then she stumbled as something pushed her again to make sure she noticed through the sensory fog.

She tried to expand her senses, and then realized that there were no extra senses to expand. She put her hand on Demi's arm. "Something's wrong."

Movement out back– out in the forest. Lina ran to the rear windows, Demi outracing her, and they caught sight of a red glowing residue hanging over the trees, like a jet trail. It stretched away into the afternoon sky while dispersing.

Ragin stood behind them, peering out. "What is it?" he asked. "It looks like something the Galactic Guardian would leave behind."

The women looked at each other. "Is he supposed to be following us?" Lina asked.

"No." Demi's mouth set in a grim line. "He's not supposed to be here at all. I don't like this. More and more Granger acts on his own agenda, not the Network's. Or even the Sentinels', I suspect."

"I said we should have channeled. I suggest that we channel now."

Demi looked at her with an expression that showed how much she didn't like the situation.

"Am I going to have to protect the place from a Galactic Guardian?" Ragin asked hesitantly.

"If he's after anything, he'll be after her, not the house," Demi said. She reached behind Ouroboros and Lina braced herself for transport.

25

Lina reappeared with Demi on what could only be the ParaNet satellite headquarters. It looked all space-age and acrylic, as if they were standing in midair when really they stood on a clear floor with fibre optics sparkling through it. Gravity was on, thank goodness. How did they do that?

The White Puma sat at the monitors. "*¡Híjole!* What the hell?"

"Change of plan," Demi announced.

"The others have been gone for hours," the Puma said, trying to anticipate them.

"We know," Demi said. "Granger's still around. What's his position? Track him, please."

The Puma studied her control board and activated some areas. "What's he done now?"

"I don't know. But he followed us."

Puma's head snapped up. "Followed you? He claimed he had an all-out Brigade emergency to attend to; that's why he didn't go with the others. He's supposed to be two galactic sectors away by now."

Demi breathed out noisily. "Do you have his position yet?"

"Got him. He's in Africa. The log says a demonstration turned into a small riot. Maybe the Brigade tracked their interplanetary trouble here?" The Puma gave Demi a twisted, unbelieving grimace.

"A poorly-constructed ruse. He was definitely following us."

"Should I try calling the Sentinels? Report him?" She worked some controls. "Do we even have a way to contact them?"

"Demi," Lina said suddenly. "You trust me, right?"

She studied Lina. "Yes, I do."

Lina held up her arm. "Then take this off. Please. I'm not afraid of the Guardian if I can port."

"I don't have the key to it."

"So take it off without the key."

White Puma stood up at her station. "I vote in her favor, Demi. Do it."

Demi studied the Puma, then Lina. "I agree," she decided. She wrapped her powerful fingers around the wrist edge and pulled it apart– or tried. "I'm afraid of hurting your arm," she admitted.

Next she threaded her snakeskin between the suppressor and Lina's arm. The rope slithered and then contracted, vibrating with tautness as it tried to shatter the bracelet. Lina trembled as the end of the rope budded with that snake's head. It bit and bit at the bracelet with the lightning snapping all around.

Nothing happened.

Demi tapped the snakeskin and let it retract to her hand.

"There must be more than a bit of impervion in the structure of the bracelet. I don't think even Hal could shatter it."

"Jae could, if he were here," Lina said. Jae… and Aldierra. "Look," she told Demi and the Puma. "I have a duty to about twenty billion people, and as much as it gives me the screaming willies to think that a Galactic Guardian may be gunning for me, I have to think of them, too. Can you establish communication with Aldierra?"

The Puma shook her head. "I never heard of that planet before this week. It's pretty far away, even on a galactic sector scale."

"Then can you call the Legion and have them relay me through? I really have to speak to Jae so we can establish a failsafe plan. Please."

"That we can do. Give me a minute."

One of the TV screens flared to life: Mega-Legion Headquarters, the Comm Room. Lina recognized the young Legionnaire on the screen.

"This is Legion Headquarters." The Legionnaire looked up and saw where the communications was coming from. She recognized Lina.

"It's Proto-Mite, isn't it?" Lina said in Lingua. She had no idea if the ParaNet had translators or not.

"Yes. Mrs. Valiant." She eyed her suspiciously. "Should you be communicating with us?"

Demi stepped into the picture. She spoke in perfect Lingua. "We have a situation here. Not yet an emergency, but there is a chance that it could become one. Are there any Legionnaires who could help us?"

"Route to Earth?" Proto-Mite checked her boards. "None within a few days of you. And you know about the operation going on. That's taking most of the membership for an estimated three days minimum from Earth once they emerge from hyperspace. Do you want me to send a message to Valiant?"

"No. Don't put any more on him than he has," Lina said quickly. "Can you patch me through to Neutrino on Aldierra? This communication *is* an emergency. You can monitor it if you wish."

"I can do that. Hold." Proto-Mite clicked a few switches, pressed a few points on her board. "Neutrino? Emergency message coming through from Earth for you. I'm recording."

Jae's face filled the screen, pushing his hair out of his face. He raised up out of bed as soon as he saw Lina, the sheets falling around his waist, leaving him bare from there up. "What's going on? Did they put that device–"

She showed him her arm. "Done and done. There's nothing we can do about it, either. It contains a lot of impervion."

"So you'll have to wait until the group gets back."

"They estimate at least five days until then. Jae, I seem to have pissed off the local Galactic Guardian. Or maybe…" She remembered the phrase "Valiant's own house." "Or maybe he doesn't like Londo," she said in wonder. "That's it. He's angry at Londo, and I think he may be considering using me to get back at him. I didn't help things, either. Anyway, he's acting very suspicious–"

"And he has become noticeably unstable of late," Demi said from behind her, where Jae could see her.

Lina nodded and swallowed. "But I thought we needed to make an emergency plan. A provision in case anything happens to me."

"What? Are things that bad?" Jae reached for his tunic.

"I don't know. Let me just make a plan. Jae, we all know that with a little training, you could take over for me to speak to Aldierra and the other two worlds. Lon could probably do it, too, given a while."

"I don't have the training," Jae said.

"So if something happens, you come to Earth. I'll tell you where to go. Are you getting all this?"

"I'm recording," he said, his face unreadable.

Lina gave him instructions on how to find the woman who taught her how to channel higher entities.

"She can be trusted?"

Lina sighed. "It used to be she could be trusted with about anything. She'll want to charge you a lot of money–" Lina let her smile linger over her beautiful lover. "And she might want to jump your bones, but other than that, she's okay."

Jae gave a faint smile.

Lina added directions to another instructor. "He'll do almost as well and your virtue will be safe with him."

"Lina–"

"I've told Aldierra already about the possibilities. She's not pleased, but she approves of you or Londo as substitutes."

"You can talk to her with that?"

"She's very faint but I can listen hard."

"Should I come there now?"

Lina deferred to Demi, who looked grim.

"It might be advisable. Yes. Come now. This Guardian could be mentally disturbed. I'm beginning to suspect he's criminally egomaniacal."

"A Galactic Guardian?" Jae's lips twisted into a snarl. "Granger. Lon's never liked him."

"We're only operating on some strange behavior he has displayed lately. He attempted a mental assault on Lina this morning. Twice today he's followed us, thinking himself unnoticed."

"Twice?" Lina asked, and Demi nodded. Lina's mouth went dry.

Jae pulled his tunic over his head and reached for his vest. "I'm two and a half days out from Earth at top speed." He snapped his fingers in the air as if for attention.

"You should come; others are at least that far away and currently in hyperspace, so we can't get communications through," Demi stated flatly. "If you're not needed, then we will all breathe a sigh of relief and look sheepish for you. But if–"

"I'm on my way," Jae said, nodding to someone else in the room. "Two and a half days, maybe three depending on what ship I get. I expect the Speaker of the Three Worlds to be hale and healthy when I arrive."

"I'll make sure of that," Demi replied stiffly.

Lina frowned at them both. "Good grief, don't everyone get all huffy. That's what got us into this mess in the first place. Jae, you have a safe trip and apologize for me to the Aldierrans for dragging you away. I'm sure that Granger can't stand up to the both of you. I'll port you back just as soon as I can. In the meantime we'll do whatever needs to be done on this end."

Jae worked his jaw in that way he had before he finally nodded. "I don't see anything else to do. I'm leaving right now, Lina. Don't worry. And be careful." His beautiful blue eyes and slightly parted lips said "I love you," and she tried to convey the same back to him without revealing any secrets.

The screen cleared, leaving Proto-Mite's face on it. "An insane Guard?" She looked to Demi for confirmation.

"It's a definite possibility," the heroine confirmed.

Proto-Mite bit her lip. She really was very young, in Lina's opinion too young for a para-military organization. Both Jae and Londo had been younger when they first joined. "I'll put a notice up here and in the outposts. The first Legionnaire back who could stand any chance against a Galactic Guard will be on their way to Earth first thing. But– there just aren't that many who could even dare to…"

"Understood," Demi said. "Thank you for the attempt. ParaNet out." The screen blanked completely.

"I'm going to feel very foolish if there isn't something going on," she said softly. "Lina, you said you could channel about this?"

"I think so."

"Maria," she addressed the Puma, "is Damon at home?"

The Puma pressed a button and nodded her head. "Dragonwing's there, too. There are some other life signs; don't know who."

"Then signal him, if you would. See if it's clear."

They waited for a minute. "We've got a green light," the Puma said.

"Beam us there. But before you do, establish a false beaming signal somewhere else. And after you beam us down, make about five or six false beamings."

"Got it." The Puma fiddled with the controls. "False beaming completed. Good luck."

The world first fuzzed out and then turned very dark. It smelled of motor oil. A few ceiling potlights focused on cement walls in the distance behind all the concrete columns, while too few others cast pools of light on the floor. Rows of parked cars, motorcycles, even an armored truck, stretched into the semi-darkness. The wall to Lina's left held a line of tinted windows revealing a great room inside lined with computers and monitors.

Lina turned in a circle to see it all. This must be the Dragonlair, home of Dragonlord. Londo's estate stretched for miles and miles and must have cost a fortune and a half. This was all state-of-the-art equipment. Plus judging from what she'd read and seen of Dragonlord's organization, most of it would need constant replacement. Likely it cost as much or more than Lon's set-up, *caching*. Was this a building? A sub-basement of some kind? Or maybe under a parking garage?

In addition to his heroic persona, Dragonlord ran ParaNet Security. Maybe the Dragonlair was at the bottom of the ParaNet Security Complex in Alexandria, Virginia.

"Demi."

The male voice echoed through the garage. People watched them from inside the computer room.

"Come along," Demi snapped. "This is the Dragonlair."

"Yes." Lina trotted to catch up to Demi and hoped that the inky shadows on the floor didn't hide any sudden drops or stairs. They entered the computer center through a hall not unlike the Legion Security corridor on Sarastor, which was lined with scanners and mysterious identity checks.

Inside, monitors towered overhead in all directions, slanted so people at ground level could see them undistorted. Most of the screens were on, scrolling strange and exotic information, and sometimes displaying people's faces. Many were mug shots.

Dragonlord waited expectantly in a central chair with his hood thrown back. Dragonwing stood by his side. Here was Talon. He was shorter than his photos. Two middle-aged men, one in a suit and one in tee shirt and jeans, plus a civilian woman stood next to a table of disassembled guns. Another woman sat in the shadows. Lina realized she was the Silk Stalker, but wasn't she a bad guy?

Then from out of the darker shadows behind the Stalker emerged a gray horse. No, it was a *centaur* dressed in a green tunic, one of those poufy medieval caps set upon his white head. A leather bag hung from a studded leather sash.

This was the fabled Green Mage of the Timeless Realms.

"Damon–" Demi started, but the magician stepped forward, his hooves clopping metallically though he wore bagging boots.

"So the Speaker for the Three Worlds has made her appearance at last," he intoned as he stepped around Lina to view her from several angles. Demi gave him room. "She heralds the official beginning of the New Age– if she can survive the tests."

Whoa. Not to be species-ist or anything, but that was the first word that came to Lina's mind as her reaction.

In the past few weeks she'd met paraheroes and seen alien worlds. She'd made friends with people with blue skin, orange skin, seen people who looked like humanoid boulders as well as giant insects and space-faring octopi. But she'd never met a centaur.

"Mage." Demi drew herself up.

"Champion." The Mage regarded her coolly though he seemed wary of her.

The Green Mage was from the Timeless Realms, where he held some high position. Lina squinted at him, trying to see his face through all the harsh shadows cast by the overhead lights. He was an older man, his white hair tied into a neat ponytail. His horse's bulk stood him four feet higher than she.

Cool. Uh… What had he said again?

"Mage, you've never looked like the Archangel Gabriel to me," Dragon-lord/Damon said.

The old centaur's nose wrinkled when he smiled, his eyes shrewd and calculating. "There's quite the hubbub on many mystic planes over this Three Worlds experiment. You," he told Lina, "are the heart of the Three Worlds, one of the three Chosen." He laughed. "The Sagittarian. We have something in common after all."

Ah, he was doing an Obi-Wan impression. She could deal with that. "Everybody's something," Lina said. "I'm pleased to–"

"Not everyone." The mage shook his head at her, his hat bobbing. "No, while others only pretend to fly, some few soar far above them all. Remember, there are *they* and there are *we*."

Lon had said something similar, but his meaning had been quite different. "Are you including me in your 'we'?"

That made him laugh once again. "So few actually attain their potential," he said. "But you– You bear watching."

"If I live so long."

He shrugged. "Tests are the universe's way of eliminating the impostors from the truly great figures of history."

Sounded like a case of ego to her. Here Lina had heard stories of him for years and shivered in delight at his mystery and power, at the very figure he cut with his centaur self straight out of a faerie tale.

But this operations center didn't work well as his backdrop. Behind him, screens changed, street maps appeared. Light upon light blinked. The theme for a news show played at low volume.

Lina exchanged glances with Demi. She had a sour expression.

Lina scrutinized the Mage as she tipped her head to meet his gaze. "No one stands above another in the eyes of God." Maybe a reminder would do him good.

"Oh, now she dares to know the mind of God. What an interesting Speaker you will be– if you survive."

"Enough," Demi said. "Granger's still on Earth," she told the group. "He's following us."

The humans in the room regarded each other gravely. "Granger."

"Can you magick this off?" Lina asked the Green Mage and held up her shackle.

"What kind of test would it be then, my dear?"

"It was a mistake for us to let you be locked up in that," Demi said bitterly.

"Oh no, Champion," the centaur declared. "A blade must be forged and tempered; so must the Chosen of Worlds." He tapped on the sharp metal of the shackle and leaned down almost in a bow so he and Lina were eye to eye. "You have all that you need to survive, Speaker. The Worlds have returned your birthright. Whenever you find yourself in one of these," he continued in a low voice, "you must remind yourself that it is only a test."

With a sudden movement, he stood tall, all four feet spread defiantly and his arms raised in fists. "The jealous inferiors can blind us, they can torture us and worse, but they cannot wither the genius that can never be theirs!"

The room seemed to shift without moving; he disappeared. Only a whiff of fog remained to quickly dissipate. It smelled ever so subtly of sulfur.

Egomaniac but impressive even so, Lina thought. There in the middle the magician had seemed to be sympathetic to her plight. She could use all the help she could get.

"I thought he'd never leave," one of the men muttered, and Lina turned to face the group.

Damon spoke up for the benefit of the others. "The Klingon Ambassador there that the Mage insisted on calling the Speaker for the Three Worlds is Carolina Starhart, Valiant's new wife."

This came as a shock to some, blatant in the way they stared at her. For once being head-blind was a comfort, for Lina couldn't read their minds: **How do they–?**

"Lina for short," she said.

"Everyone knows Demi, right?" Damon/Dragonlord looked around the room and introduced the circle of his company. "Talon. Georges Arques. Dragonwing. Cookie Kane. Silk Stalking. Mac Waterson." Georges hadn't been surprised at the news of the marriage. He nodded his head at her. "An interesting workplace you have," he said, cracking a smile.

"Past tense," she said, and he chuckled. He must have been the one who'd been upstairs at her house, investigating with Damon.

"Tell us about Granger, Demi." Dragonlord motioned for the two of them to empty chairs.

Demi gave them the condensed version. She finished, "So I decided that Lina should try to channel somewhere away from the satellite, in case he should return there. We need to find out what's going on."

"You trust this channeling?" Dragonwing spoke up.

"The priests of my people do something similar," Demi said. "I've always trusted them."

"I know many channelers," Silk said. Her accented voice was like her name. "Most are frauds, but a few seem genuine."

"The test of channeling is within yourself," Lina said, repeating what she'd told many people many times. "If the advice conflicts with what you want to do, you should question it. If it conflicts with your personal ethics, you should ignore it. Free will remains with the individual. Channeled information can come from low sources or high, but it's only information, not orders direct from God."

"So the nearest megapara help of any magnitude, besides you, Demi, is two and a half days away," Dragonlord mused. "In that case, what choice do we have? Let's see what kind of info we can get."

Great. Nothing like performing under pressure. Lina settled herself in her seat, making sure her feet were firmly on the floor. She was tired from all the stress and the shackle's burden and being around strangers. "I don't give out any guarantees anyway," she told the people staring at her, "but with so many of my senses being wonky this may be a lot more iffy than usual."

Someone in the room grunted, obviously skeptical and wanting others to know it. Lina tried to ignore him.

"What we're looking for here are some answers, some perspective, some tactics." Having announced her goals to the universe, Lina inhaled; exhaled. She reached for the white light to protect her and all within the room. Her chakras should be lined up, like soup cans strung on a string that ran down her spine. She breathed down the length of them, then back up. How faint were her guides! How quietly their whispers came. Was that her mind muttering or was it them? One presence moved closer, their voice rising from the gathered so she could understand it. She repeated their message word by word.

"Is there a clear and present danger? *Hell, yes! He's freaking crazy, out of his mind...*" Lina frowned at herself, then took another deep breath and another. The energy sent her up to purer planes.

"Could I get somebody on a higher level, please? Okay, thanks." Her words came slowly as she sought clarity. "*Yes, a very real danger. He is unstable and has been since before he became a Guardian. The Sentinels should have known, but they– their attitudes are sloppy.* Not sloppy. No, that's not right. *They suffered a moment of... inexactitude. Now they suspect that they have made a mistake. If the Network were to contact them, they would listen, given enough evidence.* What kind of evidence do they need? *The ruby records everything. Give them the ruby and the evidence will all be there.*"

A picture of Dorothy, her ruby slippers, and the Wicked Witch of the West came to her. No help in that. Besides, the word "ruby" might have triggered that memory in her. Her guides might not have anything to do with it.

Damned shackle.

Lina took another cleansing breath. Focus. "What kinds of things has he been doing? Why does he hate Londo so much?" she asked and then listened. "*Londo's received the glory for things he considers himself responsible for. Granger wants publicity, wants adulation, and again and again he finds that the big credits, the headlines, go to Londo and for good reason. But he doesn't see it that way.*

"*He thought that the ruby would be his path to riches, to women, to power, but all that has been spoiled.*" This time it was a faerie tale image that came to Lina's mind. "*Yes, like the beautiful queen looking into the magick mirror and being told that Snow White is more beautiful than she, so she turns spiteful, vengeful and ultimately murderous."*

There were two more contacts, but Lina dismissed those. They didn't make sense. They were too murky to trust. Another one furnished her imagery she couldn't make sense of.

"Another speaker," she announced. *"Granger has been taking his anger out on women for the past seven, eight months. Violence.* Is that rape? Not sure. It's definitely violence. He's hitting them. *Again and again he strikes, cowing them with threats of death if they speak out against him. The few who did report it went unbelieved because this was a Galactic Guardian.*

"Oh. Earth speaks. *He steals from mines for precious stones to enrich himself, he levels a forest...* Ah... he's peddling accident insurance? Like the mob, a protection racket. I think that's the concept. *There was a ship. Not long ago.* Something happened to it."

"What was its name?" Demi asked softly.

"Let me guess," Damon muttered.

Lina could see the picture in her mind, taste the tang of the actual metal of the ship, the sour oil floating on a smooth sea. Focus in on the name, painted there. "The... *Fff... San Francisco.* No, something's wrong there. *Francesco,* the *Francesco,* out of South Am– Venezuela, they're pointing at a map. Jeez, the *Francesco?"*

Lina remembered the story plastered across all the headlines two months ago. She had to center herself again.

"Yes, that is the one. Then in Australia six weeks ago... southwest, no, southeast in the continent. A horrible fire, *many animals and some people killed. Land laid waste to teach someone his power over them.* Earth says: *Tell them he is not welcome on my world any more. Tell the Sentinels.* Okay, we will."

Lina opened her bleary eyes and wiggled her toes to get herself back into her body. "I'm sorry but I'm really tired," she said. "This thing–" she raised her shackled arm in the air– "seems to suck my energy. I shouldn't be channeling when I'm like this. Can we take a break? I need some water."

Dragonlord and Demi looked particularly grim. "A break, then," Demi said.

Lina breathed a sigh of relief and thanked the entities, then firmly grounded herself, shaking her arms and feet. She felt herself sinking into sleep. She tried to stay awake by shaking her head and listening hard to the activity around her, but speech began to buzz unnaturally loud and then quiet, in waves. It couldn't be that late. This shackle must drain her more than she'd suspected. It felt like it weighed thirty pounds.

"We need to search assault reports, especially on women," Damon said to the Kane woman, who nodded as she typed. "Can you narrow it down, Lina?"

"Try Germany first," she said. "One place just had a German feel. Northern Germany, maybe. And Thailand. He thought they'd be easy."

Damon nodded.

"I'll check on the *Francesco,*" Dragonwing volunteered.

"I'll take Australia," Talon said.

"Double-check the Network files on the *Francesco,*" Damon said with menace in his tone. "Granger was the one who handled the investigation on that. He volunteered for the job. At the time I thought that was odd."

Georges brought Lina a glass of water. "Would you like to go somewhere to lie down?" he asked quietly.

"Thank you," she said. "I would. It's been an unusual day."

He led her upstairs instead of the elevator. Her left arm hung from her like dead weight. Down dark, twisting hallways and into living quarters, they finally came to a bedroom. "You can sleep here as long as you want, Ms. Starhart," he said. "No one will bother you until they need you."

"Thank you. Very much." She collapsed on the bed and immediately fell asleep.

An hour, two hours out– how many left?

Jae paced the cabins of the ship he'd been lent. It contained minimal housing but at least it attained some semblance of top-level speed. He hugged and then pounded himself back to alertness, hopping to increase his circulation on his next round of the ship.

Lina was in danger and he wasn't there to protect her.

She was such a neo to all this. Wouldn't hurt a *neechi* even if it was out to kill her. Now they'd cut off her senses and what power she had.

How could Londo have let them do this to her?

All right, Londo couldn't have known a Galactic Guardian was going to go crazy. He didn't know that the power of the black hole that swirled at the center of the Milky Way would be held like a blade over Lina's head, waiting for the will of an insane Guardian to loose it. Londo would tell Jae that in this one instance it made sense to do this to Lina, so they could stop the emperor in his tracks and save entire worlds.

Jae threw himself down on the couch. They should have sent Lina to him! He'd protect her better than anyone. She'd be safe next to him in the light of day or in his bed at night.

He tapped his wrist, releasing a dose of tranks. Five deep breaths later, he could feel it take effect.

Lina in his bed. In his mind, he replayed how she had finally given in to him. She'd come so alive in his arms. So responsive. She wasn't afraid of him. She didn't worship him like some had, and she wasn't after him because of his fame or prestige.

Her touch was electric. It awakened his senses. Her kisses burned through to his soul, setting him afire in ways he'd never been aroused.

Not only had they loved together, but they'd laughed.

That sweet, innocent heart of hers funneled the universe into his own. He could almost grasp it when she was in his arms. He could almost connect to a part of himself that was purer than he'd ever let himself be. She held a seed of Feith in her. Jae was the one man in the universe who could nurture it to blossom.

How perfect it would be to end each night in Londo's brawny arms and to begin each day within Lina's. When he imagined it that way, even without the forests or his family, a part of his soul grew warmer. "Home," it whispered to him. He felt protected from a hostile cosmos.

If they got married–

Jae opened his eyes and then closed them again, forcing himself to imagine. If they married, Lon and Lina would have to deny him in public to protect Lon's image. No getting around that. But in private, Lina and her songs and her sweet smile would be there for him. He'd have her woman's body warm and willing and next to his.

Their children would be beautiful. With him teaching her, they would show their babies how to be truly Feithi. Jae wouldn't be the last one of his kind any more. He'd have others around him who saw the universe in the same way, unconstrained by barbaric beliefs.

Long ago Londo had bewitched him with the elemental fire of his passions and the magnificence of his body. He'd grown into the very image of Feith's long-ago kings. Nowhere was there a greater tactician than Londo. Nowhere was there a man with emotions and ideals that ran as deeply as his. Nowhere did anyone understand Jae the way Lon did.

Walking in Lon's footsteps Jae had wanted to be swept away by Londo's stories. He so wanted to help Lon build a life independent of Hal, yet anchored by him into a loving family– even if they were Terran barbarians.

They were nice barbarians.

Jae pictured himself among friends, among the Legionnaires, walking in the sunlight in public with Lina on one arm smiling up at him, Londo on his other side with his arm wrapped around him. Of their families welcoming Jae as a full member. Of a world he could finally call home. Children playing, calling him "Daddy" in the same way he'd done with his own father, and his father with his father before him.

But Londo couldn't share that vision. It would kill Lon, and Jae would do anything to protect him, even if it meant killing himself. Killing his own pride, his own joy in life. Anything for Londo, his love.

No, if they married they couldn't go public. But Jae was Feithi. His father had always told him that a Feithi could handle anything with patience and understanding.

Without opening his eyes, he reached for the box that sat on the table next to the couch. **Change to glass,** he ordered it and oversaw the shift as the box's deva obeyed his command. With one movement Jae hurled the box across the room. It crashed spectacularly on the wall.

26

Lina awoke with a start, no idea how much later it was. She'd had some kind of nightmare. A red sky… *Danger coming, act now,* her mind whispered to her. No, it must be the sentinel angel she had placed downstairs. Or had she imagined it? So difficult to tell.

Best just in case to act. She hurried out of the room, trying to remember her route. At one point she had to retrace her steps, and at another she stopped at a blank wall. She channeled, and a faint hand hazily pointed one way, then another, then the original way. *Trust yourself more than ever,* she told herself firmly and took the first direction.

There was the staircase they'd come up. She stumbled, caught herself and then held the wall, trying to wake fully and ground, so aware of the absolute urgency.

"It won't be much of a test if you kill yourself on the stairs," the Green Mage's voice said from the bottom of the stairs. He wasn't there. Then he was.

"I hope you know the way from here," she replied.

He let her lean on him, slowly clip-clopping through the darkness until Lina saw the familiar pool of light ahead.

"You must get some sleep," the Green Mage said quietly. "You cannot protect yourself or her without some sleep."

"So she *is* in danger." Lina spotted Demi working over a keyboard. "I thought she might be. I think I dreamed about her."

She felt more centered now that she'd been moving around. She wasn't surprised to find that the Mage had disappeared. When she reached the computer center, the people gathered watching the screens looked solemn.

"Excuse me," she said. Talon and Silk both jumped, even though she had pitched her voice low. They all turned toward her.

"I think it's time we moved on," Lina said, trying not to let panic into her voice.

"We found the attack reports. Rape in two instances. We're fairly certain about the ship," Dragonlord reported.

"We should get out of here. Now," Lina told Demi. "Or just me. But it should be *now*," she repeated urgently.

The heroine nodded and touched the signal at her belt. The room faded around them. Once again they stood on the satellite. Black Magnum handled the controls.

"Where's Granger?" Demi asked brusquely.

"One second; I'm checking." he said. "Washington."

"Just in time," Demi breathed.

"Can you beam just this shackle somewhere and leave me behind?" Lina asked.

"Now that's a thought," Demi said. "Kun-woo? Try it."

He fiddled with the transporter controls. "I can't get a fine-tune lock on it," he said. "Something about it screws up my rangefinder."

"Let me try," Demi said, moving to his spot. "Damn."

"I take it that's a 'no,'" Lina said.

"Correct."

Lina couldn't think straight with this thing on. She slid down the wall to sit on the floor. Why couldn't Granger take off as much as Londo did, or Maximus? They were constantly busy with their missions. If he were them, he'd probably be off-Earth now and not bothering her...

Demi was staring at her. Oh jeez, she'd been mumbling to herself.

"We'll fake a distress call," Demi declared.

"Distress call?" Magnum cocked his head. He scratched his bristly chin. "Give us some time to regroup, you mean? How could we be sure he'd answer it?"

Demi smiled savagely. "Have it appeal to his ego. Glory for him and him alone if he responds to the call. Easy pickings. It must come from two or three days out. Make him run until he drops."

Black Magnum considered the console. "Too obvious?"

"This is Granger."

He grunted. "Wish I'd thought of it."

"Can you do it?" Lina asked.

Magnum checked his communications circuits. "I'll have to bounce it off somewhere, to make it seem like it didn't come from here. Demi, some help here…"

They called up the Legion again and got permission from Proto-Mite to utilize their communications lines so the transmission wouldn't have a Network signature.

"Here goes," Demi finally announced. The distress call went out on the frequency for Galactic Brigade emergency messages, slightly garbled as if from equipment problems. Proto-Mite rigged a cunning space-time echo to it as well. A yacht of some spacefaring royalty, carrying Crown Prince somebody– Lina didn't catch the name– had been attacked and looted. Help, please, before life support ran out.

Magnum kept track of Granger's ParaNet tracker. "He bit," he said. "Heading out of solar system. There he goes into hyperspace. Can't track him there."

Demi blew out a sigh. "That might give us a day or two unless his brains overcome his greed and he figures this out." She arranged with Proto-Mite to update the messages as needed.

Lina tried to stay awake, but the flood of relief was too great. Her eyelids began to droop.

"How about a message to the Sentinels now?" Magnum asked Demi. "Did you collect any info we can show them?"

"Plenty, but it's not the hardest of evidence. Highly circumstantial. Damon and his people are working on refining it."

"Maybe we've got enough to convince them to suspend him from active duty at least," Magnum said.

"I doubt if anyone would do that just for unsubstantiated accusations," Demi began and then looked around at Lina.

Lina smiled grimly back at her. "No," she agreed with all the sarcasm she could muster. "No one ever did anything on the basis of unfounded accusations." The shackle weighed heavily on her arm and she leaned back against the acrylic wall.

"Let's call it a night," Demi decided. "C'mon, Lina. He's gone for at least a day. I think I can guarantee you that."

Lina tried to figure how to stand. "Okay," she said. "Where to now? I hope it has a bed."

"We can arrange that." Demi helped Lina up. "Does the shackle really drain you that much?" She didn't need an answer; Lina's face was blotched with fatigue. "Let's get you some sleep and maybe things will look better tomorrow."

"*Tomorrow, tomorrow...*" Lina tried to sing, but it came out a croak. "Just point me somewhere where I can lie down and you'll have my eternal gratitude."

"Scythia, please," Demi directed Black Magnum. His fingers played across the control board.

The room went gray around Lina and she didn't think it was all the transporter's fault. Scythia. She should be excited to see the legendary nation that surrounded and guarded the Gateway to the Timeless Realms, but she couldn't summon any extra energy right now.

They materialized in deep night outside what looked like a sprawling ancient Egyptian or Babylonian temple, its painted walls so brightly spotlit that Lina had to squint. A fine rain fell like mist.

"Here we are. Let's get you out of this." Demi nodded at a woman guard with a ceremonial lance standing by the front entrance. She looked like she'd stood alert even before she spotted the materialization. She wore highly decorated armor over a tunic, with high leather boots that looked hot in the mugginess of the night.

Shouldn't it be cold here? Scythia bordered the Black Sea, didn't it? It should be a late continental winter here. Instead Lina stood under the overhang of the roof and wiped warm rain off her forehead.

The guard said something to Demi and she answered back, both of them looking at Lina. "Go with her," Demi directed. "She'll take you to a room where you can sleep."

"Thanks," Lina replied gratefully. "You get some, too."

"I need to check in with my sister," she said. Lina remembered that Demi was the co-queen of this country, though the other queen held the real governing power.

Demi snapped her fingers in front of Lina's face but it took a moment before Lina realized it. "Are you still with us?"

"Yes, Demi."

"Get to bed."

Lina followed the guard into the not-a-temple. It sprawled like Starhaven, except it had solid interior walls. Was this the royal palace? It was beautiful enough to be with paintings and statuary, frescoes of dancers on the walls, intricate mosaics on the floors. Every now and then the outer wall would open into a balcony overlooking the lights of a small city with tall hills beyond. She could hear and smell an ocean nearby. The openness of the building let the breezes through. It admitted the aroma of night-blooming flowers and the songs of frogs singing for their mates.

But it should be winter. Did living so close to the Gateway to the Timeless Realms affect the climate?

Lina dully decided that she'd consider the question tomorrow when she was awake.

The guard opened a double door and gestured for her to enter. The room was spacious, with a floor tiled in one of those beautiful mosaics. It was accented with statuary and plants. Two balconies led off from adjacent sides of the room. Over there was a blessed bed, surrounded by mosquito netting.

The guard pantomimed: if you need anything, just yell. Lina smiled and nodded her head, thanking her. Once the guard left, Lina wasted no time stripping off her clothes and climbing in. Sleep overtook her in seconds.

Lina woke slowly. Behind her eyelids, she could sense sunlight streaming onto some nearby surface. The smell of flowers combined pleasantly with the sour salt of the sea. A distant choir seemed to echo birdsong that came from just outside.

The air was cleaner here than she'd ever noticed. It was energized, like a hundred ionizers filtered the room. Was it her imagination, or was it because the Gateway to the Timeless Realms sat nearby? What magicks did the Gateway leak into the real world? Some people said that it was the Gateway that caused so many megas to appear on Earth. If that were so, how would living so near the Gateway affect Scythia's people?

Lina's musings lulled into daydreams of possibilities that could lurk just beyond the fabled link to magickal worlds. Londo had been there. What had he found? Did he have full powers there? What were the Realms' peoples like?

Wake up. But doing so was annoyingly difficult. Five more minutes. An hour. Or two. No, she had to get up. It was some time before Lina realized that it was the suppressor that was throwing her off her morning routine.

Or at least that was a good excuse.

She stretched, luxuriating in the comfort of the bed, the romantic mosquito netting that enclosed it. How wonderful it would be to have Londo in here with her. Or Jae. She could think about him that way now, and she did, smiling. Jae here with her– or both of them. She slid on the sheets, imagining that it was someone's hands sliding across her. Oh yes. Sweet Jae, blond over blue. Wonderful Londo with those luscious dark eyes and strong arms.

Jae was on his way to her rescue. Had he gotten off Aldierra safely? Or had he been caught up in another riot and hurt– or killed? Would his ship blow up in transit like the *Travern* the other day? That ship had been sabotaged by the Aldierrans. Aiko had died.

By now Londo might be at that war against the Empire, wherever it was. Londo had died before. People could make weapons that could kill him. Would they have those kinds of weapons where he was? Who would care for him if he got hurt?

Would another hero like Aiko die this time? Would many?

Clutching the sheets over her mouth, Lina lay tightly curled for some time before she realized that Demi was sitting across the room. She could barely make out the famous costume through the thick netting around the bed. Lina turned over, wrapped the sheet around herself, and then sat up.

"Good afternoon," Demi said. She set down the book she'd been reading.

"Have I slept the day away, then?" Lina scrunched to the side of the bed. She'd dropped her clothes here last night, but now they were gone. There was a pile there, but they weren't her clothes. Light blue fabric, jeweled pins. Sandals.

"Only part." Demi said. "Remember, we're on the other side of the world from your home. Bathroom's through there, and it has a shower. Let me show you how to use it. It's a little tricky for Westerners."

Lina swept the netting aside and stood up, rubbing her eyes and blinking as she rose. She looked at Demi. Her face was contorted in agony, surrounded by a red glow. Lina blinked again, and Demi's face was calm and peaceful; the light entirely normal.

"Did you get any sleep last night?" Lina asked. She picked up the pile of clothing and took it with her toward the bathroom, the heroine leading the way.

"A little." Demi showed her the shower, which was actually a small but powerful waterfall that turned on and off, complete with flowers and moss growing in a rock wall. Demi left Lina to get prepared in private.

When Lina stepped out of the bathroom, she was still fastening the pin on the shoulder of her tunic, trying to get the feel of this Scythian underwear. The tunic fell to just below her knees. It was of a light, gauzy material, open at the sides to her hips. Sandals laced up to her knee and wonder of wonders, the ties actually stayed up when she had tied them.

"What's on the agenda?" she asked Demi, who had been waiting patiently.

"We can do whatever you wish to. Since when do you know Scythian songs?"

"Hm?"

"I heard you in the shower, singing along with the chorus."

Lina smiled. "They sounded so wonderful, I couldn't help myself."

"But–"

Lina pointed at her head. "Part of the Three Worlds musical library, locked in here. Londo seems to be acquiring the same thing. Jae, too. Here," she said, tapping her heavy shackle. "No telepathy. Nothing up my sleeve. Pick an obscure tune. Any song."

Demi thought a moment, and then started to sing. She was a contralto. Lina joined in with harmony. When they finished, they laughed in delight.

"Did you understand the words?" Demi asked.

"Flowers in the springtime, blooming on Scythian mountain slopes," Lina said. "It's very pretty. You have a nice voice."

"I wouldn't have taken you for a soprano."

"I can fake my way through a soprano line if it's low enough," Lina said. She considered Demi. "Are you sure you've had enough sleep? Have you eaten lately?"

"I was just going to suggest that we go down for some dinner, Mother." Demi smiled and then stopped. "You foresaw Orenya's death, didn't you?"

"Yes," Lina said quietly. "Demi, he's going to come back before Jae can get here."

"You've seen this. And me–"

Lina shook her head. "I don't know. It's a battle, though, a rough one. The strange thing was that last night the Mage was telling me that I needed to protect you, so I should get some sleep."

"Perhaps you misheard him. You were almost walking in your sleep last night."

"Maybe." Lina blew out a frustrated breath. "Well, let's both make sure we rest up for whatever, shall we?"

"That sounds wise." Demi squared her shoulders. Lina saw the warrior in her then, the inner core of her being, ever alert for attack. Then she was just Demi again. "Eating is part of being prepared. Shall we?"

They paused at one balcony. Flowers bloomed everywhere here, in the hallways and along the hillsides outside the palace. Deer grazed fearlessly on the afternoon slopes alongside the citizens of Scythia. Some were in armor, some in more modern uniform fatigues, but by far most wore loose tunics and pants.

Beautiful buildings shimmered bright white or jewel tones in the afternoon, often with columned facades. Lush, blooming vines grew along their walls. In a square just outside the palace splashed fountains. They blended their song with the chorus that always seemed to be part of the background here like a breeze.

"It's magickal," Lina sighed, breathing in the pungent, salty air.

"Of course it is," Demi said as they resumed their walk. "It's Scythia. We've been magick since history began. We are the children of the Goddess. We guard the Gateway."

A long, wide patio with a stone railing overlooked a dramatic cliff drop to the sun-struck ocean. The waves murmured below, sea gulls dropping down to the narrow shore. It was a magnificent view. There were only a few streaks of high clouds in the azure sky.

Here a table had been set with crystal goblets and silverware that was probably real silver. A little black-haired boy ran shrieking with laughter down the length of the patio, outrunning an older girl.

"Mashy! Mashy!" the girl shouted, laughing. She put on a burst of speed and grabbed the younger child. As Lina watched open-mouthed, the girl jumped up into the sky with her playmate and performed a flying loop-de-loop.

"Children!" a firm voice ordered from behind them. "Come down! Time to be civilized now. We have a guest."

Lina turned to behold the most beautiful woman she'd ever seen. Long black hair fluttered in the sea breeze. That wasn't a thick silver streak down her left side, but one of true gold. She had bright blue eyes that could turn green if you looked at them right. Proud cheekbones, superb confidence; sun-kissed skin. Was she thirty? Forty? Or a thousand years old? Time could not touch her.

"Carolina Starhart, this is my sister, Otrera, Co-Queen of the Scythians."

"I am very pleased to meet you, Ms. Starhart," the queen said graciously. She didn't extend her hand.

Lina ducked her head, knowing that she should be curtsying or something. But Demi was a queen, too. No one bowed to Demi. "Pardon me for not knowing how to act in your presence, Your Majesty," she said. "I hope you won't take anything I do as an insult. But I'm honored to meet you."

"It's quite all right not to stand on ceremony in an informal setting like this. I wanted to meet the Speaker for the Earth, as my sister calls you. And I wanted my little hellions to learn how to treat a guest from Outside. We get so few here."

She eyed the two children with a raised eyebrow. "Juno! Shamash!" Immediately the children swooped down to the patio, cowed and polite. "That's better."

The queen presented them to her. The girl was Juno; the boy, Shamash: both probably adopted. Juno looked to be Indian while Mashy was of more eastern Asiatic origin. Parahero families came in all shapes and sizes, Lina supposed. Maximus had adopted Londo, too.

They settled down to lunch. In this setting, Lina had expected something off a gourmet TV show, but servants appeared with simple fare. She concentrated on spreading preserves on her bread the way she saw the others do, laying her knife obliquely across the bread saucer at the same angle as they.

"So you have become a megapara almost overnight," the queen observed.

"Yes ma'am," Lina said, making sure she wasn't speaking with food in her mouth. *Smaller bites, Lina, even though you're hungry.* Society bites.

"You had no powers… before?"

"No, ma'am. Well, I was a telepath. I trained in psychic healing and clairvoyance. But those are things that everyone can do, really."

That evoked a chuckle from Demi. "I don't think that everyone can—"

"Sure they can," Lina said. "I've trained a number of clairvoyants myself. It's just practice— lots of practice. The more you sit still and listen, the better you are."

"That's probably the problem right there," Demi said. "So few people nowadays can bear to sit still, much less listen."

"Mashy, Juno, you listen to this," the queen remarked almost offhandedly to her children. "Sitting still and listening. You could use practice in those areas."

Juno reached for more fruit. "'To everything there is a season,'" she quoted blithely. "'A time for sitting still and a time to jump up and down. A time to listen and a time to shout.'" Surreptitiously, she glanced at her mother to see how she was taking this.

"And a time to study literature more closely." The queen smiled. "I don't believe those are the correct words, but the message comes through."

"Where's Valiant now?" Juno asked Lina. "Where's Maximus and the others?"

Lina kept her eyes on her plate. She knew she lied horribly. "I suppose I wouldn't know," she said. "They said it was classified information."

Demi and the queen exchanged amused expressions. "I hardly think you're in a position now to spill the beans," Demi said.

"Where're the beans?" Mashy asked, rising up to examine the table's serving plates.

"It's a figure of speech, darling," Demi told her. "The megas of the Network, and some of the paras, have joined with the Affiliated Systems Mega-Legion to launch an attack on a nearby world."

"What world? Schwann?" Juno asked eagerly. She was in her middle teens. "Will the war reach here? How long will they be gone? Are you taking care of things by yourself, Demi? Do you need any help? I'll help you."

"We hope things will be very quiet here during all this, at least for a few days," Demi reassured her. "As for the war, it's on… Now what was the name of that place, Lina?"

"I wasn't supposed to be told," Lina repeated and Demi laughed outright.

"Wasn't supposed to, wouldn't know," the queen said. "How interestingly you put things, Lina. You don't say you don't know, you just say that you aren't supposed to know."

"I'm not," Lina said. "Stoan made that very clear. It would be a breach of Legion security for Londo to tell me too much. Stoan already blessed him out for telling me there'd be a war."

Lina pushed the food aimlessly on her plate. "Would you truly call it that? Lon said… Lon's told me in the past," she corrected herself quickly, "that sometimes you don't have to think about it as a war. Sometimes, he said, it's like a surgeon cutting out something with a laser. The earlier you get it, the less you have to cut, the quicker the operation, and the quicker the healing afterward. Is it like that, Demi? Quick and easy?"

Demi considered her. "Even with a surgeon's laser, the aim can slip; things can go wrong. You can never tell for sure. The quicker in and out they are, the fewer people will be hurt. Surely Valiant would be the last one to be harmed in a war."

"Yet Aiko was killed just the other day," Lina said slowly. "She was almost completely invulnerable. She was a legend."

"Who's… who was Aiko?" Juno asked.

"She was also known as Orenya, wasn't she?" the queen said. "The woman the interstellar nets have been talking incessantly about. There was a funeral for her the other day."

"Yes," Lina said. "A funeral."

"Londo spoke," the queen continued. "I recorded it; I've been meaning to show it to the children. A very stirring speech. A great tribute to his friend and a call for action on the part of all who admired her. Lovely. He has a true flair for words."

"And he knows the human heart," Lina said softly. "I worry about him. I know he's Valiant but I'm worried sick about this. I'm worried about Jae, too. We left him there on Aldierra, and there's no way of knowing if he even got to his ship alive. The other day there was sabotage on board a hyperspace liner— that's how Aiko died. How do I know that Jae's ship hasn't been sabotaged too?"

She twisted her napkin tightly in her hands before she noticed and forced herself to stop. "Stoan is an idiot. I should be with Jae on Aldierra, helping him talk sense into a bunch of silly old men there who are more interested in posturing than in saving their world. Instead I'm stuck here." She gave a start. "I didn't mean—"

"I know how you meant it," the queen said kindly. "I too have been shackled in my time, and I didn't like it one bit. I wished death on the man who had put me in those shackles."

"He lived to regret it." Demi chuckled softly.

"He did indeed. Well. Is this shackle permanent, Lina? Or is it coming off soon?"

Lina looked at the metal encasing her arm. One of the tiny lights on it seemed to be keeping time with her pulse. "Um, I sort of told Wiley that I was going to start considering how to get rid of it after four days," Lina confessed.

"Only after four days?" Demi asked. "You haven't started thinking now?"

Lina said slowly, "I was going to sit down today and really put my mind to the problem. But I wasn't going to try anything for another three days, really. I promised. But circumstances have changed."

"Where would you start?" the queen asked, considering the suppressor with its dimly blinking lights. "An electronic shackle, mightier than the cold iron I had to put up with for those long months. This is a scientific apparatus designed to neutralize a megapara. If I were you, perhaps I'd–"

"Trery!" Demi exclaimed. "Let's wait before we encourage her, shall we? I don't think we should take her into the Realms. She's in enough danger here. If it should follow us…"

The queen nodded in a soft bow of her head. "Perhaps. Then again, with something this seductively powerful– it's a beautiful design, and I've learned that they are the worst– it's best to consider all options. One should think about them as far in advance as possible so that when the time comes to strike, one is ready."

This time it was Demi's turn to nod. "The Mage is interested in her," Demi informed her sister.

"The Green Mage?" The queen pursed her lips thoughtfully. "Is that a good thing or a very bad thing?" She shook her head. "No, the Realms are definitely out of the question."

The table was silent for long moments.

"I'm surprised the television networks haven't exposed the marriage yet," Queen Otrera said in a lighter tone of voice. "I had it figured out two days ago, and considered myself lax in taking that long. They must not be paying their reporters well enough at E! and CNN."

Lina went along with the change of subject. She needed to put "getting rid of suppressor" in first position on her goals list. "You get CNN? Here?"

Demi laughed. "We aren't primitive, Lina. Quite the opposite in fact. Here."

"Let me," the queen said. Lina didn't see her touch anything or even gesture, but an all-angle screen appeared over the table. Onscreen a reporter read the news while the CNN logo and running headlines scrolled along the bottom of the screen.

Otrera played a report from Iowa, those two ambulance personnel talking about Carolina Starhart, the teleporter, who had rescued so many injured from the wreck. And then came the cardiac doctor, who spoke about her saving the life of an elderly man who had been having a heart attack. Warm relief washed over Lina, that she hadn't botched the job.

"And here were previous reports," the queen said as she nodded to the screen. Clips of Lon and Lina on the town in Montreal as well as the apartment attack, flashed by before the screen faded from view. "So we began with reports of Valiant being involved with someone in Montreal. Internet gossip columns reported a torrid dinner between the two of them, obviously smitten with each other. I believe news reports called her 'Lena.' A day and a half later, Valiant shows up at a train accident with a woman named Carolina Starhart. No one's linked any names yet. It won't take them long, I suppose, but with Valiant off-planet it might take them a longer while."

"My sister," Demi leaned over to tell Lina, "spends her days keeping track of everything and everybody, sticking her nose into anything she can."

"When it's quiet here in Scythia," the queen said archly, "it is far too quiet. I play what games I can and learn a little more about human nature and the outside world. So how is he in bed, Lina?"

"Trery!" Demi was shocked. Lina was more than shocked.

"I just wanted to know if they really, truly–" The queen glanced at the kids, who were paying rapt attention now.

"You two are excused. I believe you are scheduled for your Japanese lessons."

"Oh, Mother!"

"Right now. Go."

They reluctantly did so, disappearing inside.

"Trery, really." Demi shook her head.

"I've had my own theories about Valiant for years," the queen said haughtily. "At first I thought he could have sex with a human if he used control, like Maximus must. But since he's so rarely been seen with anyone, male or female, for so many years, I postulated that maybe he didn't have that degree of control, couldn't finish the act if he indeed ever began."

"I'm not sure I want to be involved with this part of the conversation," Lina said carefully. She didn't want to insult the queen.

"Indulge me." Queen Otrera gave a crafty grin. "There's nothing like a real-life soap opera to liven up things around here."

"The tapes the Legion furnished us mentioned a double-feedback telepathic loop." Demi's eyebrows raised expectantly at Lina.

"Good golly, did they show you that, too? I'm surprised they didn't have Wiley upload his tell-all files for y'all. Well, in that case you have all the information you need, don't you?"

"She was," the queen told Demi. "Absolutely."

"Was what?" Lina demanded. These people!

"You were a virgin. He was your first man," the queen said.

"The Legion tapes would also tell you that," Lina said irritably. "They had an office pool going."

Demi laughed. "You poor thing. And now everyone's staring at you and wondering about it."

"And they have a new question, too. 'Is she pregnant?' Maximus asked that, right after he, ah, caught us…"

"Oh dear," the queen laughed. "He interrupted you?"

"We were just in bed. Sleeping." Lina blushed to assure them. "The first time I meet Maximus, and it's like that."

Demi joined the queen in laughing.

"So it isn't just telepathic? And was he a virgin, too?" the queen asked through her laughs.

"Trery…" Demi warned.

"That's okay, Demi," Lina said. "I've read how the gods were always interested in the affairs of humans."

The queen regarded her. "Gods, eh?"

Lina shrugged.

"She's good, Demi. I like her. I like how she changes subjects and attacks. It shows a warrior spirit," the queen said, settling back in her chair.

Before the uncomfortable conversation could continue, a courtier joined them to remind the queen of an appointment. Otrera excused herself and Demi accompanied her, leaving Lina alone on the balcony to admire the view.

The atmosphere here was different somehow. Eternal. Perhaps it was just a mood-altering effect of the suppressor. She felt the delicacy and power of her own life flowing through her, making her aware of each moment. She knew that both Jae and Lon were trying their best to get back to her. It saddened her that they wouldn't make it in time. If something happened to her, they'd blame themselves. She should leave them a message, just in case, but otherwise try not to obsess about it.

Her focus had to be to protect Olympia. More and more the Mage's words repeated in her mind. She asked her guides what it meant. Through that far-off space where they were now, they told her to take care of herself and do her best. Huh, a lot of help they were– but sometimes they were just like that. Maybe it was just a bad communications link. Blame it on her shackle.

She turned as Demi came back.

"You're looking much more awake now. Do you feel up to a tour?"

"Could I?" Lina's heart surged with excitement. Scythia! "That would be wonderful. I just need to make sure I don't get too tired. And you do, too."

"Any idea when he'll return?" Demi asked quietly as they left the palace out into the streets of the city.

"No. The guides tell me not to worry, just to make sure we're both rested so that we'll be ready when it comes. We know it'll be between now and when Jae can get here, at least. Not very long." That was, if Jae had gotten to his ship safely. And if his trip was unmarred by sabotage.

They bicycled through the city. It was like stepping back to some faery-tale version of Ancient Troy or Egyptian Thebes, with splotches of modern technology that blended in with a Golden Age ambience. Computers were part of wooden fishing boats' equipment along with tri-shaped sails. Ancient temples were still in use.

Lina visited the temple of Gaia, where a priestess poured honey and wine over a bowl of pomegranates and set it ablaze at the feet of a statue of an obese woman.

"We knew that Gaia's voice was coming here, but we did not know what form it would take," the High Priestess told her. "I was afraid that it would come as a waterspout or earthquake. You know how the gods are."

From there they cycled to the rim of an almost perfectly circular valley. In the rock face along the far side, an archway had been carved, high enough to frame a giant. Inside that was a double door, its handles barely visible from where Lina stood, so they must be huge. A spectrum of light shimmered upon the doors' surface like pictures Lina had seen of the Northern Lights. And there was definitely music in the valley, or perhaps that was from the lights, *shhh…* She'd read that the aurora had a music of its own.

Thick stone walls from which iron spikes protruded lined the edge of the valley, looking like a lethal row of thorns. Attentive Scythian guards stood watch every two hundred feet or so atop the wall, guns holstered. Eight intricate, equi-distant cannons hung over it, all aimed at the Gateway.

Scythians had guarded the Gateway since history had first been recorded.

Lina tore her gaze from the landmark. The sun had begun to sink in the western sky. No trace of a ruby flight trail– yet. How long before he came back? How long before Jae arrived? Could even the Last Feithi handle a Galactic Guardian?

"I need to write some letters," Lina said.

"Do you swim?" Demi asked.

They cycled to a quiet beach. Demi's niece and nephew joined them. Lina watched the three of them play, first swimming, then flying through the air in a game of tag.

At first Lina felt like she was admitting weakness when she thought that she'd like to take a little nap out of the late sun. Then she realized that she absolutely had to take care of herself now. She took that nap under a half-tent set up on the beach, with the soothing sound of the surf beside her.

When she woke she found Demi dozing nearby– good. She was getting her rest, too. Lina didn't want to disturb her, so she went for a walk on the beach.

Juno and Mashy still played aerial tag, though now with some teasing birds. They looked down and waved.

"If you want, we'll come down and walk with you," Juno said graciously, but plainly she wanted to chase the birds.

Lina cocked her head at them. They seemed to be hanging in the air, almost as if they were… levitating.

She tried to port to them, just to see what would happen. Instead she rose up. A wobble turned into forward rotation until she caught herself, trying to balance as if she wore Lon's Legion array. The kids watched from just above her.

Lina smiled nervously. "How about that? I can do it, too." But she kept no more than eight feet above the sand.

Juno gestured to the ocean. "We train over the water so that if we fall, we'll only get wet."

"Oh, that's a good idea." Lina slowly made her way out to sea, but not too far from shore. Non-porting was weird. Her snail-paced flight swooped unwillingly as she sought control and didn't quite have it, especially against the brisk breeze. Levitation was not quickie transportation. Juno flew in next to her.

"You should let the winds carry you most of the time," she suggested.

"The wind?"

"Uh huh. If you just float, the wind will carry you, and you don't get tired so quickly. A hand-sail gets best results. We have tournaments with those."

Lina tried floating in place above the water. The ocean-powered wind picked her up like a kite, propelling her on a breathless ride. She laughed, tumbling through the air, landing in a wave and then rising up to try it again. She could spread her arms out like a freefaller and tuck them close to her body to temper the wind's effect.

Did Lon feel like this when he flew? Did Jae? Maybe they wouldn't like not being in complete control of their flight path.

After a while she headed back for shore, where Demi was awake and watching through the dusky sky. Lina landed in a sprawl next to her.

"I'll never be a Valiant," Lina laughed, soaking wet and sandy, "but at least I can do it a bit." Little Mashy "helped" her with the sand by slapping it out of her tunic, and nearly beat her legs black and blue. Demi reached to stop him.

"Gently, honey. I'm glad you two showed her how to do this. It may come in handy soon."

Juno looked to the sky as well. "Do you think he's back?" she asked.

"The Network will call me at the first sign of his signal," Demi said.

Lina shook her head. "I don't think it'll be long now."

"We've rested. Let's get some dinner," Demi said.

"Do you have any writing materials around here?" Lina said lightly, though the need was beginning to become urgent. "I want to make some notes."

"Why don't you save that until after dinner, when you're alone in your room?" Demi suggested. "You can have some privacy then."

They attended a communal dinner in one of the city's great open halls. Hundreds of Scythians dined there, and Demi explained that while many ate in their own homes within a family/friends unit, this was where they came for community and entertainment. A small but enthusiastic chorus sang to them while they ate. Then came dancers with breathtaking grace, followed by acrobats the likes of which Lina had never seen. Bursts of fire, ribbons of light, leaps that were far more than ordinary mortals could achieve. After dinner many of the guests got up to dance to a band.

But all Lina could do was worry about her own precarious situation. Guilt piled on top of that. She should be worried about Lon and Jae, shouldn't she?

They walked back to the palace in the warm night. Demi hesitated at Lina's door.

"I'll assign guards here in the hall," she said. "They'll be equipped with powerful rifles based in magick. I don't think the Sentinels can be well-versed in magick, do you? If you sense anything, if you think Granger's back you come out and they'll bring you to me. If you call out, they'll come in firing. Make sure you're down low."

Lina mustered a ghost of a smile. "Let's hope it doesn't come to that. You get your rest, too." She closed the door.

Another shower to wash the sea, sand and sweat off her. She found her own clothes folded neatly in a corner of the room, cleaned for her and smelling of flowers. The Klingon ambassador tee had never looked so good.

Paper and envelopes lay inside a desk drawer. Lina pondered what to write and came up with two letters that she hoped would help if anything happened to her. Londo would be devastated, she knew. He'd already lost so many in his life. And Jae– he'd lost his entire world. But they had each other.

She folded them and sealed them in envelopes. One she labelled "Londo," and the other, "Jae" in Lingua. Leaving them on the table would probably assure that they'd get them if the occasion arose.

On impulse, Lina took another piece of paper and wrote "Dear Queen Otrera: Thank you and Olympia for your gracious hospitality. You can't imagine how much I've appreciated it. Please don't read these." She left it covering the envelopes.

Not knowing if she'd be alive in the morning, she went to bed.

27

Londo woke fifteen minutes before the alarm. He lay on his back on his cot listening to Gary's gritty snore from the one next to him. This was all wrong. It had only been a few days, and it didn't seem right to wake up without Lina or Jae snuggled beside him, someone's arm draped around him. Here in a ship full of his friends he felt alone, cut off from his two warm lovers.

Damn, he wished he could have overridden Stoan and left the two of them together. Lina was so new at this. Lon knew she'd be scared. She needed someone to protect her from her own fears if nothing else.

Jae was a mountain of fear, too; Lon knew that now. He covered it up by flying in the face of the universe and using sheer audacity to throw everything else off-balance, leaving him in control.

And Lina called Jae "sweet." Londo had to chuckle quietly at that. Lina saw things in different ways than anyone else he'd ever known. It didn't mean she saw false images; she just viewed the universe from another angle. And now he was beginning– just beginning– to see some things from there as well.

He was discovering that some loyalties should be turned down a notch to make way for more important ones. Maybe now he could hope that he really could make a difference in his special spot in the universe, where he'd fit all along and never known it. Where other people were fitting in with him, loving him like he'd never been loved before.

He settled back on his thin mattress, a contented smile on his face. Life would be good once this mission was over. No, life *was* good now. He had this much. Life would get even better once he was back, but it was good now.

"Newlyweds," Gary grumped as he looked down on the way to the bathroom at his smiling companion. "Five minutes, Lon."

"Five minutes." Lon stretched. "Jealous."

Forty-three manned ships, one ParaNet and the rest Mega-Legion cruisers, linked up just out of standard system sensor range from Deseed. Their replicators had been kept busy. They now had enough telepathic suppressors and dampers to fill several good-sized compartments. Their supplies increased as a ship solely loaded with that equipment arrived from Legion HQ.

"Our first and foremost job," Stoan instructed the linked fleet, "is to protect the innocent. We've seen footage of so-called 'terrorists' and their families in front of firing squads or marched into death camps. Deseed's presidential council have been reported to be in favor of the transfer of power, but so far no one's actually seen any of them make that announcement, so we may assume that they're in the process of being controlled, they're out of the empire's reach, or they're dead. After we take out the mind controllers from government and military positions, that will be our next priority: to find the legitimate government, and if they are whole, to return it safely to power. Let them decide their own world's fate.

"Our continuing parallel mission is to locate, isolate and eliminate the artificial telepaths who are behind all this. Once they're out of action, we should see a snowball effect that will solve most of the other problems. Psyche and Valiant will be in charge of that."

Londo gave a start. Stoan could surprise him sometimes. He nodded at Mimik. The insectoid Legionnaire, Lon's second in command, nodded back, understanding that she was now in charge of Lon's Alpha team.

"Sunstorm, you're an official telepath now. Can you spot mental control?"

Erik's mouth opened, caught off-guard. "I doubt it, Commander," he finally said.

"He can," Psyche/Chimrin declared. Her sharp look brooked no protest from Erik. "I'll show him how."

"Valiant," Stoan said, "you say *she* told you how to control minds?"

"Yes," Londo said slowly, and he heard Chimrin suck in her breath.

"All right. I want you to take over some of the telepaths you find so we can trace 'em back to the source. You show Psyche how to do it, unless you know already, Chimrin?"

"No, I don't," she said stiffly. "Mind control is not something they teach at the Academy."

Londo crossed his arms in front of his chest. "No," he said.

"No what? You won't teach Psyche?"

"No, sir. Respectfully. I won't do it. I respect your command, but I won't take control of someone's mind." Lon lowered his arms. "It's not right. Lina said that taking away free will from someone could scar your soul."

"Soul? Valiant, we don't need any witchdoctor ideas now." Stoan scowled. "What's the use in having someone who actually knows how to do this if they won't?"

"Because then you know that they won't betray you or anyone else. And they won't betray themselves, either. I wouldn't trust anyone who's ever consciously controlled someone else's mind. Who knows what else they're capable of? Who knows if you're safe from them? No, Commander, there's got to be an alternate method to get you the information you want. We'll find it, sir."

"This is direct refusal of an order."

"Yes sir, I know." Lon clenched his fists at his side. "I'll find another way to accomplish the mission."

"Psyche?" Stoan turned to Chimrin.

The Legion's ex-commander considered Londo for a long moment. Her hawklike gaze slowly turned back to Stoan. "I've never known Valiant to refuse an order or not follow his commander to the utmost of his ability," she finally said. "But I won't try it either. I have to agree with him; how could you ever trust me again if I did this? Look at how much you trust Lina, and it's never been proven that she's controlled minds. Imagine what it would be like if you could prove someone had done that. And..." she stumbled over this next part, "it's just wrong. It makes my skin crawl to think of it."

Stoan turned to Erik, who had been staring at Londo and Chimrin with amazement. The Legionnaire suddenly looked very young, as if he hadn't served with honors on an Alpha Team for two years.

"Okay, Sunstorm, we know you've done a little control in your time…"

"But Commander, I don't even know how I– ow!" Erik rubbed his red head of hair, looking up at the air. "*Skurn,* I wasn't going to do it. I was going to say no. Cut it out!"

"What the orb– Are all my people mutinying?"

"Sorry, sir, but Lina's sicced some guardian spirit on me. He's keeping me out of trouble. Apparently he considers me doing any kind of mind control 'trouble.' And well, I have to agree. If I can be frank, sir."

"There are lines ethical people don't cross," Londo told his commander.

"Guardian spirits. Metaphysical claptrap." Stoan grunted, his face turning one shade darker blue. "Very well. The telepaths in the group refuse to mind control the enemy. Let the record so show. Perhaps they give a good reason. You three are in charge of finding a way to neutralize these controllers. I want them out of action, however you manage it, and I want it done fast."

"We can do that, Commander," Chimrin told him calmly. "Just let us find our own methods."

"All right," Stoan said coldly. "Let's get some survey teams together, check out the current situation for ourselves. Let's set up for war."

The landscape opened wide under Londo as he rose through the atmosphere after planting supply caches on the surface. Buildings and vegetation became city blocks and then became acres– large rectangles that turned into wide, blurred patterns of subtle earth colors. Londo didn't focus on that. Instead he saw missile silos embedded in the ground miles below him. Their crews stood at alert, watching their instrument panels. Sheens of nervous sweat covered their bodies.

The horizon shifted with troop movements, battalions of atmospheric craft filling the skies. Some of the aircraft contained atomic weaponry that looked very makeshift. Lon didn't recall Deseed having huge arsenals of atomics. These had to have been scraped together at the last minute.

Which made the chance of an accident that much more likely.

Faster than any rocket, he flew higher still, above the atmosphere, to carom behind an uninhabited moon and then take a new course. He entered the airlock of the linked hyperspace ships and gave his report.

Hal was already there with most of the other team leaders. The rest of the scouts returned within a few minutes of Londo and added their reports of all-out panic and chaos in the cities.

Most of the people of Deseed realized that they were being lied to. They didn't know whom to trust or what was truly going on. They only knew they were in imminent danger from both their own troops and Yanist-Glory's. Entire armies had mutinied, refusing to come under the command of the Emperor. They had been declared enemies of the state, to be shot on sight.

Power was mostly off-line; transport of food supplies had halted. Water treatment was spotty. Now with Lon's reports of atomic weaponry it looked like Armageddon could happen by accident.

Stoan carefully considered the reports and opinions of his high-ranking comrades before he finalized strategy. They would take the capital city of Karjar-Re first and purge it, track down all controlled people, all Imperial telepaths, all troops loyal to Yanist-Glory. Suspects would also be detained. Only then would the beta teams get food and water if not power back to the people. Karjar-Re was the hub of all planetary activity, both military and governmental. If it fell the rest of the insurgency would suffer the blow as well.

Stoan called for more suggestions and contingency plans. An hour later sixty-five teams beamed down to the planet, their missions clear.

Blinking hard, Londo paused to regain his balance. Spinning so fast was usually a dizzying process, but spinning inside sheer rock was even more so. He waited until his brains stopped rotating, checked his GPS, and twisted into another tight spin.

His Legion ring relayed occasional reports: He was making too much noise; slow down. He wasn't progressing fast enough; speed up. The frequency made by his actions was too high and might be picked up on the surface. He angled his impervion plow differently, and the frequency dropped.

Finally his head emerged from the rock into a sub-basement room. The Legionnaires there stood back as a rush of dirt erupted along with him. Lon climbed out of it and brushed what he could out of his hair.

He checked behind himself. A human-sized tunnel now connected this governmental center with a similar one a few hundred miles away. Legionnaires behind him were hauling the debris away, clearing the transportation route as only they could.

He snapped to attention in front of Transit. Transit might be only a Beta Team member, but he was in charge of this particular project, so for the moment that made him Londo's superior officer. Even if Transit was a prick. Legion ranks were fluid. Most Alpha Team members were working as individuals to help the lesser teams that wouldn't be involved in the final assault.

Transit walked to the tunnel opening and made a show, Londo thought, of examining the work. While he waited, Londo ran his fingernail over the edge of his plow to re-sharpen it as he could, since impervion was so, well, *impervious,* and kept his peace.

"Good work, Legionnaire," Transit finally allowed. He nodded at Londo. "The team at New Mengore is waiting for you. Dismissed."

After fifteen long, dizzying tunnels, Lon was glad to be a mere but stationary assistant in one of the final pre-Alpha operation projects. He held massive sheets of polysteel in place as IceForge combined them into a seamless tank, big enough to hold half a city's water supply. To keep boredom at bay, Lon tracked numerous reports coming in on Legion frequencies, tales of prep work taking place across this world to ensure that the majority of the civilian population would have basics for survival afterward in case this wasn't solved cleanly.

He joked with Tara, who was still digging tunnels and reported from the other side of the planet that she was sure she'd never get all the grime from under her fingernails. Stoan broke into their conversation to make an offer of allowing Tara to use the Legion Lifestyle section when this mission was completed. Lifestyle could clean anything. More voices chimed in on that to give their own exaggerated stories of the mission grime they'd encountered over the years.

Finally the tank was done and potable water began to spill in. Through layers of earth, Londo watched the Beta and Gamma Teams on the surface secure and camouflage the area. He checked in with Mimik. She was also finishing up, but hers had been a spying mission. Now she rejoined his team to lead it while he reported to special duty.

The morning was partly cloudy but still bright over Karjar-Re. The city was laid out in a neat grid of low buildings. Spacious public greens gave the place a feeling of openness. It reminded Lon of Sydney.

"There." Disguised as civilians, the three Legionnaires lurked behind a stand of trees. Chimrin pointed at a Deseedan woman. She stood on white stone steps to the side of a group of armed soldiers receiving final orders from Imperial officers. "She's a controller."

Erik tensely stared at the scene. "I don't get it," he said. "How is that woman different from the soldiers?"

"Just look inside her mind," Chimrin snapped. "You can see the obvious artificiality of the telepathic implant. There's a black cloud around her, a foulness of… spirit." Chim glanced at Londo. People tainting their souls. His glance matched hers and returned to the woman.

"Try a different tack," Londo told Erik. "Use your imagination. Don't try to push it, just let it do what it wants. Pretend that someone is going to help you so you don't have to sense the controller yourself. Just imagine someone who's going to point them out to you. Maybe it's that guardian angel of yours."

Erik gave Londo an incredulous expression. "Now's not the time for games," he told him.

"Take three minutes and try it. If it doesn't work we can try something else."

Lina had said to call on the white light. Lon tried to imagine a white light surrounding the three of them. He had little idea what he was doing, but he kept the image of the white light in his mind.

Erik scanned the crowd. "I'm sorry, sir," he told Londo, "but I don't– ow."

"What?" Londo leaned forward.

"I was just looking around and I'd swear that spirit guy tapped me on the forehead. Not as hard as before."

"Who were you looking at?"

"I don't know. I think it was– ow. That one there, the second one in the third row. He's looking at the statue."

Londo chuckled softly and glanced at Chimrin. She just shook her head. "I hadn't even noticed him," she said. "Yes, that's a controller. Not artificial, though," she said, puzzled. "But I don't think he's a natural telepath."

"Lina said anyone can do hooks," Londo said. "You don't have to be a tele-path."

"I bet it helps if you are," Chimrin said, and put her hand on Erik's shoulder. "Congratulations, Sunstorm. You're now able to spot controllers. Make sure you include that on your resume when we get back."

Londo took a breath. "Only two in this bunch," he confirmed. "Don't let them get you when you grab. Chim, let's remain on this route. The other teams have the rest of the city well-covered now. You find us another likely group. We'll return in a few minutes."

"Waitaminnit, waitaminnit," Erik said hurriedly. "How do I not let them get me? How do you protect yourself from a controller before you get the shackle on?"

"Think of a white light," Londo said. "*Strong* white light. Let's see if that helps."

"White light?" Chimrin humphed. She shook her head. "I think I'd just attach those shackles as fast as I could." She thoughtfully tapped her cheek next to her nose. "Bring back a damper when you come. That way we can blank out an area once we know who's who, and then attach the shackles at our leisure."

"Good idea," Londo nodded. "But for this time," he turned to Erik and pointed his finger at him, "think of the white light."

"Yessir, white light."

"Now."

Both men took off into the air, sweeping in low and grabbing from above the squad. The two controllers let out yelps of surprise and wrestled with them as the Legionnaires clamped the shackles on them. As soon as the shackles snapped shut, the controllers fainted dead away.

The soldiers took aim at the flying paras, but they dropped their weapons with sharp cries as they suddenly turned red-hot. One had the presence of mind to pick up a comm unit but snatched his hand away when it burned his fingers.

Erik laughed as they flew their captives away from the city. "See, Valiant? Heat is the way to go. You point and direct it; so much more direct than this telepathy business."

"So it is," Londo agreed. "Good work."

It only took two minutes to get to the designated holding area. Lon kept his speed down so as not to lose Erik, who could only rely on his Legion array for flight. Wilder awaited them with dampers already in place. He wound an energy binder through a circuit on the prisoners' shackles. Now even if the prisoners woke up, they wouldn't be going anywhere

Londo and Erik took two dampers and an armload of shackles with them as they left, following Chimrin's telepathic instructions.

There and there, she pointed as they neared. Londo spotted another one she'd missed. She frowned at her sloppiness.

Must be one of the new kind, he assured her. **Leapfrog controllers, the new wrinkle in the game.**

She nodded. **Remind me to apologize to Sunstorm. Leapfroggers: controllers off-planet seize minds who then control others.**

It increases the domino effect, the number of people one controller can ultimately handle.

Apparently. I see what they feel like now. Don't think I'll miss many others.

Oblivious to their conversation, Erik scouted ahead and found a small pack of controllers as they worked their way further into enemy territory. In a burst of speed, Lon flew around the small park, blocking access to it. Erik set off the dampers. Again they swept in, this time all three working so they could attach shackles quickly. Londo and Erik carried off the prisoners as Chimrin upchucked into some bushes.

Their plan was to make their way deep into Karjar-Re's main military complex until they'd reached its central core. The faster they could move, the less opposition they'd run into. Surprise was their ally.

Just off to the west, troops dragged off captured rioters. The three watched them for a moment before heading on. The safety of the rioters was not part of their mission. The gates to the complex lay just ahead, but Chimrin's ring beeped with a message from Wiley.

"I've intercepted communications forming a firing squad," he told her. Londo and Erik patched in on their own rings. "A hundred dissidents are scheduled to be executed in a few minutes. You're our closest team."

"Coordinates," Chimrin barked. She was in the air and streaking there before Wilder signed off.

"We make this quicker than quick," Londo reminded them.

They flew in low to the edge of an amphitheater. Once it had been a beautiful place of marble and grass, but blood stains and tramping boots had destroyed anything but its bare bones. Armed soldiers spread out in front of the throng of bound prisoners. These were different people from the ones they'd just watched. They ran the gamut of age, gender… and acceptance of their defeat.

Londo tossed active dampers to either side of the stage below them.

Guns dropped. Some of the soldiers fainted. Most looked around in confusion, lowering their arms. Then the questions came: Where were they? What were they doing? Who were these people?

Valiant, Psyche and Sunstorm landed in their midst. They grabbed five people and snapped suppressors on them. Their victims immediately crumpled.

Valiant pointed at the ragged line of soldiers with his fist, so that his ring projected the Legion symbol large enough for all to see and recognize. "You've been mind controlled," he told them in a voice that carried well across the amphitheater. "Does anyone think that these people deserve to be executed?"

"I don't even know what they've been accused of," one woman called.

"They've been convicted of trying to save Deseed from the Yanist-Glory Empire," Chimrin explained, using her own ring to amplify her voice. "You people were going to eliminate a threat to the emperor."

Consternation broke out in the ranks, and above it all another soldier cried, "The hell with that!" He stepped forward with an electronic breaker to cut through the bonds of one of the prisoners. "Come on, come on!" he urged his companions, and soon everyone was free.

Londo returned from delivering the mind controllers to Wiley and helped Erik place two more dampers so as to affect the widest possible area. "We'll establish this as a neutral holding area," Londo told the soldiers. Chimrin set up guard rotations at the entrances to the amphitheater's grounds and cautioned all the people who had been controlled not to leave.

"This area is free from mind control," Londo explained to everyone. "Anyone who comes into range of the dampers loses contact with whoever's controlling them. Any controller in the area is rendered useless. We'll bring more controlled people here and we'll get you supplies. Just hold the area and keep people calm. We or other Legionnaires will be back."

Chimrin found a bathroom and got thoroughly sick in it. She felt a little better for having done so, but still swore off all food for at least a week.

Why did the dampers inhibit non-telepathic controllers as well as teeps? Perhaps the nausea it produced was enough to break the concentration needed. But non-telepaths being mind controllers– Chim had always assumed it was the addition of artificial teep tech that allowed that. How could a non-teep have the power? Why did you never hear of a full-blown natural teep being a mind controller?

Perhaps it wasn't the artificiality of the teep implant, but the nature of the training that accompanied it. Chimrin had trained to know the auric, or energy body, and now Londo had told her that it was what controllers might be using to secure their victims. Controllers had been trained in some fashion to manipulate their own auras as well as others'. This was something to think about and relay back to Tishan. The University there might unwittingly be a prime spawning ground for controllers.

Chimrin let out a sigh of blessed relief when she felt the final edge of the damper's area of influence fade behind her as she met up with her teammates again.

"We're close to the central command," Londo said. "We need to move fast before they can figure out what we're doing. Reports must be coming in."

"We *have* been moving fast," Erik protested. "Surely they can't have a handle on us yet."

"Never underestimate the enemy," Londo told him as they walked as briskly as they could and still seem a normal part of the capital's population. "Quickest way in– Any ideas?"

The high security areas of the planetary defense complex were underground and clad completely in impervion, which fogged Londo's clairvoyant paravision. He could tell directions in general for them to follow, but not specifics. Erik checked tourist information maps on the world's Internet, and showed them to Chimrin. Of course they didn't display any of the secured areas of the complex, but this place had to be set up in a logical pattern. Chimrin's finger traced several possible routes and settled on three to try.

"We're go for attempt number one," Chimrin announced as they neared a security gate. A large warning sign glowed next to the manned entry point: ALL VISITORS MUST BE ACCOMPANIED BY OFFICIAL PERSONNEL.

The civilian clothing the Legionnaires wore was a hindrance now. Chimrin sent a mental suggestion to three likely-looking, uncontrolled personnel and guided them into an equipment room. The door *shushed* behind them. Londo triggered his Legion symbol projector against the wall. The Legion was well-known even on these non-AffSys worlds.

"We need your uniforms," Chimrin told the boggling threesome. "It's a planetary emergency."

From there it was easy enough to use telepathy to gain passwords, parapowers to trip secured locks. They moved in and downward through the complex.

"Grigach, look at them all," Erik hissed.

At these lower levels there were the controlled, the Imperials… and mind controllers by the dozen. Several had been leapfrogged.

"How are they making them all?" Chimrin asked Londo. "Have they perfected a new surgical procedure? In the past, the normal operation's success rate has been low." But if it weren't the operation but rather the training that made a true controller…

"We'll find that out after we secure the planet," Lon told her. She nodded.

People moved at a brisk pace through the wide, low-ceilinged hallways, single-minded in their duties. The Legionnaires didn't want to attract attention by slowing to consider their course, so Londo drew them into an empty bathroom.

"Where to?" Chimrin asked.

"I can't see much at all," Londo said. "And everyone echoes down here. I can't figure out who's speaking where."

"There's got to be online security maps," Erik said. "Can we get Dr. Mem-Bazer to break through their passwords?"

Londo chewed his lip. "I don't want to risk communications from within this complex," he decided. He rubbed his nose as he looked into the distance and then back at Erik. "Can you ask that guardian angel of yours?"

"Sir?"

"See if you can get some information from him."

"Uh. Okay. Just tell me how."

"I don't know. Turn in a circle and ask directions. See if you get a *thwunk.*"

"Yessir."

Chim crossed her arms in front of herself but didn't say a word as Erik closed his eyes and slowly turned around. At one point he lost his balance.

"Whoa. Sorry, sir. I must be a little dizzy from all the dampers today."

"Turn again," Londo said.

Erik did and again at the same direction point he stumbled. "Is he trying to tell me something? It felt like someone was pushing me."

"Good enough," Londo said. He held his finger in the air for a long moment and then nodded. "Tink agrees," he said. "Thanks, Tink."

"Who's Tink, sir?"

"She's someone Lina told me how to use. A deva of temperature, I suppose you could call her. She likes that direction."

"We're going to go just on this?" Chimrin asked. "On his imagination and your… whatever? Temperature deva?"

"You got better info?" Londo asked her.

She sighed and rolled her eyes. "I suppose not."

"Then check your dampers and your stomachs," Londo told them. "We're going in."

Erik spotted three controllers as they waited to clear the next checkpoint. Being *thwunked* on the head increased the speed of his learning curve.

Chim nodded. **We'll leave them until after we take care of the main group,** she said. **We can't afford the time to take them out now.**

A bright corridor ran in the correct direction. Only higher-ranking officers walked this way. Londo rounded a corner, then returned with three more bars of office for them all to attach to their uniforms.

It'll take them an hour to wake up, he told them.

That should be more than enough, Chimrin said.

Looks like the main action's right through there, sir, Erik said and his companions both nodded.

They watched more controllers entering the area.

We need more dampers for an area this large, Chimrin said. **Londo?**

Lon set his jaw. He didn't like to leave his team in such dangerous surroundings. **It'll take me time to get out of the building and then back in,** he said. **I'll make it fast as I can. Estimate fifteen to twenty minutes.** He lagged behind just before they reached the complex's main chamber, then turned smartly and began to retrace his steps at a brisk yet casual pace.

Central Control was set up as a typical planetary war room with wall-size optical maps of the planet and its defensive systems. Holoviews of the star system and galactic sector served as background screens. The Yanist-Glory Empire was delineated in the same color on the starmap as Deseed's system.

They must be very sure of themselves.

But there were so many controllers here– at least fifteen mingling with the rest. Chimrin and Erik made sure they knew who was who. Ten minutes in. They faked business, doing what others seemed to be doing.

"What's that?" a voice demanded from behind them. Chimrin's hand closed about her small damper, but a set of arms reached around to grab her while another set took the damper from her. They turned her to face a hulking brute of a man who held the damper in one hand, studying it.

Erik edged away from the group, trying to look like he wasn't associated with her. He hid his damper in the crook of his arm.

"Look! He's got one, too!" someone said, and both he and Chimrin sprang into action.

Chimrin kicked back at her captor. With a shout of pain, he released her. She jabbed him in the ribcage and whirled to block the nerve centers in his neck. Reaching out with her mind, she held the big second man rock still, his body paralyzed, as she took care of the other.

A wave of heat rolled off Erik. Not enough to burn, but enough to keep people at bay even in this crowd. A breeze, then a wind, sprang up around him. He tossed balls of heat on that wind into the crowd even as he searched to find who had taken his damper.

There: one of the controllers held it curiously before eying him. Two others turned to target their gazes upon him. Ominously.

"Psyche, watch out!" Erik called over his shoulder. White light. He could feel it like bright liquid, reaching down to flow around him. He imagined it as a wall between him and them.

He glanced back. Chimrin's eyes were squeezed shut, sweat breaking out on her brow. She was fighting something inwardly.

"White light, Psyche! White light!"

She cried out, her body spasming as more people, more controllers approached. They smiled, confident and cruel, their eyes fastened on Chimrin.

Erik touched his ring. "Valiant!" he said tersely into it, not waiting for an answer. "Psyche's down. Controllers all around. The white light works. I'm going to try to get her out at least. They have our dampers."

I'll be there in two minutes with new ones, Lon's voice rang in his mind. **Hold on. I'm almost there.**

Chimrin fell to her knees and shook, screaming, clutching her head. Erik couldn't stand it. He fired controlled blasts of heat and ice from his hands, knocking the crowd back as he made his way through them to Chimrin's side. He didn't want to hurt the innocents who were controlled, but–

"Get away from her!" he shouted. Even the controllers retreated now, but he saw people using the comm lines. They were reporting to their superiors that paras were trying to infiltrate Deseed. The Mega-Legion's plan was rapidly becoming public.

Chimrin lay crumpled on the ground. Erik reached down, his eyes on the crowd, threatening them with a gesture, holding a nimbus of flame around his hand. He pulled her up with the other hand. "Psyche? Chimrin? Are you all right? Chimrin!"

He loosed his arm in horror as the realization struck him. Control wrapped around her mind like a blanket; he could feel it. The shock of it sent all other thoughts from him. The white light dropped away.

She opened her eyes and smiled at him. "I'm perfectly all right now," she said. The voice was not hers. It was some man's, deep and doubly shocking coming from her.

Erik took two steps back. Someone kicked him in the throat, though there was no one there. They slammed him in the abdomen. He cried out, falling backward.

Chimrin pulled herself up and stepped toward him, slightly off-balance as if she were new to walking. "It's always so much easier if a natural telepath does it," her man's voice laughed.

Erik couldn't catch his breath. Slowly he crumpled to the floor, catching himself. The world contracted on him, the light in the room narrowing into a tiny dot...

And suddenly there was light again. Erik lay on the floor as feeling flooded back into his body. The floor grew cold beneath his hands and cheek.

"Sunstorm!" Londo called. "Chimrin! Are you all right?"

Erik shook his head as he pulled himself up. He took a blessedly deep breath, but that damned buzzing was really getting to him this time. He might throw up. Deciding to sit on the floor, he soon became aware of all the puzzled people milling about.

Where was Valiant? A commotion within the crowd drew Erik's attention. He watched Valiant beating up some officers who had pulled guns on him– "beating up" being tapping them on the chins and watching them fall. They'd be Yanist-Glory's troops who were mixed in here among the Deseedan.

A helpful hand reached down to help Erik get up.

"Thanks," Erik said. He didn't have to turn around to know that that was Chimrin getting ill in someone's trash bin behind him. He thought he might join her in a few minutes.

"What's happened? Who are you?"

"Sunstorm," he identified himself. "That's Psyche behind me." He didn't turn to point her out. "We've set off telepathic dampers that are blocking all forms of mind control in here."

"Is that what this is?" the big guy who'd taken Chimrin's damper examined the silver globe in his hand.

"Yes," Erik said as he retrieved it from him. He finally turned to give Chimrin a hand. She looked decidedly green under her regular lavender hue, and very pale.

"Whatever you do–" her voice came in a hoarse whisper but at least it was her own, "don't turn that one on. I don't think I could take three of these things in one room. They're… quite efficient."

"Watch out, Valiant!" Erik called suddenly, and flew up over the crowd to blast one soldier about to fire at the Legionnaire. Dropping the gun, the woman cried out as her skin blistered.

Erik examined the crowd, looking for more weaponry in the hands of Yanist-Glory personnel, trying to remember who had been the controllers. He couldn't sense them now that his telepathy wasn't working.

Something went *thwunk!* on his forehead, and he noticed a man was staring at Lon. Lon had spotted the man as well and looked curiously at him.

"Watch it, Valiant! White light!" Erik fired a blast of hot air around the man, enough to knock him out without seriously damaging his lungs.

Londo shook his head. "He can't control me, not with the damper in effect," he told Erik, but there was astonishment in his voice. "I think– I think I saw a hook," he said.

Chimrin came up to them. "Are you sure?"

"It could have been my imagination," Londo said. "But I thought–just for an instant– that there was a hook."

"You don't have to be a telepath to control," Erik said. He brought the white light back to himself. "If this guy isn't a telepath, then he might be controlling you."

Londo pondered the situation. "But the dampers stop the controlling."

"Maybe when you get outside the field, you'll be controlled," Chimrin said quietly. "We will be. I got the impression that the people who took us were in turn controlled by others, I don't know where. That means that even if we shackle the controllers in here, we'll still be under someone else's control if we leave."

"How badly were you controlled?" Londo asked.

Chimrin met his gaze levelly. "Completely."

"She didn't even have her own voice anymore," Erik reported. "And I think they got me just as much. I was totally out of it for a moment."

"But this guy was firing off hooks– or doing something– while the field was on," Londo mused.

"He could have set a trap for you," Chimrin said. "As soon as you step outside, a teep controller could utilize it."

Erik said, "Maybe it's the maintenance that requires some kind of artificial telepathic connection. So control doesn't work inside a damper field."

"Lina said that everything that's alive is telepathic to some extent," Londo said. "Maybe the initial control is low-level and the maintenance is high-level. The damper only catches the higher level of telepathy."

"All we have is theory," Chimrin said. "I'd like Wiley to check that out– and test it– before I'd trust it." She looked around at the confused crowd. "Are we stuck here with them? Or can you get out of the field? Will you be controlled when you leave this area, Londo?"

"Ow." Erik rubbed his forehead. "What was that for? I wasn't looking at anyone."

"What, that angel of yours is still hitting you– in here?"

"Yeah," Erik said, giving the air a dirty look. "That's how I saw that guy trying to get you."

A light dawned to Londo. "That's because that's psychic work, not telepathy. Lina was able to communicate with her guides with the damper field in place." He smiled at Erik. "I want you to ask your angel some questions."

"Ask my angel?"

Lon thought quickly. "One knock means yes, no knock means no."

Erik looked at Chimrin, and she shrugged. "If it doesn't work, we'll try something else," she said.

"It's not *your* head," Erik grumbled. "Okay, sir, what do I ask?"

"Repeat after me," Londo instructed. "It's safe for all three of us to go outside the damper field."

"It's safe for all three of us to go outside the damper field," Erik said, and cringed the tiniest bit, expecting a *thwunk*. He relaxed when nothing came. "Nothing," he reported.

"It's safe for me to go outside the damper field," Londo said.

"It's safe for Valiant to go outside– ow!" Erik rubbed his forehead.

Chimrin gave a small smile. "Another item to put on your resume," she told Erik.

"Let's double-check this," Londo said. "Only you and Chimrin of us three need to stay inside the field."

Erik sighed. "Only Chimrin and ow! Hey, a little softer there!"

Londo nodded. "All right. We have a new center of operations. You two do what you can here. It's a pretty good spot to direct the army, isn't it? If you had to get controlled anywhere, you picked the right place."

"Gee, thanks," Chimrin said sourly. "Okay, Thwunking Boy, let's get to work." She pulled Erik along with her as they waded through the confused crowd.

Eventually the controllers were safely shackled and stacked unconscious against a wall, out of the way and well-guarded. The Legionnaires herded the Imperial sympathizers into a corner and set armed guards on them. The milling people organized again, but now worked for Deseed and not the Empire.

28

Jae stretched out on the long couch, a glass in his hand and bottle on the floor beside him. The Aldierrans might serve poor food, but their liquor was strong enough to make them forget about it.

Randomly, he brought the video out of its flash-forward mode. It cleared to a scene of Londo, bundled in civilian Terran clothing, darting about a bounded area of outdoor ice. The people around him glided on bladed boots. They stopped to watch Lon.

Someone had fallen and Londo now swooped upside-down on the ice to circle them. It was Lina, flat on her ass on the ice. Jae chuckled and raised his glass in a silent toast to the two.

But his brows contracted to a frown as he watched them in each other's arms, flying over the Terran city. They'd had so much time together. They hadn't included Jae.

Londo was his! Lon had been his for years, and then Lina had taken him away.

But. But. Lina was his, too. She'd opened up her mind for him to see her soul. She'd spoken to him with the voice of Feith itself. *"Shalla dyem, ta fal." Follow your heart, my son.*

And there they were, leaving him behind. Pushing him out.

"Random shuffle," he told the screen and took another swig of the burning liquid.

If Feith were still alive, Jae would have brought Londo home to meet his family years ago. They would have drawn on Feithi knowledge to discover how the two of them could touch safely. And then they would have helped talk Lon into marrying him.

Lina was right. Lon's own fear of losing others' love would prevent him from ever going public that he was actively bisexual. If he did, some of his friends would turn from him. Some would disown him, deny him altogether. Londo couldn't stand that.

Lon and he had made boyish daydream plans of Lon marrying a woman and Jae bedding her since Londo couldn't. It was an almost-marriage to Lon that Jae had begun to take to heart. But then came Lina. Lon could complete the sex act with her. He'd secured her in marriage.

Then had come a moment when Jae realized that perhaps this was indeed the woman of their plans only more so, and he had given Lina new consideration. And again she had risen above his expectations of what a Terran was. She was spectacular.

Jae took another long pull at his drink and lay back as the screen continued its scene, unwatched. Yes, he could make this decision easily except for one thing.

Londo wanted to keep the honorable Triune a secret.

So they returned to an altered plan of Londo marrying a woman and having her by day, while Jae and he had her by night. No one must know, no one could be told. There'd not even be hand-holding in public, no blissful gazes across a room, no shared whispers in a crowd. Just hiding and sneaking and closed doors.

He couldn't do it. He would not reduce himself to living such a lie.

But with Lina there would be children to carry on his Feithi line. She was adamant that children would arise only from within a legal marriage. And though thousands of women had volunteered over the years to have the Last Feithi's children, to his mind there was only one possibility: the wild beauty who communed with worlds, who made love in the wilderness, who would carry a child within herself before giving birth. The woman who sang like the very angels and loved him like one, too.

Cherished Lina, whose life hung upon his getting to Earth in time. How much longer now? A day of this choking inhibition? More?

He turned over so he could reach the bottle. The liquor sloshed as he refilled his glass.

The Deseed control center personnel had to represent themselves as still loyal to the Empire. No one could remember what they'd told anyone outside about paras and infiltrators, so they reported that the paras had been captured and the threat ended. They claimed to have closed off the war room from the rest of Central to neutralize any further threat of paras getting in during this crucial window of time.

It was a splendid command post for Londo, Erik and Chimrin to coordinate Legion activities. Here were many of the planet's own command personnel as well, at least the ones who were still in place before the Imperials could replace them.

"How is the atomics recall coming?" Londo asked.

Major Krokor responded, manning his screens himself instead of having an aide– unavailable here– do it. "Undersea vessels are all returning to port, Valiant. We've locked land-based silos still in operation. Satellite nukes have been neutralized. It's just the atmospheric fleet that's causing trouble. Two squadrons report Maximus attacking, and they won't stand down."

Londo nodded and fished his ParaNet communicator out of a pocket. "Hal," he said into it.

"Here," Hal's voice came back after a moment. "What's up? I've got a good two dozen planes out here packed with atomics. I don't like the looks of two of them. Whoever put this stuff together did a lousy job."

"They think you're attacking," Londo told him. "They aren't going to retreat until you're out of the sky."

"And leave these to go off at any minute?" Hal's voice sounded incredulous.

Londo glanced at the major, who transferred his screen information to the room's main screen. Londo raised his communicator and added translation so Krokor could hear. "Which are the two?"

Hal gave the identifying codes of the two planes.

Two dots on the screen blinked red in identification. The major thumbed his communication controls. "Stamol 314, 569," he said briskly. "This is E-Fig Control. Respond."

"E-Fig Control, Stamol 569."

"E-Fig Control, this is Stamol 314."

"Stamol 569, 314, our telemetry shows that your cargo is going unstable. Repeat, unstable. Get out of there; eject at once. Maximus is standing by to keep the atomics from exploding prematurely."

"Sir. We saw him attack Bench Squadron," one of the pilots started.

"Bench Squadron defected to the other side and were targeting civilian objectives. Maximus is acting as a neutral party here. He wants no atomics used. Yours are going unstable. I repeat, eject at once! We're giving Maximus orders to take care of your planes with you or without you." The major lowered his voice. "I hear the vacuum is pretty thin today, kids."

"Stamol 314. Crew is ejecting, sir."

"Stamol 569. We're out of here."

"Londo, a little help?" Hal's voice came through on the communicator.

"Right." Lon considered his options. The planes were just a minute or three away, as he flew.

"I'll take full command here if you think it's safe for you to go out," Chimrin assured him.

"All right, Team Leader." He added in muttered tones, "Here's where we see if Thwunking Boy was right." He nodded at Security to unlock the war room doors, and then flew off down the halls of Central Control at a speed that flattened personnel in its tempest.

The clouds raced by like leaves in an autumn windstorm as Londo flashed by. His mind didn't feel any different out here. He breathed a sigh of relief. No mind control, thank god. He remembered to ask for some white light just in case.

There– ahead. A squadron starting to turn northeast from a westward course, six escape pods parachuting down to the surface, two planes moving steadily westward, and Hal. Another figure flew into the area, much slower than Londo: Stoan. Sometimes Stoan liked to oversee important phases of missions in person.

Always good to have some help, but Lon and Hal could handle this alone as long as the rest of the squadron kept to their flight plan.

Hal nodded at Londo and grabbed one plane, sinking his fingers into the very metal of its hull. He tilted its axis up with a little grunt, and gently accelerated so as not to alarm the fragile atomics inside. Londo took hold of the remaining plane and did the same. They'd have to haul them far above the planet to avoid environmental and electromagnetic damage. If the bombs exploded prematurely, parts of the planet could be plunged into a temporary stone age until computer circuitry could be replaced.

It was a potential disaster that could be easily avoided with a light touch.

Londo waved Stoan off. Stoan wore a pressure suit as if he'd been working in thin atmosphere or less.

But he kept coming.

Lon rubbed his ring against the adjacent finger, opening a comm circuit. "Stoan, we've got it," he said. "Get back down there and make sure the crews land safe, why don't you?"

"I've always wondered if the two of you could be destroyed by atomics," a voice replied through his ring. With a shock, Londo recognized it as the voice of Emperor Yanist-Glory. Lon looked at Stoan, and the voice matched his mouth movements. "I certainly hope it's true."

Suddenly the plane gave a jerk, almost ripping itself out of Lon's grasp. Magnetism! The plane shuddered. Though the Emperor held Stoan's mind, Stoan retained his mega-magnetism powers.

The controlled Legion commander was trying to slam the two planes together to set off the atomics.

Lon's fingers sank deeper into the skin of the plane, straining to fight the incredible force. The metal shredded between his fingers as the plane tore away from him.

"Isn't this fun?" the voice from Londo's ring said. "I'll kill the Legion commander at the same time. Efficiency is a wonderful thing."

Lon dove under and then up to the side facing Hal. He used his entire body surface area to brace against the plane. The force was unrelenting. Unstoppable.

The plane felt like an asteroid as it strained against him. Lon groaned with the effort to slow its attraction to the other.

The two planes closed in on each other. Hal sprawled across his plane, locked in his own struggle. They were less than a mile apart.

Could these bombs kill them? They weren't just atomics, they contained sub-atomics for a strong-force reaction.

Hal, Londo called desperately.

"Any last words?" The emperor's voice mocked them over Lon's Legion ring. "We're standing by here to record. It's a historic occasion."

Lon and Hal dove through the metal of their respective planes to grab the atomics in their arms, three bombs apiece. Hal wrapped his extra in his cape; Lon finagled his vest to sling his third. They kicked their ways out, keeping the vehicles between themselves and Stoan's line of sight. Then they streaked up through what remained of the atmosphere. Behind them the planes collided in an erupting fireball– but nothing else.

The pull between the atomics wasn't nearly as strong as it had been between the planes, but each load of three now held the same charge, and they wanted to repel each other. Londo kept firm grip on them as they left the planet's atmosphere behind. He hurled the extra one toward deep space. After a few beats, Hal threw one in the same direction. Then they took turns. When all had been dispatched, they waited.

Now? Hal mouthed, and Londo checked with his vector scanner.

Now.

A whoosh of parabreath in airless space, directing not air but pure heat, and the final bomb exploded... setting off the further bomb, which set off the further bomb...

Hal shaded his eyes from the pure-white glare, but Londo turned and dove back into the atmosphere, through the ball of smoke and flame that remained from the plane collision. Stoan was flying away at his top speed, which was dwarfed by Londo's. Lon overtook him. He grabbed him by his belt.

"You're not going anywhere, Gloryboy," Lon said with a snarl.

"I am not his Glory," and sure enough, the voice had changed. But it still wasn't Stoan's.

"Then inform Gloryboy that it's all his plans that are dead, and not us," Londo said. He nodded at Hal, who flashed by. "And do tell him to have a nice day."

Londo didn't trust taking a controlled Stoan down to a metal-filled planetary surface. Stoan— or whoever that was inside Stoan— actually physically fought against him. Lon didn't want to hurt the body of his friend, so he tore off Stoan's glove, unscrewed the array ring from Stoan's finger and let Stoan fall through the atmosphere. Maybe that would scare the mind controller enough to pull out.

As soon as Lon let go, Stoan seized the magnetic field of the planet to sling himself along a line of force. Lon was hard-pressed to catch him. Whoever it was controlling Stoan was too-quickly able to tap into his personal knowledge. Were Legion secrets immune from a controller's mind-tapping?

Better a headache than Legion security compromised. Lon slid up behind Stoan and *tocked* him— lightly for Valiant— on the helmet. The metal buckled and Lon tapped again on Stoan's skull. "Time to go to sleep," Londo said as Stoan fell unconscious.

Hal returned with a suppressor shackle. "Thank god impervion's non-magnetic," Hal said as he snapped the shackle around Stoan's arm.

Londo frowned at his unconscious, controlled friend.

"See any hooks?" Hal asked.

"I… dunno. *Peut-être*. Maybe they're my imagination. Maybe I just want to see hooks, and they aren't really there at all. Maybe there's more than one way to control someone."

Hal sighed. "I'm tired of all this mind control," he said. "Are we about to wrap things up here?"

"Let's see," Londo said, and they headed back.

Subcommander Andri and her team were mopping up some Imperial troops on the continent to the east, which left Chimrin the next-ranking Legionnaire and within the communications section of Planetary Central Control. "Even with the dampers, I don't trust myself," Chim told Londo, so he handled the planetary telecast.

The Legion teams that had worked to squelch planetary communications now jury-rigged them to override all networks and clone-feed giant holographic images to cover the skies of the world.

"People of Deseed," Londo said. "I'm pleased to tell you that the Affiliated Systems Megaforce Legion and the Terran Paranorm Network have worked together today to rid your world of illegal annexation from the Yanist-Glory Empire. Up until today, numerous high-ranking officials have been mind controlled by Imperial forces and have introduced Imperials into the upper echelons of your government.

"They've murdered thousands of people, but there will be no more casualties. We're rounding up the mind controlled and placing them in areas where their controllers have no hold over them. They will have to remain in these areas until we can come up with a cure.

"I don't want to raise any hopes, but we're following one very promising lead along that line. In the meantime, we'll be setting up as many of these control-free areas on your world as we possibly can. We will leave Legion reserve units on Deseed to continue this project, as well as to ensure that you don't receive any Imperial 'help'"– Londo frowned and raised a meaningful eyebrow– "as you get back on your feet.

"We have supplied you a way of keeping the mind controllers totally helpless. It will be up to you to decide what to do with them, according to your own laws of justice. Be aware that some of these controllers are in turn controlled by others within the Empire and may be entirely innocent. Judge them carefully.

"Central government is now operating in a control-free zone."

Londo went on to inform them that as people recognized that they'd been controlled, they should report themselves to living quarters within control-free zones. He gave the camera an encouraging smile.

"Things might become more confused for a while, but it will only be a short time. Normalcy is just around the corner. Legion forces will leave when the planetary government reorganizes to the point where it can request that they do so. Please bear with us, have patience and try to live your lives as you normally would as much as you can. Thank you. Valiant out."

"Time to hand over the last of the dampers," Wilder announced. Deseed would need every damper they could get their hands on to contain the mind-controlled until something could be done with them. The damped refugee camps already held over ten thousand people. There were certainly more out there who needed to be rounded up.

The camps were overcrowded, and the few replicators Deseed possessed capable of making such complicated electronics as the dampers were overburdened with the chore.

Londo stood within the dampered security area outside the lead Legion hyperspace ship. He held two shackles in his hands, both open. Wiley stood behind him to supervise.

Chimrin frowned at them. "I don't like the idea of spending the rest of my life on Tishan in the hospital," she said. "I hope you saw hooks, Londo. I really do. And I hope that wife of yours can get rid of them. But then, I've always had an unfortunate tendency to believe in faerie tales."

"Lina says she's been doing this for years. Gotten rid of thousands of them, no problem. Kids' play." Londo tried to make himself sound confident. So many ifs…

"If nothing else," Erik said, "maybe Wiley can modify the damper so that it can be, I don't know, clipped to a belt or something."

"It's miniaturized already," Wiley said. "I'm not sure how much smaller I can make it, but I'll work on it."

"A clip-on damper would be nice for you," Chimrin told Erik. "Not so nice for someone whose only claim to fame is telepathy."

"Worry about that when it happens, not before," Londo insisted. "Now, don't fight this. Just let yourselves sleep. If you wake up on Earth, you know that you're no longer controlled."

"And if we wake up on Tishan or Sarastor, we still will be," Chimrin said. She took one shackle from Londo and held it in place. "Here goes." She hesitated a moment and then clicked it shut. She fainted backward into her medi-cocoon.

Erik had already laid down in his. "I don't want anyone making jokes about me while I'm out, sir. And I want people to stop calling me 'Thwunking Boy,'" he added. He snapped his shackle shut before he could have second thoughts.

Londo and Wiley closed the covers on the cocoons, sealing the occupants into suspended animation. Wiley checked the cocoons' readouts and then nodded to Londo.

"Just two more things to do," Lon said, and sat down at the camp communications console. He activated a screen. Londo knew the codes for this particular recipient. The screen lit up to display a narrow-faced, suspicious-looking older man.

"Tell him I want to talk to him," Londo ordered. The man's eyes widened as he saw who he was talking to, and then they went down to slits.

"His Glory does not take common communicator calls."

"He'll be very angry to miss this one," Lon growled.

The screen went to a holding pattern for a minute, then two. Then that face appeared on it: the spring-like curls of hair, the cunning eyes, measuring everything. Above the jutting chin, thin lips, not even bothering to pretend to smile. "What is it?!" Emperor Yanist-Glory demanded. "Why are you always bothering me?"

"You keep changing your personal codes." Lon smiled evilly at him. "I want to make sure that the ones I've got are the correct ones."

Glory muttered an oath at being disturbed.

"Oh, and one other thing. I just wanted to tell you that your war ministers are going to be calling a meeting with you very soon. First they've got to find a way to break it to you that you've just lost two star systems today: not just Deseed, but Jorter as well. So sorry about that, old boy. Hope you weren't planning on paying off anything expensive with those new imperial taxes."

"Are you and your friends now overthrowing the duly-elected governments of systems? Interstellar court will not permit that. They might call for the Mega-Legion's dissolution. The Legion is a threat to worlds outside the Affiliated Systems."

"Come on, Glory," Lon said. "You know just how duly-elected those governments were. We have the proof; we have the mind controllers tracked. Let me warn you that all systems around your little empire will been shown what to look for and given equipment to prevent anything like this from happening again. Do you understand?"

The emperor merely looked at him as if he'd just told him that the skies were clear that day.

"I wouldn't begin to know what you were talking about."

Lon smiled. "Of course not. Listen, Glory, you may want to check on things along your borders. You'll notice a lot of new treaties, new alliances starting. Including one called Three Worlds. Earth's part of that one. That makes it even stronger than it was before, so don't even bother to think about doing anything there. You got that?"

"Three Worlds." The emperor considered the name. "Ah yes, I believe I have heard of that one, just the other day. Which reminds me that congratulations are in order, dear little Londo. You got married. A very pretty girl, very pretty indeed." He clicked his fingernails together as his eyes grew sharp on Londo. "It would be such a shame if something happened to her while you were interfering in the legal affairs of my empire."

Londo's face went stony. "When I was a child, Glory, I swore that I would kill you some day. People talked me out of it over the years. I've put the thought to the back of my mind. But if even one hair on her head is ever harmed by anyone, anyone at all that I can trace back to you… I'd be considering officially naming my successor, if I were you. Starheart out."

"It was an empty threat, Lon," Hal said softly behind him. "She's probably fine."

"Probably isn't good enough," Lon said. **Lina!** He put all the force he could behind the call. **Lina! Are you all right?** Damn! She was still wearing that shackle; she couldn't hear him.

And it made her that much more vulnerable to whatever Yanist-Glory could throw at her. As he fumbled to patch through a call to the ParaNet satellite, Londo's mouth went dry.

29

Lina dreamed of scenes from *Saving Private Ryan* with soldiers Londo and Jae running in slo-mo. Echoing gunfire pelted them and they fell slowly to the bloody ground. The sky glowed red with incendiaries behind them. However hard she ran, she couldn't reach them while they cried to her for help.

Lina screamed from a soundless throat.

A swarm of enemy helicopters swooped overhead. They aimed powerful searchlights into the night as they searched for the fallen. Closer. Closer–

She jerked awake.

Bright moonlight streaked through the netting of her bed. For a moment it looked like fisherman's nets, and she was still in the movie along the shore. She managed a small sound and then realized where reality was.

Oh. A dream. She gasped from the sheer terror of it. God, got to stop having these dreams. They weren't *déjà vu*. Lon was Valiant. Chances were very good that he hadn't been hurt. Yet. And Jae, as strange as it was to think of her love that way, was a top Legionnaire. He'd fought off how many men the other day? He could fight his way to a hyperspace ship if he had to. No one would have thought to sabotage it.

She closed her eyes and deliberately breathed into her gasps. She needed to sleep if she were to be prepared for whatever lay ahead. Goal A. To sleep she needed to relax. Come out of the dream.

After a while she opened her eyes and turned over into the moonlight. Soft and silver; timeless and female. It illumined the empty half of the bed.

Lon, wherever you are, be safe, she willed. Maybe she could channel, discover how whatever battle he was in was going. She closed her eyes and reached for the white light. Immediately she saw misty spiritual beings, so much further away than they usually were.

Danger, danger, they whispered.

Yes, I know Lon's in danger, she responded. But they pointed at her. **Me?** They kept pointing at her, excitedly. **When? How?** She visualized a TV screen, and they pointed at its picture:

Granger.

Is he back already? The picture changed to a closeup of the fist-sized ruby at his throat, with something sliding over it, making its ruddy glow stop. What? What was it?

She heard a voice say, **Talk to it.**

Whatever it was, she had to tell Demi immediately. Granger was back. She opened her eyes and took a deep breath, preparing to roll over and get out of bed, when she saw it. Just outside the balcony door: a red glow made hazy through the curtains. It lowered from the sky. Soft footfalls barely sounded against the solid floor of the balcony, then on the interior tiled floor. Behind her now. She heard the mosquito netting around the bed draw back.

She lay very, very still.

A body settled onto the bed behind her. He ran a gloved finger from her bare shoulder to her neck. Softly. Slowly. He began to stroke her hair. A harsh red glow suffused the netted space of the bed.

"Is this what he does with you?" he murmured, the cruel laugh hidden in his voice.

"There are guards just outside the door," she replied in the same tone, "with weapons that can bring down even a Galactic Guardian."

"Then we'll just have to be quiet, won't we?" One of his red gloves settled on the sheet over her leg. She tried not to flinch. She could understand the sound now as the other glove came off and fell somewhere.

"One loud noise and you're dead meat." He started to pull the sheet down off her. "Turn over and let's see what you've got."

She turned toward him, making no attempt to cover herself. She felt her breasts roll with her, and shrank from the thought that that might excite him even more. *I am a limp dishrag,* she ordered herself. *That's the only way I'm going to get through this.*

He was fascinated by what he saw, leering at her up and down. "Nice tits," he said. "Very, very nice. Valiant's got himself a pretty little Southern gal."

"What do your bosses say about their employees raping people?"

"It doesn't have to be rape, babe." He began to run his hands up and down her. He squeezed her breasts and made a little grunt of satisfaction. "It doesn't have to be that way at all. You and me, we can just have a little fun before I hand you over to…"

"To whom?"

"Um. I haven't made up my mind yet. You're a valuable piece of property, Carolina Starhart. I've got so many choices. You're Valiant's wife, and there's some people who would pay very well just to get a piece of that." He stared at her like an owl. "Of course there's Emperor Yanist-Glory. He told me he'd pay a star system to get his hands on you. That might be fun, owning a couple of populated planets. Then again, I've been thinking that I could maybe rent you by the hour, or maybe by the night. See how long you'd last that way." He laughed. "I could set up a photography session for each client, you know, make picture postcards to send to Londo. I think he'd like that."

He ran his hand down her left arm until it hit the shackle, and lifted it up to examine it. "And then there's the idea of having your own personal psychic wonder, all locked up and under control. I hear you're pretty powerful– in the mega-power range. You were an idiot to let them chain you. But that works to my advantage. It makes you easier to transport.

"Of course there're also the people who might pay big bucks just to have their hands on this lovely little body of yours. There's a booming trade in women among the stars, you know. Humans are very popular. Even tattooed ones." He ran a fingernail around the outline of the symbol emblazoned on her bare breast.

"There are perverts," he clucked in mock rebuke, "out there who might even like to get their… hands… on a singer. Oh, I'll try to find you a good home. Of course, I've got to test the merchandise first." He leaned down toward her, but she gave him pause with her glare.

"Once the Sentinels find out–"

"But they won't, will they? I'm not going to tell them, and neither is my ruby, are you, ruby ol' boy?" Granger patted the ruby medallion at his neck and laughed softly. He reached for her breast and pinched it until she winced. He laughed. "What, Valiant never hurt you? Never touched you too hard? All-mighty Valiant? Well maybe he don't know how to treat a woman." He bent down and kissed her harshly, still squeezing and massaging her breast, pulling on the nipple.

I am a limp dishrag, she ordered herself, trying not to fight or squirm. *I am a limp dishrag.* And then through the panic, the horror, it occurred to her:

He had talked to his ruby.

She gasped as he released her mouth, automatically pushing away at him until she remembered that she was a dishrag.

"Not much fight in you, is there? I'll remember to tell Valiant that. Afterward. Or does he like his women passive?" As he bore down for another harsh kiss, his hands explored her body. He moved down her. She caught glimpses of the ruby medallion up close.

Limp, limp, she used as a mantra behind her screaming thoughts, hoping that it would affect him as well. What if the medallion were sentient? Was it too much to hope it was telepathic? She squirmed as his hands dug between her legs, his fingers rubbing her roughly. The Guardian laughed again.

Easing up over her, he pushed her legs apart. His brutish hand fondled her. Then he put a finger inside her, pumping it. Under the white terror, she writhed at the uncomfortable feel.

"Not too wet yet, are we?" He smiled and added another finger, pumping harder. "Get wet, girl. Get dripping wet for me. I'm a big man. I don't want to damage something I could get some big bucks with."

She wasn't going to whimper. She wasn't. But she tried to squirm away from him, get his fingers out of her.

"So there's a little fight left, is there? Good, good." He removed his fingers and wiped them on her breasts. She closed her legs hurriedly. "Now, lovely little

Lina, let's not have any of that." He pried her legs open again and sprawled on top of her– thank heavens he was still fully clothed– to work on her breasts with his mouth, still rubbing her vulva. She lay there as limply as she could.

Granger slapped her hard across the mouth. "I like my women to respond more than this," he commanded.

She used the slap as an excuse to roll her shoulders away from him, hiding herself and yet watching the ruby closely. Without psychic impressions, how could you tell if a stone were sentient? Stones had presence, but did some have… thoughts?

In a swath of ruby light, Lina's body rose in the air. Granger lounged on the bed. "Down," he told his ruby, and the light turned her over to sit on him, her breasts at his mouth level.

She gritted her teeth as he began his horrible work again. Lord, she was going to have to encourage this man to get to the ruby. Arching her back, she faked a tiny moan, a little gasp.

"That's better, bitch. Now, you just tell me if I do anything Valiant would."

She twisted in his grip freely now, grinding her hips into his crotch. Maybe he'd believe she'd gone passionate on him. His head was in the way for her to reach the ruby.

Lina pulled herself away from him so she could set her hands on either side of his face. She raised him up for a deep kiss. A devouring kiss.

"C'mon, baby, let's go for it," she growled into his ear and kissed him hard again.

"Ooh, yeah. Bitch, that's good. That's real good."

She pawed at his uniform as if she wanted to rip it off him. She kept on kissing him hard, not letting him think, and he sat up straighter to unfasten one shoulder. Lina inserted her tongue into his ear and he shivered.

"You're warming up to me, I can tell," he smirked. "Maybe I'll just keep you for myself." He pulled his uniform jacket off both shoulders, pinning his arms for a moment.

"I don't think so," Lina said. She shoved her fist over his throat so the medallion bit into her skin. It slid under the lip of the neutralizer that protruded over the back of her hand.

The red glow extinguished.

"What—"

Every fiber of strength she had went into the groin kick. He doubled over, gasping as if she had delivered a death stroke. She leaned with him to keep the shackle over the ruby.

Her shrill scream curdled even her own blood. "Help!" she shouted. "Help! Somebody, for the love of god!"

Someone clumped heavily against the door. Lina tried to pry the medallion off Granger's throat, while keeping it under the edge of the shackle. It was secured onto a wide band that circled his neck. There were little hook things in the back. She couldn't get at it one-handed.

"Ruby, help me," she said to it urgently. "I need you to get off him so we can take you to the Sentinels. This man is a criminal. You can't let him use you like this!" Another clump at the door, as if someone were trying to ram it. There—one of the band's hooks let loose—

But Granger kicked her off himself, rolling on the mattress. He grabbed the band around his neck tight with a groan. Lina fell off the bed and scrambled to regain her footing. She heard him vomit across the sheets. Any second now the ring might recharge—

The bedroom doors finally crashed open. Two armored Scythian guards ran into the room, their weapons raised. They paused for a micro-second as they took in the scene: her naked on the floor. Him. His ruby glowed feebly as it recovered from the shackle's effects.

"Now, while the ruby's still weak!" Lina cried. She flattened against the floor, trying to get out of their target area. Two huge *cracks,* and the guns flashed with white-hot energy beams that hit the Guard square in the chest. They met a feeble red glow. He stumbled but did not fall, anger livid on his face. The ring glowed brighter and brighter.

More Scythian guards joined in the energy barrage on the Guard. Six guns continued to blaze against him. Grainger staggered against the conflagration. With a howl, he launched himself from the bed and took off into the night sky. Five more energy beams caught him from outside.

Lina raised herself on her hands and watched him retreat, a red trail wobbling off toward the horizon. *Go away to hell, Guardian!* she screamed at him, but with the shackle on, she knew he couldn't hear her. She reached for a clean sheet and wrapped it around herself. She was too angry to faint.

The Scythians spoke quickly to each other in their own language. One helped her up.

"Thanks," she said, hoping the woman understood English. She understood the intent at least, and smiled with despair. Glancing over her, she asked something: probably, "Are you all right?"

Something wet ran from the side of Lina's mouth. Curiously Lina wiped it away with her hand. Blood.

Olympia skidded into the chamber. What took her so long? Lina realized that it couldn't have been more than two minutes since she had first screamed.

"What's going on?"

"Granger," Lina gasped. "He just tried to kidnap me– but he wanted to do a little rape first."

One of the guards sucked in her breath, looking at her partner. "Rape– in Scythia!"

"Well, he didn't get a chance to carry it out. Thank goodness for this damned thing." Lina indicated the shackle. She looked at Demi triumphantly. "It seems that Galactic Brigade rubies work telepathically," she said.

Demi's lips set in a grim line. "Get your clothes, Lina. We're teleporting– now." She produced a ParaNet communicator from her jacket even as Lina grabbed for her clothes and shoes, making sure the sheet was secure around herself. Then the world pixilated around her. It re-focused into the quiet, acrylic monitor room in ParaNet satellite headquarters.

At the small control console sat Dragonwing, a Networker who had no para-powers. There were no heroes with big powers left on Earth. Jae wouldn't be back for another day, plus. All the paras were gone except her bodyguard, Olympia.

And the Galactic Guardian.

30

Dragonwing opened his mouth to say something, but Olympia interrupted.

"Granger's gone off the deep end. Attempted rape, attempted kidnapping. Move over, Rich, I want to try something. Lina, get dressed. Now."

Dragonwing, or Rich apparently, moved away from the control console and asked questions of Lina with his eyes as Demi busied herself there. Lina just made a face at him and raised her eyebrows, wiping another drop of blood from her mouth. He looked abashed and turned toward the wall.

Demi snapped, "This is no time for modesty, woman. Get dressed."

"Yes'm." She did, almost as fast as porting a new outfit. "Done," she said for Dragonwing's sake, and he turned back. "If we could just figure out how to unlock this thing, it sure would save a lot of trouble. I could keep away from Granger easy, no need for bodyguards. I could go to Sarastor and lie low until this all blows over."

"The only key is with the Legion, and they're off wherever the battle is. They've taken our only hyperspace vehicle with them, so we couldn't just lose you to the void for a day or two."

"Which means another day, maybe two?"

"Maybe less. But you're right; all we have to do is stay on the run until Neutrino or the others get back. We'll have more manpower then and the shackle can come off. We can take care of Granger as a team. He can't stand up to all of us at once."

Something made Lina's hair stand up on the back of her neck. She thought it best not to think about what that might mean.

Dragonwing answered a beep on the console. "He's trying to beam on board."

"Block it," Olympia ordered. "Take away his Network authority. I am revoking his membership."

"Right." Dragonwing concerned himself with the part of the console that Demi wasn't working at, then glanced at what she was programming. "Done. What the hell is that, Demi? You can't be serious."

"I am. Just because no one's ever done it doesn't mean it can't be done. I'm taking her back to Scythia by a roundabout route. He won't think to look for us there again. Probably. It's still the safest place, especially now that we're warned about him."

"What? What?" Lina tried to make sense of the console's odd labels.

Demi trotted out of the room to return no more than two minutes later with a bundle in her arms.

"Stand down there." Demi pointed at the middle of the plexiglass room where the circles on the floor were, and Lina obeyed. "We're beaming down… now!"

The room pixilated again.

Lina would have noticed the focusing of materialization if she hadn't been slammed against a wall.

"Ow! Hey! Watch out!"

Demi hit right next to her. Lina rubbed her sore neck and looked around.

An airplane! They were in one of the big ones with two aisles. They sprawled in the service area in the back, next to rest rooms. Down the darkened aisle in front of her, two attendants serving drinks looked back in shock to see the new arrivals.

"I think I needed to compensate a hair more for velocity," Demi said next to her. She, too, rubbed her neck and shoulders. The two women looked at each other and laughed weakly.

"Don't sweat it," Lina said. "I'm still trying to get the hang of this porting thing, too."

One of the flight attendants quick-stepped back to them, glancing back and forth at the passengers with quick smiles, as if not to alarm them. She closed the curtain to the service compartment. "What's going on here?" she demanded of Olympia. She spared Lina a curious glance: *Who the hell are you?* it said.

"This is a ParaNet emergency," Demi said tersely. "This plane should not be in any danger. We're just using it as temporary transportation."

"Temporary?" Lina asked. She didn't like the sound of that.

Demi's eyes narrowed on her: *Shut up and let me talk.* Lina looked heavenward.

"We won't stay around for landing," Demi told the attendant. Lina didn't like the sound of that, either. "Is there any place for us to sit, out of people's way?"

The attendant could think on her feet, Lina gave her that. "You could stay back here. We have to take our seats again for landing, but if you're not going to be here then, Olympia, you're welcome to them."

The pilot's voice buzzed on the intercom, announcing a cruising altitude of 35,000 feet. He gave the projected weather conditions in Istanbul.

"Istanbul?" Lina repeated involuntarily.

Demi stashed her bundle under the seats and then nodded to the flight attendant. "Thank you; that will be fine. Could I bother you for some water? My companion here doesn't look so well."

Lina realized that she was shaking. Everything was starting to hit her. She sat down heavily and rubbed her face. "Oh god," she said.

Demi sat next to her to pat her free wrist. "Are you all right?"

"Let's see. I'm wearing the shackle from hell, a Galactic Guardian just tried to rape me, and now I'm on a plane to Turkey that I'm not going to stick around long enough to land in. No, I'm not up to my usual levels."

The attendant paused at this information as she handed Lina a plastic glass of ice water.

"Thanks," Lina said, very gratefully. The water was heaven. "Guess I'm not Scythian material," she said to Demi. "Minor emergencies like this scare the shit out of me."

"I wouldn't call this minor," Demi said and dismissed the attendant with another nod. She stood up to look for a blanket in a cabinet, then wrapped Lina in it. "You have about an hour and a half before we depart," she said.

"Do I have to ask? Is this departure going to be by transporter?"

Demi smiled without humor. "No. It's not. Don't worry about it."

"Destination?"

"We should be passing near Scythia in about 90 minutes. If Granger eventually traces us to this plane, perhaps he will follow it for a while after we've gone so that we can reach Scythia and its defenses before he realizes that we've bailed out. But really, I don't think plane travel will occur to him. He won't connect the dots. He's not that imaginative."

"Oh boy. Listen, is there any reason why we can't use the transporter for this?"

"We are buying time. Taking a moving, roundabout route gives us 90 minutes more than we would have had. Using the transporter puts out a signal that can be easily tracked by, say, a Guard's ruby. By now Rich has made several false transports to disguise our trail. So I would prefer to keep teleportation to a minimum. Neutrino could arrive very soon."

"Yeah."

"You can still levitate, yes?"

Lina tried it on her cup. It hovered wobbily in mid-air. "All systems go in that department," she said.

"Good. When we jump you'll use that to slow your fall."

"When we—" Lina's mouth dried to dust.

"We'll bail out over the Black Sea."

Lina leaned back in the seat and closed her eyes. "Yeah."

"Get some sleep if you can. I'll wake you when the time comes. Or sooner, if it's needed. We will not put these passengers in danger."

"I'm sorry to put you in danger, too," Lina said as her eyes closed.

"This isn't your fault," Demi replied. "We should have seen this coming. We could have been prepared if we had."

"Coulda, shoulda," Lina said in her sleep.

"Wake up," Demi commanded. "It's time."

Lina blinked herself rapidly awake. Time for what? Oh. Oh no. How had she managed even a wink of sleep? She felt exhausted, and now... She unwound herself from the blanket and folded it slowly, trying to work up her nerve. The attendant from before was there, conferring with Demi.

"Batten everything down here; there'll be a drop in pressure. You go up front and inform the pilot he should tell the passengers that the plane is running into turbulence and they should buckle in. Warn them that that the engines might roar. Say anything so they can convince themselves that this is normal."

The stewardess nodded uncertainly.

"We'll jump out and I'll secure the door behind us. Once we're gone, you can tell the passengers whatever you want. You'll be out of danger and we'll be gone. Don't let anyone back here until then."

The attendant nodded again and conferred with another one, who helped another stow all loose items in the rear compartment. Demi took her bundle and began to unfold it. At its center was a heavy jacket she handed to Lina. The rest consisted of stiff gray material and rods, which made a framework when locked together. The first attendant went forward at a leisurely pace toward the cockpit. Demi then sealed the material to the frame and the walls of the plane.

Demi turned to Lina, oblivious of the remaining attendant. "When I open the door, you jump. Got that? Jump as far as you can. If you can aim yourself by levitation, aim far away from the plane. Be quick."

"Got it," Lina steeled herself, refusing to give in to the jitters. She was *not* going to be a coward in front of Olympia! She had to be brave to protect her, whatever was coming. "Jump away from the plane."

"Good. You may black out, but that's okay. I'll make sure you miss the engines, then I'll refasten the door and come after you. It's going to be cold."

"And probably windy, I'd say."

Demi gave her a warrior's grin. "Yes, that too. Don't worry; in another half hour you could be sleeping in comfort in Scythia again."

Lina locked gazes with her. "I wouldn't put money on that if I were you. This is the battle, and you know it."

Demi looked away. "You should be able to see a string of five islands once we get down below the clouds. They mark the entrance to Scythia and the Great Barrier. If I'm not there, head for them. Take your time; conserve your energy."

"You, too."

The final attendant had locked everything up while trying to listen to them, and Demi shooed her toward the front. There were three rows of empty seats at the back of the passenger compartment. The attendants had lured the passengers forward somehow, away from the rear door.

Demi secured the barrier across the section, cutting the two of them off from the rest of the plane.

The pilot's voice come on the intercom. "Good morning, folks, those of you awake, that is. This is Captain Alexander. We've got reports of some very unstable air in front of us, so we're putting on the fasten seat belts sign as we go below it. Please stow any loose items in the overhead compartments and buckle in as quickly as possible. Some of this turbulence consists of pockets of air, so it may sound a little loud as we go through it. It shouldn't last long. We'll tell you when we're through."

"Let's give them two minutes," Demi said quietly.

The plane gave a sickening, backward-seeming lurch as it slowed to lose altitude.

Demi paused ready before the emergency door. Lina looked at the floor. She gathered what shreds of courage she could find. There weren't many.

I can do this, she told herself. *Demi said so. She'll be there for me if I black out. I can levitate or fly or something now. I won't fall and splat.*

It's going to be noisy. Just imagine you're at a rock concert, that it's the crowd going crazy. It's going to be windy and cold. Imagine you're in a blizzard. A blizzard with a rock concert going on.

I'm not going to embarrass myself in front of Demi. I'm going to do this for Londo and Jae and not embarrass either of them. Okay, I can do it for them. I can do this.

"Lina."

She looked up to see Demi nod.

"One, two…" On the count of three Demi pushed open the door. A roar filled the cabin. Uncontrolled suction pulled Lina toward the opening, but she grabbed at the door's sill with a death grip. Just a second more to gather her courage–

Demi kicked her butt from behind.

Jesus! What am I doing?!

Lina screamed– but it was too late. She floundered outside the plane in a raging torrent of wind.

The tail jet loomed suddenly.

Automatically, she tried to port away. She shouted words that she didn't know she knew, phrases describing her situation in combinations of four letters. The plane streaked past, farther away from her now through her own maneuvering as well as its engines. She tumbled through the sky. Lina pulled herself as level as she could, but upside-down. She could see Demi securing the door behind her.

Christ, it was cold. And windy. Breathlessly she tucked her jacket up around her ears and then wrapped her arms around herself, shuddering with fear and frost. Rock concert in a blizzard. Rock concert in a low-oxygen blizzard. It would be warmer below. More air below. She turned over to non-port herself downward as fast as she could. She didn't want to black out and be more of a burden. Demi would be behind her in a moment.

Lina broke through a thin, icy layer of cloud back into the early-morning sparkle of something below her. It must be the ocean, but it didn't look like water. It looked solid and hard.

She checked around and paused. The air was still cold, but not nearly as windy here. She sucked in a long breath and felt as if she were getting a little oxygen. She held her position, she thought– it was hard to gauge if she was still falling or not– and checked the landforms below. Where were those islands?

Five bumps stuck out of the shiny hard stuff near the horizon. Those had to be it. She aimed herself for them and crossed her frozen fingers. Fortunately, the wind blew in that general direction. She could float and glide, using the least amount of energy. If they could get to Scythia, they could get hold of those guns that had done such a good job against the Guardian.

A human-shaped shadow darkened the cloud layer above her, and she turned around to give Demi a smile.

But the body glowed red and left a red trail behind it.

He swooped down on her. "You're dead, bitch," he growled, pulling her roughly against him. His palm glowed red, the very image of his medallion in its center, and he pressed it against her head.

"What," she said quickly, "you're not going for the big bucks? You don't want a little fun first? A little vengeance?" Play for time.

He ripped open her jacket. Grabbing one of the straps of her top, he pulled it down to reveal her bra. He glanced from her breast to her face, considering.

She arched her eyebrow at him cockily. "You said you liked the merchandise, didn't you? After all, I'm Valiant's woman. He only takes the best. What have you earned lately?"

Granger's mouth turned into a snarl. He pointed his red-gloved finger at the air before them. In answer, a red platform appeared with a railing around it. It was a standard Galactic Guard transport, seen many times on the evening news. He threw her onto it. She rolled until he landed on top of her, pinning her arms down to the decking.

"Here's where you get yours." He laughed. Red tentacles sprang out of the decking to hold her in place as he reached for the zipper on her jeans.

Demi swooped in behind him. She swung on him as only Olympia could, sending him flying up and over the railing.

Lina took the interruption to try to slip out of the tentacles. She managed one arm, then the other, but the one around her waist was too tight.

"C'mon ruby," she said to the air. "If you can control this, you can hear me. Let me go. Your master has gone around the bend. He's a criminal. A psycho. The Sentinels will take you away from him when they find out. Ruby, let me go!"

She didn't know if it was because of her or because the Guard's attention was now divided, but the last tentacle weakened to the point that it went plastic, and she barely wriggled out. She stood up, adjusting her clothing automatically, leaned over the railing to see what was going on–

And ducked as the two flashed by her. Granger wove out of the way at top speed of the unbound Ouroboros. He hid crouching on the far side of the platform. Before Lina could shout a warning, Demi flew into view. A red, solid sledgehammer of gravitic energy slammed her across the sky. Like a hawk after his kill, Granger followed.

Could the ruby hear her from there? It could maintain the platform. "Ruby, he's a criminal," Lina said. "You don't want to serve a criminal. He stands against everything the Galactic Brigade represents. Look at him. Look at what he's making you do. He's bringing you down to his level. Don't work for him, ruby. Stop working for him."

Demi seemed to have recovered, though she looked shaky. She faced down the Guard again. Ouroboros raised up like a snake ready to strike. It fanned out to form a head and hissed between its great fangs. Lightning crackled all around it.

Lina kept up her patter, not knowing if the platform were going to dissolve at any moment and not really caring. "You're a good ruby," she said, talking to it like she would a dog, "I can tell that you are. But he's making you do bad things. You don't want to do bad things."

Demi landed a solid punch against the red shield that protected the Guard. It shattered with the blow. The Guard fell back, summoning a new shield. Ouroboros reached behind it and struck, tearing a long rip in the back of his jacket.

Granger cried out. The platform swayed uncertainly.

"That's right, ruby." Lina decided that she'd pretend the ruby wasn't losing energy, but rather the will to fight. "That's a good ruby. Don't work for him. Stop working for him. You don't want to do this. We'll return you to the Sentinels. You can tell them what he's been forcing you to do. They'll understand."

Granger sheltered underneath the platform right below her, firing bursts of red energy at Demi. The snake's head flashed back and forth, deflecting the bolts. Each time Granger fired, the air for a hundred feet around turned red as his ruby sucked up all the other wavelengths. Then the colors returned. Granger fired again and the world turned red.

Lina gritted her teeth in utter determination and took hold of the railing. Using it as a pivot, she jumped. Her feet drove straight at Granger's head. She knocked him from his secure position, sending him reeling. The air turned red again. An energy blast ricocheted from the platform back to her. It hit her on the arm– but the shackle caught its full force.

The metal shredded like paper, leaving a wire framework with a few blinking lights, the metal still there on the opposite side of her arm. Telepathic static assailed her. It came as screaming white noise, hitting her as if she'd just come out of hyperspace. An on/off pattern drove into her head like a jackhammer.

"Don't work for him, ruby," she managed to plead.

Lina clung to the railing as the world spun around her. She slipped on her strut– had it blinked out of existence for a moment? She held on, chanting her litany for the ruby. *Hear her! Hear her!*

Demi dove for the Guard, but he rolled mid-air in a loop-de-loop. He came up behind her to bash her in the back of the head. It must have dazed her, but Ouroboros struck as she recovered. Granger dodged and repositioned for a second strike when he saw a better weapon.

Lina tried to levitate to the center of the platform, but he grabbed her in mid-air. "Sweet little bitch," he cooed to her. "Come to papa." He forced her head back and held his red-glowing palm to her throat.

"Hey Olym-pussy," he yelled. "Listen up! One more move and she gets it!"

Demi froze where she was. Lina whispered, "Ruby, don't listen to him. See what he's making you do. You're not a bad ruby. I know you aren't. Stop working for him. We'll take you back to the Sentinels. They'll let you help–"

He jerked her around her ribcage, cutting off her air. "Shut up, bitch," he hissed at her. "I'll kill you right now."

His ruby's glow faded.

The platform dissolved above them. They began to fall. Granger's grip lessened on Lina as he grabbed his ruby medallion.

"Listen, ruby! I'm the Guardian here! You'll do as I say, exactly as I say, and when I say it! You are my servant! Do as you're told!"

The glow strengthened as Lina twisted in the Guard's grip.

Demi's fists came down hard on the Guard's jaw, barely missing her. He slacked and released Lina. She dropped away from the two of them so as not to get in Demi's way, but the Guard fell with her. He grabbed her and formed the platform again by pointing. Throwing her onto it, he encased her in a red translucent dome.

Lina beat on the substance to no avail. She tried to use her levitation to make it explode or expand, but it wouldn't budge. What could she do?

The ruby had heard her. It had heard her! She began to talk to it again: insistent, mothering, commanding, understanding, commiserating.

Yet it still worked for Granger.

The battle wore on, the sky punctuated by blood-red flashes as the ruby recharged to finish the fight. Granger encased himself in red energy armor. He manifested a thick wedge of solid gravitic energy. It sprouted a handle like an axe. He grabbed it and swung. Though he missed Demi, he caught Ouroboros, which wrapped around the weapon. Its lightnings turned red. Granger swung the axe and loosed it. It carried Ouroboros in a long arc, falling toward the hard ocean below.

Lina kept talking to the ruby.

Weaponless, Demi's feet touched down on the platform. She used its support to kick off as she launched herself at Granger. He was bruised and bleeding; there was something wrong with his left arm. But she bled from great gashes as he materialized slivers of hard energy to slash her by remote control. A long-bladed mace appeared in his good right hand. He used it to keep her out of arm's reach. From all angles he struck her again and again.

Demi was badly wounded. The deck she now used as a base was slick with her blood. She lost her footing and went down, hitting her head hard against the decking. Granger took advantage of his position. He bashed her head, lifting her up and pummeling her against the decking until she went unconscious.

"No!" Lina screamed. "No! You want me, not her. Let her go now! She's out of it, probably dead. You want me, do you hear? Me! Let her go!"

The Guard looked back at her and grinned. "You're next." He pointed at her, then cockily turned back to Olympia. He ripped what shreds of costume remained on her off.

"Ohmigod, stop it! Stop it! Ruby, stop him! Don't let him do it!"

He tossed Demi's legs outward like a rag doll's, pulled his pants down to his knees, and then masturbated with quick jerks.

"Ruby, don't let him do it! Stop working and he won't be able to hurt her anymore!"

He thrust forward like a rifle, tearing into Demi with a roar of laughter. He backed out and did it again, just to see the body jerk and spasm under him.

"Wake up, your highness," the Guard sneered. "Wake up so you can enjoy this." He did it again, and then changed to hard thrusting, trying to bury himself in her every time.

Demi groaned and let out a cry. Granger smacked her hard across the face. Lina could see a glow around his penis, something he was doing to make it even worse. The great Olympia screamed pitifully with every thrust and flailed arms that had lost all strength.

"Ruby," Lina sobbed. "You don't want to do this. Stop it and he won't be able to hurt her any more. Please stop it. Please stop it. Oh God in Heaven, please stop it."

Granger paused. He rose up from Demi, mewling in agony on the deck, and turned to Lina. He pulled his pants back up, although he was still hard. "You stop talking to my ruby, slut," he said. "Shut up."

"Ruby, he's scared now. Did you hear him? He's scared because you can stop this. You can stop this right now. Just don't work for him anymore. We'll take you back to Aum to the Sentinels. You can rest and recover. They'll find you a new master if you want one. I'll make sure of it. I'll make sure it's a good master. You'll like that, won't you? Being able to help people again. It feels so good to help, doesn't it?"

The thick rubine dome around her shuddered as Granger stepped through it toward her. She cowered against the railing, and he backhanded her hard. She fell down on the floor. She didn't even try to get up.

"Ruby, see how he's scared. Listen to yourself. Listen to your conscience."

He slapped her again and again, then pulled her head up to beat it against the railing–

And the railing disappeared. The entire platform disappeared.

They fell, all three of them– toward the ocean, a long, long way below.

"Good ruby!" Lina cooed through her swelling lips. "Such a good ruby! Don't worry; it won't be long now. I'll take you now. I'll take you away from him."

She reached for his throat, for the ruby, and Granger pulled away from her with an expression–

Of fear.

"Get away from me! Witch! Get away!" He bared his teeth as he pushed at her, both falling, and covered his medallion with his hand.

"Ruby! This is Galactic Guardian Paul Granger talking! You will obey me! You will obey me!"

Lina launched herself at him in cold fury, wrapping her arm around his neck just above the medallion to choke him. She beat his hands away as best she could. When he got a firm hold on her, she brought them into a tight spin and then reversed it. His hands dropped away and he sputtered. She tightened her grip.

The ocean became distinct below them. She let her concentration expand to Demi, to try to slow her descent below the two of them. She couldn't do much. It was all she could do to levitate herself through the screaming static of her shackle, and here she was trying to handle all three of them.

It was then she set herself to kill Granger.

She used both arms, forcing his head back and squeezing as hard as she could. He gasped and then made no sound. She kept him that way for ten long seconds, not certain that he was really unconscious. And then she looked around to see where Demi was.

She was almost at impact. Lina reached out to stop her, but all she did was slow her. Demi disappeared under the waves. Had it been slow enough? Whatever it was, Demi was going to drown.

Lina pried the medallion band's hooks apart and off Granger's neck. They hovered just above the water. She'd heard that Galactic Brigade rubies needed occasional recharging, and the "red-outs" during the battle seemed to confirm that. Please, oh please, don't let it have run out of juice!

"Ruby," she said desperately. It operated telepathically, but she was still wearing that damned on/off shackle. She concentrated as fiercely as she could, hoping something was getting out in between the shackle's shrieking cycles. "Come on back, ruby. I've got you off him, but we're in deep shit trouble here. I need you to help us. Please ruby. Come on, you can do it for me. Please."

She realized that the ruby was glowing again. "Thank you, ruby," she said, wrapping the band around her arm because there was no other place to put it. "Can you retrieve Demi? Hurry! She can't drown after all this!"

Lina felt that the ruby needed something else. The ruby operated on gravity forces and advanced Guardian tech. How to use that? She visualized a giant magnet hovering above the water and sucking Demi up. It happened, just like that. A ball of red energy appeared and Demi floated up into the air. Lina groaned from the effort of concentration.

She levitated Granger and herself up to Demi's level. First one would drop, then the other as she sought to correct. Then they all dropped, only to steady suddenly. Or so it seemed.

"Is she alive?" Lina breathed. "Ruby, how about some kind of platform here? It's a standard Brigade vehicle, isn't it?" The flying platform appeared. Lina dropped the Guard onto the floor without even thinking as she hurried to Demi's side. Demi wasn't breathing.

"I need a raised area," she said. "And ruby, can you get us to the nearest Networker… to Dragonlord," she corrected. "Washington, DC. As much speed as you can get, please."

She put her fingers on Demi's neck, testing for a pulse. Good. It was there, barely. She gingerly positioned her for artificial respiration and began the process, stopping every now and then to make sure she still had a pulse. A minute passed. *Breathe!* She willed Demi. *Oh please, breathe!*

Demi coughed and coughed again, wheezing horribly. Blood ran in rivulets from her mouth. Lina held her while she threw up overboard, but she was still breathing. She laid her down on the platform. "A blanket," she told the ruby. "Something to keep her warm. Can you elevate her feet?"

The platform shifted to accommodate, and a thin blanket encased Demi. Only then did Lina look back at Granger. He had collapsed in a heap, his costume torn in great patches, bruises and cuts all over him. His nose bled freely, and his lower lip seemed to have been half-ripped from his face, but she could see that he still breathed. She had the ruby make a prison around him, just as he had done to her.

But the platform hadn't moved.

Her shackle was shredded, but still attached to her arm. Telepathic impressions of the world came through like bullhorned static. "Ruby, can you get this thing off so I can–? No, forget that. Save your power for getting us to Dragonlord as soon as possible. Do you need an image?"

Washington. It had been a couple years since she'd been there. The curved walls of the Native American museum, so different from the other structures of the Mall, stood out in her memory and she tried to build a picture of that.

The platform moved.

Lina sat down heavily on the deck, leaning against Olympia's platform. "Hurry, ruby," she whispered. "Hurry, please. Best speed." She felt as if her life were draining away through the shackle.

Redness seemed to envelop the world and she blinked against it. Something was happening, but she wasn't sure what. The fog left, but now dark clouds hung overhead and they hovered over the Washington Mall. What time was it here? The threatening storm made it seem like dusk.

"Oh. Oh my, that was quick. Thanks, ruby," Lina said. Her palm was wet. It was blood. Demi was bleeding profusely. Which pressure point would help the most? Lina chose one of the legs and leaned on it.

"Ruby, can you follow ParaNet signals to find Dragonlord? He'll know the best hospital for her. Find him as quickly as–" The platform moved again, at first uncertainly but then darting across the Washington sky in a straight line.

She looked down at Demi, injured so horribly. The only bits of her costume remaining were her belt and boots. She tried to send out a telepathic call through all this horrible static to Dragonlord, wherever he was, to warn him of her arrival. For a moment it occurred to her that wherever they were headed he might not be in his Dragonlord identity. She'd try to be circumspect to protect his secret, but she didn't really care at this point.

They raced to the north of the city, barely dodging buildings, swooping in low over cars that had turned their lights on in the early darkness. Their passage caused consternation in the streets. A high building loomed ahead with a small plaza in front of it filled with people. Camera spotlights focused on a group gathered at a podium.

"Is that him?" she asked the ruby, and the platform slowed to a stop above the crowd.

These people were the press. This was some kind of press conference, and Dragonlord stood center stage, staring up like all were at her flying platform. Despite the crowd, Lina had to report in to him, find out where to take Demi, what to do from here. Quickly. She kept the platform floating just above everyone's heads while she grabbed the Guardian by the collar of his costume and levitated down to Dragonlord.

She flung Granger at Dragonlord's feet. He stood there, stunned as silence hung over the crowd.

"It's the Galactic Guardian," someone said, their voice ringing too loud.

Dragonlord stepped around the body. "What's happened?" He squinted at her. "Are you all right? Where's–" He raised his eyebrow at her significantly.

"It's over," she told him. Her footsteps left a bloody trail on the pavement. "We got him. You can have him now." She was aware of all the flashing cameras, all the microphones around them and spoke as softly as she could. "But I need to get Demi to a hospital. Fast. I need one that can handle major, major injuries. You need to give the ruby a picture where it can go."

She could feel Damon's shock blast out like a wave through the on/off sensations, his eyes darting back and forth between her, the ruby on her arm, and the vehicle floating above them. He turned to the microphones, the cameras, and said, "I've got to go. We have an emergency here."

31

Someplace deep inside herself, Lina laughed bitterly. He hadn't called it a situation; it must be serious. Disasters were always called situations. She was beginning to get the hang of this.

Uproar swept the plaza. What a scene she must make: a strange woman covered with blood, her face badly bruised, and commanding a Galactic Brigade ruby on her arm, had just delivered the bloody husk of a Guard to Dragonlord's feet. They could vaguely see a body of some kind through the translucent floor of the platform, but that was all.

"Where do we take her?" Lina asked again.

"Who are you?" the reporters all demanded. One in particular stuck a video camera practically in her face. She glared at him and he backed off.

"I am Carolina Starhart," she said fiercely as three camera flashes went off around her. "I am Speaker for the Earth. The Galactic Guardian Paul Granger is no longer welcome on the planet. *If* he's still alive." She could feel the planet's anger pulsing through her.

"I know a place," Dragonlord said, and she nodded. As carefully as she could, Lina levitated the three of them up to the platform. Even so, it was a shaky ride. Dragonlord rushed to kneel over Demi, taking in her injuries.

Lina brought the platform around in a sharp turn so he had to clutch to the railing. She stood in the center of the platform, her feet wide apart, controlling the platform with her sheer will as he directed her. She held onto only her own determination for support.

They swooped to the emergency room entrance, and she dispersed the platform as they arrived. The ruby constructed a capsule around Olympia that hovered in midair next to her. "Thanks, ruby." Lina regarded Granger, collapsed and now moaning on the pavement next to her, and had the ruby draw a gurney to him. He rose to settle on it.

Dragonlord said, "I'll see to him. You follow Demi." They burst into the emergency room together. All business there stopped as people swiveled to stare at them.

"I have a victim of a terrible attack here," Lina said to the on-duty nurse. "She needs immediate help." The nurse boggled at Lina with her ruby glowing, the red capsule hovering next to her, all covered with blood. "Move it, *now*," Lina ordered. "Her life is at stake!"

"Over here!" the nurse called to attendants, running around the desk.

"I can transport her," Lina said, an unnatural curtain of calm settling over her. "Just show me where to take her."

The attendants led her down a white-linoleum hallway, running as they went. She kept up until they came to a room lined with medical electronics. Lina deposited the capsule gently on the examining table and dissolved it. After gasping at what was left of Demi, one nurse began taking vital signs while the other quickly began stanching the bleeding. Two doctors brushed through the curtains on the side.

All the personnel gaped when they saw the extent of injuries.

As the doctors began their examination and the nurses started to feed tubes into Demi, one asked, "Do you know the name of the victim? Have you notified the relatives?"

"This is– She's Olympia."

"Olympia?" The woman doctor paused in shock and glanced up at Lina, who bit her trembling lip hard so she wouldn't cry.

"Holy Jesus," the doctor said softly and returned to her duty.

They called for more help, stat. Equipment came barreling in. More tubes went into her. They used tourniquets and pressure bandages to try to stop the bleeding. Others mopped up the blood while Lina sat there in shock. She should be helping, but she couldn't move from where she'd stumbled back into a chair. She had to move; she must help.

The static from her shackle cut through her like knives.

Within the tempest Lina centered and called the white light for herself, blue and green healing light for Demi. She began to move her hands over Demi's feet, hovering in her imagination above Lina's lap.

Smooth the etheric field. Remind the net of the form, of the function of the body and its systems.

Static crackled through her mind, random thoughts from around the room, cut off in mid-idea to be overrun by others.

White light. The blue net went deep, through the body and out again on the other side, larger than it was by a few inches. It held the blueprint of physical life.

Her hands stroked Demi's etheric body. Without her full senses, she had no idea if she was doing any good at all.

Sometimes you had to operate on faith alone.

When they wheeled Demi to X-ray a nurse gathered up Lina and led her to an empty waiting area. Lina's hands still moved, now farther up the body. Steady, deep strokes. The etheric body held Demi together but it was also with Lina now as she molded it and reminded it of its true shape and healthy function.

Dimly Lina saw them wheel Demi out of X-ray and down the hall toward the elevators. She snapped out of her healing trance. How her head ached from the noise of the shackle! Lina stumbled to the elevator, but the door closed in front of her. A nurse or aide or someone still stood in the hallway.

"Where–?" Lina asked.

"She's being taken into surgery," the woman said.

"Is– Is she–"

"The best thing we can do now is pray."

Again Lina was guided back to the white-walled waiting area and the aide left.

Lina wished she was numb. The incessant telepathic static grated against her bruised and battered mind and all she could see was blood, blood. She sat in her vinyl chair and cried. Then she slid down to the floor and curled into a ball, pressing her knees against her forehead, trying to muffle her sobs. Even with her arms wrapped around her head, she couldn't shut out the world and its infernal, undulating racket.

When someone knelt down beside her and took her by the shoulders in a hug, she leaned against them, against Dragonlord, and sobbed into his shoulder. She cried past her fear of the battle, past her pity and fear for Demi. She cried out her fright of the last few days and cried for the life she could never go back to, the changes that forever made her different.

Rain began to patter at the long line of windows along one wall. A bright flash of lightning and nearby roll of thunder made her jump.

How long had she been here like this? Ohmigod, this was Dragonlord here. She sniffed, and he handed her another tissue.

"How many boxes have I gone through?" she asked weakly.

"Not more than a dozen," he smiled and squeezed her. "Feeling better?"

She nodded, not willing to speak much, and took another tissue. "I'm sorry," she started.

"I think you had reason enough."

She snuffled for a minute or two. "Any word yet?"

"No news is good news. It will take some time, I think."

Lina detached herself from his shoulder and just sat there on the cold linoleum floor, her face in her hands. "Oh God, please help her. Angels, please help her." She unwound the ruby from where she'd wrapped it like a bandage around her arm, and shoved it into her jeans pocket so it wouldn't remind her of the battle.

After a minute she took a shaky breath. "Is there a sink around here so I can wash my face?"

"Bathroom over there," Damon said, gesturing.

She pulled herself up and went in, making sure the door shut tightly behind her.

In the empty waiting room the sound of water running in a sink came through clearly. So did the sound of her sobs through the water. After five minutes of this, Damon knocked softly on the door.

"Lina?"

The water stayed on for a few more beats, then shut off. "Just a minute," she called in a small voice, but it was three more before she came out.

Her eyes were still puffy and purplish-red, as was her nose. Her face was free from blood, but cuts marred the skin and great purple welts swelled along her mouth, cheek and jaw. Her hair lay wet from where she'd rinsed the blood from it. Her clothes were still stained with sickly red. Granger had left his very handprints in bruises all over her exposed skin.

"How are you doing?" Damon asked.

She shrugged and then put her hand in her pocket to draw the ruby out. "I think it needs to charge," she told Damon. Her eyebrows knit in concentration. "Okay, ruby, do whatever you need to do."

The air of the room seemed to contract. All color except red leeched from it to concentrate into a swirl, a draining into the ruby medallion. Her legs leaden, Lina braced herself as best she could against the influx.

Then it stopped. "Is that enough?" she asked. The other colors of light came back, punctuated by another flash of lightning from outside.

"I guess it is," Lina said, and stuffed the ruby in her jeans again. The ends of its band flopped outside the pocket. "Thanks, ruby," she whispered. "You're one of the good guys." She dropped into a chair and looked at her shackle. It hung in shreds on her arm.

Her consideration of it drew Damon's attention. "What, does it still work? In that condition?" he asked.

"Wiley did a good job with it. Mostly it's just making the world emit static, as if you'd only half-tuned into a really bad radio station and kept it at full blast." She rubbed her face roughly and turned away from him, her unfocused gaze for the storm outside.

"Tell me about it," Damon urged.

"He was an animal," Lina said as an introduction. She stopped many times to blow her nose as she told him what had happened: the attempted rape, the flight over the Black Sea, the battle, the rape, the ruby refusing to operate for the Guardian.

She sniffled and went back to the bathroom, this time leaving the door open as she washed her face again. When she heard the room door open she came out. A doctor in blood-spattered green scrubs stood talking to Dragonlord.

"What?" Lina demanded. "How is she?"

"We took her out of the OR. She's been put in ICU. We have our best staff with her."

She hadn't been in surgery long, Lina knew. Not long at all.

"How do we contact her relatives?" the doctor asked.

"She can't die."

"I'm afraid it doesn't look good, Miss. If she weren't Olympia she would have been dead by the time she'd arrived here. As it is–" The doctor glanced away and shook his head.

Even Dragonlord seemed lost. Olympia had been a parahero for generations. "No," he said in a dazed voice.

Lina covered her head with her hands to close herself off from the world. Not Demi. Not like Aiko. It couldn't end this way– could it?

"Do you need a counselor, maybe a minister?" the doctor asked her. "Has a doctor seen you yet? I'm afraid we don't even know your name."

Lina tried to speak from under her enveloping arms and couldn't. The only thing she could think to say was, "Someone needs to call Queen Otrera. She shouldn't hear this from CNN. Is there any way we could get her here?"

"Yes," Damon said. "Yes, Queen Otrera. I'll have ParaNet Security place the call. I've got it, Lina."

Lina, he echoed.

That wasn't his voice.

"Londo?" Lina asked.

Lina, the air whispered to her in Londo's low tones.

"We can't contact him," Damon said. "They're operating under communications blackout."

"Hush." Lina lifted her head and closed her eyes.

A bad radio half-tuned to a shrieking station. Someone was trying to call through it.

She shook her arm with the shackle on it. "Shut up, you stupid thing, I'm trying to hear. Londo?"

The doctor and Dragonlord watched her curiously. Lina opened her eyes. "Lon's calling me. I think. They're getting ready to go to hyperspace. Don't. Don't go there. That'll make you gone for days."

She reached into her pocket for the ruby and wrapped in around her hand. "C'mon, ruby," she urged. "You gotta get me out of this." She concentrated and nothing happened.

Dragonlord watched the renewed fierce determination, the sweat breaking out on her as the ruby encased her arm in a rubine glow– but the shackle remained.

The glow vanished. Lina took a breath, then another, her shoulders falling. She closed her eyes and Dragonlord sighed.

"That's a Galactic Guardian's medallion," the doctor whispered to him.

"It took Granger months to learn how to use it," Damon answered. "She'll have to wait until the megas of the ParaNet return to Earth to get out of that shackle."

He lifted his cell phone to call ParaNet Security, but paused. Lina wasn't slumping; she was bending over, her arms flexed. Hands curled into fists. With a shout she jumped up, flinging her arms up and out. Red light exploded around her like a nova. The windows burst outward with answering screams of shock from outside.

Red bolts of lightning crashed close around the hospital. A bolt of pure red light splintered through the remains of the window to splash against what still covered Lina's arm. Dragonlord shielded himself and the doctor as best he could from the blast. The sheer pressure of it threw them across the room.

A tornado of lightnings ripped around Lina's silhouette. The thunder hissed as metal dissolved in splatters. In the midst of it all, Lina shrieked.

The shackle burst apart with a roar in a shower of sparks that slammed her into the wall. Books and metal bric-a-brac showered off shelves next to her. The door banged open, wrenching itself off its hinges. A line of chairs rose up and flew out the window. Damon and the doctor held on for dear life. Somewhere nearby a fire alarm went off.

For a moment all went silent. Then color returned. Then sound.

Lina crouched on the floor. Damon hurried to her. Trickles of blood ran down her forehead. She cradled her charred and pitted arm against herself– raw skin and muscle with no trace of the shackle remaining.

"Don't go," she whispered, her words indecipherable to anyone else. "I'm here now." She paused to catch her breath, holding her head as best she could. "One, two, three… eight, no. Less. Can you make it two? No. No. Okay, three. Hurry."

The doctor tried to lift her protective arm from her burned one and Lina hissed.

"Away," it sounded as if she said. She batted at him and Damon pulled him back.

"She needs medical attention," the doctor said.

"Give her a minute."

Lina's eyes unfocused.

"She's going into shock."

"One minute. Or maybe it's two."

She shifted to lie down flat on the floor. Her white face slowly turned a warmer ivory color.

"Let me elevate her feet at least," the doctor decided and then sat down himself in complete surprise. Maximus, Valiant, and a blue man with purple hair stood in the room, looking around as if to catch their bearings.

"Lina!" Londo pushed the others out of his way to get to her. He paused over her as her swollen eyes fluttered open. She looked like pale death: bedraggled, covered with blood, lying on the floor.

"Lina!"

The veins throbbed on her half-closed eyelids. Horrible bruises and swellings disfigured her face, her shoulders and arms. Purple fingerprints mottled her chest above the scoop neckline of her tee. Trickles of blood dried on their path down from her forehead. And her arm…

So gingerly he gathered her in his own arms. "Lina, *ma chère.* Tell me if I'm hurting you. What happened?" Distantly he took note of his surroundings: the remains of some kind of hospital. Damon and a man in scrubs with "Dr." on his nameplate. "What happened to her?" he demanded of the doctor.

Lina pulled at his vest. "L-Lah…"

Three medical personnel entered, picking their way into the room past the splintered doorway. Pausing as they recognized the ParaNet members.

Londo cradled Lina to his heart. "She needs help," he cried. "What's happened? What–"

Lina was patting him on the chest, trying to say something. If she'd had any strength to her, the pats would have been pounding.

"Deh," was the only sound she could make, though her lips continued the motion.

"What? What is it, *chérie?* Demi? What's the–" In shock, he raised his face to his father. "Demi's dying!"

Lina passed out.

Hal stood momentarily paralyzed by the condition of his daughter-in-law, by his son's declaration. "What's going on here?" he asked, turning in a circle.

"You're in Washington," Damon told him brusquely. "Demi's in critical condition, not expected to live. Granger's been taken care of and his ruby confiscated. I don't know how badly Lina's injured, but I suspect–"

"Wilder! Here! Now!" Londo commanded, but Wiley had already fished into his pockets and bags for medical monitors and supplies.

"It looks worse than it is," Wiley lied. Lina jerked back to consciousness.

Londo nodded. "Then we need to get Demi to Sarastor, stat. Hal– Call Legion Medical, have them standing by for both of them. Let's get Lina to Demi while you work on her, Wiley. Does anyone around here have a gurney?"

Distantly Lina knew she was in a wheelchair. Doors rolled past her but the shadow of a man stayed by her side– Wiley. Londo steered her with his reassuring presence. Londo was back. Londo was safe. She fainted again.

"Just get her fully conscious for three minutes," Londo was saying as a room came into view again. "Gorgeon will fix her up if we can just get to Sarastor in one piece."

"Um."

"You with us, Lina? Wiley says you're beat up, but you'll be fine in time. We have to put you on stims, *chérie.* Just a little more so we can save Demi."

"S-Sarastor."

"That's right. You port us to Sarastor. Direct to Legion Medical. You can do this. I've got the picture for you right here."

Lina blinked. A full-sized screen spread out in front of her showing a room with a big black cocoon split in half laid out on a table. There were Riz Gorgeon, head of Legion Medical, and three other doctors, looking alert but calm, wearing coverall bunny suits.

"We're prepared for quarantine conditions," Riz said. "Don't worry about filtering contagion. Put her directly into the cocoon."

"Do you have the picture, honey?" Londo asked. He tried to help her focus her clairvoyant link.

Lina shook her head. "More stims," she said.

Riz grimaced at that but nodded at Wiley.

Wiley administered one more to her neck.

Lina licked her dry lips. "Where's Demi?"

"Here." Londo picked her up in his arms and swung her to see the bloody gurney with the body on it. A swollen mass of flesh peeked out of one end of a sheet, brown straggles of hair flowing from it. That must be Demi's head. The medical techs disconnected the last of the plastic lines, needles and sensors that had been attached to her.

"She'll–" one doctor said, but the three disappeared as if they'd never been there. They left Wiley staring at the screen while the sheet on the gurney slumped over empty air.

"Good girl," Londo whispered to her as they arrived. He waited for Lina's "Arf," but instead she closed her eyes. Her head dropped to her chest.

But she still breathed. "Hang on," he pleaded.

The Legion Medical team settled Demi more securely in the cocoon, and then snapped it closed. Benton, a doctor Londo knew, knelt at Lina's side to tend to her. Almost immediately, Lina stirred. Slowly her eyelids peeled open. She searched for Londo. Finding him, she then sought Demi.

"She'll stay in suspended animation until they can diagnose," Londo told her, knowing that the screen would also send his words to Earth. "They can work on parts of the body in real time while other parts stay frozen in stasis. When everything's fixed, they pop her out.

"You did it, Kitten. It might take a while, but she'll be fine."

As if in answer, Riz straightened up from where she'd been leaning over the cocoon's readouts. "I've seen worse," she told them, though that could very well be a professional lie. "We'll have a stream of casualties from the Deseed action coming through in the next few hours, but that's the nice thing about the cocoons: you can put a patient on hold and it doesn't harm them. We can give this lady our full attention later."

"How long do you think–?" Lon asked.

Riz shrugged. "Depending on the total number of other casualties, estimating Legion Med remaining at full strength for this effort... I'd say she'll be conscious in two, three weeks, Sarastoran, Valiant. Up and walking is another matter. She registers as a physical mega, so that will condense recovery time. Back on duty in three months, perhaps. Maybe more. If she's like most Legionnaires, she likely needs a long vacation anyway."

"Oh, Londo." Relief washed so hard over Lina she began to cry. Demi was going to be all right. She wasn't going to die because Lina had messed up so badly.

"Shh. Shh. You did great." Lon cradled her head in one hand and wrapped his other arm around her. He held her until she cried through to sniffles. "You're safe now." He closed his eyes in thanksgiving. Awful knots that had plagued him for days melted away just because she was near. He bunched her hair through his fingers and rolled his head against hers. "You're safe. I'm here for you. God, I missed you so," he whispered. His reward came from the way she clutched him tighter.

She blew her nose on tissues that appeared out of nowhere.

"I'm going to start packing those things in my vest," Londo told her and was rewarded with a tiny smile. He turned to the screen and said in English. "Olympia will be fine. They'll uncork her in a couple weeks, estimated recovery time six, maybe eight months." **Let's give her a real vacation when she's well,** he told Lina.

His announcement was greeted by a buzz of excited speculation and tears on the Terran end. Hal had joined the group. The relief that glowed upon his face was matched by the pride in his eyes for his son and the pale lady by his side.

"We'll be back in a little while," Londo told him. "I think we've got some experiments to carry out there. Wilder, direct the personnel at Base Camp to launch for home except for our three Legion mind control casualties and Bolt. I'm sure he'd like to take the quick route once it's available."

"Yes, Valiant."

32

The two were still clutching each other when they appeared in the demolished waiting room back in Washington. The original group gathered there as well as a few more ParaNetters. The White Puma hung out the hole in the wall that used to be a bank of windows, peering down at the wet streets below before she eased back inside to shake her head at Lina and Lon.

"Oh shoo," Lina said as she surveyed the damage. She tried not to rub the scratchy bandage that covered her left arm where the shackle had been. "I made a real mess. It couldn't be h– Oh."

"What?" Londo asked as she disengaged herself from him.

Lina reached into her front pocket and dragged out the medallion. "I think it needs to do its thing again," she said. "Hang on. Hang on, everyone." The spiraling drain of color began again, slower than before. This time Lina could sense the suction on all levels as the ruby drew energy into itself. She braced against the flow and Londo steadied her.

Damon held on to Dragonwing and Reedbuck, who watched the process, mesmerized. "I thought it only needed recharging every few days or so," he said.

"This isn't recharging," Lina told him. "It's priming itself, like a well pump. Apparently large surges can cut it off from its power source–"

"The black hole at the center of the galaxy," Lon said.

"Right. It does this so it can get back into the flow again. Whuff. It's done. Feel better, ruby?"

A full spectrum in the room faded back in. People caught themselves as if they'd been on a train that had just stopped. Lina stuffed the medallion back into her pocket with a final pat for safety.

"And what are you doing with a Galactic Guardian's medallion?" Londo asked her softly. "Does it belong to anyone I know?"

"Not any more. Poor thing needs a vacation too. We have to take it back to Aum."

Londo glanced up to trade facial comments with Hal. "Of course we do, *chérie*. We'll take it later." To Hal: "Where's Granger?"

"In ICU. He'll live. He's under Scythian and ParaNet guard."

Londo nodded grimly. "I don't have the full story yet, but I think we need to deliver him to Aum as well. They have a courts martial body there, don't they?"

"I'm sure they'll arrange one once they find out. And they'll probably reserve a space in Daq-qu-a for him."

"Daq-qu-a?" Lina asked.

"That's the prison run by the Galactic Brigade themselves," Hal told her.

That sounded secure enough. And if Scythian guards were here, that meant Queen Otrera had been notified. Good.

"Feel up to a few more ports?" Lon asked.

Those stims were good. Doctor Riz had given her enough to keep her awake for a while. Lon had said Lina needed to be debriefed and there might be something else. Riz warned that after Lina crashed she'd be out for a good day at least. Lina now wore Sarastoran adult diapers under her jeans. The one pair would last her long enough, but even though they didn't show, they were embarrassing. Less embarrassing than having to have her brand new husband have to change her, she admitted to herself.

She ported in Andri, Bolt and Tara, along with three man-sized black cocoon-capsules like the one Demi had been put in. She sensed people inside them.

"Andri?" Wiley asked in surprise when she appeared.

"I should be returning with the fleet, but I wanted to supervise this," Andri told him, looking expectantly at Lina and Londo.

"The other ParaNetters are bringing our own ship back after they finish getting patched up," Tara reported. She sported a square bandage on her temple. Her right eyebrow was mostly missing.

Bolt had a thin cast on his left arm, and a solid bandage circling his right thigh. He looked chipper enough, though, and he carried Lina's plastic cookie bin.

"Didn't want to leave it behind. I know how valuable these things are," he said as he handed it back. The bin was empty even of crumbs. Bolt checked out the room. "Eff. I see Londo's been living here. When are you going to hire a maid?"

Lon grabbed the bin from him with a growl. Gary laughed before the Puma and Damon dragged him away.

Lina cocked her head to the side. Something was… She squinted at Lon. She took the bin from him and set it down. Then she held him by her good hand at arm's length and examined him up and down. "What's happened to you?"

"I'm all right," he said.

"No you're not," she accused. "You haven't been using the white light."

"Yes I have."

"What do you mean?" Hal rushed to their side. "What's wrong with Lon?"

"He's… he's… Is that what mind control looks like?" She traded concerned looks with Hal and then saw past him to the black pod next to Tara. "Good god," she breathed. "No, *that's* what mind control looks like."

"Lon's under control?" Hal wanted to know.

"I– I don't think it's nearly enough to do it, but there's a start here. Honey, how do you feel?"

Londo just felt confused. He tried to test if anything felt different in his mind, but everything seemed normal. "We thought I might have caught something once, but Erik's guides said–"

"Can you do anything about it?" Hal demanded.

"Of course I can. It's just hooks."

"Just hooks." Again, Lon exchanged glances with his father. Andri moved closer. "How about Chimrin?"

"Is that who it is? Oh yes, that would explain that. I should have known." Lina walked over to the pod, so much like the one they'd put Demi in, and examined the astral level.

"Lots of hooks," she said. "All these are black hooks, same as in you, Lon. I've never seen a black hook before. They're going to take a little time to untangle."

"But you can do it?"

"As long as Riz' stims hold me up. I can give you the names of some people who might be able to do a reasonable job if I go to sleep on you." She returned to Londo's side.

"All right." Hal chewed on his lip, his gaze considering the pod, considering Londo… considering Lina. "How'd you get the ruby?"

"It stopped working for Granger," Lina told them. "It knows that a ruby's supposed to stand at the call of a Guard, but it knew that Granger was evil. It refused to work for him. He went off the deep end, just went crazy."

She clutched Lon's vest. "He attacked Demi– oh god, Londo, he was trying to kill her! He hacked her and he– he *raped* her and he laughed and he–" Lina buried her head under Lon's chin as she fought off the sobs again. Not now! Not in front of these people when she had to help Lon!

Lon made clucking noises to her, petting her hair. Here inside his arms the world seemed so safe. She snuffled against his chest.

Tell me, he whispered to her. **Real quick, an overview. I'll get the full story later when you're feeling better.** He gasped as images poured out of her. The wave of fear washed over him, igniting pure rage toward Granger. He stanched it as best he could. See to Lina's health first, then these others and Demi, and then Granger would get his! "I'm here, I'm here," he chanted softly. "Everything's going to be all right."

"Oh, Londo!"

"Give us two minutes," Londo told the crowd in the room, who tried to look everywhere but at them.

Finally he nodded and she disengaged. "Are you sure you're okay?"

She nodded. "Yeah, I'll be– whoa!– another stim just kicked in." She smoothed her hair back and wiped her eyes. "Sorry. I was pretty tired."

Hal's face was stern and set, his fists braced against the room's desk. "Wasn't Granger off-planet? He said there was a Brigade emergency."

"He lied," the White Puma told him. "So what else is new? Can we all troop down to ICU and throw him out into the street? After what he did to Demi–"

Lina swallowed. "I saw it all. I couldn't do anything about it. I'm sorry. I'm so sorry." She kicked at a shard of glass. "And I'm sorry about this mess. I just knew that Lon was leaving and Demi's only hope was on Sarastor, and that stupid shackle was making me half-crazy. I couldn't focus."

Lon wrapped his arms around her. "Kitten, the hospital's still standing. I think you focused well enough. No one blames you for anything."

"Oh."

Hal said, "Tell us what happened." He held one of those camera eyes in her direction.

She didn't want to relive the experience again. "I need to work on Lon while the stims are working. And then on Chimrin. And the others."

Hal's gaze shifted on her. Finally he nodded crisply and said, "Later."

Damon said, "I recorded her," and Hal nodded again, this time including the rest of the ParaNetters, who gathered in a circle to watch the recording Damon had made on his tablet of Lina's debriefing.

Lon and Lina stood apart from them, at arm's length from each other.

"Try to feel the hooks as I pull them out," Lina told her husband.

"Is this going to hurt?"

"I don't think so. Let me concentrate. Feel your aura– not just the part around you. It goes all the way through and out the other side…"

Lina centered herself, calling on the white light for protection. She made a few large sweeps of his body, magnetic passes, just to get a covering of general aura muck off him.

There were the hooks: three of them, two in his solar plexus, one in his throat, all black and thick and strong.

She reached to grab the larger hook. It was well-ensconced, wrapped around something so it wouldn't pull out easily. She pictured it as a very long Christmas tree ornament hanger, as if someone had enlarged it until it was about two feet long. She held one end of it. The other end was the hooked one. She told the hook to relax, to become flexible, to straighten out. Hesitatingly, it did, and she eased it out. It tried to hook up again before it completely left his body, and she had to deal with it some more. But within another minute it slid out all the way. She loosed it and let it snap back to whoever had placed it.

"One down, two to go," Lina said.

Wiley stood between the two groups, recording both Damon's recording and her technique. Hal watched Lina as he listened to Damon's screen.

The second, smaller hook in Londo's solar plexus didn't want to unbend so Lina had to take some more time with it. Eventually it came loose. The one in his throat was smaller still and pinched with tension. She had to work with it, hum to it to try to raise its vibration. She anthropomorphized Lon's throat chakra and enlisted its help. Finally she puffed three times at the hook, sending it pure white light, and it was so surprised that it released. She pulled it out before it could clamp down again.

"Hey, I felt that," Lon said, surprised.

"Did it hurt?"

"No; I just felt it."

She nodded. "That one was tricky," Lina said. "I've never seen a hook so well-crafted. Well, it's gone now. You're clean. How are you feeling, darling?"

Lon's eyes shifted, unfocused. "I don't feel any… Well, maybe I do feel a little different. More in control of myself, come to think of it." He rolled his shoulders, loosening up, and then gazed at her with that crooked smile of his. "You're looking a little better now. Not as pale."

"Good," she said and reached for him. He took her in a tight embrace and they kissed, then broke apart. "Welcome home, Lon," she said softly, stroking his cheek. "Are you feeling okay otherwise? You didn't get hurt, did you? How'd it go?"

"For the most part it's over. Just some cleaning up that other people will be doing. Look, I'll tell you all about it later after we both get some sleep. I'm fine, so don't worry about me. Chim's next. You feel up to it? We can always keep her in the bottle until tomorrow or whenever."

"Bring her on. I've got my rhythm going now." Lina wagged her hips side to side, revving up.

"That's my girl."

Tara propped the pod that held Chimrin against a desk and broke open the lock with a loud *pop,* like a jar unsealing. The Legionnaire lay like a mummy inside, unconscious.

"You've got a shackle on her, poor thing. She looks like a pincushion."

Lina examined Chimrin carefully as Wilder followed her, recording. Damon paused his own recording. He was near the end anyway and the others watched her curiously.

Lina shook her arms out, letting excess energy dissipate into the earth. She instructed Wilder on what she saw and how it fit into the various levels of the human aura.

Londo watched over Lina's shoulder. She asked, "Is she okay physically? All I can see when I look are these blasted hooks. If she's hurt, that should be cleared up before I do anything. "

"She's fine."

"All right." Lina shook her head. "I don't know how that damned shackle on her is going to affect this, but I'd hate to have her running around in this condition without it."

"That's why it's there," Lon said. He sat down to watch her work and to keep track of how she herself was doing.

Lina made some large passes around Chimrin. "This time I'll start with the small hooks. They seem to be the most stubborn ones. Maybe after they're out the others will be easier to do."

"Sounds good to me," Lon said helpfully.

As Damon came to the climax of her story, Lina proceeded carefully, beginning at the tiniest of hooks embedded like needles in Chimrin's throat chakra. Twice she cursed at the stubbornness of the needles, but she took a breath and tried again.

She'd hum as she worked, sometimes raising her vibration, and sometimes, to Lon's surprise, hum along with the muzak that came into the room from the hallway through the curtained divider that someone had placed at the ruined door.

Every now and then she'd blow or puff into Chimrin's throat, and then either make the motion of quickly pulling something out, or cock her head and reconsider the problem. Three times she extended her left hand above herself like an antenna, and reached with her right to extract something that had been causing her trouble. Once she laughed and whispered, "Gotcha!" and plucked some invisible thing, flicking it away from herself. When she got through with the throat chakra, she balanced it quickly and gently, nodding satisfaction at the job.

Lon tried to sense what she was doing. Wiley gave him a quick jerk of his chin. He looked on Wiley's padd: the screen showed Lina and Chimrin, but Chimrin had a whitish-blue double-image around herself, a silhouette marred by hundreds of spines sticking out of it. Lina's fingers were around one spine.

Hal joined them along with Tara, Andri and Damon to look. One by one the spines disappeared as Lina gingerly pulled them out and tossed them toward the open outer wall in a dispersing gesture. The spines remaining were larger now than the ones she'd already handled and sure enough, they were easier to get rid of.

"I'll need an aluminum basin with salt water to de-energize," Lina managed to say as she was finishing the third hook to the last.

"I'm on it," Tara told her and trotted off.

Londo's shock at returning to an injured wife began to wear off. Lina was safe now, and so was Demi. Now anger filled his gut coupled with white fear from what he'd heard of Damon's story.

God, he'd almost lost Lina! That menace… that *savage* Granger had tried to rape her–twice! The list of crimes Damon and his team had come up with was horrendous. And what he'd done to Demi… It could have been Lina, so easily. And he'd let Stoan put that stinking shackle on her.

Never again. It was time Valiant grew a backbone.

Hal asked Damon, "She still wore the shackle when she took out a Guard?"

"For the most part. I think it being partially on was worse than it being whole. It didn't come off all the way until just before she ported you people in."

Londo studied Lina. Gorgeon had programmed timed stims to allow the amount of time Londo had guessed they'd need for debriefing and beyond. How much longer would Lina last like this? Her hands shook. She had to hold herself up with one hand on the armrest of the chair next to her. He left to find her some drinking water.

When he returned, Damon was finishing his story. "And then she glowers into the camera like some avenging angel– very dramatic– and says, 'I'm Carolina Starhart, Speaker for the Earth.' I guarantee you that that sound byte is going to be on all the networks tonight."

Lina finished the job. She shook her arms out, looking around for the basin and saw it, immersing her limbs into it gratefully, feeling the energies draining. She thanked the angels for their assistance. Her knees started to buckle, but Lon was right behind her to catch and support her.

"C'mon, Kitten, why don't you sit down," he suggested.

"I'd rather sleep for a week or two," she said as she collapsed into the chair he'd set beside her. She nodded at Chimrin as she accepted Lon's water. "You can take the shackle off now. Someone did bring a key, didn't they? It takes a little effort to get the ruby to do it. Hoo y'all!" She gave a great jerk.

"Stim?" Lon asked.

"Good one. Fifteen on a scale of ten."

Lon managed a half-hearted chuckle.

Wiley produced an electronic key from his utility bag and unlocked the suppressor. Chimrin's eyelids fluttered. Her hand flew to her mouth. "I'm going to be sick," she announced. Forte picked her up and ran her into the bathroom, closing the door behind them.

The wall didn't offer much soundproofing. Lina glanced up at the ceiling and around the debris-strewn room. "I'm up now. Who's in the remaining ones?"

"Erik and Stoan," Lon confirmed.

Lina had to laugh. "Sorry," she said. "The idea of Stoan under mind control. So I'm a vindictive person. Sue me." She laughed again and the laugh became a choke. She covered her face and shook her head as Londo reached to embrace her.

"Can we get this over with?" she said. "I have a feeling that in a little while I'm going to be really, really tired."

The bathroom door opened. "Shards, what happened to me?" Chimrin moaned like she was coming out of a hangover.

"A little mind control," Wiley replied easily. "Do you remember? We had to put the suppressor on you."

"Oh yes. Ah, shards," she repeated, looking around. "Where are we?"

"Earth," Lon said. "Lina just de-controlled you."

"How are you feeling?" Lina asked. "Control-wise, I mean?"

Chimrin checked herself. "I feel… normal."

"Good. You're going to fix Stoan and I'll get Erik. All right?"

Chimrin frowned at her. "And how am I going to do that? I don't know how to de-control people. It's supposed to be impossible."

"Then welcome to your first day of psychic healing class," Lina said with an encouraging smile. "Okay, Lon, how do we pop 'em out?"

Hal broke the locks this time. Erik the budding telepath remained asleep under the suppressor's influence, but Stoan sat up, trying to say something that came out only as a mumble. Even so, he got up the strength to point accusingly at Lina before Wiley tapped him with a mild sedative.

"Thank you," Lina said.

Stoan sat there, blinking and wobbling.

"I'm not going to touch Stoan," Lina told Chimrin. "You know what he'll say if I do."

Chimrin sighed. "He's a very fine man, Lina. You've just–"

"Caught him on a bad decade," Lina finished for her. "You're doing him; I'll do Erik. Can you see what's going on here?"

Chimrin frowned at the two of them and shook her head. "All I get is that there are two layers of consciousness in each of them, indicating control. Strange how the overriding layer is so faint on Erik, but it's definitely still there. I suppose that's the suppressor's work. How do you get rid of the control layer?"

Lina nodded. "They're hooks. You pull them out." She walked Chimrin through the mechanics of the human aura, surprised at how she couldn't visualize it when she knew of the levels in theory. What did the Tishana teach, if not the basics? Chim was quite a powerful and skilled telepath.

"If you get into trouble, just ask for more of the white light," Lina told her. "Focus on my hand." She held her hand about four feet behind Erik. "Stay focused on it but try to see what's going on around his throat chakra. You know chakras?"

"I know chakras."

Well, that was something. "Don't focus on it, focus on my hand. Just split your attention, not your vision–"

"Oh!" Chimrin blinked. "Just for a moment there, I thought I saw–"

"What?"

Chimrin shook her head. "Something. Like hooks, going in."

Lina smiled. "That's it."

Chimrin frowned. "But I can't see it anymore."

"Then imagine them. Feel for them." Slowly Lina ran her hand down Erik's aura, stopping as she felt a hook. "You can feel them if you tune into the aura, mental level."

Chimrin nodded. "Mental level." She ran her hand down Stoan's aura and stopped at his throat. "Shards," she breathed. "What, just pull them out now?"

"Ease them out. You don't want to damage anything as you do so. Tell them to let go, to straighten out. Take the little ones first; they're the hardest. If they won't give, then blow some white light into them."

The two of them bent to their work, oblivious of the others talking in the room. The hospital director joined them to talk to members of the ParaNet. She gave Chim and Lina the merest of glances, not realizing what they were doing. Two doctors arrived to report on Granger's condition. Four police officers took statements and made a cursory examination of the room's damage. A ParaNet photographer arrived to move through the crowd, taking pictures for their records and possibly a press release.

Lon made sure that Lina wasn't overtaxing herself. And Wiley paid full attention to both groups, recording all the time.

Lon noticed that Chimrin was having trouble on one. "Lina," she said, but Lina was too engrossed to hear her. Lon moved to Chim's side.

"What's the problem?" he asked her.

"This one... it's very fine," she said, unable to quite describe it.

"A higher frequency?" That's what it sounded like to Lon, like when he'd investigated Lina's mind that time.

"I can't seem to get a handle on it."

"Hum, and then hum a third or a fifth higher. It raises your own vibration," Lon said authoritatively.

"A third? What's that?"

He hummed and then took it a third higher. "Like that."

Chimrin shook her head. "Too voodoo for me."

Lon tried to center himself, imagining himself surrounded by brilliant white light. He reached out, testing the air to see where it felt denser. Just imagine… Just imagine… There. That must be Stoan's aura. He patted the air six inches from Stoan's throat and felt around.

"Stop that," he told Stoan, who'd backed away from his hand. There was something sticking out, Londo thought, but it was insubstantial. He hummed, then took it a third, then a fifth higher. Now he could put his fingers around it. He tugged and whatever it was felt stuck. **Loosen up,** he ordered it. **Relax.** As it joggled he could feel a hook on the end of it. Another firm shake and it straightened out. He could pull it out easily, and held it in front of Chimrin's eyes. She looked from it to him.

"Terran shamanism," he said smugly.

She took it from him and released it to the air. "Well, fire, if you can do that, help me with the rest of these."

So he joined in, working hesitantly at first, then more confidently as he got the hang of it. "Hey, look at me," he said. "I'm a psychic surgeon. Just call me Doctor Ra– Starheart."

Across the room, Hal watched his son. He and Chimrin were working carefully, slowly, taking the hooks one by agonizing one, while Lina worked quickly: gesturing, puffing, doing strange-looking things that somehow let her get the job done sooner. If he could count every time she seemed to loose something as if she'd successfully taken out a hook, she'd done about three times the amount of hooks that Lon and Chim together had accomplished in the same amount of time. And Erik hadn't flinched every now and then as Stoan had during the process.

Lon was doing psychic work. Lon was a telepath. And he'd married the girl who'd saved his life.

Hal scratched the back of his head. The world had changed overnight. Where had he been? Had he blinked?

Then again, it had changed for the better. Number one, Lon was alive. Demi would recover. Lon was happy. Lon's bride was a nice girl who loved him. She was brave. Able. And it seemed she could get rid of mind control.

The head of ParaNet Media arrived to check out the room and its occupants. Hal turned away from watching his son. The Network had immediate needs that needed attending to.

"Finished," Lon announced loud enough for Lina to hear. She came up for air then and looked at Stoan, smiling at the satisfaction in Lon and Chimrin's faces.

"Very nice, but I think you've missed some," she said. She left Erik to approach Stoan. Lina swiped the air a foot away from him in large sweeps, clearing out invisible debris. "Now check again," she said, and returned to Erik.

"Aw shit, there's more," Londo muttered. He and Chimrin both sighed and resumed their work.

Since she finished Erik first, Lina supervised Lon and Chimrin on Stoan. He blearily regarded them as he leaned on his cocoon. He gave a start when Chimrin hesitantly hummed at one point, then hummed a higher note before she reached and plucked *something* from the air around him.

"What's going on?" Stoan grumped.

"You were under mind control," Chimrin told him. "We're on Earth. Now be quiet while we finish."

Stoan eyed Lina as she sat behind Chimrin and Lon.

"She hasn't touched you," Lon told Stoan. "Chim and I have been working on you."

Wiley unlocked Erik's shackle. He woke quickly, his hand immediately going to his mouth.

"Bathroom's in there," Wiley directed, and Erik ran. Wiley turned to Lina. "Interesting reaction," he observed. "Did that happen to you?"

"I didn't get mine off in one fell swoop," she told him.

Stoan was looking at the blood that covered Lina's clothes. The bandage where the shackle should be.

"Who unlocked hers?" Stoan demanded to know. "I should have been the one to give the order."

"I got rid of mine on my own," Lina told him. She could see him grit his teeth in response. Too bad for Stoan if he didn't like it.

"She gets crabby when she's tired," Lon said.

"Oh be quiet and finish," Lina snapped. Lon laughed at her.

"I want a report on how she got out of it, Wilder," Stoan said. "I want it fixed so that no others can do the same thing."

"I doubt if the same circumstances will ever come up again, Commander."

Lina rinsed her arms in salt water, thanking the angels for their help. **While you're at it, help me figure out what to do about Stoan,** she asked them.

The other two finished. She showed them how to release the energies using the salt water and their own intention. Chimrin laughed in delight.

"You know," she told them, "that was a lot of work, but it was basically very simple." She stood there with her hands on her hips, looking at Stoan. "How about that: mind control is curable!"

He grunted.

"Where's a drink machine?" Lon wanted to know. "I want a Coke. Who else is thirsty?" He dug into a pocket of his vest for money.

"You don't get a Coke." Lina pointed at him. "We three need to drink water to get rid of toxins. Maybe two glasses, then you can have your Coke if you're still thirsty."

"*Jawohl.*" Lon gave her a smart salute.

"You can dish it out, but you can't take it. Whoa." Lina jumped.

"Another stim, just in time," Lon smirked at her. She stuck her tongue out at him and he returned the favor, though not as innocently.

A hubbub in the hallway drew their attention. Three civilians entered the room carrying small cases. A woman pointed at the desk Stoan sat on. She wasn't deterred by Stoan's bluish skin but asked him politely to move so they could set up.

"Are we being thrown out?" Lina asked Londo. He was sitting on the arm of her chair.

"That's ParaNet Media Support," he said. "I suspect there'll be a–"

"Press conference."

They both turned to Hal, striding into the room. "It's all set up," he told them. "Starts in twenty. Better get ready."

Lina smiled as she stroked Lon's arm. "Can I watch?" she asked.

Lon flashed her a smile and then scowled up at Hal. "She needs her rest," he said. "Doctor's orders."

"A stim just kicked in, didn't it? Gorgeon told me she had one more after this. When that one's done, she's out for the night."

Lina blinked. "Excuse me?"

"She's not ready for a solo press conference."

"She's ready enough. All she has to do is tell her story– in condensed form– and answer questions. Give her a padd so she can read Demi's condition to them."

"Um, hello? Do I get a vote?"

"Lina, I hate to do this to you but you were there. You witnessed everything. We've got rumors flying out there tonight; the channels are full of special reports. I just heard one that said that it was Demi who'd gone rogue and beaten up Granger."

"No!" Lina squeezed Lon's arm. "That's a lie."

He patted her hand silently.

"So we need you to get out there and tell your story. Damon says that the press already has footage of you concerning this story."

One of the civilians came over to Lina. She held out her hand, motioning to the desk, which had been set up as a makeup table. "Come along, Miss. We'll prep you."

"But I can't! You tell him, Lon," she begged. "Tell them to leave us alone. Too many people are getting hurt or being threatened–"

"Sorry, *chérie.*" Lon took her hand in his. "Just a little while longer. The stims will hold. I suspected this would happen," he added sheepishly. "Don't worry. You can take it." He stood up and pulled her with him. "I'll be right behind you. There's going to be a few still cameras there, so–"

"I don't care about the cameras." It was only then that she noticed the ParaNet photographer, who snapped a shot of her before she could react.

"Good," Lon said.

A sharply-suited middle-aged man breezed into the room, gave the destruction a quick glance, and approached Lina even as he nodded at Hal and Lon. "I've got your opening statement here," he told Lina and introduced himself. "Niloy Sarkar, ParaNet Media Services."

"Good. Tell them to use a ParaNetter for this."

"You were the one who brought Olympia and the Guard in. You're the new face in the crowd, the one they want to see. Not any of them." Pogue gave Londo the evil eye. "And you didn't inform us of certain *matters,* sir. We're running hard enough trying to cover that as it is. We had to coordinate with–" his mouth tightened in distaste– "*your* PR people for this. Apparently you saw fit to furnish them with the needed information and not us."

Londo gave him a sour look and held out his hand. "Let's see this statement of yours."

They strode down the hall at a trot: Mr. Sarkar alongside Londo, who steered Lina in a wheelchair, with Hal and Damon trailing behind. Everyone else had returned to the ParaNet satellite except for the Media Services personnel, who hung around.

"I tell you, I want her in a suit," Sarkar insisted.

Lina's hair was neat and loose; her eyes were clear. The ParaNet makeup artist had wanted to do extensive work on her face and neck, but Lon had nixed anything other than what they absolutely needed to make her show up under the television lights. One bruise was a striking purple-blue mark on her face, though another showing above the neckline of her tee stood out almost as much. The bandage covered her arm burns. She still wore the bloody garments she'd been in for hours.

"I want them to remember that she's been in a fight, too," Londo said.

"It's unprofessional," Sarkar retorted.

"And I'm just an amateur," Lina said. She used her padd to coordinate information from two different screens into one organized list. "Lon, is there any way you can find out when Jae's due to arrive?"

She'd already told Londo about the emergency call to Aldierra. Londo heaved a sorry sigh. "He's probably frantic about you. Easy enough to find his hyperspace schedule. Likely it'll be between tomorrow or the day after. That's if their tech is equal to Sarastor's. We'll both be there to tell him everyone's alive and fairly well as soon as he hits normal space."

"Good."

A sign marking the cafeteria loomed just ahead. The Network's media people had cleared out the place so that every major newsgroup on the planet could squeeze in a reporter. The only video feed would come from three ParaNet cameras.

When Londo stopped the chair, Lina made no move to stand up, but stared at the closed swinging doors that marked the temporary press room.

Londo gave her a squeeze here, out of sight of the cameras, as Sarkar went on ahead. They had agreed that they would not introduce her as his wife, not yet. Leave that for another press conference. "You'll do fine, Kitten. You're a Sagittarian, remember? Jump. I'll be right behind you."

"Even Sags can stretch only so far, love." Lina drew a shaky breath and he helped her up.

"That's why you married me. I'll make sure you don't snap."

Sarkar was already at the podium with the ParaNet insignia front and center, microphones clustered all around it. A background had been set up on tripods. It was patterned in smaller insignias that also included those of Network members. Sarkar gave the ground rules for the conference, which included the fact that the speaker, one Ms. Starheart (he carefully spelled it with an "e" for the audience) was on stimulants to keep her awake, and when she finally crashed, the session would be over.

A murmur through the crowd went up, interrupting Sarkar: "Maximus! Valiant!" The reporters had expected Dragonlord's presence but not them. But all eyes were on Lina.

"Oh god," she said, and Lon squeezed her hand.

You'll be all right. Cuppa.

"What?"

"You know. That Klingon thing. 'Cupcake.'"

"*Qapla'.*"

"*Oui.*"

He let go, and she made her way to the podium as Sarkar stepped away. The three heroes followed Lina to form a solemn line behind her. She was heartened to realize that her step was steady and her demeanor calm although the pit of her stomach was literally shaking. She reached the microphones. ParaNet Media had measured her so the podium was already adjusted to her height, the reason why Sarkar had to stretch to reach them. The room went dead silent, but the deep breath she took before she spoke was not heard by anyone except Londo and Hal.

"As I said before," she began, "My name is Carolina Starhart, and I am Speaker for the Three Worlds, one of which is Earth. I was a witness to today's terrible events. Earth's Galactic Guardian, Paul Granger, brutally attacked, mauled and then raped Olympia with the full power at his disposal."

A murmur swept through the crowd of professional reporters, not easily shocked.

Lina continued, "By the order of Earth herself, Paul Granger is no longer welcome on this planet as a Galactic Guardian or in any other capacity. I have his ruby in custody—" she held the ruby medallion high to show everyone "– and when he is able to be moved, I shall take him to Aum and the Galactic Sentinels to have an accounting. I should not think that the Sentinels will choose to keep him in their ranks."

Her pause opened the way for a couple of reporters to shout out questions, pointing their hands in her direction to flag her attention. Suddenly everyone was yelling questions at her. She remained silent until the room quieted again.

She triggered a screen and enlarged it to more than life size. "When Olympia arrived here she was dying," Lina told the room, "We managed to transport her to a world called Sarastor where they employ very advanced medicine. Sarastor is the home of the Affiliated Systems Megaforce Legion, which has teamed up with our own ParaNet in the past few days for a major mission. The Mega-Legion is to the galactic sector to which Sarastor belongs in the same way as the ParaNet is to Earth. Valiant is a part-time member of the Mega-Legion." Behind her she knew Lon was giving the slightest of affirming nods.

"I would like to introduce you to the Legion's chief medical officer, Dr. Riz Gorgeon, who will fill you in as to Olympia's condition. Please note that we're using a translator unit on this live feed. She's going to be dubbed instantaneously and your questions will be translated for her to understand. Dr. Gorgeon?"

The screen brightened to show Riz in her office. "Thank you, Ms. Starhart," Riz began, her friendly round face so serious.

Lina stepped back from the podium and shook the tension in her shoulders out slightly.

"Has Gorgeon ever appeared at a press conference?" Hal whispered across to Lon.

His son shook his head. "This is her first."

"If they need first-hand information from me about the attack, they need first-hand info about Demi's medical condition, too," Lina said, so glad she'd thought of including Riz in this. Riz had such a calming authority.

The doctor kept her remarks brief and answered all questions. There weren't many; this crowd was reeling at what they heard.

"There are a lot of words that aren't translating," Lina told the group, "because they concern concepts that Terra hasn't discovered yet. But we get the gist: Olympia was as injured as a person can get without actually losing their life, but she should be back to full physical health in a few months, is that right, Dr. Gorgeon?"

"That's correct. We have excellent psychological therapists on Sarastor as well, and I hope that your great hero Olympia will take advantage of them to heal the mental trauma such an attack produces. We will care for her as if she were one of our own." With Riz's nod, the screen blanked and disappeared.

Now Lina settled to reading the statement that Sarkar and Londo had prepared, with her corrections, describing the attack and the events leading up to it. The reporters listened raptly, but even before she was through there were hands in the air for her to choose questions. Most were not that polite as she finished. The renewed hubbub was deafening, but a few shouted questions stood out.

"Was the alleged rapist–"

"There was no *alleged* rapist," Lina stated grimly. "I am not a lawyer or police officer to bandy words about. It was rape, it was an attempt to murder, aggravated murder, and Paul Granger was the perpetrator. I'm a witness to the event. An event I had absolutely no control over." She had to swallow then to control the roil of her emotions, and her eyes dropped away from the crowd. The control she had held with them was broken. Questions broke out once more.

"Are you telling us that rocks can think?"

"Yes I am, and apparently the Galactic Brigade's stones can think in ways that interact well with human thought. Perhaps you'd classify them on the level of a dog. Or maybe that's all a human can understand of them and they're beyond us. I was able to get through to this stone that Granger was acting contrary to what a Galactic Guardian is supposed to do, so it stopped functioning for him. It's a very nice ruby."

"Does this make you the next Galactic Guardian?"

The question surprised her, though she should have expected it. "I think one of the traditional qualifications for being a Guard is to be very brave. That definitely leaves me out of the running. I was terrified most of today."

"What was Olympia guarding you for?"

Lina slyly looked sideways at Londo. "Perhaps Valiant," she drawled the hero name, "would care to explain?" She stepped back from the mike and heard a cough cover Damon's soft laugh at Lon's uncomfortable position.

33

Lon frowned at Lina as he advanced to the microphones. "The Network and Mega-Legion have been battling a threat to this region of the galaxy. A squad from the ParaNet has just returned from a decisive victory on another world. Maximus has already scheduled a joint press conference for tomorrow concerning that.

"A *few,*" he stressed the word, looking back at Lina, "a very few members of each organization had been disturbed at Ms. Starheart's sudden appearance two weeks ago as a mega paranormal." He gave a short, vague description of the kinds of preparations against rogue telepaths that had been made, and how Lina had been shackled.

"There has been no shred of proof that she was part of this invasion force. Instead, she has cooperated fully with both the Network and the Legion. She has saved the life of Olympia and brought the renegade Guard to justice. After this, I don't think that any member of either group will do anything but apologize to her. Ms. Starheart?" He gave her a little bow as he stepped back.

"Thank you, Valiant," she said as she returned to her place. She had kept the sea of reporter faces, the camera lights and cameras all massed together in a blur so they wouldn't look like people. That way she wouldn't be so nervous. Now she tried to single each of them out, meet their eyes.

"The important thing today that I'd like to impress upon y'all," and she realized that her southern accent had leaked out despite her best efforts at anonymity. "is that a great woman is recovering on a distant planet after doing her absolute and amazing best to stop a very evil, very powerful man. We are all here, all children of the earth, and she is our sister. When she returns, I'd like for you to treat her with the kindness and understanding you would afford your own blood sister in such a situation. She is a Scythian; her body will recover from this. But she needs our good thoughts and love to help her through the tremendous emotional battering she's been through."

Questions, Lon beamed to her.

"I think I have about a half-hour before my last stimulant wears off. Are there any questions?" she asked smoothly.

All hell broke out. She started sorting through the queries and answered them to the best of her ability unless they asked things like where exactly Scythia was, information that had to be kept secret. There were lots of questions that asked for information she had already given. Perhaps she dismissed those quicker than others would have at a press conference, but she didn't have time to fool around. Time was money.

Whenever they asked her about herself, she turned the question around so that it pertained to Olympia. When one asked if she was the same person who had helped out at the Iowa train wreck, she just answered, "Yes," and went on to take the next question.

There was one reporter who got in a question about her that she felt needed answering. "When you say you're Speaker for the Earth," the reporter asked. "What does that mean? Who appointed you?"

"I am Speaker for the Three Worlds," she said clearly. "One of the Three Worlds is Earth, one is Sarastor, and the third is a world called Aldierra. I hear the Earth and repeat what she tells me to say. And as for who appointed me, the Three Worlds themselves did. I do not speak for the humans of the planet; I speak for the planet herself, the living entity whom we all inhabit."

"Maximus! Maximus, is this true?"

Hal stepped up to the mikes as Lina stepped aside. "As far as I've been able to figure out, it's true. Strange, but absolutely true. We're still examining records made on the world of Sarastor and using some interstellar telepaths to confirm, but every last preliminary report seems to indicate that it's real." He held his hands up to deflect questions. "Don't ask me to explain it. I've been trying to adjust my thinking in these past few days to consider that *things* can be sentient. Not just sentient, but even more intelligent than humans. And that some humans can tune into that intelligence."

That brought a pause to the questioning, as Londo nodded his agreement behind them. Apparently none of the ParaNetters disagreed with the Speaker's mysterious statement.

"Ms. Starhart, can you furnish us with proof?"

"There will be a videotape made available in the next few days of the investiture of the Three Worlds. I think it will have various scientific corroborations along with it for those who need quantitative proof. For those who choose not to believe, no amount of proof will ever convince them."

"What were these other crimes that Granger is accused of?" one reporter asked. Interesting that the reporters were now referring to him as Granger and not the Galactic Guardian.

Lina read through the long list of accusations, researched in her absence. She ended with, "In the last three months, six women have identified him in rape reports to police and went unbelieved– just because Granger was a Guard. I hope that the police departments involved will begin thorough investigations to see how this could have happened. No one should stand above anyone else in privilege or justice under the law."

One reporter raised her hand. "You said you were Granger's original target," she said. "Do you know why? Did he have a reason?"

They weren't going to make the announcement yet. Time to fudge a little. Lina cut her eyes to Lon and checked in with him to make sure she said the right thing. "Granger has a vendetta going against my husband," she told the reporter. "I believe his plan was based on revenge." She looked for other questions, but the woman quickly placed another.

"Who is your husband? Would we know him? Is he a paranorm, too?"

"We prefer to keep that information private right now." How long would it be before anyone put it together? Another fifteen minutes? Ah, but Londo wanted another two weeks. She'd give him that.

She fielded queries about how Granger would be taken to face judgment before the Galactic Sentinels and watched the clock. Her right hand was trembling and her knees felt wobbly.

There were some repeat questions that she pointed out as such. "If there are no new questions, I'd like to thank you all for coming—" Lina began, but Londo gently pushed her away from the mike. He kept his hands on her shoulders.

"Um, if the main conference is over," he said, leaning into the mikes, "I have a small unrelated item, just a detail." The reporters hardly paid attention to him, aware that the big story had already been told. Some looked up expectantly, others merely paused in turning off their recording devices.

"I wanted to make a correction and a note for the record, " he said. "First, Ms. Starheart's surname is spelled S-T-A-R-H-A-R-T."

Lina stared at him wonderingly before her face blossomed into a smile.

He only looked at her long enough to check her expression. "Second, please add that name to my own now. Londo Rand Starhart, no hyphens. Thank you."

With a perfectly straight face, Londo stepped back in line with Hal and Damon. The three turned as if they'd rehearsed choreography and double-timed toward the exit.

Lina closed her eyes and shook her head as a billion camera shutters clicked. The raucous sound of three men's hearty laughs came from beyond the door even over the shouting from within.

She turned back toward the reporters, their electronics coming back to life after being shut off, and sheepishly raised her left hand so they could see the wedding ring. The room quieted.

"Well. So much for, 'Let's wait two more weeks to announce,'" she said, lowering the hand. The room suddenly began to spin. She gripped the podium with something considerably less than her normal strength. "Whoops. It's spurdling now. Blenk."

Lon jumped back into the room in time to catch her in his arms. "Wooffle," she clearly told him as her eyes closed and her head fell against his chest.

Londo blinked a moment and then took in his silent audience. "I think it's time to take her home and tuck her into bed," he told them. "Good night."

Things would never be the same again.

Right now that seemed a very good thing.

Londo's face seemed so innocent when he slept, so free from care. Lina lay on her side watching him. A floater of dust kept trying to settle on his nose, just to rise in the air again. He snored ever so slightly and she smiled. This was married life.

She didn't want to wake him. He'd been at war for how many days? He'd come home to chaos. He must be exhausted. Worst of all, in the middle of last night when she'd come out of her doze, they'd only had time for a couple of kisses before he had to change her IV and then she'd conked out again on him.

Thank goodness for those diapers. Her brain was still asleep enough to make figuring time zones against what the clock showed her a problem, but likely she'd been out for about eighteen hours. Maybe twenty.

When she'd awakened not only had she heard his small snores, but those of the cats, tucked into their own little nooks all over the bedroom. He'd brought them all in. They didn't seem like they were starving, and she was willing to bet that a snug kitty door was already installed downstairs.

A beautiful new vase of roses sat on a small table to her side of the bed. Next to it was a note that said, "Forever." On the back of it was jotted "DON'T EVEN THINK OF GETTING UP."

It was late afternoon. Londo's guides told her he'd be out for at least another hour, so she eased out of bed, took a shower, and checked the ruby medallion that sat on top of Lon's dresser.

"Are you okay?" she whispered to it. "Would you like me to put you in sunlight? I could get some ocean water for you to soak in, or bury you." These were things you did to cleanse crystals. Lina wondered if a Galactic Guardian's ruby would like the same treatment.

It seemed to want the water, and at the image Lina clapped her hand over her mouth.

"Just a minute first," she told it, and together they ported across the world.

It was barely sunrise here. She hovered unevenly above the waters of the Black Sea. Now that she could port again, levitating was extremely difficult. The ruby offered to hold her up.

"That's okay, thanks," she told it. "I need you to find Ouroboros for me. Demi lost it somewhere around here, remember? Do you know where it is? Can you find it?"

A reddened image of the battle appeared in midair before her. There were Granger and Demi battling, Ouroboros whirling past Granger, wrapped around the giant red axe. It had fallen into the ocean– there. The image hovered above an ocean swell.

Now what? Tides and currents must have carried it away. Lina reached for her inner white light and asked some water devas if they had seen it. They pointed east. Lina let the wind blow her, wobbling her way after the trail.

"Somewhere around here, I think," she told the ruby. "Can you find it now?"

A tracking screen like sonar appeared in the air: technology of the Galactic Brigade. It showed levels below them, fanning out, blinking as areas were searched and discarded. One screen lit up. A coiled outline showed on it: Ouroboros!

"Great!" Lina exclaimed. "Now what? Can you, um, part the ocean down to it, just so I can see it?"

Quicker than a blink, the air turned rubine and the sea under them became the color of blood, sloshing unnaturally. "Easy," Lina cautioned. "Let's not cause any tidal waves. Leave the spectacle to Cecil B. DeMille." Still the sea groaned as it opened, caught between gravity matrices, a narrow wedge of air slicing down and down and–

"There it is!" Lina exclaimed as she could see through the red light. The snakeskin still sparked, which helped her locate it. She ported it above herself and caught one end, wrapping it as she would a garden hose. "Hey!" This hose had a life of its own. It fought her. "Hey!" Lina yelled again. "Settle down! Whoa– Easy! I'm trying to rescue you!"

But Ouroboros struggled against her, whipping her back and forth in a tug of war, lightnings crackling all around. Lina held on for dear life. Underneath her the ocean slapped itself shut with a clap of thunder. Pocketed air burbled forth in multiple pops and then an enormous belch. "Excuse you!" Lina gritted her teeth against the bucking rope. "Oh hell, let's just get out of here!"

She ported to an elegant hallway in the Scythian royal palace and let Ouroboros drop to the ground. It slithered upon itself, then reared into the air like a snake, slashing at her. "Hello!" Lina cried as she hastily retreated. "Anybody home? Help!"

Lina almost stumbled as she back-stepped, but then she heard the sound of running on the marble floors. Princess Juno rounded a corner at top speed.

"Ouroboros!" Juno exclaimed as she skidded to a stop. She had eyes only for the snakeskin.

"I was trying to return it," Lina told the princess. "I don't think it wants to be returned."

Juno gave her a quick glance before returning her attention to the problem at hand. "Ouroboros! Here!" She patted her hip and stepped determinedly toward the coiling rope. The rope didn't want to come. It stood up high on its own coil and struck at her.

Almost as fast as Lina could see, Juno reached out and grasped the snake by its head, then grabbed an arm's length beyond. Slowly she began to wind it up, heaving on it, stopping every so often to catch her breath.

"Very good, Ouroboros," she muttered through strangled teeth. "Good Ouroboros." The muscles of her arms worked hard as the last of Ouroboros looped into a tight mass. Seat dripped from her brow as Juno took the final loop and drew it around her waist, then secured the rest of the rope with it.

"Ouroboros is tamed again," she said with a satisfied smile. "Thank you for bringing it home, Speaker."

"You're very welcome." A little girl– well, a teenager– had tamed that bronco bull of a snake! Lina tried not to blink in amazement. On TV she'd seen Ouroboros pull down semis, even planes, but it couldn't best this Scythian princess. "You're also quite impressive."

Juno gave her an impish grin. "I've always wanted to try my hand at Ouroboros," she admitted. "Demi would never let me near it. She said…" Juno's face twisted. "Is she truly going to be all right? Mother said–"

"She is." Lina hugged the girl, who hugged her back with enormous strength. "She's going to need recuperation time, maybe a long one, and she's going to need to see some good psychiatrists, too. Your people have those, don't they?"

"We do." Otrera's voice came from behind her, and they both turned. "Tamed Ouroboros, have you, daughter?" she smiled. "Demi said it wouldn't be long before you'd have the skill. Yes, Lina, we have medical facilities here that are just as good in mystical healing as the more scientific ones in the outlying world."

Lina breathed a sigh of relief. "Good. I feel better knowing that Demi can recover at home. She saved my life. There's no way I can ever begin to–"

Otrera nodded. "And you saved hers."

"If you want to pack some luggage, I'm awake enough that I can port you to Sarastor. Lon can get permission for you to stay in our apartment there. But–"

"They have explained that there won't be a bed to sit by for another two weeks," Otrera told her. Her pained eyes belied her calm expression. "At that point the Mega-Legion will provide us with transport and lodging. But thank you."

The queen straightened her shoulders. "And thank you for returning Ouroboros, Speaker. That part of my sister's legacy remains with us now. I won't have to break the bad news of its loss to her."

She patted the rope at her daughter's side and it seemed to relax. "Control it but respect it," she instructed as she knelt next to the two. "Be firm but gentle also." Otrera looked up at Lina. "I have had the occasion to use Ouroboros myself. It's a magnificent creature."

"Does this mean I can sub for Demi?" Juno asked hopefully.

The queen frowned as she stood. "Ouroboros' keeper would be the logical successor while Demi recuperates."

"Oh boy!"

"We'll see. It would have to be on a very limited basis, young lady. If I decide you will, it will consist of a learning curve; no earth-shaking missions. We'll talk about this later tonight. Lina, would you like some tea? And oh–" the queen produced Lina's two letters from her pocket. "I found these in your room. I thought you might like to have them back. Unread."

Lina took them quickly. "Thank you," she said.

"Isn't it odd," the queen mused, "that you would write two letters. One to your husband, that's understandable. The other not to the rest of your family, to your mother or father, but to your partner in the Three Worlds." The queen tapped her chin with two fingers.

"Tell me, Lina, is he as handsome as Valiant?"

Lina paused. "I thought you had access to interstellar TV. Surely you must have seen Neutrino."

"But I wouldn't be able to get my next question about him answered."

Lina knew she shouldn't ask what that would be, so she didn't. But the queen asked anyway.

"How do they compare in bed?"

"You do love to ask personal questions, your majesty."

"Call me Trery. Forgive me, but I pry to liven my days. Life here can be quite humdrum, unlike the life you're just beginning. With things as they are now, you must be…?"

"Very content, Trery. I should be getting on my way. Jae is due home in a few hours, I think. Londo and I *both* have to get ready."

"Oh." The queen's mouth dropped open. "Why… why, you've given me an entirely different angle to think about. Oh my, yes. We'll talk again, Lina, of many things."

Jae hopped in place to rid himself of excess nervous energy. Four minutes to go. He'd limbered up with stretching and reviewed yet again Legion records on known battle maneuvers of the Galactic Brigade. He'd practiced his cho-klain moves for three hours straight. He'd meditated to calm himself. Now he'd stretched again and felt ready to meet this Galactic Guardian, even if he should be waiting just outside the hatch when Jae regained normal space.

If anyone wanted to harm Lina, they'd have to do it over his dead body. And Neutrino was notoriously difficult to kill.

Outside the low moon shone wide ribbons on the snowy mountain vista. Londo lit a fire in the bedroom fireplace. He adjusted the furniture they'd placed here: a love seat, chair, and hassock from his place. Lina finished setting the small table with hors d'oeuvres, arranging some candles in the mix. Lina's afghan draped over the back of the small sofa. One of his smaller Persian rugs covered the unfinished floor. Lina's candles were placed in every empty nook that wasn't accessible to cats.

The queen-sized bed had suffered fatal injury hours before, once Londo had awakened and Lina formally welcomed him back home. Its pieces had regretfully been assigned to the trash, but Lon's king-size bed from Montreal had replaced it in here, a temporary measure that increased the elegance of the unfinished area.

He'd tucked her into it twice already, insisting that she nap.

Lina stopped to admire the view outside and inside. They had both changed to the formal wear they'd worn in Montreal. Londo was absolutely irresistible. "Has there ever been a time or place as magical as this?" Lina asked. She leaned her head on his shoulder, her arms around his waist. How lovely to have someone looking after her!

"Every place is magical when you're there," he said as his kissed her forehead. "Ah, he's arrived."

Argh, feedback. Lina! Lina!! Arggh, Lina! Ah, shards!

Here, Jae! Londo's here, too. All clear. Everything's okay. Take a minute to get over the post-hyperspace feedback.

She ported him in, and before she could even react to his presence, he dropped his duffle bag and took her in a tight hug which became a frantic kiss and then a longer, more leisurely one.

You're alive, you're here...

The worry swept out of him like a tide as he pressed her to himself. He eased back to look at her. "Are you all right? Great *grigach,* look at that bruise." His thumb traced the outline of what had once been a handprint on her neck. "How long has it been healing? Are you okay?"

"I'm fine. I'm perfect now that you're here. Oh, Jae!" She enfolded him in her arms again. Now Starhaven was truly home.

Jae took a deep breath and turned to see Lon. With one hand extended, he invited him to join their embrace. "Thank the universe you're here," Jae said. Lina eased away so they could welcome each other as thoroughly as she and Jae had.

Three long kisses later, Jae stepped back. "I need something," he said.

Londo scooped him up to take him downstairs and Lina followed in her own way. The wall down here that Londo had slammed Granger partially through– Lon placed Jae in front of it.

"Go to it," Londo invited.

Jae slammed his fist into the wallboard, making a hole. Then he hit it again. And again.

He stood there staring at the damage. "Good enough?" Londo asked.

"Yeah. Yeah, just needed to get rid of some energy. Thanks."

Lina ported them back upstairs as Jae rested his cheek against the top of Lon's head and closed his eyes. Then he backed away a step to look at the two of them in their obviously formal Terran wear. "It must have been a hell of a fight," he said. Lina was covered with almost-healed bruises and she wore an arm bandage in familiar Legion Med configuration. "You're sure you're all right? I see Lon picked out the dress."

"Like it?" Lina asked. She wiggled her shoulders coquettishly.

Jae took her into his arms again. "I like who's inside it just fine," he said as he moved in to receive one of her glorious 'hello' kisses. They made him tingle down to his toenails, happy to be there. Another part of him in particular wanted to welcome her right back.

"Thanks for rushing to my rescue, Jae," she said softly. "My knight in shining armor."

"Whatever the orb that means," Jae replied, although he could sense the general meaning. "Well, Lon, tell me about the fight."

Lon caught Jae's offered hand. "I missed it," he said. "Wasn't here."

"What?"

"I was off fighting Yanist-Glory's invasion troops a dozen systems over," Lon reported.

"Then how–"

"Neutrino! Where are you?!" Stoan's voice came out of Jae's Legion ring.

34

"I'm here, Commander," Jae reported. He glanced about the room. Candles. Moonlight. Bed. "Earth. At Starhaven, I think."

Lon nodded.

Lon, we're going to need a new bed. I don't want to sleep all cramped up. Great orb, look at that view! "My mission here was an emergency, so I was checking the situation status. All clear."

"A few of us are still on Earth, at the ParaNet's orbital station. We need to be getting back so we can coordinate from Headquarters. You can come with us. A ship's due to arrive here in a half-hour."

They could hear a voice in the background, but it wasn't clear.

"*Grigach,*" Jae said. "Are we going to have a Legion meeting by ring communicator? Lina, why don't you just port every Legionnaire here?"

"Not here," Lon said quickly. "Living room."

Jae glanced around at the candles and gave a half-smile. "Give us a minute," he said into the ring. It beeped to show that communications were turned off.

Lina reached for a tissue to wipe a smear of her lipstick off Jae's mouth. "Stoan's ordered you and me to stay clear of each other when you're on Legion business," she told him.

"When did this happen?" Lon demanded.

"When he was here, before you all took off for god knows where. He said he'd talk to you both about it."

"Shards and splinters," Jae muttered as they flew downstairs to the living room. Now Jae looked around with lively interest. Everything was in an early state of construction. He certainly hoped that the wobbly steps between stories were temporary. Ember bounded out of the shadows to greet him, and he bent down to pet her. The rest of the cats were locked in the east wing for the night. "Just on Legion business?"

"That was a compromise," Lina told him. "He wanted the Three Worlds to appear always as either three or individuals."

"He can't have any say in Three Worlds."

"Damned straight," Lon agreed. "You and I'll sit down with him—"

"Oh, Lon, how often am I going to be in on Legion business?" Lina asked. "Almost never. So this ten-foot-pole rule won't come into play. Let's just leave it, all right?"

"At least until Stoan comes around." Jae shrugged his shoulders. He picked up the cat and she wrapped one paw around his neck, allowing him to rub an ear.

"Is he ever?" Lina asked. She stood at the opposite side of the room from Jae, with Londo halfway between them. "Ready?" The men nodded as she got a mental picture from Wiley, and suddenly Wilder, Stoan, Chimrin, Andri and Erik stood in their living room. The three who had never been there took in their new surroundings.

Conversation switched to Panlingua. The newly-arrived Legionnaires stared at Lina and Lon's formal clothes, so different from Lon's usual. "We just got in from a late dinner," Lon lied.

Stoan looked from Jae to Lina, then to Lon. All were scowling faintly at him, and he gave them a pleasant smile. "Good evening, Starharts… and Jae. I just wanted to gather the group that's going back to Sarastor so we can take one ship."

"A ship?!" Erik exclaimed. "Excuse me, Commander, but why take a ship, when Lina's here? We can be back in a few minutes."

"It does seem unnecessary," Wilder added. "I recommend we set our ship on automatic and let it waste its time getting back. Me, I have better things to do.

Legion HQ's seriously understaffed right now until everyone returns from De-seed." He seemed almost to be urging Stoan. "It'd be for the good of the Legion if we took the teleportation route."

"I'll be teleporting back to Aldierra," Jae began, but Lon interrupted.

"We'd rather you didn't."

Jae looked at him.

"We've got things to do tomorrow. And we have to go to Aum in a week or so."

"Aum?!"

"I need to return a ruby," Lina said from across the room. She tipped her glass baking dish so Jae could see the great red-stoned ruby that sat within. It had been soaking up sunshine in seawater all day, and glowed contentedly.

"Great orb," Jae breathed. "What the *kick* happened here? How'd you get a Guard's ruby from him?"

"Let's just say that Paul Granger, former Galactic Guardian of the Terran sector, is in the hospital tonight under lock and key," Lon explained. "That's his ruby. Despite us stripping her powers from her, Lina defeated him. Perhaps next time, Stoan, you take a hard re-think before you start making orders. I won't stand for–"

Subcommander Andri had been watching them all, only her eyes moving. "There won't be a next time," she said quietly. "Lina's passed all of Stoan's tests for her. Some of us have directly experienced mind control in the past few days. We all know that she's not guilty of that. We should vote on formal security clearance for her at our next meeting. I suspect Lina would like all the suspicion put to rest."

"We need to approve Legion security forces for our tour at that meeting, too," Londo told them.

Stoan put his fists on his waist. "Tour? A honeymoon with Legion security?"

"No. Lina wants to teach others how to get rid of hooks. I told her the best way to do that was a fast tour of the Unaffiliated Worlds on the Empire's bound-aries. We port from world to world and Lina gives classes. We eliminate the threat of mind control forever."

Stoan just stood there. To his credit, he seemed shaken.

"Valiant, sir," Erik choked. "Do you have any idea how long people have wanted to put the threat of mind control behind them?"

Londo nodded.

Chimrin said, "You have to bring Tishan in on this, Lon. If you don't, you'll make a terrible enemy."

"Tishan?" Londo rubbed his nose at that.

"How many years are you going to be teaching?" Andri asked Lina. "They'll exhaust you. Everyone will want to learn."

Lina shook her head. "I teach a few and they teach a few and they teach a few. Eventually everyone knows."

"It will take too much time," Wilder said. "Assassins will eliminate the few who know before they can teach anyone else."

Jae settled on the back of the couch that faced the large fireplace. "Wait a minute," he told the group. "If I understand this, Lina really can follow through on her claims that she can counter mind control. Is that true?"

"Believe me, Jae," Erik said, rolling his eyes. "You don't want to be controlled. It is not a pleasant experience."

Jae nodded. "All right. Lina can't teach others fast enough. The Tishana need to be involved or there'll be shards to pay down the road. How about you deputizing a squad of Tishana as teachers to assist you, Lie?"

"I don't want this to become classified information," Lina declared. "Those Tishana want to keep all knowledge to themselves. No offense meant, Chimrin."

"None taken." The ex-commander waved off the statement.

Lina continued. "What if I took some of my friends along to teach? And if we have to have Tishana, then they can help– but they've got to be part of the team, not just Tishana Thought Police. They've got to be there to spread the word."

"Your friends?" Stoan asked.

"The Wednesday Evening Psychic Bowling League," Lon hazarded. "Yes, that would work if they're really up to the job, *chérie.*"

"Of course they are. We do it all the time. Well, on a minor scale. I started fooling around with this technique when we were all in Sue's class. It's changed a bit since then. They already know how to balance chakras and such. I can teach them ninety percent of the rest in fifteen minutes."

Londo nodded at Stoan. "We want Legion security. If the border worlds are secured, so is the Affiliated Systems' most vulnerable side."

Stoan clasped his hands behind his back and paced in a circle behind the couch as he considered. "Starhart," he finally said, "if you want Legion security, you have to open this to Affiliated Systems participants. The technique gets spread to the AffSys as well."

"Done," Londo said quickly.

"And I want every last Legionnaire to learn this."

"Yes, Commander."

"If we can make a tape," Lina said, "we can distribute it as well. No security anything on the tape."

Stoan chewed his cheek and then nodded. "No security. Open to anyone who wants to see it."

"How much is this going to cost us?" Lina asked Londo.

"Kitten, they'll be paying us for the privilege."

"I repeat, Londo, we need another bed." Jae reached for another nacho.

Lina shooed Bran away from the cheese cubes. Somehow the cats had all gotten out of their confinement. Katie and Fafhrd were both snoozing on the hearth. Ember had one paw on Jae's thigh, looking hopefully at the nacho.

The rest of the Legionnaires had been ported to Sarastor, leaving them in peace.

"We were waiting for you," Lina told him. "We'll go shopping for one. Tomorrow, tonight, whenever you want."

"Tomorrow," Londo said, pouring champagne for them all. "Tonight we have things to discuss." He passed out the glasses, and Lina took a seat on a cushion on the hearth. Jae dropped his cape onto the rug. He picked through crackers and vegetables, ignoring the joined chopsticks there for his use. Using his fingers in the barbaric way, he set everything on a plate for himself. Then he sat on the floor next to Lina,

The flames were truly fire and not a fakery. The wood smelled like it was burning. Londo pulled the hassock next to Jae and sat.

"Jae," Londo began, "Lina and I have been married now for, what, a few weeks now, mostly not together. And we both find that although our marriage is complete, it is at the same time missing a major piece. Join us in a Triune marriage. I love you, Jaeson Rheoboth Rallene. You've been my truest friend, there for me through thick and thin. You've gone out of your way to help me and listen to me through all these years. You're always surprising me, and I can't imagine life without you. We're the ultimate team. Our love has lasted over a decade now. You know how I feel about you. I love you now even deeper than I ever thought I could, and I know I'll love you forever. Please marry me."

"I love you, Jae," Lina said softly. "Somehow it happened with you, just as it did between Lon and me, but differently. You were a friend, and suddenly you were so much more than that. You helped me, you made me your friend when you didn't have to. You listened to me and made fun of me and you petted my cats. You came to my rescue as fast as Londo would have if he had known the danger."

Jae glanced at Lon, who sat tensely as if awaiting mission orders. Then he turned back to Lina.

She said, "In all the illusion of the world, only love is real."

"Ah," Jae murmured. Terrans knew this, too. He didn't notice Londo relaxing now, confident that Lina had caught Jae from a side that he couldn't.

She touched Jae's jaw. "I don't want to be just friends any more. I want you to marry me so we can be more than friends forever. I want to help you to see the spark of God that lies within yourself. I want to love you as only a wife can. Please say you'll marry me."

Jae smiled softly as he wiped a tear from her cheek with his thumb, but then he turned to stare at the fire. After a while he said, "I need to know a few things." He looked up at Lina. "Children."

Lina sat and thought about the future while Jae offered Ember a chunk of cheese.

Londo took Lina's hand. "You promised me two children," he told her.

"Yes. Two. With others to be negotiated. I take it we're negotiating now?"

"I give up my second one," Londo declared quietly, glancing at Jae. "One for me and one for Jae."

Jae's mouth opened in surprise.

Lina's mouth was busy with her chewing on her own lower lip. She said, "We'll revisit this. Definitely one child for Jae, but we have to set up this Three Worlds thing and get it going, so there won't be any children in the near future. But I will bear no bastards. Kids come within a legal marriage, not out of it. I want to revisit this secrecy pact."

"And I want to talk about fidelity," Lon added. Jae had such a history…

A deep, eerie wail drifted through the air.

"Moose!" Lina called. "We're up here, Moosie! I was wondering where he'd got to. I bet you he's lost. Let me call him; he's shy in his own way. Until he's not."

She called again. Within a minute the burly black cat skidded into the room, looking around suspiciously until he spotted the other cats and Lina. And the strangers. He began to back out. But when he saw the food, he galloped in to jump on the table. Lina had to rescue their snacks.

"Where's the other one?" Lon asked. "Obiobiobi? Wait, there's another– where's Fat Cat?" He pointed to Katie on the hearth. "Isn't that Fat Cat there?"

"You're getting your Fat Cats mixed up," Lina pouted. "Learn their names or face my wrath. Obi and Molly are hiding under the bed. Strange places scare them."

"I know the feeling," Jae said as he added, "Lon shouldn't be rude to the cats" to his list of negotiations he was recording on his padd. He tapped the screen. "Security," he said, and his eyes slid to Lina.

"You make this place impervion, and I'll set up a security corridor," Londo promised. "No air traffic, no traffic of any kind allowed within the bounds of Starhaven. I'll hire our own squadron of guards just to patrol the perimeter."

"I want Sarastoran protective devices as well," Jae insisted.

"Of course. Easy enough to get."

"How about a kol-vanasche?" Lina piped up.

"Forbidden technology," Lon replied. "Sorry, Kitten."

"How come the cleaning equipment is forbidden, but the stuff that can blow people up isn't?"

"I want Lina taking defensive lessons from Kuttr."

Lina blinked. "Whatever for? I can port out."

"You can't port when you're upset, *chérie*," Londo pointed out. He nodded at Jae. "I agree. We'll ask Kuttr. If we can't get him, we'll get someone on staff."

"Kuttr will do this for me," Jae assured him, and the discussions went on late into the night.

"I'm not sure I understand," Dr. Gorgeon said as she checked the healed burns on Lina's arm.

"I want you to record this for Demi to see when she wakes up," Lina told her. They were in the medical section of Legion HQ. Lina flipped the camera into the air with her good hand, and below it a communications screen flared to life. "Are we coming through okay, Londo?"

"Loud and clear, kitten. Absolutely no one else is to see this, Gorgeon. This is Need to Know security."

"Yes sir, Valiant."

"His name is Londo. And hers is Riz, dear. I insisted on having a guest of my own this time, so that's you, Riz," Lina said as she adjusted the screen for Riz to see better. "And we all picked Demi. I wish you could attend in person, but I understand that you're needed here. Oh, it's the first day of Spring. What a perfect date. I'm not nervous at all. Do I look okay?"

The orange-skinned doctor studied Lina. Her gown– make that gowns– were shockingly strapless, the undergown a gray satin, the belled overgown in white lace made up of those Three Worlds symbols and cascading in back to form a long train. A halo of pink and white flowers rested on her upswept hair, and Lina's green eyes glowed in anticipation.

"You look quite the beautiful bride," Riz smiled. "Glad we could get rid of those bruises in time. Congratulations. I'm not sure I understand why you have to do this again. Is it Terran tradition?"

Lina beamed. "I feel like a bride, not like the first time; that happened too fast. We'll start in about twenty minutes, I think. I'm coming, Londo!" And with that, she disappeared.

Riz settled back at her desk to read reports on the latest casualties to arrive from Deseed, and to watch the screen out of the corners of her eyes.

"Are they ready yet?" Lina asked from final placements of the flower pots around the podium. She'd hot-glued white satin and masses of ribbons to it, tied a bouquet in front, and it looked quite striking. Lon had rented some lovely candelabra that now arched behind it. Everywhere they could find a space, they'd put the pots and pots of flowers. These were forced azaleas for the most part, in shades of pink and white. They could plant them in the yard after they were through here. Right now some of them sat on pedestals. Lina prayed the cats wouldn't jump up and send them crashing.

Jae had set up the chairs here in the marbled entrance rotunda. Hundreds of yards of fabric cascaded from the balcony above, successfully hiding all the construction with tasteful grace– well, maybe it was the tiniest bit ostentatious– and creating a snug, sun-drenched wedding chapel.

Two of the chairs were taken with cats, snoozing away despite the hubbub, and instead of shooing them off, Jae just went to investigate more chairs amid Londo's things.

"Londo!" Lina cried again. He hovered high above the floor in starched shirt and not-so-starched briefs with dark socks, taking a hydraulic nailer to the final trim for these windows.

"I'll be done in a minute!" he yelled back amid *pthoom, pthoom, pthoom* in a headache-producing flurry of activity. He glided back twenty feet above the flooring, and judged the results.

"This is being taped for Demi!" Lina reminded him and Londo turned to the screen looking into Riz's office, seeing that the doctor wasn't paying him any mind.

"She'll be wearing less than I am when she sees this. *Salut,* Demi! Hope you're feeling well. It won't be long now, Riz. There's the signal, Lina."

"You go get dressed first. I'm not having guests see you like that!"

"*Mais oui,* Lina love." He flew off.

One by one the guests were ported in. Wiley wasn't in his lab coat uniform. Lina had been adamant about that. Instead he showed up in a Terran-style morning coat, complete with striped cravat, and bowed to her as Jae laughed at him.

Jae of course was in the outfit the Three Worlds had provided him for the first wedding: a comfortable, layered bit of gray trousers tied at his ankles with matching slippers, a long-sleeved shirt under a looser tunic. Andri came in what she'd worn to the original wedding: a knee-length tunic over a bodysuit, narsaws in her short pink hair. She made a fuss over Wiley's outfit, and Lina was extremely pleased when Wiley took Andri's arm and steered her to seats front and center.

Damon was next, arriving through Lina instead of ParaNet transporter services. They did want to keep this secret, after all. He was so sharply suited, so perfectly *GQ,* that Lina bit her lip. She was *not* going to tell him that he should have so much taste when it came to his antennaed costume as Dragonlord! That wouldn't be polite at all.

Damon and the others talked quietly as Chimrin arrived, dressed in a bright red jumpsuit with black trim and diamond jewelry. It was quite flashy, something that Lina would never have guessed she'd be the type to wear. Wiley got up from his chair and bowed to her grandly even as Chim made some rude comments about his own choice of clothing. He escorted her to her chair. "These are traditional Terran manners," he told her. "Apparently women on Earth are too stupid to know the way to their seats."

"I heard that!" Lina barked. "Londo! Are you coming sometime today?" She tipped her head to the side for a moment and announced, "He's working on his *hair.*"

"It'll be another half-hour, then," Chim told the group sourly.

"Kitty, kitty, kitties!" Lina called. She whistled, and those cats who had abandoned the stranger-populated room returned suspiciously, joined by their brothers and sisters. "You cats are invited, too. You're from the bride's side," Lina said, and produced a plate of catfood to ensure that some at least would remain. Molly had already been bothering the guests, rubbing up against them and demanding to be cooed at– although these off-worlders didn't know how to coo to a cat.

Lina showed Chim what Molly wanted. The three Legionnaires went to work fussing over the chubby orange showoff until she was satisfied that her perfection was sufficiently acknowledged. She then plopped down in a splash of sunshine to snooze.

"I hate to say it," Damon said of the scrawny black cat lying in the chair next to his. It hadn't moved even at the whistle. "But…"

"She's not dead, she's just old. Let her sleep," Lina instructed. "Jae?"

He reappeared from behind some silk hangings. "Sound balance, check," he reported, and then bellowed. "Lon-DO! Get your ass down here! We'll start without you, I swear it!" He turned to the crowd. "Everyone on best behavior now. Lina?"

Two minutes later Admiral Bracken stood before them, his chest a marvel of medals and finery. He bowed to everyone as he was introduced, and looked curiously at the cats.

"Are these for the wedding feast?" he asked, his translator hanging next to him.

"These are pets," Damon explained, as Jae and Lina had disappeared behind the draperies. "I doubt if Lina would like it if you even thought of eating them." Bracken nodded gravely and took his seat.

The "Venus" movement from Holst's *The Planets* began so softly almost no one noticed. Then Jae emerged from the drapery with his minister's stole around his neck to take his place at the podium.

"Here we go again," he smiled at his audience, nodding at Riz' screen. The doctor sat alert to the proceedings. "As we told all of you, there was a minor mistake made during the first ceremony of the wedding of the Starharts. We are gathered here today to rectify that and celebrate this deepest of loves that has bloomed in the past few weeks."

"I did some research on the subject this afternoon," Wiley announced from the audience, "and I didn't see any mistakes. Where is Hal, by the way?"

Jae regarded his longtime friend. "It is quite permissible for the audience to take part in Feithi ceremonies," he said frostily, "but it is not polite to be rude. Let us proceed. Londo and Lina? Are you ready?"

Both wearing excited smiles, the two stepped out hand-in-hand from behind the drapery. Londo's hair was perfect, as was his gray and white Napoleonic wedding costume with high-collared jacket and tight silk pants that tucked into boots. But as Lina's white lace train slithered across the marble floor, young Bran pounced on it.

Lina came to a halt. "Oh no. No, Bwan-Bwan! That's not a toy, Bwannie! Get off! Get off, baby!"

Londo reached down and disconnected the cat from the train. Lina cautiously began to walk again, and again the cat pounced.

They handed the squirming cat to Wiley, who gingerly held him until the cat lost interest in the proceedings.

Jae checked the room to see that all was in order. Then he said:

"As a minister of Uriel, I officially proclaim the marriage of Londo Rand Starhart and Carolina O'Kelly Starhart... annulled."

He slammed a fist into his open palm. The vibrations from a great, invisible gong seemed to shake the room. Even Fafhrd stirred at it.

"What?" Damon and Andri asked at the same time, in different languages.

"Their slate is wiped clean. We begin again, a fresh start. Let the cosmos so witness."

With that, Jae reiterated his officiating speech of the first wedding, but kept the frou-frouery he'd done then out of this one. A white-draped table next to the podium held a jug of wine and wineglass, bitter herbs, sour wafers, and salt which would be tasted in turn as symbols of the different fortunes of life running in cycles that must be faced together now.

With instrumental music from the speakers, Lina sang to Londo a different song from before, an ancient French song of love that permeated the innermost crevices of her soul, and Londo sang Lina a new American song about how love was not enough to describe how he felt about her. They took their vows, exchanged rings, and kissed a long, heartfelt kiss.

The Sarastorans in the audience familiar with the ceremony waited for Jae to ask who witnessed this marriage, but the line never came. Instead, Jae took off his stole. He turned to Wiley. "This is the part we didn't do right the first time," he said.

None of Wiley's minds understood, even as one scratched the head of the dozing cat in his arms.

Lina accepted the stole from Jae and moved behind the podium as Jae took his place beside Londo, who had positioned himself to be to Jae's left.

"We three have a directive to keep the traditions and dreams of Feith alive," Lina announced to the audience. "With the greatest joy we do so. Jaeson Rheoboth Rallene and Londo Falcon Rand stand before us—"

"Ah," Wiley said before he knew he'd said it out loud.

"Yes?" Lina blinked expectantly at him.

Might as well ask. "Ah." It couldn't be, though. Surely they didn't… Hadn't he warned Jae about Prisoner Watch Syndrome! One of his minds bulled ahead. "May I assume that this is a Feithi dual-Triune?"

Lina smiled kindly at him. "You could assume that, but you'd be wrong," she told him, and went on with her lecture. She told the audience of an unfulfilled love that had started well over a decade ago, that had grown and been tested through the years and now could be celebrated in all ways. She didn't look over to Damon, whose mouth hung open for much more than a moment as the import began to sink into his famous lightning-quick mind. Andri let out one syllable of surprise, but then was silent.

Lina repoured wine for Lon and Jae to drink and supervised them dipping a finger into the salt and placing it on the tips of each other's tongues, of eating the bitter herbs and then the sour wafers, and back to the wine again.

Londo sang to Jae in French and Jae almost cried, holding himself still with great effort. And then Jae sang to Londo in English, telling him how long he'd hungered for his touch and needed his love. They exchanged rings. Londo actually blushed and hesitated only a moment before they kissed before their guests. Sniffling with happiness, Lina blew her nose.

Now it was Londo's turn to take on the mantle of priest. "I am authorized as a brand-new priest of Uriel," he announced, and then added in a stage whisper to Wiley, "We told you it wasn't a dual-Triune."

"Now I know why Hal wasn't invited," Wiley returned. "A Triune. A Feithi Triune! Do you have any idea what a complete Triune involves?"

"They do, Wilder," Chimrin retorted, giving Wiley a start. "Be quiet. This is their wedding, not yours."

Jae took Lina's hand and stepped up to the front of the podium. Londo spoke to them of possession and its dangers, of the balancing of egos and the patience that they would all need in the coming years.

"Isn't he a wonderful speaker?" Lina asked Jae.

"He always has been. Now let him finish."

They tasted the wine and went the round of fate. Lina sang to Jae in Feithi and this time he really did weep openly. That triggered tears on her part that almost– but not quite– interrupted her love song. Then Jae sang to her in English about the springtime of love that would always be theirs.

They took their vows: "I promise to love and cherish you in heart, mind and body through the cycles of time and fortune's wheel. I promise to help you face the challenges of life, to aid you in leaving the universe a better place for having been here, and to better enable you to see the spark of God that lies within you."

They exchanged rings, completing the double rings that the Three Worlds had gifted them: "This ring is a material symbol of my vows to you and commitment to any children resulting from our union in this lifetime. Wear it and remember."

Jae turned to the audience. "The line of Feith will continue," he announced. "It will go through me to my child or children, but it will also continue through my husband and my wife and their children. We are one now. If we all are not strictly Feithi, then we are of Feith. We will return the balance to the universe that was missing." In the silence of the rotunda he kissed Lina.

Londo stepped forward to join hands with his spouses as new music rose from speakers around the room. It was a traditional Feithi wedding song:

Our hands are now entwined, Lon sang.

Jae sang, *Our hearts join together.*

Lina joined in: *Creation notes our vows…*

They harmonized to finish with, *Together our souls soar beyond forever.*

Lina shooed the cats from the two-layered chocolate wedding cake loaded down with pink and white icing roses. She laughed, so happy, and Londo and Jae were laughing too. At their happiness, at their guests' surprise, at the Admiral who wasn't surprised at all… until he found out that this wedding meant that Londo and Jae truly loved each other as well and planned to have as much marital contact with each other as they would with Lina.

"It's… blasphemous," Bracken confided in Wiley.

Wiley shrugged. "Perhaps blasphemy is overstating the situation, Admiral," he said. "Surprising. Quite the scandal."

"Nonsense." Riz said. Lina had ported her away from her patients for a few minutes so she could have some cake and champagne. "It's about time someone stepped up and did something like this. I'm rather disappointed that Valiant's not going public."

"He will in time," Wiley confided. "I'd be willing to bet money on it."

"It will be a very long time," Londo said as he passed by with drink refills.

"He's married Lina," Andri said even as he left. "He'll have to come out soon. I can already see that he's catching some of her honesty."

"I agree," Wiley said.

The Admiral mulled the situation over. "I think it would be best if they didn't announce this part of it on Aldierra," he said slowly. "The Speaker is almost a goddess to the people of our world. If her husbands were to say that they… love each other…" He shook his head. "It would cause culture-wide repercussions. It would shake the entire world's foundations."

"More than they have been already, Admiral?" Andri asked. "I'd say all three worlds are going to be shaken with this, but perhaps not in a bad way. Have some faith in your people."

"Hm," was all Bracken would say before he returned to the buffet table. Wiley followed him, asking questions about the culture of his world.

The newlyweds made the rounds of their guests. Lon was in charge of drinks and Lina of food; both were determined that Jae would not have to lift a finger for the reception that focused on him. After a few drinks his laugh degenerated into the rat-tat-tat machine gun bray that signaled his extreme enjoyment. Lina hugged him. Maybe someday that sound might grate, but for her right now it meant that Jae was happy, and thus was sublime music. Jae's happiness was the most important thing in the world. Anything for Jae.

Everyone looked up when Katie climbed one of the drapes hanging from the balcony. Her mouth opened wide into a kitty-grin even as she held on tightly when the material slipped, swinging her all the way across the rotunda. Jae rescued her, but she climbed right back up, perhaps hoping for another ride.

Lina showed her ring to Andri. "It was what the Worlds wanted from the beginning," she said. "See? It splits into two, one for Londo and one for Jae. They knew. They managed it so we all met. They think they're so smart! They're sitting around gloating now. Yes, I'm talking about *you!*" and she laughed at a comment the others couldn't hear.

Chimrin joined them and the two Legionnaires teased Lina about her new situation. Lina was shocked at how ribald their jokes were but... different cultures. She laughed because the jokes were funny, if embarrassing.

"Fantasizing about me?" From behind her, Londo wound his arm around Andri and gave her a peck on the cheek before he came around to Lina and gave her a satisfying kiss. "Girl talk," he said. "I love spying on it. You're all so devious and conniving."

"I beg your pardon?" Lina replied icily.

Lon put his arms around Lina and tipped her gently back and forth to the rhythm of the soundtrack playing. "Listen, An, you want to know what Jae's like in bed, I can tell you. I not only know myself now, but he's spent the last ten years regaling me about each and every one of his conquests. And he hasn't done the *entire* Legion, has he, Chim, hm? But I believe he's gone through all the zero-G's. It gets lonely on those far Outposts. If I remember right, he took on the entire Perfectionist team in one night." He squeezed Lina. "That's one of our intramural teams, *chérie.* They gave him a medal for it."

"I so do not want to hear this," Lina said as she leaned happily on her groom.

Andri took a sip of her champagne. "But Jae's going to be monogamous– or whatever it is when you have two– now?"

Lina patted Lon's arm, encased in his warmth. "All Jae ever really wanted was Londo and everything else was to try to make up for that."

"He's an over-achiever," Londo said.

"And we decided that our marriage is one that will adapt as needed," Lina said. "With three-way discussions and compromise."

"Ugh, I hate that word," Londo groaned. "Here, I'm neglecting my other guests. You ladies continue your gossip." He made his way over to the other group. The women watched him silently as he put his arms around Jae from behind and floated a few inches in the air so he could rest his chin on Jae's shoulder.

"So now Jae has his Londo… and you," Chim told Lina thoughtfully. "And Wiley and Dragonlord were brought in because they'd be the first to guess."

"The Admiral was brought to test the Aldierran waters?" Andri guessed, and Lina nodded. "Olympia… As a reward?"

"We owe her big time," Lina explained.

There was respectful silence for a few moments. "This cake would cost me ten demerits if I reported it," Andri said as she reached for a second slice.

"What cake is that?" Chim asked.

The edge of Andri's mouth twitched. "Chimrin was invited because obviously she already knew. I think Riz was invited so you could make a statement. I understand your viewpoint, Lina. Perhaps it *is* time to reassess how the Legion treats its staff. So why am I here? Or do I have to ask?"

"You're our official Legion ace in the hole," Lina said. "You've been so nice to Lon and me, and we sure as hell weren't going to invite Stoan. We needed someone high up who would know what was going on. We're going to make some mistakes; we don't want to harm the Legion in any way because of all this."

"Hm." Andri's eyes slid to Chim's. Chimrin had been commander before Andri had even joined the Legion. "It sounds like the slightest kind of blackmail as well."

"It's insurance to make sure we don't embarrass the organization," Lina assured Andri.

("We need Andri on our side, all the way," Londo had told the two of them this morning when they were figuring out the guest list. "An will pull strings for us if we need them. She's good people. And she's powerful; she's going to be the next commander." Jae had agreed.)

Chim regarded Lina. "It's also a sneak play on your part," she surmised. "One more person to know. You don't want to keep this secret, do you?"

"I promised them I would until they both give the go-ahead," Lina said. "We know we'll make mistakes. More people will find out over the coming months. Even Londo admits that."

"But you believe you can keep it from Hal. You believe you can keep it from the Legion and the media," Chim said. "I think I'm going to start a top-secret area of the Betting Boards. I don't think you can do it."

"Neither do I," Lina whispered, "but we're going to give it one hell of a shot. Heaven help us if it comes out before Londo wants."

"Heaven help you when Yency in Protocol finds out." Andri nodded, looking over at the other group. "Isn't Wiley rather dashing in those clothes? It's such a different look for him."

Lina gazed around at this hotel of a house, all unfinished, sitting lord knew where in the Rockies. At these friends whom she hadn't even known before all this.

At her husbands. Plural. A month ago she'd never met either. Her life had been uneventful. She'd hidden from the world.

Now newspapers from every continent were stacked on the breakfast table on the other side of this gigantic house. On each of them, above or below the fold depending on whether they led with the good-news story or the gory one, lay her picture. Many had her in both positions.

No, this wouldn't be a quiet marriage. This wouldn't be any kind of marriage like she'd ever imagined. None of them were entirely stable. Lon tended ever so slightly to the bossy side and Lina knew she had more than a bit of a stubborn streak to counter that. And Jae– oh dear, was he getting tipsy from the champagne? Poor Jae had so much to try to forget. But she'd help him. She'd help Londo, too.

Dishes were piling up. Dust was creeping into the room from where Katie had dislodged the hanging. Who was going to keep this place clean? How was she to take care of her cats when she had so much to do?

Admiral Bracken eyed Molly like she was slated for supper. What were Aldierrans like? How could the Chosen of the Three Worlds help them?

And when were these people going to leave so that the three of them could have a well-deserved and extremely anticipated wedding night? They needed to break in that big bed they'd bought this morning. (Lina amended that thought to make sure it was figurative. There were two lovely new beds, one in the master and one in the back-up master, and Jae had given both impervion structure.)

Okay, so she'd have to endure a little publicity. It wasn't like she was going to explode or anything in front of a camera. If people wanted to take pictures of Muttbutt, Muttbutt pictures would be what they'd get. She wouldn't give them any false expectations. Maybe they'd be satisfied.

With this Three Worlds business she had a big job to do. She'd have to juggle career and family. Lots of women did that. It wasn't a run-of-the-mill marriage, but it was probably going to be a lot more interesting than anyone else's she knew. After all, no one else had both Lon and Jae by their side.

On this first day of spring, Lina felt like Creation was drawing back a curtain she'd never noticed before, unveiling a vista that invited her to discover her true self, a future full of promise. Now she had family and new friends by her side to come with her. It beckoned with dazzling joy.

She could hardly wait to jump into it!

Art by Colleen Doran. Copyright the artist.

Don't miss the next chapter in the Three Worlds saga...

Mind Shift

Three Worlds vol. 5

by Carol A. Strickland

"**P**oisoned?!"

Carolina Starhart stared at the three Affiliated Systems Mega-Legionnaires who faced her, looking remarkably blasé about their findings at the food-laden break table set up in the back of this teaching amphitheater. How could they be so calm when she boiled with anger at the situation?

Poison! How *dare* anyone try to–

After all she'd been through these past three weeks. Damn whoever did this anyway! She'd been run through the universe's wringer, "treated" to tests that had left Demi– one of the most important heroes in Earth's history– encased in a stasis cocoon back on the AffSys capital world of Sarastor, waiting for the medical staff there to have time to crack the thing open and start piecing her back into a human being.

Aiko hadn't been that lucky. The legendary interstellar parahero had died in Londo's arms.

Lina had been unjustly arrested– twice!– and stashed for a short while into a hyperspace cell by Minzier here, the hulking blue Legionnaire whose left eyebrow merely twitched at her as he relayed the news. Minzier was a member of Jae's Alpha Team and a friend of Lon. Chimrin, the lavender-skinned woman with wary features and mind, always seemed unruffled; this was nothing unusual for her. She'd been Legion Commander when Lon and Jae had been in their early teens and new to the Legion, so she'd likely seen everything there was to be seen.

Lina didn't know who the third person was, other than that he was yet another Mega-Legionnaire she had to learn, clad in the same general type of clinging costume the others wore. Powers up the wazoo and used to hell breaking loose.

But Lina wasn't. After her experiences she deserved a little rest from the wrath of the chaos gods.

Oh, she hoped there weren't really chaos gods.

Then she realized what the three were telling her.

Someone had *poisoned* the food this other-planetary hotel had set out for the innocent people who were going to attend her seminar. The worlds of both the Affiliated Systems and unaffiliated planets wanted to learn how to get rid of Mind Control once and for all. She could teach them. Meanwhile the Yanist-Glory Empire was keen to extend its borders, and Mind Control was its favorite weapon to accomplish that.

So someone thought they'd just kill off everyone who learned how to counter them, tra-la.

Lina had been afraid down to her very cells at too many points these past weeks, but now she discovered she was still uncalloused enough that fear could rip its way through her. She could feel the blood begin to drain from her face. The room started to spin, just a trifle, before she set her jaw.

She was *not* going to faint in front of Legionnaires!

Four days ago she'd managed to faint in front of most of the cameras of Earth. In retrospect: mortifying! No, there would be no fainting now.

Especially since– wonder of wonders– they were looking to *her* to tell them what to do next. This was her project, not theirs. Chimrin squinted at her. Without reading her mind– or vice versa– Lina knew Chim was urging her on to her new position as Speaker of the Three Worlds.

"How'd this happen?" Lina asked the three. "I mean, the Legion was supposed to provide security for all this. Somebody miss a training day?"

"Some things can slip through," Chim told her in clipped syllables. "This is why you have to keep your guard up all the time, from all directions."

Chim was hounding the three of them: Lon, herself, and Jae, to take self-defense classes and more since their new relationship had changed everything. Here was something else to bolster that idea. Gah.

The third guy started to gather up the food in bags. "How're the drinks?" Lina asked.

"Poisoned." As if *of course*.

Coming soon! Find out more here:
http://www.carolastrickland.com/fiction/index.html

ABOUT THE AUTHOR

When you think of strong women and strange worlds, think Carol A. Strickland.

Although born in a small town in Illinois noted for its Nineteenth Century demonic possession cases, Carol claims that all those voices inside her head are a result of having stories to tell and books to write. Even so, her strange devotion to and study of Wonder Woman would seem to indicate an abby-normal brain.

A one-time comics letterhack and outspoken member of various comics message boards, Carol has found herself the basis for two comic book villains (at times her opinions have not been taken well by the books' creators) (both villains were soundly thrashed) (and both, for some perverse reason, were male) and had one superhero wear her costume design. (Light Lass!)

Carol has also become an award-winning painter. Along with her writing, she exercises this skill in her secondary hours (both of them) as she waits for the lottery to free her 9-to-5 time to more fulfilling pursuits.